Assault on the Vatican

by

T. R. Haney

authorHOUSE

1663 LIBERTY DRIVE, SUITE 200
BLOOMINGTON, INDIANA 47403
(800) 839-8640
www.authorhouse.com

First published by AuthorHouse 09/09/04

ISBN: 1-4184-7490-8 (sc)
ISBN: 1-4184-7491-6 (dj)

Printed in the United States of America
Bloomington, Indiana

This book is printed on acid-free paper.

TABLE OF CONTENTS

PROLOGUE

He paced back and forth almost as mindlessly as a caged cheetah.

"How could they?" he muttered in heavy-breathing exasperation. "This isn't the way it was to happen! My God, an assassination! How could they?"

He fingered his pectoral cross as though he were rubbing a Genie's bottle. He always did that when he was on the verge of exploding over something he couldn't control.

"How could they?" he kept muttering over and over.

He had taped the first report and now he listened to it again:

> Pope Charles was found dead outside his summer mountain resort shortly before dark on Wednesday. Although there is no confirmation, it seems he slipped and fell into the ravine. As is the custom, there will be no autopsy. Further details will be reported as they are made available. Pope Charles, who was elected on June 29, 2030, died on January 16, 2031. He reigned for less than seven months.

Then there was the usual background of this unusual Pope.

> Pope Charles will no doubt be remembered for his liberal leaps away from the traditionalist stance taken by his predecessors. Theological exploration into the possibility of lifting the ban on birth control, allowing pastoral consideration into the possibility of a married clergy as

well as the ordination of women are just a few instances of his embattled disagreements with conservative clergy and laity throughout the Catholic world. He entered the papacy as a well-known conservative, but within months the conservative Cardinals who had elected him were in a holy uproar. ("Nice touch," he sneered).

Viri Lucis had promised that it would be some form of blackmail, forcing the Pope to resign. "Men of the Light?" he muttered to himself. "Or are they disciples of darkness?"

This was out-and-out murder.

Oh sure, "slipped and fell" will be the official stand taken by one and all on the top rung of the hierarchical ladder.

He waved his hand over his Viewphone to activate it. He punched in the sacrosanct number. Even though he was alone, he would not recite the number aloud. After all, that is why it was called sacrosanct. Possibly the most guarded number in the world. He clicked on his viewscreen.

"Yes, Michael," came the smooth voice on the other end. The man at the other end never clicked on his viewscreen so that Michael could not see him or his expressions.

"What in God's name have you done?"

"Ah, Michael, I've been expecting your call. I was concerned about the strength of your commitment."

Michael grabbed his pectoral cross. Was it nervousness or fear?

"I dare say that I have contributed more to Viri Lucis than anyone else in the Church. You know damn well what my commitment's like."

"And in return, my dear Michael, your career has been assured. Have we not told you that as soon as his Eminence goes to meet his Maker, you will ascend his throne? You wouldn't want to spoil it now, would you? Let's just say that we shoved the church back to a balanced center. What is one man's life — or death — in the universal scheme of God's plan of salvation?"

"I'll tell you what his *murder* means. It means you'll not get one more cent out of me."

"Calm down, Michael, take some time to think things over. Pray."

Michael held the phone in his white-knuckled hand while he fidgeted with his pectoral cross with the other. There was his career to think about. Once he became a member of the College of Cardinals, he'd be able to wield far more influence than as a mere Auxiliary bishop. He might even be able to take control of Viri Lucis.

"I will pray, Mentor. Perhaps God will direct me to see your light," Michael said reluctantly.

"I feel much more assured, Michael. I'm certain that once you come to visit us, you too will feel more certain that what has been done was done for the greater glory of God."

The next day Michael listened to the feigned regrets Churchmen throughout the nation were expressing over Pope Charles' untimely death. With few exceptions like the Archbishop of Rockville Center, he knew that the hierarchy of the United States was secretly thrilled that God had intervened.

Then again, who was to say that God did not intervene through human agents who wanted to 'shove' the church toward the center?

By evening two representatives from Viri Lucis paid him a visit. The premonition he had all day now became a physical pain in the pit of his stomach.

"The Mentor sent us," one of the priests said, "to see if we can be of any help. We know you're quite distressed and we're here to assist you in any way we can. We don't want to lose your allegiance —that's from the Mentor himself."

"I'm feeling a bit better now," he smiled insincerely. As a matter of fact, he was still feeling furious beyond words. Late that afternoon after all the routine daily work had been done, he had told his secretary, Monsignor John J. Travine to take a few days off just so he wouldn't see him in such a perturbed state of mind.

Johnny has assumed that he was upset about the Pope's untimely death. That was all he needed to think for the time being. Before Johnny left, Michael had him witness a personal affidavit to be appended to his will. He had noticed that Johnny had been deeply disturbed by the contents of the affidavit, but he had not said a word to Michael.

"It was thought that as a sign of your good faith, your, ah, fidelity, you might want to make your quarterly contribution," the other priest said quietly.

"I've already made the check out for the usual amount," he said as he handed them a check for a quarter of a million dollars. "No matter what I decide, this should take care of my dues for the near future."

"Thank you so much, Your Excellency. We're certain that all involved will be relieved by your donation to the ongoing cause of orthodoxy."

Then one of the priests took out a small revolver and shot Bishop Michael McCann in the forehead. He slammed against the wall, slid down to the floor, his eyes snapped upward as though staring at his eternal destination.

THE EXECUTOR

Joseph Walter Daniels or "Father Joe" as his parishioners called him, sat in his small study. Stunned and mystified.

He and Michael had been best of friends in the seminary and in the early years of their priesthood. But in the years since they had lived in two separate hemispheres of the Church. They would meet from time to time but the conversations were kept on a level as superficial as a passing greeting. Mostly they talked about Michael, his ambitions and plans for himself and of course the Church.

Funny, he thought, how the Church officialdom always warned about avoiding close relationships with women, but never a word about having intimate relations with ambition.

"You know, Danny (the nickname all his friends and close acquaintances used as a spinoff on his last name, Daniels), when I take over the Archdiocese the first thing I'm going to do is get you out of this inner-city dump."

Danny would always smile indicating his conviction that when Michael "took over" the last person on earth he'd be thinking of was Joseph Walter Daniels.

Now here he was learning for the first time that he was the executor of Michael's multimillion dollar estate. As far as his quick calculations indicated, the estate was worth about $500 million after taxes.

Michael had never told him about being his executor. Of course Michael probably envisioned himself living to a ripe old age in the Archbishop's mansion.

That was something he admired about Michael: even though he came from one of the wealthiest families in the State while Danny came from a middle class family, there was never a fiscal barrier between them. Michael never flaunted his wealth.

Once in a while Michael would joke about his father buying him a diocese one day. As it turned out, it was more a prediction than a joke. His father was what is called a "heavy hitter" and made huge

1

contributions to the Archdiocese and to the Vatican. His father was not the type who gave without expecting in return.

Joseph Walter Daniels was 49. He stood over a six feet. He was losing some of his brown hair. But he was slim, almost athletic. He buried his ruggedly handsome face in his hands and sat back. Just thinking about being the executor of this vast fortune left him feeling desolate.

First the shock of Michael's murder and now this added burden of being Michael's executor. Added to this was his clawing dismay over the untimely death of the new Pope, Charles. There had been such an effusion of hope. The Commission he had set up to study the possibility of optional celibacy not just with theological justification but far more importantly from a pastoral point of view was one of the most momentous decisions in the history of the Church.

Pope Charles seemed to be unique among Church leaders in recognizing that the mandate of Jesus, "Do this in memory of me," was essential compared to the man-made law of celibacy. A law which caused so many parishes to be Eucharisticless. No Masses, no confessions.

Had Pope Charles been elected a few years ago, Joseph Walter Daniels' life might have been as different today as a slab of granite from a beating heart.

His memory drifted back to his third grade. There was Janie, a beautiful girl, smart and well-mannered. He had just moved into the area and was attending a new school. Janie sort of took him under her protective wing, making sure he knew what was expected of a student at St. Anselm's. They became close. His father would kid him about having a girlfriend.

Then somewhere in the year Janie died.

Even now he could not remember how he had reacted. He thought he had gone to see her in her casket, but he really wasn't sure. Even now he could not recall what emotions, if any, he had felt. Certainly he didn't just go through the third grade as if nothing had happened.

But he could never relive that time in his life to the extent of remembering what he had experienced. Had he just automatically blocked it out when Janie died? Or had he been too young to understand?

There would be no blocking out of Michael's death. That was for sure.

He opened the envelope addressed in Michael's handwriting to him. He read the note.

> Dear Danny,
>
> As you go through my papers think kindly of me.
> One section in my will refers to leaving the residue of my wealth to Viri Lucis. I want nothing left to them—absolutely nothing!
> The bulk of my estate is to go to the charities I've already designated in my will.
> Danny, pray for me. I am heartily sorry for any part I may have had in the death of Our Holy Father.
> Yours in Christ,
>
> Michael.

The note was dated the same day Michael had been killed.

Danny sat there, his mind churning like a whirlpool. Viri Lucis? Men of the Light? The death of Our Holy Father? What in the good God's name was this all about? Who was Viri Lucis? Where was Viri Lucis? Men of the Light? What did that designation mean? Why did Michael change his will? And why had he changed it on the very day he was killed?

One thing for sure. Bishop Michael J. McCann was not the victim of a random burglary.

Danny decided to call Leno Cappelli.

Joseph Walter Daniels and Leno Cappelli had been friends for many years. Along with Gene Shilling, Leno often served as Danny's confidante.

Danny knew that if anyone would have a lead about Viri Lucis, it would be Leno Cappelli. Some regarded Leno as the Church Universal's Premiere Gossip. Others as a thorn in the side of the Mystical Body. Whatever, he was the most informed member of that Body. There was even a quip: As soon as the Vatican knows, Leno knows.

Danny used to kid Leno about the Mafia. He'd say things like the Mafia was genetic. And just because men of a particular nationality ascended the ecclesiastical ladder in the Vatican, that didn't mean they forsook their Mafia mindset. They may not, he'd tease, shoot somebody down on the Church steps, but they did excommunicate and that was certainly a form of dealing out death. He hadn't kidded Leno like that for a long while. Hitting too close to home? he wondered.

"What can I tell you, Danny. My mind is an open book and matches my mouth," Leno would laugh heartily.

Leno answered the phone and clicked on his viewscreen. "Hello, Danny," he said in a soothing, almost musical, tone.

"Hello, Leno. I need some information," Danny said without preamble, indicating the urgency of his request.

"Leno, what can you tell me about an organization — I think it might be a Church organization — called Viri Lucis? Men of the Light?"

There was silence on the other end that seemed eternal even though it was only a few seconds.

"Leno, did you hear my question?"

"Where did you hear about that?" Leno asked in an obviously perturbed voice.

"For the present, that's neither here nor there. All I want to know is what you know," Danny responded curtly.

"I don't know anything," Leno answered just as curtly.

Danny surmised that the usually glib, smooth-talking Leno was holding something back. No use pushing him, at least not just now.

"Okay, Leno, I just thought that if anyone would have heard about Viri Lucis, it would be you. Thanks, anyway. Talk to you later."

"By the way," Leno spoke in his usual spirited manner, "condolences. We're all pretty upset."

Danny suspected the condolences were being offered because word had got around that he was the executor, not because he was especially close to Michael.

"Yes, it was quite a shock, Leno. To be honest with you, I'm overwhelmed. A little frightened in fact. This is a lot of money to try to handle. And there's some fishy stuff involved like this thing called Viri Lucis."

"You'll handle it, Danny," Leno said in what sounded like a forced upbeat tone.

Leno waved his hand over his phone and disconnected. He sat back, his face a dark, furrowed worry. "God help us," he sighed heavily. He knew he would eventually have to tell Danny something. But what? He activated the phone again and punched in the sacrosanct number.

Danny sat there almost in a stupor. What did Leno know? What was he holding back? And why?

He had to visit the hospitals. He hated this part of his work. People stabbed. Shot. Beaten. He wished that he could visit someone who merely had an appendectomy or a mother in the maternity ward. Then he had to stop at the homes of some shut-ins. That too was depressing. So many of the people in his parish lived in hovels. They had nothing. Well, not quite nothing. They did have their faith or religion as the case may be.

He reached over and pushed around in one of Michael's boxes. Another shock. Among the piles of papers he found a diary.

Once again Michael had never mentioned keeping a diary. How superficial their conversations were, he thought. He knew next to nothing about Michael. Why hadn't he chosen someone else to be his executor like his secretary, Father What's-his-name, that careerist with a Roman collar.

Danny sat and stared at the diary. Then he opened it. He was perplexed that Michael had written it in longhand instead of putting it on a telecomputer disc as most people would have. Michael's penmanship was small but painstakingly clear. It bordered on being a work of art. Opening it was like invading Michael's soul. It was like hearing his confession and not being able to give him absolution.

It could be like exploring Michael's Shadow Self except Michael probably never averred to having a shadow side. He was a pure pragmatist. A careerist of the umpteenth order. He would never have been accused of being a profound thinker, or, for that matter, a thinker unless he was involved in some kind of political quagmire.

He set the diary aside. Then he picked it up again, put it in his top desk drawer and locked it.

Political? Danny wondered again about Viri Lucis.

He got up, put on his coat, checked for the keys to his ancient Chevy, turned off the light and locked the door behind him — something he had never done before.

Later, he thought, he'd give Celine a call.

"You fools!" the white haired man, with steel gray bushy eyebrows that emphasized his drawn, ascetic face, roared from behind the heavy desk in the dimly lighted room. "You God-forsaken idiots!"

"But you gave us distinct instructions to evaluate him. To see if he could be trusted."

"And," the other priest joined in, "you implied that if we had any doubts, we should take what measures we thought were necessary.

"We could tell that he was desperate. He was still in a state of angry shock. There's no telling what he might have done. Gone to the media or God knows what."

"I didn't tell you to kill him in such an obvious manner, you insufferable lamebrains! You could have at least made it look like an accident like we did with our departed brother, Pope Charles."

"But, Mentor," the first priest persisted, "it's being reported as the result of a burglary. We took all kinds of expensive things out of his apartment. His ring and pectoral cross alone were well known to be worth a half a million dollars."

"Fortunately for us," the elderly man rasped, "we will gain most of his money."

The older man behind the desk pushed some papers out of the way. It seemed to the two men standing in front of his desk like a gesture of his ability to discard anyone he wanted to.

"What do you have on this Father Daniels?" the elderly man asked in a grilling tone.

The two were visibly nervous. They knew well that there could be more than a verbal reprimand. One of them shuffled his feet and put his hand to his cheek.

"He was a classmate and one-time close friend of our brother, Bishop McCann. He's the pastor of a poor, inner city parish. From what we can gather he hasn't been close to our departed brother for years. Our source tells us that he was shocked to find out he was the executor. He is a lamb. There'll be no trouble sheering him."

"If I let you two numbskulls loose, he'll end up being a lamb led to slaughter. May the Mother of God preserve us," the elderly man whispered his prayer.

"I'll dispatch Brown as soon as possible. He can get a first-hand measure on this 'lamb.' Meanwhile you two monitor whatever the police are doing in their investigation of poor Michael's demise."

The white-haired man made a sweeping gesture that told the two that had been dismissed.

With sighs of relief they bowed and headed for the door.

The man behind the desk called out after them, "I appreciate your efforts."

The two men acted like they had just been handed the key to the Vatican. They smiled at each other and went through the door.

"Mentor," the remaining and most trusted of the elderly man said, "did I have an inaccurate impression? I thought you intended Bishop McCann's death."

"Poor Michael," the white-haired man mused aloud. "He had such ambitions. Never to be realized, I'm afraid. After we discovered he had left his fortune to us, his will became his death warrant. "I needed his fortune. How else could I ever get the document from those infidel Iranians?"

"But if you had already decided McCann's death, why were you so upset with the two Attendants?"

"I was upset not with the fact of his demise but the way in which it was done. What was done was God's will and that is that. That is why I didn't punish them. Sometimes, as we say, God's ways are not always ours."

"'Man proposes, God disposes,'" the young man smiled as he offered the Mentor a glass of Burgundy.

"Thank you, Rolando. You are indeed a good and faithful servant."

CELINE

Danny finished his soup. Ran the water into the dish and left it in the sink.

He looked at his watch. Celine would be home by now. He unlocked the door to his study and went in.

He was still reeling from the impact of Michael's murder and the news of Pope Charles' sudden death. For someone like him, Pope Charles was pure hope. He had been so forward-looking, so pastoral in his concern.

Yet, there were many, perhaps most of the Church membership, who considered him a maverick or a traitor. Too liberal. Too headstrong. Disrespectful of tradition. It would be interesting, Danny thought, to read the commentaries on Pope Charles as to why and how he made the change from a moderate conservative to what many thought was a wild-eyed liberal.

The next Pope would be the fifth since Danny was ordained 25 years ago in 2006.

Danny waved his hand over his phone, activated it and recited Celine's number. The screen was blank as he listened to the recorded message. "We're not at home now. You know what to do. Be happy." He sat there staring at the phone. Remembering.

The first time he met Celine Kreel was in the winter of 2026 at one of those repetitious meetings in The Alley on Southside where the do-gooders from the land of the upper crust paid a brief visit to his inner city parish to discuss how the problems of these poor, marginalized people could be solved.

It was the first time Celine had been at one of these meetings.

As always, those present who had all the suggestions did all the talking. Danny, who lived with these problems day in and day out, sat there saying nothing.

His silence, it was obvious, annoyed Celine. Visibly. "Don't you have anything to say?" she had asked as pointedly as a dagger.

9

"Yes," he had replied as pointedly, "there's too much talk and too little action."

He could have gone into a tirade about their being tourists, about the need to go into these places and see seven or eight people crammed into one room, smell the urine, feel the draft, but the others had heard it before. No need to introduce this lawyer woman to his obvious ingratitude or was it wrath?

Shortly afterwards the meeting broke up. Nothing much to show for it except the minutes. What was that his friend Bill, who worked among the migrants, says? A committee keeps minutes and wastes hours. Or that ditty he had heard somewhere, "In no park or city is there a monument to a committee."

He thanked everyone as graciously as he could, put on his coat and headed for the door.

Celine caught up with him. "You're certainly a walking downer," she said without preamble.

"I guess I just get tired of all these miraculous suggestions and all the dead ends," he answered without paying much attention to her.

"Look," she said, "I have some time and if you do, would you like to go somewhere for a drink or a cup of coffee?"

They walked through the frightening winter wind in the icy steel rain that slanted against some abandoned buildings standing like lonely sentinels keeping watch over a dying ghetto. They came to a nearby coffee shop. Like so many other shops in the area, it was rundown. Danny assured Celine that the coffee was the best in The Alley.

From his six foot two perspective he judged her to be about five feet seven or eight inches. She was statuesque to say the least. Shapely long legs, thin waist and attractive, full breasts.

As they sat across the table from one another, Danny looked at her not intrusively but in a respectful manner.

She was a beautiful woman. Very. But her body language sent a clear message: Don't lust after my body — respect my mind. Yet she wasn't cold or distant. Quite the contrary, she was as warm as a spring day. She made you feel comfortable in her presence. Her voice was low-pitched and delicate. She was articulate but not pedantic.

Celine Kreel, the lawyer lady from up town, seemed persuasively interested not so much in what he did here but in him being here. He soon discovered that the mind she wanted respected was one of a sensitive thinker who came by her sensitivity by being an empathetic listener.

Her long thick ash brown hair fell loosely around her face like an expensive frame enhancing a priceless work of art and reminded him that the world is not just a place of ugly destitution but also of bountiful beauty.

Her soft emerald eyes which moved with waltz-like grace seemed to gently absorb him, to nurture him with an assurance that life is worth the risk of living. Her translucent soul seemed to sparkle in her gleaming eyes. Her smile was wide and spontaneous, warm and inviting. It seemed to say, "You are a worthwhile person."

There could be no doubt, Danny thought, that she was a graceful, self-possessed, very confident woman, capable of raising or demolishing anyone who dared to enter her lair. She looked like she worked out regularly.

Danny concluded that Celine Kreel was an obsessive-compulsive which wasn't the worst characteristic a person might have. Yet, Danny mused, she probably could be quite flexible when necessary.

Or was his assessment merely a figment of his overactive imagination? Was he seeing only what he wanted to see? Was he reading into her smile what he wanted to find there? Was he romanticizing her far beyond the reality of who she was? It was all a first impression. He didn't know her at all. He was being stupid. Still he knew from experience that he was intuitive, that his first instincts about people usually were accurate.

She also talked easily about herself in response to his questions. She was wonderfully unselfconcious.

Like him, she came from an upper middle class family. She graduated *maxima cum laude* from college. St. Bridget's, an all-female school. She finished in the top three percent of her class in

Michigan Law School and as a result, landed a good job with the firm she was presently working for, Lambert, Hudson and Greer.

She was never married. "Too obsessed right now with the icy glamor of pushing my career to the limit," she had said honestly. Wasn't attached but did have someone who was interested in her. His name was George Korbach. He was a vice president in charge of marketing.

She admitted they went out together more for convenience than for serious planning for the future. "I guess," she said laughing, "we're just a couple of misplaced pilgrims."

Self-deprecating humor, he thought. Not bad for a successful lawyer.

Something else was obvious. She had a kind of laid back aggressiveness. You knew what she wanted without her telling you.

"May I ask," she said with a pixy smile, "how old you are?"

"Forty-nine," Danny answered. "Ordained almost 25 years. Why? Do I look older?"

"No, just a bit worn," Celine laughed.

"And you? How old are you?"

"Women are never supposed to tell," she teased. Then she added promptly, "Thirty-four."

"Why did you come here to the inner city?" Danny had asked. He was trying to understand this beautiful young woman's reason for what might be called an on-sight experience of attempting to do something to not only help the poor but to untangle the problems that caused their poverty. After all, she could have just as easily sent a check and let it go at that.

"I don't know for sure. Maybe it's because I had such a good life — and still do. Or it could be an impulse that may not last for long so I'm doing what I think I should while it does last. Or maybe it's an escape from whatever.

"At the firm I do my share of pro bono work and I truly enjoy doing it. Maybe it's seeing those people in such dire need that has made me want to do more. Those people at the meeting tonight …. they have to have reasons for taking an interest in the plight of the people down here in The Alley. Or do I have to have a reason? Can't you be satisfied that I'm trying to do something?"

"Look...." Celine hesitated, not knowing how to address her new acquaintance.

"Danny," he supplied.

"Look, Danny, can I be brutally blunt?"

"It's your date," he feigned a laugh.

"I work hard at my job. I derive a great deal of satisfaction from practicing law. These people tonight at the meeting? They're acquaintances of mine who asked me if I wanted to come along. They said I might be interested.

"All I'm trying to do is give something back. I came here full of good will and, if you don't mind my saying so, I encounter a man who in my judgment is smug and a bit self-righteous about living and working in the inner city among society's downtrodden.

"I don't think it's fair of you to assume some kind of a moral stance of superiority just because you're involved with the stereotype of poor people," Celine said quietly if not gently.

"I never thought of myself as being morally superior," Danny said defensively. "I don't know. It could be that I see you people discuss the problems of the inner city, annex God to your noble words of concern about the poor here in The Alley and then get into your expensive cars and drive back to the land of Upper Crust. Or maybe I resent it that I can't follow you."

Celine picked up her cup and blew on the coffee. "Sure," she said with noticeable sarcasm, "Sure and I spend all my free time in the Loop shopping on Michigan Avenue. Then with what time is left, I go to the top of the Sears Tower and survey my world. What would you have me do, Father Daniels? Give up my lifestyle and move into the slums to prove I care? Perhaps become a self-styled martyr like .... like you?" "Don't you realize," Celine continued with more empathy, "that it's through these people from 'the land of Upper Crust' that you are able to bring groups like the Spychalskie String Quartet here to give your people the opportunity to enjoy them. An opportunity they would not otherwise have?"

Danny sipped his coffee but did not respond. Celine moved and settled down in a more casual or comfortable way on the wooden bench of the booth.

"Do you have to stay here?" she asked. "Aren't there other parishes you could go to?"

"Sure but I guess I have this compulsion to do what I can to help these people. They are poor and I wonder if we of the Church really care about them besides writing a few pastoral letters on their behalf and then it's business as usual.

"It's like this. When I see their faces as they come up for Communion, I'm filled with wonder. There they are with so little yet their faces are full of light and joy. Their faces are peaceful. I don't mean to say anything negative about the people of suburban parishes.

"All I'm saying is that my people have no bragging rights when it comes to material possessions and yet they seem so quietly boastful of their faith."

Danny called to the waitress. Then looked at Celine who nodded. He ordered a second round of coffee for both of them.

"Another reason — and I guess this is a more selfish one — is that no matter what I do for them, no matter how much or how little, they are always so grateful," Danny said quietly. "They seem to be more than satisfied to get just a ray of hope from me. I must admit there are times when I have to fake my own hope for their sakes.

"I guess my own feeling of hopelessness stems from the fact that I don't think the Church really cares about the poor. Our bishops have their own economics to worry about. The bottom line doesn't seem to include people like the ones here in The Alley."

"Frankly, Danny, I think you're being unfair. Even judgmental. There are a lot of sincere people who are concerned about the disadvantaged, including bishops. And besides, there are all kinds of poor people. Don't you think a couple on the verge of divorce are poor?" Celine stirred her coffee absently. She put her spoon on the saucer and continued.

"Aren't parents who are financially well-off but who are in the throes of anguish over a son or daughter who is incorrigible or who

14

is deliberately failing in school or who is on drugs — don't you think they are poor? Aren't their kids poor?

"What about a client who comes to me, someone who is obsessed, addicted to greed or ambition? Isn't that person poor? What about us professionals, caught up in this insane rat race? Aren't we poor?

"The poor are not just those who are hungry for food. There are thousands of people out there who are starving for love, for appreciation, understanding, support.

"I'm not trying to put you down. I'm trying to open your eyes to a broader vision of reality."

Danny sat there in silence for the longest time. Celine didn't know whether he'd respond with harsh anger or just get up and walk out. Finally he said, "Food for thought."

"Speaking of food," Celine said, "do you accept invitations for dinner?"

"Yes," Danny answered rather sheepishly.

"So," Celine said, "if you accept invitations to dinner, would you like me to give you a call sometime? We could have dinner at my place. I'm not a kitchen magician but the food's edible."

"Yes," Danny replied. "In fact I'll be looking forward to it."

That's how their relationship began.

THE RELATIONSHIP

During the next two years Danny and Celine had dinner together from time to time. Most of the time they ate at Celine's apartment.

Sometimes, in a secluded, intimate restaurant. The chances of his running into any of his parishioners was as probable as a sandstorm in the Atlantic Ocean.

Danny let it be known that he preferred Celine's apartment. It was cozy and yet exuded class. So very different from his shabby rectory.

In the living room there was a powder blue couch with a matching chair. A soft rose recliner. Against one of the wall were gold etageres with glass shelves where Celine had placed what seemed to Danny to be very expensive wooden statuettes and a few pictures. The carpet was a deep blue shag.

The lamps on either side of the couch and near the recliner had cream colored shades. On another wall was, as Celine told Danny, an original painting. It was from her friend, Raymond Gauth. It was a modern piece which, as far as Danny was concerned, could mean anything you wanted it to.

A combination downlink televisor and stereo set filled the corner opposite the couch. The third wall boasted ceiling to floor book shelves crammed with books on a wide variety of subjects other than law.

The kitchen off the dining room was compact. Her bedroom and bath which Danny only glanced at since it was the most personal section of her apartment were spacious. Danny felt comfortable there in Celine's company.

"The pictures?" Danny had asked.

"This one is of my mother and father, very much alive. This is my younger sister, her husband and their three children. This is Bob, my former fiancé. I don't know why I keep it. Lingering affection or as a symbol of my need to get on with my life.

"What does your father do?" Danny asked.

16

"He's a lawyer too."

"He must be very proud of you."

"Yes. When I was in college and law school, he'd write to me about every three weeks, encouraging me, telling me how brilliant I was. He'd always end by urging me not to take a back seat to anyone. The word, anyone, was always underlined."

"That's great. A father affirming his daughter that way."

"Yes. My mother and I enjoyed a good relationship, even though she hovered to the point of suffocation. If I told her I was dating some boy, her immediate question was, 'You're not sleeping with him, are you?'"

"Sounds like a close knit family."

"Yes it was …. is."

"Your sister?"

"Yes, Joreen. A free spirit. She didn't care if our parents ever affirmed her. In fact if they encouraged her to do something, she'd do the opposite and then blame them if she failed. Now she's the quintessential mature woman. A devoted wife and most solicitous mother of three. Sometimes I envy her."

"Why?"

" Oh, I don't know. I guess it's because she has a family. Lovely children, as you saw from the picture, two girls and a boy. She rules the roost but in a subliminal sort of way. She doesn't manipulate. Her husband, Paul, has his own construction company. Works hard and is a very good provider. Really loves the kids.

"I'm not saying they're the ideal family. They've had their share of problems. One time she even left him. Came back because of the children. Since then their relationship seems to have grown stronger."

"What happened between you and Bob? If I may ask."

Celine sat on the couch with her long legs crossed, revealing the full impact of her sultry sensuality. "Well, Bob and I went together for a little over a year when he proposed and I was thrilled. He was a lawyer and we had that in common.

"I had the usual dreams of having a family and trying to balance my career with being a wife and mother. All our friends were happy for us and I guess we were ecstatic. Making plans and dreaming dreams.

"Then something began to change." Her eyes flew open as if in befuddlement. "What was at first his consideration and thoughtfulness degenerated into control. He became unbearably possessive. Her finely chiseled hand swept the air. Her full breasts heaved with emotion.

"So eventually I decided to call it quits. It was rough. Bob was taken completely off guard. Said he had no idea he was controlling or possessive. Wanted to have a second chance. He even cried. I felt horrible. He was so vulnerable. So I said okay we'll give it another chance.

She uncrossed her legs and reached across the couch for the other pillow which she held tight to her chest. She was silent for quite a while and Danny allowed her this private time.

"For a few weeks," she finally continued, "he was back to just being thoughtful. Then it started all over again. When I tried to tell him about it, he accused me of nitpicking and imagining things. Reading into his words. We began to argue. Finally we both agreed to go our separate ways. It was terrible.

"I really did love him and I know he loved me. I never experienced such sadness. I was demolished. I couldn't bring myself to date for months after that. I just threw myself into my work with such intensity that I became obsessive. I decided then and there I would never go through that again. Gun shy is the description, I guess. Even now I wonder if I'm capable of a life-long commitment."

Danny saw tears welling up in Celine's eyes. His heart went out to her. But there really wasn't anything he could say. She had weathered the storm for the most part. Who knew how long the pain of the aftermath would last?

"I tried to learn something about myself," Celine continued. "From that experience, you know. Especially about how I deal with intimate relationships. I know I am demanding of myself and I had to find out if I was too demanding of others, especially the men I dated."

Danny stood up and walked over to the couch. For the first time he sat down next to her. He wanted to put his arm around her but he didn't know how she might react especially since she was reliving a part of her life that was so emotionally painful. This was obviously not the time for any show of emotion on his part even if he only intended it to be supportive.

At the same time Celine did not react either with surprise or vexation when Danny sat down on the couch. In fact, Danny surmised, she seemed to be reassured.

"How are you feeling now?" Danny had asked. "I mean, do you feel you've recovered your emotional balance? I don't mean to presume ...."

"I understand. I'm not sure. As I said, I seem to have this fear about making a life-long commitment especially with so many of my friends getting married and divorced. There are times when I feel threatened by the future even though I am successful in my profession.

"I'm not certain if I want to plan ahead any more. Sometimes I feel like just letting time carry me along. I am an orderly person and I do like to plan ahead. Maybe this .... no, I *know* this will pass."

Danny reached over and gently squeezed her hand. "It won't pass, Celine. You will make it pass."

"Thanks, Danny, for being such a good friend," Celine said without looking at him.

Danny got up. "I'll see myself out. I'm sorry that I brought up unhappy memories."

"No, that's all right," Celine smiled. "A purging now and then is healthy."

Danny went to the door and as he was leaving, he merely said, "Good night. I'll be in touch."

"Fine," Celine said.

Then abruptly Danny did a turnabout. "You know, Celine, ever since I met you and we have become close friends, I have been coming more alive. Alive to my emotions. Alive to the wonder of an intimate relationship. Alive to the mystery of growing love."

"I have to admit," Celine responded, "I've been having some of the same feelings. But my feelings only cause me to question celibacy the more. Why is celibacy an absolute condition for getting ordained? Why can't someone be a priest and be married at the same time?

"You have friends who have left the active ministry to get married and who still want to serve in the ordained ministry, don't you? Why shouldn't they? Why should people have to do without the Mass and other services because of a shortage not of priests but of celibate priests?"

Danny didn't respond but he was wondering why he and Celine couldn't be married? Their love, he was certain, was genuine and mutually supportive, comforting and growth-producing. He knew in his heart that the love he had for her yearned for a life together. Or was this just infatuation?

Hadn't she just told him about her fear of a life-long commitment? Or was that something she would eventually grow away from? To Celine he had said, "Celibacy is the law to be kept if you want to continue in the active ministry as an ordained priest. You can question it but the law's the law. Celibacy has been called a gift. I think that's the way I always thought of it. I never questioned it until …" His voice trailed off as if he couldn't bring himself to say, "until I met you."

"I'm sorry," Celine had said as though reading Danny's thoughts, "but I have trouble accepting the abstract intellectual arguments about celibacy being a positive value. It may be for some but isn't that all the more reason for supporting the idea of optional celibacy? I mean other professionals marry and raise a family."

"But how many priests end up being comfortable, if not selfish, bachelors? Their hobbies or trips more important than the people? Or am I being judgmental? I probably am. I only know the situation from the outside in. And I'm sure what I said doesn't apply to all priests."

"No it really doesn't. There are many zealous priests around," Danny replied quietly.

"I was being judgmental, Danny." Celine stood up. "As in every line of work, there are the beavers and there are the drones. Is that some kind of a mixed metaphor?" She laughed.

Danny felt so comfortable with Celine, so understood. She supplied the kind of response he could never get from the priests who were his friends.

Celine gave him a soft, gentle kind of support that made her all the more attractive not only as a woman but as a person who was able to offer insights that escaped Danny because of his closeness to his way of life. Or because of his maleness.

THE DETECTIVE

The phone sounded. "You have an incoming call. Do you wish to go on line or do you want me to take a message?" the phone butler voice asked. Danny was jerked out of his reverie as though the phone signal were a shock wave. "On line," Danny said quietly.

Danny saw the image of Detective Lou Mc Dermott. "Hi ya, Lou."

"Halllo, Danny, as you can see it's your favorite homicide detective."

"And my favorite missing parishioner."

"You know how it goes, Danny. I'm on my way to church and someone plugs somebody and I'm out sleuthing."

"There must be one heck of lot of murders on Sunday mornings, Lou," Danny laughed.

"Well, I'm just calling to find out if you know if the bishop had any known enemies. Routine, you know." But Lou sounded hopeful.

"I really wouldn't know, Lou. Michael and I weren't that close. I never expected that I was his executor. How's the investigation coming along?"

"Not too good. There's so little to go on. Danny, honest to God as crazy as this sounds, it looks like a professional hit. That's why I'm calling. I don't suppose from what you just said that you would know if the bishop had any ties with …. well, with unsavory types. Now don't get your nose out of joint. It's just that a hit like this one does raise some sordid questions."

"No, Lou, I don't know anything like that. Michael had enough money in his own right that it would be hard to think …"

"Yeah, I heard. The McCann family and their billion dollar fortune. His brothers are all over us. And they got clout. Still I was thinking you never know what kind of investments are being made."

"Frankly, Lou, I think you're heading for a dead end. Speaking of the underworld, have you ever heard of an organization called Men of the Light? Its Latin title is Viri Lucis. Maybe you've heard it referred to as Vir or Lucis or something?"

"Can't say that I have. Why? Does it have something to do with the bishop's death?"

"No. I just heard about it from around here in the last couple of days. I thought it might be a gang moving into The Alley," Danny lied.

"There's something else, Danny. There was a robbery. Some very expensive stuff. Right now we're thinkin' it's a cover. It looks too much like a professional hit, like I said. I can trust you not to hold back on me, can't I?

"Sure you can," Danny really didn't know what to say or how to react.

"Would you know anything about the meaning of a red cross?"

"No. Except for the organization that goes under that title. Why?"

"Well, a cross was traced with the bishop's blood on his right cheek."

"What do you make of that, Lou?"

"I'm not sure. Was he a victim of some religious fanatic? Or did the burglar, assuming it was a burglary, try to make it look like some religious thing?"

"Michael couldn't have done it as some kind of sign, could he?" Danny asked.

"He was dead before he ever slammed against the wall. We have a couple of guys who are known religious nuts with violence documented in their files. We're goin' a haul them in. We don't have much else to go on, like I said."

"What about Monsignor Travine, Michael's secretary?" Danny asked.

"Only that he had gone away for a few days and high tailed it back as soon as he heard of the bishop's death .... murder."

"What did he have to say about the bloody cross?"

"We didn't tell him. In fact you're the only one I've mentioned it to. And for the time being, it's like the confessional, okay?"

"Okay."

"It's just that we don't want any crazy copy cats to start some kind of a religious war. I was just hoping you could give me a lead.

"Was your friend involved in any kind of dispute with some religious organization? Did he tramp on the toes of someone in the Church? Any fanatic he might have insulted?"

"As I said, we weren't that close. But I can assure you, Michael was the quintessential ecumenist."

"Whatever that means."

"It means he got along with everybody. Inside and outside the Church. He worked with ministers and Rabbis on social issues like helping the poor and homeless. That's a matter of public record. I wouldn't be surprised if he sunk a lot of his own money into causes like that. He certainly tried to help me here."

Danny paused. "I'm afraid I can't help you on this score either. Maybe you should go back to your idea that the bloody cross is a false trail."

"Yeah, I guess that's about it. It was just too smooth an operation to be the work of a fanatic. Unless the fanatic is an accomplished operator," Lou sounded hesitant as though he was distracted by some other piece of the puzzle that had just popped into his mind.

"You remember that stabbing that happened outside the Plaza hotel a few weeks ago?" Lou asked.

"Yes," Danny said. "I heard it on the evening news. Some very well-healed gentleman."

"Very. Completely stripped of everything on him. But what we didn't release was that there was a cross traced in his blood on his forehead."

"A serial killer?"

"Or a copy cat. We have no way of knowing. I'll tell you, Danny, you may get frustrated trying to get people into heaven but I get real down trying to catch people so's I can begin their hell on earth."

"Lou, if I think of anything, I'll call you."

"Good enough. And, Danny, stay away from anybody whose eyes look glazed over. Oh, by the way, that guy that was stabbed was a Catholic. Bantram. Name mean anything to you?"

"No, his name doesn't ring any bells."

"Well, thanks for your time, Danny. Take care."

"You too, Lou."

Danny waved his hand over the phone. He had decided during the conversation not to mention the note to Lou. Mainly because he had no idea yet how it did or did not fit into Michael's death. His murder. Lou was having enough trouble without complicating matters.

On the other hand, the note could be an important clue. Later, he thought, after there was some kind of clarification, he would tell Lou. Lou would probably be mad as hell but Danny had made his decision for the time being at least.

DOUBTS

Danny went back to his reverie. He recalled how his and Celine's friendship grew. He was able to be comfortably self-revelational with Celine and self-revelation didn't come easy to him except when he wrote his poetry. Yet he had confided his doubts to Celine. Doubts about his priesthood. And about the work he was doing at Old St. Matt's, his parish, or as most people referred to it, Poor St. Matt's. Even doubts about his faith.

From time to time Celine would visit Danny at his rectory as she did today. She wanted to "spruce up" the place but Danny only allowed her to bring some small things like plants or napkins.

Danny, who had purchased the makings of a dry martini, Celine's favorite drink, was busy in the kitchen mixing her a very, very dry martini. Celine sat down at the kitchen table where Danny did all of his entertaining and unwrapped a cocktail glass.

"This will be mine when I come here, okay?"

"Great," Danny replied graciously.

"I didn't bring you one since you're a bourbon drinker and all you need for that is one of your 'fancy' water glasses. Frankly I prefer my martinis in something other than a water glass," Celine laughed.

Danny took the cocktail glass and poured Celine a drink. He had a strange tingling sensation about keeping the cocktail glass here at the rectory as though it was a kind of a part of Celine. Something more permanent than the smell of her perfume after she had left. He suddenly wondered why they had never exchanged photos of each other.

"It seems strange to me," Celine had said as she sipped her martini with obvious relish, "that someone who is so dedicated could be plagued with these kinds of doubts," Celine was picking up on a recent conversation in which Danny had been confiding some of his doubts.

"I'm not so sure it's dedication. When I returned from my studies in Rome, I was assigned by the Cardinal as Vice Chancellor of the Archdiocese. My friends were effusive in assuring me that my career was on the rise.

"After two years in that job, the Cardinal sent me back to Rome to study for a doctorate in theology. He wanted me to be his personal theologian. I studied under one of the most scholarly theologians in the Church. Alessandro Percussi. He is now the Cardinal Archbishop of Milan," Danny had said.

" I returned after two years with my degree and worked in the Cardinal's office for four years.

"Two years to get a doctorate?" Celine interrupted. "Am I in the presence of some kind of genius?"

"Not quite. I just worked harder than most," Danny replied with a mischievous glint in his eyes. Celine knew he was feigning modesty. "Go on," she urged.

"Well, finally I asked the Cardinal for an assignment to parish work. That, I believed, was why I got ordained. He was reluctant but most gracious. And so I spent the next three years working in a parish as an assistant. The old Monsignor was a godsend to my priesthood. Everyone called him 'Muntz,' an nickname for Monsignor. He's still alive.

"Then St. Matt's opened and no one seemed to want it. I applied for it. And I got it. Maybe it's because no one else applied," Danny smiled. "The point about dedication is that I am not sure if I really wanted an inner city parish or I just wanted to be a pastor. Just wanted to be able to call my own shots."

"But you've stayed there," Celine countered. "You could have applied for another parish years ago, couldn't you?"

"Well, to be honest, I never knew what this parish would demand of me. There have been far more heartbreaks than consolations. Sometimes the loneliness is unbearable. I have a few priest friends but they're busy with their own parishes. We do get together from time to time, but it's not a time to whine about your problems. Most of the time they're good intellectual companions."

27

It was then, he remembered, that he had told Celine how much he appreciated her friendship and how much her affection meant to him. He noticed that Celine seemed uneasy so he didn't pursue it any further.

Celine continued to press him about his doubts.

"Maybe I'm too susceptible to the ways of success and failure," Danny had said. "And so I often wonder if I'm really making a difference. I try to draw inspiration and strength from gospel images like the Widow's Mite.

"You know, it's not the amount of good I get done but the selflessness I do it with. Sometimes it works, sometimes it doesn't. I hate to sound like I'm throwing a pity-me party but most of the time it doesn't work.

"After I've done everything I can to help somebody and failed, I'm thrust back into the realization that I'm not some supernatural force in people's lives. I'm just another struggling pilgrim on the way.

"I don't like swallowing my limitations but if I don't I'll have to eat my frustration. I have to step back, give myself some breathing room, some distance until I can convince myself that the person I failed to help has freedom of choice and is responsible for the choices made."

"It's tough, Danny, isn't it? To have to admit that you're not a messiah."

Celine got up and went over to the sink where she rinsed out the cocktail glass and placed in the cabinet on the first shelf.

"I know," Danny turned from the table and directed his response to Celine who was standing at the sink. "I have to come to grips with the reality that there are times, more times than I'd prefer to experience, when I have to stand in my desert with my promises of hope, for a better life, caught in my throat while I watch people walk away from me."

"Like Jesus," Celine offered. "And like him, you've got to let go, Danny. Let them go."

"I know this intellectually but when I try to put it into practice, that's when the doubts hit full force. Doubts about why I am needed at all. I find myself asking, Am I needed only for failures? Oh, I do help people but when it's failure most of the time, I wonder if I make a difference. If my life, my being a priest, makes a difference."

"Trying to lighten the mood," Celine said laughingly, "What you need, Joseph Michael Daniels, is a good workshop on self-esteem."

"How many of us make that much of a difference?" Celine asked. "I mean really. A Pope, a President .... they wield such power but the world doesn't change that much, does it? You know the saying, Cemeteries are filled with indispensable people.

"The world just keeps spinning along, casting off all the important people into eternity. The thing is .... oh, I know you've heard this many times, but we each do what we can. You know, if each of us does a little bit, it becomes a lot.

"Perhaps somewhere in the future, all our little bits will come together and there will be the impact for good we all hope for. For now, dear Danny, stick with that image of the Widow's Mite."

He wanted to tell her about his doubts about celibacy but decided this was not the time. Celine was still suffering from her broken engagement and all the devastation that can have on her self esteem. He certainly didn't want to appear as if he was taking advantage of her vulnerability.

Despite her obvious demonstrations of competence and her outward show of self-assured confidence, there was about her a mysterious fragileness as if she wasn't totally convinced of *her* worth as a person.

Yet it worked like magic luring him into the depths of her winsome personality. She was elusive. He was becoming more and more captivated.

Celine's visits were not just social calls. She would come over to St. Matt's usually to do some counseling of battered women and try to get them to go to a shelter. Her success rate was no better than Danny's.

Still she hung in. Danny was astounded at the way she could look at a situation and see any number of possibilities. She was willing to live with ambiguity while he more often than not felt stymied. It puzzled him how she could seem so ethereal and at the same time be so practical.

Another thing that allured him to her was her detachment. She most certainly had to be in a high income bracket — he never asked and she never volunteered. But it seemed to Danny that she was blithely indifferent to material things.

She seemed almost carelessly unimpressed by either wealth or power. Yet she was neither harsh nor judgmental about those who lived in the luxury of affluence. The more Danny contemplated this aspect of her attitude, the more impressed he became.

Once again he wondered if he was idealizing her.

One evening after everyone had left, they sat at the kitchen table having a beer. Both were visibly exhausted and worse, feeling despondent. They talked for a while about the people who had come to them for help and then seemed to refuse it.

"I remember," Danny said, "when I first started working in a parish. I'd take everyone's problems to heart. One time when I was home on a visit, I was telling my mother about my feelings of depression over people's problems. She told me to try to be a bit more clinical. 'Those people come to you, dump their problems on you and go home whistling. You end up in your room alone feeling down and out.'"

"She sounds like a very wise woman," Celine said with obvious admiration.

"She was but I don't know how well I've absorbed her wisdom over the years."

"She's dead?" Celine asked.

"Yes, both my mother and father," Danny answered with no visible emotion.

TORTURE

Danny recalled how there were nights when the questions Celine raised about celibacy would yank him out of a sound sleep and not allow him rest. Was he wrestling with celibacy on an intellectual level or was it an unbridled emotional reaction to Celine. Whatever it was, it was torture.

Those nights when he awoke he would pray. Pray out of sheer anguish. Pray for guidance he really wasn't sure he wanted. For control over his emotions. He would challenge God right there on the spot. "Is such a lifegiving relationship a near occasion of sin to be avoided? If you created us out of love for loving, why can't I love Celine with my whole being, with all my passion?

"Please, dear God, give me just one sliver of your light in this darkness of my ambiguity. Fill the emptiness of my longing for Celine. Heal my pain. Lord God, strengthen my faith that I can believe that celibacy is your will and not just a manufactured demand of those who feared the sacred gift of their own bodies. Give me direction."

"Lord," he would cry out the agony of his conflict between what he knew and what he believed, "why have you led me into the experience of my passion only to leave me standing immobilized? Every vein of my body is bursting with desire. Every beat of my heart pounds on the closed door called celibacy.

"Why? I need serenity in this treacherous torment. I surrender all my emotions to you. Return me to the emotionless existence I once had before I met Celine."

There were times when Danny yearned to be released from his body, if not into ecstasy, at least into total detachment where nothing and no one could touch him. He knew this was irrational. It was just part of the torture he was enduring. He prayed something good would come out of all this. And soon.

Deep in the night of the silent screams of his prayer, Danny tried again and again to slip into the silence of peace. But all he had, all he endured, was more turmoil. "Why am I here? Why is the heartbeat of life still mine? What do you want for me? From me?" Then as always back to the core of his heartache: "Why am I allowed to feel such craving love for Celine only to be denied its full expression because of this ecclesiastical law?"

There were times when his soul felt hardened and dark like an old walnut.

Surprisingly, or maybe after all it was a grace, even though he was plagued with these afflictions, these ordeals of torment, Danny noticed that he was approaching his ministry not only with hope but with renewed zeal.

It wasn't that relentless spirit-breaking drudgery anymore. He woke up most mornings with a desire to live each day as a new life. And on the days he knew he would see Celine, he actually experienced exhilaration in the pit of his stomach.

He still had his lapses. Times when he would question whether the people he was serving were merely practicing their religion or living their faith. He wanted so much to be able, through his sacramental ministry, to reveal his personal mystery. To what avail he wasn't sure.

He wanted to diminish the pain of those who feared the future and those who hated the past. Yet he was plagued with doubts. Must he, because he was a priest, feign competency to deal with every problem?

He would begin to sink into some kind of a dark night. But then Celine would appear like a dawn-enkindling fire dispelling the gloominess of his doubts. How often she had challenged him saying things like, "There is joy when you persevere. There is hope when you don't take yourself too seriously. There is strength in laughing at your humanness."

Celine was not just a beautiful woman physically. She radiated a beauty of soul. Lying there in the dark night of his soul, he remembered how she once had confided to him that her favorite scripture quote was from John's gospel. "I have come that they may have life and have it to the fullest."

And with all her vivacity, all her eagerness to affirm even the dregs of humanity, all her optimism that life was worth living, she seemed to live that gospel verse to the fullest. And her spirit, as far as Danny was concerned, which was as lively as a child with a heart filled with wonder, was melding with his.

"Do you believe in miracles?" Celine asked him one evening when they were alone after having delivered clothing she had conned her colleagues into donating.

"I guess it depends on what is meant by a miracle," Danny had responded. "I think there a lot of miracles in ordinary people and events of everyday living. At least that has been an intellectual conviction of mine even if it hasn't been something I've lived."

"I see a miracle in you," she said as simply as if she were saying she saw a star in the night sky. "You remember one of the first things I said to you? That you were a walking downer? That's tucked away in the archives of your life now. You've truly come alive. You're so full of hope.

"I see it making a difference in the people around here, whether they are parishioners or vagrants. You're giving them more than duty-bound service. More than handouts. You're giving them yourself and in return you are growing again, becoming more of who you are."

"It's because of you," Danny said honestly, "and our friendship. You've affirmed me in so many ways. You've treated me as if I were already what I could be. As a result you've enabled me to start becoming what I can be."

"Well, you certainly laugh a little more," Celine said. "You're don't seem to be afraid of your vulnerability anymore. You don't always have to be in control. You're not trying to be the proverbial answer man as you did when I first met you.

"I used to think, If only he'd quit trying to have all the answers. If only he would learn to live in the mystery of it all, he'd be so much more open to the possibilities of life."

"You know what I think?" she had asked. "What?" "I think you were living a kind of schizophrenic life. You knew all the things I've been saying to you. You believed in life to the fullest. You understood that you are a limited human being.

"But on the other side of the split, you weren't putting your knowledge into practice. You weren't living your beliefs. As a result you were looking to blame something or someone. And your blaming was shattering your bond with reality. You weren't being a realist and so you couldn't be an idealist. You were a self-made defeatist."

"That's what I love about you," Danny laughed. "You're so articulate. You really are wise beyond your years. And you toss off your insights like they were common fare."

The word, love, didn't go unnoticed by either of them. And there was a long moment of silence as if a decision was being made as to whether or not they should probe how they felt about each other. But the conversation took another direction, exploring other matters less self-revelatory. For the first time there was an uneasy timidity between them.

QUANDARIES

Monsignor Leno Cappelli punched in the sacrosanct number. "Yes, Leno," the smooth, confident voice came from the other end with no image on the viewscreen.

"Father Joseph Daniels, Michael's executor called me. He wanted to know what I might know about Viri Lucis."

Silence on the other end. "I denied having any knowledge. But I think he suspects I do what with my reputation for being in the know, as they say." Still no response.

"I strongly feel that I should say something. I could tell him it's a pious society that prays and fasts for the benefit of the poor in the world. Something like that."

"And how would you explain your initial denial? If it's just a pious society, why wouldn't you have said so in the first place? While you are at it why not tell him that Jesus was a member of the Royal House of Windsor. You've put yourself in an irretrievable position, Leno. We will handle the matter at this end. You know how we operate, Monsignor."

"He's a friend. I don't want anything to happen to him."

"All that will be done will be God's will," the voice on the other end of the line said soothingly. "This is not your province. It is not your area of expertise. You don't have the skill."

Leno felt like he had just gone from being a star performer to a season ticket holder. His ego was as deflated like a balloon stuck with a pin.

"I know I could get him off the trail."

"You don't know enough about the matter to do anything. My dear Leno, you are one of my most prized colleagues. You keep us so thoroughly informed. That is where you inestimable value lies. You also know loyalty means obedience to my decisions."

Leno's heart felt like a sailboat rising and falling on the Mentor of Viri Lucis's affirmation and rejection. Recently his trust in the Mentor had waned. He had doubts. His objections were coming too regularly. Now once again the Mentor's rejection far outweighed his affirmation. A steel door had been pulled down on the entrance to any compromise.

Only yesterday, before Danny had called him, he had called the sacrosanct number and vehemently objected to what happened to Michael. He didn't mention Pope Charles although he had his suspicions. He was appeased by the Mentor's assurance that he would be Michael's replacement. The carrot had been too inviting and so once again he had capitulated to Viri Lucis' plan of action which, in effect, was the Mentor's plan.

"I just thought …."

"I forbid you to do or say anything," the Mentor's voice was low like the sound of a steel file on rough wood; his words were as hard as a fist.

In a more mollifying voice, the Mentor said, "Why don't you wait until I send my emissary to you? He will be able to dramatize the ramifications of this situation for you."

Leno's strongly felt reluctance to capitulate finally crumbled.

"All right," he said with a heavy sigh. With that they both disconnected without so much as a goodbye.

The Mentor turned to the young priest sitting in front of his desk. "Go to him at once. Do not mention the will or the note." Then with a sigh that sounded more like exhaustion, he said, "Our brother has become too troublesome of late.

"Try to persuade him. If that doesn't work, assess the situation and do whatever has to be done. Do it with utmost prudence. Not like those two imbeciles I sent to our brother, Michael."

Three mornings later Monsignor Leno Cappelli was found dead in his bed. He had apparently died of a heart attack in his sleep.

The phone sounded. Gene Shilling, pastor of St. Gertrudes, viewed the face of Monsignor Richards, Secretary to the Cardinal.

"Father Shilling," Richards spoke in a solemn tone, "I have some very sad news for you."

Gene felt his heart skip a beat. What now?

"Monsignor Cappelli was found dead this morning," Richards continued sounding like the most sympathetic mortician, "and he named you as his executor."

Gene was stunned beyond belief. "Are you sure?" He realized what a stupid question that was as soon as he had asked it. "I mean how?"

"No autopsy yet, of course," Richards had switched into his usual brisk, business-like voice. "But it seems he died of a heart attack. You, of course, will be making arrangements for his funeral. Please come by as soon as you can to pick up Monsignor's will."

"I will, Monsignor," Gene was still in a daze. "Later today."

The phones were deactivated and Gene sat back hardly able to process the information he had just received about Leno. Leno was such an alive person. Bubbling over with enthusiasm for life. He and Joe Daniels were his closest friends.

Gene continued sitting, not touching his cup of coffee. He was a short and stocky man. Even though he was getting a bit flabby, he was still obviously muscular. His red hair was thick and unruly. His eyes sparkled with magnetic compassion. He was lost in thought about his friend Leno.

It was Leno who had encouraged him when he was thinking of applying for the seminary. "Try it, Gene," Leno had said, "if you have any doubts about becoming a priest, the doors always swing out. No one will force you to stay."

The priesthood for Gene was a second career. He had been a successful businessman. At age thirty-five he was vice president of a small but flourishing import-export firm. A big fish in a little pond, he used to say. He was generally credited for the 'flourishing' aspect of the company. He enjoyed his work but he always felt something was missing.

Or more accurately that there should have been something more, something lasting. He wasn't especially a people person. More a flitting, hail-fellow-well-met. He could listen to people's problems easily enough and forget them just as easily. He had a good resume and knew he'd be moving on from Schleisher and Corbash Import-

Export. He had wisely invested his money and owned his own home. Life was good. But his life was hollow.

He was a regular church goer and contributor but that was about it. Yet he suspected in more pensive moods that there was a lot more to his faith than going to church. And so he had taken Leno's advice and applied for the seminary. He was accepted with no problem. Eventually he was ordained and now he was pastor of this sprawling, well-to-do suburban parish.

Gene sat there sipping his morning coffee without actually tasting it. He sort of expected things to go on. There would always be Leno. Now Leno was gone. He'd have to tell Danny. Danny was as close to Leno as he was.

Gene wasn't someone given to sentimentality. It's just that first there was Michael McCann's horrible murder and now Leno's sudden death. It wasn't sentiment as much as a feeling of anxiety about the precariousness of things, about the mortality of it all. He wished that when he was confronted with mortality, he could live the words he prayed each day during Eucharist, " …. as we wait in joyful hope for the coming of our Savior, Jesus Christ."

Gene prided himself on being an orderly, efficient administrator. He had taken a parish that had potential and made it fiscally sound. He had organized it and made it a center of service at least for the parishioners.

But, he wondered, when he died, would that be all people would say of him? An efficient administrator? Had he died suddenly of a heart attack today, would people say he had been a loving pastor? He doubted it. Yet he was sincerely concerned about his people. He did what he could to help whenever he could. But there was always a distance.

Perhaps the distance was due to the fact that he had been in and out of love several time before he had entered the seminary. There had been Gloria who was delicate and caring, a lover of beauty, gentle and loving. They could have been happy together but he wasn't ready for a lifelong commitment and he didn't want to lead Gloria on. She was just too good for that.

She had thought there was marriage in their future. He felt miserable because he knew he had broken her heart when he told her he wasn't ready for marriage. She had cried quietly but there had been no accusations, no lashing out. Gloria just went away. He had felt so selfish, so cruel but he was realistic enough to know that marrying Gloria would have been even crueler.

There were several other women he dated. Nothing serious until Rebecca came along. He had fallen head over heals in love with her. Rebecca was strong-willed, determined, opinionated, coy, elegant, beautiful and most of all, elusive. He never felt sure of her. There were times when he believed she really loved him. Most of the time all he knew was that he was absolute crazy about her.

Rebecca seemed to enjoy his company. They had mutual interests, the main one being that they both wanted to get ahead, be successful. But Rebecca was ambition personified. A workaholic. Nothing would ever interfere with her career as managing editor of FashionNet, a women's channel that did a hundred million or more annually. She made no secret about wanting to be executive editor.

So when Gene had proposed to her, her response was simply, "No." She had said she was too busy to even think of getting involved in all that marriage required. What goes around comes around, Gene had thought at the time. You break a heart and get your heart broken in return.

Those experiences coupled with the intense indoctrination on celibacy in the seminary had left him, he surmised, emotionally empty. He felt incapable of relating to others on a deep affective level. Yet as a priest he could always help people without getting emotionally involved. The priesthood allowed you the luxury of being clinical.

He filled his days with work. He enjoyed reading. He had some friends with whom he played Bridge. He knew he was likeable, had an easy laugh and, in fact, was quite charming. There were enough things to keep him busy. To keep his mind off himself.

Most of all he was a problem solver. He enjoyed being challenged. And once he got his teeth into something, he had the jaws of a pit bull. He couldn't rest until he reached the bottom line. And that filled his days. His ability at problem solving was the source of his self esteem. He convinced himself he didn't need close-up affection to reassure him.

Emotional involvement, he was convinced, would rob him of the control he felt he needed to be an efficient pastor. There were times of regret because he didn't relate to people on an affective level, that he was so abstract about human emotions. But then he would just get busier. And he did accomplish a lot. His people admired him. He knew that. And admiration would have to fill the gap in his emotional life. There were days of joy and days of heartbreak. But that was true of everybody's life.

From his experience as a layman, he had a deep respect for those who knew the stress of the workaday world. He knew what it was like to come to church on a weekend searching for some peace having been distracted by all the troubles and problems of the preceding week. He would never manipulate his people. He would always try to help them to find that peace they so desperately desired.

The one thing that bothered Gene the most was that so many people did not have problems with spiritual development although that is what they called their problems. Most people had deep-seated psychological problems. So instead of being a spiritual director, Gene found himself in the role of psychological counselor.

It wasn't, for example, so much a problem of being unable to live the gospel dictum of loving others as Christ loves us as it was a lack of self-esteem and self-acceptance that blocked the living out of Christ's command to love.

He remembered telling this to Danny and how Danny had found the same difficulty. Danny had said, "If grace builds on nature, then spiritual growth must be rooted in psychological health. What we need is more emphasis on psychospirituality."

Gene liked being a priest. He relished the work and truly liked the people he served. He sincerely believed what he was doing was meaningful. He tried to live up to something he had learned from Danny. Danny had told him not to be satisfied with challenging people's minds but to be intent on replenishing their emotional commitment.

If he had died suddenly of a heart attack, he was sure there would be enough good things people would say about him to make his life as a priest worthwhile. There wouldn't be any tears for him but people would speak kindly of him and no doubt praise him.

Then again, praise and admiration from the people were not the ultimate criteria of his worth as a priest. When he stood before God, as Leno had done, it would be his dedication, perseverance, hopefulness and caring that would stand him in good stead, whether he was emotionally involved or not. In his own way he was, he felt, a loving pastor.

Gene roused himself from his musings and spoke Danny's number into his phone.

"Danny," I have sad news. Leno was found dead in his bed this morning. Apparently suffered a heart attack."

"Oh my God! I can't believe it. I just talked to him the other day. He sounded great." Danny decided not to tell Gene about substance of the conversation he had had with Leno at this time. "I can't believe it. He was in tip top shape. He worked out two or three times a week."

"I know. I'm still in a state of shock. He made me his executor"

Danny thought of his own situation as executor. "Welcome to the growing league of hypertense eager beavers."

"Yeah, I know."

"As a matter of fact, I was going to call you this morning about something in Michael's will I wanted to talk to you about. Have any time?"

"Sure, come over for brunch. We'll raise one in both their memories."

Danny and Gene had become very close friends over the past several years. They were around the same age. Danny had a few years on Gene. It was because of Gene's business acuity that he was assigned to St Anselm's, a sprawling, suburban parish filled with upward mobile executives and professionals.

Despite the potential wealth of the parish, it was on the verge of financial disaster. Gene's predecessor was a strange mixture of fiscal

41

incompetence and arrogant autocracy. The people he hadn't driven away showed their displeasure by withholding their contributions. Gene was a whiz with money matters and had a pleasant, outgoing personality. The affluent crowd seemed to have been coddled satisfactorily.

Danny remembered the day he went to welcome Gene to the deanery. Gene seemed gracious enough. But Danny thought Gene was a bit wary too. As the conversation progressed, Gene had said, in what Danny had later come to know as Gene's guileless integrity, "You're considered to be a maverick by the powers that be."

"A maverick?" Danny had smiled playfully. "How so?" He had asked as if already knowing most of the answer.

"Well, you don't often wear clerics."

"Complete with French cuffs and diamond studded links?" Danny had been obviously enjoying this.

"There are rumors that you have contacts among the brethren of organized crime."

"And I've invited prostitutes and tax collectors to dine with me." Danny had been toying with Gene and Gene knew it but he persisted as if he were a surgeon doing an exploratory.

"It's alleged that you make anti-institutional statements about the Church in your homilies."

"I've never advocated tarring and feathering the Cardinal or burning all his cronies at the stake. What's that line from Commencement addresses? 'Dare to be different.' The reality of that challenge is, Go ahead I *dare* you to be different."

"It's been said," Gene persisted, "that you go out of your way to prove you don't fit in."

"I wonder how anyone came to that conclusion," Danny smiled impishly.

"You don't respond to mail from the Cardinal's office."

"Oh, I have. I remember one such missive asking what His Eminence could do for his priests. I suggested His Eminence hire a full time psychiatrist."

"Actually, under present-day circumstances, that's not such a bad idea." It was Gene's turn to smile.

"But at the time I got called in and was told I was a smart ass and if I didn't keep a bridle on my loose tongue I could be buried. I can't cite the gospel value he was living when he threatened me. I'm sure he could have given me chapter and verse. Do you think St. Matt's is a tomb, Gene?"

"If it is," Gene had replied sincerely, "with you there, it's the tomb of resurrection."

It was an affirmation Danny never forgot. He received so few from his peers and none at all from the top. As time went on, they became through wit and humor and some very serious conversations closest of friends.

Danny remembered telling Gene in a more serious vein that he felt empathy for the bishops, even for the Cardinal. Those little bureaucrats in the Vatican who are positioned in powerful offices wreck havoc on a bishop's authority in his diocese. The bishops are as controlled as they control us.

"Those bureaucrats," he remembered saying, "can even manipulate the supreme priest, the Pope, by deluging him with incidentals. While he thinks he's busy running the Church, they're running him. It's a game and the name of the game is Religion. It has nothing to do with living their faith. I know that's a judgment that could be rash except for the historical evidence," Danny had concluded.

Danny arrived at Gene's around eleven. After greetings and mutual commiseration over the deaths of Leno and Michael they sat down to a light lunch. Gene poured two glasses of Chablis, raised his and said, "To our two departed brothers."

"To Michael and Leno," Danny said with obvious sadness.

"Now what is it you wanted to tell me about Michael's will," Gene said as though he was starting up the computer of his mind.

"It's not so much telling as it is showing," Danny responded as he handed Gene a copy of the note.

Gene read it, put it down and said, "Well?"

"Viri Lucis. Does it sound like some kind of secret organization to you?"

Gene smiled. "Not necessarily. It could be some kind of pious society."

"I have my doubts about that, Gene. We have priests in favor of the ordination of women, priests for an end to celibacy, priests for the preservation of the life of the preborn, priests advocates of peace and justice.

"All kinds of groups of priests for or against this or that, but at least you know what they stand for. Viri Lucis seems to be as anonymous as an unsigned letter. Why? If they're a pious group or a group dedicated to some social work, why does there seem to be a shadow of secrecy enshrouding them?"

"Maybe they want to keep their good works hidden. Maybe they're elitist and they just don't want any Tom, Dick or Harry joining. The Knights of Columbus have secret initiations. That doesn't make them subversive."

"Okay but what about Michael's reference to the Pope's death?"

"Remember, Danny, Michael was an ultraconservative. Even more than I am. Maybe he was praying for the Pope's death and felt guilt because his prayers were answered."

"I called Leno and asked him if he knew anything about an organization called Viri Lucis."

"And?"

"And I thought or at least I got the impression that he knew something but wasn't about to tell me."

"Danny, you know Leno. He always acted like he knew more than he did. Now, of course, he knows far more than he'll probably be able to handle. May God give him rest. Personally I wouldn't react on what you have read into Leno's response to you.

"For all you know he was putting you on. After you called he probably scrambled all over the place looking for information on an organization called Viri Lucis.

"If I were you, Danny, I wouldn't manufacture problems for myself. Talk to Celine. She can give you legal advice or refer you to some lawyer who's up on these things. Forget about secret societies."

"I do have a call in to Celine. She's away, I guess. She hasn't gotten back to me yet."

"Good. And follow her advice. Forget about secret societies and ecclesiastical intrigue.

How is Celine, by the way?"

"Good. We're still very close. It has its advantages but also its stress." Danny didn't have to go into detail. Gene knew and had done more than enough to help Danny through his trauma three years ago.

INTIMACY

As Danny drove home from Gene's, he began to think again about Celine, probably because Gene had asked him how she was. Well into the second year of their friendship, after they had finished dinner and Danny was getting ready to go, they stood at the door saying goodbye. It happened as spontaneously as a bird chirping. They kissed.

At first it was a tender almost innocent kiss between two friends. Then it became a searching passionate exploration.

That's when their friendship turned into intimacy.

It was rapturous. Physical. And despite the sage moral opinions to the contrary, Danny believed it was spiritual.

Danny went home that night in ecstatic wonder. How long had he known that he was in love with Celine! But now… Now he knew she was in love with him or at least that she loved him. His emotions were kaleidoscopic. Joy, exuberance, happiness, unbelievable wonder at himself, at Celine. Still there was anxiety, dread, a feeling of betrayal too.

How would they respond the next time they saw each other? Would they be embarrassed? Would Celine apologize and say they shouldn't see each other anymore? Oh, God, he prayed with all the energy of his new-found emotions, don't let that happen.

Maybe they would just talk the whole thing through. Certainly after their tender, passionate lovemaking they couldn't act as if nothing ever happened.

Celine was so practical. She would be able to work them through this. But he didn't want some kind of closure which would bring the physical expression of their love to an end — a love that had grown slowly and steadily from the soil of mutual concern for others and for each other.

Theirs was not a one night stand. Danny was absolute on this. It wasn't superficial physical passion. There was far more to it.

Something deeper, richer and their entwined bodies were a symbol of souls that long ago had become one.

It was sacred, damnit! How many people in their lovemaking were as selfless as he and Celine had been?

Danny knew in his heart that Celine's happiness was all that mattered to him. Still if she said that it would make her happiest if they would never see each other again, would her happiness be truly of supreme importance to him?

Oh, God! What was happening? Was he in fact being selfish? Was he only concerned about what he wanted? How did he know that Celine didn't want what he wanted too? Why was he putting himself through this self-inflicted torture?

What was wrong with him? He was once again manufacturing problems. This was immature. I'll just take what happened between us for what is was, he thought, a beautiful act of love and forget it. I'll just put it in a compartment of my mind and get on with my life. I'll just be nonchalant. Things like this happen.

Who was he trying to kid? His love for Celine was sincere. Profound. Real. And he was certain her love for him was the same. They could love without being physical, couldn't they? Oh, God, what a mess! Yet what an enthralling mess! He felt so alive. Filled with the wonder that someone as beautiful and talented, as tender and clever as Celine could actually love him. It had to be love.

It wasn't mere physical attraction. Not just blind passion. That would trivialize what had grown and been so carefully nurtured between them. The love he felt for Celine was so worth treasuring that hoarding it seemed like a virtue. Yet there was a premonition, an ever-present ache that his love would be beyond the reach of total realization.

He had to stop this. All this thinking and questioning. He had to wait. The best thing to do was wait until he and Celine could sit down and talk this through. He was certain that her insights would guide them, elucidate the situation, if not offer a solution — if a solution was warranted or necessary.

The next evening Danny went to Celine's apartment. No sooner had Celine opened the door than she threw her arms around him and kissed him in a long sustained expression of love. Suddenly like the stone tablets rumbling down Mount Sinai in an avalanche, Danny, as somber as a tomb, whispered, "We can't continue a physical relationship." He said this not so much with determination as with pleading.

Celine looked as if a bomb had exploded. Her face crumbled from free floating joy to soul wrenching shock. "Second thoughts?" she almost sobbed.

"You do understand?" Danny whispered.

Celine gathered herself. "I don't but if that's what you really want, then shall we be close, dear friends?"

"I want that very much," Danny had tears in his eyes as did Celine. "We don't have to give physical expression to our love for one another," he said, but without much conviction.

"So you're putting me in the position of seductress?" Celine sounded harsh.

"No, I'm putting us both in the position of being loving friends," Danny said soothingly.

"A one night stand?" Again Celine sounded harsh.

"That's cruel," Danny said plaintively. "I still want a relationship with you, you know that. Do you … want a relationship with me?"

"Well, if that's the only offer on the table, I'll have to take it, but not without horrid disappointment," Celine spoke more softly now.

"Then it's friends … forever?" Danny tried to smile.

"Friends forever," Celine sighed.

With that, Danny gave Celine a peck on the cheek and excused himself and left.

Still Danny was surprised at his renewed tenderness toward his people. He couldn't do enough for them. And with Celine coming to help him, having her there, working together, he wouldn't even touch the decision made.

PARISH ROUNDS

The next day Danny decided to make some parish rounds. As he drove down the street toward the hospital, he couldn't help but admire the pride some of the people took in their homes. Not all lived in hovels. But like his church building, these homes were fighting a losing battle against time and its legion: pollution, wear and tear, heat and snow, aging and collapse under constant usage.

Still, for Danny, the neighborhood was like an antique shop that stretched for blocks. The Alley, as the area had been nicknamed long ago and beyond memory as to why, was not a slums. Perhaps two or three steps above. But, as with beauty, so with The Alley: Ugliness is in the eyes of the beholder.

There was a kind of comfort in the crowded row houses. Each one seemed to lean on the next. It was a kind of metaphor for the interdependence of the people here who were struggling to survive or hoping to leave one day.

The Alley was a sort of way station on the road between poverty and solvency. The road was like the journey of a soul from original sin to holiness. The point of departure was well marked. The destination was never too clear but you knew somehow it was somewhere.

Danny knew, of course, that his analogy broke down because only a few would make the whole journey out of The Alley. Most would stay.

He tried so hard, so diligently to extend a healing hand to the oppressed in The Alley. But, he realized with acid desperation, he couldn't even speak a healing word to the oppressors.

He returned to the rectory in the late evening. Exhausted and depressed.

At the hospital there were three stab wounds. He asked one of the victims how he got stabbed. What he was actually asking was, "What kind of a brawl did you get into?" The man stared at him for the longest moments, then he growled, "How did I get stabbed? I got stabbed because somebody stabbed me!"

At the last shut-in's home he encountered the woman's daughter. She asked if she could talk to him for a few minutes. The few minutes lasted for three quarters of an hour.

She sobbed and broke down a few times as she wove a tale of tragedy about her marriage. Her husband was an alcoholic. There was no marital relationship with him. Basically he was a good man. She didn't hate him. She disliked him with all her heart. How could she go to Communion feeling the way she did. She was trapped.

What did her future hold for her? She didn't care anymore. Maybe if she tried harder. He didn't respond to her except with sarcastic name-calling. She had no marketable skills. She was trapped. She had been for counseling and that helped some. "I need help. Some advice," she cried.

He knew what she wanted. He had seen it so many, many times. She wanted him to wave that good old supernatural magic wand. Make it all nice again.

He was honest with her. Told her she was in a destructive situation. Suggested that she try to get involved in some charitable work. Maybe she could get a part time job and work herself into a position where she might become financially independent.

Even as he was saying it, it sounded like pie-in-the-sky. He knew from experience that she wasn't going to make any kind of a change. As with so many of these situations, hers seemed hopeless.

As Danny neared the rectory, it began to snow. He parked and got out of his car. He stood gazing up at the dark sky watching the white flurries floating down to the ground. He put out his tongue and caught some of the snowflakes on it in a kind of holy communion with Nature.

Strange, he thought, how falling snow had a warmth about it. Perhaps it was the warmth of peacefulness like the quietude of God's blessings. For a few moments the snow buckled from an enormous gust of wind as though a reminded that peace is never lasting, that life is always being disrupted, that beauty can be disfigured.

Soon there would be icicles drying their way back to empty clouds. The cycle would continue, the creative force of divine sustenance was captured in snowflakes on a winter night.

Now sitting in the kitchen he was feeling helpless. A feeling that was becoming a habit lately. His words, his advice, seemed so unrealistic, so useless. And that was another feeling he was experiencing more often than not — uselessness. Or was it a hopelessness that matched the situations he was encountering?

If he had any hope at all, it was a hope that sought security in a flight from reality. In his life to date the pulse of things as they are was abandoned under the pressure of things as they might be.

Then he shuddered. Could it be as radical as a lack or even an absence of faith? If faith is the religious expression of trust, perhaps he was not trusting in God's power working through him. All the training, all the reading, but when push came to shove....

It could be a crisis of faith. Another one. Still without a crisis there is no growth. Without questioning, there is no maturing. But when push came to shove....

That phrase brought back the memory of the woman whose husband had been electrocuted at work. The inevitable question, "Why?" from the man's wife had evoked words from him like mystery, the overall scheme of things, God's ways are not out ways. Bland words, empty words in the face of this woman's disaster.

"You priests," she had all but sneered. "You're so glib in the pulpit while you're quoting scripture or rules or just feeding us pabulum. But when push comes to shove, when reality comes crashing in on you with a flesh and blood impact, you stand there muttering pious bromides from the sideline of life."

Her empty eyes wounded him, cut through to the deepest dark recess of his self-preservation.

It had been a harsh encounter. It left him emotionally debilitated weeks after. Was what that woman said true? Not totally. There were times when he didn't strike out. Times when he heard those precious words, "Thank you." And it made the struggle seem worthwhile.

As he opened a can of soup and buttered a couple of slices of bread, he decided he was just having one of those bleak days. The only thing that worried him was that bleak days were coming more and more frequently.

He recalled something his first pastor had said to him, "There's nothing more pathetic than someone taking himself too seriously." Maybe that's precisely what he was doing, taking himself to the conclusion that some problems are unsolvable?

Still, it was the people. The ones who were suffering. The ones he couldn't help.

How many times had he sat in Church not saying a word of prayer for fear he might scream at God. How easy it is to talk about justice. But when you meet injustice in the flesh time and again, what's left but a scream? Then he remembered a line from somewhere, God doesn't hear the cry of the poor, God is the cry of the poor. Is the whole thing a screaming match between us and God?

He remembered his friend Steve Rinko telling him to lighten up. Telling him to be more clinical. "I haven't heard you laugh in months," he had said. Danny had muttered something about there not being much to laugh at. Steve, in his usual direct, unvarnished manner, replied, "You'd better get your ass out of that inner city before you end up in an asylum somewhere."

What was that he had read? When you're locked in the cellar of an asylum, look around for the wine. How often he had preached about celebrating your humanness? Some celebrant he was!

Of course it had been a bleak day. The news about Michael was still griping his heart in a vise of sadness. Then having been called in by the Chancellor and told he was the executor. Being given Michael's will.

"We will take care of the funeral arrangements," the Chancellor had said. "His Eminence will give the eulogy. It's a very touchy situation. You understand. Diplomacy and all that involves," the Chancellor had said.

Even though he was made to feel that he was incapable of handling it and given the impression that it was only with deep regret that the will was being handed over to him, he had felt relieved.

Then the people he had met this afternoon, their hopeless situations or situations they were making hopeless, he deserved a bleak day. He found himself smiling at his own wry humor.

He wondered if the people had any idea of the feelings of inadequacy a priest experiences. With few exceptions most of the people see him appear on the weekend as if out of nowhere. They see him in control or even as a controller.

Do they have the slightest inkling of what goes on in his daily soul — his doubts, his questions, his desperation, the wrinkled torment of his regrets, the heart-withering loss of passion?

Or did they just see a priest as someone who does or does not appear on time or is there at the time of a death or at marriages? Some, of course, did realize that a priest was human, born into a family, liable to moral failures, with his own developed or underdeveloped social abilities.

But in general, he was convinced, people usually regarded a priest as someone who treated them nicely or gruffly, who did or did not have time for them no matter how trivial their concern might be.

What did it mean, To love the people? How do you love "the people"? You can give them service and hope your motive is love. Sometimes you even felt something like at a baptism or a wedding. But were you *feeling* love?

Besides, did the people want you to love them? Or did they just want you to be there when they needed you for whatever? He'd been over this before, many times. He never came up with a satisfying answer. For now as before, he would just keep on trying to be helpful. Nice when he could be. Challenging when he should be.

Oh well, at least he had listened to that desperate, trapped woman. Then again his listening wasn't as keen as it once was. Perhaps he just didn't want to hear these tragedies anymore. Maybe he was blocking out any emotional response. Maybe he was far more clinical than Steve had given him credit for.

Yet, he wondered, isn't his concern, even his discouragement over the sufferings inflicted on people or those they inflict on themselves a form of love? Perhaps, after all, love is a rapturous torture. In the end mortality wasn't just the limitation on a life span but the limitation on life's energies and possibilities.

He thought of Janie from third grade again. Did he cry? He couldn't remember.

Time for some more positive self-talk.

Still was he taking these negative feelings, these doubts, these imponderables too seriously? How many times had he himself said that he wasn't on this earth to solve everyone's problems? Wasn't this all part of what it means when you say God is Mystery?

Another day had come and gone and he still had not heard from Celine. Perhaps, no, certainly, what had gone on between him and Celine was weighing down his whole emotional system.

As exhausted as he was, he decided that as soon as he finished eating he would take a "stroll" up in The Block.

The Block was two streets north of the rectory. It was actually made up of four or five blocks. This was the hell hole of The Alley. The center of drug dealing and prostitution. He was known there. He would walk around, greet people and sometimes even get into a conversation if anyone was willing to talk.

Sometimes he was even able to help.

There was one drug addict who had just got out of prison. Danny was able to get him to come around to the rectory. Through several conversations he finally got the addict into Common Ground, a residence where thirty day programs were held for alcoholics or the drug addicted.

Once he had got a young prostitute into Vision 90. This was a ninety day program which helped to reinforce people's sense of dignity and self-worth. They were able to teach some basic skills so that a prostitute, for example, wouldn't have to go back on the streets. The people at Vision 90 also helped dropouts to get their G.E.D's.

In all the years he was at St. Matt's, he had helped just a few people. The drug dealers were beyond redemption and were a threat because they didn't want Danny to be taking away their clients.

Most of the houses on The Block were boarded up. They were owned by Allan Pendington, a dean at Chicago U. He had inherited them from his father. He was an absentee slum lord. Danny had tried to contact him to ask him to fix up these houses and perhaps sell them for low cost housing.

Pendington never responded. These houses were easily entered and were used for drug deals and prostitution.

In The Block, Danny had experienced everything from jovial curiosity to outright belligerence, from being greeted with smiles to being cursed at.

One day during Danny's second year at St. Matt's a Black man came to the rectory. He wore an outlandish fur coat, gold chains hanging from his neck, glittering rings on each finger.

"I am Kingpin," he announced with a wide toothful grin like someone who knew that he was the victor and to him belonged all the spoils.

Behind him were two scrawny looking younger men. They looked treacherous. The kind who would knife you while they were waiting to buy an ice cream cone.

"I have come on behalf of the free enterprise system we so dearly treasure and delightfully enjoy in this great nation of ours," Kingpin stated as though giving the State of the Neighborhood address.

"You, Reverend, have been interfering with this system. You have been responsible for the loss of two of my best workers. Not to mention untold numbers of clients. I should sue you for breech of contract. The contract, although unwritten, is that you don't interfere with me and I keep hands off your labors in the Lord's vineyard."

Danny had just helped two young girls to get off the street and into a program to help extricate them from a life of prostitution.

"I am here to tell you that if you continue this interfering, I can't guarantee your safety," Kingpin rolled the words around as though he were a wine taster.

Danny stood in absolute silence. His eyes did all the talking. They said, You're a lousy rotten pimp. And, The line has been drawn.

Kingpin became flustered at Danny's refusal to respond. "Do I make myself clear?" Kingpin asked.

"Perfectly," Danny finally answered. With that he began to close the door. The two rat-faced hoodlums made a move toward Danny. Kingpin held up his hand signaling them to back off.

"I'm glad we have come to an agreeable understanding, Reverend." With that Kingpin turned and walked away.

Danny put a call into his detective friend, Lou Mc Dermott. "I know you're homicide," Danny said, "but you have contacts with the narks. I have an address of the kingpin drug lord in The Block. He just made a threat on my life. So I figure the best offense et cetera."

"The sonofabitch. Excuse me, Danny."

"My word of choice under the circumstances," Danny tried to sound lighthearted without much success.

"Give me the address. A couple of guys over at nark owe me. I'll push them from this end and you lay low. Stay away from The Block."

"Thanks, Lou. It's not just me. I worry about our kids here at St. Matt's. Their parents just don't want to get involved. I can't blame them — retribution is no farther away than their front stoops. Still noninvolvement is like an open invitation for the drug pushers to swoop down on these kids like vultures."

"Don't worry, Danny. Something'll be done."

Three nights later there was a raid. Kingpin and a number of his Board members were hauled off to prison. For how long Danny didn't know. What he did know was that Kingpin could be heard for blocks screaming he'd get that goddamn priest.

As far as Danny knew Kingpin was still serving time.

The drug dealing was still going on in those boarded up houses the esteemed dean of a prestigious university didn't want to bother with.

Danny left the rectory not knowing which dwellers of The Block he would encounter this evening. People living on the edge of existence, morose feelings, their constant companion, despair, the thrust of their belief that they were unlovable.

Will they ever realize that human love is the reason for the universe's standing ovation? In The Block Danny found it more difficult than anywhere else to believe that in the slow motion of life's hopeless drudgery, God's eternal music beckoned his children to dance.

Could his presence there be the transparency of God's love for these Block dwellers who are God's children, perhaps his most precious children? As he looked into the faces of these poorest of the poor, he could see the isolation and loneliness of a dead spirit. Could he cause a resurrection in any one of these people who never pondered God's Poem made flesh.

Danny walked along the street. The clouds were resting on the black velvet of the winter sky. The sun's explosions were unechoed on earth. The frigid embrace of the winter wind sucked the air out of his lungs into ghostly puffs of haunting reminders that he was alive, that he was here for a purpose.

Danny found himself longing for the more sumptuous weather of Spring and Summer when he would take a drive out of The Alley into the countryside where the unfurled blood-red vermilion waited for his reverence and appreciation. Where the courteous grass would invite him to leave behind the barren pavements of the city and feel life curling through his toes. Where the sensuous sweep of a ripening field beckoned him to enter vulnerably into the many resurrections of his life.

But for now he pulled the collar of his coat tighter around his neck. The snow that had followed him home had now gone back to the steely clouds to await the opportunity of an ambushing onslaught.

The people of The Block would be there. They were the people of all seasons. Tonight the Arctic cold would find a refuge in their winter souls. Concetta, the premiere prostitute of The Block, would be there. She would babble on about how she could make more money in two nights than a clerk in a store makes in a month. Her dispassionate eyes would squint as though the bright vision of a better life would blind her. And Danny would feel her unadmitted outrage at her way of life cutting through her apologia like a razor-sharp blade.

He knew that the severest cross of all was not bitter opposition but pleasant indifference. The burdening feeling that what he did would make no difference. The realization that the situation would never change anymore than a river changes its flow toward the ocean.

Danny prayed that he could marshal his zeal or his routine commitment, whichever it was, against malice not against human frailty. He prayed for the courage not to fear failure.

He tried to identify himself with the Eucharistic presence of Christ in the tabernacle hoping to stimulate his belief that his presence in The Block, in The Alley, would be power.

He made his way through the snow to The Block.

THE UNRAVELING

As exhausted as he had been, Danny woke up in the middle of the night. His mind was churning like a turbine. Memories of Celine were still flooding his half wakened consciousness.

Why were these memories coming back now? Was it Michael's murder that suddenly switched a conscious spotlight on and focused it on the most devastating loss of his life? The loss of Celine.

He remembered how it gradually dawned on him that loving each other was not all that mattered.

After the ecstasy, reality began to set in. Some mystic said, "After ecstasy, the laundry."

What was obvious, as they tried to maintain a "loving" friendship, was that their easy conversations had begun to turn into edgy disagreements. They weren't the kind of disagreements that people have and patch up with sincere apologies. Rather they dug deep into the very soul of their relationship.

"Where are we going with this 'friendship' Danny?" Celine had asked petulantly as she stood in the center of her living room one evening.

"I don't know," he had answered guardedly.

"I think you do. Nowhere!" she almost shouted. "I told you when we first met that I had doubts about entering into a lifelong commitment and then I was talking about marriage." Celine had turned her back on Danny.

"With our situation being what it is," Celine had turned now to face Danny, "I certainly don't have to worry about a lifelong commitment, do I? I mean, what do we have? How long does it last?

"Up until now neither one of us has even spoken about the future. Our future. On the bottom line of practicality, we're living a fantasy. I told you I like to plan ahead. How do I do that with this relationship?"

The disagreements had become open, harsh arguments. At first Danny was bewildered. He had thought things between them had been going well. When he voiced this feeling, Celine had accused him of being a typical man. "You're so insensitive that you can't see what is right in front of your eyes," she had cried.

In return Danny had accused Celine of being naive. "You agreed to keeping our relationship on a 'friends forever' basis," he had said in the most wounding way he could. "Don't forget, Celine, you were the one who extended the initial invitation. Why did you get involved with me in the first place?" He couldn't believe he was capable of being so harsh.

"Look," Danny persisted, "I thought it was working. Our just being loving friends

"So I'm the one who can't control her desires? Very human desires," Celine sobbed.

"Not every human desire can be gratified," Danny was challenging.

"You've had years of training and living a celibate life. I haven't," Celine retorted. "And I don't at all relish the idea of being in a celibate relationship."

They were both relentless. Things they had previously overlooked or tolerated now poured out of their mouths like corroding acid, disfiguring all the beauty of what they had had together.

The arguments became more frequent and rancorous. It got to the point that they weren't even bothering to call each other. It had been a brutal time for each of them. When they did infrequently get together, the vibes between them were more like death-dealing rays.

Every time one or the other had tried to broach the matter of their ending their relationship, the arguments exploded like a volcano.

"This just isn't going anywhere," Celine complained repeatedly.

"Where the hell do you expect it to go?" Danny retorted. "What do you want from me?" Danny fired back.

Each one felt the other pulling away more and more. Each felt emotionally battered. Each one refused to make a move either toward a solution or toward ending the relationship. It was like being damned forever in Limbo.

On another occasion when they met for lunch if for no other reason than to fulfill a mutual obligation, Celine said in a muted tone, "I gave myself entirely to you. You took and then went back to your priestly duties." She pronounced the last two words with venomous sarcasm.

"And you," Danny retaliated, "are so afraid of an honest relationship that you thought you could use me to escape it. You knew from the start that I couldn't make the kind of commitment you're saying you now want from me," Danny almost pleaded.

"You're a real study. Trouble is I don't know enough psychiatry to deal with you," Celine was vociferous.

"This is the gentle, caring Father Joe all the poor in The Alley love. I never met anyone who could be as cruel as you. You talk commitment. Well, what about yours?" Celine began to sob. Danny could feel nothing but anger.

"How did we get to this point?" Danny's voice was choked. "My God, Celine, all we have meant to each other and here we are tearing one another to shreds. We're like two predatory animals. Celine, we have the most wonderful, the most beautiful friendship ...."

"We did for a while. But it's going nowhere." They were both talking in more subdued tones now. "Danny, you just can't give me what I want. Or you won't. Can't you see I'm torn. I don't want you to leave the priesthood if you don't want to. At the same time I can't go on with this .... this makeshift love we claim to have for each other.

"We can't go anywhere in public. To the symphony or to a cocktail party as a couple. For those occasions I 'use' George. God help him." She raised her hand and brushed her hair back. "God help me."

"It's .... well, it's like two kids sneaking around when they've been grounded," Celine complained. "I can't take you home to meet my parents. What would I say, 'Hi, Mom and Dad, this is Danny. He's my dear, dear friend. He's a priest. We almost had an affair, but we just did it once."

"And it was once followed by regret and remorse," Danny's eyes shot anger like a saber.

"For you," Celine shot back with the same sneering anger. She was fury. A woman spurned…

"I guess the strain, the unreality of it all is getting to me," Celine's voice was a rasp. "I don't know how to handle it so my frustration erupts in outbursts of anger. We *are* tearing each other apart. Neither of us deserves that. What we have …. had …."

"Is too sacred to, in your word, desecrate," Danny finished Celine's thought. "The question is, What are we going to do?"

"Danny, we can't just keep pretending we're friends. That's unreasonable. Irrational. Impossible."

"Then, to use your words again, we call it quits?" Danny couldn't help inflicting another hurt. He was hurting with such unbearable pain he just wanted to make absolutely certain Celine was too.

"Why don't we wait for a while?" Celine said ignoring the way he had phrased his last comment. "Wait until we can be certain that we're basing our decision on more than emotional pain."

"Okay. Shall I call you?"

"Please."

For several weeks Danny could not bring himself to call Celine. His premonition of an end turned him into a coward. During this time he prayed. He was shocked to realize that his prayer was becoming more focused, more intense.

It was as though the love he felt for Celine was being transferred to God. Or was it that he was seeking some substitution for the lack of response from Celine? He felt empty but not depressed. Perhaps he was asking God to fill the void somehow.

He wasn't quite aware what he was praying for. He just sat there in the dim old Church and kept repeating, "I love you, Jesus, my friend." He just wanted someone to say back to him, "And I love you." Celine hadn't said that in ages. He felt so tortured, so alone. Was this a kind of dark night of the soul? Was he being prepared for something he couldn't begin to comprehend? What was God doing in his life? What was he doing in God's life?

He sat there in silence. Not just the silence of the empty Church but the silence of his soul. A silence that veered from anxiety to calm and back again, over and over. He wished he could chuck the whole thing. Start all over again. Clean slate and all that involved. But he knew that was daydreaming not prayer.

Finally, one evening Danny went, unannounced and uninvited to Celine's apartment.

Celine pushed the button and the door became transparent. She saw Danny standing there like a disenchanted nomad. Celine pushed the other button and the door slid open. Celine did not get up but watched Danny walk into her apartment as she slid the door shut.

"Hello, Danny," Celine said in a tone as close to neutral as it could be.

Danny noticed that her dining room table was covered with printouts and note paper. She undoubtedly was plunging headlong into her work. He envied the way women could do that or at least appear to be able to do it.

"What's up?" Celine asked with transparent indifference.

"Nothing much. Same old routine. Hanging in."

Silence.

"Celine...."

"Look, Danny, we've got to talk this through."

He felt like saying, "It's about time," but he stood there immobilized.

"Sit down, please, Danny." Her tone had shifted into that caring, concerned way that had always attracted her to him.

"Danny, this relationship.... well, it's just not going anywhere." How many times had he heard that. But this time she sounded prepared as though she were addressing the jury with her closing argument.

"I mean it's obvious to me that there's nothing for us in the future. It's obvious that you're married to the Church and, well, I just can't spend the rest of my life being your friend. I want something more out of a relationship. I want — I need — a love that gives me a feeling of security. A hope for the future. Not just the feeling of a high school crush."

Then in a rush of words, Celine said, "Danny, it's time to call it quits. The relationship is over, caput, ended. There's nothing in it anymore for me or for you. To continue it would be a charade."

"I know this sounds cruel to you," Celine was already on the verge of tears and this time Danny's heart was breaking, "and you're probably ready to clobber me with a remark like, 'Quitters are losers and losers are quitters.'

"I wanted to say something to you long before this but I was afraid of hurting you. And now I can see from the expression on your face that no matter when I said what I've just said, you would end up wounded.

" I know my behavior lately has been a breach of the first rule of effective communication: Speak out on an adult-to-adult level. But in the last several weeks you haven't made much of an effort to communicate either. And so it's been building up in me since we last talked. I just have to get it out in the open once and for all."

Danny felt his emotions freeze. Even though he knew what Celine would say to him, he was stunned. It was like expecting someone to die and yet being shocked when death finally arrived.

He got up and started to leave.

"Aren't you going to say anything? There were tears in Celine's voice.

"What's to say? You've given me your bottom line, your decision, your conclusion. I've given you my heart *and* my soul." With that Danny turned and walked out.

Now it was Celine's turn to be stunned.

Danny had no idea how he would react. Never even thought about his reaction.

What was he supposed to do? Sit there and argue her back into the relationship? He had seen a sign hanging around her neck: My mind is made up. Don't disturb me with discussion.

He was crushed beyond words, beyond feelings. He walked for what seemed hours, not even noticing the ink-stained clouds draped over the stars as though hiding in the darkness his feeling of humiliation. Later he could not remember one thought he had.

And that is how their intimate relationship ended in the Fall of 2028.

Danny saw Celine's image as he answered the Viewphone and heard, "Hi." It was Celine's familiar greeting. "Hi," he responded as he clicked on his viewscreen.

"I'm sorry, Danny. I was at home visiting my folks for a few days. I called as soon as I got back and heard of your friend's murder. "

"That's okay," Danny said pleasantly.

As Danny looked at Celine's image, he couldn't help but feel a stirring of his emotions. She was even more beautiful than when he first had met her. Was he experiencing regret or longing? Whatever it was, he was conscious that he had never gotten over her. That he still loved her. It wasn't torture. He was beyond that. But the emotions he was feeling were sharp and real.

"I saw that horrible story about the bishop being killed on NewsNet," Celine said sympathetically. Also there was the statement from the Cardinal's office saying that although you were the executor, that office would handle all arrangements."

"Yeah, the story's been all over the NewsNet," Danny said.

"It sort of gets you off the hook, doesn't it?"

"As far as the funeral arrangements go," Danny laughed nervously.

"Well, all you have to do is get yourself an efficient lawyer and turn the whole thing over to her or him."

Danny paused. If there was anyone in the world he could trust, it was Celine. Quickly he told her about the note. About Viri Lucis — Men of the Light — and Michael's asking for forgiveness for the death of Pope Charles.

Celine let out a heavy "Oh my God!"

"Is the note witnessed?" she asked immediately.

"Yes by his secretary. Monsignor John J. Travine. He's a young, up and coming priest."

"Was it notarized?"

"Yes."

Sounds legit to me," Celine still sounded overwhelmed or perplexed. Danny wasn't certain.

"It's not so much what the note directs me to do," Danny said, "but what is Viri Lucis? And what in the hell is he talking about as far as the Pope's death goes? There's also a diary. Michael's. It's in his own handwriting."

"You've got yourself a problem there," Celine sounded like what she was, a lawyer. Are you free to tell me what the bishop's worth was? I've heard he was quite wealthy in his own right."

"I'll tell you but it's in strictest confidence. Approximately $500 million or maybe more."

Celine left out a low whistle. "He was indeed quite wealthy."

"The McCann family," Danny said simply.

"I hate to sound crass on such an occasion, but as executor, you could come into several million yourself."

"I hadn't thought about that," Danny said almost in a distracted voice.

"You never were swift on finances, Danny," Celine laughed pleasantly. Whoever said it was right, Danny thought, laughter is the shortest distance between two people.

"There'll have to be grants set up.... trust funds.... for the kids...." Danny's voice drifted off . Celine didn't know whether he was lost in thought or just totally overwhelmed.

"You were always supersonic when it came to generosity," Celine said sincerely. "What are you planning to do with this matter about Viri Lucis?"

"I haven't the slightest idea, Celine. I did call someone I thought might be able to help, Leno Cappelli. He's a close friend and someone I entrust confidences to. I think he knew something but whatever it was, he wasn't talking. And now I just found out Leno died suddenly. Apparently of a heart attack."

Celine paused as she wondered if Danny had told Leno Cappelli about them. She shrugged.

"Danny, how important is it for you to find out what Viri Lucis is? Or what the bishop meant when he denied involvement in the Pope's death? I mean does it matter as far as your fulfilling your obligation as executor?"

"Probably not. I guess it's just my accursed curiosity."

"Can't say I blame you. That note would arouse the curiosity of a manic depressive."

"I'm not sure what to do, Celine."

"Why not go through the papers and the diary. See what you can find. Then make a decision."

"Sounds good. I'll get back to you as soon as I find out anything that may throw light on the damnable note."

"Okay, Danny, and, Danny, watch out for that obsessiveness." Celine laughed quietly but empathetically as they disconnected.

THE FUNERAL

"I'm standing here in front of the Cathedral of the Holy Name," the magnetically attractive blonde, pixy-like, well-endowed, driven reporter whose humble goal was to become the premiere anchorwoman, Dawn Sylva of Channel 22XL, intoned solemnly, "The Archdiocese of Chicago is still reeling from the murder of one of its most outstanding churchmen, Bishop Michael McCann.

"As most of our viewers already know, Bishop McCann is from one of the wealthiest families in the nation." Dawn Sylva stepped to her left so that there was a view of the procession going into the Cathedral. The cameras focused in on the Cardinal who looked devastated.

"The murder of Bishop McCann remains a mystery," Dawn Sylva had put on her most intense expression. "Sources high up in the police department have said little except they are continuing their investigation. Other sources from the Cardinal's office have revealed that apparently it was a robbery. Police did not confirm this.

"There is a rumor of a possible serial killer being involved in Bishop McCann's murder. Many in the Archdiocese considered the relatively young bishop as a probable successor to the Cardinal who will be retiring within the next few years."

Dawn Sylva paused as the camera made a silent panoramic shot of the last of the procession and all the people standing outside the Cathedral. "It is obvious from the expressions on people's faces that there is deep sorrow over the sudden death of this beloved bishop.

"Once again the citizenry is wondering if this will be yet another unsolved murder in the city of Chicago. The feeling that the police are more interested in taking care of their own affairs, threatening, as they did last year, to go on strike if they did not receive an eight percent raise than they are in solving brutal murders of prominent citizens like Bishop McCann." Dawn Sylva seemed to wince a bit at her last convoluted sentence.

She recovered immediately. "The Cardinal himself will preach the eulogy and 22XL will bring you that sermon live. A Father Joseph Daniels is the executor of Bishop McCann's estate which is rumored to be in the hundreds of millions. We tried earlier to get a statement from him but he refused to go on television. We do have an interview from Monsignor O'Henyeu, the archdiocesan spokesperson which was taped earlier today." Sylva nodded. On screen appeared Dawn Sylva and Monsignor O'Henyeu, the archdiocesan Secretary for Communications.

O'Henyeu stood a little under six feet. Too heavy but despite his weight, his face was handsome with twinkling eyes, a head full of wavy silver hair, a perpetual grin that quickly flashed into a congenial smile No one, except the media snipers, would ever guess that behind that carefully carved veneer of sophistication was a buffoon.

Sylva: Monsignor O'Henyeu, can you tell us of any further developments in the case of Bishop McCann's murder?

O'Henyeu: One development, Dawn, is the overwhelming sadness that has enveloped the entire Archdiocese from the Cardinal down to the lowliest member of our church....

Sylva: I mean about the solving of the murder.

O'Henyeu: Thanks to the efforts of our fine police force I think this horrendous murder will be solved within a week or so.

Sylva: What basis do you have for that judgment?

O'Henyeu: Oh, I have my sources just as you do, Dawn. Of course I can't reveal them just as you can't, Dawn. There is no doubt in my mind that Bishop McCann's murder is the result of a carefully planned conspiracy. Confidentiality oozed from his squinting eyes.

Sylva: A conspiracy? That's the first I've heard of a conspiracy. You can elaborate on that, can't you? (Disbelief and doubt dramatically scarred her lovely, classic features. She fluttered her long eyelashes in a please-stop-the-bullshit gesture).

O'Henyeu: Now, now, Dawn, you know I can't. But I will say this about that. There are a number of disaffected liberal Catholics who have made secret threats against the lives of some prominent clergymen, myself included. He knit his brow in austere bravery.

Sylva: Your life has been threatened? What possible reason would anyone have for killing you? (Sylva's face registered genuine amazement and she gave all the appearances of trying to stifle a smile or perhaps out-and-out laughter).

O'Henyeu: Well, as you know, Dawn, I hold a very prominent position in the Archdiocese, open as I am to full public view. When I speak the truth of our religion on behalf of his Eminence, the Cardinal, there are those — and their number is growing by leaps and bounds — who would like to silence me even by the most violent means. (He swept his hand in a huge semi circle to indicate the vast number of liberal Catholics who would like to bring his life to a sorry end).

Sylva: I find it hard to think of anyone who would want to stop you from talking, Monsignor. Is there any truth to the rumor that you may be appointed a bishop to take Bishop McCann's place? (She looked too eager for any kind of an answer. The smile on her face seemed to be an facetious endorsement).

O'Henyeu: I myself have heard that rumor, Dawn, and may I say that I am humbled by the thought that there are so many in the Archdiocese who are convinced that I would make a fine bishop. It is, of course, an honor I would never seek but if the Holy Spirit should reach out and tap me on the shoulder, I would humbly serve in that august capacity. (His demeanor was that of total self-effacement).

Sylva: Well, you are probably the best known clergyperson in the entire Archdiocese except for the Cardinal, of course.

O'Henyeu: Thank you, Dawn. Even though I try to keep a low profile, the duties of my Office force me to make myself as available and public as possible. And may I say that, thanks to my strenuous efforts in this direction, the relationship between the Archdiocese and the media has the best record in the entire nation. Wouldn't you agree, Dawn? (A large toothy smile).

Sylva: We seemed to have strayed from the purpose of our interview. What I want to know and what our viewers are eager to hear is what is the Archdiocese going to do about solving this murder?

O'Henyeu: We will support the police in their efforts. I myself am working on offering a substantial reward for any information that may help us to solve poor Bishop McCann's murder. I am thinking of going on NewsNet and pleading with the culprit or culprits to give themselves up. I can be most persuasive as you know from interviewing me so many times, Dawn.

Sylva: Well, thank you for taking time out from your busy schedule, Monsignor O'Henyeu.

O'Henyeu: Thank you, Dawn. And remember, my time is your time anytime.

"And there you have it," Dawn Sylva reported with a straight face. An in-depth official report on the murder of Bishop McCann. Monsignor O'Henyeu is convinced that the murder of Bishop McCann will be solved within a week or so. All the police have to do is find the conspirators if they are aware of their existence.

"And all the people will be given an equal opportunity to help the police because of the reward the good Monsignor, who we may soon be calling Bishop, is offering.

"This is Dawn Sylva. Now back to the studio where the live coverage of the funeral will begin to be broadcasted." She smiled captivatingly as though trying to live up to her coveted epithet, The Golden Girl.

Homicide Detective Lou Mc Dermott sat in his office staring at his T.V. set. "Shit!" he moaned. "That crazy O'Henyeu has set the investigation back by God know how many months. Conspiracy! The guy is the biggest bullshitter since Barnum. Solved in two weeks? Thanks a million, you crazy …. Shit!"

Michael's funeral was exactly what Danny had expected. All pomp and circumstance.

Danny, as he also expected, was excluded except for being an altar concelebrant. The Cardinal had been most gracious to him.

"How is everything going at Saint ….?" the Cardinal had asked, standing there in the sacristy. Danny hadn't seen him for a long time. He looked thin and drawn and his thinness made him appear taller than his five feet ten. He looked preoccupied but that had always been a trait of his. In two years he would be retired and then what? What for him and what for the Archdiocese?

The Cardinal's worn look reminded Danny of a poem he had written, "What Price Power?" Part of the poem ran:

> "Gulping down divine flesh not in communion of holiness but in the destitution of craving like that of First Parents who haunt us with their appetite to be gods for which All Power crucified paid the nailed down price for meanest people's haughty ambition placed at the service of a haughtier God."

Danny looked again at the old man who had had such plans for him. "One day, Joseph, you may take my place here in the Archdiocese." Thinking of his poem in reference to the Cardinal had been an act of rash judgment — a sin Danny still had to conquer.

"Everything at St. Matt's is going as might be expected," Danny had answered courteously.

"What a waste," the Cardinal has murmured. Danny wasn't quite sure if the Cardinal meant St. Matt's or him or both. He decided he'd treat himself to a shot of self-esteem and conclude the Cardinal meant him.

The Cardinal spoke in glowing terms about Michael. "A priest's priest." "Someone who was destined to be a great Church leader." "Struck down in his prime." "God had other plans for him and now he would lead us through his intercession at the throne of the Almighty." "Death is always a mystery but this kind of murderous atrocity is beyond human comprehension."

Danny was beginning to think His Eminence should have quit while he was still making sense. On the other hand, Danny thought, the Cardinal was the master of the sound bite. Anyone of his descriptions of Michael would have made a grabber of an opener on the evening news. "Truly a martyr," the Cardinal continued.

Danny couldn't help but notice that the Cardinal never explained how Michael's murder was the equivalent of or even analogous to martyrdom. Another solid sound bite.

The Cardinal concluded by thanking Monsignor John Travine for his loyalty to Bishop Michael McCann and asking prayers for those who martyred this sterling, outstanding, holy bishop who never flaunted his wealth. Danny couldn't help but wonder how much of the wealth the Cardinal hoped to dump into the archdiocesan coffers. Why was he so intent on rash judging the Cardinal? An authority figure? His own lack of power?

During the rest of the Eucharistic celebration, Danny's thoughts wandered. Why was Michael killed? He was so non threatening, so unobtrusive. He never ruffled a feather in his life. Was there a relationship between Michael's murder and Viri Lucis? If so, what was it? If not, why the note? Would he find any answers in Michael's diary?

How much would Michael be missed? Had he been destined to be a leading churchman? He hadn't heard a word from any of Michael's brothers. Strange. There they sat. Stoics. Wealthy. Emotionless. Powerful. Should he contact them? Who killed him? Not a word from any of the Cardinal's gofers except that one call to tell him he was out of the circle.

There was no doubt in his mind that all zeal for spreading God's kingdom through word and action ends here in a somber casket.

He wondered what he would be thinking about as he lay on his deathbed waiting for the end of the beginning. A beginning of what? The formal teaching is eternal happiness or eternal punishment.

Wasn't that strapping God into the simplistic straitjacket of either/or? How typical of our human fear which rushes to lock God into our flimsy, choke holding definitions. Oh, there was purgatory to stave off giving into the temptation of final despair over our habitual failure to live up to the ideals set before our human frailty.

It's all so neatly wrapped. The fact is, Danny mused, that no one knows. Not even in the Resurrection did Christ ever tell us what it's like to be dead. Once again he would pray for the strength to face what he did not understand. That seemed to be his habitual prayer lately.

Danny thought of a story he had read. A woman approached a priest about her son who was into selling drugs and prostitution. She suspected that her son had been involved in a few murders too. She was worried sick that here son would die and be sent to hell.

The priest asked her to picture herself sitting beside God on his judgment seat. He told her to visualize her son standing before God. After she had done this, the priest asked her what she was feeling. She cried out loud and said, "I feel such pity for my son, such love, such a desire to forgive him."

"And what is God doing?" the priest asked.

"He's getting up. He's taking me by the arm. We walk down to where my son is standing. Now all three of us are in an embrace — and we're all crying."

"If you, a mother, have such love for your son that you're willing to forgive him, what about God who is infinite Mercy itself?" the priest concluded.

To die is ultimate sadness, Danny thought. But to be killed is inexplicable waste. How many had he seen killed, or as it is commonly referred to, "wasted" in his years at St. Matt's?

Drug overdoses, drug wars, young lovely girls murdered while plying their trade as prostitutes. Life snuffed out before it was even begun to be lived.

Like a cloud pierced by a mountain peak and rendered motionless, Danny's imagination dwelt on all those who had been and are being massacred in the "Holy War" between Christians and Moslems over the past forty years. The wasted blood. The stockpiled bodies.

What was it the legendary twentieth century scientist, Einstein said when he was asked what weapons he thought would be used in a third world war? He said he didn't know but he was certain the fourth world war would be fought with stones and clubs.

When you think of the hundreds of thousands killed and being killed, it's numbing. But when you think of just one individual whose fledgling hopes are ground into the dust of death in a nonsensical war, it's devastation beyond bearing.

What irony! Here we are at the beginning of the twenty-first century preparing to send human beings to explore the planet Mars while here on earth the mythical god of war, Mars, reigns.

Then there are those trapped in loveless marriages whose asphyxiating boredom is broken only by occasional fits of hatred. Many die. Murdered by their loveless marriages. Death at the hands of hopeless desperation. Death of the human spirit, once proud and courageous, now like a fortune squandered in the effort to keep up the appearances of success.

Death is the context of life. The moment we are born we begin to die is the axiom. Danny shuddered at his morbid thoughts and images. Yet death somehow keeps our maverick imaginations from carving passageways into a pastel never-never land.

Danny turned his head slowly. He stared at the casket so stately positioned in the middle aisle. Here lies Michael McCann. Why? Michael, Michael, you moved in and out of our lives with such careless ease, leaving us to stalk your memory.

What dreams, hopes, ambitions, sacrificial commitments, joys, laughter, images lay in that solemn box. What happens to them in eternity? Are they all satisfied and disappear into some ecstatic NOW? Or do they grow in intensity, expanding in their influence on us who are still here?

The rituals of burial force us to face the sadness that life is experienced only in its incompleteness. Perhaps that's what keeps us striving to live life to the fullest. A defiance of mortality in the hope of gaining the tranquility of immortality.

Whatever else, death should be the reminder of immortality. Of the fact that we are homeless and that death is the doorway into our everlasting home. Danny'd have to meditate on this image more. He needed the hope it gave. The hope that life is worth living whatever else it may be.

After the burial, Monsignor Thomas O'Henyeu, Diocesan Secretary of Communications, approached Danny. O'Henyeu had been all over the television screens for the past week or so. He obviously loved it. In his most sonorous tones he had entreated the guilty parties to step forward and accept God's forgiveness — never alluding to their having to accept death by lethal injection together with that forgiveness.

His facial expression on NewsNet was a professional mix of bewilderment, sorrow, serenity under excruciating circumstances and trust in God to whom he reverently lifted his eyes as if on cue. He too was a master of the sound bite — probably trained the Cardinal. "An incalculable loss to God's people." "… now he is heaven praying for the forgiveness of his murderers …" " …a legacy of love and service …" "mourn the dead by serving the living …"

Danny wondered if O'Henyeu believed in anything but the mellifluous sound of his own voice. Word was the media vultures wouldn't believe him if he told them rain was wet. Mouthing deep sincerity was their castoff phrase for him. Still they buzzed around him like flies around a manure pile.

For them O'Henyeu was a jig step on life's arid way. Trying to get substantial information out of him was like trying to eat Jello with chopsticks. At least that's what Danny had heard. He couldn't help but smile and hope he wouldn't burst out in laughter.

The media loved O'Henyeu precisely because he never caught on to what an obvious pompous ass they were able to portray him as on the tube. Danny wondered if O'Henyeu ever heard the snickers of the cameramen.

From what Danny knew about him, O'Henyeu was a man of average intelligence who was clever enough to parlay his mediocre abilities into the brilliance of opportunism. He thrived on frenzy. He exploited every chance he could to make himself glamorous in the steady, gaudy lights of T.V. cameras.

O'Henyeu's entire record as the P.R. person for the Cardinal could be summed up in one word: Advancement. He filtered all reality through his fantasies of self importance. In fact his fantasies were his reality. How well, Danny thought, O'Henyeu worshipped the god of firecracker fame.

"Joseph, my boy, I'm so glad we were able to meet even if the circumstances are so unutterably tragic. I was so hoping I'd run into you. There's something urgent we must talk about." Danny winced.

76

O'Henyeu was only two years older so where did this "my boy" come from? Besides, O'Henyeu could have picked up the phone days ago and called him.

"It's the business of Bishop Michael's will." Danny always laughed inside himself at the insistence on the use of titles. He had said to Leno one time, "How come we have to address everyone in the hierarchy by his title and yet we can call the Son of God made man by his first name?"

And just because O'Henyeu was one of those who all but demanded he be addressed by his title, Monsignor, Danny said, "What's so urgent, Tom?" Danny took fiendish delight at O'Henyeu's discomfiture.

Danny thought of that story about the bishop who told his priests he had had a vision of Jesus. One of priests asked, "Did Jesus talk to you?"

"Oh yes," the bishop answered with sincere gravity.

"Well," another priest asked, "what did he say to you?"

Steeped in the most profound humility, the bishop answered, "Well, Jesus said to me, 'Your Excellency ....'"

"Well, now, Joseph (O'Henyeu retaliated by emphasizing Danny's first name) it has been decided that the amount of Michael's fortune would not be released to the media. I tell you this so that you'll be on your guard. Of course, according to archdiocesan policy, you are to refer the media folk to me."

"Thanks for letting me in on the know, Tom. It's the first time anyone has given me any consideration since it was announced that I was Michael's executor."

"Yes, well, I always try to accommodate, as you know. I must take my leave now. The media folk will want a few words about today's ... about this tragic event."

Danny smiled as he watched O'Henyeu strut away as though he were heading for the other side of the stage.

No doubt there would be rumors flying around about who would get Michael's job as Vicar General\ General Secretary. What a shallow scene we play on the stage of life, he thought. And barely has the actor left the stage than the audience is off to another studied distraction.

MEMORIES

After Celine's brief conversation with Danny, she sat there for the longest while remembering. Every so often after a conversation with Danny, she would fall into reveries of what had been and how it came to an end. The winter twilight softly enveloped the room like the presence of a cherished memory.

She remembered how she felt after she and Danny had called it quits as far as any physical exchanges went. At first she had felt bitterness as never before in her life even when her engagement with Bob ended. Now her whole world had collapsed again.

At the same time she wondered if she wanted what Danny wanted. Had she set out to be deliberately cruel? Had she subconsciously planned to start a relationship only to end it? Or did she sincerely want a total commitment from him or nothing at all? Did she expect Danny to leave the priesthood and marry her? Maybe and maybe not. She loved him because of what he was, a priest.

She knew she had been deliberately nursing her bitterness in order to keep her resolve to join in the ending of their relationship. She had been right. The relationship was going nowhere. She had given her total self to him.

What is it with men? It's just like in a sexual relationship. A woman gives her all. Her entire body, her most intense affections, a complete surrender whereas men are satisfied if they have their obsession with their orgasm satisfied.

Afterwards it's as if nothing had happened. A woman lies there craving further signs of affection that seldom or never come. Well, maybe that wasn't true of all men, but it was certainly true of the men she had been with, including Danny who thought he was so damn affectionate. Men don't even know!

Could she have been experiencing some guilt? Not at all. As far as she was concerned she had long ago liberated herself from what she considered a pathological need for total control in Church leaders.

The Church or at least some of its members in the ruling class had a perverse hang up on sex. She and a multitude of other women would have nothing to do with it and didn't see this as interfering with their relationship with God and his people. If Aborigines could get into heaven without the control of the Church, why couldn't she?

Hadn't she seen Danny come alive through their affection, their love? And not just for himself but for all those poor, miserable, lonely, unwanted people he dealt with endless day after endless day.

She had missed his rugged handsomeness. Those piercing blue-green eyes. That half smile that hid his sense of humor rather than revealing it. His thinning brown hair that always seemed a bit tousled from his nervous habit of running his hand through it.

But most of all she had missed his easy wisdom. It wasn't that of a know-it-all guru. It was so simple that it could go unnoticed until later when what he had said dawned on you. The time he talked to her about her relationship with her mother after she described her mother as a private eye watching her every move, wanting to know each detail of her life, personally and socially.

"Do you think you relate to your mother on an adult-to-adult level?" he had asked.

"I don't know. I guess I'll always be her little girl. And I don't want to hurt her."

"Sometimes you have to take the risk of hurting her feelings if you ever want to escape bondage. You don't have to hurtful. Only honest. When she asks you something personal, just indicate to her that you don't want to go into that. If she gets hurt, that is her problem. Don't always try to be a fixer. She treats you like a child because you allow her to do it."

Danny never went into a long verbal dissertation. He would just say enough to trigger your own thinking. He let you fill in the spaces and come to your own conclusion or course of action. It was one of his most charming attributes. He respected people's freedom and didn't need to control them.

Then there were times when he would smile and toss out little gems of wisdom during the course of a conversation with the ease of skipping a pebble across a pond. They were aphorisms that might make you laugh for a few seconds and think for a few hours. He'd say something like there are people with calloused knees who also have calloused hearts. Or many people who are closest to the Church may be farthest from God.

There was always his underlying preoccupation about the practice of religion without the living one's faith. But even in this preoccupation Danny displayed dismay more than anger. After all, he would say, we're the ones who trained the people.

He talked one time about a movie he had seen. In one scene the captain of a police precinct was excoriating a detective for being too sensitive when dealing with criminals. The captain, in a low, threatening voice he used to emphasize his point, said, "I go to Church every Sunday. I go to two or three prayer breakfasts every week. But when I put on my badge and gun, God is out of my life."

"That," said Danny with a sound of futility in his voice, "is a perfect example of practicing religion but not living your faith. Too many people, I'm afraid, put religion in one compartment and faith in another. Religious practice should flow from internalized faith values. But what should be and what is are generally two different stories."

And that was something else she had missed: his stories. Danny was a mesmerizing storyteller both in his preaching and in conversations.

Celine smiled suddenly as she thought of Danny's dry humor in many of his stories. They made her laugh not as you laugh at the punch line of a joke, but at the irony of the human situation.

There was one story Danny told her shortly before their.... the end of their relationship. It was about a priest — real or fictional, he never said —who was meticulous to the point of absurdity.

As Danny often said, "If you can't cope with absurdity, find the humor in it."

This priest liked to set everything up in a familiar pattern: his razor in the little flat dish to the upper right of the sink, his toothbrush hanging in the glass stand, the hand mirror, by which he checked the balding spot on the crown of his head, over to the left of the sink stand, the soap and dish next to the sink on the left-hand side, his shaving cream off to the right of the sink stand and so on.

Once he had set everything in its place and provided the cleaning lady put things back where they were after she cleaned, there wasn't much to think about.

He prided himself on the fact that he ran his life like he set up his bathroom. He'd organize the routine things, like where his notebook and favorite pen were, and then never have to bother looking for them.

In fact, he'd try to simplify routines. His communion call list was scheduled in such a way that he had to do the least amount of driving. He always made sure he had three of everything. Three tubes of toothpaste so that when he finished one and began the second he'd buy a new one, thus always three.

He liked to reach into his desk drawer and know that his paper clips would always be in the same familiar place.

One day he was out in the parish taking census. He expected this census call to be routine like all the others. He had a set of questions from which he never deviated. It was more orderly and the information he received was uniform. People rarely asked him questions in return. They would comment on the weather or mention how nice the decorations at Mass looked. If someone did ask something, for instance, about the parish council, he would quickly direct them to the minutes of the meetings published with robot-like regularity each month.

This particular census call was going well. "Do you and your family attend Mass each weekend?

"Yes," the attractive but slightly overweight woman replied politely as she glanced indifferently out the window.

"Do you and your family frequent the Sacraments?"

"Yes."

The priest smiled as he made the proper notations on the card.

"Where do you live?" the woman asked suddenly as her eyes seemed to burn away his shield of self-protection. Her tone was almost nonchalant like that used in small talk.

He was stunned by her question. Totally flustered. "Pardon me."

Where do you live?" she repeated with no sign of impatience.

"Uh, well…. in the rectory." He felt embarrassed because he couldn't control the trembling in his voice.

"Yes," she said almost absently, "but I mean, do you live in a room or an apartment or what?"

"In an apartment," he answered feeling more and more defensive. "I have a study, a bedroom and a bath." He could not for all the world figure out where this was going and he was now feeling invaded. Privacy was always paramount in his well-ordered life. Not just physical privacy but the kind of privacy that kept people at a deferential distance and cloaked him in an aura of unapproachable majesty.

"A bath?" she tilted her head in a way that made him feel that her whole body was curled into a question mark. "Do you mean a bathroom?"

"Yes," he found himself almost stuttering. "Yes…. a…. a…. full bathroom. Why?" With that word he seemed to regain his composure. Now he would put her in the position of self-revelation. He would invade her privacy. So in a louder tone he repeated himself, "Why do you ask?"

She gazed out the window as if she had not heard the question or was ignoring it.

"I have five children," she said in a distant voice that sounded more like a sigh than a statement of fact. "This isn't a very large house as you can see. My husband and I share one bathroom with our five children." She paused as if she didn't particularly care whether he responded or not.

He could feel the heat of a flush reddening his face. He was perplexed and embarrassed. Now why should he feel embarrassed? What in the world did this conversation have to do with his census call? What was this woman who was becoming increasingly annoying trying to say?

And why in God's name was she talking about bathrooms of all things?

"You asked if my family and I go to Mass every weekend," she looked away from the window and back at him. "Do you know how long it takes for the seven of us to get ready for Mass? Can you imagine what goes on here in the morning?

"Well.... I....I" He wanted to say he had never thought of it, but he knew intuitively that that was not the appropriate response. So he just sat there feeling stupid or ridiculous, definitely at a loss.

"I read a line the other day," she said as though talking out loud to herself. "It went, 'When others cry blood, what right have I to cry tears.'?"

"I'm.... I'm sorry, I don't understand. I...."

"No, I'm sure you don't," she cut in blithely, her confidence seeming like a velvet arrogance compared to his ragged discomfiture.

"Last week," she continued, "in your homily you said in effect that it wasn't enough to be charitable. You said we had to identify with the oppressed and feel the injustice that 'man's inhumanity to man' had so ruthlessly caused. She arched her brow as though she was seeking his concurrence on the accuracy of her rendition of his homily.

As though sensing the unspoken question, he quickly agreed while shaking his head affirmatively. "Yes, that's what I said and may I say that I'm flattered that you should remember so accurately. It's really most reassuring." His voice trailed off into silent embarrassment.

She was gazing out the window again. "It was nice of you to visit, Father," she said with a note of sincerity and the sound of an obvious dismissal reserved to those in charge.

He bolted as though the door of a dungeon had just been unexpectedly flung open. After a brief exchange of pleasantries he headed quickly to his car, never looking back as though he feared being sucked into that house with its solitary bathroom.

As he drove directly back to the rectory, he shook his head repeatedly. "My bathroom?" he exclaimed aloud. "My bathroom?" "Semi classic," he demanded and relaxed as the soft, soothing music flooded the inside of his huge Oldsmobile like warm, uterine water.

Soon he was humming along with the music. This afternoon, he thought, he would put his index cards of quotations in better order. He would double his efforts on his homilies. He felt quite satisfied. Imagine how that lady had remembered so much from his homily! She had really affirmed his efforts.

Celine wondered why she thought of that story from among so many Danny had told. Perhaps like the priest in Danny's story she had missed the point. The point of their relationship. Did she subconsciously want too much order in their chaotic romance? A place for everything and everything in its place?

She shrugged her shoulders. Maybe she had been too rash. Should she have talked to Danny about eliminating the physical from their expressions of love? Sure, and she could have also discussed with him the possibility of building a one rung ladder to the moon!

Celine had poured herself a very dry martini and began to pace slowly back and forth from the dining room to the bedroom, trying to put things into perspective. She went into her bedroom and took a box from the shelf of her closet. Perhaps because of her methodical way of handling her life, she made copies of what she considered important letters she wrote. She placed those letters in this box. Seldom did she retrieve any to re-read. This time she wanted to read a letter she had written to her sister at the time she was deciding to bring her relationship with Danny to an end.

> Dear Sis,
>
> I'm writing to you not to burden you with my problems. I guess I'm just trying to sort things out. I don't expect you to respond to what I'm saying in this letter. You've already expressed your opinion on my relationship with Danny. As harsh as it seemed at the time, I have to admit you were right.
>
> What is it about love that makes us so vulnerable? How can I feel so much

pain and exuberance at the same time? Why can't love be simple? Why is it that love is what we want most and understand least? Why is it that I know that loving Danny is a dead end and yet I can still love him so desperately?

You can see why I said you don't have to respond.

I've decided that love isn't a mystery, we are. I know what you're probably thinking at this very moment. My sister, Celine, is schizophrenic. Aren't we all to a certain degree? One part of us wants all the love we can absorb. Another feels terror at the slightest movement of love that someone offers. Maybe I'm exaggerating. Maybe it's me. But this is the way I'm feeling right now.

And, as you always say, feelings are neither good or bad. They are just there. I guess that's why I'm writing to you. To express my feelings.

I know how hard you have worked at your marriage, Sis. Love has to be worked at. But what motive do I have to work at this relationship I have with Danny? None!

I remember when I first confided in you about Danny and me and who and what Danny is, you said something to

the effect that it's better to be friends
for a long time than lovers for a short
time. Does that ever fit my situation!

Do you remember what Mother used
to tell us? "Girls, don't take sex too
seriously. It's not that it's frivolous.
It's just so crude." I'm still not sure
what she meant exactly. Maybe she
meant "rude" as in sex is a rude
awakening.

There are times when I truly feel
sorry for Danny — the poor celibate.
He was indoctrinated to relate to
women on a pragmatic level not on
the heart level. As a result he comes
from an exclusively male mindset.
He can't feel with his mind. Then
again how different is he from other
men? It seems there are always two
problems: the one you talk about and
the real one. I don't know which one I
am addressing in this letter. Maybe it
doesn't matter.

Danny and I have had some brutal
arguments. Even knock-down-drag-
out fights. When I think of the scathing
words, the verbal pummeling… On
both sides. I'm in no way excusing
myself. But I can't help but wonder
if what we had was love or just a
repertoire of passions. We certainly
were friends before we became
lovers. Although lovers is not exactly
what we were. As I told you, we made

love once. Or, perhaps, we just had sex. Afterwards he was a wreck, filled with guilt.

And so here I am writing to you, Sis, telling you that now there is nothing to soften the hard-edged despair of poisonous estrangement between Danny and me. The ocean of enthusiastic love has become a muddy rivulet of unresponsiveness except for the constant argumentative harping.

What have I done with what we had felt for each other? Did we dig so deep into our emotions only to use that depth to lay the foundation for the unscallable wall of separation?

There was one argument (read fight) when I told him outright that I wanted all I could get out of life for myself. And Danny retorted, "And who gets that?"

"Who gets the whole loaf in this life? Do you actually believe that couples, married or not, have all you imagine life will give you?"

I feel so selfish, Sis. Then he said, "I want your happiness as much as I want my own salvation. Tell me, before you met me, did you ever experience total happiness?"

He was so aggravatingly logical. All it did was to infuriate me more. And yet as I sit here writing you, it's becoming clearer that he was right. Is right. With each of my accomplishments I've felt a compulsion to climb another peak. There is in the very happiness of my satisfaction a feeling of emptiness which no craving can ever fill. There is no such thing as total happiness. How stupid I am. How utterly stupid!

It's all ended now. I must admit to you that I have been trying to keep a manufactured bitterness alive if only to help me to stick to my resolution. But there are times when I feel trapped. It's like that line Woody Allen made classic. "Never before has humankind stood at a crossroad like this one we have today. One direction leads to despair and utter hopelessness and the other leads to total extinction. May we have the wisdom to choose correctly."

See, I haven't completely lost my sense of humor. And I'm not bonkers either. I remember something my literature professor had said to me when he was returning a poem I had written. (Remember how we used to love to read our homemade poems to each other?). He said, "In the heart where memories dwell, there are tears, sometimes of delight, sometimes of sorrow. I see no tears in your poem."

Now is when I could write dozen of poems with tears in them. How's this for an opening line? "There is the sweetest torment in the uncertainty of love and the bittersweet yearning in the consummation of loving."

I'm sorry, Honey, if I've burdened you with my problems. I'm a big girl and I should have known better. I guess I just wanted to say, You told me so. But at least in writing this, I have been able to get some things off my chest and find some clarity.

Please pray for me as I do for you and your family.

With all my love,
Celine

REUNION

Celine put the letter aside and wiped tears from her eyes. She never did get a response.

After Celine had put the letter aside she called out, "Table light on." She sat in the long shadow which matched her thoughts. What strange twists life takes, she thought.

She remembered how she had been standing at the perfume counter right inside the department store. It was a few days before the Christmas of 2029 and she was getting a bottle of her mother's favorite perfume. In walked Danny.

They hadn't seen or talked to each other in little over a year. She couldn't believe her reaction. She tightened up. Her stomach did a roll. She couldn't control the thrill of anxiety she felt at seeing him. Danny, on the other hand, seemed rather composed just as though he had seen Celine the day before.

"Hello, Celine, how are you? You're looking wonderful."

It was awkward though. They both seemed to act like two seventh-graders at their first school dance. Celine had rushed through her explanation of why she was there. Danny had managed to get out something about last minute Christmas shopping.

Finally after preliminary comments that said little, Celine said, "Look, I'll be finished here in a couple of seconds. I know I did this before but how can life be an adventure without risks? I have the time if you have the time. We could go get a drink or a cup of coffee."

"Why not?" Danny smiled.

They strolled down the Mall to a small cafe. It was almost like the walks they used to take when they were so madly in love. Danny even thought he felt Celine bump against him but decided it was his imagination.

"I thought…" they both said simultaneously as they sat down at the cozy table in the cocktail lounge.

"You first," Danny feigned gallantry.

"I thought you might have called sometime," Celine said with visible discomfort.

"Same here," Danny failed at hiding his obvious uneasiness.

""Foolish, huh?" Celine half winced.

"Not really. Given the circumstances," Danny said reassuringly. "I think we both ended up convinced we were going nowhere. You just happened to hit on it first. You are incisive, Counselor."

They both made an effort to laugh.

"So," Celine asked as if she was searching for a clever way to bring back the easy feeling that always had existed between them, "what've you been up to?"

"Same routine, same problems, same rewards, same absurdities. If you can't cope with absurdity…."

"Find the humor in it," Celine finished the statement.

This time they both laughed out loud, sincerely.

"There's still Mr. Rosak to keep me on my theological toes," Danny said, trying to keep the conversation on the light side.

Mr. Rosak was one of Danny's favorite tales. Mr. Rosak was a shut-in. Danny brought him communion every month. Mr. Rosak's theological opinion on Danny's always being three of four minutes late was, "You know, Father Joe, I'm glad you weren't with Jesus on his way to the cross. You'd have made him late and we might never have been saved."

One time when Danny had encouraged Mr. Rosak to make a mature confession of his sins by searching out his predominant fault. The next time Danny heard Mr. Rosak's confession, his penitent switched the order of his sins and made up new numbers to go with each one.

When Mr. Rosak was complaining about the loss of Latin, even expressing doubts that his sins weren't being forgiven what with the absolution spoken in English, Danny tried to explain to him the beauty of using our native tongue and how that enhanced the Sacrament of Reconciliation.

"Hee, hee, hee, I got you there, Your Eminence. My native tongue isn't English. It's Hungarian. Hee, hee, hee."

"Then there's Bess the Bag lady and part time Prophetess

"Dear Bess," Celine sounded almost whimsical. "Does she still come around with her sage prognostications?"

"Yep. 'Father Joe, if you eat the intestines of a cat boiled with hairs of a bat, you will come into so much money that you will never have to worry about those poor street people again.'"

" '*Those* poor street people'?" Celine laughed uproariously. "God love her."

"And you.... how have you been?" Danny asked with genuine interest.

"Well, you remember George Korbach?"

"The man you dated for the convenience of having as escort?"

"The very same. Danny, we were married during this past year."

Danny drew a deep breath, quickly regained his composure and said, "I'm so glad, Celine. I really am.. Are you happy?"

"We're quite comfortable. There won't be any children, though. George is 47 and I, as you know, am pushing into the vestibule of 36.

"Danny, I went into therapy. Not just because of us but .... well, you did say quite a few hard things to me. I resented them at first and for a long time, but then I began to reconsider.

"What if what you had said to me had any validity? I had to find out. Why was I having difficulty maintaining relationships with men? I had to know if there was anything radically wrong with me.

"I found out a great deal about myself. It wasn't easy. It wasn't enjoyable. Still I remember you telling me that without self-knowledge there can be no authenticity in our relationships with others, including God.

"That motivated me to keep going no matter how traumatic the experience was. Remember that song, 'Me and my shadow'? Well, let me tell you my Shadow Self was not anywhere near being my friend."

Celine stopped talking and fidgeted with her napkin. Then she continued.

93

"The therapist took me back to when I was a little girl, to the time when my kitten died. I was in first grade. I remember lighting candles after Mass and asking God to take her to heaven so she could wait for me until I would get there. I was heartbroken.

"I asked my father why God would take my kitten away from me like that. He said, 'It's God's will and that's all you need to know. You must be resigned to God's will.'

"I didn't know what 'resigned' meant so I decided it meant that I shouldn't ask my father any more questions about my kitten.

"As time went on, being resigned meant not ever questioning my father. Through some kind of spiritual osmosis God's will became my father's will or vice versa.

"With the help of the therapist I began to understand that I spent most of my life being resigned. I finally grabbed hold of something I could not admit or didn't think I had to admit.

"My father was dominant in my life. He was a lawyer. I'm a lawyer. He was a perfectionist. I'm a perfectionist. He was demanding of me. I'm demanding of myself. Duty was preeminent for him. I'm predominantly duty bound.

"And when I finally rebelled against resignation to my father's will, I struck out at the men in my life instead of against my father."

Celine's voice once again drifted off into silence. She looked around as if to see whether anyone was eavesdropping.

"Please go on," Danny said gently as he pushed empty his glass to the side of the table.

"You remember what I said about Bob." Danny winced internally as he recalled how cruel he had been to her about her decision to break off her engagement. "Well," Celine continued, "I came to realize that he really wasn't that much of a controller.

"He made suggestions and I interpreted them as demands. Unconsciously I was rebelling against being resigned to what he thought might be good for me. Objectively, he was thoughtful and considerate.

"And you, Danny, dear Danny, you didn't deserve …. I wanted to call or write but my therapist thought that it might not be healthy for me at the time. She was concerned about my inability to deal fully with the resignation thing, with my fixation on authority figures. You of all people know what that's like, Danny. You have plenty of problems with authority."

"More than I care to admit," Danny sighed. "And I'm guilty of many, many rash judgments in that area, I'm afraid."

"Danny, for me you were one of those authority figures."

"I'm not sure I ever thought of myself as that — an authority figure," Danny smiled.

Celine ignored Danny's comment and proceeded to reveal the results of her therapy sessions like someone who was rushing through a list of sins in the confessional.

"My therapist said that no matter how intimate we were, if I still perceived you as an authority figure, even unconsciously, I might, again unconsciously, submit to some kind of resignation to your power over me. Does it make sense? I don't want you to think that I wasn't concerned about us, about you."

"Certainly it makes sense, Celine."

" I guess my problem has been that I've always believed in what I consider God's greatest gift to us, our freedom. I've thought that people could take control of their lives and relationships if they wanted to. When I hear someone say, 'That's the way I am' or 'I can't change' I assume they're into a cop-out. What they're saying in effect is that they refuse to grow.

"I could never figure out why people would let their past hold them prisoners in their present. I realize that people do bury past experiences that can break out in other negative forms later in life.

"I know about complexes, Oedipus, inferiority and so on. But I've consistently believed that people could somehow deal with the cause and change the resulting behavior. Maybe that's being simplistic."

"But don't you see," Celine said as she continued to tear her paper napkin into small pieces, "that's exactly what I did. But I needed help. The therapist. Sometimes the cause is buried so deep you can't find it by yourself.

"Or as in my case, I just couldn't bring myself to admit that my wonderful, loving, affirming father was the most manipulative force in my life. I'm certain he never thought of himself as a manipulator.

"Danny, it was a scary experience. I never knew how much a person could bury. I had so much to let go of. I needed the support of a professional to help me. And then to change. I prayed so hard I thought I was becoming a latter-day mystic.

"But you know what? You were with me through the whole healing experience. All you gave me, your wise insights. Like when you talked to me about my mother. That was transference. I accused her instead of my father. That's why I interpreted her interest as being a private eye.

"I was hiding my really real self. When I tried to let that real self out, as I did with you, I couldn't handle me so I took it out on you, on others. At least that what my therapist and I decided.

"I should have contacted you, if for no other reason than not to let you hanging out there feeling whatever you were feeling. And to apologize. I really think I would have contacted you eventually. I just wasn't sure of myself. I may not be even now.

"My only control over my life was separation. And yet meeting you like this today, I feel secure, comfortable. I should have known. You are the one person I can trust absolutely."

"Thanks, Celine. Believe me I always wanted your happiness even more than my own. You embraced your Shadow Self and now you are in control of your happiness. Even if there are lapses, you will know what to do."

Danny nodded after he had paid the tab and they both got up from the booth. They went outside the Mall where there were pathways through the snow. They walked along slowly. Finally, Danny broke the silence.

"I remember a spiritual writer from the late 90s talking about what he called 'the hole in the soul.' By that he meant our feelings of powerlessness, our poor self image, our capitulation to our limitations. He said there was no other way to come to freedom and wisdom except through the hole in the soul.

"From what you've told me, you've regained your own power and broken through you limitations. I really feel so good, a kind of my own freedom, because you've dealt with all this and are coping. I am happy because you are happy. I feel right now like I'm babbling."

"Tough men don't babble, Danny. And you're one tough man. Behind all your sensitivity there is a backbone of strontium. It was your toughness that got me through that therapy, that helped me get an honest hold on myself. I knew you were suffering just as I was. But you were hanging in and that helped me to dig deep. I guess I'm pretty tough myself."

"You're tough all right. Whatever the reason, buried or not, you took a stand. You called it as you saw it. And you acted on your conviction despite the pain."

"You'll never know how much pain, Danny."

"I think I know."

"Of course you do. It was just an expression."

"Danny, my therapist said something I thought was so good that I went right to my journal and wrote it down. In fact, I committed it to memory.

"She said, 'In the hopes and dreams that encourage and sometimes afflict us, we seek to strip away the many layers of our self and of another's self. We continually search for our mutual core, believing that in the depth of my self, the other self is present.'"

"It's the mystery of being human, isn't it?" Danny mused. "The humanness that extends beyond the boundaries of the individual self, beyond a person's flesh and even his or her most secret thoughts."

"Exactly. The way I interpreted it is that I am a self but not existing in the midst of a multitude of other selves. I am a self infused into all others and they all reside in me. That's kind of heavy but I know what it means for me. And that's a source of help too."

"I'm pretty sure I know what you're talking about, Celine."

"And what about you, Danny? I mean about coping."

"I made a 30-day retreat after…. well, after we…."

"And were you able to get it all together?" Celine smiled with beautiful sympathy for a suffering soul mate.

97

" Eventually. Celine, it was thirty days of pure torture. All I could do is think of you. Morning, noon and night. I tried praying but next to nothing in that department. Gene Shilling, you remember him? From over at St Anselm's, you know, the Prince of Suburbia. Well, he helped me to recoup enough of my interior resources to keep going. As the saying goes, If you can't get over it, get through it."

" Was Gene shocked when you told him about us?"

"Not in the least. He was pure empathy. Of course he's been dealing with my doubts for so long I don't think anything I would say to him would even cause the arch of a brow."

"He said that real love is not based on illusions but on the reality of the two people who love each other. Love, he said, is rooted in truth. And truth means that no two people can satisfy all the needs of the other."

"We can only satisfy each other's needs partially and live with the rest, right?" Celine sighed.

"Celine, I'm sorry I couldn't give you more." Danny's eyes had filled.

"I think I knew that from the start, Danny. I guess I was angry with myself for not…. well, for not being more understanding of our situation. More compassionate. For, you know, blaming you. Wasn't I the one who told you that blaming destroys the bond we have with reality?"

" I always liked Gene," Celine had spoken in a way that sounded nostalgic for the times when the three of them would get together. There had always been such warmth among them. "There is a tenderness underneath all that glamorous bravado of his. Tell me, does Gene still do what he did with the Christmas flower money? "You know donating the money collected for Christmas flowers to the poor and then placing one huge poinsettia in front of the altar?"

"No. His people were in an uproar. They told him they donated the money for flowers not for the poor. They said if he wanted to donate money to the poor, he should take up another collection for that purpose. Gene didn't want a collection for the poor. He wanted his people to experience sacrificial giving. Sacrifice their Christmas flowers for the benefit of the poor."

"He told me," Danny went on, "that he had mentioned the idea several times in his homilies during Advent. I guess they weren't listening. Anyway they got to him. They told him they could afford both, money for flowers and for the poor, which is true. So Gene capitulated. It seems they missed the point.

"The irony is that we were the beneficiaries. We had enough money left over to buy a few poinsettias for our dingy Crèche. I told my people that the flowers were the gift of the people of St. Anselm's. They were thrilled at the thoughtfulness and generosity of the suburbanites."

"Religion versus faith?" Celine smiled as if reading Danny's mind. Danny just smiled back.

Finally Danny said, "Celine, there is something I need to tell you, and I would have called you long ago to say it, but I just couldn't face the possibility of a response of icy indifference from you."

"Maybe you would have gotten that kind of a response too. I would hope not but there just was no telling back then."

"What I need to tell you is that ever since that night, ever since I've known you, I've carried your spirit of love within me. It has made the difference between actually loving my people and merely giving them perfunctory service."

Danny paused and then continued. "What we had was treasurable for me these past years. Love brings its share of problems but the wise learn from them."

"Danny, I still love you, too. I think, no, I know I will always love you. Not with the same physical passion as I once wanted but just as passionately. And I owe you, too. Because of you, your dedication, even if you deny it as such, at least twice a week I take time out from my upward mobile rat race and help out at a half-way house for girls with all kinds of problems. I'm still trying to do my little bit."

Maybe, Celine thought, it had been the Christmas spirit or it could have been a maturer understanding of what love really is which both of them had come to realize over their time of separation, but she had recognized that they felt drawn to each other in a much more intimate, self-giving way.

Maybe they had been able finally to strip themselves down to the absolute nakedness of their souls. And through the alchemy of forgiveness they were able to turn the dross of egotism into the gold of authentic love. Maybe each one of them had been asking less for love and was willing to give more of love to each other.

There had been a long moment of silence between them. Not the kind of silence in which there is nothing to say, but a silence in which a conclusion to say something decisive was being reached. Abruptly, Celine had broken the silence. "Danny, I'll always be there for you but I won't be here with you." Danny had nodded in understanding and agreement. It was a Christmas gift neither would ever forget.

That day their forsaken intimacy had become genuine friendship.

That was almost a little over a year ago. Since then their affection for one another was truer than ever before, but the boundaries they had so carefully set were respected at all times. Theirs was a comfortable friendship of mutual concern and support. And George had been more than gracious. In fact, Danny and George had also become friends of sorts. One thing Celine felt she knew about both men in her life, neither had a jealous bone in his body. At least she hoped she was realistically perceiving the situation accurately.

Celine shook herself out of her reverie and began to think of the recent reality Danny had confided in her. She got up and began to pace. Anxiety tore at her stomach. If that note Danny had mentioned was as foreboding as she thought it was, Danny could be in for real danger from the ones the note cut out of the will, the Viri Lucis.

Celine waved and activated the Viewphone. She recited Danny's number. "Hi," she said. "Hi" came the response. Danny clicked on his screen.

"Look, Danny, I've been thinking. Why don't you make a copy of the note and put the original in a pneumatic tube in the bank for safekeeping."

"Good idea, Celine. I'll do it first thing tomorrow morning. Any other thoughts on this matter?"

"Not yet but I'll call you when I get some."

"Thanks, Celine. I'll be talking to you."

"Okay." Celine waved the phone dead. Danny's image faded from view. She went back to her worrying.

After Mass and breakfast the next morning, Danny watched NewsNet for a while. He usually scanned the lead stories, listened to the editorial comments and concentrated on the sports results.

He checked his watch. The bank should be open by the time he got there. He went into his study. He made two copies of the note and placed them in a strong box which he locked. He took the original and carefully placed it in an envelop, sealed it and put it in his inside coat pocket.

When he got to the bank he was greeted cordially by the Teller. He told her what he wanted and went through the process of obtaining a pneumatic tube.

"Collections going up?" the Teller teased laughingly. Danny just smiled.

After Danny inserted the note into the tube, the Teller recited the bank's code which changed each day. Danny then made an imprint of his palm. They left together chatting about nothing in particular.

THE VISIT

Archbishop Brown entered his office, pulled the drapes, spoke into his intercom. "I don't want to be disturbed for the next half hour," he growled.

With an indifferent wave of his hand he activated his Viewphone and punched in the sacrosanct number.

"You wanted me to call, Mentor?"

"Yes," came the smooth-sounding voice. "I want to see you here at your earliest convenience."

Archbishop Brown commanded. "Computer, access calendar." Then to the Mentor, "I can be there at seven this evening, if that is suitable."

"Fine. I'm looking forward to seeing you, David."

"Till then." Archbishop Brown pressed the intercom. "I'm now available."

That evening at seven o'clock promptly, Archbishop Brown was ushered into the office of the Mentor.

"Ah, my brother," the Mentor smiled graciously. "Please have a seat."

Dismissing all amenities, the Mentor got immediately down to the business at hand.

"It seems, David, we have a problem," the Mentor said heavily.

Archbishop Brown was visibly ill at ease. He said nothing. Just waited.

"Viri Lucis stands to lose millions of dollars. You are informed about our brother, Michael McCann's untimely death?"

"Yes."

"In his will, he left Viri Lucis approximately 95 percent of his fortune which is estimated at over 500 million dollars. But there is this note which purports to have cancelled the stipulation in his will. At this point the note seems legal enough. That, however, remains to be seen if we allow it to get that far which we won't. Am I clear?"

"Very."

"The note is presently in the hands of the executor, Father Joseph Daniels. Here is his complete dossier. You will notice that he was a student here in the Eternal City. Study it thoroughly. Father Daniels is very bright and as with most intelligent people, he is consumed with curiosity. He is not to be taken lightly. He is clever."

"What is it you want me to do?"

"David, you are one of the most — no, the most skilled diplomat and negotiator in Rome — in the Church today. That is why I prize you so highly. What is it they say about you? You could sell refrigerators to Eskimos." The Mentor laughed quietly but also forebodingly.

Archbishop Brown sat in frigid silence. What was this leading up to? What demands would be made of him? Would he have the ability or more to the point, the courage?

"David, I need you to visit our brother, Father Daniels. I need you to retrieve that note."

Archbishop Brown sat there wondering for a moment if he belonged to a well-oiled machine or was he just a victim of an oil spill? "And how do I do that? Retrieve the note?"

"Read the dossier. You will come up with some creative way of doing what needs to be done," the Mentor's focused eyes were as threatening as loaded pistols.

Archbishop Brown studied his calendar. "I have to go to the Holy Land and from there to Australia. When I am finished there I can fly directly to Chicago."

"Fine. And, David, pleased be assured of my humble prayers for the success of your mission," the Mentor smiled but the word, Obligation, was written all over his face.

As always, Archbishop Brown was as obedient as a shadow.

One morning Danny was getting ready to make the rounds at the hospitals. He had been trying to keep busy with parish concerns but he knew in his heart he was looking for distractions to keep his mind off Michael's note and all its ramifications.

Just as he was about to leave, the phone sounded. It was about ten o'clock. It was Monsignor Richards of the Cardinal's office. He had just been made General Secretary, filling Michael's post. He appeared on the screen looking dapper and well-groomed. Not a hair out of place, his relatively handsome and youngish looking face an immovable tableaux of self-confidence.

"Father Daniels," the cultivated voice on the other end purred, "we are honored to have with us Archbishop Brown, President of the Supreme Council of the Pontifical Missionary Works. He is currently visiting the United States. He would very much like to come and see you since you are a pastor of one of our …. shall I say, most inner of our inner city parishes." Monsignor Richards use of the words, inner city, sounded as though he was referring to a contagious disease.

"When does he want to come?" Danny said in his best disinterested tone.

"He could be there by 10:30. I think it would be in our best interest to be available to him at that time."

How urbanely the bureaucrat can turn a request into an order from on high, Danny smiled to himself.

Archbishop Brown arrived exactly at ten-thirty. He was a man in his early sixties. Dressed flawlessly in black as contrasted to Danny's jeans and pullover sweat shirt. His sparse hair was groomed carefully and he smelled of a luxuriant after shave. His eyes sparkled and he had an easy smile. His whole demeanor advertised graciousness.

"Good morning, Father Daniels. May I call you Father Joseph? Thank you for seeing me on so short a notice."

"Most people call me Danny. You may, if you wish to, Archbishop." Danny noticed that the Archbishop had quickly evaluated his dress without a hint of a change in expression. "Please sit down."

"Thank you."

"You're from what office?" Danny asked politely.

"The Supreme Council of the Pontifical Missionary Works." The Archbishop emphasized the word, Supreme, to assure Danny of his importance.

"Well, what can I do for you?" Danny asked again with a politeness that revealed that he was far from impressed with the man or his position who sat on the other side of Danny's worn and cluttered desk. Whether or not the Archbishop got the message, Danny would never know from the expression on his face.

"We are interested in getting a hands-on experience of what inner city parishes are up against in terms of our efforts to help further missionary activity throughout the Church."

"Sounds interesting. I know of no such effort in my own Archdiocese," Danny was doing all in his power not to sound glib.

"May I say that we are particularly interested in the work you are doing?"

"Rome is interested in what *I* am doing? Not even my own Archbishop has given any evidence along those lines. And the Vatican is interested?"

"Well, you are one of our more illustrious students to have come from the Eternal City. And, to be perfectly blunt, you have piqued our curiosity. A man of such intellectual ability and potential for a leadership role in the Church. And to be spending your life here." He made a sweeping gesture that, to Danny, seemed a bit melodramatic or was he too indicating some kind of disdain for the inner city? Hardly, after all he was from the *Supreme Council*. Danny was again smiling within himself.

"I must admit my surprise," Danny tried to sound as blazé as the Archbishop, "that out of the thousands and thousands of priests in the world, you would take such a personal interest in me."

"Well, as a matter of fact, there will have to be a replacement for dearly departed brother, Bishop McCann."

"The Supreme Council of Pontifical Missionary Works is involved in the selection of bishops?" This time Danny's astonishment was genuine. He also felt a caution flag go up somewhere in the back of his mind. Since when did the death, even the murder, of an Auxiliary bishop become a concern of a Pontifical Council? And "dearly departed brother"?

"I am but a humble emissary," the Archbishop said without seeming to be very humble.

"I'm perplexed, to say the least," Danny said in all sincerity. "Other than my academic record which I'm sure can be matched by hundreds, perhaps thousands of others, there's nothing in my resume that I know of that could possibly recommend me for the episcopate."

"Ah, who knows the inner workings of Holy Mother Church?"

God, Danny thought, where did this guy come from? Out loud he said, "With all due respect (he always said that when no respect was intended), you seem to be familiar with such inner workings."

"Only an emissary," the Archbishop smiled benignly. Then he continued on an entirely new line of thought. "It was quite a shock. What happened to our dearly departed brother, Bishop Michael."

"Yes," Danny repeated, "quite a shock." What was going on here? To the Archbishop he said, "Would the Supreme Council be interested in helping St. Matthew's? I mean after all, I am involved in missionary activity, as you seemed to indicate at the beginning of our conversation."

"Not exactly, Father Joseph. There are channels for such help."

"Okay, then, why does a man of your prestige and power visit the pastor of a nondescript, ecclesiastically neglected parish? I hate to be blunt, Archbishop, but I am, to say the least, totally bewildered." He didn't believe for one moment that the Archbishop bought it.

"There is another matter. It's rather delicate and I don't want to appear calloused. It has to do with your being our brother, Michael's executor."

"What, may I ask, has that got to do with World Missions?" No sooner had Danny got the question out of his mouth than he knew the answer. The mission people wanted a chunk of Michael's estate.

Danny verbalized his hunch. "Does the Supreme Council of the Pontifical Missionary Works want something from Michael's estate?"

"Only what justly belongs to it, Father."

The Supreme Council is Viri Lucis? Danny wondered as he began to realize he was losing the control he thought he had over this meeting.

The Archbishop took a deep breath. Whatever he was going to say, Danny knew it was going to be a plunge. He could never have dreamed what depths of shock that plunge would bring him to.

"There is a note…."

"How in the hell did you know about that?" Danny exploded.

"Come, now, Father, you are not so naive as to not to be cognizant of Rome's capacity to gather information from all over the world. In every nook and cranny of this world, the Vatican has its listening posts. Dare I say we, that is, the Vatican is all-knowing?"

"I thought that attribute was reserved to God," Danny smirked, his voice filled with sarcasm.

"My dear Father, if the will is contested, there is every reason to believe the note will not stand."

"We'll just have to find out, won't we?"

"Not necessarily. You could simply give me the note and forget about it."

That makes three who have told me to forget the note. This one though …. Danny's thought was interrupted.

"As I said, someone will have to fill the place left by our dearly departed brother."

"You son-of-a-bitch! Bribery?"

"Think of it more as reward," the Archbishop's composure was sheer ice.

"If the note won't stand up in court, why would you want it?" Danny felt like he was regaining his control, but it was no match for this Archbishop whose procedure was like that of a precision-like surgeon.

"Caution," Archbishop Brown replied blithely, "is the hallmark of the Vatican's existence."

"Which chapter of the gospel is that taken from?" Danny could not rattle this granite of ecclesiastical diplomacy. He merely smiled at each of Danny's attempted forays.

Then suddenly the Archbishop's face darkened.

"My dear brother, there is the matter of you and Celine Kreel Korbach."

Danny sat there. Stunned was not the word to describe his reaction. Nor was blindsided. It was more like death-dealing blow. He could feel his composure, which he had struggled so hard to keep intact during this meeting, drained out of him like water gurgling out of a tub. It was only by a sheer act of an indomitable will that he was able to whisper in a horse, gasping tone, "How dare you!"

It was a feeble attempt at repartee. In his effort to put the Archbishop on the defensive, Danny knew his entire body language spoke paralysis.

He felt his stomach contract in convulsive pain. A shock of anxiety shot through him from head to toe. He wanted so much to display anger but anger required strength he no longer had. He thought he might pass out.

"Nook and cranny," "listening posts." The Archbishop's words. They were like electric nodes fastened to his brain, terrorizing him. No one — no one but Gene and Leno knew about him and Celine.

Gradually he began to regain his composure. Perhaps the Archbishop knew only about his and Celine's friendship. It was impossible for him to know more.

Just as Danny started to recover from his terror-stricken feelings, the Archbishop, in a move like a master chess player, whispered in an acrid tone, "There are ways of destroying not only you but your whore as well."

Tears blistered Danny' eyes. That word to describe Celine? This suave Churchman would make the Inquisitors look like scout leaders. Danny was beyond recovery. The Archbishop did know.

"There need not be an immediate decision, dear Father. We shall allow you time to pray over the matter.

"Go to hell!" Danny whispered back putting whatever energy he could muster into each word, trying to make each word sound life-threatening. "I will never give you that note!"

Slowly, not abruptly, Archbishop Brown rose, bowed slightly, graciously toward Danny and without another word made his departure, leaving Danny riveted to his chair.

What in God's name would he do? What could he do? Brown's word smashed into his brain, "There are ways of not only destroying you ...." Danny couldn't bring himself to repeat, even mentally, the word Brown had used to defame Celine. Could they, whoever they were, actually harm Celine? He couldn't care less about what they could do to him. But Celine?

He sat there. He wanted to feel anger in the worst way but all he could feel was devastating depression. Bribery. Blackmail. Gospel living. Christian community. He could feel new tears welling in his eyes. What could they do to destroy Celine? Destroy. Church leadership. God. Jesus. Shit. That's all the whole thing is.

No, no it isn't. It's people. Christianity is relationships. It's that or nothing. He had to hold onto that. It's what's for others is for Christ. It's loving and serving others just because they are. Oh Christ, what am I going to do? He sat there for what seemed like hours. Thoughts meshing. Not making sense. He felt caught in a turmoil of emotions. Anger, humiliation, embarrassment swirling out of control like an ocean attacked by a typhoon.

He had to hold onto the distinction between the Church as institution and the Church as the Body of Christ.

Finally, he roused himself, walked out to the kitchen and got himself a drink of water. "…. time to pray over the matter." That damn pious fraud! What the hell did Michael get him into? He would call Celine and Gene and arrange a meeting.

THE EVALUATION

The next evening the three of them sat around the kitchen table in Gene's rectory. "I can't believe it!" Gene all but shouted. Celine sat stiff and erect . Stunned beyond words. Beyond comprehension. The word, destroy, stuck in her mind like a steel blade.

"Whoever they are, they can't destroy me," she said without much conviction. "But they may be able to destroy you, Danny. What have I done to you?"

"Celine," Gene intervened, "this is no time for blaming. This is a time for retrenchment. Planning."

Danny sat exhausted. He had told them the whole episode about Brown's visit and was drained of every ounce of energy. He felt like a balloon pricked by a pin. Flat and empty. Finally he spoke up. "I won't let anything happen to Celine. I'll give them the damn note. You both told me to forget it, didn't you?"

"But that was before the illustrious Archbishop's visit," Gene countered.

"I knew my intuition about that note's being dangerous was on target." Celine could barely be heard. It was as though she was talking out loud to herself.

"The frightening thing about Brown's composure is that it emanated from a serene sense of supreme power," Danny said. "Brown said, 'destroy,' and I'm convinced that he and whoever he represents have that kind of power. It's scary. God, it's like the Inquisition. Worse."

It was obvious that both Danny and Celine were emotionally overwrought. It was Gene who had to be the logical guide, easing them out of the shroud of their emotional distress into the light of reason.

"Let's see what we have here," Gene adopted a very professorial tone which fastened both Celine and Danny's attention on him like jurors listening to the opening argument.

"One, World Missions isn't Viri Lucis. A well known Congregation has no need of subterfuge.

"Two, the Archbishop is most likely a member of Viri Lucis. Why else would he want the note which excludes Viri Lucis from Michael's will.

"Three, Viri Lucis apparently has power. Otherwise the threat of destroying you two would just be a bluff. That is a possibility. On the other hand, a bluff would serve no purpose in Viri Lucis' getting that note from you. A bluff would only indicate impotency. So, as I said, Viri Lucis does have power.

"Four, someone had to tell Viri Lucis about you two. Since it wasn't me and Leno was the only other one who knew, it had to be Leno. Therefore, Leno, as you suspected, Danny, was a member of Viri Lucis."

Celine interrupted. "My friend Margaret knows a little about .... about how I feel but she knows nothing about .... before."

"Five, Michael was also a member of Viri Lucis.

"Six, how Viri Lucis found out about the note remains a puzzle."

This time Danny interrupted. "But who knew about the note? You two did and ....Of course! our dear Monsignor Travine, Michael's trusted secretary."

"So Travine is also a member of Viri Lucis," Celine said with no special emphasis.

"Seven," Gene continued, "what Viri Lucis is, who belongs, what it's purpose is, are all unknowns."

"Big unknowns, essential unknowns," Celine said. "So what do we do? Go to Travine and say, 'We know you're a member of Viri Lucis. Now tell us all about it or we'll' .... what? We have no evidence, no proof."

"If he is anything like our Archbishop," Danny said, "he'll just smile and wave us off — with lighthearted graciousness, of course."

"And, too," Celine added, "if he is a member, he'll report back to Viri Lucis we are on his trail and the danger will only become more formidable, more immediate."

Gene spoke up. "There are eight and nine."

"Which are?" Danny asked.

"Eight, why was Michael killed? and Nine, was Leno's death really from natural causes?"

"If Viri Lucis did have anything to do with their deaths," Celine said, "they could just as well kill off Danny, and on the assumption that he told me about the note, kill me too. The will would be executed without any reference to the note and that would be that. They'd get their money and spend the rest of their lives lighting votive candles."

"Except that Viri Lucis doesn't know who else Danny may have told. No, they'll use whatever means they have at their disposal to get that note from Danny," Gene pointed out.

"But if they publicly disgrace or destroy Danny — and me —what assurance will they have that they'll get the note?" Celine asked.

"It's the power of threat," Gene responded. "They may think Danny will not risk your public destruction, Celine, and give them the note. It's reasonable in a twisted sort of way."

"Which," Danny said with a heavy sigh, "seems like the commonsense thing to do. Why the hell should I care?"

"Look, Danny," Celine spoke up, "if, as we suspect, Viri Lucis has something to do with the Church and is as powerful and dangerous as we think it is, then you who have dedicated your life to the Church cannot walk away, leaving the note with them."

"That's a strange thing for you to say," Danny retorted. "You're the one who from the beginning told me to forget the note and hand the whole thing over to a lawyer. In fact, why not turn it over to a lawyer. Once it's in his hands, what can they do? I don't have it anymore."

"They can still put enough pressure on you, Danny," Gene said, "to retrieve the note from the lawyer, just as they're trying to get you to pull the note from wherever you've stashed it."

"Besides," Celine said determinedly, "we could be putting the lawyer's life at risk. Look, Danny, I'm willing to take whatever risk's involved to keep them from getting that note."

"But," Danny replied with more than a little annoyance, "I'm not willing to put you in any kind of jeopardy and that's that. What kind of a Church produces somebody like Brown?"

"Danny," Gene answered, "you of all people should know that where there's religion there's always the possibility of fanaticism. It isn't the Church. It's always a fanatical element within or outside the Church. You're not being logical. You're drawing a much larger conclusion than the premise allows."

"But we must be doing something wrong, Gene," Danny said trying to cool down. "Our primary work or ministry, if you will, is to help people to grow in and develop their faith, to live by gospel values in every area of their lives. That's what we're all about. Everything else is secondary. All Brown's done is remind us again of history's lesson, that the gospel can be interpreted to fit any self-serving ideology that those in power want it to."

"Soapbox, Danny," Gene warned. "there are far more examples of people who have lived the gospel sincerely and with genuine self-sacrifice. Don't you get the feeling at morning Masses that you are in the presence of many mystics, to our embarrassment?

"Brown's an aberration. Look at the people in your own parish. They don't have much but there they are running a soup kitchen to help people who are worse off they are. Isn't that living the gospel?"

"But," Celine interrupted, "Danny's got a point. The gospel can be twisted to serve personal ambition. And that, it seems to me, is what Brown's all about and whoever he is representing. But, Danny, Gene's right too. Brown doesn't represent the Church."

"If there are people, even members of Church leadership," Gene said, "who have made an idol of the Church or their version of the Church, sure, I'll agree with you, Danny. They can go through the gospel with a scissors and glue pot and paste together the kind of gospel that will serve their purpose. That's reality. That's the human condition. Church leaders are not immaculately conceived no matter how hard they try to act as if they were.

"There have been men in the hierarchy who have served the people heroically. Romero, for instance. Or Helder Camera. With time we could come up with an inspiring list."

"Are they aberrations?" Danny asked almost with disinterest.

"Danny," Gene pleaded, "don't go cynical on us. You've had a hellava traumatic experience with Brown. Don't let that color your whole attitude. Excuse the pun."

For the first time that evening, they all smiled.

"I think we're all emotionally drained," Celine said. "Let's call it a night. Maybe after a night's sleep ….as the saying goes, A problem is only a decision waiting to be made. And we're not in any shape to make decisions especially about taking risks. Anyway I told George I wouldn't be gone for long.

" And speaking about George, Danny, Gene, I've got to tell him. I've got to tell George everything and that includes us, Danny. I probably should have told him long before but I felt he had no need to know anymore than I had a right to know about his past with other women. I don't know how he's going to take it. Pray that it goes well. But I do need to bring him in on this." It was more a request for reassurance than a statement. Both nodded assent.

They said goodbye and Danny and Celine drove off in different directions, their fates entwined more intimately than that one-time love-making had ever been.

Archbishop Brown punched in the sacrosanct number observing the Mentor's rule that no one was allowed to speak that number aloud.

His report was three brief words, "He won't budge."

"I am very disappointed in you, David. You know we need that money. Those with money create reality. And our reality is impatiently waiting to be instituted. The time is now."

Silence.

"Where are you now?"

"I'm still in the U.S. I told him I'd give him a grace period to reconsider."

"Let us pray that it will indeed be a time of grace."

"I used every persuasion including the matter of Miss Celine Kreel. I will be calling him in a few days."

"And I will pray that for your sake he will change his mind."

With that the Mentor disconnected.

Archbishop Brown felt weak. He may never be a member of the College of Cardinals.

THE SCHOOL

The next morning Danny decided to visit the school. One aspect of his ministry he prized above all others, except perhaps that of preaching, was the children of his school. For that matter, he loved all the children in the neighborhood. The children loved him in return. It was the one tangible reward he could depend on.

He wondered if his love for the children was somehow influenced by his experience with Janie back in the third grade. Past experiences, conscious or unconscious, do affect present realities. Something like Celine's dead kitten and her father's refusal to say more than it was God's will. What a simple exchange and yet what a negative impact it had had on Celine.

Strange, Danny thought, how Celine had asked about her kitten's death. She had only been in the first grade. He had been in third grade when Janie died. He could not remember ever asking his parents or anyone about why Janie had died.

If his parents or someone like Sister Thomasita, his third grade teacher, had told him that it was God's will that Janie had died, he wondered what effect that would have had on his image of and relationship to God.

He remembered how Janie had given him all the books he would need in his new school. How she had encouraged him to practice the piano when he didn't even want to take the lessons his mother insisted on.

One time, after school, he had walked Janie home. As they walked along, Janie reached down and took him by the hand. A strange feeling came over him. Excitement like he felt on Christmas morning. Puzzlement like that he experienced during a Easter-egg hunt.

Then he squeezed her hand back. Not hard but sincerely. Janie had giggled. "I like you a lot, Joey," she had said. "I hope you like me."

"Yeah, sure I do. Why do think I'm walking you home?" he had replied. "We'll always be good friends won't we?" Janie had asked. "Oh sure, always," Danny had replied nonchalantly.

She was so pretty. The prettiest girl in the class. and she wasn't snooty either like some of those other girls. "Aren't you afraid your friends will make fun of you because I'm your friend?" Janie had asked, keeping the conversation going.

"Nah," he had said although he hoped they wouldn't run into any of his friends just now.

"We'll always be friends," Janie repeated, this time with a little sigh.

"Yeah, I like you a lot, Janie."

How could he remember that so clearly and yet he couldn't remember how he felt when Janie died. Why hadn't he asked anyone any questions about Janie's death. Maybe he had but couldn't remember anymore than he could recall his baptism. Had he coped through denial? He couldn't remember.

Strange how now he felt so sad over Janie's death. He even felt like crying. Why did such a lovely little girl have to die She apparently got sick. He couldn't even remember what sickness she had. God's will? No, just the human condition.

He did have a vague memory about Sister Thomasita's taking him under her wing after Janie no longer came to school. He knew for certain he had had a crush on that beautiful Sister. He loved her at least all through the rest of third grade.

Then Danny thought of little Sally Winters in third grade here at St. Matt's. She died too. Of complications, the doctor had said. He had gone over to the third grade class and talked to the children about how God loved Sally so much he wanted her with him right away. He explained how happy Sally was now. How she would never get sick again.

He wanted the children to remember Sally. They just sat there staring at him as if he were explaining Quantum physics to them. That was his impression, anyway. He asked them to remember Sally by praying to her.

He said, "Let's say a prayer to Sally." Then he began, "Dear Sally, Jesus always loved little children and he blessed them. Ask Jesus to bless your classmates, please, and me too, Father Joe. We will always remember you, Sally. Amen" All the children repeated, "Amen." He had left in silence. He wondered how much Sally's classmates would remember. Maybe God blesses little children with random amnesia.

Danny was glad that Celine was able to deal with her demon. He wasn't sure if he knew who or what his demon was.

Danny went over to the school. He desperately needed a studied distraction. He had six grades and 154 children. Eighty-five to 90 percent were not Catholics. He had five teachers and a teaching principal, Joan Cromlic. Two of the teachers were volunteers who were on Social Security. Even though their love for the children was enduring, their physical stamina wasn't.

Any day now, he thought, and I'll have two resignations on my desk. Three teachers were paid almost minimum wages. And the teaching principal was Joan Cromlic. She was a former nun and asked only enough to live on. If anyone ever lived the vow of poverty, she did. Whenever Celine sent some money which she "collected" from her colleagues, Danny would always try to give a little bonus to his principal and faculty.

Despite the fact that the bureaucrats kept telling him that his school was not up to par and that there were not enough Catholic students to justify keeping it open, Danny tenaciously fought to keep the school going.

There was all this rhetoric about Evangelization, but when you attempted it, there were the ever-present bureaucrats announcing from on high that your efforts were a waste. Perhaps not that harsh but the message was the same.

Besides, wasn't a little education better than none? Where was their trust in God? Isn't trust the religious expression of faith? What is it, faith in one compartment and educational excellence in another? Or again, is it the practice of religion as contrasted with the living of faith? The very people he would expect support from were the ones who were undermining his efforts.

Naive was the word they used on him. He knew they wanted to close down his school but what about presence?

Danny recalled a story he had read about an international gathering of students who had come together to discuss ways of making evangelization a reality in their respective countries. One young woman told the group about the procedure they used in her country.

When it was decided that a certain village was ready to hear the Good News, they didn't send in missionaries or books. They sent a Christian family to live in the village so that the villagers could observe first hand what it meant to live the gospel. In this way, she said, the opportunity for conversion was made available to the villagers. Presence, Danny said under his breath. Presence.

Joan Cromlic, his principal, was living faith in the midst of these children. Whether these children were baptized or believed in the Catholic Church was not the point. Through Joan's efforts and those of the other faculty members, these children were being exposed to values they would never get anywhere else. The children were his "villagers."

He tried so desperately to keep his school open and viable. He did this without any support from the education office. As a matter of fact, he kept the school open in the face of opposition from that office.

There was the day when Sister Regina Pacis, the Superintendent of Schools, came to the rectory after her visitation to the school. He remembered Leno's comment about her name being the most obvious misnomer in the history of the Catholic Church. "Regina Pacis?" Leno had roared with laughter. "Queen of Peace? My God, I wonder if she has any inkling at all that the priests call her 'The Terrorizing Terrier.' Again Leno let out a boisterous laugh, "I'm afraid that little lady has been educated beyond her intelligence."

She sat erect in the wooden chair in Danny's office opposite his desk, her heavy shoulders expanding to fill it. Her face was a mask of passivity. No emotion. Just a bottom-of-the-line implacable practicality. Regina Pacis was a woman who knew she was in charge and used her control to intimidate.

She was not a handsome woman. Her face was pocked-marked and was as plain as cellophane wrapping. She overcompensated by assuming an arrogant stare. It was next to impossible to read the coded message that was her face. Her hands were large and fleshy and as motionless as the inflexibility of her attitude.

Regina Pacis looked like someone who spent her life dealing with urgencies rather than with what was really important. She seemed to relish a crisis to the point that if none existed, she would conjure up one. The people in her ministry as well as in her life were all cases to be analyzed not persons to be cherished.

When she spoke it was like a dictator who used the position of power to define the situation for the common people who were incapable of understanding anything but what they were told to do. She dominated every scene. The front and center of the stage of life was hers. Everyone else was a member of the supporting cast.

Danny wondered where and how she had acquired the moral savagery of a prophet of vested interests. Was it from an exaggerated sense of duty or was it from her being habitually at odds with the reality of her inner self? How could a person be so sincere about her duty and so calloused toward people who did not live up to her expectations which would fulfill the requirements of her duty?

Whatever else, Sister Regina Pacis was formidable and her position in the hierarchy of the educational bureaucracy made her as severe as a Grand Inquisitor. With her there were no relationships, only confrontations. What was obvious was that she had about as much of a sense of humor as a swaying cobra.

When she began to talk about the necessity of closing the school "for the benefit of all concerned" — whoever they might be, Danny had tried to slam-dunk her.

"Sister, we're not talking here about the physical decay of the school. We're talking about the prime disease of our nation, spiritual decay. And that's precisely why we need a school here. To teach spiritual values.

"We're trying to change the lifestyle of these children whether they are Catholic or not," Danny spoke as firmly as if he were delivering the Ten Commandments.

"You're not being practical, Father," she had retorted.

"What is more practical than trying to teach these children gospel values?" Danny said in a seething tone. "With insights from the gospel they can, we hope, arrange the information they're getting in a meaningful way so that it will have an impact on the way they live in the future.

"If each child who goes through this school can do a little bit to change the environment around here, it will become a lot. Surely, Sister, that is the most practical approach to education? Even you must be able to see that." He couldn't help himself. He had to get that personal attack in.

"How long have you been here, Father?" Regina Pacis asked with obvious disdain for someone who was not initiated into the finer nuances of Catholic education.

"Going on thirteen years."

"And how much has changed?" She spoke like a gambler with a full house. "How much has changed in the Alley because of your school's graduates?"

"The numbers game?" Danny sounded indifferent. He had been through this so many times before. "Measurement, Sister, that's what's killing the Church. Facts and stats. We've given up on Mystery — if we ever embraced it in the first place. Quantity. Right? The hell with quality. We measure our effectiveness not by fervor but by numbers."

"Please Father, your language," Regina Pacis interrupted as though she was about to take a ruler to Danny's knuckles.

"The mystical is for the few," Danny pursued, ignoring her plea about his language. "For the rest it's religion in its best form of routine. The controllable. The measurable. If you want to play the numbers game, I know a pastor who is turning children away. He has empty classrooms and money in the bank. Why aren't you over there pounding on his head?"

"Are you through, Father?" Her tone by now was pure acid. "Is every graduate from your school an exemplary Catholic? We know that the non Catholics certainly are not."

"Let me ask you, Sister, how many graduates from any of our Catholic schools are exemplary Catholics? Would you be willing to risk letting Confirmation go until graduation night at our high schools? Would you risk asking the graduates to come forward if they wanted to be confirmed?

"Most of our schools, if not all, indoctrinate for dependency and insecurity, Sister. Don't deny it." It was no longer a game of one-upmanship. Danny was deadly serious.

"You're throwing out a Red Herring, Father. You will not face up to the problems you have here and as a result you're perpetuating mediocrity."

"What we're doing, Sister, is trying to help our youngsters to become creative problem solvers especially for problems that have no predetermined outcome as happens in real life. We're trying to help them to come to terms with the realities of their lives and not just reinforce the 'right' answer. These kids in the ghetto cannot live on catechism answers alone, Sister."

"No one will deny the sincerity of your intentions, Father, but it is unreasonable to expect the outcomes you're hoping for without the proper environment. Call it measuring or whatever, but you do not have the wherewithal to put forth a school that measures up to the standards set by the Archdiocese and the government.

" You have five — five — compuinfomers. None of which are on the Pannet. You don't have one piece of virtual reality equipment. To pursue your course is irrational and will undoubtedly lead to mass disillusionment."

"You're talking scientific equipment," Danny countered again. "I have some feelers out. We'll get equipment." Danny knew Celine was working over some of her well-heeled friends and she had already made a personal donation. "In fact, I can guarantee you we'll have some of that equipment by the end of the school year."

Regina Pacis sat in what seemed to be disdainful silence.

"Besides," Danny pursued his point. "You're talking science. You and I both know that no sooner do children begin to talk than they're scientists. They ask questions like, Why is the sky blue? Why is water wet? Why is snow cold?

"They are also philosophers. Why does it hurt so much? Why doesn't my father live with us? Why was my sister crying all night? If God is good, how come the people in my neighborhood are sad?

"But you and I also know, Sister, that when these kids come to a school, the teachers will program all their curiosity out of them. The regimentation will kill their creativity. And these kids will grow up to be productive, conforming citizens. Uniformity will be the supreme virtue of the drab reality of their lives.

"That is not the philosophy of St. Matt's school. It's our hope that our children will rebel. Not against their inner city background so much as against the socializing indoctrination of a neurotic culture. I want them to rebel so that they will become inventors, artists and even poets."

"You are a very dangerous man, Father. You have a reputation for being a maverick. But I had no idea how unbridled you really are."

Danny felt demoralized. She was like a tungsten wall. He knew that if he was to be honest, he had to give her the benefit of the doubt. He had to credit her with her sincere belief in what she was saying. But sincerity was not the final word because sincerity could go awry. Sincerity is too often the spark that flares up into the uncontrollable blaze of fanaticism. And, Danny had thought at the time, Sister Regina Pacis, despite her name, was conducting what must be considered a Holy War.

To her Danny had said, "Sometimes we reach our goal and sometimes we don't. Don't you find it that way in your work, Sister?"

"The difference is, Father, that our goals are practical. They are attainable. While yours ...."

"There's Juan," Danny interrupted. "Juan de Garcia. He was nine when I came here to St. Matt's. He's currently a pre-med student. And next year he'll graduate from college."

"One student, Father?"

"There are others. Not many but we're not into the numbers game. These others may not have a high profile but they are working and are productive. Our school is worthwhile as long as every so often we can produce a Juan or a Ramone who is working at the Post Office.

Sister Regina Pacis sighed heavily. "You're like a bull dog with its teeth clamped on a bone. You make it very difficult. You just won't listen to reason. Why can't you accept the evaluation of an objective observer?"

"Because, Sister, as an objective observer, visiting our school for a day, you can't possibly understand that we're not indoctrinating our children with blind obedience. What we're trying to do is help our kids develop the optimal use of their imaginations so that they can break out of this ghetto.

"We're also attempting to give them a sense of ethical concern for the good of others. As I said, sometimes we succeed, sometimes we fail. But we're up against an environment here that's like a deadly virus. If we don't do something …."

Danny's voice trailed off as though he was wrestling with his own feelings of frustration at the enormity of the challenge.

"That's all well and good, Father, and I do admire your efforts. But what you say you want to do and the facilities you have to do it with …. well, the chasm is just too vast. There's no bridging it. You need to be realistic."

Suddenly Danny began to lose it. "Frankly, Sister, I find pretended perfection sickening. You sit in stern propriety, in learned educational circles, back there in your academic fortress and you hurl anathemas at our little school that's struggling to stay in existence.

"You'll go home to a comfortable convent and write your report in a high tech office. But what about these children who go back to rat infested houses, to street corners where drug pushers conduct their nightly business — what about them? Are you going to snuff out the only ray of hope they have? Is that why you became a

Religious? My God, Sister, have you surrendered your faith values for educational priorities?"

"I'm not here, Father, to have my spirituality evaluated by you. I have my position and I am trying to do God's will in that position. I do indeed live my faith values but, unlike you, I am not a stained-glass idealist. And sometimes our faith values must be adapted to the reality in which we find ourselves."

"Adapted or compromised? Don't our faith values demand that we teach our children how to love the world and contradict it at the same time? Isn't that reality, Sister? Doesn't our reality challenge us not to teach a religion that is preoccupied with avoiding evil rather than doing good?"

'We're talking standards, Father, educational standards."

"Standards or institutional sclerosis, Sister? You've just visited our school ...."

"And found so many things that are lacking."

"Tell me, Sister, is it lacking in eagerness? Or joy? Or vitality?"

"Noooo ...."

"I rest my case. If you're a true educator, you will not, cannot, kill creativity. That's what we're about, enabling our children to be creative enough to discover the divine meaning of their lives and their relationships.

"We want to develop their creativity so that they won't abandon their responsibilities and wait around for God to do it all for them. To perform miracles that releases them from any effort. If we don't foster the creativity of these kids, then their potential for being creative will explode into destructive activity. You know that.

"When parishes were consolidated St. Matt's was allowed to stay open as the only Catholic presence here in The Alley," Danny argued.

"But wasn't there a provision, Father? That you could make it financially?"

"We may be floundering, Sister, but we're not drowning. There are two parishes that are helping us."

"Father, you're a dreamer."

"Where would we be without dreamers, Sister? Maybe that's the problem with the Church. We've given up our dreaming for the pragmatism of the bottom line. I have a stanza that I take refuge in. It goes,

'We are the music makers,
      We are the dreamers of dreams,
Wandering by lone sea-breakers,
      And sitting by desolate streams;
World-losers and world-forsakers,
      On whom the pale moon gleams.
Yet we are the movers and shakers
      Of the world forever, it seems.'

"And the poem ends with the lines, 'For each age is a dream that is dying/ Or one that is coming to birth.'"

"Poetry," Sister Regina Pacis all but sneered. "There's nothing more impractical."

"On the contrary, Sister, as the saying goes, 'Poetry may not save the world, but it makes the world worth saving.'"

"Dreamers, despite your poem, Father, are not practical. And practicality is what is needed here at St. Matthew's."

"Tell that to Columbus or Francis Xavier or Madame Curie or Martin Luther King. Remember, 'I have a dream?' It hasn't come true yet but life is a process, isn't it? Even Jesus' dream hasn't been fulfilled. But we keep dreaming, don't we?"

"You may but I don't."

"Well, Sister, then try this for a nightmare. You try to close this school and I'll have every able bodied person here in The Alley park on your doorstep. I don't think His Eminence would care for that kind of publicity, do you? I mean it, Sister. Try these initials, NAACP and ACLU. I have friends in both."

Sister Regina Pacis laughed a short, brittle laugh. "You are a dreamer. You're also out of contact with reality. I will submit my report as I see fit. And don't you ever dare threaten me again. I have the full weight of the Cardinal's authority behind me."

With that she got up and abruptly left.

Danny's reverie was disrupted by the part-time maintenance man who volunteered his services. "It's the main solar cell again, Father Joe. Looks like we'll have to replace it this time." Danny knew he'd end up calling Celine and asking her to make the rounds of her friends. Danny suspected that the money he received from Celine came mostly from her own pocketbook.

STELLA MC CONKLER

Danny went into his office. His office was not much different from his study upstairs. It needed wallpapering. The two windows needed caulking. He had a desk and a chair. To the right was his telecomputer as indispensable as light bulbs even in this poverty stricken dump that was St. Matt's rectory.

There were two straight wooden chairs in front of the desk where people sat as they begged a handout or told a tale of hopeless desperation about a wayward daughter or a drug addicted son or cried their heartbreak into reddened eyes over a deceased loved one. Sometimes the parade of tragedy seemed unending.

Even happy times like baptisms and weddings were marred with worriment. "Another mouth to feed, Father Joe." "We'll have to live with my parents for a while and they're not happy about it, Father Joe. They keep saying, 'If he can marry you, why can't he support you?'"

Often Danny found himself counting the small holes in the carpet just to help him get through whatever gloom was spreading over his office.

Upstairs his study had an easy chair. A small computelevisor. A two seat couch with a battered old coffee table. He had books on three walls of the study ranging from theology and sociology to fiction and poetry. All accumulated over his years in the seminary and during the first years of his priesthood. Now he depended on scholarly printouts from the computelevisor. There were boxes of printouts stacked in the small study like pilings for future skyscrapers.

He had no desk in his study. He used a writing pad for working on his homilies or composing his poetry. Later he would put his poems in the telecomputer in his office. The drapes in his study were old and musty. He had a floor lamp that cast three hundred watts of indirect lighting. He had one air conditioner in his bedroom which rattled like tin cans being kicked down the street. He didn't use it much.

There were only five pictures on the mantel of the inoperable fireplace. One of Father Henning, his philosophy professor. Another of his deceased father and mother. A picture of "Muntz," his first pastor. One of Professor Percussi under whom he studied for his doctorate in theology at Rome. And most recently, a picture of Celine. He used to laugh and say far from living in the lap of luxury he didn't even make it to the knees of comfort. Still the rectory was comfortable in an early American junk sort of way.

Danny sat down at his telecomputer and switched on the local internet. He spoke the words, "Computer, access outstanding bills." He stared at the list of bills begging to be paid.

He clicked onto the first one, High School Assessment. A hollow voice spoke in a clipped cadence: "Your assessment for Lower Central Catholic High School is three months overdue.

"You can do one of the following: Pay one third immediately and the rest on a weekly basis. See file #3056. Pay in full over the next month. See file #1782. Contact the Office of Fiscal Management. See file #82 for instructions."

Danny continued to click onto the other bills and heard the same metallic voice over and over. "You still owe ...." "You still owe ...." "You still owe ...."

There were times when he wished he were Moses. Only when he struck the rock with his rod, instead of water gushing out, it would be money tumbling out in a tumultuously clinking rush like it does when you hit the jackpot at the slots.

If what Celine had said about his getting some money for acting as Michael's executor was true .... Oh, God," he whispered, "please make it true."

Oil had gone up. The electric was out of sight. There was a third notice from the officious bookkeeper at the high school telling him he was three and a half months in arrears in his assessment. This would be the fourth time this year he couldn't take his salary.

Was this what it is all about? What was it some low-level Chancery official had said to him long ago? "The good priest is the priest whose books balance at the end of the fiscal year." All that stuff they taught in the seminary. They never mentioned that most of your time would be taken up with money matters.

All those pious talks on The Good Priest never included a word about the bankrupt priest. Pray regularly. Meditate. Say your rosary every day. Don't let your breviary go to the last minute and then rush through it. Go to confession each week. Spend 15 minutes each day doing spiritual reading. And you too will be a true shepherd of souls.

Besides not mentioning money worries, they never talked about prayer as a personal faith experience of God. They were too busy reminding you of your obligation to *say* certain prayers. Talk about the slots! You puts your spiritual exercises in and you gets a harvest of souls out.

His current problem, however, was trying not to go down for the third time in this ocean of bills. He'd have to figure out again how much he could pay on each bill. Was he just staving off the inevitable?

Danny's phone sounded. It was Stella Mc Conkler. Her face on the viewscreen screwed up in torturous apprehension as usual. "Can you come to see me, Father Joe?" Stella pleaded. She would call him three or four times a week asking him to come by and hear her confession. He had assured her time and again that confession once a month was more than sufficient but to no avail. Stella wanted to "make sure." "I'll try, Stella," Danny promised with an appropriate mental reservation.

What image of God did people have? he had wondered then and he still tries to puzzle it through now. What kind of an image of God did people have that they actually found security in a fear-ridden religious practice? Someone confessing missing Mass because he or she was sick in bed and there was six feet of snow outside and besides he or she is 87 years old. No sense in telling them they didn't commit a sin and they didn't have to confess it. They wanted to "make sure."

One afternoon Stella made her call, asking him to come by and hear her confession. Danny hated going to her apartment. It was polluted with cats. Polluted was the accurate term. The stench was unbearable. He would try to hold his breath but Stella always wanted to talk for a while. Cat urine was the all-pervading putrid stench throughout the apartment.

He remembered thinking at the time that one way of waging modern day warfare without causing a nuclear holocaust was to fill cylinders with cat urine and drop them on the enemy. In the first strike the enemy would surrender before you could say Tender Vittles.

Once again he pictured himself as Moses. He looked for all the world like Charlton Heston. He would strike the rock and out would pour cat urine. The people would be so preoccupied with getting away from the stench that they'd have no time to make demands on him. Everything would be wonderfully relaxed until, human compulsion being what it is, someone would demand, "What are *you* going to do about all this cat urine, Father?"

Before Danny could even give another thought to going to see Stella, he had been called over to the school to officiate at a knife fight between two sixth grade boys. The police had been called. Danny ended up at the police station begging to have the boys released into his custody.

He got back in the late afternoon. On his door was a note stuck there with a pin. He read the note. "Stella McAllister died this afternoon." Then appended to the bottom of the note were the words, "Without benefit of a priest." People could be so piously cruel in the practice of their religion. Danny immediately called Stella's niece. "I'm sorry about your Aunt Stella," he said to the niece.

"Oh Father Joe! Did you hear?"

"Yes, I just got a note informing me that she died this afternoon."

"No I mean did you *hear*?"

"Hear what?" Danny asked with resignation. Was she going to tell him that Stella had died without benefit of a priest?

"We didn't even know!"

"Know what?" Danny was becoming annoyed.

"We didn't know Auntie Stella had money. I mean she lived in that one room all these years. Father Joe, Auntie Stella left 34 thousand dollars. Father Joe, she left 34 thousand dollars to those goddamn cats!"

Danny knew he'd have no difficulty in choosing which loss to console the niece on. In fact it would probably turn out to be mutual commiseration. Thirty-four thousand dollars would have gone the distance in helping the parish get back on its feet and make a dash toward some kind of viability.

SAM'S WAKE

Two weeks later Danny had a wake for Sam Jordan. Sam had been a quiet, pleasant sort. His wife Gertie was a character.

It was strange, Danny thought, how death always seemed to nudge him toward the mystical. Perhaps it was the finality of death that captured his imagination and inspired him with the desire to immerse himself in the God with whom he would spend eternity.

After all, the flowering of God's grace is mysticism and mysticism is not reserved for the chosen few. Isn't mystical experience rooted in wonder, the ability to see through the commonplace and glimpse the sacred? Isn't mysticism the experience of the poetry of our faith? The recovery of our sacred stories which were mutated by being "elevated" to abstract theological statements or robbed of their richness by being reduced to oversimplified catechism answers. We're so insistent that our people have all the answers. When are we going to inspire them to live the answers?

To be a mystic is to be able to experience the extraordinary in the ordinary. Sounds almost glamorous. But there is always torture in the mystical experience. The realization of how finite we really are. The cruel limitation of our ability to express the Inexpressible even to ourselves, never mind to others.

And perhaps this was the reason that the mystical had only a fleeting attraction for him. He didn't want to risk living the paradox of being so infinitesimal and yet so priceless. The plunge into ultimate Reality might mean drowning in the absence of his control over his relationship with God. Sometimes he wished he could settle for living on the surface of his faith. It would be so much more comfortable.

It was these repeated reflections in one form or another on the lure of the mystical that provoked the doubts that seemed to plague him. He lived with doubt as habitually as he lived with his faith. In fact his faith was often nothing but doubt. And his doubts went to the core of all he was taught to hold sacred.

Not things like the Pope's infallibility but the teachings of Jesus or even the existence of Jesus or the very existence of God himself or the true presence of Christ in the Eucharist. There were times when he was elevating the host at Mass and all he experienced was doubt.

Danny knew that if he lived on the surface of his faith, if he was content just to practice religion, he wouldn't be troubled by these doubts. He also knew that only those who don't think don't doubt. He took consolation from a line by Tennyson, "There is more faith in honest doubt than in half the creeds."

The only thing he could do for the present, he was convinced, was to keep giving service to his people. And, as he told Celine, his service was less an act of the will fulfilling duties. It had become an expression of love emanating from his heart. And for now that had to be the reality of his experience of God and of Jesus' teachings no matter how often he felt like chucking the whole thing and going off to a monastery or just going off.

He could see himself riding off into the sunset on his faithful stead. He looked a lot like John Wayne whom he didn't particularly care for. The lonesome cowboy who rides into town, shoots all the crooks and refuses the proffered love of the town damsel, preferring his freedom in the wide open range.

He began humming a song he had heard on the Golden Oldies station, "Don't Fence Me In." Then for the first time in a long time he laughed out loud. He remembered an axiom he had read somewhere, "Blessed are they who can laugh at themselves; they will never cease to be entertained."

That evening Danny went to the Jordan home.

"I didn't want anything to do with those funeral parlors, Father Joe," Gertie said in a plaintive tone. She and Danny were sitting at the kitchen table. "Do you think those people in there think it's terrible that I'm sitting here having a beer? I just got tired of people telling me they're sorry for my trouble.

"My 'trouble' is over. I love my kitchen, Father Joe. In a funeral parlor you can't go to the kitchen, I guess a lot of people will think

I'm strange 'cause I wanted Sam's wake here where I could get a cold beer when I wanted to.

"Yes, my trouble's over now. God, when I think of these past years... It was like having to care for a baby. I had to feed him, wash him, change him. Imagine! Change him like you change a baby's diapers.

"The real trouble, if you want to call it that, was that bit by bit he didn't even know who I was. Sometimes he called me Maria — his mother's name. Sometimes, Judy — that's our daughter. You met her when you came in. You knew her before though, didn't you?

"The blank stare. That's what I'll remember most. He'd look at me and he wouldn't even see me. Know what that's like? It's like caring for a shell. You know you can hear the ocean if you listen hard enough but you know the ocean's not really there. My daughter, Judy — you met her before — she said it was like the living dead. You know, like those zombies.

"They wanted me to put him in a nursing home. I said they're not 'homes.' I said it was for better or for worse. We had a lot of better years, believe me, than these last ones.

"Sure you won't have a beer with me, Father Joe? I said, let Judy greet those people in there. I guess I sound bitter but they never came around when I ... when he was fading out of life. Now they're here when he's gone, saying, 'Sorry for your trouble.' Now it's really my relief.

"When you watch a big, strapping man who worked all his life on the monorail — I mean, hard work — just dwindle before your eyes, well, you know, Father Joe, you brought him Communion. It will be a relief not to have to watch that anymore, believe me.

"When he was still able to talk and make sense, he'd say, 'When I get better, we'll go on a long trip. Maybe out West to see the deserts.' I think he was remembering how much I like cactus plants or something.

"When I hear how people gripe about such stupid little things and how they split up like Judy — that's our daughter — just because they have differences, I guess I feel a bit bitter. Why don't you split a beer with me? No? Okay.

"When Sam finally died, a neighbor said to me, 'You've been very courageous, a real heroine.' I wasn't courageous at all. Most of the time I resented the whole thing. A lot of times I felt angry at God and, you know, I told him so. I was no heroine, believe me, I just did what I had to do. That's all.

"As soon as I finish my beer I'll go back into that room. People will expect that. They'll want to tell me how sorry they are for my trouble. Don't know why I feel so thirsty. You know the problem is that most of them in there won't ever know how much trouble I've had. Probably couldn't care either. They come and they go.

"It's like driving through the desert, I guess. They come to see what it's like and then hurry off to get back where the noise makes them forget.

"Sure you don't want a beer, Father Joe?"

"No thanks Gertie," Danny said courteously. "I have to go now. I'll see you in Church tomorrow."

"Ah, dear Father Joe, you know what Jesus should have said?" Gertie downed the last of her beer. "'Blessed are they that mourn, they'll always have their beer to cry in.'"

On the way home Danny found himself smiling. Gertie was coping well. God love her. And despite her denials, she was a courageous heroine. Gertie's holding Sam's wake in their home was a metaphor for their years of companionship and of her refusal to parade her sacrificial love and care for Sam.

He thought of a line from the poet, Rilke. "We are all beginners." There was Gertie beginning a new life without Sam. And Sam was beginning a new life with God. Maybe he would use that in his homily tomorrow. He would amend Rilke's line to read, "We are forever beginners." Life after all is a series of new beginnings, as the seminary Rector used to say after each marking period.

The only reason we stop beginning over is that we become so discouraged about our many failures that we decide what's the use of trying. He remembered reading somewhere that out failures are not excuses for discouragement but reasons for continued growth. The only real failure in life is to have learned nothing from our failures.

He wondered if the process of growing continued in eternity. Who knows?

Of course, the answer he would receive to his query would be no. We stop growing because all growing takes place here on earth. There are no further opportunities for growth in the afterlife. That cancels out his idea that we are forever beginners.

The problem with religious formulas is not only that they give us the presumption that we have all the answers including what God has in store for us in eternity but that we can reduce infinite Mystery itself to our finite, paltry definitions. Is it our need to control? To control God himself? Why do we fear to accept God as Mystery? And what does such control and fear say about our mental stability? These are thoughts he would *not* use in his homily.

For his own spirituality Danny preferred the thinking of Process theologians that in eternity we continue to grow and develop. An eternal evolution. An everlasting becoming of all we can be. Eternal life as a never-ending process.

What he needed to stress tomorrow was a faith that doesn't soar from the realities of life but plunges into the messiness of living. That certainly was what Gertie had done. He doubted he could get that idea across tomorrow. People just wanted to hear the well-worn clichés about this world's not being our true home, about eternal rest and being happy ever after.

Then again he may be selling the people short. It's difficult to preach. The congregation is such a mix of so many different kinds of people. Different educational backgrounds. Different vested interests. And they were all capable of selective listening.

He'd look for a story. Stories seemed to be able to reach all stages of human development. He thought of one he would not use. It was about this old Jewish man who was lying on his death bed. The family was all gathered around. "Are you all here?" the old gentleman asked. "Yes, Papa," the oldest son answered. "Well, then, who's watching the store?"

In the long run, Danny decided, the breaking and sharing of God's Word could only be done with the fractured words of limited human understanding. And you prayed that some hope would slip through the cracks in those words.

It's always the same, Danny mused. Someone dies. His or her loved ones grieve. And the priest has to suppress his emotions in order to be the proverbial pillar of strength for the mourners.

The priest sees deaths, wakes and funerals again and again but he is to remain distant enough from the sorrow so that he can offer the insights of faith to the bereaved. He is not allowed to be caught up in the swirling sadness. He is not supposed to cry or weep or become despondent.

Does anyone ever think of saying to the priest, "This must be difficult for you. Going through all this sorrow, trying to mend all these heartbreaks so many, many times in your life"?

Danny wondered how he would cope if Celine were to die before he did. Is the pain of loss like the ache of wanting to be the one gift bestowed on someone you love? How would he live without her sensitive mind, her heart ever open like a cove offering shelter from life's chaotic storms? Unlike his failure to recall how he felt when Janie died, he would spend the rest of his life with thoughts softly holding the gift of love remembered.

He wondered if he could even bring himself to attend her funeral. Would he have enough faith to celebrate her entrance totally into God? We make such demands on our people, telling them to *celebrate* a loved one's death. Yet if we truly lived our faith, we should be able to celebrate. Still he doubted he could celebrate his loss of Celine.

He recalled something Celine had said to him sometime after they renewed their friendship that Christmas. "I cannot forget what we had but I must forget the fantasy of our ever going back to it. Still wherever I am, you will be there with me in my affection for you." He had responded that theirs would be an intimacy beyond the body. She seemed satisfied. It was hard to tell. Love and grief are twin travelers.

One thing for sure, until he met Celine all he ever did was talk about feelings. Now he was able to experience them.

MARGARET

After Sam's funeral, Danny went into his study and closed the door. He picked up Michael's diary. He still felt uncomfortable about reading what might be Michael's most intimate thoughts and dreams. But it was essential that he did if ever he was going to discover the meaning of that note.

He opened the diary and flipped through it looking for references to Viri Lucis. There were many but when he stopped to read, there was nothing to tell him what Viri Lucis is or who belonged or what it did. Frustrating to say the least. He'd have to read the diary slowly and thoroughly.

Danny began to make notes in a tablet he bought just for that. **Viri Lucis? Pope's death?** Great! Danny thought. The two questions that have been plaguing me for days. A real breakthrough. Then he wrote, **Pope — Michael? Connection? Pope and bishop. Death and plea for understanding? What meaning?** This is ridiculous. But he persisted. **Michael's state of mind? Was it burglary? Then why the note? Michael and Viri Lucis? Connection?** Enough of a connection, he thought, to leave the bulk of his estate to Viri Lucis. Then why the note? He tore the page out of the notebook, rolled it up and tossed it into the wastebasket. "Two points!" he cheered. He got up and retrieved the note and straightened it out. He'd show it to Celine.

Danny called Celine. "Hi," he said. "Hi," she answered. "I was wondering if we could get together for lunch today." "I can't today, Danny. I'm having lunch with Margaret. How about tomorrow?" "Fine," Danny said. "At Toolie's?" "Toolie's it is." "See you there about one?" "Okay." They disconnected.

Celine met Margaret "Margaret, not Marge, not Peg. Margaret." for lunch. Margaret was an interior decorator. After George and she were married, Celine had hired Margaret to refurnish and redecorate their apartment. There had been an immediate attraction between them and since then they had become good friends. "An open

139

window in a musty old legal library," she had told George. Margaret talked like she had a Pod double parked with the meter running.

Margaret was a handsome woman. A little too much makeup, perhaps, and always dressed flamboyantly. She had an attractive figure. A little too big-busted for Celine's taste, but men would certainly take a second glance. They always did. Something to do with being suckled, she supposed. Or not being suckled. Either way, men had an obsession with big breasts. Margaret was in her early forties and was quite 'artsy.'

She had eyes you could dance a jig to. Still the gray shading of her eyes was at one time inviting and at another, forbidding, depending on the shifts of her moods. She was a vivacious extrovert who always seemed to have twenty different things on her mind at the same time. As a result, it wasn't always easy to get her to focus on what you were saying to her. In fact, talking to her often seemed like interrupting a psychotic episode. Although, Celine conceded, as of late, Margaret seemed to give Celine her undivided attention for some reason or another.

Margaret's flaming red hair was piled on top of her head as usual. It was aided with heavy tint to distract people from studying the lines in her otherwise attractive face. Those who knew her recognized the lines as scars from worry, disappointment and anger over the hand dealt her at the poker table of life. Her divorce had all the ingredients of a soap opera and raising her son was more a burden than a blessing.

Worst of all she hadn't yet met another man she would ever consider having a lifelong relationship with. She enjoyed success in her work as an interior decorator but she would not equate it with fulfillment. At times her face was a bit puffy. Probably, Celine surmised, from too much night life and too much booze.

Margaret was always the life of the party. No doubt a cover up for the torture she experienced from knowing that chances for intimate love were growing rarer. Her constant nervous smile seemed to be Morse code for don't look at my sharp nose. She was witty in a crude sort of way but it was studied crudeness for effect rather than for self-revelation.

The transparency of her flippant remarks revealed all the more the opaque mystery of her heart. She was in general a delightful person to be around and there were occasions when, in a street-wise fashion, she could be quite insightful. She bore herself with regal dignity, as she told Celine, "I always advocated Eleanor Roosevelt's advice of entering a room as though you were wearing a crown and all that."

It was amusing at times to watch her accept the obeisance of waiters as due her majestic role. All in all Margaret was fun. She was wise and unpredictable. But above all she was a loyal, loving friend.

Celine enjoyed Margaret. She relieved the intensity which was Celine's way of life. Margaret reminded Celine of the humorous in life's tragedies even though Margaret could strike the tragic pose better than anyone.

It was the old bromide of opposites attracting. Celine was glamorous but taut. Margaret was fashionable and loquacious. Celine was prim. Margaret was carefree. Celine was analytical. Margaret was intuitive. But what they had in common was that both were appealingly vulnerable.

Despite her studied flippancy, Celine appreciated the undivided attention Margaret gave her. After her divorce, Margaret had undergone therapy. It was a common bond that offered them immediate entree into one another's lives, worries, hopes and disappointments.

Margaret, like Celine, had emerged from therapy with a more realistic appraisal of herself, her life situation and a release from the past which had been holding her hostage. At least to some degree.

When pressed, Margaret could be as sensitive as a kindergarten teacher although she'd no more shed her impudence, often peppered with saucy vulgarity, than she would have her head shaved.

Celine knew that Margaret's impudence was her way of venting. A cover. A defense against allowing anyone too close for fear that her slowly healing wounds would rupture all over again. Celine was the exception. Margaret treated her as a truly intimate friend.

Like most people, Margaret was vulnerable. There were times when Margaret was venting that Celine saw her eyes water. Sometimes there was even a hint of tears. Celine was convinced that Margaret's guise of impish humor was her way of trying to be humble and honest about herself — and brutally honest to others. She was the essence of practicality. And Celine knew that if she wanted the truth, Margaret was the one to come to. She would give you the truth, unvarnished and as blunt as a sledgehammer's blow.

There were times when Celine was able to plumb the depths of Margaret's soul where she found a luscious wellspring of empathy. Margaret's compassion had been forged in the crucible of the personal pain she had endured during her divorce and the heartbreak of an apparent alienation from her son. Her empathy was genuine and for Celine it was a source of comfort.

"How's your son doing?" Celine asked.

"Fine. He's with his father right now. God knows I need a break. It's so hard raising a boy … by yourself. Sometimes I feel like a bug on the windshield of life. You know, being a woman and all that."

"Margaret, would you mind if I asked you why you broke up? I mean we didn't meet until after that and we never really talked about it."

"No, I don't mind. I'll tell you this, though, after the divorce my life was as unplanned as a doodle. I try not to talk about the divorce and life ever after. I hate women who are forever talking about why their marriages didn't work out. Dull as dust. So filled with self-pity. I mean how many shoulders do you need to cry on? I guess it's therapeutic and all that" Margaret took a sip of her Bloody Mary and a deep breath almost at the same time.

"You know how men are," Margaret continued. "Lousy communicators. I swear to God they can't get in touch with their feelings anymore than they can kiss their ear. You try for some in-depth conversation and all you get is 'Uh-huh' or 'What?' Talking to my EX was like bobbing for apples in a bucket of mud and all that.

"I swear he wouldn't have told me if my bra was on fire. After a while I began to think my only choice was between being dysfunctional and being absolutely psychotic. Sometimes I think men have all been hired from central casting. He has a girlfriend, you know. Saw her once. I may not be the world's most enviable beauty but she looked like a soup kitchen blew up in her face.

"Men are so damned busy bonding with the fellahs that they don't even think they have to talk to the 'little woman.' It's so demeaning. They supply things and think that's all you want. They take you to bed and by some erotic alchemy they're tender. Until it's over and then it's roll over and sweet dreams and all that."

"Men use tenderness to get sex and women use sex to get tenderness," Celine uttered off-handedly.

"Something like that." Now that Margaret got started she was just rolling along. "Maybe women expect too much. Maybe we're not realistic about wanting romance in a relationship. When they say you have to work at love, do they mean sweaty, exhausting work and all that?

"Anyway, all we talked about was our jobs, friends, our son, our in-laws, money, neighbors and all that. I mean there was little or no self-revelatory communication. I asked him repeatedly what he wanted out of relationship. You know what he finally came up with? He sat like a cherub and said, 'I want to be alone with you there.' Can you believe the gall?"

"Sounds like a title for a manual on marriage," Celine said trying to lighten things up a bit. "Who knows, maybe that's the answer to all marital problems. Alone with you there."

Undaunted, Margaret continued her delightful gushing. "And then, of course, men have to always be in control. They have to be the cock of the walk, if you'll excuse the Freudian sex reference. They're so obsessed with being macho. They come on like the last reel of one of those old John Wayne movies but the longer you live with them the more you realize they're just a tower of Jello.

"And the one place they think they can be in total control is in their own homes. God, I could puke at the thought. The one thing I want to make sure about is that my son, Brian, doesn't grow up thinking he's Lord and Master. I want to help him get in touch with his feminine side without becoming effeminate."

"I really don't think you have anything to worry about in that department," Celine tried to sound encouraging. Brian's father is so macho that I can't see him turning out any way but like that." No sooner had Celine said that than she knew she had gone beyond a stock phrase.

"God forbid!" Margaret all but shouted. "Honey, I know we're all grass and God is the Big Lawnmower but he'd never mow me down like that, would he? Come on, Celine, you're the one who played footsie with a priest."

Without letting Celine answer or even register dismay at the footsie remark, Margaret plowed on. "Anyway, we just grew apart. At first it was two miles past terrible but then we just grew calluses on our feelings and shared the same address.

"It got to the point that we didn't even get on one another's nerves anymore. Whoever said the opposite of love isn't hatred but indifference was right on target. Our divorce was as casual as saying goodbye, see ya later and all that.

"It wasn't until later that I felt anger. Maybe it's because things are no better now than they were then. The grass really isn't greener. Talk about caviar dreams and champagne wishes. I date around but I'm lonely.

"Sometimes I wish I could come home and have somebody to talk to about my job, friends and all that. Maybe I was angry because I didn't try harder or just settle for what I had. You know, growing old comfortably together. I mean I wasn't a battered woman unless the lack of sensitive communication could be considered psychological battering.

" Sometimes, dear, I think happiness is like trying to catch tadpoles with your tongue."

"I read somewhere," Celine said, her statement more like talking out loud to herself than to Margaret, "that happiness is making a bouquet out of the flowers nearest to you,"

"Well, yes, that too," Margaret didn't seem too interested in a positive spin.

"Shit, Celine, I don't know. Men say we're bitches and maybe we are. What's that old saying, 'Women get married thinking their husbands will change but they don't. Men get married thinking their wives won't change but they do'?

"I like that joke I heard at a wedding. The minister or priest or whatever, I get them mixed up, told it. Adam and Eve were the only ones who had an ideal marriage. Adam couldn't tell Eve what a great cook his mother was. And Eve couldn't' tell Adam about all the other guys she could have married. How come we have to shave our arm pits and they don't?"

"I'm sorry, Margaret. I didn't mean for you to open up old wounds. I was just wondering about close relationships. How they begin and how they end. I'm married to George. That's one close relationship. Then there's Danny.

"Still," Celine's voice seemed to come from some distant cavern of introspective thought, "I do worry about Danny."

"What's to worry. He's a busy priest working with the poor and downtrodden and all that. Is it the neighborhood?"

"Not really. He's pretty much in control, if you'll excuse the expression."

"Then what?"

"Oh, nothing." She couldn't take Margaret into her confidence about Danny and that note. "Nothing really."

"Well, I'm telling you, Honey, and I know I'm unloading this on you like a ton of cement, but drop your relationship with Danny. As long as you insist on maintaining this 'friendship' you'll never be at peace. And I'm not at all sure that George is all that pleased with the setup. He may just be accommodating you.

"You know, my dear, George may not be the best but you can certainly settle for what's next. In fact, you know better than I that you should be talking this over with George instead of with me. I only wish my marriage had been based on a more open and honest communication. At least give it a try. If it doesn't work out, then you can spin a tale of woe for me."

"I'll think about it, Margaret." And pray, she thought to herself. On her way back to her office, Celine thought that the best one to talk to about her and Danny was definitely not a woman with a broken relationship. She thought she might visit her sister, Joreen. There was a woman who had a happy marriage.

Oh, she had her days and her problems but they both worked at it and except for one time it wasn't a sweaty, exhausting workout. She had to smile. Just as her mother played the sleuth with her, all she did about Joreen was worry.

Maybe that's what mothers do when the nest is empty. Her smile disappeared as quickly as a shadow in sunshine. She felt depressed. No, angry. No, befuddled. Damn you, Danny, why did you have to happen to me? "I'm not a happy camper," she muttered aloud.

The street was teeming with workers making a last minute dash back to their offices from lingering lunch breaks. Celine's head was bowed, her coat collar pulled up against the cutting wind and the interior frost of despondency, lost in thought. She bumped into someone but barely heard the caustic, "Why the hell don't ya watch where yer goin'?"

She wished she could just let go of the sphinx-like riddle of human relationships altogether. She felt adrift on a turbulent sea of the touch-and-go friendship with Danny. Battered by the hit-and-run desperation of what might have been had it not been manufactured restrictions.

Sometimes, she thought, she lived in a Technicolor fantasy world as spectacular and as unreal as a Disney cartoon production. She knew that what she needed was a close-up awareness of reality as familiar as the morning buzz of her alarm system.

Would she ever experience the oneness of a single soul dwelling in two bodies, as someone had put it? She was lost, she had to admit, in the luscious grief of self-pity over an abandoned love. She yearned for a moment of insight that would make all her experiences with Danny disappear.

The next day Danny and Celine met for lunch at Toolie's. Toolie's was dark and intimate. The booths were made of heavy oak with real leather. On each table was a small oil lamp. When it was time to study the menu, the waiter would turn up the lamp. When the waiter served the entree, he would ask if you wanted the lamp turned down.

There was a large mirror that spanned the far wall and added a depth to the room that seduced patrons into a feeling that reality was not so important as fantasy. As a result, there was a kind of quiet, restful gaiety about the place. Despite the fact that Toolie's was usually crowded, patrons always enjoyed the cozy privacy of their booths which made them feel as though they were the only ones there.

After a few warm exchanges between them, Danny showed Celine the paper with his questions written on it.

"Danny, why don't you just let it go. You are not Chesterton's Father Brown. You don't even read detective novels. Turn the whole thing over to a lawyer. I have a friend who will take care of all this for you. You men. You think you have to shoulder every burden."

"Women do their share, Celine," Danny said smiling. "Look at how you try to fix everything."

"I guess that's a reference to our parting."

"It was more like your departure." Danny could feel himself getting annoyed. "I thought we had all that settled."

"Oh, sure, that's the way you want to think about it. You never called me in over a year. It was all settled. You had your fling and that was that. Back to your priestly duties."

"What's going on here, Celine?"

They kept their voices low which only added to the intensity of what they were saying.

"I don't know. I feel like I'm watching a tennis match being played without a ball. I'm so tired trying to do everything with triple efforts to prove I'm just as competent as men. Just as deserving. Just as intelligent. What do you want me to do? Gush with enthusiasm? Gee whiz, men have allowed me into their law firm.!"

"So you're taking it out on me?"

"Do you realize, Danny, that since we've become 'friends' we've never discussed *us?*

"I thought you were satisfied, even happy, that we were able to establish a friendship."

"I guess I am. It's just …."

"Just what, Celine?"

"Oh, I don't know. Margaret told me I should drop our relationship and get on with my life."

"Ah, Margaret! The font of all wisdom. She tosses off her Sunday Supplement psychoanalysis and you're back to letting someone control you. Maybe it's time to go back and visit your therapist. At least she's licensed."

"You always have all the answers, don't you?"

"No, I don't. I'm just trying to figure out how we got from my concern about the note to….to this."

"Concern? *Concern?* Try obsession. Danny, don't mess with this. I have this premonition that it could be dangerous."

"I just don't understand this premonition of yours. About the note. About me and the note."

"Call it one woman's intuition. One shrewd woman."

"Celine, do you want our relationship to end – again?"

"Why? Can you just walk away again?" By now Celine's eyes were filling and her voice was breaking.

"I didn't walk away. I was sent away."

"You do have to make points, don't you? You'd have made a fine lawyer."

Danny was torn. He wanted to take her into his arms. But right now he was too angry. He just wanted this to stop. "Look, Celine, let's stop this wrangling. It's going nowhere." No sooner had he said it than he regretted it. That was Celine's line, going nowhere. He hoped she missed it.

"Maybe that's what we've always been about, going nowhere," Celine countered.

She hadn't missed it.

"Celine, why are we having this argument? I think we should drop this right now. You seem to be out of sorts."

"Out of sorts? You've ruined my life and I'm just out of sorts."

It was as if Danny had been shot in the stomach. "I didn't realize you felt that way, that I've ruined your life."

"Who the hell do you think I'm thinking about when I'm with George? That's not good for me, for him, for us. Oh forget it. You're not ruining my life. No one is. I was thinking of you even before we got back together that Christmas. Maybe I should hightail it back to my therapist."

"Celine, what brought this on? I just don't know where you're coming from. For the last months I thought we've been so close, so supportive of each other. We've enjoyed each other."

"Maybe I just care too much, love you too much."

"Celine, what we have for each other is precious. Don't you think I feel pain? Sometimes I get up in the middle of the night filled with regret. Then I soothe my feelings by realizing that at least we have what we have. Then I'm plunged into depression by the thought that I should had chucked the whole thing and married you. I don't know what's keeping me where I am. Hell, I'm not making that much of difference anyway."

"Yes you are! I don't want to take you away from that. It's just that sometimes my emotions go haywire. I guess Margaret just pushed some buttons that set me off. I'm truly sorry. I wouldn't hurt you for all the world. I guess I just don't have your kind of faith."

"Is it faith?" Danny asked dolefully. "It could just as well be cowardice. Maybe I'm clinging to the illusion of security. In my weaker or clearer moments I think I'm a magician for the superstitious. I hate the thought. Yet by some strange twist of irony, I derive security from it. And that security is a source of most of my doubts. I don't know if this makes any sense. It probably sounds like the rankings of a psychotic."

"Danny, you are the most endearing man I've ever known. You're street smart and so naive in the ways of the world. You're brilliant but not pretentious. You're wise but you don't manipulate."

" Celine. I'm just like everyone else. A mix of shadow and light, fear and courage, doubts and hope. Strong and weak, as you well know. I fight my demons and pray that in the process I don't become one. I want you to know, though, that in this desperate fight, Celine, I owe you so much. I will always be grateful to you — for you."

149

"Thank you for saying that, Danny. It means so much to me. Maybe I was just indulging in regret for what might have been, what can never be."

"Celine, don't you think I've had the identical regrets? The anguish of unfulfilled love. And yet the space between us now needs two hearts that can blend without breaking. I think we're capable of this. We had romance and we're doing our damnest to supplant it with heartfelt concern. It's more depthful. More lasting. Our feelings are still there but what we have now is the result of a well thought-out choice.

"You've caused so many resurrections in my life, Celine. You know that. You've seen the transformation. We can still be close, affectionate friends. I will never hold you so close that I'll stifle what you want, what you need, believe me. Can't we treasure this together?"

"But what if I can't have the same feeling for my husband as I do for you? Do I spend the rest of my life faking it?"

"Celine, you know love is not reduced to feelings. My God, feelings are as fleeting as clouds. Sometimes they're strong, sometimes they're not. If we based our relationships on feelings only, we'd be like a boat without a rudder tossed any which way by the waves of our changing situations."

"I know, Danny. I've said it to myself hundreds of times. Love is a conscious choice. I can't say that often enough. It's a choice to make the other person's happiness highest on your list of priorities. I'm not so naive as to believe married couples live on perpetual romance like the advertisers for Big Business would have us believe."

" Celine, you and George have made a choice to love each other and that's what matters most, isn't it?

"I guess so." There was an obvious sound of resignation in her voice. "Usually, I am so in control. Maybe I'm angry at myself for allowing my emotions to take over. You know how strong I am."

"I know. Just keep thinking about love as an attitude. And you are in control of your attitude. If someone's attitude is that there should be romantic feelings at all times in his or her relationship, that attitude can be changed to one that's more realistic. That's taking charge with your strength."

"I know, 'To change your life, change your attitude.'" She didn't sound totally convinced. "I guess I'm being self indulgent. Do you think I'm a bitch? Margaret says that men think we're bitches. "

"No, you're not a bitch but you are being bitchy. Hell, men can be just as bitchy. We just call it by different names. Moody, indifferent, aloof, emotionless, uninvolved, superficial, whatever."

Celine dabbed her face and smiled. "You're either the most sincere man I've ever met or the flashiest word wizard." Suddenly they both laughed out loud.

"I'm sorry, Danny. I guess Margaret's bitching about her EX just threw me off.

"Look, Danny, getting back to the note, let it go. Hand the whole thing over to a lawyer. As I said, I can get you someone who's an expert on these matters, someone you can trust. Do it if for no other reason than for your own peace of mind."

Danny wasn't so sure about peace if he gave up on his investigation. He would talk to Gene.

READING THE DIARY

Eventually Danny decided it was time to sit down and read Michael's diary methodically and not just glance through it as he did before. The first thing he noticed was that it was not a daily record. Sometimes there was a date, most of the time there was none. Danny began to read:

I am so thrilled. I received the telegram today. I am to be a successor of the Apostles. A bishop in the Church. I thank God for this grace. God has used the instrument of Viri Lucis to bring this sacred honor to me. I have already placed a call to express my thanks. When I survey the kinds of weak and even liberal bishops recently appointed, I am certain God has very important work for me to do. This is but the beginning. In a few years I will ascend to the Red Hat. I will be a Prince of the Church. All I have to do is wait until his Eminence is called to his eternal reward.

I will meet with him tomorrow to set the date of my ordination. I know my father will want to do it up big. I'd prefer a more simple reception, but my father has so many friends among the hierarchy. I will accede to his wishes. I only hope he will live until I am made a Cardinal. It would be the crown of his achievements. I wish my

mother were alive but I know she is
smiling down on me this day.

I intend to make a retreat before my
ordination.

I want to lay my plans for the future.
This is essential since I am to be one
day the most influential Churchman
in the U.S.

Danny stopped reading. This didn't sound like the Michael he
knew. Good natured, almost happy-go-lucky. Ambitious, yes, but
always within reasonable limits. This Michael of the diary sounded
like a megalomaniac.

What could Michael have possibly meant? He was just informed
he had been appointed an Auxiliary bishop and he's writing about
becoming a Cardinal? The most influential Cardinal in the United
States? Where did all this come from? Did he think all his wealth
....? Maybe. Danny continued to read:

The Church needs to be purified.
Obedience must be restored especially
among women. Not all of them but
too many of them are rebellious
and their influence on children is
breeding a generation of heretics.
Their insistence on the ordination of
women is in direct attack against His
Holiness, Pope John Paul II of happy
memory.

As the Vicar of Christ, Pope John
Paul II's pronouncement on the
impossibility of ordaining women
was infallible. He fulfilled the
four requirements for an infallible

statement: he spoke as the Vicar of Christ, on a matter of faith, to the whole Church, for the purpose of absolute obedience. These women are in fact heretical in ignoring Pope John Paul's infallible teaching.

Then there are women who openly advocate abortion. They too are no longer members of the Church. We need leaders who will excommunicate them once and for all. Women need to be restored to their primary God-given role as procreators and nurturers. They must be taken out of the work force and be returned to their proper places in the home. The whole Church is just too loose from the top to the bottom. What is needed is either a violent persecution or a drastic reformation. The decisions of Vatican II were obviously misguided and are being taken far beyond what was even then enacted. I know I will be able to do a great deal to heal the Church I love.

Danny paused. He was trying to absorb the outlandish statements made by his friend, by a man he realized he did not know, by a .... a fanatic. Danny actually felt physically sick. He didn't know if he could continue reading but he knew he had to if he was going to find out what Michael's abstruse note. He read on.

We must begin with priests. The older ones don't care anymore and the younger never did care. A purge is necessary. Let there be a holy remnant. Better that than all these people who are Catholics in name only. There has been absolutely too much emphasis on the mercy of God. As a result people are convinced they can sin anyway they want. What is needed is a new sense of penitence.

Public penance must be reintroduced. The gospel is being distorted. The woman taken in adultery has become a metaphor for the immorality of our day. Emphasis needs to be restored to the plucking out of an eye, the cutting off of a limb. The Iranians and others have the healthier idea. Someone steals and his hand is cut off.

Danny picked up his pen. He wrote in his notebook. **Megalomania. Mercy vs. Public Penance. Heretics. Excommunication.**

He sat there staring at the carefully written script. He wasn't sure he could continue reading the diary. Never before in his life …. The phone buzzed. "You have an incoming call. Will you go on line?" "Yes," Danny answered. It was Gene.

"Danny."

"Yes."

"Danny, I was going through Leno's papers. I came across a number of references to something called the Ardentes. The Ardent?"

"I remember seeing something in a footnote. The term is more accurately and perhaps more insidiously translated as the Vindictive," Danny replied.

"What's that all about?"

"Not sure but I'll tell you what. I'll dust off some old text books and see what I can come up with. Or better, I'll take a trip out to the seminary library."

"Good and when you find out something, let me know. Okay?"

"Okay."

"By the way I've been reading Michael's diary."

"And …?"

"To say the least it's hair raising. I'll fill you in on that, too."

"Okay. Talk to you later."

THE OLD PROF

Danny got out of his car and walked toward the Administration building of the seminary. Here is where he studied philosophy before he went to Rome. It still boasted a first class library. As he walked along the corridor, he smiled. Here he was walking in the middle of the floor. In his student days they were obliged to walk on the right or left but never in the middle of the floor.

No one ever explained why. Maybe it prevented getting too cozy with the person you were walking along with. Maybe it was to preserve the sheen in the center. Maybe it was just a matter of training you in obedience.

He decided to stop in and see Father Henning, his old History of Philosophy professor whom he admired so much and should have visited oftener. He had to be in his early nineties. Danny wasn't sure if the old boy's mind would have the same legendary keenness as he was once famous for.

"Ah, Joseph, my boy. Didn't think I'd recognize you? These days I look in the mirror and have trouble recognizing the face I see." Father Henning laughed until he coughed up phlegm.

"I'm on my way to the library and thought I'd drop in to drink at the fountain of wisdom," Danny smiled. "You're looking quite fit. How do you feel?"

"As fit as anyone can expect at 93," the old priest smiled back. "What is so important as to drag the likes of you to a library, not to mention a seminary library?"

"The Ardentes," Danny said simply.

Father Henning's face lit up. "Ah, 15th century. An ugly little group."

"I only recall it as a footnote," Danny said.

"And a footnote would have pleased them. They were so secretive," Father Henning replied.

"As I recall," Danny said, "Ardentes stood for the Vindictive?"

157

"Quite. They were a sneaky bunch of subversives. Ah, Joseph, you're the only student I ever taught who had a more retentive memory than I."

"A flatterer's throat is an open sepulcher," Danny laughed. Father Henning joined him in the laughter. "Savanarola, that little Dominican reformer turned fanatic," Father Henning warmed up to the subject. "In Florence. He preached against every conceivable immorality, even the most delectable. Bitchy sort, he. Attacked the Medicis and Lorenzo the Magnificent in particular. Attacked Pope Alexander VI of the Borgia clan.

" Not that Alexander didn't need attacking. Poor man. A freelance ecclesiastic who regarded almost every woman as an ambulatory sex organ. God must have created him to make everyone else look like a saint.

"You don't go around attacking members of two of the most powerful families in Italy without getting into hot water even if it does have a cleansing effect. Savanarola in the beginning was filled with zeal and self-sacrifice, but then he went fanatic. Disobedient to the Pope and obstinate in his attacks.

"Alexander censured him. But Savanarola kept chuggin' along. His preaching episodes which in the beginning made the people's blood shiver and their flesh ache, eventually turned into emotional carnivals. Anyway the people's initial fervor in the heat of conversion, like milk left out in the sun, turned sour.

"So one morning when poor Savanarola sat down to his Eggs Benedict an ad hoc lynch mob dragged him out into the square and hanged him. Then they burned his body. Talk about ashes to ashes.

"Interesting," Danny said, "but the Ardentes?"

"Ah, yes. Apparently, and this has never been confirmed, they were a band of Savanarola's followers who took his rigorism over the edge of properly approved piety. Good carried to an extreme becoming evil, you know. And as Savanarola became more violent in his verbal attacks, this particular group of followers became physically violent in their assaults on anyone they considered heretical or even unworthy."

"Killings?"

"Oh, killings were the least of their atrocities. They kidnapped, incarcerated, tortured, flogged, mutilated, dismembered, castrated, depending on the sex of the offender."

Danny couldn't help but notice that even at 93 the old priest visibly shivered at the mention of the word, castrated.

"It was a wonderful mélange of cultic inhumanities," Father Henning continued almost oblivious of Danny. "And all done in the name of purity of doctrine or just plain purity. How they loved to get their hands on adulterers and fornicators. Had they been around when Jesus delivered his immortal line about casting the stone first, that poor woman would have looked like a rock pile. Being around them must have been like a tour of Bedlam Hospital."

"What happened to them?" Danny asked.

"Oh, they got caught up with the Enthusiasts of the Reformation. And thanks to the impetus Luther gave them, they went rushing pell-mell right into the sink hole of excommunication and disappeared or so the story goes. Who knows?"

"Rumor has it that they're going to canonize Luther. Wouldn't surprise me after they exonerated Galileo. Why bother with today's problems when you too can solve century-old problems?" Henning gave a short laugh.

"They're not going to canonize Luther," Danny said. "And besides Galileo was wrong. The sun does revolve around the earth and the earth is flat."

Father Henning laughed uproariously. "The very picture of the sun circling around a flat planet. You're quite the astronomer."

"You know about Jansenism?" the old professor asked. "Of course you do."

"Seventeenth and eighteenth centuries," Danny responded. "Obsessed with sins of the flesh. Protested against frequent communion because no one was worthy. Preparation for communion should take months, maybe years."

"Jansenius was a sophisticated theologian. Non violent except perhaps on the intellectual level," Father Henning continued his instruction. "Seems, and you probably won't find this in any of the scholarly tomes approved as authentic history from on high, that Jansenius was a descendent of one of the Ardentes. Sort of a religious Rip van Winkle who woke up one day and decided we were all inherently depraved, incapable of good.

"And God, according to him, dished out grace to some and refused it to others. Poor Jansenius. A triumph of miscasting. Meant well but don't all fanatics? He started out seriously enough but ended up being meticulously insipid. His was a grab bag of Manichaeism, Predestination, Quietism and Pelagianism, all very fine heresies whose atmospheres still cling to the faithful to this very day,"

"Like people still going to communion as a reward for their good lives?" Danny smiled wryly.

"Exactly. If nothing else Jansenius gave the Ardentes a veneer of theological sophistication albeit with verbal bloodletting. Condemned eventually. Sometimes I wonder if condemning heresies doesn't abet their becoming atmospheres for succeeding generations."

"There's another formidable group. The Fidelists," Father Henning teased. "Late 18th and 19th centuries."

"The Faithful?" Danny asked.

"Would that it were that innocuous. More insidious. The Orthodox. The Fidelists or Orthodox were the most insidious of all. They identified with Church authorities who wanted to restore law and order, if you'll excuse the Nixonian expression. They were in the vanguard of accusing others of unorthodox practices from out and out open rebellion against the papacy for changing a word or gesture in the liturgy.

"They went after theologians who were teaching the Mystical Body, accused them of heresy and had their license to teach as Catholic theologians revoked. Eventually they were condemned for their fanatical attacks on just about everyone from Princes of the Church to the blind, the deaf and the lame. But I'm getting sleepy now. That's all I do anymore, eat and sleep. That's why your visit has been so energizing," the old man said graciously. "How's our young bishop, Michael?"

"He's fine," Danny lied. No need in going into what had happened. Why upset the old boy? "I'll give him your regards."

160

"Well, remember, Joseph, for those who feel, life is a tragedy, for those who think, it's a comedy."

Before Danny could leave, old Father Henning was fast asleep.

Danny proceeded to the library. His original research had been taken care of thanks to Raleigh W. Henning, Ph.D., S.T.D. But he wanted to check up on details especially the connections, if any, among the various groups. Probably there is only one heresy and the rest are variations on a theme.

That evening Celine, Gene and Danny were once again gathered in Gene's kitchen. Danny gave them a rundown of the Ardentes or the Vindictive, the Jansenists and the Fidelists or Orthodox.

"Do you think Viri Lucis could be a continuation or development … a modern day version of these fanatical groups?" Celine asked sounding bewildered.

"I don't know," Danny answered. "I really don't."

"There's nothing in your research to make a connection?" Gene asked.

"Not really. Even what 'Pops' Henning told me was couched in cautions about his information or theories not being in history books."

"It sounds like another conspiracy theory to me," Celine said.

"Still it may be a lead," Gene didn't sound very convinced. "And then again there is that reference to the Ardentes in Leno's telecomputer."

When Danny arrived home late that night he found the door to his office open. He had been locking it and wondered if he had forgotten to do so when he left to go to Gene's.

When he entered the office he saw immediately that it had been ransacked. It looked like a cyclone had blasted through it. As he slowly examined it, he saw that everything had been destroyed.

Even his miniature Hummels which people had given him over the years and which he treasured as a contact with the world of beauty were pulverized. His office had not been searched. It had been destroyed.

Just then the phone sounded. "Incoming call," the butler voice recited. "Do you wish to go on line or should I …." "On line," Danny commanded.

Danny expected to hear the familiar "Hi" but instead he heard a soft-spoken voice which he immediately identified as Archbishop Brown's. The Archbishop had failed or deliberately not turned on the viewscreen.

"Good evening, Father Daniels."

"Is having someone's office torn to shreds the ultimate touch of ecclesiastic diplomacy?" Danny responded with all the sarcasm he could muster.

"I have no idea what you're talking about, dear Father," Archbishop Brown purred.

Danny let it go, although he was seething. He knew he'd get nowhere.

"As you might expect, I'm calling to hear what you've discerned with regard to my request."

"You could have saved yourself the effort," Danny responded with sarcasm still ringing in his voice. "You got my answer. Now live with it."

"You'll never know how much I am disappointed in you. Let me assure you, you will regret your decision. The condition of your office is just a foretaste. As for your companion in sin, you have put her at grave risk also."

"Just what gospel are you following, Brown? I may have sinned but at least I admit it. How do you sleep at night? What image of Christ do you have?"

"I didn't call you for an examen of conscience," Brown retorted abruptly, matching Danny's sarcasm. With that the phone went dead.

Archbishop Brown physically shivered. He knew for certain he would never be a member of the College of Cardinals.

Danny waved his phone off. His anxiety was so aggravated that he thought he might go into hyperventilation. He distracted himself by trying to clean up his office. The first thing he did was look for his strong box. There it was over in a corner, broken open. The two copies of the note were gone.

If I had only placed one copy in the box, he thought, they may have been convinced that they had the original. That might have gotten them off his back. He doubted it. They would have soon discovered that it was not the original.

As he gathered up the fragments of his Hummels, he could feel tears smarting his eyes. He had so few possessions and these were his pride and joy.

He wondered what Viri Lucis might be planning for him, and worse, for Celine. He ached for her. "Damn you Michael," he said aloud, "what did you get me into?"

He decided not to call Celine. No purpose would be served except to upset her more. He recalled her face from earlier that evening. She looked as though she was waiting wistfully for a larger destiny to loom before her. What would be her destiny in all this? What would be their destiny?

THE CANDIDATES

"The Cardinals are here in the Vatican, gathered in the shadow of St. Peter's dome and in the bleakness of their dismal quandary," Charles Weakley of World News Broadcast spoke solemnly. "Not since the sudden death of Pope John Paul I have the Cardinal-electors been called to Rome as quickly as they have been after Pope Charles' accidental death."

The debonair commentator was well known for using words like a brush dipped into the colors of current events. His forte was analysis. He preferred to step on opinions rather than on toes. He did not always succeed.

He was an agnostic who enjoyed dabbling in religious matters much like a concert pianist might sit in from time to time with a jazz group.

Charles Weakley stood before the camera braving the February winds in thirty degree weather, his coat collar pulled up around his neck, a red scarf wrapped loosely over the collar. The snow covered Apennines in the background only added to the mystique of a panoramic view that emphasized the universality of the Roman Catholic Church.

A real hero. His ambiguous smile expressed neither warm empathy for his Catholic viewers nor subtle disdain for their beliefs. His eyes were kindled with curiosity about a solemn event but displayed no sign of respect for the religious importance of what was happening.

He had a mountain look that made the election of a Pope seem microscopic compared to his stature as the premiere commentator of GlobeNet's WNBM who boasted not only of a legion of devoted followers but of three Pulitzer prizes.

"The dilemma for the Cardinals, it seems, is that they do not want to have another ultra conservative reactionary nor do they want another ultra liberal revolutionary. Apparently they want someone who can walk the highwire between the two extremes. Whether or not there will be a safety net below, no one is saying."

Charles Weakley smiled graciously as if he were letting his viewers learn secrets he alone could share.

"The Roman Church today seems either to be yearning for a vital dream or praying to be delivered from the rack of its recent past.

"There are those among the Cardinals who, from what we understand, hope they can participate in the healing power of their founder and stop the slow heavy drops of blood dripping from the open wound inflicted by their last Supreme Pontiff, Pope Charles.

"There are others as up-to-date as the jetliners which flew them into Rome. Their aim, it seems, is to make certain their Church has enough jet propulsion to enable it to land safely in the 21st century."

He paused again for effect. Those who worked closely with him knew well he was making this pause to relish his own words and the sound of his deep, resonant voice.

Standing there with his microphone in hand, against the backdrop of St. Peter's, he continued. "There is a third segment among the Cardinals, perhaps the largest, who has no other desire than to see white smoke fill the Vatican sky so that they can get back to the comfort or problems of their own archdioceses.

"For all of them, one fact seems certain. There will be no feasting on hope's immortal food." He paused again to allow his picturesque words to sink in. "The solemn procession of the Cardinals moving slowly into the Sistine Chapel seems to be a metaphor for a Church that is convinced that it does not have to do today what can be put off until the next century.

"The question that has the religious professionals buzzing not only here but throughout the Catholic world is this: When the door of the conclave is closed, will the gates of possibility be flung open?

"From a mere layman's view, for days now there have been trysts among various members of the College of Cardinals in which, apparently, a great deal of politicking has been going on. Although the Cardinals themselves would undoubtedly prefer to call it discussion. Yet, we are informed, once they enter the conclave, they put their trust in the Holy Spirit to guide them in their choice of the next Vicar of Christ on earth.

"If trust is the religious expression of faith, then these must be men of monumental faith. Or on the other hand, perhaps the gospel could be rendered for them to read, 'Where two or three are gathered in my name, there is politics in their midst.'"

Charles Weakley signaled to the cameraman to cut. Despite the cold weather, he took out a handkerchief and wiped his brow. Then he glanced for a long time over Vatican City as though he were surveying the universal Catholic Church.

"Let's continue this later," he said to the cameraman. "I've got to do some brushing up on the front runners before I go on the air."

The next morning, Charles Weakley stood in front of St. John Lateran, the Bishop of Rome's cathedral. It was, he thought, a most appropriate place since this segment of his commentary would be about the front runners for the position of the next Bishop of Rome and Pontiff of the Roman Church.

"As the Cardinals' perseverance trudges through the snowstorm of frigid determination, there are several who appear to be front runners. It must be noted, however, that there is a saying that he who goes into the conclave as Pope exits as a Cardinal, his heart as empty as a wheat bin in a draught.

"Rumors of front runners are running through Rome like solemn whispers. This is what we were able to overhear. It's the only information that has filtered through high level sieves.

"First, there is Cardinal Giambattista Martino of Naples who is 63. He is known for liberal stands on birth control which would put him in sync with Pope Charles. He is renown for involvement with the poor and as an advocate of justice. He has extensive pastoral experience, having served in parishes for 17 years of his priesthood. He is outgoing and charming, not an intellectual but a very empathetic man.

" The story is that he appears at times to be torn between old loyalties and new commitments. There is about him a casualness that cannot quite extinguish the aura of his brash elegance. Associates say that he draws his strength from his refusal to fear failure. There are those who criticize him for having fervent ideas but poor judgment. He is a man who seems to enjoy his humanness and through it serve his people generously.

"He is not much of a linguist and has not traveled except to several European countries. He is well known among many Cardinals and his charm could carry him to the throne of Peter. After Pope Charles, however, his chances seem slim.

Weakly paused to study his notes. The human touch. He had everything committed to memory.

"Then there is Cardinal Alessandro Percussi, 78, of Milan. He is considered moderate. An introvert but a very patient and sympathetic man. He has little pastoral experience other than that of being bishop, having spent most of his priesthood teaching at the Gregorian University. He is a renowned scholar.

"Little is known about his stands on current issues. Most of his scholarly writings dealt with esoteric kinds of theological research. He is known for helping Pope John Paul II in the composition of his encyclicals and was duly rewarded by being appointed Archbishop at the age of 61 by Pope Leo XIV in the year 2014. Later that year he was made a Cardinal. He is not a linguist and has never traveled outside of Italy.

"He appears to be a mountain of obscurity that must be mined. He apparently prefers to be interpreted than interrogated. Associates say that he usually reacts as if he had just been told of an unexpected death. They point to this as a sign of his genius.

"He gives the impression that he is uneasy with life as exemplified by the way he stands with militaristic rigidity as though he were about to refuse the blindfold. If the Cardinals are looking for a stay-at-home moderate, he's the one, although he has little else to recommend him."

Weakley stopped. The midmorning winter sun was beginning to seep through the lead-colored clouds causing small beads of perspiration to dot his broad, finely chiseled forehead. The tiny beads were a result more of his perfectionism than of the weather.

In the late afternoon Weakley continued to parade the ones he considered to be the front runners.

"The third Italian Cardinal is the best known among the three. He is Camillo Tamacci, the 64-year old Secretary of State. He is a linguist not unlike John Paul II. He, like him, is well traveled. Probably best known for his successful efforts to bring the Israelis and the PLO to a peaceful settlement of their angry hatreds, he is acclaimed as not only one of the most prominent Churchmen of the era, but as one of the keenest statesmen.

"He too oozes with charm although he does not seem comfortable in huge crowds. He has been the trusted confidant of four Popes. He handles the verbal formulas of a career diplomat like someone who never turns over a stone he doesn't have to. Like most arbiters of elite groups he has a knack of couching his statements in brilliantly humble phrases. He is, it is said, sensitive to every subtlety and immune to every emotion. He has the kind of detachment that enables him to contemplate the unthinkable and often act upon it with success.

"He is criticized for diverting the flow of accurate information in the Global Village of communications. He is secretive but that makes him most trustworthy in his service to the Popes. It is also said of him that power for him is an addictive drug. With all there is to recommend him, this last could be his downfall.

"Front runners on the perimeter of Church politics are Cardinal Joseph Rawmanda of Zaire, Africa. Also an American, Cardinal Joseph McMurtrie.

"Rawmanda, 57, has been a dynamic leader in the last three Roman Synods. He is known for his many proposals on behalf of women's rights within the Church. He is a scholar and dedicated to the education of all peoples but especially those of the Third World. He has been a open critic of the *Revised New Catechism*.

"He has claimed that religious education should concentrate on helping people to live their faith rather than providing easy answers that foster comfort with no challenges. He has a phenomenal relationship with the people of his archdiocese. But he is an outsider as far as the Vatican family is concerned and outsiders have been given short shrift since John Paul II.

"Finally, America Cardinal McMurtrie. He is only 49. His star rose so rapidly that there are those who fear an early burn out. He is internationally known for his ecumenical work and his mediations between the Vatican and the world Jewish community. He is the most moderate of the front runners mentioned. As an American, he stands no chance or so the odds at Vegas indicate.

"All these men are honorable and have fine records but will they be steady ships in a tumultuous sea? That after all is what the Church in general seems to be looking for — peace and stability even if it means a return to severe authoritarian leadership."

Weakley put down his microphone and smiled. He knew he had given a run down no one else would come near. They just don't to their homework, he thought with a swell of self-satisfaction.

Danny had been half listening to the report on International GlobeNet. Imagine that, he thought, my old professor, Alessandro Percussi, a front runner for the Papacy. Danny smiled to himself. If he would be elected Pope, he'd probably spend his pontificate prowling around the stacks of the Vatican Library searching through all the sealed documents.

In his study, the Mentor sat with his chosen few watching Weakley's performance.

"It is obvious that we do not have enough members among the College to swing the vote to one of our own. Still there is always the Holy Spirit," the Mentor spoke in a heavy tone.

"We are at a crisis point in the life of the Roman Catholic Church. Heretics abound even in the sacred precinct of the College of Cardinals. And if they are not heretics, they are all weak sisters. They run for shelter in the moderate camp, some even in the liberal. It must be breaking the Good Lord's Sacred Heart.

"But," one of the Attendants was bold enough to speak, "the Church does have you, Mentor. Surely God is blessing your efforts."

The Mentor rose from behind his desk, approached the Attendant who had just spoken and embraced him. "If only we had members in the College of Cardinals like you, my son. We would save the Church from its demise with so little effort."

"Thank you, Mentor."

"One day you will wear the Red Hat. You have my word on that."

"Oh, thank you, most holy Mentor."

"I only hope the rest of you are as faithful," the Mentor said as his eyes swept over them in a ferocious glare.

"We are," came the choral response.

"I only wish we could have found more skeletons in the closets of those front runners. I think my choices of front runners is far more accurate than that atheistic loudmouth on the television. You have spread all the negative information I prepared on certain possible candidates?

"Yes Mentor," they replied in unison.

"Good. Now we will wait for God's will to be done. And if God's will is thwarted by those imbeciles in Conclave, we will have to clarify his will for them."

INTERACTIONS

Margaret sat across from Celine. Margaret's office was comfortable in an artsy sort of way. She poured coffee and sat back relaxed. Margaret was wearing a garish multicolored vest over a hot pink blouse with an off-gray skirt. Her hair as usual was swept up and as usual her makeup was a bit too heavy.

"So what makes my lawyer friend take time out from her busy life to come here and see me?"

Celine had decided to take Margaret into her confidence, at least partially. If nothing else, Margaret was worldly wise and Celine felt the need to confide and seek an outside perspective.

"Margaret, I never told you this but Danny and I …."

"Had an affair? Don't you think I suspected it all along? So what? Just because he's a priest? Honey, right now I'm so tired of being alone I'd have an affair with the Pope himself provided he wouldn't embarrass me by making some kind of a public confession with his rear end planted on a pile of ashes."

"I wouldn't denigrate what we had with the word, 'affair,' Margaret. We didn't have an affair. Just once. We were lovers in the truest sense of the word love. And I think the fact that we stopped being lovers and have become loving friends proves that it was more than your idea of an affair. "

" Sorry, Celine, dear. How thoughtless of me. But thoughtlessness is one of my strengths. Why would God make me thoughtless if he or she, as the case may be, didn't want me to use such a charming quality. Now tell me, why did you decide to tell me this and all that?"

"Well, because something pretty terrible has happened. There are some people in the Church who want to expose us. Or in their words, 'destroy us.'"

"Why on earth would they want to do that? I mean 'destroy' is such a nasty word. It kind of reminds you of the Mafia and all that. What do they plan to do? Sell you into bondage? White slavery is just too beneath you, Honey. If I were to sell myself, believe me it would be to the highest bidder among a bunch of certifiable billionaires. Why would they want to destroy you?"

"Because Danny has some information they want and he refuses to give it to them." Celine decided not to go into detail. She would keep it in the general term of information.

"Celine, Honey, how many time have I told you …."

"I know, get rid of my relationship with Danny. But, Margaret, this is certainly not the time to abandon a friend."

"Your relationship, as you call it, has caused you nothing but heartbreak and now it might cause you your life if I'm reading the word, 'destroy,' accurately. It all depends on who 'they' are. Whatever, your friend has chosen to put your career and perhaps your life in jeopardy. When you're in a destructive situation, get out."

"He didn't choose to put me in any kind of danger. I made the choice. I will not walk away from him. He can't go against what he believes in and I feel that I have to stand by him. It's just that …." Her voice trailed off.

"I'm lost and all that, Honey. Why do you have to stand by him? Because he's a friend? I admire you but there's a limit. I consider you one of my closest friends but I would no more think of standing by you standing by him than selling myself for ten cents a roll and all that."

This was not going well, Celine thought. She did not quite know what she had hoped to gain from this get together with Margaret but she was certain it wasn't to be told to leave Danny hanging in the wind.

"Margaret," Celine sounded as though she was pleading for understanding. "A friend is not someone who has all the answers. A friend is someone who, when no solutions seem possible, doesn't walk away from you. A friend doesn't tell you to do this or say that. She says in effect, 'No matter what happens I'll always be your friend.' Can't you see that?"

"I'm sorry," Margaret responded sheepishly. "Of course you have to stand by him if you feel that's the right thing to do. Don't always listen to me. Maybe down deep I am a quitter and all that."

" No you're not. You're someone I can trust. That's why I guess I wanted to bounce this off you. You're not involved and I thought maybe you might be able to give me an objective appraisal."

"This 'destroy' you mentioned. If it's about your position at the Firm, maybe it would be a prudent move to go the Head Honcho and tell him outright about you and Danny and the possibility that something untoward might happen because of your former relationship.

"You know, Honey, 'The best defense is a good offense.' My Ex used to say that about us. I was never sure how it fit into our marital bliss and all that but I guess it had something to do with 'To the victor goes the spoils.'

"Hell, Celine, I still think you should go to whoever — whomever — and tell him what might be brewing."

"That makes sense except what if these people are just bluffing." Celine replied nervously. "If I go now and nothing happens, the Head Honcho, as you call him, may feel that I'm a liability. No matter how good a lawyer I've been, the Firm is the idol and I'm just another worshipper. If I tell him about the threat, it'll hang over me like a sword on a thin string."

" True. Maybe you should just bide your time. If these Church people do make a move against you, what can the Firm do? They're not going to fire you for something you did in your private life."

"Unless the Firm's name is dragged through some kind of a public mud. And what about my parents? My father…."

"Well, as far as the Firm is concerned, they'll probably just slap you on the wrist and make you stand in a corner until you learn to behave like a good little girl. Damn men! They can go around whoring and then brag about their conquests in the locker room and that's considered as normal as an April shower and all that. It's a man's world and God help us if we dare try to break through the glass ceiling.

"As for your parents, they'll stand by you, no matter what. How many times do I have to tell you? You're a big girl and it's your private life. No one's going to brand you with a Scarlet A or F for fornication which, if memory serves, is what you were involved in. And the operative word is, were. You've seen the light. You've repented. Praise the Lord and all that."

"Margaret, I'm torn between loyalty and fear. I've been praying so hard these past days. I don't want anything to happen to Danny to ruin him either. He's so good. I've never met anyone who tries to live the gospel like he does. I mean his value system is unimpeachable. He doesn't deserve to be destroyed."

"Why doesn't he just give them the information they want?"

"It's a matter of principle. Besides, we don't know who these people are exactly. And they have no legal right to the information. There is something sinister about the whole thing."

" I'll say. If they're threatening to destroy the both of you. You've got yourself into some fix, Honey. I'm not one for prayer and God and all that but if you think it'll help, by all means pray up a storm. 'More things are wrought' et cetera, I think the line goes."

"I know you don't believe in a personal God, Margaret, and I'm not too sure about my own belief. The therapist I went to suggested that my father is my image of God and if that's true, my image of God isn't great.

"I think I treat God the same way I treat or used to treat my father. I'm always trying to please God, too. I try to rebel but I'm right back begging his forgiveness, more like groveling in my guilt feelings.

"Or I try to be indifferent, talking myself into believing that God doesn't even exist. Then I become shattered with fear. What if he does exist and one day will demand a complete tally with the power to damn me forever?

"Sometimes I wish I had reacted totally against my father and ended up a tramp. At least I would have been free of him. Although, I must admit, that my therapist has helped me a great deal. At least I know that a lot of my problems with men stem from my unadmitted desire to please my father in every damn iota of my life. He's not to blame. No one is. What's the bumper sticker say? 'Shit happens.'"

"Celine, dearest, aren't we all daddy's little girls? I think our fathers wanted to get into our pants. You know all that Freudian stuff. Our mothers were too routine for them and we appeared on the scene as a new conquest. For most fathers, they were able to deal with their incestuous desires by making demands on us to be the ideal women they could never conquer and all that."

"My God, Margaret, you are preposterously Freudian. I'd hate to live in your world of fantasies. Besides, I don't think Freud ever said any of that."

"In fantasyland it's a different man every night, Honey. That's the trade off. No one to hug but you can get screwed by somebody new every night if you want to and all that."

"Well, anyway, Margaret, I envy you. I envy your sincere disbelief in God."

"How did you ever get hooked up with Danny? I mean he represents everything that tortures you."

"No, in Danny I found the soft underbelly of God. I discovered a God of kindliness and caring. A God of love. But, God help me, I couldn't handle that kind of God. Consciously or unconsciously, that may be why I couldn't maintain my original relationship with Danny. And when he left, I was able to hate God again like I guess I have hated my father. I think I felt more comfortable with a God who devastates me. I truly do envy you, Margaret."

"Well," Margaret said, "I never knew my father. He abandoned us when I was only two. I often wonder if that's why my marriage failed. Maybe that's why I can't establish a lasting relationship with another man.

"And yet, look at you, Celine. You now have a deep, loving bond with Danny and, I suspect, a comfortable, permanent relationship with George. You're twice blest. Somehow that has to tell you something about you and your God. If I were in your shoes, I'd be accused of bigamy and I sure as hell would be enjoying it."

"Thanks for listening, Margaret. I've taken up enough of your time. And I've got to get back to my job while I still have it."

"Listening is love in action, Honey. Who knows, maybe I'll even shock the Almighty with a prayer of my own for you …. and Danny."

Celine joined the crush of people heading back from their lunch break to their posts as small cogs in the gargantuan mechanism of American Big Business.

As she walked along with head bowed against the wind and in deep thought, she once again bumped into a man. This time the man was more genteel. "Take care," he said cordially, "and watch where you are going."

Yes, Celine thought, I should watch where I'm going. Life is not neatly mapped out. You set up a destination and then you're detoured. Sometimes these detours take up more of your time and energy than the actual journey.

The unnerving paradox is that you spend so much time trying to accomplish the goals you've set for yourself that you fail to attain the human goal of just sitting back and letting the wonders of the world and life settle on you.

What was it someone had said? The eighth wonder in the world is the person who thinks there are only seven. She smiled at the truth in that statement. Was she one of those who thinks there are only seven wonders in the world?

Our problem is that we stand in wonder only at the unusual or the extraordinary. We haven't yet learned the wisdom to wonder at the fact that something — anything — exists at all.

She would, she decided, have to watch not only where she was going but to observe the wonderful gifts that surround her on the way.

Danny had just sat down to a cup of coffee after morning Mass when the door bell rang. He got up and went to the door. When he opened it there was a young man standing there.

"Good morning. I was wondering if you might have some time to see me. I don't know if you remember me."

Danny did remember him. He couldn't put a name on him right away but he recognized him as a parishioner or a former parishioner as the case might be. He hadn't seen him at a weekend Mass in months. The young man was one of the few dozen Anglos who came to St. Matt's.

"Yes I recognize you." And then his name popped into Danny's mind. "You're Donald Johnston."

"Yes," the young man responded with no show of any warmth or friendliness.

"Come in," Danny said graciously. He led the young man to the kitchen. He liked to use the kitchen more than his office. It was more informal. "Coffee?" Danny asked. "No thank you."

Danny couldn't help but notice that the young man had not called him Father Joe or even Father.

"I don't know if you remember but I came to you some time back with a problem about my marriage."

"Yes, I do recall," Danny said. Danny remembered some of the details. Donald's obvious depression, his halting words of helplessness. Days in his marriage with no vital communication. Arguments over trivial matters. Stubbornness on her part. Indifference on his. Routine, often unaffectionate, sex. Complaints of boredom from her. Complaints about unreasonable demands from him.

Danny was not surprised that he remembered. He had a very fine retentive memory which had stood him in good stead when he was going through school since intelligence was measured only by what you could memorize and recall.

Danny was surprised that the young man had come back because Danny did not pride himself on his counseling skills. It wasn't that he didn't care or have concern. And it wasn't because he didn't have immediate insights at the tip of his tongue. In fact that was precisely the problem. He could grasp the other person's story so quickly that he too often jumped in with advice before the whole story had been told.

Maybe it was impatience. Maybe intuition. He guessed that people got the impression he wanted to be done with it, that he didn't want to waste time listening. He tried to control this compulsion to give ill-timed responses but not with much success. So he decided long ago that one-on-one counseling was not his forte.

Years after he came to that conclusion, he had read somewhere that there are people who can see through a problem so quickly that their power of intuition made them unlikely candidates for the lifetime work of being a psychologist or counselor. If nothing else the article had relieved him somewhat of his guilt feelings. It wasn't lack of interest or concern. It was just that his mind moved too fast and his tongue even faster for him to be good at counseling.

"I feel I owe you an apology," Donald said without any indication of remorse. "You've noticed that I haven't been here for Mass since then?"

"Yes, I've noticed," Danny said wondering what this was leading up to and why an apology was in order.

"When I came to you with my problem I was deeply disappointed at your response. And I've said some terrible things about you. Things like you aren't very religious. That you really don't approach a person's problem from a spiritual point. And other derogatory things along those lines."

Danny sat there not knowing what was coming next. He felt annoyance percolating through his veins. He may not be the best of counselors but irreligious was a bit too much. He had given this young man the advice he thought was appropriate at the time. As far as he could intuit it, Donald's problem was not spiritual but psychological. The fact, he thought, is that too many people don't know what their real problem is or they don't want the help they need.

In a flashback, he remembered the time he was at a cocktail party thrown by one of Leno's upper crust friends in his 'simple mansion.' A pretty young woman had approached him. On this particular occasion he was in collar. Leno had admonished him that it was a high class gathering and he didn't want Danny showing up in jeans.

For no apparent reason other than she recognized him as a priest, the young woman pronounced her personal dogma. "When you really have to talk to someone," she had said, "really have to tell somebody about something that's really bothering you, to *whom* (she had emphasized the 'm' as though to assure him that she wasn't just another beautiful air-head) to whom do you go? I mean *really*?"

Danny had muttered something about a lot of caring people around to which she countered, "No one really cares. That's why I just keep my problems to myself. Just between you and I (Danny repressed the impulse to correct her by inserting the word, "me.") I tell you I really have no confidence in you clergy. What do you know about sex?"

She darted away as quickly as she had appeared, no doubt moving on to find someone else with *whom* she would not share her problems.

"Do you remember the advice you gave me?" Donald asked.

"No, I don't." Danny was finding this more than a bit annoying but then he remembered his promise to try to be a patient counselor and listen. So he did.

"After I told you all about the problems my wife and I were having, you went on about how I should discover my worth qualities. You said that if I made a serious effort to discover and develop my worth qualities, I might be able to relate to my wife with a more positive self-image. That this would bring about more understanding and might even re-introduce some of the romance back into our marriage."

"Yes, I seem to recall now that that's what I said. And I think I suggested that you talk to your wife about doing the same thing."

"Well, I have to tell you that I was truly disappointed that you didn't even mention Jesus once. What you told me any marriage counselor could have said. That's why I quit coming here for Mass. I didn't leave the parish. I just didn't think you had anything to offer me. My wife and I went somewhere else and as a result, we joined a charismatic prayer group. We have found Jesus, the Lord! And now our marriage is like a miracle of rebirth."

Danny couldn't help but wonder if the young man seated across the table from him had ever addressed his real problem, if indeed a poor self-image was his real problem. Danny hoped that the prayer group was not just an escape from the need to face up to whatever problem needed remedying. If not, after the first fervor of finding

Jesus, the Lord, wore off, Donald and his wife might find themselves in worse shape than they were before.

To Donald Danny said, "I'm very happy to hear this."

"As I said, I spoke quite scathingly about you and your failure to talk to me about Jesus. I know Jesus wants me to apologize to you."

"Thank you," Danny said without much enthusiasm. "And I wish both you and your wife the best of God's blessings." There, Danny thought, I said something really pious.

"Oh, by the way, Father, my wife and I are planning to adopt and we need a letter of recommendation from our pastor. If you wouldn't mind."

I'll have it ready for you on Sunday after Mass." Danny couldn't help but get the dig in.

After Donald left, Danny went into his office to try to finish putting it in order. Fortunately, he thought, he had put Michael's diary in his briefcase and locked it in the trunk of his car. He thought he would share what he had read with Celine and Gene. As it turned out, there wasn't time so he had left it in the trunk of his car. If these people knew as much as they seemed to, they probably knew about the diary. He'd have to find a safe place to hide it. What a hell of a life. He felt like he was trapped in some kind of a detective novel.

THE ELECTION

Whether Charles Weakley was truly breathless or was feigning it for effect, no one would ever know. He was not only an astute commentator but quite the showman.

"Contrary to predictions, this conclave turned out to be one of the shortest in history. Less than seventy-two hours. It is also the first time since Cardinal Montini, Pope Paul VI, that a prospective front runner was elected.

"The white smoke announcing the new Pontiff swirled into the gray Roman sky at 2:30 this afternoon like an angel ascending back to heaven after having delivered its message." Even Weakley seemed to wince at that analogy. "The speed of the election caught everyone off guard including this commentator.

"The announcement was made in its usual dramatic fashion but the drama unfolded to a small audience in St. Peter's Square. As if by some lemming instinct, people began to fill the Square like the rush of a river into a basin. The new Pope had barely begun to speak when he found himself addressing a throng of believers who cheered a choral *Deo Gratias.*

"The new Pontiff is," Weakley paused for a moment as though he were announcing the new Miss America, "Cardinal Alessandro Percussi of Milan. He has taken for his name, Pope John Paul IV. From what we know of the new Pontiff, he may be more like Paul VI than John XXIII.

"Of course the last time the College of Cardinals chose an elderly man as a transitional Pope — Percussi is seventy-eight — which appears to be what they have done here, John XXIII called a Council. You never know. And believers are convinced it is the work and inspiration of the Spirit.

"As I reported earlier, the new Pope is a scholarly introvert. He is not a linguist except in the most classic languages of the scholar and has done next to no traveling. He gives the impression that he is not comfortable with people. How he was chosen and why, no one will ever know. We can only speculate. He is considered a moderate and after the last two pontificates, this perhaps is what the Cardinals were desperately searching for.

"One thing we do not have to speculate about is the Church John Paul IV has been elected to rule. According to highly placed reliable sources who wish for good reasons to remain anonymous, it is a troubled Church. A Church battered by storms from all sides. Or perhaps it would be more accurate to say typhoons.

"The gales of unrest sweep in from conservatives who are sick of innovation and still horrified at the direction Pope Charles took. They are still reeling at his attempts to change the ancient teaching against birth control and at the commissions he set up to investigate the possibility of a married clergy and of ordaining women.

"Then there are the aggressive left-wing liberals who are convinced that their Church will decay if it continues to cling to the dead past. They insist that the updating begun at the Second Vatican Council must continue.

"The Church, they insist, must be in touch and deal realistically with current problems or it will run the risk of losing its younger members to total disillusionment. They wonder aloud not if but when the Barque of Peter will sink in the tumultuously troubled waters of modern times.

"At the same time this is a Church which, under the banner of social justice, is so involved in world politics that it cannot claim the right of sanctuary when it is attacked.

"There are those who are convinced that this era is a time of a crucifixion of the Church and question whether there will be a resurrection. There is a growing number of people who refuse to give blind obedience to the Pope and his minions. They have questions about the claim to absolute authority and do not want catechism answers to soothe their anxieties about an ultra secretive institution. Apparently democracy has taken its toll on the monarchical structure of the Roman Church.

"At the same time there is an even greater number of members of the Roman Church who are convinced that obedience to every utterance of the Pope or his representatives is the only way to salvation.

"It seems that a leap of faith must be taken. The question is, Who will take it? The people of God or the new Roman Pontiff? There are those, including a growing number of bishops, who are saying that this is the time for the Pope to kneel and literally wash the people's feet rather than being satisfied with a formal ritual on Good Friday.

"These same bishops are becoming increasingly aggravated not at the Pope as such but with the various Prefects of Congregations who seem determined to usurp the authority and jurisdiction of individual bishops.

"Once again, so the complaint goes, there is a perceived lack of trust in the Vatican bureaucrats. As one unnamed member of the Church's hierarchy put it, 'Are we descendants of the Apostles or just the servants of unelected, episcopal bureaucrats?'

"From this commentator's view, this is a time when a Cardinal needs to think twice before assuming the mantel of supreme authority in the Roman Church with its almost preposterous burden.

"Still it is a burden that each Pope believes can be borne with the help and power of the Most High. It most certainly is not a time when any Pontiff can utter the words of Leo X, 'Since God has given us the Papacy, let us enjoy it.'"

Charles Weakley put down his microphone with an ingratiating smile as if to indicate to his audience that they would not get a clearer picture of the situation anywhere else in the world.

"You were a bit tough on them, don't you think?" Weakley's producer asked with due respect.

"Not at all," he answered with a tone of annoyance in his voice. One thing Charles Weakley detested was the second guessing of an up-and-coming producer. "What I gave was a commentary of the current state of the Roman Church as I was able to get it from reliable sources. If Catholics don't get the information from me, they certainly won't get it from their leaders in the Church."

"But do you think you gave an apt description of the majority of Catholics who go to Mass and try to live a good life?" the young producer persisted.

"They are the most affected by the tribulations of their Church. They are just not aware of it yet."

"Well, it's your call."

"To date," Weakley spoke with near disdain, "my calls have served me well and have served the people's interests and concerns just as well. Let's get packed up. I don't have to stay around for the pageantry of the crowning."

"Well," the Mentor spoke in a soft, self-assured voice, "Percussi is not the worst choice they could have made. He's a stuffy intellectual and he's indecisive. He won't do much harm. He can be kept on a harness. All we have to do is manipulate him until he dies."

"Is there any possibility that he, like John XXIII, might do something foolish like calling a Council?" one of the Mentor's Attendants asked.

"Not a chance," the Mentor almost shouted. "Unlike John XXIII, he has had no experience of the Church outside of Milan or beyond his scholarly books. I doubt if he even has any idea of the extent of the turmoil in the Church. Unlike John, he truly will be a transition pope. May God grant that the transition will be long enough to allow us to strengthen our position."

"What do you think he might do about Pope Charles' misguided efforts to renew the Church? I mean, will he reverse Charles' decisions?" another of the Attendants asked.

The Mentor smiled. "I think he'll spend his remaining days on earth anguishing about what to do. He's at home in the abstract. The practical is a foreign country. In his own Archdiocese he let the day-to-day matters up to his six auxiliary bishops. They made him look good.

"There's a story told about three of those six approaching Percussi and asking to have the Central Administration computerized. It took old Percussi over two years to decide to get one telecomputer. They were asking for dozens. Then another year before he capitulated. The story has it that they even got him one. He found it very useful. On hot summer days, when the window was open, he would place his telecomputer on top of a pile of papers so the breeze wouldn't blow them away.

"He's an incidentalist. He wasn't a great Archbishop and he won't be a great pope. He's the type who will sit on the Papal Throne and count the number of jewels stuck in it. He's not only indecisive, he's spineless."

"How ironic," another Attendant said. "At the very time when the Church needs a strong hand to pull it out of the dregs of liberalism, we end up with an empty glove."

"Yes," the Mentor smiled humorlessly, "the Holy Spirit has plunged into the whirlpool of Church affairs nothing but a woodchip. This is all the more reason we have to do what needs to be done, gentlemen."

"All our confidence is in you, Mentor. You have our unconditional loyalty. All you have to do is ask and it will be done," the first Attendant said.

"Still, as I said," the Mentor seemed to have regained his composure, "this can bode well for us. It gives us time to reinforce our efforts and extend control. It's costing us to keep our three Cardinals in the Vatican happy and compliant.

"That's why we need Michael's money. The pittance Browning's been able to siphon off to us and other donations are absolutely insufficient for what we want to do. And we keep spending that money to have our men named bishops. Of course, the more that are named, the wider our influence spreads." The Mentor sat back as if relaxing yet a dark concern clouded his face.

Then in an unexpected burst of anger the Mentor exclaimed, "I must have that document. And it will cost. Hundreds of millions. That's why Michael's money is essential. With it I can buy back what legitimately belongs to the Church."

"Are the Iranians willing to sell?" another of the Attendant asked.

"For the right price," the Mentor said as if thinking aloud. "They want half a billion dollars. That's what Michael's money will bring us. As soon as we have the money, we can start negotiating with those damnable infidels. Damn that note. Damn that nobody priest who's the executor."

One of the Attendants cleared his throat as though he was fearful of bringing on the Mentor's wrath with his question. Nevertheless he spoke. "If the document is everything it is reported to be, I'm surprised the Iranians will let it go for a half billion."

"The Iranians know there is only one customer. The Vatican. And the Vatican has shown no interest. That leaves us. They either sell it or they're stuck with what is totally useless to them. Those God-forsaken infidels." The Mentor spoke harshly.

Danny heard the news about the election of the new Pope on the morning Globenet news.

So, he mused, Professor Percussi was now Pope John Paul IV. He didn't know whether to feel elation or despondency. He deeply admired the theologian Percussi but Percussi the Pope?

He remembered something Percussi had said to him about ecclesiastical power before he became one of its brokers. "When power is used to subjugate people or when power enslaves the one who holds it, then power corrupts the gospel and perverts the mystical tradition of our faith."

He would write the new Pontiff a note of congratulations. He felt he knew him well enough to remind him of his aphorism.

He worried about Percussi. His old professor was far more sensitive than most realized. Danny thought of the lines of the Irish poet, Thomas Moore:

"The heart that is soonest awake to the flowers

Is always the first to be touched by the thorns."

Nothing is incidental to the person who feels with keen sensitivity, Danny mused. He hoped that the new Pope would not get bogged down in the incidentals of the universal Church. He prayed he wouldn't.

The doorbell rang and Danny went to answer. It was a Knight of the Road looking for a handout. Danny gave him a coupon for a meal at the local diner.

He came back to the kitchen and sat down in front of the television set. "...nothing much is expected from this new pope according to sources high up in the Vatican," the newscaster was concluding.

It's hard not to fall into cynicism, Danny thought. "Nothing much is expected ..." Sounds like a summation of the history of the Church. You get somebody like Pope Charles who did try to make something happen and all hell broke loose. If ever we tried to live up to all the theories put forth in Church documents, we'd revolutionize the Church — the world.

Then an inner voice whispered, Just serve the people. Yes, Danny decided for the umpteenth time, that's what it's all about. It's the only way to stave off cynicism. The only way to keep going with any kind of hope. "Damnit," he muttered to himself, "why do we have to hope in spite of the Church?" If you keep busy enough, you won't have time to indulge in cynicism. You may not have that much hope but at least you won't be hopeless.

And yet, as he continued his musings, hope is what people so desperately want and need. Danny recalled something he had read some time ago. "Life with Christ is endless hope. Without Christ, life is a hopeless end."

And where will they find Christ? Obviously in the Eucharist. But on a day-to-day basis, it's in people that they encounter Christ. And if people have little or no hope, what kind of an encounter with Christ would it be? If I am lacking in hope, what can the people I serve expect of Christ?

It's not theological gibber-jabber, Danny believed. It's out-and-out hard-nosed practicality. The problem is that those of us who are most aware of this on an intellectual level are the very ones who don't live it on a practical level.

We get so tied up in the daily routine of administering a parish or we're so trapped in all the rules and regulations of the Church that we don't allow the people to experience our reflective values. We don't let people see Christ in us.

The image of another friend of his popped into his mind. Steve Rinko, pastor of a suburban parish who was dying of cancer. You never know, Danny thought, how much time you have.

Who am I to squander the time I have left on cynicism or skepticism. If I were told, like Steve was, that I only had six months to live, I surely wouldn't waste my time being obsessive about Church leadership.

I should be treasuring every minute given to me and using my time caring for these poor people here, many of whom are the living dead and some, living saints. I would be doing my damnest to let Christ appear to these people through me.

My God! Danny's mind swirled, did Michael ever think for a moment that he would be dead at his age? That his life would be snuffed out like it was? Who am I to be negative? Who am I to be anything but a hope-filled pastor? Isn't hope born of the most desperate situations? Situations like my own? Of anybody I should have the market on hope cornered.

He would have to pray more for hopefulness. It is one thing to have the infused virtue of hope but quite another to be hopeful. Still as he knew from his experience he had too often heard the echoes of his prayer bouncing back at him like ingratiating babble. He would have to pray if for no other reason so that the lyrical innocence of hope would not be lost in the heavy drumbeat of cynical depression.

If his experience had taught him anything, it was the awesome fallibility of his prayer. What he certainly did not want in his prayer was a religious enthusiasm that cries out, "Jesus is Lord!" and then rushes on to where the action isn't.

Danny recalled the story of the man who was walking through the slums of somewhere. The inhuman misery he witnessed prompted him to cry out, "Why doesn't someone do something about this?" Then he heard a voice within him whisper, "I have done something. I created you." Or the other ending to the same story: Suddenly he realized he was that someone. Whichever ending you choose, the result is the same: the Vine depends on us branches to produce the fruit of good works.

How he needed to be more hopeful. How he needed the creative hope that can see around the corners of life's impossibilities. "Lord," he prayed, "grant me the revolutionary virtue of hope that I might not be carried through each day by the blind momentum of routine existence."

Still, as he came back to the news of Percussi's election, his predominant emotional reaction was despondency.

The despondency was only intensified by his thoughts about Michael which prompted Danny to go back to the diary. He felt like reading it straight through but he worried that he might miss some innuendo, some coded hint about Viri Lucis. And he wanted to find out about that more than he wanted to finish the diary.

> Today I was ordained a bishop. There is no way to describe the experience. I actually felt the Holy Spirit descend on me and take possession of me. I, in union with all the bishops in the world and with the supreme Bishop of Rome, am infallible! It is no longer my opinion. It is the Holy Spirit speaking through my opinion with infallible truth.
>
> Although I still do not have jurisdiction, being an auxiliary bishop, I will wait my turn. My turn will come. I have the Mentor's word on it.

Danny paused. This was the first mention of the Mentor he had come across in Michael's diary. What or who was the Mentor? Was he someone in Viri Lucis? If so, what position? Was he the head of Viri Lucis? It certainly sounded from what Michael wrote that he was someone of power, someone to be reckoned with, someone who was able to bestow grandiose gifts.

Danny continued to read.

> With the infallible truth of the Spirit,
> I will lead the attack on those liberals
> who think that they possess all truth:
> making the liturgy relevant, using
> inclusive language, advocating
> women's ordination, a married clergy,
> birth control — I will rid the Church I
> love and serve of this brood of vipers,
> these whited sepulchers. And God will
> be with me as he was with Samson.
>
> No one knows what it is like to be
> a successor of the Apostles except
> someone who is. May Christ be
> praised for his foresight. He who
> preached the revealed Word made
> certain that there would be those of us
> who would keep that Word pure. I will
> place myself in diametric opposition
> to those who would twist that revealed
> Word into their own version of the
> truth which supports their man-made,
> evil-prompted ambition.
>
> How I pray for guidance, for strength.
> There are so many demons in the
> Church parading around in such
> righteousness. They think they are
> the only ones who are right. That they
> alone have the truth.
>
> Then there are those who harp
> constantly on social justice and
> peace issues. They are a detriment

to the Church. They are wild-eyed liberals who don't care one iota for the sanctity of God's truth. They only want to make huge waves to drown good, God- fearing Catholics in. They must either be converted or be expelled from the Church, leaving good religious people to worship God in silence and genuine peace. Rabble rousers! God put certain people on earth to suffer that their reward in heaven may be all the greater. These liberation theologians who are stirring up the poor, giving them illusions of a better life here on earth are disrupting God's will for them. "The poor you shall always have with you." The liberals of the First World need to recognize the benefits of capitalism just as my father has. Without people like my father where would the works of charity be? Such liberals should feel the sting of Rome's vengeance. But Rome has become so weak. These liberals offer destitute people neither theology nor liberation. They foster fantasies and disillusionments. No one can play God with people of simple trust. They need authentic leadership according to the orthodox teachings of the Church. I feel called by God to give that kind of leadership.

The Mentor has more than hinted that I will be his personal authority here in the United States.

Once again Danny put the dairy down. He could feel himself tremble. What he had just read was again unbelievable, coming from Michael. His world view. His personal ambition. His absolute intolerance. His vindictive attitude. His hard-heartedness toward the poor. This was not Michael!

But it was Michael's handwriting. How did Michael get to this point in his priesthood? And again who is this Mentor? Michael sounded like some brainwashed fanatic. "Think kindly of me," Michael had written in his note.

CARDINAL TAMACCI

Cardinal Camillo Tamacci was a relatively short and a definitely heavy man of 67. He stood about five foot six and his eyes flashed with nervous energy. He was a man who relished power as a gourmet cook enjoyed consuming a meal he had just concocted. There was about him an air of efficiency and the demeanor of someone who had known success in every undertaking throughout his life.

Even in his quieter and more restful moments, he gave the impression he could spring into action with the alacrity of a tiger pouncing on its next meal.

His smooth face told anyone looking at him that worry had never been one of his problems. Anyone who knew him knew that pragmatism was his altar and accomplishment, his god. He was an indefatigable worker and was ill-at-ease when there was nothing important to do. As a result, he always managed to create work even out the smallest details of his position as Secretary of State.

He was very domineering over those who were accountable to him but subservient when in the presence of the popes he served. He had the instincts of a professional gambler and always played his cards to win not caring the least that others had to lose. There was little joviality in his personality. Everything for him was serious business.

Despite his overweight problem, he moved swiftly through the corridors of power within the Vatican fortress. As the saying goes, he was a legend in his own mind. He was a master manipulator and everyone, including popes, was his pawn on the chessboard of ecclesiastical politics.

He had his favorites and they always fared well. His enemies knew the scathing wrath of his vindictive hatred. He was, above all, a survivor. He had enough information on every member of the Vatican bureaucracy and even beyond to threaten blackmail if the need arose.

He used his unfettered ambition to serve the Church well and, in return, the Church had served his ambition just as well. He lived the conviction that if he pushed enough of the right buttons on the Vatican's control panel, he would one day hold the supreme position in the Church.

He prepared now to enter his first meeting with the newly elected pope.

"Ah, Camillo, come in, please," Pope John Paul IV invited most pleasantly.

Cardinal Camillo Tamacci stood respectfully before the new Pope.

"Please, Camillo, sit down. We have a great deal to talk about."

"Thank you, Holiness," Cardinal Tamacci all but whispered.

"Please, Camillo, call me Alessandro when we are together as we are now. As to your letter of resignation, it is a mere formality. I have already reappointed you Secretary of State. I can not think of anyone who should hold that position more than you. In fact, Camillo, let us clear the air right from the beginning."

"Whatever your Holiness desires," Tamacci seemed just a bit too obsequious.

"Camillo, there is no doubt in my mind that you should be here where I am sitting. I should not have been elected Supreme Pontiff." Tamacci began to protest but the Pope raised his hand. "Please let me finish. You have been Secretary of State for so long that no one can remember who your predecessor was. They would have to look it up in some almanac.

"You are far better versed in world affairs, far more experienced in diplomacy. You have a wealth of knowledge about the behind-the-scenes maneuverings of nations, great and small. You have served my predecessors with fidelity and wisdom. It should have been you. And I want you to know how aware of this I am."

"Who can fathom the workings of the Spirit?" Tamacci spoke sincerely.

"Yes, the workings of the Spirit," the newly elected Pope repeated with little or no conviction in his voice.

"Camillo, I have never felt so helpless in my whole life."

194

"God will provide, Holiness. He always has. Others have had the same feeling you are now experiencing and God has seen them through. He always will."

"Camillo, as far as I am concerned, God has already provided by giving you to me, to be my right arm, my eyes and ears. You are my treasured advisor, my confidante. You will stay on, will you not?"

"If that is your desire, Holiness, then that is God's will for me. I will stay on."

"Let me be totally honest with you, Camillo. I don't know where to begin. After what Pope Charles initiated what do I do?

"May I suggest, Holiness, pondering the gospel. Does not the Good News transform our self-understanding?"

"Sometimes, Camillo, I fear the gospel for what it reveals to me about me, about what I have failed to become. I feel I have too often evaded the demands of love."

"The people of Milan loved you, Holiness, and the people will support you by and large."

"Ah, Camillo, our people are so sick with the inability to feel happy. The panic hidden away in their hearts only causes them to construct a make-believe world where they escape to — the world of religious piety. Too many, I'm afraid, are obsessed with living good lives when what is needed are saints."

"But, Holiness, you are a brilliant scholar. You have the resource of knowledge which you will be able to use in leading our people.

"I have spent most of my life — all of my life, actually — probing the doctrines of our religion. Now I must model them with every breath of my life. It's no longer academics. It's flesh and blood reality.

"I have to take the finely formulated creedal statements of our religion and search them for their human meaning in the lives of the faithful. I wonder how faith-full they are. Somehow I never felt this compulsion to be a model when I was Archbishop — there were so many of us. But there is only one Pope."

At that point, the Pope began to cough. His coughing lasting for well over two minutes. Camillo noticed that the Pope had pulled out a red handkerchief to cover his mouth. He wondered if the Pope used this color of a handkerchief to hide any blood that might be coming from the his lungs.

" I understand, Camillo," the Pope said while trying to get his breath and still sounding as if he was choking, "the media are already calling me a 'Do Nothing Pope.' And perhaps they are not far off the mark. Perhaps I am to stay here and do nothing until the Angel of Death beckons me."

"Holiness, I have watched men in your position rise to the challenge with more will than they ever believed they had. No one with your power and influence could ever do nothing. Time will present you with the challenges and the opportunities to fulfill your destiny."

"Thank you so much, Camillo. And may I say in all truth that it will be *our* destiny. With you at my side and with the help of the Holy Spirit, perhaps I can do something worthwhile with the last years or days, as the case may be, that God gives me here on earth — and, Camillo, I meant what I said about calling me Alessandro when we are alone here or anywhere."

"Thank you …. Alessandro," Tamacci smiled for the first time. "And once again, let me pledge my unconditional loyalty to you. My meager talents and experience are at your disposal."

"May God bless you, Camillo. Thank you. I feel somewhat relieved if not confident. You have been so affirming and honest. I will be depending on that honesty in the near and who knows? — far future." The Pope went into another spasm of coughing. He held his red handkerchief to his mouth with one hand while waving off Camillo.

"God bless you, Alessandro, and please take care of your health," Tamacci bowed slightly as he took his leave.

Cardinal Camillo Tamacci, Secretary of State of the universal Roman Catholic Church, second in power to the Supreme Pontiff, entered his office, closed the door, unlocked the bottom drawer of his desk, took out a phone and punched in the sacrosanct number. No one was ever to speak it.

He was contacting the only man on earth whom he feared — the Mentor.

ANOTHER CLUE

Danny got up from his desk. He went upstairs and put Michael's diary under a floor board in his bedroom. It was a copy. After his office had been turned into a city dump, he decided to put the original version of the diary in the safety tube with the original note at the bank. He honestly didn't know if he was paranoid or prudent.

He decided he needed a break. So he went over to the school and visited the fourth grade.

As he entered the classroom, all the children rose and in sing-song fashion greeted him, "Good morning, Father Joe."

"Good morning, children," Danny replied smiling. This is what makes it all worthwhile, he thought. "Continue with your work, please." He had noticed that they were very busy writing. The children sat down at their desks and continued their writing.

Danny proceeded to walk around the classroom observing what they were doing.

He stopped at one desk and looked over the shoulder of a little girl. She was writing a list:

"I can't get out of here."

"I can't get Marie to like me."

"I can't do arithmetic."

Danny went to the desk of one of the boys and examined his list.

"I can't get out of here."

"I can't hit a ball into left field."

"I can't get along with my brother."

Danny walked up to the teacher's desk. Mrs. Campbell was also writing a list.

"I can't get my daughter to clean up her room."

"I can't get Barbara's mother to come in for a teacher's conference."

"I can't get the children to sit still."

Danny was perplexed but said nothing.

Mrs. Campbell, the teacher, was a small, grandmotherly type, whose face was always bathed in a smile. She was a widow with a comfortable income. For the small pittance Danny was able to pay her, she might as well have been a volunteer

Mrs. Campbell asked all the children to fold their papers and bring them up to her desk. When they approached her desk, they put their folded papers into a small box. Mrs. Campbell put hers in too. Then she put the lid on the box, picked it up and led the children in procession outside to the back of the school.

There she and a few of the students took turns digging a hole. Mrs. Campbell placed the box in the hole and they all scooped the earth over it. Then Mrs. Campbell put a sign on the mound of ground that covered the hole. I read: "Here lies I Can't. May he rest in peace."

Mrs. Campbell gathered the children around her and said, "Now, children, we have buried I Can't. He is survived by his brother, I Can and his sister, I Will. But always remember, I Can't is dead and buried."

Before she led the children back to their classroom, Danny said, "That was most creative, Mrs. Campbell."

"Oh, Father Joe, I don't deserve any credit. I read this in a book and thought I'd give it a try with my boys and girls."

"But it is an extremely important lesson for them and for all of us, Mrs. Campbell. Thank you so much."

"You're welcome, Father Joe. Have a pleasant day." And she led her children back to their classroom.

Danny stood there gazing at the mound of earth and the "tombstone" that stood so stalwartly as a sign of hope. Then he took his notepad out and with his pen he wrote, "I can't solve the riddle of Viri Lucis."

He rolled the paper, pushed his finger into the mound and made a hole. Then he pushed the little scroll into the hole, covered it up and walked back to the rectory.

No sooner had he walked through the back door than he heard the phone signal. "You have a call. Do you wish to go online or should I take a message?" the butler voice spoke in a grace note cadence.

He waved his hand, activating the phone while he flicked on the viewscreen to see Gene's image. "Hiya, Gene. What's up?" Danny sounded if not exuberant at least refreshed at his visit at the graveside of I Can't.

"Danny, I just came across another reference to the Ardentes on one of Leno's discs. It's in a letter to Leno."

"Another reference?" Danny exclaimed.

"Yes. Savonarola's happy fanatics."

"Right," Danny replied, his new-found determination draining from his voice.

"It's a letter from a Jerzy Yakablonski," Gene said. "He's …. well, maybe we ought to get together. You can read it, okay?"

"Okay."

"I'll come over as soon as I'm finished with a one o'clock appointment." Gene disconnected. Gene showed up at two O'clock. "Here," he said to Danny, "just read through it.

Danny took the letter and began to read:

> My dearest Leno,
>
> In my last letter, I told you to remember the Ardentes. The spirit of the Ardentes is being preserved in Viri Lucis and must be preserved at all costs.
>
> Sad to say, your attitude of late has been most troubling. The Ardentes have left us a glorious tradition. A tradition that has always kept the Church pure in doctrine and practice according to the mind of Christ.

There have always been those who have closed their eyes to the light of Christ shining through this tradition. Their refusal to accept the teachings of our tradition has led to violence against us and those who have gone before us. I only need to mention the sacred name of our patron, the saintly Savonarola.

Church authorities down through the centuries, crazed with their power, have used the weapon of excommunication to sever those who have advocated nothing else but the orthodoxy of God's truth from the ranks of the faithful. We who have imbibed the spirit of the Ardentes have been caricatured as being unfaithful.

But those who have been so excommunicated are the authentic saints of the Church. There are times when each of us has had doubts. These doubts are temptations from the Evil One who goes about like a lion seeking whom he might devour.

Leno, my dearest son in the Lord, you must renew your faith in the Mentor. He knows what he is doing. He is a man of deep belief in the purity of doctrine and practice. He takes into his heart all the inflictions and suffering of good souls, pious men, who want only to live by God's revelation freed from all the tribulations that so-called theologians infest us with.

There may be times, Leno, when you do not understand what the Mentor is about. Trust in him. God has given him special insights into the evils within the Church. He himself has told us of his visions of the most blessed Michael the Archangel.

Leno, my dearest brother, you have been given a great grace by being included in Viri Lucis. You have been designated to enter the ranks of the hierarchy. Do not squander the gifts you have been given on frivolous doubts. Your many talents will be used to purge Holy Mother Church of her many enemies, wolves wearing sheep's clothing, pious fools, blind guides who are leading our people to perdition.

Think of your glory when the Just Judge will come and give you your crown of eternal reward. Think of how you will feel when Our Lord Jesus says to you, "Well done, good and faithful servant." In the meantime purge yourself of these doubts you have nurturing. The Mentor is deeply saddened by your questioning his decisions. He depends on you so much. Look at him and see Christ your Savior. Put total faith in him as you would in the Lord Jesus.

Remember the words of the prophet. Micah: "….walk wisely before your God." How much wisdom you would show if you walked in the footsteps of the Mentor without doubt, with complete allegiance. How certain you would be that you are walking before your God. To follow the Mentor without reservations is to walk in the footsteps of Christ himself.

Remember, dearest Leno, Our Blessed Mother's words, "He has put down the mighty from their thrones." Those thrones must be filled. You will be one of those who fill them. You are suffering at present but what is your suffering compared to that of our spiritual ancestors, the Ardentes? Refuel the passion of your belief in the Mentor by fasting and prayer. Our new day, the Mentor assures us, is about to dawn.

May God bless you,
Jerzy
Translated from Polish to English by your most humble servant, Josef Bezelskie.

The letter was dated September 22, 2030. About five months before Leno's death.

"Who is this Jerzy What's-his-name?" Danny shoved the question at Gene like a camel poking its nose into a tent.

Gene handed Danny the envelope. In the upper left hand corner, Danny read:

JERZY CARDINAL YAKABLONSKI
CRACOW, POLAND

Danny sat with the envelop clutched in his fingers staring at it like a surveyor squinting off the inches. "My God," he finally exclaimed, "an Encyclical to the Elect. It's terrifying. A Cardinal who sounds like a raving fanatic. Even God is defended with nonsense."

"Not that terrifying, Danny, when you think about it. It all depends what the Cardinal is fanatical about. Ours is a fanatic about finances. No one should know that better than you," Gene was talking quietly as if to soothe Danny. "Face it. I got St. Anselm's as a financial transaction."

"Who is this Mentor, Gene? The way this Cardinal Whatchamacallit writes about him you'd think he was the Son of God reincarnated. We still don't know what Viri Lucis is. And now it's the Mentor."

"Let's review, Danny. Of course, not everything we have is fact, some things are just suppositions.

"Fine," Danny agreed. "Go right ahead."

"Well," Gene started, "number one, there is an organization called Viri Lucis.

"Two," Gene continued, "The Mentor is the leader.

"Three, Viri Lucis is somehow related to the Church."

"Then there's four," Danny added. "Four, Leno and Michael were members of Viri Lucis. And both of them seemed to have had their doubts or at least questions. And both are dead.

"Five, high-ranking officials like Cardinal What's-his-name and Archbishop Brown belong to Viri Lucis." Danny paused.

"Six, Viri Lucis is a fanatical organization obsessed with some form of orthodoxy, something to do with purity of belief," Gene spoke evenly.

"Seven, Viri Lucis wants Michael's fortune for what, we don't know," Danny added

"Eight, as a result, Viri Lucis desperately needs to have that note of Michael's," Gene said.

"Nine," Danny offered, "Viri Lucis is anonymous as far as the general membership of the Church goes.

"Ten, Viri Lucis claims some kind of affiliation with the Ardentes and presumably with other heretical sects over the centuries." Danny's disbelief was as clear in his tone as a drumbeat.

"And eleven," Gene dropped his voice a whisper as hushed as monk telling his beads in chapel, Viri Lucis is ruthless to the point of murder."

Danny exhaled a sigh as final as a boxer who had just been knocked to the canvas for the ten count. He felt his stomach constrict as though it were in a vise. "Gene, I feel sick. How long has Viri Lucis been in existence? Where is Viri Lucis? Is it world-wide? Who belongs? Who and where is the Mentor? What's the exact purpose of Viri Lucis? Why does it need money, and so much of it, so desperately?"

"I think we need a number twelve, Danny. Pope Charles was not a member of Viri Lucis."

"Do you think ….? Did Viri Lucis kill ….?" Danny was obviously exasperated.

"Remember number eleven. Ruthless to the point of murder," Gene said, knowing that he was only adding to Danny's experience of dry martyrdom. "Why else did Michael protest he had nothing to do with Pope Charles death?"

"On my God, my God!" Danny was physically rocking back and forth on the kitchen chair.

"Danny," Gene spoke in a pleading tone, "this is just too big. What was it you told me Celine said to you? You're not Chesterton's Father Brown. It would take ten Father Browns to unravel this thing."

"Who do we go to, Gene? We don't know who is or who isn't a member of Viri Lucis."

"There's Travine, Michael's dapper secretary."

"Yeah, but like Celine said, what do we do? March in on him, tell him we know he's a member of Viri Lucis and force him to spill his guts?"

"I'm stabbing, Danny, but what about the highly-polished Archbishop Brown?"

"You'd get as much out of him as smoke from a camp fire in a downpour, Gene."

"We do have the Polish Cardinal's letter."

"And judging from it, he would wow us with profuse dribble about a pious society dedicated to the spread of God's revealed truth," Danny was worn to the core of his being. "Face it, Gene, we're probably up against the most formidable organization in the history of the Church — maybe in the world. Who knows? We certainly don't."

"I remember reading," Gene said with an encouraging smile, "'When David picks up his slingshot, no one cheers for Goliath.' We've got to have hope. We need to be creative enough to at least be ready for a break of some kind."

"Hope," Danny growled, "hope. I wish to God I were an atheist. How do I live with I Can and I Will?

"What's that?"

"Oh, nothing, Gene. Just something I thought I had learned this morning."

They sat staring at the table like two paralytics, totally incapacitated.

THE MENTOR'S PLOT

"Mentor, how are you?" Cardinal Tamacci asked as he greeted the man behind the huge desk. Tamacci sat down on the uncomfortable wooden chair in front of the desk.

"I am fine, thank you for asking, Camillo. How are you? We haven't heard from you in some time."

"I didn't want to bother you, Mentor, until I had some good news."

"Which is ....?

"We are in, Mentor. Our new Pope has placed his unqualified trust in me."

"That *is* good news, indeed, Camillo. Very good news. After your failure with our dearly departed brother, Charles, you could use some redemption. It is because of your failure, Camillo, that what was done became the only viable alternative.

"You and you alone, Camillo, were responsible for Charles' untimely demise. You will have to answer before God for that unless you redeem yourself by your handling of our new Pope."

"Mentor, I can assure you that this will not be a repeat. Charles, as you well know, just dismissed me. Treated me as if I were non-existent. Then he moved so fast that no one was able to derail him. That is, until ...."

"Let us not rehash old errors, Camillo. We look to the future with hope, do we not?"

"There is no possibility that John Paul IV will be another Charles, Mentor. If anything, the mantel of the papacy is a straitjacket. You yourself labeled him an incidentalist. I can keep him buried in peripheral paper work while making him feel he is fulfilling his papal obligations with astute fervor."

"Being the scholar he is," Camillo continued, "I'm certain he will want to write some encyclicals. But he is so obviously scrupulous that I will be able to keep him writing for months. His scrupulosity will fit into our hands like a magic wand.

"And besides, Mentor, I don't think our new Holy Father has much time to spend here in the Lord's vineyard. His coughing spells are frequent and I'm rather certain he is spitting up blood. He either has consumption or cancer."

"What our Church needs, Camillo," the Mentor, as Tamacci suspected, was gearing up for one of his tirades, "are more wrathful prophets and no more consoling therapists. I am sick and tired, my soul aches. All this liberal talk about trust, honesty and friendship as the bond of the Christian community. We need a clear statement of regulations and total obedience to law."

How often had Tamacci listened to this and other tirades. The Mentor was right but did he have to grind it into the ground? There was no need to convert the Secretary of State, the already converted.

"We need a war to destroy our enemies within and outside the Church. That is a divine imperative. It's time to delete in whatever way possible those who mouth syrupy sentiments about Jesus eating with sinners and telling us that as the Church we can do no less.

"We must not only hate the sin but the sinners as well. Those who refuse to keep the laws set down for their salvation. We are defined by our distance from those who ignore or sneer at the orthodox teachings we represent. I read the other day some so-called scripture scholar who said, 'Our image of God tells us more about ourselves than about God.'

"That's sheer rubbish. God has revealed himself as Judge. And he will sit in judgment on the woman who wrote that trash, trying to prove that women can be as learned as men. We must cleanse the Church of all vanity for the love of Christ. And we will do it by reestablishing the Holy Inquisition."

Tamacci sighed within himself and tried to look attentive. This was the reason he stayed away. The Mentor just couldn't deal with the business at hand. He had to lecture and lecture.

"I assure you, Camillo, that God will soon bless me with all the power on earth to rule. And if I do not rule by subjugating everyone to orthodoxy, I am an idolater. God's will is our will. And the sooner these liberal anarchists in the Church learn this, the sooner will the Church be the Kingdom of God on earth.

"To claim that the Kingdom of God is the realm of human freedom is heresy. Blasphemy. We must rid the Church of these evil people even — no, especially — if they are members of the hierarchy."

There could be no doubt in the mind of anyone listening to the Mentor that he believed that the Church was as emptied of orthodoxy as a reservoir in a draught. He was firm in his conviction that current Church leaders had reduced the challenge of keeping the laws of God, as he interpreted them, to the soft sentimentalism of a Christmas crèche.

The Mentor had carved his one and only expression of orthodox practice in the stone of judgmentalism and he had no qualms about casting that stone in furious condemnation. He was convinced that the straight and narrow way to heaven had been cluttered with detour signs to the back streets of heresy.

He hated all the liturgical reforms since Vatican II calling them carnival sideshows. For him the connection between his vision of what the Church should be and God's will was as obvious as a line drawn from one dot to another. As far as he was concerned the laws and rules of orthodox Catholic living had been bypassed on the beltway of antilegalism.

Legalism, as he so often said, was not a vice as so many of the Church liberals claimed. Rather legalism, the letter of the law for the sake of the letter, was like traveling on the monorail of God's divine prescriptions.

Those liberal anarchists had draped themselves in the fashionable garb of self-deception. Their religious practice was like a stained glass window in the dark. The god they made to reinforce their liberal views was as obvious as the Golden Calf was to Moses.

The Mentor's God, the true God, he knew, would cut these unorthodox heretics off as a farmer snaps away an unproductive branch. These damnable liberals were trying to make the Church a funhouse of escapes. Their sinful teachings, they would find out, were a bolt lock against God's truth.

The Mentor was dedicated to his continued efforts to stab the sharp splinters of orthodoxy into the ballooning illusions of these love-gushing, liberal free-thinkers who scoff at or ignore God's truth as revealed to the Mentor and his followers.

"Now is the time to put yourself in the international spotlight, Camillo."

"I thought I did that when I was uniquely instrumental in settling the long-running dispute between the Israelis and the Palestinians. Apparently my brother Cardinals were not sufficiently impressed to consider me for the papacy."

"Camillo, what you did in the Near East didn't gain you a wisp of admiration from those within the Church. It's what you do in and for the Church that matters. Never forget, we are not promoting Christianity. We are the saviors of Churchianity. More is needed."

"What do you suggest, Mentor?" Camillo asked with a hesitation that telegraphed gloomy symptoms of a fear that the Mentor's suggestions might be too delightfully guileful. As it turned out, his expectation was not denied.

"See to it that you manipulate our new Pope into excommunicating some well-known liberals," the Mentor spoke with the silky elegance he used when he was about to hatch his notoriously tantalizing plots.

"There is," he purred, "our brother, Archbishop Perez of San Antonio in the United States. He is a God-forsaken aberration, surrounding himself as he does with those heretical liberation theologians. Even his brother bishops cannot tolerate his incendiary liberalism. And the Captains of industry and business consider him the anti-Christ with all his predatory pronouncements about the poor having equal access to the material goods of this world.

"Camillo, we have talked about Perez before. You know the plan. Follow that plan and the Pope will be forced to suspend him, render him useless. It's the equivalent of excommunication. You have that young reporter. Tell him he will be paid $100,000 plus all expenses to blackmail Perez. The accusation will be Perez's homosexual advances to him. Although false, everyone will believe it. People love to think the worst about men in power.

"Louis Gabler?" Camillo asked as if talking out loud to himself.

"The very same. He is just waiting for the go ahead. He has been instructed on the matter. He knows what is wanted. Tell him, through your emissaries, $30,000 down and the rest when the work of the Lord has been completed satisfactorily. He will need a photographer. We will pay him $35,000.

"Why could we not dispatch one of your Attendants to assassinate him?" Camillo asked more to test the Mentor than to offer an alternative plan.

"Because, my dear Camillo," the Mentor explained, feigning patience, "we need an international disgrace that will bring an avalanche of harsh contempt down on these privileged liberal hoodlums. We need a scandal that will arouse the savage energy of every God-fearing ultra conservative reactionary in the world-wide Church."

"Sounds plausible to me," Camillo said in a subservient tone.

"What does or does not sound plausible to you is of no consequence," the Mentor replied harshly.

"I will see to it at once," Camillo sounded as he should, as if he had been given a command.

"And, Camillo …."

"Yes, Mentor."

"Do not leave a paper trail. In no way must this reporter's activity be traced back to you."

"Yes, Mentor." At this point to say Camillo was subservient was like saying water was wet.

"There is another ministry you could work on, Camillo."

"And that is …." Camillo sounded either wary or exasperated or fearful. The Mentor was not sure, but he continued.

"Your most formidable opposition in the next Conclave will be Rawmanda from Zaire. He came very close to being elected this time around. Thank God for his liberal tendencies. But, being African, he could emerge the next round."

"Too many of the Cardinals are overly preoccupied with giving the appearance that they are very sensitive to the equality of all races. They have abandoned the proven fact of the inferiority of certain races, Rawmanda's most especially at the top of the list."

"And what do you have in mind for my brother Cardinal?" Camillo sounded almost insolent as though he was convinced that his head, not the Mentor's, would be on the block if anything went wrong.

"We have Matubu in Rawmanda's inner circle. He is Rawmanda's finance minister. What needs to be done is to fix the books until it is obvious to everyone that our beloved Black Cardinal has been stealing his Archdiocese blind. Here, a paper trail is essential and it must lead right back to Rawmanda.

"Here again we need a full blown scandal. Rawmanda must be disgraced not only as an out-and-out thief but as a fiendishly smooth manipulator of sacred Church funds. Add to this his public statements opposing the *Revised New Catechism* and I think we'll have him where we want him — out of the race, Black or otherwise." The Mentor chuckled at his own twist of irony.

"Is that it?" Camillo asked seeming to indicate with as much respect as he could muster that he would like to be able to get about his work as Secretary of State in the Holy Roman Catholic Church.

"And, Mentor, please be patient. I have much to do. I have to gather my 'emissaries' as you call them. They have to make the contacts and report back to me and I have to indoctrinate our new Holy Father with abject fear, if not suffocating terror, of the liberal wing of the Church."

"Camillo, my dearest Camillo, I have all the respect in the world for you. I hold you in the highest esteem of all our members. And I have promised that when I come into my own, you will sit on my right hand. Is not all this true?"

"Yes, Mentor," but Camillo could not help but remember how the Mentor had lashed out at him for his failure with Pope Charles, accusing him of being responsible for Charles' death.

"There's one more matter, Camillo."

"Yes, what is that?" Once again wariness crept back into his voice.

"It's that new, young so-called Catholic President in the United States. His pro abortion, pro euthanasia stance is diametrically opposed to his tongue-thrusting Communions each Sunday. It's not enough that there is opposition from the conservative party to all his policies.

"He is not only considered a liberal politician but an ultra liberal Catholic. You must do something to bring him into moral disgrace."

"His niece?" Camillo asked, knowing that was exactly whom the Mentor was thinking of. "But she is a confirmed drug addict," he added as if to head off the Mentor.

"All the better for our plan, Camillo. Imagine how thrilled she will be to be able to maintain her habit with $150,000. When she accuses her uncle of abusing her as a child, the drug addiction will be seen as the ultimate ruination of her life which began with her uncle's abuse of her. As I have so often said, people will believe anything derogatory about men in power."

"She is not the most stable person to persist in her accusation. She may break under the spotlights of the media and recant. I don't know if or how much we can depend on her to carry off this accusation of pedophilia against the President of the United States."

"Camillo, just keep her in an ample supply of drugs. I repeat, her drug addiction will only lend greater credibility to her accusation.

"When the President is brought down from his mighty throne in total political and moral disgrace, the Catholic liberal movement will have nowhere to go but into schism." the Mentor spoke in such reassuring terms that Camillo could not but feel confident.

"As you wish, Mentor." Camillo sounded genuinely gracious.

"Remember, Camillo, I am depending on you as a vine depends on its branch. You will produce the fruit of these good works. I leave all this in your most sacred hands. You know I have other pressing matters, most important of all being this matter with our brother, Father Daniels. Camillo, I .... we must have that money. Without it the document will not be ours and without the document, well .... need I say more?"

Camillo felt a pang of empathy for the suffering of the Mentor. "I will pray diligently for you, my friend," Tamacci whispered. "I am certain God will see you through to a successful completion of our work in his vineyard." With that Camillo got up, said good-bye, bowed slightly and left.

A JOLTING REVELATION

Danny lifted the floor board and took out the copy of Michael's diary. He flopped on his bed and began once again to read. There had to be some lead to the identity of Viri Lucis and the Mentor.

He read rapidly through a number of pages that were records of Michael's routine activities. Michael had made notations of Confirmations he had administered. Then there were banquets for the Archdiocesan Council of Catholic Women, the Knights of Columbus, the Serra Club and so on. Then there were ground breakings, commencements, political rallies, fund raisers. Michael also recorded names of people he had met. Sometimes he described the influence some of these people had and how he might be able to use them in the future.

> Samuel Packston has been a stalwart supporter of the Republican Party. He is a fervent advocate of the conservative philosophy. He would make a very valuable resource for me as I guide the archdiocese once I am made Archbishop.

Danny continued to skim over these pages with little interest. Then he came to one of Michael's more reflective entries. Danny wanted to try to get inside Michael's mind. Perhaps there he might discover a clue to the gnawing questions he had about Viri Lucis. Or had Michael deliberately disguised any information about that organization? Only one way to find out — keep reading no matter how disillusioning Michael's revelations might be.

> I remember back in the seminary how everyone treated me with such deference because my father was one

of the wealthiest men in Chicago. It was so easy for me to be likeable. If I merely greeted someone, he felt so privileged that I took notice. But I must admit I never used money to buy friends.

My father was so proud when I was ordained. He expressed himself in the only way he knew. With money. He added $100 million to my already bulging account. "It will assure your independence," he said. "It will give you leverage."

I really shouldn't say money was the only way he had to express himself. He had a definite philosophy and articulated it very well. We had many in-depth conversations usually about bottom-line pragmatic things.

"Son," he said to me shortly after I was ordained a priest, "I worry that you are not ruthless enough. I realize the because of your priestly training, you may have difficulty seeing the connection between being a priest and being ruthless. But there is one.

"As in any profession, you can be satisfied with just being another priest. But you have leadership qualities. They won't be recognized unless you are ruthless enough to demonstrate them. In no walk of life that is worth taking is there room for humility. Humility is the virtue of the worthless. I'm not saying you have to change your personality. Far from it. You are very charming and charm is the best face you could ever put on ambition. You know about the velvet glove and the iron fist. Continue being charming but let it be the glove that covers the iron fist of your ruthless spirit."

My father wasn't especially pleased with my objection. "I don't know, Dad," I said, "ruthless sounds …. well, so ruthless." I laughed at the way I always came off sounding so "profound" when I tangled with my father. "As you yourself said, ruthlessness doesn't fit into what a priest is all about," I parried.

"You've made your commitment, haven't you?" my father replied in his usual persuasive tone that hid the power of his own ruthlessness. "Isn't there a kind of ruthlessness in keeping that commitment?" His logic was always flawless if you accepted his premise. "You want to be effective, don't you? You want to rise in the ranks of Church leadership' don't you? You want to make me even prouder of you, don't you?"

I, of course, nodded my assent. But my father was always open

to compromise. "Compromise,"
he used to say, "is the art of letting
others have your way." And so we
compromised and he was willing to
use the synonym I offered in place
of the word, ruthless. We settled on
single-mindedness. Although my
father had to have the last word. "It's
all semantics, son. What is essential
is the attitude behind the words. And
your attitude will determine the kind
of behavior you employ."

Danny put the diary aside. He lay there, his mind more or less a blank. He was having difficulty trying to absorb what went into the making of Michael McCann. His father's guidance not only created a goal-oriented individual out of Michael but a goal-driven person.

That brief record of a conversation between father and son revealed how Michael had arrived at his ambition. But his father's influence, as far as Danny could figure, did not account for Michael's ruthlessness toward those in the Church whom he disagreed with. A ruthlessness that Danny had read in previous pages. Or was it, in Michael's word, single-mindedness?

Danny flipped through a few more pages and then began to read again.

Today I buried my father. He was far
more than a father to me. He was my
guiding light. How I will miss him!
No doubt there will be those who will
tell tales of my father's ruthlessness.
He was a man of abrasive power who
could not abide fools. But I always
found him to be demanding but
understanding. He recognized human
weakness but would not tolerate

stupidity. I so agree with him. And, God knows, there are so many stupid fools in the Church. Their name is Legion.

My father was known as the King of Takeovers. Many hated him for what he did to the businesses he bought out and the changes he made. But isn't that the blessing of capitalism? He was truly a genius and a very religious man. He would say, "Power does not corrupt the powerful. Power demoralizes the pretenders to power." I agree with him. Those who pretend to power, such as those liberal demons who are trying to destroy the Church, must be crushed. Crushed under the heel of orthodox belief. To be in my father's presence was always to feel power throbbing in your own veins.

My father, God give him eternal rest, left me well-off. As I calculate it, my worth comes to over 500 million dollars. I guess I can say I am set for the rest of my natural life. My two brothers and my sister, of course, inherited my father's businesses. They're welcome to them. I have my money and am freed from the daily drudgery of taking care of my father's legacy. Besides, I have my own work to do. My father understood this and made certain that I would be financially independent enough to accomplish my goal of purging and renewing the Church.

I will use this money to further our sacred cause. I will not give it to Viri Lucis during my lifetime. I want to keep most of my money toward the time when I am in a position of power in the Church. I will further our cause here in the United States. I know this is what God wants of me. Viri Lucis will guess at my worth as will others but no one but my lawyer and investment consultant will know.

I thank God that my father lived to see me ordained a bishop. I only wish he had lived long enough to take pride in my being elevated to the Red Hat. His dream for me always was that I would be a Cardinal. Jokingly or seriously, he often addressed me as Your Eminence. He repeatedly said, "When you take over the Archdiocese, you will be able to restore the good order of God's law. Our present Cardinal is a nice enough man but he's allowed things and especially priests to slip out of his control. Control, Michael, is the supreme virtue of a leader," he would always say. He was so proud when the Cardinal made me one of his Vicars General and then appointed me General Secretary, a position second to that of His Eminence.

I intend to set up an investment fund
for Johnny. I don't know what I
would do without him. And yet he is
so appreciative of the slightest thing
I do for him. He is so debonair and
cultured. Very brilliant. A delightful
sense of humor. The least I can do for
him is to make certain he is financially
independent. I really don't know what
I would do without this Godsend,
Johnny Travine.

Danny wondered why Michael hadn't made John J. Travine his
executor. He would have privy to much more about Michael than he
was. Danny hoped that perhaps here he might get some information
about Viri Lucis. After all, it was evident from Travine's witness
to Michael's note that Travine was a sure bet to be a member of
Viri Lucis. Danny's eyes drifted down the page. Suddenly he bolted
upright.

He sat there for the longest while in a state of shock and
bewilderment. Then he reached to the phone. His hand was trembling
as he waved it and called out Gene's number. "When can you come
over?" Danny asked without prelude or expectation. Gene obviously
caught the urgency in Danny's tone.

"I probably could make it around seven this evening."

"Good. I'll see you then."

Then he spoke Celine's number at her office. After waiting for
her secretary to put him through, Danny, almost breathless, said,
"I've discovered something in the diary. Gene's coming over at
seven. Can you be here then?"

"Let me check. Yes," Celine whispered as though to calm Danny
down, "I'll be there at seven."

"Good. I'll see you then." Danny waved off without a goodbye.

When Celine told George about meeting with Gene and Danny
that evening, she was taken aback by his reaction.

"Celine," George said with not a little annoyance, "do you have to go over to Danny's this evening? I was looking forward to a quiet evening at home — together."

"Danny sounded so urgent, George. I really feel I must. Gene's coming too."

"I really get puzzled, Celine. All Danny has to do is call and you drop everything and run." George was not trying to disguise his annoyance one bit.

"Look, George, Danny's in a very vulnerable position right now and needs all the support I can give him. I've explained the situation thoroughly to you. Whatever it is that Danny has discovered could have a very negative impact on me as well as on him."

"I've tried to be understanding," George said, less with annoyance now and more with the determination of someone who wanted to make an unmistakable point. "But this whole thing is disrupting your life and our life."

"Well, what do you want me to do? Tell Danny not to bother me anymore with this nonsense? Or tell him to keep his discoveries to himself until I can clear it with you whether or not I can listen? Now it was Celine's turn to sound annoyed. She launched a preemptive strike. "George, Danny and I are not lovers. I have been absolutely faithful to you from the moment we pronounced our vows."

"There are other kinds of infidelity," George sounded uncharacteristically peevish. "You don't have to go to bed with someone to be unfaithful. It can be a matter of attitude, too."

"What exactly are you saying, George?"

"What I am saying is that while you may be physically faithful to me, your affections, concern and …. well, your love can be given to someone else. I think I've been more than understanding of your prior relationship with Danny.

"I've even gone out of my way to become friends with him because I knew that would make you happy. But I don't want to be made to feel like a house pet — someone you come home to after you've given all your quality time to another man."

"This is ridiculous. Outlandish." Celine's eyes filled. "How can you possibly accuse me of not giving you my very best. I love you and I've made what I hope is a lifelong commitment to you. What I feel for Danny is a different kind of love. It's not the same as our love."

"Are you sure you're not still in love with Danny?" George's voice was at a low, factual pitch as insipid as a priest in the confessional trying to pry enough information out of a penitent to decide whether the sin was grave or slight.

"George, do you want me to call Danny back and tell him I won't be there?" Celine asked, ignoring his question.

"No, I don't want you to do that. I just thought you might want to examine your priorities. Not the ones you mouth but the ones you're living. I am a tolerant man but I have my limits."

"And I am an independent woman. The priority I am living is twofold. When I married you, I did not surrender my independence to you. And secondly, when I married you, I pledged my first loyalty to you.

"My philosophy, if you will, is that the love we share should expand us both to be able to love others, not in some kind of clinical disinterest but with genuine affection. All along I thought you subscribed to that philosophy and regarded it as your own. One of the qualities I admired in you was your total lack of a jealous attitude. Don't disappoint me now."

"Am I disappointing or am I just expressing what any husband would expect from his wife? Perhaps your own choice of words is what makes me doubtful."

"What choice of words?"

"You said you pledged your loyalty to me. Somehow I would rather have heard the word love."

"George, for me, unqualified loyalty is the preeminent symbol of authentic love. If we're going to get bogged down in semantics, nothing of value will be communicated between us."

"On the contrary, Celine, and you should know this from your legal background, the clarification that takes place in communicating depends a great deal on knowing that we both mean the same thing by the words we use. When I say, 'I love you,' and you say, 'I love you,' I want to know that we both mean the same thing by the word, love."

"All I can say is that I love you, George. And my loyalty is my pledge of a lifelong commitment to you. On the other hand when I say I love Danny, I mean that I consider myself to be a dear friend of his. There is loyalty and commitment in friendship but it's not the same as what we have together."

Even as she spoke, Celine wasn't certain that what she was saying was the total truth. Down deep in her heart she felt she was still in love with Danny. She would have to be careful in the future to see to it that what she felt for George was expressed more explicitly, with more affection if not passion. She did love George and the last thing she wanted was a failure in her marriage. But now was the time for her to assert herself.

"George, I am going over to Danny's this evening. I'll try not to be late getting back."

After Celine left, George sat on the straight back desk chair, strumming his fingers on the desktop. In the aftermath of his outburst he was enveloped in a flush of red-faced embarrassment.

He remembered something Danny had said, "When you fail, celebrate your humanness." He didn't feel much like celebrating. He had always controlled his emotions with the skill of an animal trainer. He felt humiliated over his loss of control this evening.

He considered himself a fair-minded man. He was convinced that it wasn't jealousy that was the catalyst of his confrontation with Celine. It was more a premonition as tangible as the embarrassment he was feeling that Celine's relationship with Danny could prove traumatic if not disastrous.

Celine's relationship with Danny, he felt, was as dangerous as an amateur gymnast tiptoeing across a high wire with no net underneath. Still he didn't give much credence to feelings, premonitions or intuitions, for that matter.

On the other hand, was he in fact trying to convince himself that possible danger to Celine was the cause of his flare-up? Was he denying feelings of jealousy to justify himself?

He knew that his marriage to Celine was not the passionate romance that she apparently yearned for. Yet they were friends. Very good friends. He was reasonable enough to settle for her less than passionate response to him.

He was also calculating enough not to measure Celine's affection for him against her love for Danny. He had long ago surmised that Celine's love for Danny was more a pining for forbidden fruit than it was passionate desire.

In a way he felt sorry for Celine. She was torn between the worlds of what is and of what could not be. Perhaps that was actually the hazardous high wire she was walking.

Standing at almost six feet with a well proportioned frame and a full head of black hair, graying on the sides, George knew he was attractive. He sensed how women responded to him. He was socially reserved and quietly cordial enough to project an aura of mystery.

But, he also knew, there was no electricity in his personality. He wasn't dull but neither was he a dynamo. He was a steady ship plowing through all kinds of tumultuous waters.

For Celine, there was no challenge, no adventure, no risk in her relationship with him. He was, in the words of Celine's friend, Margaret, too predictable.

He recognized that he was as cautious as a beast of prey hunkering up to the object of its hunt. He was also as conscientious as a cloistered nun in prayer. It was these qualities that had made him successful in the business world. He was respected by competitors and colleagues alike. As the cliché goes, he was not a bad catch.

Yet for all his caution and predictability, he had taken the most inexplicable risk of his life when he fell in love with and married Celine.

He knew all this. Yet he cared for Celine more than anyone in the world. Still he knew that sometimes we care more for others than they do for us.

If anything, he was her protector. For the most part he protected her from her own perfectionism. With Celine it was always all or nothing. And in the most important choice of her life, her decision to marry him, she had neither. This saddened him and yet he had to admit that Celine responded gently, even lovingly to his caring.

Was he jealous of Celine's love for Danny? He hoped not. But he wasn't introspective enough to pry open his heart and find out. He'd just continue to go along. Surprisingly, he was convinced that he and Celine would stay together until death.

It was the paradox of their love. The lack of wild rapturous passion held the reins tight on capricious discontent. He and Celine just seemed to be gliding over the placid lake of life. That is, until this evening.

George actually smiled to himself. What must Celine be thinking about her predictable, cautious husband? A confrontation once in a while, the stirring of the waters of "Lake Placid," wasn't all that harmful to a relationship. In fact, there had been some in-depth communication in their "exchange."

George suddenly felt aroused. There would be a kind of eroticism involved in the reconciliation with Celine, he thought. Perhaps even passion. He hoped she would not delay too long with whatever it was that the two "Father Browns" had discovered in their quest of the unholy Grail, Viri Lucis.

"Celine, my dearest, I am truly sorry about this evening. I love you and I worry about you," he practiced aloud. Again he smiled, quietly laughing at himself.

Shortly after both Gene and Celine arrived, Danny who looked like he had just stepped off the electric chair after a power failure, opened the copy of Michael's diary. He began to read aloud.

> I intend to set up an investment fund for Johnny. I don't know what I would do without him. And yet he is so appreciative of the slightest thing I do for him. He is so debonair and cultured. Very brilliant. A delightful sense of humor. The least I can do for him is to make certain he is financially

226

independent. I really don't know what I would do without this Godsend, Johnny Travine.

Danny paused. He looked from Gene to Celine, left out heavy, exasperated sigh and continued.

The other night when we were in bed together Johnny professed his love for me so beautifully it brought tears to my eyes. I never have felt so loved in all my life. And I, in return, love him more than my own life. What a loving God to have given me this wonderful young man. I am certain that no matter what ever happens, we will always love each other till death and beyond.

Danny stopped reading. The silence was sepulchral. Gene and Celine looked at each other in stark shock as if words at that moment would be nothing if not contrived.

Then Gene broke the silence. "No wonder Michael asked you to think kindly of him."

Celine spoke next. "Look, I can't get exercised over someone's sexual preference. Ray Gauth, my artist friend, is gay. I can only say he's one of the most tender and caring people I know. His sensitivity makes the machismo of straight men seem ludicrously barbaric."

"But why did Michael write this in his diary?" Gene asked as though his favorite pastime was contemplating the paradoxes of the universe.

"I don't know," Celine answered. Maybe he was purging himself. A confession."

"In a way," Gene said, "I feel sorry for John Travine. How or to whom does he express his grief? I saw him at Michael's funeral and he looked as composed as a Stoic philosopher. He looked for all the world as Michael's secretary and nothing else. His heart must have been breaking and all his energy was being poured into keeping up a good appearance."

"Something Church*men* are so adept at doing," Celine couldn't help but squeeze out a bit of her invective.

"But," Danny spoke with new-found fervor, ignoring Celine's innuendo, "don't you see? John Travine's homosexuality could be the chink in Viri Lucis' armor."

"Oh, sure," Celine sounded exasperated. "What do we do? March in on Travine and tell him we know he's gay. Tell him we have proof from Michael's diary? He'd laugh at us. He'd accuse Michael of fantasizing and he would deny Michael's fantasy as ridiculous adolescent sexual narcissism. Then he'd tell us if we spread this slander, he would sue us for defamation. We wouldn't have a legal leg to stand on."

"But even if he did sue us," Gene offered, "his reputation would spin down the drain."

"Is that what we want?" Celine countered. "Or do we want information on Viri Lucis?"

Danny sat there. His fractured expectations carved deep furrows in his brow. "Maybe I jumped too fast into a conclusion without following the logic Celine just mentioned. Still it seemed like such a ready-made opportunity. I guess I thought we could blackmail Travine into spilling his guts. I was convinced his homosexual relationship with Michael would give us some leverage."

"Not with what we have," Celine reemphasized. "I'm sorry, Danny, but that's the reality."

"God, we've got to find out who and what Viri Lucis is before …"

"Before," Celine interrupted Danny, "they get us."

"But what if we just approached him," Gene suggested, "and …. no, that wouldn't work. And it's not just Viri Lucis," Gene made no attempt to hide his frustration. "Who or what is this Mentor?"

"It has to be someone with power in the Vatican," Danny offered. "Someone who is ultra conservative to the point of insufferable harshness. There's Cardinal Krantz, Prefect of Congregation for the Doctrine of the Faith. He's a living reminder that that Congregation was once the Inquisition. He'd love to drive us back to the days of the Council of Trent."

"There's Cardinal Tamacci, Secretary of State. He's a suave diplomat in public but little is known about his private ideology."

"Why does it have to be a bureaucrat in the Vatican?" Celine asked.

"It doesn't necessarily," Gene agreed. "There's our Polish friend, Cardinal Yakablonski. In his letter to Leno, he all but canonized the Mentor. He could have been writing in the third person."

"Hell" Danny exploded, "it could be anyone in power."

"Why does it have to be a Church official?" Celine wondered aloud. "It could be a layperson. A powerful politician or a czar in industry who thinks the Church is going to hell in the proverbial basket."

"If it's not somebody in the Vatican," Gene mused, "the Mentor could be anywhere in the world."

They sat in silence. Then Gene laughed more out desperation than humor. "And I thought the Trinity was a mystery." Both Celine and Danny seemed to relax momentarily.

"No matter what," Danny said with determination, "I will honor Michael's memory. I will not let go of that note. If there was only some way we could get Travine to tell us about Viri Lucis without doing any damage to Michael."

"I have to get back," Celine said with a nervous smile. George wants to have a quiet evening at home and I've already cut into that."

"Sorry," Danny said. He felt a twinge of anguish at the thought of Celine and George having a "quiet evening" together. He knew he would never get over his feelings for Celine no matter how hard he tried, no matter how diligently they both worked at just being friends.

He wondered if Celine had said that to punish him for not forsaking everything for her, for quiet evenings with her. He put that thought out of his mind at once. He was reading into her remark again far more than what she had said. Still he wondered if she would have preferred to have had a quiet evening with him instead of George. He put that thought out of his mind too.

For her part, Celine decided this was not the time to pull Danny aside and tell him about the "discussion" she and George had. Instead, her parting comment was, "Maybe we'll be able to come up with another idea later."

Celine said goodbye and left. A general feeling of dejection hung over the room.

"I really don't think Celine has anything to fear from Viri Lucis," Gene said as he and Danny lingered around the kitchen table, having a nightcap.

"I hope you're right, Gene, but did you notice how she shuddered when she was referring to Viri Lucis? She's going through too much. I honestly think I should tell her to pull out of this now and stay away from it."

"You're the one I'm worried about, Danny," Gene sounded just like what he said — worried. "Celine belongs to a very prestigious law firm and they usually rally around their own especially when their own is someone like Celine who helps to fill their coffers to overflowing. You, on the other hand, could be hung out to dry.

"Church authorities, especially when they're convinced they have been publicly embarrassed, are legendary for sweeping the 'guilty' party under the sanctuary rug. And as you know so well, there is nothing so embarrassing as sexual misconduct that reaches to the outer limit of public scandal — at least as far as the authorities perceive it."

"If it is Church authorities we dealing with," Danny countered.

"I'm worried," Gene continued, "because, from what we have been able to gather, Viri Lucis is pernicious and destructive. They won't kill you. They can't. Not if they want that note. "And even if they did kill you, they wouldn't know what provisions you've made about using the note to stop them from getting Michael's money.

So they need the note. They need to destroy it. Still, they could ruin you. And that could be even worse."

"I've tried to read through Michael's diary in one sitting," Danny said apparently ignoring Gene's worriment, "but I can get only so far and I have to stop. There's his whole attitude toward the people he considers dangerous to the Church. Now there's this 'relationship' with Travine. I just can't absorb it except in bits and pieces."

A FRANK DISCUSSION

Danny got up and poured another glass of bourbon for each of them.

"Remember, Gene, when we first met, you told me all kinds of stuff you'd heard about me? None of which was especially flattering."

"Yeah, so?"

"So I want to ask you what you think about me? Honestly, as a friend."

"You're a troubled soul, Danny. Perhaps even a divided soul."

"Celine once said I lived a kind of schizophrenic life."

"Maybe," Gene sounded tentative.

"I've often thought I am in psychological schism with the Church."

"You're one of the most brilliant thinkers I've met, Danny. And you have this charming quality of not being a know-it-all. You respect what others think and say no matter how pedestrian it may be."

"I don't know it all," Danny said. "I don't even know a little bit. There's an aphorism I picked up in high school. 'The wise man is the man who knows that he knows little.' I like to think I'm a lifelong learner and I honestly believe I can learn something from everyone."

"Still, you're tortured, aren't you. I can sense it in your dark moods. Not just over this rubbish with Viri Lucis but more or less on a regular basis. It's as though you're searching for a phantasm or maybe a panacea.

"You asked, Danny, so I'll tell you. As much as I like and admire Celine, I think your relationship with her is just further dividing your soul."

"I'll be honest with you, Gene, sometimes I feel so trapped. I love her with every pulse of my life. I'm not that certain that I love my priesthood as much. Yet I covet it with the fierce greed of a miser. I can't let go."

"Well, to continue. There is a mystic streak in you, Danny. And I think this also contributes to your torture. You seem to want to close yourself down to everyone and everything but the lavish waste of the divine and you can't. I'm not so sure you should. I'm just too pragmatic to understand the workings of the mystical."

"You've hit on something, Gene. Sometimes I wonder if when I'm being most contemplative I am most manipulative. Do I use my insights to manipulate others? Myself? God? I don't know. It's just a feeling I have from time to time. It may be that proverbial division between role self and real self. Do we spend our lives making contact only with roles instead of with persons?"

"I guess we're most comfortable," Gene responded thoughtfully, "when each person stays within a predictable role. We hate disruptions. Maybe that's why we don't grow all that much. We're too busy extending or expanding out roles."

"I don't want to end up," Danny spoke with what sounded like quiet desperation, "in the grand finale of a conscientious life feeling nothing but emptiness. At the same time I want to continue being a utopian dreamer with the hope that I might shine light into tomorrow."

"Well, I'll say one thing on your behalf," Gene smiled, "as I've said before, you don't spend time trying to fit in instead of speaking out. And you're not afraid that speaking out will mean losing out."

"But maybe I'm using up too much time crusading for lost causes like my school or the whole messiness of The Alley."

"But isn't that what we're about, Danny? The lost? I don't mean those who deliberately walk away. Let them go. Who knows what they'll find? Maybe a better way to God if that's what they're looking for. But the lost — those who are starving to belong and don't know how or to what? Isn't that the shepherd angle?

"Or maybe that is too grandiose a figure. Maybe we're just signposts. I don't know. I do know that the lost don't all live in The Alley. There are probably more of the lost in my affluent suburbia and maybe your people are looking for a signpost more sincerely, more eagerly, than my people. Sorry, I didn't mean to run on like that."

"Some psychiatrist said that more therapy's accomplished over a drink than hours on a psychiatrist's couch. I appreciate your insights, Gene. I really do. They're helpful. I may never escape the labyrinth but you help me feel a little more comfortable being lost in it.

"Why is it that we human beings are so willing, even eager to think the worst of others? And what does that say about us?" Danny paused, wanting Gene's insight.

"Maybe we're afraid that if we give others the benefit of the doubt, we'll let them get away without being properly punished," Gene spoke slowly, thinking through what he was saying.

"Or maybe we have a perverse desire to participate in God's judgment. We think that by judging others we'll be more Godlike. Or maybe we don't want to give others the benefit of the doubt because we think that will take away from us, lessen our self-esteem or whatever."

"Interesting," Danny said, "how easily, how cleverly we find justifications for our suspicions, judgments and condemnations." Danny smiled. "Maybe we're all paranoid schizophrenics."

"Just don't become bitter, Danny. Whether it's over your work at St. Matt's or over Celine or that crazy bunch, Viri Lucis. As you have so often said yourself, if you feel you're in a destructive situation, get out of it and that goes for all three categories I just mentioned."

"I'm not sure if it's a destructive situation or a challenge. Celine pounced on me one time about the different varieties of the poor. It was enlightening as so much of what she says is.

"I've come to realize that the poor are not just those who clothe themselves in newspapers against the winter wind or those whose stomachs a bloated to the size of a huge empty bowl. The poor for us is someone who is hungering for a well-placed word of affirmation or an unobtrusive gesture of support."

"True," Gene responded, "but the usual image of the poor as hordes of the destitute milling around a Third World country is as realistic as a famine, as accurate as decimation."

"But still," Danny insisted, "just as urgently poor is the person standing right in front of us knee-deep in an inferiority complex or someone suffering from malnutrition because of being fed nothing but spiritual pabulum or someone cramped with the acid indigestion of bitterness."

"I know what you're saying, Danny. Whether the poverty is physical or emotional or spiritual, we've got to put out our lives like a well-worn welcome mat. It certainly helps me to think over my position in the suburban land of milk and honey."

"Sometimes, honestly, Gene, I think my involvement with the poor in The Alley is more a sign of my own needs than really caring for those people."

"You're so typically Irish, Danny. You seem to enjoy luxuriating in the anguish of self-torture. Who has pure motives for doing anything? What you're doing for your people makes them part of yourself. And, I hope, the same is true of me."

"I know. 'To pray for others is to become those for whom we pray.'"

"You're the one who told me that you read somewhere that we don't serve people. We serve the movement of the Spirit in people. We do what we can to discern that movement of the Spirit in others. Sometimes we're right on target. Other times we miss by miles."

"Gene, I want to believe so much in the possibilities of people. But then I get impatient. Celine told me to stick with the image of the Widow's Mite and I guess that's my greatest struggle — believing that my small contribution will have an impact for good on the whole world or even on the whole of my world. Maybe I am too utopian. Maybe I should settle for being a flicker instead of a bright light.

"Be patient, Danny. It'll keep you from rushing into false hopes as a way of escaping from the pain of your people or your own pain in trying to solve their problems. Not all problems have solutions. They're there to challenge us to continue growing. And maybe we just grow into the crucifixion.

"The 20th century mystic, Thomas Merton, said, 'Jesus was crucified because he wasn't holy in the right way.' Who's to say who is holy or who isn't? If you really believe in the possibilities of people, you have to be willing to risk frustration. Isn't that the symbolism of the cross? Frustration crucifying our hope?" Gene fell silent.

"And the Resurrection is the startling surprise of passing through frustration to renewed hope, right?" Danny added.

"I think so," Gene said thoughtfully. "Look at it this way. There is no record of Jesus doing a sociological analysis of how the poor or the outcast got that way. He just cared for people because they were in need. Can't we do as much? I mean without tearing ourselves apart looking for the purity of our motives."

"Yeah, I guess we try too hard sometimes," Danny offered. "I know I torture myself with introspection when it's not necessary. It's so easy to convince myself that my efforts are all that count. I should dwell more in the gospel image of 'One sows, another reaps.' Anything I'm reaping comes from seeds sown long ago by someone else. And what I'm sowing will be reaped by someone who comes after me.

"Why is it, Gene, that we know all this stuff but it takes almost forever for it to get into the sinews of our souls? Into our emotions so that we'll act on them and not just give intellectual assent to them?"

"Danny, you just used the word, surprise. Maybe you need to get back to a sense of childlike surprise and wonder, which can take the edge off disillusionment or even lead to humor over frustration. A sense of surprise can serve as a catalyst to transform the theory into motivating emotions."

"I know. Sometimes when things don't go the way I've planned them I cave in like a sink hole. I need to react with a capacity for surprise that'll keep me believing that God brings beautiful butterflies out of ugly cocoons."

"Exactly. Danny. Remember, if you're too available to others, you won't be available to yourself. Maybe that's what's causing you these bouts with depression. You need refueling."

"Is it depression or burn-out, Gene?"

"Danny, you're very creative. Creative ventures stir up the embers in a burn-out, if that's what's ailing you. Don't let your creative spirit dry up in you. I know I'm a great one to say this, but break away from the pragmatic.

"Hang a little looser. Learn to be more carefree and less somber. Life is too short. And God doesn't expect us to be perfect. He just wants us to try to keep growing. The operative word is try."

"You're right, of course, but it's hard not to be somber what with this stuff about Viri Lucis and Michael. I feel so heartbroken over Michael and I don't know for sure why."

"When was the last time you wrote a poem, Danny?"

"When Celine and I …. when we were madly in love."

"Get back to some creative writing."

"I was thinking of keeping a journal."

"Like Michael's?"

"Not in content." And for the first time that evening, Danny laughed.

"No, I suppose not," Gene joined in the laughter. "God forbid."

"Gene, I won't ever judge Michael. Who am I to judge anyone?"

"If you're referring to you and Celine, Danny, let me make an observation. Your sin is far more pardonable than the ambition of those who use the Church to advance themselves and then play the role of the humble but rewarded steward.

"Or the self-righteousness of those who sit in judgment on people who are frail and weak human beings struggling and failing more than they succeed.

"You're a good man, Danny. You're worth a hundred Michaels. I'm not just saying that. You're a good priest and I'm proud to have you for a close friend."

"Thanks, Gene, I really appreciate your affirmation even if it's a bit of an exaggeration."

"Danny, may I change the subject?" Gene asked in a weary tone.

"Certainly. What's up?"

"Well, I have this teacher. We'll call her X. How can I say this without sounding like a character assassin? I've never met anyone more destructive than she is.

"Why don't you just get rid of her?"

"It's not that easy. She's known to be one of those wonderfully fervent, exemplary, orthodox Catholics."

"So what's the problem?"

"She has a tongue as destructive as a hydrogen bomb. She demolishes reputations with the ease of a professional marksman shooting clay pigeons out of the sky. At the same time at religion department meetings she is the enthusiastic herald for teaching the children the true doctrines of the Church, of making sure orthodoxy is observed in every jot and tittle. And God help anyone she decides is unorthodox.

"She talks …. well, a conversation with her is like listening to a monologue that rushes with the force of flood waters. And she is not out to get just liberals, which from her point of view, is anyone who doesn't agree and go along with her. She'll demolish anyone she doesn't like, anyone who steals one ray of the spotlight from her, anyone who makes her feel inferior. At the same time she is as pleasant as a Spring morning, as ingratiating as a professional politician. She's not harsh. She is 'concerned.' She is the self-anointed defender of the faith. She has the parents bamboozled. Totally. They love to gossip with her and she's only too eager to oblige, giving them the inside story.

"I hate talking about her like this but I'm trying to get an handle on it. I'm talking to help myself think this through."

"I understand," Danny said sympathetically.

"Danny, I don't think this woman would know a gospel value if it bit her on the ass.

"Let me give you a couple of examples. My principal is one of the most Christian gentlemen I've ever met. He often comes to daily Mass. When he does he serves as minister of the cup. Some mornings he has to consume quite a bit of the Precious Blood. One morning X smelled his breath and before you knew it there was a story going around that the principal was an alkie"

"A lie can travel half way around the world before truth has even put its shoes on," Danny sighed.

"I called in the teacher who told the principal that X was spreading this about him. And do you know, the teacher claimed she must have misunderstood. X has raised intimidation to a new art form. You either go along with her or you're her next victim.

"Then there was the situation of one our teachers who was having dinner with a book salesman. X and her husband walked into the restaurant and saw them. Next thing you know there's a story going around that the teacher was involved in an adulterous affair. X doesn't' even know what adultery is. Neither the teacher nor the salesman are married.

"I called X in. I told her in no uncertain terms that her gossiping had to stop. You know what her reaction was? She told me that if I were a true pastor, I'd be more involved in the school and would be doing something about all the immorality among the faculty members. Can you beat that?

"I told her her job was on the line and that I was writing her up. She told me the children's spiritual welfare was at stake and that I would burn in hell for not fulfilling my moral duty, and that she would have no qualms about going to the Cardinal and telling him about my 'moral lassitude.' They were her exact words. God knows what stories she'll be spreading about me now."

"There's nothing so malicious as self-righteous judgmentalism parading itself under the halo of virtue," Danny said with empathy for Gene's plight in this matter.

"The problem is that I can't get through to her. Her self-righteousness is like the pupil of an eye, the more light that shines into it, the more it contracts. Like you said, Danny, there is a viciousness about people who pride themselves on their orthodoxy."

"I've found," Danny said pursuing the thought, "that self-righteous people become more and more bitter precisely because they think their happiness depends on their wanting to be known as more virtuous than everyone else. They go through all the pious rituals of religion and then turn around and sit in judgment on anyone they choose.

239

"I'm not a psychiatrist, Gene, but this woman must be suffering from a neurotic lack of self-esteem. And the only way she can compensate is by condemning others. Hatred is the expression of the lowest kind of self-esteem. And you can't hate someone else unless you hate yourself first. Anyone who is obsessed with evil in other people will find no outlet but violence. And that's what she apparently has done."

"I swear to God, Danny, I think she is psychotic. Or a sociopath. No conscience. No feeling of regret. Not the slightest hint of remorse. She just goes along her destructive route on the way to her God who, I'm sure, she envisions as the vengeful Judge who will get us all in the end. All but her."

"The damnable thing, Gene, is that if she is psychotic, then she's not morally responsible for all the destruction she causes. Hatred has a way of consuming and destroying the one who hates. And so the question is, Is she hateful because she's psychotic or has her hatred brought her to the destruction of psychosis?"

"Sometimes I think she's possessed," Gene sounded like he was reaching into the depths of his soul.

"You hit on it earlier, Gene. She practices religion flawlessly but she wouldn't know faith values if Jesus himself handed them to her which in fact he does through the gospel. There are people, fervent practitioners of religion, who minimize their own sins by exaggerating the faults of others.

"If we become like the God we worship, what kind of a God does she have? It would have to be a God whose only function is to condemn everyone he has created," Danny said answering his own question. Danny got up and stretched. He walked around a little then sat down again.

Gene spoke softly, "The condemnation of others that finds satisfaction in condemning has to feel supported by a God who is a ruthless, unloving, vengeful judge — a God who is out to get us and throw us all into hell. My God, Danny, there are people who act with the deepest religious fervor and they're nowhere near the gospel. It's frightening, to say the least."

"Maybe the system is neurotic," Danny said in all seriousness. "I don't mean to sound cynical but look at the emphasis placed on humility in our seminary training. The corollary, whether intentional or not, was that anyone in authority had to make certain that all his or her subjects were kept humble, even if that meant humiliating them. There's a saying that fits here: 'Those who love to be feared fear to be loved.'

"Is it any wonder that there is so little affirmation within the Christian community? If we go around telling people they're doing a good job or they're using their talents well, then they'll become proud. The next thing you know they won't be obedient and there goes the control."

" I don't know how I'm going to handle this mess," Gene sounded exasperated.

"You'll handle it, Gene."

"Danny, she's the type who could go to someone in authority and with that sugar-sweet pietism of hers make a case that I'm the one who is a self-righteous, judgmental bastard."

"I don't know how much consolation this adage will hold for you but it goes, 'The roaring fires of fanaticism eventually consume the fanatic.'"

"Sort of what goes around comes around," Gene said. "Trouble is sometimes the coming around is very slow. In the meantime the person in question goes around damaging and destroying all kinds of really good people."

"I don't want to come off with my own sugar-sweet pious bromides," Danny said, "but it's the crucifixion episode at the hands of the Pharisees all over again, Gene. After all, if we participate in Christ's life, who's to say we won't share in his sufferings? But there is always resurrection if we have the courage of our faith convictions."

"God, I hope so. I pray so. You know what scares me most, Danny? That X is not an isolated case. There may be many 'good' Catholics out there who draw energy from despising others as being morally inferior.

"They go to Church, receive the sacraments, say their prayers, keep the rules and everything a 'good' Catholic should do except live the gospel maxim, 'Judge not ....condemn not.' I'm afraid we have a lot of work to do unearthing whited sepulchers."

"Hypocrisy is all the worse for being sincere," Danny said evenly. "Even if the sincerity is a cover for mental imbalance."

"You know what?" Danny asked rhetorically. "What we don't dwell enough on is that living the gospel values is a skill. It's an acquired quality. It's a habit learned by repetitive acts like learning how to play a musical instrument."

"Yeah," Gene responded. "And if you don't acquire the skill, your desire to live the gospel values, to improve, to grow spiritually will merely be a wisp of smoke fading into the air."

"How often do we preach on learning the skill of being hopeful or optimistic?" Danny asked, pursuing the thought. That parable about not building a tower without first sitting down and figuring out how much it will cost, for me at least, speaks to the need of having a strategy."

"You mean," Gene said, "you've got to envision your goal like wanting to be more forgiving or compassionate, then sit down and calculate the means you'll use to accomplish that goal."

"Right," Danny said with unexpected enthusiasm. "Without some kind of a strategy you may end up putting out titanic amounts of energy just to spin your wheels and go nowhere. I don't think you can acquire the skill of living the gospel values without a strategy for learning that skill.

"It's just my opinion. But I'm convinced it's the right way to go. Too many of us approach our spirituality with wishful thinking. I'd like to be more understanding or if only I could be more involved in the needs of others. You know how it goes, Gene.

"We may even have a stern determination but what good is it if there's no strategy to make the determination a reality? Will without skill is nil, as the saying goes."

"I guess I have to work on developing the skill of dealing with this teacher in a more compassionate way. That's going to be tough. Real tough. I'd like to kick her ass from here to kingdom come.

"Anyway, thanks a million for listening, Danny. I really appreciate it. And take my advice and forget that note. After all, you've had two of the most brilliant people you know tell you to do this." Gene laughed and some of his tension seemed to dissolve.

Gene finished his drink. "I've got to get going. Gotta see if I can find some of those 'lost' we were talking about. And I hope I wasn't out of line about what I said about your relationship with Celine."

"I thank God for you, Gene."

"You're a gold mine, Danny. Dig deep.

Gene sighed, got up and, as he was leaving, said, "I'll pray, Danny. I'll pray real hard."

Danny got up and went outside for a brisk walk. He was lost in thought. The matter with teacher X made him so angry that he wanted to scream out loud to himself. She was a metaphor of all he hated in religion.

He knew he was to love the sinner as long as the sinner admitted her sin. But if the sinner is a psychopath, must he also tolerate her absolute irresponsibility for the sins she commits and doesn't even recognize as sins? It was the same for Viri Lucis. He hadn't let on to Gene how violently he was reacting since he didn't want him to feel any worse than he already did.

A person like madam X can get so used to judging what appears to be wrong that she starts fabricating wrongdoing. In effect, she has assumed the judgment seat of God. And she is convinced she is doing the work of God. Her image of God, as he and Gene had discussed, is undoubtedly that of a ruthless, vindictive judge. And she has become like the God she images.

Without even thinking consciously about it Danny had come to a decision. He would take Celine's and Gene's advice and contact the lawyer Celine had in mind. He'd forget about the note and its contents. Celine was right. He was not Chesterton's Father Brown. It was a decision he would have stuck to had it not been for the events that occurred later.

That evening Danny dreamed. In his dream he heard Janie, his third grade sweetheart, calling to him from a faraway distance.

"Joooey! Joooey!" He looked across a beautiful green hill near a forest but couldn't see anybody. Then closer, "Joey." He turned and saw a little girl but not clearly. Her face was shaded by trees in a forest but he could make out blond hair.

She reached out to him and he gave her his hand. "Joey, why didn't you cry when I went away? Then before he could answer the forest burst into flames. "Janie! Janie! Where are you? He couldn't see her. The flames were blinding him.

"In here, Joey. In the burning forest. Come, get me."

He took one step into the forest and the fire disappeared. He called out, "Janie!" But she wasn't there. He sat down and cried uncontrollably.

He woke up with a jolt. He could feel tears dripping from the corners of his eyes.

What did the dream mean? Realizing that dreams are open to all kinds of interpretations, he decided to try to delve into the symbols of his dream.

Was Janie some kind of a divine call to him to be courageous, to take a risk?

Was he crying because he lost Janie again. Was he crying over lost innocence? His own? Viri Lucis'? Was he crying because of Celine?

What was the fire? Destruction? Purification? Was it the flames of hell? Or Elijah's fiery chariot ascending into heaven? Why did the fire go out when took one step into the forest? He didn't know. Perhaps something about overcoming? A courageous risk winning victory?

Was it the first step of a long journey not into destruction but into a labyrinthine problem where he might get lost in a forest with no paths but only the overgrowth of perplexity?

Was Janie's call to come a get her a challenge to take the risk of persevering? Did Janie's disappearance tell him one step was sufficient and he need go no farther for the time being?

Or did his dream have nothing at all to do with his preoccupation — or, as Celine called it, his obsession — with Viri Lucis and now with the Mentor?

244

Perhaps his dream was a call to persevere in his vocation. Not only his vocation as a priest but as a priest working in the slums of the inner city. Could his dream be a call to plunge into the fire of mystical experience — an experience of destructive confusion? And after that, there would be security just as the fire had gone out? And then he would enter deeply into the delights of the forest, God's creation?

There was something else in the dream which he could not recall. He tried. Nothing. Maybe it would come to him. Maybe not. He didn't usually remember his dreams.

THE MEETING

The four men sat around the heavy table in the middle of the room. One lamp hanging over the table provided the only light. The rest of the room was enveloped in an eerie darkness.

Cardinal Camillo Tamacci, Secretary of State, Archbishop Brown, Secretary of the Supreme Council of Pontifical Missionary Works, Cardinal Rudolph Krantz, Prefect of the Congregation for the Doctrine of the Faith (formerly the Inquisition) and Cardinal Reginald Modenna, Prefect of The Congregation for Bishops. They all spoke ponderously and slowly as though their time was measured by some eternal clock

Cardinal Krantz had been appointed Prefect of the Congregation for the Doctrine of the Faith in 2016 by Pope Pius XIII who reigned from 2016 until 2030. His tenure as Prefect was dedicated to keeping a steel grip on all progressives in the Church. There were enough conservatives and reactionaries in the Church to make Krantz a hero, the leader of the cause, the savior of all that was dear and sacred.

The liberal element in the Church simply ignored Krantz. Some went so far as to mock his pronouncements which had become more rancorous in their demands for uniformity through the years. Some even compared him to the twentieth century despotic director of the F.B.I., J. Edgar Hoover. Their opposition, whether in public disagreements or quiet disregard, didn't faze Krantz at all. He had the power and the limelight. He was the one who had to be reckoned with.

Cardinal Krantz had been a member of Viri Lucis from its beginning in 2016.

Cardinal Tamacci had served as Secretary of State since 2014, appointed by Pope Leo XIV. In this capacity, he had served Popes Leo XIV, Peter II, John Paul III, Charles and now John Paul IV. For the most part he was preoccupied with world affairs especially the Israeli-P.L.O. problem which was finally settled in 2027.

He too enjoyed international limelight which was much more favorable than that of Cardinal Krantz. He never made any public statements about the tensions among various factions in the Church. But behind the scenes he was well known for his ultra conservative stances.

Cardinal Tamacci was a member of Viri Lucis since 2017.

Cardinal Modenna joined Viri Lucis in 2018. Through the influence of Cardinals Tamacci and Krantz, he was appointed to the very important post of Prefect of The Congregation for Bishops in 2019.

He wasn't known outside the Vatican but his impact on the Church universal through appointments of bishops was incalculable. He made every effort possible to see to it that as many worthy members of Viri Lucis were appointed to the hierarchy as possible. Michael McCann was one such appointment. Or lacking that, men who at least had the attitude of Viri Lucis.

Archbishop Brown, who exuded self-confidence in dealing with others, shrank like the proverbial violet when he was in the company of these three men, anyone of whom could be the successor of John Paul IV. His lack of confidence could have been traced to the fact that as yet he had not received the Red Hat which he coveted with his whole being.

Tamacci had been responsible for Brown's appointment to the Supreme Council of Pontifical Missionary Works in 2020 shortly after he had been recruited to join Viri Lucis. In return for his appointment he was to filter as much money as reasonably possible to Viri Lucis for its activities.

The faces of these men were etched in the harsh lines of cynical idealism. They looked for the world like a pride of lions waiting for some angelic annunciation telling them to attack.

Each one was worn from bearing the burden of what they considered a Church mortally wounded, languishing in its final death rattle. It was as though they were surgeons speaking in muffled tones, trying to decide the exact procedure of the only operation that would restore health to the expiring Body of Christ.

Somewhere beneath the collective layer of casual arrogance there were soft spots of vulnerability which each hid from the other. Krantz was vulnerable because, despite his outward show of disregard for those who hated him, he really wanted to be admired, even loved.

Modenna's vulnerability was his feeling of inferiority because of the color of his skin. Tamacci feared he would never be elected Pope and Brown that he would never be raised to the honor of the College of Cardinals.

Like a scavenger, each one had dedicated his career to the search for a pearl of great price buried somewhere beneath the rotting garbage referred to euphemistically as the People of God.

For these men the future was not something to be shaped by human manipulation like a potter molding clay into earthen bowls. Rather the future was to be received from the hand of God as a gift to be hoarded. This was one of the fundamental reasons why those who advocated insane changes in the Church were their mortal enemies.

As far as they were concerned, it was no longer a matter of their enemies being tamed like wild beasts. They had to be exterminated like carriers of a plague virus. These enemies, in the estimation of the churchmen gathered on this evening, were fanatics threatening the sensational destruction of the Church.

Outside snowflakes like miniature white meteors streamed down from the dark sky. But it was the frigid wind of paranoia that cut through the hearts of these church leaders making them shiver in the quaking apprehension of the Church's demise.

These four men had also dedicated their careers to controlling, manipulating and shaping all information coming from the Vatican. They produced allegations against those they considered to be dissidents within the Church. Allegations that were commonplace and meticulous, spread without doubts or scruples. Allegations that were all false. It was difficult to discern whether their motivation was personal ambition or pathological legalism.

In their avowed legalistic approach to Church discipline they rested complacently in the smugness that a nearsighted faith offered them. With unimpeachable self-assurance they were convinced that they had all the answers even though these answers came from viewing the Church's plight in the heavy blacks and glaring whites of extremes with no pastels in between.

On the broad map of human freedom, they had followed the route from the humble hamlet of dedicated service to the arrogant heights of bitter dictatorship.

The Christ they worshipped was a grotesque disfiguration of the simple, humble Jesus of Nazareth. Their Christ was a task-demanding tyrant who wore the mask of the Nazarene.

These august leaders were the elite who knew in their hearts that a God without the threat of eternal hell was not worthy of worship. There had to be those cast into everlasting fires and these men sitting around the table were only too eager to do the casting. Theirs was an elitism that had built a deep moat around the fortress of the Church

They didn't seem to be aware that justifying and rationalizing their actions had become an espionage agent working its way into what they prized as their noblest motives, subverting them from within their sanctimonious souls.

They enjoyed their belief in their own significance for the Church's survival against the assaults of liberal progressives. And this belief had placed them on a towering pedestal isolating them from the commonplace masses of church-goers.

As they sat around the table, each man had long ago idolized his position of power. The Golden Calf they worshipped was the control they had to give no accounting for. The only difference between them and the wandering Israelites was that the liberated Jews knew full well they were worshipping an idol which was not the true God. These four sincerely believed their idol was the God who gave his divine stamp of approval to their every decision and action.

They were serenely unconscious of the fact that their only saving grace might be that in some eternal moment the infinitely merciful God would pronounce them misguided.

"I am concerned, my brothers," Cardinal Krantz spoke in a kind of staccato tone. "I worry the Mentor's goal of purifying the Church of all unorthodox teachings and practices may be getting sidetracked.

"His goal is why we all have pledged allegiance to him. We look to him for leadership. But his obsession with that document seems all-consuming. And this obsession has produced his fixation on McCann's money. It worries me."

"He hasn't spoken a word to me since, as he put it, I failed to get that note from Daniels," Archbishop Brown whined. You would think …."

"Still," Cardinal Tamacci sounded soothing, he has recently commissioned me to discredit and destroy three well-known leaders of the liberal cause."

Tamacci then proceeded in minute detail about the plots against Archbishop Perez, Cardinal Rawmanda and the President of the United States.

The last designate brought the other three men's heads up in a sharp snap of attention as if they had just felt the sizzling pain of being struck with a whip.

"Why America's President?" Cardinal Krantz asked, bewildered.

"Because he has a reputation for being an ultra liberal Catholic. The Mentor is concerned that he could lead many American Catholics astray since he is a very popular President although he is being bombarded with criticism from the political right in his nation.

"Of course this only adds to the myth of his being a martyr and makes him all the more persuasive both as a politician and as a Catholic. It's the young Catholics the Mentor is concerned about. The President is a most charismatic figure."

"I must admit," Tamacci continued, "that he did tell me he had more urgent business and placed all the responsibility for destroying these three men who worship at the idol of liberalism in my 'capable' hands." Tamacci smiled with humble graciousness. "It was obvious to me that his more urgent business had to do with his getting that document."

"Well, gentlemen, with or without the Mentor's leadership, we are committed to more than a man. We have a cause. We know full well what God has called us to do," Krantz said as though he were a German commandant issuing marching orders.

Cardinal Modenna, who had said nothing during the entire meeting, spoke up. "Gentlemen, let us never forget even for one moment that it is the Mentor who holds us together. It is the Mentor who leads us in our quest for pure orthodoxy within the Church. It is the Mentor who has been our inspiration, who has attracted us to the risks we are taking for the sake of the truth.

"Let me remind you, gentlemen, that without the Mentor, there is not one of us who has the strength nor the charisma nor the resources to keep Viri Lucis's crusade alive and moving.

"No matter about this obsession with the document, our fealty is to the Mentor. He is the one who conceived this plan and we are here only to help him with our God-given talents to execute that plan.

"May we never forget our place in God's scheme of things." Modenna had spoken quietly but most persuasively and the others had listened.

"Camillo, my brother," Krantz's tone sounded severe, "you do what the Mentor has ordered you to do except for the time being this matter concerning the United States President. Brown and I will continue surveillance on the Mentor to make certain that he is leading us where we want to go —where the Church needs to go." Obviously Krantz had heard Modenna but had dismissed his plea out of hand.

"He will be spending a great deal of money on these ventures," Brown complained. "He will probably talk to me whenever he needs money to cover these expenses."

It was obvious that Krantz was visibly upset at the plan to involve the American President. And he voiced his reaction with professional savagery.

"I think going after the President of the United States is at best a feebly imagined idea. It's one thing to operate within Holy Mother Church but to expand into the arena of world politics could have devastating repercussions.

"If anything went wrong and it was ever traced back, the damage to the Church would be irreparable. Irreversible. No! This is not an efficient plan!" He slammed his big fist on the table top.

The other three sat in silence.

Finally, Brown spoke up. "The Mentor trusts your judgment implicitly, Rudolph."

"Yes," Krantz answered. "I will go to him."

"In the meanwhile, we four must maintain constant and open communication," Krantz snapped.

The other three nodded in silent agreement.

The next evening Cardinal Rudolph Krantz was ushered with kowtowing respect into the Mentor's presence.

"Ah, Rudolph, so good to see you. Please have a seat. A spot of cognac?" The Mentor was all congeniality.

"No thank you." It was obvious that this man of supreme ecclesiastical power felt less than in command in the Mentor's presence. Still he was a man used to control and he focused all the force of his habit of domination on the purpose of his meeting with the Mentor. His courage was bolstered by his awareness of the Mentor's respect for his observations.

"I will get right to the point, Mentor. This plan to damage or ruin the President of the United States is less than feasible."

"Oh?" the Mentor purred. "Go on, please."

"In years gone by," Krantz continued, "I traveled the United States and lectured as a young theologian...."

"A young *liberal* theologian," the Mentor interrupted with an almost sinister smile.

"I think I have repented sufficiently of my misguided youth, Mentor." Krantz's tone telegraphed his regained self-assurance as a man of power although his fidgeting fingers were not lost to the Mentor's keen observing eyes.

"I know enough about Americans," Krantz said, "to be able to state, without fear of contradiction, that they don't give a damn one way or another about their President's religious liberalism. In fact they would consider such liberal stances as proof of his refusal to be subservient to Rome.

"Add to that, Mentor, the possibility of any kind of failure in accomplishing this plan and the chance that this plan may be traced back to the Roman Catholic Church...."

"And we would suffer a setback of cataclysmic proportions," the Mentor interrupted again.

"Exactly," Krantz concurred.

"As always, your advice is most appropriate, Rudolph. And I thank you. You have my total trust. You are right. Do me the service of contacting Camillo at once and telling him to cancel the plan regarding the America President. We want nothing to hinder the progress of our cause.

"Is there anything else, Rudolph?"

"No, Mentor." Krantz felt the sting of the Mentor's dismissive tone. He was the only man on earth who could treat him this way. He was Cardinal Rudolph Krantz, Defender of Catholic Orthodoxy, Forger of the New Holy Roman Empire. Even Popes shrank in the presence of Cardinal Krantz.

"Thank you so much, then, Rudolph."

"Good evening, Mentor." With that Cardinal Rudolph Krantz rose and walked stiffly out of the room.

After he left, the Mentor summoned his two most trusted Attendants.

"We have a change of plans," he said. "We will not attempt to bring down the President of the United States in disgrace. It would seem another plan is inevitable. The President will have to be assassinated.

"Contact our Sudanese colleagues. $500,000 now in their Swiss bank account and $500,000 upon completion. If they balk, you can go as high as one million after completion. It is to be set up so that no one — I repeat — no one in Viri Lucis will ever know.

"Remind the Sudanese infidels that in the event of failure to accomplish this mission, the suicide pact is in force. Otherwise they will be exposed worldwide. If they attempt to withdraw the down payment before the completion of the mission, they will not receive the balance."

The Mentor paused. Then he glared at his two Attendants. "Tell them there is to be no failure," he rasped.

"Camillo, this is Rudolph. No worry. The plan involving the President of the United States has been cancelled."

"Thank God! I must admit I was having nerve-racking second thoughts about …. well, about the Mentor's perspective."

Krantz knew that Tamacci really meant balance.

"The Mentor is always a most reasonable man, Camillo."

"Yes, of course."

"Sleep well, Camillo. And concentrate your efforts on Perez and Rawmanda. With that plan I am in wholehearted agreement. Both of them have been thorns in the side of Christ's most sacred Mystical Body. The Mentor's selection is most astute and proves beyond a doubt that he is worthy of our most fervent loyalty."

If Tamacci thinks that getting rid of Rawmanda will assure him of the Papacy, he has another revelation coming, Krantz thought bitterly as he waved off the phone connection dead.

THE PREACHER

Danny was putting the finishing touches on his homily for the weekend. The scripture reference was to John: 10-10, "I have come that they may have life and life to the fullest."

He liked to begin his homily with a story. For him it was not just an attention grabber. He sincerely believed in Narrative or storytelling Theology.

In stories, whether sacred or not, you could always find the Author of all stories. All you needed was insight and a sensitivity to the power of story. As someone had pointed out, Stories are our environment like water is for fish.

A good story or one that people could identify with was available to everyone at almost every age. Whether you had a doctorate or graduated from the eighth grade, a story had universal appeal.

Sometimes he would open up a story to see how much it could reveal our sacred, inherited stories from the scriptures. Other times he'd use a story as a springboard into some reflection on a scriptural story.

Usually he made lengthy notes. Often he would write down or type a figure of speech verbatim for the sake of accuracy. He believed that the purpose of words was to create pictures. Picture words were, he felt, essential in a visual culture. Besides picture words kept the homilist from soaring off into the abstract with the risk of not making contact with the people. For that reason he constantly asked himself, "What is it like?"

Danny realized that his people would not remember all or even many of the words he spoke. What congregation does? He hoped, however, that some of the pictures his word drew might somehow be hung on the walls of their imaginations.

Pictures they might revisit in times of trial, tragedy, challenge or in times of triumph and joy. He recognized that, as in a gallery, not all pictures would appeal to everyone. But it was his hope that if he presented enough pictures, each person might find at least one that would excite his or her attention and retention.

A number of pictures would allow each person to choose his or her own pathway to greater involvement in the problems of the community, a pathway to a holiness that would fit his or her needs and temperament.

Danny knew he had a reputation of being one of the better preachers in the Archdiocese and this motivated him to work diligently on his homilies. He usually spent about six hours a week on his preparation. He took pride in the fact that he never brought notes to the pulpit when he preached. Sometimes he would record his homily so that he could listen to and critique it.

Danny believed that a homilist should preach. The conversational approach was just a little too cozy to inspire or move people to action. The work of a lecturer, he thought, is to inform. The work of the homilist is to inspire. Without actually preaching, a homilist runs another risk, that of failing to urge people to change, to grow, to act.

There are so many people sitting out there waiting to hear what you have to say to them, waiting for a word of inspiration to keep them going, to keep them loving. People who are hungering for support, waiting for the bread of his affirmation. People starving for love, waiting for him to offer them the food of his selfless affection.

They sit there after spending a week when the clouds of helplessness eclipsed the brilliant sunlight of hope, waiting for just one ray of encouragement. Too often in homilies divine revelation became human amputation.

These people, these dear people, need all the support and encouragement he could give them. They need to hear through his words God's word of support and encouragement not only in the reckless repertoire of crises that crack open the smooth surface of their lives but in the everyday shifts and thrusts of their efforts to do well, in their eagerness to fulfill their duties, in their hopes to succeed.

How his people needed hope. How they had to believe in their potential despite the conditions of The Alley where they lived. They needed to believe not only in God but in themselves. They had to feel self-esteem.

Preaching was such a risk. The person who stood in the pulpit had to constantly shine the spotlight on the towering ideals of Christian faith living while he himself often lived in the shadows of human imperfection.

Without being maudlin or histrionic, Danny usually tried to interject his own failings into his homily just to let people know he was in the same boat plowing along toward the same horizon. He was in no way preaching as one who had attained perfection but as one taken from among them with the same weaknesses, faults and failures.

As far as he was concerned, the greatest fault, the most horrendous failure was to be unprepared to give his people the hope, encouragement, motivation they needed so desperately.

And in return his people gave him their attention and their gratitude. As a result he learned from them because each one of them was a fragment of God's total revelation.

On the weekend Danny entered the pulpit to do the work he loved most, the work he thought was the most sacred of his priestly ministry.

> There was a old rabbi who died. As
> he waited outside the judgment hall,
> he paced the long marble lobby. Back
> and forth he paced. His hands clasped
> behind his back like a vise. His pacing
> rushed into a frenzy. His worry and
> anxiety were converging into panic
> How would his judgment go?
>
> "What if God asks me, 'Why didn't
> you discover the cure for cancer?'
> Or what if he asks me, 'Why didn't
> you write the great western novel?'
> Or what if he asks me, 'Why didn't

257

you become the Messiah?' How will I ever answer?"

Finally, the huge golden door to the judgment hall opened and an angel signaled for the rabbi to enter. With fear and anxiety he walked through the door and made his way down the long aisle to God's judgment seat. He looked up and saw God with the most beautiful and compassionate smile on his face. The rabbi stood there shaking, wondering what God would ask him.

Finally God spoke. And in a most loving voice, God asked the rabbi, "Why didn't you become you?"

My dear friends, Jesus tells you in our gospel story today, I have come that you may have life and have life to the fullest. But if you, like the rabbi in our story, do not make the effort to become you, to become all God wants you to become, how will you ever enjoy the fullness of life which Jesus still comes to give you? Jesus comes to you today and every day to give you the fullness of life not only spiritually, but emotionally, intellectually, psychologically, socially. Jesus wants you to have the fullness of life for the wholeness of life.

Think about it! Jesus wants you to be fully alive. He wants you to enjoy the life you have, even if you do not have all the material comforts of life, even if life is often a struggle.

There is so much beauty in life. The first glistening snow-fall, the first crocus of Spring, a Summer breeze on a sweltering day. The wide-eyed amazement of a child, the devoted love of an elderly couple, the generous understanding and forgiveness of a husband and wife who are caught up in the trials and rewards of raising a family. There is beauty, God-given beauty, all around you.

But it is only when you are fully alive, when you are trying to live life to the fullest, that you will appreciate this beauty. And to be fully alive you need to become you, to develop all the talents, abilities, gifts God has given you.

I challenge you today in the name of Jesus who comes to you to give you the fullness of life: Live your life to the fullest — don't just exist! Don't just exist.

People who just exist never see, for example, the wide array that Spring sets out before them, arranging flowers in the most stunning designs. People who live life to the fullest can stop at

259

one tiny crocus or one budding tulip and stare in wonder and amazement at the intricacy of God's designs in each petal.

I beg you. Live life to the fullest. Don't just exist. (Pause).

People who merely exist walk by other people with dull-eyed indifference or they regard others as endless sources of annoyance. People who live life to the fullest constantly put out the welcome mat on the threshold of their personalities.

I beg you. Live life to the fullest. Don't just exist. (Pause).

People who only exist have one foot in the swamp of depression and the other on the solid ground of hypercriticism. People who live life to the fullest dive into the refreshing waters of exuberance and swim with the currents of understanding, compassion and forgiveness.

I beg you. Live life to the fullest. Don't just exist. (Pause).

People who exist see religion as a prison cell of obligations, they feel locked into a chain- gang of duties. For people who exist, religion is not a fountain of free-flowing joy but a heavy burden of restrictions and regulations. People who live life to the fullest see their faith as a never-ending opportunity to give praise to God, a banquet to feast at, a growing friendship with Jesus.

I beg you. Live life to the fullest. Don't just exist. (Pause).

You may not have a great deal of this world's goods. But wealth and possessions are no guarantee that people live life to the fullest. Each and every one of you, no matter how much or how little you have, can live life to the fullest. You have Jesus' guarantee for that, "I have come that you may have life and have life to the fullest." That is Jesus' guarantee. You have to choose. Will you choose to live life to the fullest or will you choose merely to exist? Develop your talents, gifts and abilities as much as you can and you will have the fullness of life. Develop you appreciation for all the gifts God has spread so lavishly around you from the tiniest flower to the immense expanse of the universe to the wondrous mystery of another human being and you will have the fullness of life.

I don't want to give you the impression that it is easy to live life to the fullest. It isn't easy. It isn't automatic like breathing. You have to develop the habit of trying to live life to the

261

fullest. And a habit is developed by repeated acts like playing the piano well depends on hours of practice. You have to be habitually conscious and keenly aware of the challenge to live life to the fullest. This requires effort. This means hard work.

I know in my own life that so often I rush through a day or days without even thinking of living my life to the fullest, without even noticing all the beauty and wonders around me, all the gifts God has bestowed on me. Often too I find myself preferring security to risk. I take it easy rather than being adventurous. It takes conscious effort to respond to Jesus' invitation to enter into the fullness of life which he wants for us.

In your personal prayer life as you talk things over with Jesus, your friend, who dwells within you ask him to help to enter into the fullness of life which he comes to give you. Tell him over and over that you want to live life to the fullest and not just exist.

Jacquin Bazun entered Pope John Paul IV's private study. "Ah, the Black Pope," the Pope said with a bit of irony in his tone.

He was referring to the unofficial title the Jesuits bestowed on their Superior General to indicate his power and prestige within the

Church. The adjective, black, was used because the Superior General wore a black cassock in contrast with the Pope's white cassock.

"We've abandoned that title, Holiness," Bazun replied. "No reflection on the occupants of the Chair of Peter." He smiled widely in a very relaxed manner as one who was speaking to an equal.

The Superior General of the Jesuits was the type of man that was immediately likeable. He was a big, broad, towering man whose physical appearance paradoxically gave the impression of gentleness as though his huge arms were made for nothing but hugging.

He was bald which made him appear even more formidable. His face was full and ruddy. His gray eyes betrayed a hidden mirth that could break out into boisterous laughter at any moment. He was a man anyone could feel comfortable with.

"Jacquin," the Pope said with an uncharacteristically mischievous smile, "I am Alessandro and I am a man who has no time except for bottom lines. Please. Sit down."

"As you say, Alessandro," the wide smile seemed to grow broader as the Superior General relaxed in the company of this, to say the least, surprising Pope.

"Your fourth vow, Jacquin, is what?"

"Total loyalty to the Pope."

"And what does that mean to you personally?" the Pope asked.

"Your word is the command of the Society of Jesus." Bazun paused, smiled widely again and added, "With a few notorious exceptions which your Holiness is undoubtedly familiar with."

"Ah, yes. Aelard Grahm, the poet-protestor. Jose Juarez, the liberation revolutionary come to mind. I am not a product of some kind of academic cocoon, as many of the clever observers of world affairs have pegged me.

The Pope, who had been standing erect in front of his desk, now began to pace. It was a slow, deliberated pace, not of an old man but of someone deeply troubled, perhaps even lost.

"What I need from you, Jacquin, is information. Not the kind I can get from GlobeNet. I want information drawn from close-up

263

observation. The kind you receive from your men out in the field. The kind of information that comes with editorial insights.

"Oh I get plenty of reports from nuncios and apostolic delegates around the world. The reports are very precise and very objective. I want to know the *heart* of my people.

"I want to know what you know about the Church worldwide. I don't want mounds of detail. I want an overall picture or pictures, as the case may be." The Pope concluded his request.

"I know this will not come as a shock to you, Alessandro," Bazun said, as he played with the sash on his worn cassock, "but I can give you what you want right now without research. And what I tell you, you will already know, I'm sure."

John Paul smiled slightly as he recognized the political skill in Bazun's compliment about his knowledge. "Still," the Pope insisted, "the intelligence network of the Jesuits is legendary. Has always been. Even when, sadly, they were repressed." The Pope stopped his pacing. He looked directly into Bazun's eyes for a very long moment. "Give me the overall picture and then if I feel the need of any salient details, you can do your research or contact the knowledgeable members of your Order wherever they may be in the world."

"Well, Alessandro, where do I begin? The obvious split is between the time-honored categories of liberals and conservatives. I myself find the division rather entertaining since I, for example, believe in the decentralization of government. In the Church, that makes me a liberal. In my own country, it makes me a conservative."

"Good point, Jacquin, please continue." The Pope began his slow pacing again, his head bowed. Then suddenly he stopped and began to cough into his red handkerchief.

"Let me try two other categories, Alessandro," Bazun said, deliberately pretending not to have noticed the Pope's coughing spell. "The formalists and the creationists. These are not commonplace categories. They are just our own designation. You know the penchant the Jesuits have for analyzing and categorizing. We like things neat and tidy and sometimes we may push a little to squeeze something into a pigeonhole of logic which doesn't fit too well."

"Go right ahead, Jacquin. Let me be the judge of how well the fittings are."

"Anyway, the formalists don't necessarily want to go back to pre-Vatican II times. But they subtly want that spirit to pervade current religious practices of religion. They see the Church as chaos and want law and order restored. They see too much emphasis being placed on futurism and not enough on historical roots." Bazun paused as though he was searching his memory or seeking words to translate what he remembered into an intelligible report.

"The formalists are accused of wanting to embalm tradition rather than build on it. They almost bolted under your revered predecessor, Pope Charles. They were about to establish their own church. These people are not just labels. They are real and they are powerful. They're the heavy hitters, as we call them. Their monetary contributions are considerable. They want to conserve the tradition of the Church's teachings."

Bazun paused again as though he was deciding whether or not to continue. He continued.

"Then there are the creationists. They trace themselves back to a theologian by the name of Joseph Schoks, who left our beloved Church and joined another."

"I've read some of his works," the Pope interjected as he turned to face Bazun. "If you will excuse the pun, quite creative. There were a lot of interesting insights in his writings. I fear he may be one of those who would fit the category of dry martyrdom. Of course, some of his tenets were, how do you say it, 'off the wall.'

"Schoks seems to glaze over the radical evil in the world," the Pope assumed the tone of a lecturer. "He doesn't pay enough attention to the perversity human beings are capable of. If you follow his logic to its conclusion, there would really be no reason to live the gospel counterculturally. In fact, there is no need for salvation."

The Pope paused, lit a cigarette, coughed, cocked his head as though expecting a question. When Bazun asked no question, the Pope went on.

"We are constantly being seduced by the values of our culture, Jacquin. The question is, How to we react when our culture preaches,

'Warfare is the true route to peace'? Or when our culture says, 'Economic stability requires a certain amount of starving people in the world'?

"Look at me," the Pope pointed his long thin finger at his face. "As a professor I lived in total security. As an Archbishop and now as Pope, I live in, for want of a better word, in grandeur. Yet there are millions who live — make that, exist — in sub human conditions.

"How well am I living the gospel counterculturally? Is the Church truly countercultural? Sorry, I tend at times to slip back into my professorial role."

"No need to apologize, Holiness. Your thoughts are challenging. And if followed to *their* logical conclusion, would demand radical change. Your official life may demand a certain amount of grandeur as you call it."

"But," Bazun said, "I am given to understand that in your personal life you have achieved great simplicity."

The Pope did not respond. It was as though he was plunging into the depth of his commitment searching for a lost treasure.

Bazun continued when he realized John Paul was not going to say anything. "Someone has to teach the people to live the gospel counterculturally. *I* need to learn the lesson."

"My job, right?" The Pope smiled tightly.

"Our job," Bazun smiled back affirmingly.

"I don't want it to be, Do as I say, not as I do."

"It won't be, I'm sure, Alessandro. Sometimes being at the end of something means a new beginning."

"Well, to get on with my brief summary," Bazun continued, "the creationists are at the opposite end of the spectrum from the formalists. They're accused of being obnoxiously irreverent toward all tradition. They, on the other hand, claim they have discarded the dead past in favor of the living past.

Bazun stood up walked over to the credenza and poured himself a drink of water. "The creationists are expected to bolt if your Holiness does not follow through on Pope Charles' effort on birth control or disperses his commissions which are studying the feasibility of a married and female clergy," Jacquin said somberly.

"Who knows?" Bazun seemed to brighten. "About them or others? What's the saying, to label is to libel?" he laughed heartily.

The Pope smiled a bit. "In other words," he said, "the creationists like to think of themselves as the explorers, the innovators, the risk takers, the dreamers. The formalists want to preserve the wealth of tradition, the ancient and ever-new wisdom, the tried and provable, the security of the familiar."

"That's about it," Bazun concurred. "Still there needn't be this chasm between the formalists and the creationists. In American lore, as I understand it, there were the settlers who built the towns, farmed, raised cattle. Then there were the scouts who bid the settlers farewell and headed out into the pristine wilderness where one day the settlers would come. And then the scouts would move on again."

"And what happens when the scouts run out of new territories?" the Pope asked.

"In geography they either settle down or disappear." Jacquin responded. "In theology there is no end to new territory. We've had over two millennia of theological scouting. Somehow I believe the exploring will be eternal. If only the two groups could be brought together to draw on one another's strengths"

"Yes, yes," the Pope agreed. "But what of the spirit, the morale, the attitude out there?"

"There is anger, Alessandro." Bazun's eyes seemed to mist over. "Even hatred. In some quarters, violence. As you are aware, there are no smooth lines of demarcation.

"Ethnicity still plays a major role in the drawing of the jagged lines of divisions. You have Eastern Europeans, North Irelanders, my own people, the Basques in Spain. In the United States, it's the Spanish speaking versus Blacks and the Blacks versus the Koreans and Vietnamese. Then there's the Filipinos versus the Catholic Japanese, the Jesus Jews versus the Lebanese, the Russian Orthodox versus the Serbians and Croatians."

Bazun was about to elaborate but the Pope held up his hand for silence. After a few moments, he said, "Please continue, Jacquin."

"The tragedy, of course, is that these people are all waging 'holy wars.' They all practice their religion fervently, even fanatically. But as to the values of their faith …." Jacquin shrugged but did not smile. All the lightheartedness seemed to have been drained out of him by this gruesome recitation.

"How many over the centuries have been killed in the name of religion?" the Pope asked rhetorically. "How many have killed, convinced they were doing the work of God? This is what happens when religion is used as a weapon, Jacquin.

"There is another …. shall we call it, a faction?" the Pope asked. "By far this is the largest segment within the Church today." The Pope lit a cigarette, went through a coughing spell, offered one to Bazun who refused politely.

"Damnable habit," the Pope admitted. "I've been told it could keep me from being canonized. I think the Pope can change that little criterion. But we are to strive for sanctity not canonization, right?" He smiled broadly and ingratiatingly.

Bazun realized that the Pope's full smile could light up a room, perhaps the world. This man, Bazun thought, has a wealth of untapped charism.

"The segment you refer to, Alessandro, are deeply religious. To the best of their graces, they abide by the values of the gospel. Sadly, I must admit, even when these values clash with Church policies. And that is why these people do not pay much attention to the Magesterium of the Church."

"We seem not to be talking to them," Bazun mused aloud. "Or we are but our words are so foreign to their experience of faith that they have little or no impact, no influence on their attitude. It's a paraphrase on the old quip, My mind is made up. Don't disturb me with your teachings."

Bazun sat down again looking upward at the Pope who was once again standing ramrod straight in front of his desk. "This segment is often referred to as smorgasbord Catholics," Bazun continued.

"The problem with that metaphor is that it stops short with picking and choosing. There is no follow through to the admission that they are feeding themselves. The metaphor breaks down even more when we consider that those accused of being smorgasbord Catholics are designated such for picking and choosing with regards to moral teachings on sexuality.

"There is never the same allegation leveled at those who pick and choose among the moral teachings on hungering for peace or thirsting for justice or loving one's enemies. These latter moral teachings are considered either a superfluous or works of supererogation.

"You work for peace or justice only after you've taken care of the real work of bolstering your me-and-my-God religiosity.

"Those accused of being smorgasbord Catholics are not interested in returning to the past or in forging ahead into the future. They live in the present, within the reality that has been dealt to them."

"These are the ones who protest war and capital punishment and the plight of the neglected poor. Is that not accurate, Jacquin?"

"Yes, quite accurate, Alessandro. They are deeply concerned about the injustices in the world and they feel they do not need high level direction in trying to deal with these injustices. The problem with them sometimes is that they are more involved with worldwide injustices than caring for the person next to them."

"And there is anger also among them?" the Pope asked. "Anger at the Church?" The Pope held out both his arms as if in supplication that he would not be told he missed the mark on this one.

"Some are angry but most are indifferent to the Administrative Church. They try to live their faith values as they discover them in Sacred Scripture. They put a parenthesis around Church policies and revisit those policies from time to time to see if they can remove the parenthesis. If not they go their own not untroubled way. They're loyal but they claim creative obedience. Once again I'm labeling."

"Then there are innumerable splinter groups," Bazun continued in a hesitant tone as though he was wondering if he was unloading too much on this aged Pontiff. "I'm certain that your Holiness is aware of most of what I am telling him," he said more to reassure himself that it was all right to continue than to give the Pope more credit than he might deserve.

"Quite," the Pontiff nodded. "Please go on."

"Well, there are the piously obnoxious, the scrupulous alarmists, the pleasantly indifferent. Then there are the manipulative legalists, the vindictive orthodox, the hateful guardians of propriety.

"And, yes, there are still the simple faithful and they far outnumber all the other groups, thank God. They are the foundation of your strength."

"Sounds like a catalogue taken right from the gospels," the Pope showed a wistful smile.

"And they are your sheep."

"And I must feed them."

"How do we speak to all these diverse groups, Jacquin? Oh, I know I can say all the right words and go on talking and talking. But what good is it if our people have ears but do not hear? Or refuse to hear?

"What I mean is, How do I speak in such a way that I will be heard? That my words will fall on fertile ground and make a difference? That what I say will not only be true but be attractive, persuasive?" The Pope suddenly swung around and stared out the window, enveloped in a puzzle he knew he did not have all the pieces for.

Jacquin Bazun just sat there.

"Just look at my desk, will you?" The Pope turned from the window and pointed a long index finger toward a pile of papers on his desk. "It's piled with paperwork up to the ceiling. Well, a bit of an exaggeration, perhaps. That stack is from the Curialists. I'm locked in a paper battle with the Curia.

"Here we are at the beginning of the 21st century and the Curia still thinks it alone is the preserve of all truth. That there is no truth outside the Vatican.

"Despite John XXIII's efforts to open the Church to the world, to reach out to all people on earth, the Curalists are still convinced that such openness is against God's will. The Curialists seem hell-bent on preserving their Medieval insularity."

"In the United States," Bazun responded, "I understand the President will often bypass the Congress by going on television and appealing directly to the people."

"Yes. Well, thank you, Jacquin. I appreciate your input and I will be staying in touch. It would be unwise not to be in contact with the 'Black Pope.'"

John Paul took two long strides toward Bazun who was getting up from his chair. The Pope reached out and embraced Bazun who returned the unexpectedly strong embrace of the Pontiff.

"Alessandro, your Holiness, I am always at your disposal as is all the information gathering expertise of the Society of Jesus." Jacquin Bazun withdrew.

THE COCKTAIL HOUR

Celine had called Danny and asked him if he wanted to join her for cocktails at Bennies. She was on her way to meet George and a few friends at The Chicago Blue nightclub. George enjoyed Chicago Blues music and there was no better place to listen to it than The Chicago Blue.

It was the first time they had gotten together by themselves since their argument at Toolies.

Bennies was on the way and Celine had spare time. Bennies was almost empty so they had no trouble getting a booth off by themselves.

Danny was pleased with this opportunity to talk with Celine alone.

After exchanging pleasantries they ordered drinks. Danny had Bourbon smooth. Celine ordered Perrier — "I'll be drinking Martinis at the Blue," she explained.

"So," Danny asked, "how are things going?"

"Good," Celine answered but Danny could see that Celine seemed preoccupied.

"Is there anything the matter?" he asked with concern.

"Well, I've been thinking a lot lately about what we know about Viri Lucis. You know, their fanaticism, their apparent ruthlessness and whatever other horrendous negatives we might use to label them."

"Join the crowd," Danny laughed quietly. "I think Viri Lucis has become my Moby Dick."

"I was wondering" Celine said, "how a group of churchmen, presuming that's who they are, highly sophisticated, very well educated et cetera, et cetera, could be so .... so crass, so .... well, barbaric in their pursuit of whatever it is they're pursuing."

"Well, I guess the most ghastly shock we can encounter in the Church is a religious institution without Christianity," Danny said laconically.

"Yes, I can see that," Celine said quietly. "I started thinking about things you've said about the need for psychospirituality. You know, how can a healthy spirituality exist if its roots are buried deep in psychological imbalances or even aberrations?"

Danny had in fact given a great deal of thought to the need for psychospirituality. From his experience of dealing with all kinds of people he had come to the conclusion long ago that most people who come to a priest with so-called spiritual or even moral problems actually had psychological problems. Problems they didn't even recognize having.

Some of these people covered up their psychological uncertainties with the cloak of absolute control. For them each person was a pawn they moved at will or at whim. They were willing to go so far as to destroy anyone who might disrupt their game of hit-and-run defensiveness.

Almost every encounter for them was a win-lose situation and they had to be the winners. They will confront for the sake of the game blithely ignoring the fact that confrontation without compassion is control.

To compensate for their psychological insecurity or disturbances they become master manipulators, relieving their frustrations with themselves or their life situations by dumping guilt feelings on anyone available.

And they train themselves to be aloofly oblivious to anything being the least bit out of sync in their psychological or emotional makeup. That's an essential part of their fabricated security: denial. And, he knew, they could not be cured of something they denied even existed.

Danny was convinced that before spiritual or moral direction could be given, there had to be a clearing out of the psychological problems people have or a confrontation with unresolved emotional conflicts. If this didn't occur, people would remain in denial of their real problems and focus the searchlight on what they were convinced were spiritual problems.

A woman, for instance, who was scrupulous about sexual sins may not so much be motivated by the virtue of purity as by an unresolved emotional conflict with her father or her mother. Until that conflict has been resolved there really wasn't much use trying to work through her scrupulosity.

"I've been thinking that the members of Viri Lucis are mentally unstable," Celine continued. "Maybe it's because I underwent therapy myself. I mean you can be very well educated, train yourself to interact with others in a pleasant and even a supportive way and still not be mentally healthy."

"Well," Danny said, "I would never think of you as being mentally unstable. You just had some problems you had to work on — which you did in fine fashion. Sometimes people let their past experiences dictate their present behavior as if it were a post hypnotic suggestion.

"But I do think you're onto something. I'm convinced, as you know from other conversations, that psychological disturbances can feed into someone's spirituality. Someone, for example, who surrounds himself with all kinds of defense mechanisms might have a spirituality that is nothing more than a defense against a God who is out to get him. Or his spirituality might be a way of stonewalling God with the words of his prayers.

"Just as his defense mechanisms afford him security in his dealings with other people, so they will serve as a security blanket when he turns his attention to God."

"Or," Celine added, "if a person is habitually involved in projection …. if, for instance, she projects her anger against her father onto others, it stands to reason that in her spiritual life, chances are she'll project everything that goes wrong onto God. Then her choices are either spineless resignation or volcanic hatred of God."

"And in both examples — defensiveness or projection — the person involved doesn't want to let go," Danny said. "Either of these is a source of security for that person. It's a way to cope although to a person standing outside and looking in the coping is really unhealthy."

"So many times," Danny said, "people come for spiritual direction when what they need is psychotherapy. And so many times, as I said, we zero in on the wrong problem.

"It reminds me of the story about this guy who was bothered with continual ringing in his ears, bulging eyes, and a flushed face. Over a period of years he went to specialist after specialist.

One doctor took out his tonsils, one his appendix, another pulled all his teeth. He even went to Switzerland to get goat gland treatment — all to no avail.

"Finally, one specialist told him there was no hope — he had only six months to live. The guy quit his job, sold all belongings, converted all his investments into cash. He decided that if he had only six months to live, he was going to live it up. He'd go first class on a worldwide tour.

"He went to a tailor and ordered a dozen suits, a trunk full of casual clothes and three dozen silk shirts. The tailor measured his neck and wrote down 17. The guy corrected him: 16. The tailor measured again: 17. But the guy insisted that he'd always worn a size 16.

"'Well, all right,' the tailor said, 'but I'm telling you right now, don't come back here complaining if you have ringing ears, bulging eyes and flushed face.'"

Celine laughed out loud. She really enjoyed the story and the point it made. When she caught her breath, she said, "Well, with Viri Lucis I don't think we're zeroing in on the wrong problem," Celine had left the humor of the story behind and was speaking now with intensity. "Maybe the members of Viri Lucis are suffering from some disability like defensiveness or projection."

"Or most likely paranoia," Danny offered. "I know we're just talking examples but paranoia seems to fit. They may be men in power with unreasonable or even irrational suspicions about the direction the Church is moving in or unreasonable doubts about the leadership others in the Church are giving.

"They may well project their paranoia onto these Church leaders and try to subvert the mission of the Church in an effort to allay their own fears."

"Yes, but to do it in the name of religion ...." Celine's stopped as though she was considering the horrendous implications of what she was saying.

"Of course, they'll do this under the rubric of preserving the Church," Danny admitted. "In reality they just haven't dealt with their personal psychological problems. And worse, you would never be able to convince them that the real problem is not the Church but that they themselves are the problem."

"There have to be some horribly negative experiences in their past that cause them to dwell selfishly in these debilities," Celine said thoughtfully. "Or maybe they just grow calluses on their souls and as a result, they treat others with unrestrained violence. Or maybe it's as obvious as their being just too inflated with their own self-importance.

"That reminds *me* of a story," Celine said with a mischievous smile and in a much lighter tone. "I remember reading somewhere that during the Second World War back in the mid twentieth century, General Eisenhower was in charge of all the forces in the European campaign. His son, John, was serving on his father's staff. One time Eisenhower gave his son a message to deliver to a General on the front lines.

"When John, a First Lieutenant arrived, he rather pompously announced to the General, 'My dad says you're to watch your right flank better.' 'Really,' the General said, 'and what does your mommy say?'"

Now it was Danny's turn to laugh. That's a good one. I could use that in a homily." Then he too switched to a more serious tone. "I like your metaphor," he said. "The real terror of violence is the callousness, isn't it," Danny spoke distantly as though he hadn't yet settled the matter in his own mind. "Either that or their psychological disorders become a narcotic enabling them to escape from facing up the reality of who they really are."

"Calluses or narcotics, there are people," Celine continued her thought, "whose jealousies, insecurities and hatreds smolder so deep beneath their consciousness that the only relief they can find is to explode violently usually at an innocent bystander in their lives."

"Then there's schizophrenia," Danny added to the list. "People can cover their mental instability with the veneer of normalcy. But if you happen to push a wrong button, all neurotic hell breaks loose."

"I know mental instability allows for degrees," Danny said. "On a scale of one to ten, ten being the worst, someone may be at three or four but at any given time they can shoot up to an eight or nine."

"The trouble, as I understand it," Celine said, "is that the mentally unstable or the emotionally disturbed may not be fully responsible for their actions. But objectively the damage is still done. A wife breaks up with her husband because she hates her grandfather. We know it's projection but the broken marriage is still the reality."

"You do wonder how much responsibility and therefore culpability members of Viri Lucis have," Danny was putting his statement across more like a rhetorical question. "If they're all mentally disturbed …. but then as you said, Celine, the objective damage is still being done."

"But despite the objective evil, we're confronted with the image of Jesus on the cross crying out his passionate prayer that shattered the eye-for-an-eye tradition of his religion. 'Father, forgive them, they know not what they do.'"

The waiter approached. Danny ordered another bourbon. Celine declined.

"Even though the Roman soldiers were putting an innocent man to death," Danny continued, "Jesus said they didn't know the full ramifications of what they were doing. I guess the same can be said of Viri Lucis.

"They may have so rationalized their motives that they have no idea of the big moral picture. They don't recognize the evil they're doing. Even when they murder someone like Michael. They're convinced they're doing what's right. They really don't know what they're doing."

"But can we honestly say the members of Viri Lucis – Men of the Light! — don't know what they do?" Celine asked with annoyance.

"It depends on what you mean by 'do not know.'" Danny answered. "Look at it this way. If nothing else, they do not know how much they are exposing themselves as foolish fanatics. Or how they are revealing their mental disabilities like that of paranoia. So in that sense we can pray for them as not knowing what they are doing."

"But that still doesn't have anything to do with the objective evil they are doing," Celine quietly protested.

"Perhaps not. But if they are mentally disabled …."

"…. they really don't know how much evil they are doing."

"I think so. They're hindered by their paranoia, for instance, from having a clear-cut knowledge of what they're doing."

"I hope we're right," Celine said desperately. "I hope we're not just making up excuses to minimize their responsibility."

"As I said, it all depends on what is meant by, 'they do not know.' In their minds they may be utterly convinced they're doing what is right."

"Mitigating circumstances?" Celine asked.

"Yeah. Something like that. On the psychological level."

"So if mental disabilities diminish total knowledge of the evil they're doing, we can pray like Jesus, 'they know not what they do.'" Celine seemed to be posing a question rather than making a statement.

"They still have an obligation to examine their problems, whether mental or emotional or moral. Even if this means getting professional help," Danny observed.

"Like I did?"

"Maybe, if nothing else, we can pray that they'll get this kind of help."

"Good luck in that prayer. I'm sorry …."

"Don't be, Celine. Prayer for what seems impossible is probably our greatest act of trust in God's power. It's one of those paradoxes. Praying for the impossible empowers us to do the possible."

"The whole thing is such a hard inference to swallow," Celine objected quietly. "So what you're really saying is that we can forgive them? I don't know. Jesus was able to do this. But are we mere mortals able to forgive when there's no admission of guilt, no apology? I really don't know. But I suppose I'm willing to work on it. I've got to work on it."

"We all do, Celine. What Jesus did is our ideal. He did it. We're still striving. That's life, isn't it — a struggle? It's what makes life worth living — the struggle."

"I guess so. I hope so. I just have a lot of trouble with what Viri Lucis' doing or how they're doing it."

"We've both agreed, I think, that Viri Lucis is mentally unstable …."

"I know," Celine interrupted, "they're not responsible. 'They know not what they do.' Still I'm hung up on the objective evil like the murder of Michael. It's so damn complicated."

"It's complicated because we can see the grays and yellows between the blacks and whites," Danny seemed to be arguing with himself. "It's there in the grays, yellows, browns and blues that compassion happens — and forgiveness."

"So," Celine pouted, "while Viri Lucis in its raging vindictiveness sees only blacks and whites, we're supposed to forgive them because of the yellows and grays. It's one hell of a demand Christ puts on us."

"It's one hell of a power Christ gives us to do it," Danny half smiled.

"Intellectually I can accept it, I guess. Emotionally …."

"Well, all we can do is keep trying," Danny tried to sound encouraging. "Remember, we're human …." Celine joined in with a sing-song tone …. "therefore limited, therefore imperfect therefore disappointing to ourselves and others but we *are* perfectible."

"Well, I can say in all honesty I've come to appreciate more what you've often mentioned," Celine said, "you know, that idea about the Church's moderating influence. How did you put it? The Church prods the indifferent into zeal and restrains the zealous from fanaticism. Still, what happens when this restraining influence is in the hands of those who already fanatics?"

"You get Viri Lucis," Danny said bluntly. "Human beings differ from animals by only a little and most of us throw that little away."

279

"This whole thing of psychospirituality," Danny went back to what they had been talking about earlier, "has social ramifications.

"People who ignore or refuse to deal with their psychological or emotional problems and yet still want to have some kind of spirituality will more often than not curl up in their own piety as though it were a security blanket. And they won't even think of offering that blanket to someone shivering in the frigid indifference of social injustices."

"Without sermonizing," Danny smiled openly at his own disclaimer, "those who demean or ignore the so-called social gospel must ask themselves if they're really experiencing the Sacred.

"I say this because I've found in my own experience that the Sacred breaks me out of my own individual concerns and catapults me into the social ramifications of the gospel. If this doesn't happen then I know I might be experiencing fervor but as for the Sacred ...."

"In other words," Celine issued one of her facile and accurate observations. "people with unresolved personal problems may strive for a holiness that can be just a selfish crown of self-canonizing glory."

"Right," Danny agreed. "And their defensive piety can cause the brownout of morose living. The result can be that their relationship with God will be joyless, lacking enthusiasm, heartless and fear-ridden. They'll probably be plunged into depression. This will definitely have a negative impact on any attempt at living the gospel of social justice."

Danny paused as though making sure he had completed his thought. He toyed with his drink and looked out over the empty room.

"So," Celine added her own observation, "for people who refuse to deal with unresolved emotional conflicts, their religion or even what they consider their deep spirituality, can either be a cover-up for unadmitted problems or a defense against the need to radically change their lifestyles.

"Either way their involvement in society's problems can be a form of escape. They just won't give up all the mechanisms they've developed to cope even if those mechanisms are unhealthy," Celine sighed as though she were lost in a maze and didn't have the will to find her way to the end.

"At any rate they won't be healed," Danny added. "So if people are inauthentic themselves, how can their spirituality be authentic?"

"That's what I've been thinking about," Celine said. "Your claim that some kind of psychospirituality is imperative. Are we just scratching the surface?"

"In a way. And yet," Danny paused again, "and yet, according to the thinking of Process theologians, God takes all that is debilitating in our lives and relationships into himself.

"Then he heals all these negatives, transforms them and sends them back into our lives as positive, growth-producing forces. It's a slow evolution and we have to be patient. With ourselves and others."

"There are stories of saints who would have appeared mentally unstable," Danny said with that on-the-other-hand tone he used so often as though he was arguing with himself rather than with someone else.

"I'm thinking of Blessed Raymond Lull. Lived in the thirteenth century. Some call him the Don Quixote of saints. A strange, mystical kind of guy. He wandered around the world singing about the glories of Christ.

"Yet he found time to compile a kind of encyclopedia on mysticism. Was widely read in the Middle Ages.

"He was born of a wealthy Majorcan family. Married and had a son and daughter. At the same time he was shameless in his pursuit of other women. Then one night he was writing a poem to his latest conquest. According to the story he suddenly had a vision of Christ Crucified.

"He wasn't converted all at once. But when he was, it was a total conversion. One extreme to another as often happens in conversions.

"Anyway he provided for his family and gave the rest of his wealth to the poor. Then he spent time in solitude studying and learning. His goal was the conversion of the Muslims. He wrote endless amounts of books. Sailed to Africa several times, preached on the street corners of Tunis, got arrested and deported each time. He even sailed to Cyprus to meet the Khan of Tartary. No one, especially the Muslims, took his zealotry seriously. He was looked upon as a quaint kind of nut. He was obsessed with converting the Muslims. But every attempt to convert them turned into a disastrous failure but he kept going until he died in 1316.

"I guess the moral of the story is, Don't judge. You might be sitting in judgment on a saint."

"Another more important moral of the story as far as I can see it," Celine responded, "is that the difference between a saint who was eccentric or even severely neurotic and a person who is mentally sick is that a saint never did anything to harm others. That's a big difference."

"It's the difference between neurosis and integrity," Danny said. "It's the difference between sanctity and sanctimony. It's like the difference between gold and fool's gold."

"Viri Lucis," Celine said, "is psychopathic. I'm convinced of it. They are responsible for the deaths — make that the murders — of Michael and Leno. I'm convinced of that. It's one thing to have quirks and eccentricities and it's another to be psychotic. The saint has integrity whatever his or her neurotic tendencies are."

"Viri Lucis is embalming tradition rather than building on it," Danny said. "That's the beginning of their whole psychological pathology, I think. Probably there's a lot more to it than that. I'm oversimplifying to try to get a handle on it, I guess."

"This whole thing of psychospirituality calls for a lot of hope," Celine said reflectively. "And, as I understand it, hope has to be affirming and empathetic if it's going to work. That's why I think the members of Viri Lucis are, to say it kindly, lacking in hope. Their attacks are a cry for help from the depths of unadmitted hopelessness. Whereas the story of Blessed Raymond is an epoch of hope."

"You should have been a psychologist," Danny laughed easily. "But you are on target."

"I guess," Celine said, "that a healthy spirituality should reflect our degree of sanity. If I may invade your domain of theology, I think that psychological health and spiritual authenticity are as inseparable as nature and grace."

"My hat's off to you. Your 'invasion' is a *coup de maitre*. I might add that I think what is also needed is a more dynamic use of the imagination. You know the difference between adopt and adapt is imagination.

"For an obvious example, I think we have to spend more imaginative effort taking the external images of the gospel and translating them into psychological images.

"For instance, the open roof that the paralytic's buddies lowered him through so that Jesus could heal him. To convert that image you could think of being lowered deep into yourself, there to encounter Christ who heals.

"It's a descent that demands faith enough to be honest to yourself about yourself so that wholeness, fractured or splintered by dishonesty, can be yours again. And also you have to admit that you need people to help you to get down into your personal depth.

"I know that from my own experience in therapy. Why don't you do some writing on psychospirituality?" Celine asked encouragingly.

"Well, how are *you* doing, Celine?" Danny was obviously changing the subject without responding to Celine's suggestion.

"Talking about mental instability, you mean?" Celine laughed softly.

"Not at all," Danny said quickly. "Not by any means. You are the most stable person I know."

" Of course," Celine smiled, "we're all a little neurotic."

"The Garden of Eden thing," Danny said. "I heard or read somewhere that planet Earth is an insane asylum for some other galaxy. UFOs are the caretakers coming around to see how the inmates are doing."

"Celine laughed out loud. "I never heard that one before but it would make living with other Earthlings much easier, wouldn't it? Danny, I'm thinking of going back into therapy myself."

"Therapy?"

"I think the last time I finally faced my problems but that doesn't mean they're resolved. I think I quit too soon. You know, 'Oh, okay, so that's my problem. Thanks a lot.' Remember how I struck out at you when we together at Toolie's? There's still stuff to be resolved.

"I'm not as strong as you are, Danny. I need help to face things about myself and deal with them. You're much more introspective than I am. I'm intelligent enough but that's no guarantee that I can be honestly introspective without help."

"I don't know how honest I am either, Celine. I don't think I was being very honest when you and I ...."

Celine placed her hand on Danny's. He actually felt the shock of a thrill shoot through his stomach.

"Danny, what we had was beautiful and the residue is the love we still have for each other. Please don't sully it with regrets. In the end we were both honest and that's what really counts."

"It's all so elusive .... love, human relationships, passion ...." Danny sat silent.

"Ah, sweet mystery of life?" Celine arched her brow humorously.

"Yeah, something like that, I guess. How often I've preached that the essence of Christianity is relationality. And yet there are times when I think the way I live that relationality is the fictional version."

"It's not easy, is it? To convert a relationship into meaning," Celine asked as though the question was being directed at herself than at Danny.

"No, it isn't easy. Even when I'm trying to help people I think sometimes I extend a helping hand just to keep them at arm's length."

"There you go again, Danny. You are so hard on yourself. So demanding. You'd really make me happy if you'd just loosen up a bit. I've said that to you so often. You know that sign in some of the rapid transport pods? 'Sit back, relax and enjoy the ride.' You're too intense. I know it's your ever-churning mind, always questioning, puzzling through. Still you have to take time out. Learn to let go."

"Or I'll end up being mentally unstable?" Danny smiled.

Celine didn't respond. Danny took her silence as an affirmative. Then she smiled that gorgeous smile of hers. "We're getting into heavy stuff again, aren't we?"

The waiter approached and asked if they would like another round. Danny looked at Celine who shook her head no. "We'll just keep sipping," Danny said.

"We get into heavy stuff because you're so damn thought provoking," Danny said looking directly into Celine's eyes.

Celine smiled graciously. "Well, thank you for your generous affirmation."

They both laughed. It was the lighthearted laughter of two people whose presence to each other may not be the whole world but enough of a land grab to make whatever intimacy they were allowed acceptable and comfortable.

They didn't need to use each other as crutches. They could both stand on their own two feet, look into each other's eyes and recognize they were soul mates without embarrassment or shame but with courtesy and sensitivity.

With the exception of those times when they were chewing over the note, Viri Lucis and that whole mess, Danny and Celine communicated on a high level of unconscious grandeur and challenging energy. That was their intimacy now. And each hoped, forever.

"How's George doing?"

"Fine. Fine. We're .... comfortable. We talk a lot and that's good. He's very intelligent. I have learned through experience that love has to be balanced on the high wire of give-and-take. I guess it's true what they say that success in marriage is not so much finding the right person as it is being the right person."

"I'm glad to hear you say things like that, Celine. Following up on being the right person, as you so often have said, happiness is making a bouquet out of the flowers nearest to you. And I need to tell you again that my life rejoices in your happiness."

"I know that, Danny. And I feel the same for you. Believe me, I do. There's no such thing as perfect love, only human love, isn't that the fact of the matter? That's what makes our love so selfless, isn't it? We recognize that we are bound by the human situation we've found ourselves in and we're willing to live with it. Or try anyway."

"Someone said, 'Love's like a glass, Celine. You hold it too tightly or too loosely and it shatters.'"

"Your holy indifference again?" Celine gave a slight laugh.

Celine fell silent. She felt the suddenness of love's silent interlude. She treasured Danny's love so much that she trembled. Yet she was once again experiencing the ache of that love so far beyond any hope of consummation. It was the quiet pain that throbs in the fantasies of unfulfilled passion.

Still her love for Danny grew stronger each time her imagination moved into her heart. He, she was sure, wanted so much to offer her the tenderness of a patient heart. And, as she reviewed their present relationship, she felt he was succeeding.

More often than not she was frightened by Danny's soul-haunting love. Other times she was reassured by what she perceived as Danny's eagerness to risk life itself in his love for her. Over the years her love for Danny had traveled the roller coaster of the sadness of hopes unfulfilled and the sweetness of memories cherished.

Celine knew that both she and Danny were studying the sphinx-like riddle of human relationships.

Danny had taught her to tremble in soft wonder at the mystery, the majesty, the frailty of another human being.

She in turn, she believed, had taught him that presence *to* another can be transformed to a presence *for* another and that their love for each other helped them both to touch eternity. As long as she lived, Danny would always be loved. And his love enabled her to love George, her father and mother and her sister and many others, even clients, with greater intensity and selflessness.

Theirs was a holy love exposed in the golden monstrance of passionate self-sacrifice. Celine felt at peace, reassured that all would be well.

"What are you thinking about?" Danny asked.

"Us."

For Danny there was a cosmic beauty in the slightest stir of her smile.

"Danny, I so glad we don't take each other for granted. I think so many relationships fall apart because people take each other for granted, don't you?"

"Yes. And when people take each other for granted, there is no self-revelatory communication. That just widens the chasm."

"Why do you think people do take one another or others for granted?" Danny asked.

"I don't know. Maybe it's a case of idealistic expectations or unfulfilled romantic fantasies. And when the one partner doesn't come through, the other grows indifferent. Indifference may be a synonym for taking for granted," Celine responded to Danny's question as though she was looking for a gold nugget of a clue in a deep stream.

"The opposite of love is not hatred but indifference?" Danny arched his brow.

"I guess that's one way of putting it," Celine smiled. "There's something else I want to tell you."

"And that is ...." Danny felt no apprehension.

"You know how much I questioned celibacy back ... then?

"And I joined you in the doubt, right?"

"Well, I want to tell you that I have come to the conclusion that celibacy is a real gift. I do believe that it frees you to give yourself as total love to people. It's a gift that makes you a gift. I sincerely believe that. I'm not saying that I no longer advocate optional celibacy. What I'm saying is that I've come to an appreciation of the idea of celibacy."

"And I appreciate your saying that, Celine. It's reinforcing, believe me. And I have to admit too that my attitude has changed from questioning celibacy to embracing it. I experience my conviction in the affection I feel for my people. I'm really giving them love instead of dutiful service. At least I think I am. At the same time our love has helped me to love them."

"I'm happy to hear that."

"You know what's been happening?" Danny asked. "I've revisited the whole thing on storytelling. You know how it is. You know something but then it slips through the cracks of your awareness. So you go back to it and come away with a stronger realization of how important it is. That's what I did with this narrative theology stuff.

"I'm listening to what people are saying as their stories not as their problems. And I feel more affection for them. An outlet for my love. I'm not diagnosing and prescribing. I'm allowing their stories to become part of my life story.

"I dwell more in the images they use: the casual cruelties they experience or the urgent kindness they receive, the listlessness of their love or the exuberance of their struggles to be faithful, their bloated loneliness or the slimness of their hope.

"I had forgotten about this. I was treating people. Treating them like problems and they were becoming annoyances instead of human beings with stories to tell me. And I've been able to share my stories with them as well."

"Just as we have been doing?"

"Exactly. And it's been in the mutual story sharing that I've come to understand the gift of celibate love not in theological jargon but in terms of the humanness of our fragile existence on earth. It's our stories, personal and sacred, that hold us together."

"I love the way you say things," Celine said "'Their bloated loneliness.' You're not just a poet on paper. Your life is poetry."

"And like poetry, I'm afraid my life is an endless search to experience and express what I can't fully grasp," Danny responded.

"Is that something to be afraid of?" Celine asked "We treasure the poems that are so mysterious that we go back to them often, don't we? Poems that try to grasp reality. Isn't that what you do when you write?"

"I guess so," Danny said slowly. "In a sense everyone is a poet and if we don't take that into our hearts, our lives can clang and bang around within the practicalities of everyday activities and distractions. Or our lives can be dragged down into the quicksand of boredom."

"In other words," Celine offered, "people should take that thought of each of us being a poet and think it through until each one can say, 'Yes, I am a poet.'"

"Right," Danny agreed. "What I'm talking about is the poetry of daily life. It's the poetry that cracks open the ordinary and reveals the wonderful, that takes the unlikely and fashions it into new patterns of beauty.

"It's the poetry that winnows, confronts, startles, lubricates, verifies, refreshes and dreams. It's the poetry of living. It's not written in stanzas of iambic pentameter rhyme. It's carved in the rough edges of free verse and you take it into the open fields or crowded streets and cry out, 'I am alive! I am alive!'"

"That's such a beautiful thought, Danny. I don't think I ever considered it like that before. And the poets of daily living come to the poets of the written word for inspiration, for that refreshment you mentioned. And I appreciate your poems more than I can tell. They are a source of renewing my hope, my desire to identify with real life instead of the roles we assume to get through life."

"Speaking of which," Danny smiled, "I have something for you. It's a poem I wrote for you some time ago. I guess I've carried it around waiting for the right moment to give it to you. Don't read it now. Wait till you have some time. I'd feel less self conscious."

"Thank you so much. I can tell you without reading it that I'll treasure it. Just because you wrote it for me."

Danny reached into his wallet and withdrew a folded piece of paper. It looked like Danny had opened and folded it many times himself. "Maybe you ought to copy it on a fresh piece of paper," he suggested. "This is a bit tattered."

Celine took it and held it like a delicate flower in her fingers.

Danny smiled at the pleasure he saw in Celine's eyes.

"I'll probably end up reading it in the Ladies Room at the Blue." She put the poem in her purse and looked at her watch. I'd better get going. I don't want to keep George waiting."

"Did you drive?" Danny asked.

"No. George and I will drive home together."

"I'll call you a pod."

"Thanks and we'll get together again soon, okay?"

"Be looking forward to it," Danny continued to smile as he went to the desk to order a rapid transport pod for Celine.

On his way home Danny was lost in thought. Love is not something you plan on. It comes as an unexpected gift like the farmer in the parable who found the hidden treasure in the field. When love does happen, life begins all over again as though there had been no life before.

Love is the thrill of a roller coaster. Up into expectations, down into vulnerability. Yet it is love and you are alive as you never had been before and all is new. Now you feel rather than know that the greatest mystery of all is that anything is. The mystery that anything exists at all.

You're energized by a love that tells you that you are and that through love you are related to everything that is. And somehow you know that at the fleshy edge of life your vulnerability has become immortality because of the risk of faith and the trust of love.

It began to rain and when he got home he sat for a long time in his dimly lighted study listening to the rain. It was light and steady. He had heard rain before and taken it for granted. But this evening he was hearing it as a mystery.

All those drops. And mystery was pattering on his imagination like the rain outside, mesmerizing him with the thought of all the mysteries of life like all the raindrops. He listened in a different way this evening until the streams of raindrops became strings of a musical instrument with a haunting melody of some primordial hymn echoing from the guttural depths of eternity. And he was no longer listening to the rain but was drenched in mystery.

There are times, Danny reflected, when you are as alone as a desert monk of old lost in the deep night of your soul. Yet you are freed from all the distractions of daylight. The deep night is a time of flashes of honest insight. Times when you are pulled into the memories of all the people who have touched you life and whose lives you have touched.

Some relationships are preserved, others forsaken. You think of words you should have spoken and didn't speak. You think of the good you should have done and didn't do. And regret is your solitary companion.

Still the good you did do gives you new life, a reason to go on despite your weaknesses and fears. And you know that somehow you will still do some good as long as life and breath are yours. And you hope against all odds. You hope.

THE POPE'S PLANS

Less than a week later after his conversation with Cardinal Tamacci, Pope John Paul IV again summoned his Secretary of State to his chambers.

"Ah, Camillo, my dear friend, please come in. Have a seat. We have a great deal to discuss."

"Good morning, your Holi …. Alessandro." Tamacci smiled a most convincingly subservient smile.

"Camillo, my trusted colleague, I've always wondered about John Paul I's death. You know, whether he died …. ah … prematurely. Yet I can find nothing to indicate one way of the other. Interesting, isn't it? The Supreme Pontiff doesn't have access to recent history. Makes one wonder.

"I understand that our beloved John Paul II had many records destroyed. Would you know anything about that, Camillo?"

"No." Tamacci answered so quickly, so bluntly that the Pope's eyebrow arched in a less than subtle gesture of skepticism.

"Since John Paul's time, the records all seem to be quite intact. Frankly, Camillo, I find some of the information I have been perusing to say the least rather scandalous."

Tamacci said nothing. The scholar/researcher had been at work. Again the Pope, with a wordless rebuttal, registered surprise at Tamacci's silence.

"You have been here for a long time, Camillo. I, on the other hand, only a short stay. I am depending on you for answers to all my questions. Honest and forthright answers. At all times."

Tamacci was obviously taken off guard by the direct confrontational tone in the Pope's voice. He was feeling more than a little uneasy about how he was to fulfill his role with this new, and as yet unknown Pontiff.

His plan had been to be as non-committal as possible while giving the impression of being most cooperative. He was diplomat enough to carry this off. At least he had thought he was up until now.

The new Pope was most disarming in his directness. Could it be that the office made the leader?

"I've been thinking of writing an encyclical, Camillo."

Praise the Lord, Tamacci prayed within himself. To the Pope he said, "I was anticipating with hope that you would, Alessandro."

"Were you? Really?"

"Yes," Tamacci said regaining some of his composure, "with your brilliant academic background, you will produce a memorable, if not immortal, work, I'm certain."

"Thank you, Camillo. I feel reassured by your encouraging word."

"May I ask the nature of the encyclical?" Camillo was now speaking with some enthusiasm.

"I was thinking of expanding Pius XII's encyclical on the Mystical Body. I feel it is needed. To use an understatement imported from England's diplomatic circles, we are suffering from the breakdown of unity.

"On the one hand, you have those who seek lockstep uniformity as legalistic as that of the Pharisees. On the other, there are many, too many, who want absolute license rather than responsible freedom. Then there is the anonymous middle as slippery as mercury."

"Yes, yes," Camillo responded slipping into his non-committal, cooperative stance.

"Camillo, I am not going to have anyone write this encyclical for me. I will be the sole author."

That should take you the rest of your life, Camillo thought. He remained respectfully silent.

"But," the Pope went on, "I am going to invite as many poets as I can to come here and collaborate with me. I want this encyclical to be the most readable and enjoyable document ever produced in the Church. I want it to appeal to people's hearts and imaginations.

"I will also employ theologians. They will make certain that the poets don't go spinning off into some fairy tale fantasies. But theirs will not be the final redaction.

Cardinal Tamacci sat staring at this old man whose facial skin belied his seventy-seven years. It was smooth and even a bit luminescent. There were wrinkles only when he arched his brows or when there was a flicker of a smile. His erect stance also gave the impression of a man younger than his age.

"Camillo, my dear colleague, you have undoubtedly heard of my six Auxiliaries in Milan and how they 'ran' the Archdiocese."

"I have heard some things along those lines."

"I am a notorious delegator as you are now finding out. I suggest you do some of your own delegating. For the moment, may I suggest you start taking notes.

Tamacci almost scrambled to get pen and paper from the desk.

"Then I want musicians gathered. I want hymns that will reflect the content of the encyclical being sung immediately after the encyclical is issued. Hymns that touch the very core of people's sensitivity. Then I want experts from the cinematic arts brought here. The encyclical will also be dramatized.

"Before all this, I want you to set up meetings for me. As you know, I am not well traveled. My research will be gathered from among living people not from dusty old tomes. Bring here pastors representing all kinds of parishes. Pastors from the inner cities, metropolitan areas, suburbs, rural districts and so on. Next, theologians — representatives only — but do not exclude those who are considered on the fringe of theological speculation.

"I want representatives of religious orders, especially women religious. They are so far ahead in their formation that they are a priceless resource. Lay people. Ordinary, everyday people from all walks of life. Not just notables. Young people. Maybe we should have a special gathering of young people. I'll see."

Tamacci was writing furiously.

"That's not all, Camillo."

Tamacci actually sighed out loud.

"Would you rather come back for another session, my friend? the Pope asked.

"No, Alessandro. Not at all." The last impression Tamacci wanted to give is that he could not keep up with this old man turned whirlwind.

Tamacci's left eye twitched. Percussi hadn't noticed that twitch before. Did Tamacci have a congenital nervous twitch or did his eye twitch only when he was nervous? And why would he be nervous?

Was he a bit flabbergasted by an old man from whom nothing was expected? Good, the Pope thought. He smiled inwardly. Maybe I'll unnerve quite a few people around here.

"Immediately," the Pope directed, "I want a thorough evaluation of every Prefect of Congregations, everyone who holds a position of authority in the Vatican. Line up our young priests/careerists, too. Evaluate them. Devise a variety of evaluation instruments but I want to see them before you send them out.

"Camillo, you don't have to be here very long to recognize the waste. There are dioceses throughout the world that suffer from not having Eucharist because of a lack of priests. And here we have a glut of clergy. Maybe we will test the vocations of some of our young priests by offering them the opportunity to become missionaries.

"Who will do the evaluating?" Tamcci asked.

"As Secretary of State, you will," the Pope replied. "I will review the major office holders. I want the dry wood out of here. You remember the classic line of our holy predecessor, John XXIII, when he was asked how many people worked in the Vatican? He answered, 'About half.'"

Cardinal Tamacci did not laugh. He didn't even smile.

"I want the entire Vatican in all its offices totally telecomputerized. That people here are still using old fashioned typewriters baffles my mind. State of the art telecomputers, Camillo. And bring in whoever to train these Medieval office holders in the use of telecomputers. And I want them all interfaced.

Tamacci's face registered wonderment at the acuity of this man's mind. He kept making notes.

The Pope pointed his finger toward the door at the entrance to his office. "Then there's the Swiss Guard. They will no longer be ceremonial. Get in touch with whatever department in the United

States that is involved and ask for Secret Service trainers to come here and update the Swiss Guard. I want six of the Guard with me at all times.

Tamacci jerked his head upwards from his notepad. "Is there a reason I can give the Guard for this training, Alessandro?"

"Yes, Camillo, there is." The Pope began to pace in slow, easy steps. It seemed that his stride was that of a man who was at peace with himself not someone who was troubled or anxious.

"I don't mind when God tells me my time is up but I want it to be God not some fanatic short-circuiting God's plan. I'm not being paranoid, Camillo. I'm just being cautious or to use a time-worn ecclesiastical term that has given us more dry martyrs than anyone would care to count, I am being 'prudent.'

"After all, John Paul I died under curious circumstances. John Paul II was almost assassinated. I think I am being realistic about the tradition I joined by choosing the name, John Paul IV."

"May I ask what you intend to do with the Commissions your predecessor, Pope Charles set up? The ones on married and women clergy?"

"I will keep them, Camillo. I will keep them busy. Very busy. As our predecessor of beloved memory, Pius XI once remarked, 'What a Pope can do, a Pope can undo.'"

Tamacci had no idea what the Pope meant but decided to pursue it no further.

"Set up an appointment with the President of the Pontifical Council for Social Communications. I'll see him tomorrow afternoon at two o'clock. I realize that this is not your usual line of work, Camillo, but it is because I trust you and have confidence in your efficiency that I am asking you to take charge of all this. Use whoever you must to get it done, but, Camillo, get it done, please."

"Yes, Alessandro." And Tamacci got up to leave.

"Oh, by the way, Camillo, when you send out that memorandum about the evaluations, mention that if the Curialists keep piling my desk with nonsensical paperwork, they won't have to wait for an evaluation. They will be out on the street looking for a place to say Mass."

Cardinal Camillo Tamacci entered his office and sat down behind his desk. He threw the notepapers on his desk. For the longest time, he stared at the wall. He felt numb. Then he began to tremble. He felt his stomach twist into a knot.

He didn't know whether to be angry because he, the Secretary of State, had just been treated as an errand boy or to feel relief that he had the new Pope's unequivocal trust. Perhaps he was feeling overwhelmed. Where to begin?

On top of all the Pope had given him to do, he had the Mentor's order to make contact with that reporter, Louis Gabler. The Mentor wanted this matter with Archbishop Perez begun at once.

Then he had to make contact with Matubu to begin the downfall of Cardinal Rawmanda. He reached for a glass to pour himself some wine and his hand was shaking like a weathervane in a storm. Well, at least he didn't have to bother about the President of the United States. One thin silver lining, he smirked.

What happens to these men? Tamacci wondered. Charles entered the papacy a confirmed conservative and turned into a wild-eyed liberal. Percussi comes here a musty old bookworm and turns into a front-and-center-stage public relations guru. My God, Tamacci gasped, maybe the Spirit does have something to do with it after all.

Should he call the Mentor? Hardly. He was in no state to make a coherent report. Besides, he didn't feel like hearing the Mentor blame him for not subverting the Pope's plans. Maybe later he would meet with Krantz.

The next afternoon, promptly at two o'clock, Archbishop Jonathan O'Reilley of Pontifical Communications arrived in the Pope's inner sanctum. His red hair and ruddy complexion served only to set off his dancing eyes. He was not quite six feet tall and his lean frame gave the appearance nervous energy. He was an emerald Irishman from head to toe.

"Your Holiness," O'Reilley nodded.

"Please, take a chair, Jonathan," the Pope sounded quite pleasant. "I have called you here to tap your Irish ingenuity and your Gaelic cunning. I advise you to take notes.

"Yes, your Holiness." O'Reilley sounded wary. He took out a notepad and sat poised with pen in hand.

The Pope was impressed.

The Pontiff stood erect as was his usual posture. He laid out all the plans he had discussed with Tamacci. He noticed O'Reilley's face come alive as he spoke of what he intended to do with regards to the writing of the encyclical.

"What I want from you, Jonathan, is this: I want you to set up a translation system like they have at the United Nations. I am not a linguist. I speak Italian and I am conversant in several classic languages, but I want what I say to be understood in at least every major native tongue.

"Get people in here to do the translating. Once we get things set up, I will be holding news conferences as did my esteemed but short-lived predecessor, John Paul I. Also I'll need this system when we bring in people from all around the world. I don't want them to get bogged down in the mire of language diversity."

The Pope stopped pacing. He looked down at O'Reilley who sat with pen poised. The Pope smiled. He was truly enjoying this. The reactions he was getting to his plans were exhilarating. He scratched the top of his left hand slowly as if giving O'Reilley time to absorb everything.

"Next, I want a state of the art computelevision studio and our own communications satellite capable of beaming my messages into every home that wants to see and hear. I expect to deliver weekly televised statements. Set it up so that there will instantaneous translations. I don't know how that can be done but I'm certain you'll find a way.

"Finally, I want you to employ some the best public relations people you can fine. Make that the best and only the best." The Pope smiled warmly and said, "Nothing but the best for the Holy Father, eh?"

O'Reilley was reeling. He just nodded his head without making any effort to return the Pope's smile. Again the Pope recognized that he was in the presence of another who had expected not very much from the elderly Pope and his smile telegraphed this coded message. He was certain that O'Reilley was not able to break the code at this time. He would eventually.

"I want to undergo intensified training in public relations. Then I want other key members of the Curia to go through the same kind of training.

"Every week I want you to get out news releases on what we are doing or planning to do here in the Vatican. Anything that has an impact on the world at large and of course on our Church worldwide. And, Jonathan. I am not using the royal 'we.' By 'we' I mean what all of us are doing, beginning with the plans for the new encyclical. I believe it's called a media blitz."

John Paul IV stopped, allowing this red-headed Archbishop to be startled by his awareness of the phrase, media blitz.

"I intend to make certain that this papacy becomes the conscience of the world. I will be the living critique of the evil that is caused by greed. Whether that greed is in the form of the backbreaking, agonizing labor of peasants in Third World nations or the workaholic obsession of the wealthy in First World nations, I want to be there pointing to the values of our faith.

"We cannot allow millions to starve while tons and tons of food are being stored away and left to rot. Or cattle killed and their carcasses thrown into bone yards just to keep prices soaring. Those who profiteer from greed must be made accountable on a worldwide scale. Programs to eliminate poverty will never work until there is a conversion from greed, personal or institutional."

For just a moment the Pope's shoulders slumped as though he was feeling the weight of the global problems he was describing. Then he straightened up and continued.

"I know I'm sounding ponderous, Jonathan, but I want you to know what direction I am going in and why you are essential to what I want to do."

"Yes, your Holiness." O'Reilley was beaming.

299

"You see, Jonathan, I want to convince all people of good will that our Savior's passion is not just an historical event back then, 2000+ years ago. I want them to recognize his passion, his suffering, here and now in the members of his Mystical Body.

"I want them to see with the eyes of whatever faith they profess Jesus suffering still in the poor, the displaced, the oppressed, the marginalized. Jesus still feeling the sting of the scourges and the crown of thorns in those who are being tortured, physically or psychologically. Jesus still being crucified wherever and whenever anyone is a victim of 'man's inhumanity to man.'

"Sorry if I sound like I am preaching, Jonathan." The Pope held out his right hand as though pleading for O'Reilley's understanding. "But, as God is my witness, I want our people to live their faith and not just practice their religion. That is something I tried to drum into every student I ever taught. And I am convinced that in a world that is stupidly evil, Jesus' passion is the touchstone of living faith."

"I understand, your Holiness."

"There's no sense piling up tons of words if no one is listening, don't you agree, Jonathan?"

"Absolutely, your Holiness. And may I say I've been waiting a long time for this kind of an opportunity."

"Fine. That's what I want to hear, Jonathan. You may make a very efficient paradigm buster." The Pope smiled as he realized he had again shocked the young Archbishop with his awareness of current jargon.

"Call on whoever you need, young or old. And remember, Jonathan, when you are seeking co-workers, it's not how old they are but how they are old. Some are useless at age 46. Others in their 70s are keen of mind and energetic in imagination. Imagination and creativity are what you are going to need."

Archbishop O'Reilley put his pad aside as he realized that the Pope was talking about himself. The Pope nodded and O'Reilley stood. He was obviously fascinated by this man who knew exactly how to be old in an engagingly creative way. He was a man O'Reilley felt he could come to love. He bowed reverently as he left the presence of this most intriguing Pope.

The Pope sat back and lit a cigarette. He inhaled and went into a coughing spasm. Now this evening would be his most difficult interview.

That evening, American born, Archbishop Richard Shamansky, the Head of Banco Vaticano, entered the Pope's study.

"Ah, Richard, do come in and please be seated. I have much to tell you if you have not already heard it."

Shamansky sat down dutifully. He was a small man and with his thick glasses and sallow skin he looked the perfect picture of a bookkeeper. There was no humor in his face or attitude. He was obviously conscientious to the point of scrupolosity. He singlehandedly had put the Vatican finances in good and profitable order.

He should most definitely have been awarded the Red Hat but no one seemed to remember him at the time of a Consistory when less deserving prelates were being elevated to the status of Prince of the Church.

"No, your Holiness, I have heard nothing. I am not given to gossip, either speaking it or listening to it." He thrust his face upward and outward in an obvious attempt to accentuate the privileged self-satisfaction he took in not being a typical Vatican gossip.

"Good. For what I am about to tell you I want you to keep in strictest confidence. At least for a while. Until I get things moving."

The Pope began and told Shamansky his whole plan including what he had asked O'Reilley to do.

When he finished, he asked, "What do you think, Richard?"

Shamansky looked as though someone had just robbed the bank. In fact, that is exactly what he felt the Pope was doing.

"I think that what you are planning will take more money than we could ever afford. That's what I think." Then he added respectfully, "your Holiness."

"But you, Richard, are my financial wizard. You will come up with a plan to finance what I want done, say, by this time next

301

week. You can funnel monies that are, shall we say, being spent frivolously.

"And you have outside contacts. Use them. There are big time investors who would be only too happy to give the Holy Father a helping hand. Find them and twist their arms."

"I will do all in my power, your Holiness. It may take longer than a week."

"Report back to me in a week's time to let me know your progress. Richard, I will not have my plans aborted because of anyone's obsession with pinching pennies. Do I make myself clear?"

"Perfectly clear, your Holiness."

"And, Richard, I will not forget you in the next Consistory. You have been denied the Red Hat for far too long."

This finally brought a smile to Shamansky's face. And with what might be interpreted as a hint of enthusiasm, he said, "Thank you, your Holiness. Thank you."

Pope John Paul IV sat back after Shamansky had left and for the first time that day, he felt himself relax. He lit a cigarette, coughed and rang for his secretary, Monsignor Douglas Haynes, another American.

"Douglas, my dear comrade, would you get me a glass of sherry?"

"At once, Holiness."

"When Haynes returned with the sherry, the Pope said, "All in all, things went well today, don't you think, Douglas?" John Paul stood up, unbuttoned his cassock, took it off and threw it over the back of one of the chairs.

"Very well, Holiness. Especially with our friend, Shamansky."

"Ah yes, the promise of the Red Hat covers a multitude of hesitations and misgivings."

"And what did you promise his Eminence, Cardinal Tamacci?" Haynes asked humorously.

"My unqualified trust."

"Something I think he craves at this point in time," Haynes assured the Pope.

"And O'Reilley is probably doing an Irish jig. He was so enthusiastic," the Pope smiled.

"By the way, Douglas, how is your classmate, Joseph Daniels doing these days?"

"I haven't been in close contact with him for some time, Holiness. The last I heard he has published two slim volumes of poetry and is quite content as the pastor of an inner city parish in the Chicago Archdiocese."

The Pope was now slouching comfortably in his easy chair. "Joseph was one of the most — no, *the* most brilliant student I ever had. I thought he would certainly be in a leadership position within the hierarchy by now," the Pope sighed. "You, Douglas, achieved a doctorate in Canon Law, *summa cum laude*, did you not?"

"Yes, Holiness." Haynes seemed uneasy about admitting his own brilliance.

"I wonder how Joseph is using his doctorate in theology in the inner city," the Pope smiled. "Hmmm, a poet and an inner city pastor. See to it that his name is placed at the top of Tamacci's list of collaborators, will you, Douglas?"

"Yes, Holiness. I'll get you another glass of sherry now."

"Thank you, my son."

Before Haynes could turn to leave, the Pope continued his casual conversation.

"Do you ever wonder, Douglas," the Pope yawned, "what would happen to or in the Church if we were to close down the Vatican for a month or even a year? Do you think it would make any noticeable difference in the lives of our people? In the living of their faith?"

Monsignor Douglas Haynes did not respond. But the Pope could tell from the smile on Douglas' face that he had caught the dry, sometimes playfully disrespectful humor of John Paul.

MUNTZ

It was getting harder and harder to get up in the morning. He really had no reason to. He used to like to tell himself that the reason for getting out of bed was to celebrate the 8:15 daily Mass. Now he could say Mass anytime during the day. Whenever he felt like it. So getting up had become a real struggle.

In fact, he thought, everything was a struggle. Shaving, brushing his teeth, his bowel movements. Most of all putting on his socks. Sometimes he gave up on that and wore slippers all day. At 86 and in failing health, life was a struggle.

He looked out the window and saw that it was snowing. He'd have to put his socks on today. His room seemed to be getting chillier each winter. He could remember when he loved to take long walks in the snow. Hear the crunch under his feet. Feel the snow in his face. Watch his frozen breath wreathing his nose, red from the chill factor.

As far as he could figure it, it had been eleven years since he resigned his parish and became Pastor Emeritus. "Monsignor Peter Kerris, known to one and all as Muntz, is retiring with gracious honor and with out sincerest and most heartfelt gratitude," the Cardinal had said at the testimonial. But that was only after his young Chancellor had visited him several times and, frankly, put the pressure on him. "Age," he had said, "was not the main factor. It was his habitual forgetfulness like skipping the consecration at Mass. And there was his overall physical decline.

"You deserve a much earned rest, Monsignor," he had said. "You can remain here at St. Edward's. Keep your suite. Still stay busy in the Lord's vineyard. But as a retired priest."

"Couldn't retirement wait?" he had pleaded. "Still have a lot to do. Feel fine. Really."

The young Chancellor had ignored his tears. "The Cardinal would prefer now, Monsignor," he had countered. Now he had nothing to do. Say Mass. Go to the bathroom. Couldn't read for too long. Eyes going on him. Anyway he couldn't always remember what he had already read. Watch TV..

And that's how his successor, The Reverend Raymond Korlacki, had come here to take over.

He felt badly, he had said, that it had to be under such circumstances. Wanted him to be as comfortable as possible. Certainly keep your rooms. Will stay in touch for advice about the parish.

At first his successor would sit and chat almost each day. Or just sit and watch TV. Bit by bit he got busier. Just stick his head in the doorway and call cheerily, "How're ya doin,' Muntz?" or "Feeling okay?" or "Take care and have a nice day." Still that was something.

People said his successor was charismatic. Certainly was handsome enough. Wavy black hair, classic features, athletic build. The kind women would always wonder among themselves why he ever became a priest. "Soooo handsome!"

Now it would be a whole month between times that he saw his successor. Sometimes he wondered if his successor resented his presence in the rectory. Thought about giving up his suite then decided to wait until he was told to.

As for the new curate — ordained just a few months or a few years, he couldn't seem to remember — he had met him once when he first came. Hadn't seen him since. At least as far as he could recall. Maybe he shouldn't have started to take his meals in his room. It was so hard to go down and up the stairs. Used to bound them in five leaps. Used to walk for an hour every day too. Played basketball until he was 43. Bowled until his early sixties. Funny how his legs gave out first.

Now he could say Mass in his room. Any time during the day. Whenever he felt like it. "Just imagine, Monsignor," the Cardinal had said when he spent about three minutes in his room during a Confirmation visit, "you've offered almost 20,000 Masses in your priesthood. Almost 20,000! It's just wonderful! All those graces and merits! The whole Mystical Body! It's just wonderful!" That's about all he said except for telling him to enjoy his well-deserved retirement. Forgot to ask him how his health was. Maybe he didn't want to know. Maybe he reminded the Cardinal of his own fate.

His successor was doing a good job. Wasn't much of a preacher. A good administrator though. Of course, there had been no debt to be paid off. Money in the bank, in fact. He had heard through the grapevine that his successor had spent a lot fixing up the property. Like renovating the church. All that really had to be done was a paint job. He would have gotten around to it eventually. *Festina lente,* he always said. Make haste slowly.

His successor spent interminable hours at meetings. How could he sit through all those meetings? Parish Council, Finance Committee, Bingo workers. Priests' Advisory Council. Consultors. Priests' Personnel Board.

He himself had always been able to find an excuse to get out of parish meetings and he went to no archdiocesan meetings. Often he delegated his assistant to take charge of parish meetings. He'd fill him in later.

His poor successor. He'd have to be buried on his stomach to give his rear end a rest. He chuckled out loud to himself. That was a good one. He'd have to tell that one to Harry. Harry?

Poor Harry. He had forgotten. Harry had died. Almost prematurely. He was only 80 when the good Lord called him home. The good Lord has some strange quirks about life and death. He'd remember his joke anyway. Save it for the right moment. He always loved a good joke.

That's what he missed the most. When he was at his height, he'd insist that his three curates come to his study forty-five minutes before dinner for cocktails. They could drink soda if they wanted to, but he wanted them there. No shop talk. That was the rule. There'd be jokes and swapping stories. He'd love to hear their stories. Now he'd have a scotch smooth but there were no stories. No company. Doc said it was okay to drink one scotch a day even if he was alone.

His successor and the new curate — ordained this year or last, he couldn't remember — were always on the go. No time to swap stories. They were both very zealous. Sometimes he wondered if they were workaholics. You had to take time out, rest awhile. Even Jesus did that.

He noticed too when he was able to walk down the hall for a little exercise how they were both huddled in one or another's room. No doubt going over their next venture into their work day. It was barbaric to just keep going without taking time out to relax, have a cocktail, trade some jokes and swap some stories.

His successor had told him once when he used to drop in on a regular basis and sit for a while that the only way to cope with the pressures of today's Church was to pray on the run. He didn't tell his successor that he didn't buy that because he was afraid Raymond Korlacki might say, "Sure, you can say that. You have all the time in the world."

Actually he didn't have that much time at all. Not with the Grim Reaper moving in on him. That was a kind of joke too. Still, he believed you had to make time. Praying on the run was like making love in the back seat of a car. Now that's a good one. He'd have to remember that one. He chuckled out loud to himself. He was becoming quite the wit in his old age.

His successor, he had heard, was really involved in civic affairs and community projects. He remembered his successor telling him that the gospel had to be lived in the streets. Fair housing, equal rights, migrant workers, the militaristic culture. The list seemed endless. He couldn't recall all the issues his successor had mentioned. He had heard that his successor was often involved in demonstrations. Almost got arrested once. He was a good priest.

He had never been involved like that. Maybe he should have taken a stronger stand on some public issues. He did remember one day there was a phone call. An anguished voice bleated, "Monsignor, oh Monsignor," her anguish rang in his ears like a call from the pits of hell. "There's a colored family moving into out block, right down the street. Imagine a colored family here in our precious Sylvan Cove!"

"Oh really?" he had responded gently. "Tell me, what color?" Even now he smiled with genuine self-satisfaction. He hadn't been an activist but no one could ever accuse him of bigotry.

Once he had even preached on the theme, "I was black and you welcomed me." Harrison Davis, Jr. had abruptly transferred to another parish. He was a hefty contributor, too. Even now he felt some legitimate pride in his courage to speak out. What kind of religion did someone like Harrison Davis, Jr. practice? A kind that didn't have much to do with the gospel, he guessed.

He felt the presence before he looked up from his chair in the dim light of early evening. It was the young curate — ordained a few months or a few years, he couldn't remember — standing in the doorway, holding a sheet of paper in his hand, tears pouring out of his eyes.

The young curate walked over to him in silence and handed him the piece of paper. He recognized his successor's handwriting. There was no salutation. Just a few words.

> Sorry I didn't have time to talk with
> you personally. I've decided to leave
> the active ministry.
> Prayers, please.

No signature. No reason. He stared hard at the paper, trying to assimilate the full impact of the message. Then he looked up at the young curate who, he knew, idolized Raymond Korlacki. The young fellow was sobbing, visibly, quietly. Then suddenly, he let out a scream, "Why did he do this to me?"

With an unexpected surge of energy, he stood up, walked a few strong, deliberate steps over to the deeply disturbed young priest, put his arm around his shaking shoulders.

"Come back when you're finished with your appointments and we'll talk. Maybe swap a few stories. Tell a couple of jokes."

He never did come back.

Monsignor Peter Kerris spoke Danny's number.

"Hiya, Muntz. How are ya doin'?" Danny sounded genuinely glad to see Muntz's image on the Viewscreen.

"Danny? Is that you?"

Danny clicked on his Viewscreen. "Yes, Muntz, it's me."

"Oh, yes, yes. I can see you. My eyes aren't what they used to be. Danny, they made me retire. Did you know that?"

"Yes, I heard. I'm sorry, Muntz."

"Danny, I'm only 73."

"Muntz, you're 86."

"Am I now? My how the time flies when you're enjoying retirement." He chuckled. He'd have to remember that one. Oh, why bother? There's no one to tell it to anyway.

"Danny, how are you doing, lad? You know I always loved you as a son when you were with me. And I still do."

Danny winced. It had been months, a lot of months since he had dropped in to see the old man. "And I love you, too, Muntz."

"Last week when you were here, Danny, you didn't look too well."

Danny decided not to bother correcting him. Time for the old man seemed always to be last week. "Oh, I guess it's St. Matt's. It's such a poor place. And they're trying to close down my school." Danny thought it was wise to tell the old man this kind of news. It'd give him something to worry about and he'd feel important. Needed. Necessary.

You know Ray Korlacki, my successor?"

"Yes."

"He left the priesthood last week."

"I heard. I was sorry to hear it," Danny said compassionately even though it had been months since Korlacki had left.

"What a waste, Danny. He was so full of zeal. He never even said goodbye."

"Yes, very sad, Muntz."

"You know I was so proud of you when you volunteered to take St. Matt's. The year after you left they made me retire. I was in my prime and with you to help me .... we were a great team, weren't we?"

"Yes, Muntz, a great team."

"I wonder why God doesn't come and get me. I'm ready. This is no way to live. Would you ask God to come for me, Danny?"

"Sure, I'll ask him every day."

"Don't know who this new pastor is. Came last week."

"His name is Frank Seleski. He's a very nice priest." Danny didn't bother to tell the old man that Frank had been there for almost four months.

"Hasn't even bothered to drop in and say hello, never mind have a drink, swap a few stories. Maybe tell a couple of jokes."

"I'm sure he'll be around as soon as he's unpacked."

"Danny, I've made you my executor. Is that all right?"

"Certainly, Muntz. I'm honored." Within himself he offered a fervent prayer that Muntz wasn't a secret member of Viri Lucis, too.

"And I left you something special in my will. I want you to take a good long vacation. You seemed very tired last week. Nothing wrong, is there?"

"Nothing, Muntz."

"I heard a funny one the other day, Danny. Why did Moses wander in the desert for 40 years?"

"I give up. Why?"

"Because, just like a man, he refused to stop and ask for directions." He laughed heartily.

Danny feigned laughter. The old man had told him that joke dozens of times. "I saw an old friend of yours not too long ago, Muntz."

"And who might that be? It wasn't Harry unless you were out to the cemetery." Once again he let out a whooping laugh. Another good one, he thought.

"Father Henning," Danny informed him.

"That old buzzard. He's younger than I am."

"No, older."

"That's right but I look younger than he does. He's not still teaching, is he?"

"No."

"He always told me you were the brightest student he ever had."

"A bit of an exaggeration, I think," Danny said while a feeling of pride swelled inside him.

"I always told him that you were the best curate I ever had. Then we'd argue about who had the greater influence on you. You know, which one of us was really your mentor."

Danny heard his own intake of breath at the sound of that word, mentor. "You both had a profound influence on me, Muntz. And it was for the best, believe me."

"You're such a good priest, Danny."

What is this, Danny wondered. That's two times in just a few days he was told he was a good priest by two men he admired deeply. Was this some kind of a sign? To the old man, he said, "Thank you for that affirmation, Muntz."

"Danny?"

"Yes, Muntz."

"I think they want me to move out of here. Danny, I always dreamed of dying with my boots on."

"You'll have your dream, Muntz. You'll die with your boots on."

"Ah, yes …. dreams. You have so many of them. In the seminary you dreamed that you would really make a difference. You dreamed how your preaching and gentle concern for people would gather them around you as you tried to lead wandering sheep toward a vision this world with all its clever manipulation of reality could never give.

"You dreamed of bringing peace to broken hearts. Having just the right words that would be like a derrick lifting people out of their depression or doubts. You dreamed of loving your people and being loved in return."

He fell silent as though he was reviewing other dreams and deciding whether he would share them.

"Danny?"

"Yes, Muntz."

"A lot of dreams don't come true. We don't make that much of a difference."

"How so?"

"Oh, I don't know. Let's face it, Danny, we're squirrelly. We don't just squirrel away things and money. We squirrel away our dreams, hopes, ideals. We store them away like nuts in the cubby hole of our selfishness. After a while you become more clinical than loving.

"And the people. Some like you. Others resent the way you operate. And then there are those who come very close to hating you personally. A few love you but they keep it to themselves for the most part. Ninety percent couldn't care less.

"You preach and many don't want to hear. They don't want to be challenged. And they look at you and your lifestyle and question whether you're living what you're preaching. They were taught to idolize us priests and so they spend their time pointing and staring at your clay feet."

"You may be exaggerating, Muntz." No doubt, the old man was drawing from his experience of retirement more than when he was on the job. Still Danny was astonished at the clarity of the old man's words.

"I guess the only realistic dream," the old man continued, ignoring Danny's comment, "is to help people understand they're human and we priests are human. And the real miracle is that even though we are human, weak and flawed, God suffers with us through our struggles to become noble and holy.

"Or maybe the real miracle is God's humor, allowing us to live in one dream world after another. I don't know, even after all these years."

Since the old man was speaking with such coherence, Danny decided to join in the discussion. "Muntz, it's the dreams that keep us going and do all we can to try to share our dreams with our people. Help them understand that God works in and through our dreams.

"Remember Shaw's play on Joan of Arc, Muntz? Joan says she heard God speak to her in her dreams and the Inquisitor mocks her. 'In your dreams?' he asks her sarcastically. And Joan answers,

'Where else but in our dreams does God talk to us?' I didn't quote that exactly but the message is there.

"The more impossible our dreams, it seems to me, the more active God is in them. That's what makes God real for us. He's the God who makes the impossible possible. He keeps the whole process going. His eternity is his steadfast call to us to become all he knows we can become.

"And when we are able to help people respond to that call, we make a difference as little as it may be. We further the process of becoming more of what we are and what our people are. And that's God's dream for us. That's the beauty of it all, isn't it, Muntz?"

"It's sort of like that line from that English poet, Oscar Wilde. You know it, Danny. 'It is only through a broken heart that the Christ Jesus can enter.' Danny, I don't want to go to that old priests' home. All that moaning and groaning. Those repetitious stories. Some of them even shit themselves. That's no way to live."

Danny wondered if the old man had really grasped what he said. Probably not. Well, anyway, he was talking more to himself. Hearing himself say what he needed to hear.

"You'll be all right, Muntz."

"Danny?"

"Yes, Muntz."

"Do you remember when you were in school? As a little kid, I mean. You had to color all the tree trunks brown. You couldn't color them blue. Blue was always for the sky. You couldn't color the sky brown. And so you left the world of blue tree trunks forever. It just wasn't the right world to live in.

"Sometimes I wonder why I spent my whole life coloring within the lines. Don't do that, Danny. Don't be afraid to launch out into the deep. A risk-free life is a most pitiable expression of an adventurous God's dream for us. Don't be afraid to take risks, Danny."

He did hear what I said, Danny thought. "You took risks, Muntz. You took the biggest risk of all. You risked being human. You took the risk of abandoning the security and prestige of hiding behind the Roman collar. You risked being vulnerable among wounded people. You didn't stand on the shore of ecclesiastical certitude. You

313

risked searching for the truth as it's lived in the real world of tears and cheers, of despair and hope. You were always a risk-taker not a security-seeker."

"Danny, I'm trying to pray in a different way."

How the old man could speak at times with such logic and at other times in such meandering memory lapses baffled Danny and brought a compassionate smile to his face.

"I figure I don't have that much time. Do you remember how you used to talk to me about the mystical poems of St. John of the Cross?"

"Yes."

"Well, I thought I'd give mystical prayer a whack. I can't read the breviary much anymore. Never did like it anyway. Is that a sin?"

"Only a little one."

The old man laughed. "Well, to call it the universal prayer … every prayer is universal."

"I think it's called the official prayer of the Church, Muntz."

"Yeah, well how many inches are there between official and officious? Official is often not a too well disguised synonym for legalistic. Anyway I'm trying to plumb the depths of Mystery like you used to say. Do you do that, Danny?"

"I try."

"That's what counts, my boy. Trying. That's all God wills for us."

"And how far do we go in trying, Muntz?"

"God doesn't tell us. The Church may try to, but God doesn't. That's why he gave us his greatest gift, our freedom."

Danny couldn't believe how this man was coming off with such articulated insights, accurate or not, he was still thinking and thinking wonderfully well.

"But what if you're trying to do what you think is right, Muntz and …" Danny hesitated. Why was he bothering the old man with his problem?

" …. and," the old man picked up, "doing the right thing might be harmful to you or someone else? Like fasting. It's a good form of asceticism but taken to an extreme it can cause illness or even death. The Church calendar is filled with saints who committed ascetical suicide." He laughed. "It all depends on how extreme you want to be in doing what is right. Are you an extremist, Danny? I always thought you were well balanced."

"Wouldn't you call asking for St. Matt's extreme?"

"Noble, heroic, self-sacrificing, perhaps. But no, not extreme," Muntz answered.

"Danny, are you in any kind of trouble?" The old man sounded genuinely concerned.

"No," Danny lied.

"You know the old adage. If you've bit off more than you can chew, for God sakes, don't swallow."

"That is an old adage?" Danny laughed.

"Maybe I should jot those down as a kind of last will and testament," the old man laughed out loud. "Did I tell you I left you something in my will?"

"Yes, that is very generous. Thank you."

"I can't remember what it is and so if you're disappointed, I'll be gone and laughing it up with God. I hope it will be something to make you laugh. You sound like you need a good laugh."

"I'm just tired, I guess."

"Don't become an old man before your time, Danny. It's no fun being old. They say, 'Listen to the wisdom of your elders.' But when you go to say something, you're interrupted in mid-sentence. 'Yes, yes, well I'll see you later' or 'Take care now' or 'I'd like to stay but I have an appointment.'"

"Not a very happy situation, Muntz." Danny felt sheepish. He himself was just as guilty of not caring for his old 'mentor' as much as he should.

"Well, my boy, I've taken up enough of your time. You're one of the exceptions. Always an open ear. I appreciate it. And, Danny, you will preach at my funeral, won't you?"

"I'd be honored, Muntz. I really would." Danny felt honored but saddened by the soon-to-be loss of a very, very dear friend.

"It's time for me to get back to my mystical pursuit of the Hound of Heaven. If I can stay awake long enough. I guess we sleep a lot to get us ready for the long sleep." He laughed. Another good one. At least he had Danny to share it with.

"I just hope, Danny, that we aren't spending our waking hours being masters of fantasy."

"No, Muntz, we're not. If anything, we're dealing with too much reality."

"By the way, Danny, that young curate, the one who was so heartbroken when my successor, Ray Korlacki left, do you know how he's doing? What was his name? Travine. Yes, that's it. Travine."

"He's doing quite well, Muntz. Quite well."

"Well, goodbye, Danny."

"Goodbye, Muntz. I'll be out to see you soon." Danny hoped that wasn't just an empty promise.

Danny waved the phone dead. Travine. Was he responsible for Ray Korlacki's sudden departure from the active ministry where he was doing such a fine job? Was there a history here? Was Michael just one of a long string of partners or did Travine pick and choose?

He'd have to tell Gene and Celine about Muntz's story about Travine and Korlacki. About his hunch about Travine's history of homosexuality.

THE END OF THE DIARY

Danny really didn't feel like reading any more of Michael's diary. After the shocking revelation about Michael and Travine in his last reading, he didn't know how much more he could take.

Anyone else would have read straight through Michael's diary but Danny felt like he was exhuming Michael's soul.

Each time he read the diary, he felt like a moral wringer squeezing Michael's soul for every last drop of steaming shame.

He felt …. he didn't know how or what he felt. Was he repulsed? Filled with sadness? Or did he want to grab Michael by the throat and shake him into the realization of what he had become?

No, Danny decided finally, he felt empathy. The kind of empathy one sinner has for another as they stand beneath the Tree of Knowledge with forbidden fruit in their hands.

He felt regret not for Michael but for himself. In a different way he had betrayed what was most sacred to him just as Michael had. If there was to be any judgment made, it had to begin with himself.

And just as he had confessed and believed God had forgiven him so he had to believe God had forgiven Michael. The images of God the Good Shepherd and God the Good Homemaker came to mind. God goes out in search of us like a shepherd looking for a lost lamb. God sweeps and cleans until she finds the lost coin like the homemaker.

Interesting, Danny thought, how we adopted the image of God the Good Shepherd but not of God the Good Homemaker.

Then there was the story he had used in his homilies. The story of the young nun who lived in the Middle Ages and was reported as having visions of Jesus.

She was sent to the very skeptical local bishop. She waited for the longest time in the bishop's anteroom. Finally the bishop's secretary signaled for her to enter the august presence of the bishop. She entered, knelt and kissed the bishop's ring.

The bishop sat down, leaving the young nun to stand before him.

"I understand you are having visions of Jesus?" the bishop asked sardonically.

"Yes, your Excellency," the nun answered with deepest respect.

"And tell me," the bishop asked with sarcasm dripping from each word, "does Jesus talk to you in these visions?"

"Oh, yes, your Excellency," the nun answered respectfully.

"Then the next time you have one of your 'visions' ask Jesus what was the big sin the bishop committed before he was made a bishop."

Months passed. Then one day the young visionary was again in the bishop's anteroom. This time the bishop's secretary ushered her into the bishop's presence immediately.

"Did you have another vision?" the bishop asked cynically.

"Yes, your Excellency," the young nun answered humbly.

"And did you ask Jesus the question I told you to ask him?"

"Yes, your Excellency."

"And what exactly did Jesus say?" the bishop asked with offensive haughtiness.

"Jesus said, your Excellency, 'I cannot remember.'"

Danny's knit brow revealed how much he hoped he could internalize that story. He then thought of the return of the Prodigal Son. The image of the banquet the father threw upon his son's return. God, Danny had always said in his homily, not only forgives and forgets but actually *celebrates* our return from any journey into any kind of sin.

There could be no doubt that God had forgiven Michael just as God had forgiven him.

With that feeling, then, Danny picked up Michael's diary. He had no hope anymore of discovering anything about Viri Lucis or the Mentor in the diary. Still ....

Once again he found himself flipping through what seemed to be myriads of pages of tidbits, gossip, appointments and so on.

Then he came to the final entry. It was dated the day before Michael had been murdered.

Today while others heard of Pope Charles' death-dealing accident, I heard about his assassination. Today I have decided to end my membership in Viri Lucis.

Two of the Mentor's Attendants are coming to see me tomorrow evening. I will give them what will be my last check together with a note to the Mentor telling him about my decision to withdraw. I no longer can support Viri Lucis' actions. Actually they are the Mentor's and his alone.

The assassination of Pope Charles is a kind of spiritual trauma for me. Almost within minutes I have experienced a lightning-like flashback of my life. Before God, I do not like what I see. I don't like me. I hate my stupid ambition with an intensity of a clenched fist. An ambition planted and fostered by Viri Lucis. I hate the way I have let myself be misguided. I don't even know who I am.

I've gone along living on the surface of my faith, thinking I could buy my way to the top. And maybe I could have. But now it no longer matters. Right now I feel obscene as though someone has just dug into my soul and uncovered a cesspool of filthy compromises.

I have in fact forsaken my faith while convincing myself that I was one of its greatest defenders. Oh, my God, my God, all I was defending was the trappings of religion. I've been nothing but a ritualistic preserver of nostalgic legalism.

All I really wanted was what Viri Lucis brainwashed me to seek: an orthodox practice of religion. I have now discovered that orthodox religion can not only be tolerant of but actually active in the violation of all faith values. What I have involved myself in is nothing less than pharisaical self-righteousness. I have been heartlessly judgmental even of those who have done nothing wrong.

I feel so burdened by the weight of what I have become. I am sitting here recalling something my friend, Joe Daniels — Danny — once said to me. "Life is becoming. Life is a process in which God is the lure, whose Word is constantly beckoning us and whose Spirit is forever urging us to become all that we can be, all that God wants us to become."

Danny stopped reading as he often did when studying Michael's diary. My God, he thought, Pope Charles was assassinated! How could that ever, ever happen? Up to this point he had had no idea that the Pope's death was anything but an accident. Viri Lucis had been responsible for the Pope's murder too. Or as Michael stated, the Mentor was responsible. This is crazy! Who could be safe from

Viri Lucis? If they could murder a pope, what were they not capable of?

Danny looked back at the diary. He saw his own statement quoted by Michael. Somehow Danny felt much closer to Michael than he had realized. Perhaps this is why Michael made him his executor. Judging from Michael's own words, Danny had said this only once to Michael. Yet Michael had remembered it. Never again would he doubt his power of influence with God's grace. Never again would he doubt the significance of the good he was trying to do. He continued reading:

> As I evaluate my life this day, I realize that if life is becoming, we are all in process. And I further realize that if we do not respond to God's call, his lure, then we will continue becoming but not what God wants us to be.
>
> This is most certainly what has happened to me. I have continued becoming but I have not become my real self. I have become more and more my role self. It is so difficult to analyze this in a few brief pages. I will have to spend more time on it later. Maybe I'll make a thirty-day retreat. I need to. Desperately.

Danny put the diary aside. "Oh, Michael, Michael, may God give you eternal peace," Danny prayed aloud. Michael had not really done anything to damage the Church. How the broken hopes, the hurt, the disillusionment must have congealed into a sour lump in his soul as he wrote these words. Danny could feel tears washing over his blank stare. "Michael, what did they do to you?"

Danny went back to the diary.

I inherited my father's value system without questioning him. That was mistake one. *Big* mistake one. Then the second mistake was allowing myself to get duped by members of Viri Lucis. I felt so honored when they recruited me. Their ideals, as presented, were so lofty: the return to orthodox beliefs and practices. The problem is they never told me who defines what or who is or is not orthodox.

Members of Viri Lucis held me in such high esteem. They even invited me to Rome to meet with the Mentor. It was like being in the presence of Christ himself. I was never so much in awe. He talked with me about the need to restore the simplicity and beauty of the early Church to our times. The need to make certain that the beliefs of our people be brought into line with traditional teachings down through the ages.

The hour I spent with him was like a weeklong retreat. He spoke with me about Christ's desire to cleanse the temple of the Church. To spread the fire of the Spirit among the members of the Church. To meet heretical teachings head on with the two-edged sword of vengeance against heretics and of excommunication of Church leaders who are so soft on doctrine that they allow heresies to flourish.

He never once mentioned money to me. And as I surveyed the simplicity of his lifestyle, I realized that the things of this world meant nothing to this most holy man. Still I felt urged, no, compelled to make some donation to the cause Viri Lucis stood for. As a result, I have been sending a quarter of a million dollars each quarter to the Mentor. This is why in my will I left the majority of my personal assets to Viri Lucis. Today I changed my will.

The Mentor told me that he thought that one day I would make a most zealous leader in the Church. He said he would do all in his humble power to assure me of a position of preeminent leadership. "One day," he said, "you will wear the Red Hat. You will be a Prince of the Church. A Cardinal with all the power and influence for orthodoxy within the Church that that position afforded." I left there and I was in sheer ecstasy.

That was the beginning of my new life. Now I realize with irrevocable heartbreak that it was the beginning of the end of my true ministry to the People of God. How I was duped! How gullible I was! And tragically I didn't realize this until I heard of the assassination of our Holy Father, Pope Charles.

Granted he was tearing the Church asunder, but to *murder* him? The Church has survived other Popes and even experienced new birth after their reign was brought to an end by the Angel of Death.

Christ has promised to be with his Church even until the end of time. That is an essential tenet of out faith in him. No matter how often the Church begins to die, Christ, the risen Lord, is with her with his resurrection power to raise her to new life.

Oh God, have mercy on me. Deliver me from this desert of anguish.

Poor Leno! He saw it all first. He had his doubts. Leno said to me, "Michael, virtue carried to an extreme becomes vice."

I asked him what exactly he meant by that. "Our dedication to pure orthodoxy, our intolerance of anyone who we think is unorthodox has become the extreme of self-righteous jugmentalism, Michael. Can't you see that? We have become the persecutors as members of Viri Lucis."

"Nonsense," I said. "You're bordering on heresy. You had better get your head screwed on right, Leno. You had better get right with God. Your immortal soul is at stake."

"The Mentor is the one who guides us," I said. "You owe allegiance to him and to him alone. He will lead us through these days of the tumult of the heresy of indifference. Can't you see that?"

"All I know," Leno said, "is I am having my doubts. Plenty of them." (This was even before the Pope's "accident.") My mind was so closed that I wouldn't give Leno's doubts a second thought. He was wrong. If only I had been more open. If only I had done my own thinking like Leno did.

I have told Johnny about my decision to leave Viri Lucis. He's gone ballistic. He is violently angry at me. "You do that and you'll not only destroy yourself but me too," he screamed at me. But I insisted that he witness my directive to leave nothing to Viri Lucis in my will. He finally relented. I gave the note to my attorney who in turn will give it to my executor upon my death.

Danny is so brilliant. How I envy him. Devoting his life to the poor and dregs of society. What faith he has. If I had but an iota of his faith, I would never have gotten myself into this bind.

Danny let the diary slip to his lap. "Oh, to see ourselves as others see us," he said quietly. Michael thought I had such strong faith. He had no idea of the torture I've been going through because of this precious gift of faith, he thought.

Michael probably had greater faith than I ever did. It was just misguided. How often has my faith fizzled like a wet Chinese firecracker. How often I have been resentful because I have been given this faith. How often I have lived in a state of suspended spiritual animation because of my doubts.

Danny got up, put the diary on the table next to his chair. He stretched and walked out to the kitchen where he poured himself some bourbon, added water and ice and took a heavy swig. Then he walked back to his study, picked up the diary and went into the small anteroom he used as a living room, sat down on the couch and began reading again.

> I also told Johnny today that our relationship had come to an end. Again he screamed at me. This time not in anger but in turmoil of tears. "Don't," he cried. "Don't leave me!" I told him I would see to it that his next assignment would be much more prestigious than being my secretary. He cried out loud so uncontrollably that I thought he'd have a breakdown right then and there.
>
> My heart broke for him. We were so close and loving. But if there is to be any real breaking, it must be with what I have become. I finally calmed him down and told him to take a few days away. Still whimpering he agreed. He left a little while later. I'll never see him again except in passing

at gatherings of priests. Now my heart is breaking for myself.

I may, as Mark Twain wrote, be remembered for a day and forgotten forever. But if I do happen to leave any sign behind that I have traveled this vale of tears, I don't want it to be what I have been. I am filled with the ache of longing to be released from my past. This longing has already supplanted all the personal ambition I have had.

As I write these words, tears are flowing. But they are tears of joy, perhaps even of ecstasy. I don't know how yet but I will become all God wants me to be. Jesus' rancor was never so obvious than in his dealings with the legalists of his day. Yet isn't Viri Lucis' legalistic defense of orthodoxy the very thing Jesus condemned? I am so sad. So troubled. How can I with all my self-righteousness call out to a God of mercy? Yet it is infinite mercy and it seduces me into the hope I need so desperately.

I am now learning how easy it is for us to be as unresponsive as granite to the gospel. We are terrifyingly capable of manipulating the gospel for our own, sometimes far less than noble, ends and purposes. I hope I am not once again indulging in my habitual judgmentalism. But I truly see now

327

how I, and I suppose others, was able to go through the routines of religious practice with great fervor while ignoring the demands and challenges of the gospel.

In fact the very practice of these religious rituals was the occasion of my self-righteous judgmentalism. I felt so secure in keeping the letter of the law that I bypassed the spirit of the gospel. This was why I could sit in such harsh judgment on those who refused to be legalistic about their faith.

In my note to the Mentor I swore again my oath of secrecy. I will do nothing to expose them. Yet I have such mixed feelings. I would still like to think that Viri Lucis' fundamental purpose is worth pursuing. And then I feel disgust with Viri Lucis' methods. There is no justification for murder — especially the murder of God's chosen Vicar of Christ on earth! None whatsoever. No matter how high the ideals. All I can think of is that line from John's gospel, "The chief priests planned to kill Lazarus because many were going over to Jesus and believing in him on account of Lazarus." In striving for pure orthodoxy hasn't Viri Lucis taken the very place of those legalists and hypocrites Jesus so roundly condemned? Has not Viri

Lucis become the very ones who opposed Jesus?

I now have no desire to advance my career In fact I would very much like to get a parish like Danny's. Maybe not that destitute. But when I think of what I could do for such a parish with my resources .... No, it's not just financial resources. I feel there is something within me that is a bud in need of unfolding.

At first I thought of withdrawing from the world altogether, to imprison myself in a cell of penance for the rest of my life. But the jovial Jailor kept leaving the key laying around.

How I have spun an impenetrable web of vested interests. I know for certain now that I am uncertain. Even if, from now on, mine is not a golden age, I hope that maybe I will have a few sunlit hours now and then. Can I really turn my life around? I hope so.

My father was wrong. How I hate to write those words. But he lived in two worlds. The world of high finances where morality can be turned off with pushbutton control. Then he lived in the world of religion where piety covers a multitude of unadmitted cruel business deals.

And I, sadly, have followed suit. I have lived in the world of unrelenting, merciless, unforgiving self-righteousness. And I have lived in the world of an ordained minister of the gospel proclaiming God's unconditional love. But I've never believed in that love. I've hated sin and sinners alike. I wanted to destroy rather than heal. I never admitted that my hateful determination to eliminate the so-called unorthodox from our Church was itself a sin — perhaps a sin that cries out to heaven. I've lived in the world of stony vengeance against all those I decided were unworthy or worthless. And I've lived in the world of my relationship with John Travine — a world of despicable rationalizing.

GOD HAVE MERCY!!

Danny put the diary on the small coffee table in front of the couch. He felt emptiness. A wild rush of senselessness. Michael, poor Michael. Danny decided to fax this last entry to Gene and Celine. The note he would send had only one line.

"Where sin abounded, grace did more
abound."
(Romans, 5:20).

He took out a small notebook he used to jot down ideas and images for future poems. Lately ideas and images were all he wrote. He hadn't written a poem of any consequence or substance in ages. He wrote:

I will walk through my mortality.

Walk through the violets, daffodils and briar roses
    whose dying lingers
    in artistic mood.
Walk through long days and short years and
    know that I am a voyager
with an immortal destiny.
And while I walk, I will pray
    for the graciousness of lifelong dreams

which through the alchemy of repentance
    will burn as zeal in my heart
until my last breath breathes into open sky
as soul on homeward journey.

Danny frowned. No wonder he hadn't written any poems for such a long time.

His thoughts turned back to Michael's last entry. Viri Lucis had taken his innocent zeal and turned it into the obsession of a zealot.

They had converted his burning desire for correctness of belief into a fanatical witch hunt.

Danny could feel Michael's heartbreak. A heart shattered by the realization of his wasted passion. His love poisoned by ambition. His final disillusionment.

And yet …. There were in this last and final entry signs of hope. The pulse of heartfelt repentance.

But Michael had not sinned as a member of Viri Lucis. He had been deceived. Used. Manipulated. Not only by Viri Lucis but by his own father.

Still, like Celine in her therapy, Michael had made his own personal discovery.

Like Paul, he had been struck down on the road he was following toward the persecution of others. He had heard the words, "I am Jesus whom you are persecuting." He had overcome Viri Lucis' self-imposed alienation from the rest of the Body of Christ.

Michael had planted his anguish in the soft soil of frail hope and waited eagerly the surprise of blossoming peace.

331

Danny got up and went outside. He needed fresh air. He needed a brisk walk. The early Spring air was chilly. He shivered. Was it the air or was a frigid hand of anxiety grabbing his heart? The small garden behind the rectory was his private desert place. Here he could think without interruptions except for his own intruding imagination.

Why was a negative imagination so eager, so able to capture your total attention? And you had to work so hard on directing your positive imaginings. Bad things, foreboding anticipations, anxious images just popped up and hung around forever. But you had to put so much effort into positive visualizing. The imagination was like a wild bronco, Danny sighed.

Was it the result of Original Sin? Part of our human dysfunction? Or was it acquired? Imagining the worst would help us to experience greater relief when the worst didn't happen? Why were we so afraid to imagine the best? Because we don't want to be doomed to horrendous disappointments?

He continued his fast-paced walk. On this day the snow-patched ground had the eeriness of a cemetery. The whiteness of the snow had become discolored like old ivory. The melting mounds where the snow had been shoveled were dripping in a kind of comic monstrosity. Yet the sky was an achingly beautiful blue as though it had been created by a child's summer pastel crayon on the pavement.

Back to the matter at hand. He was no closer to the identity of Viri Lucis or for that matter the Mentor than he was when he first began to read Michael's diary.

He wanted to scream profanities or cry out in prayer.

Instead, his thoughts continued to go to Michael and how he had been taken in by Viri Lucis. The despots' promises of utopias are merely rationalizations for tyranny, Danny mused.

Michael, despite his association with Viri Lucis, had done a great deal of good.

All those pages in his diary that he had flipped through or skimmed over were stories of Michael's generous, kindly, sincere encounters with all types of people.

In contrast, Danny thought he had spent many years at St. Matt's being angry at the system that is responsible for the injustices that bred the poverty around him.

Danny knew that he had been so intent on discovering something about Viri Lucis and the Mentor that he missed another whole part of Michael. He would go back and read those pages. He owed it to Michael — to Michael the priest.

How often, he thought, I've prayed in a tense, lonely, anguished voice, asking only to be able to get through the tired sameness of my daily responsibilities. Yet from the little he had read of those pages, Michael seemed to delight in what had to be a tiresome routine of visits, dinners, groundbreakings, blessings and so on.

How often, too, Danny admitted to himself, I have offered racked prayer in profound disquiet to loosen the shackles of disillusionment with the policies of my Church especially with regard to the poor, the homeless, the forgotten.

Oh sure, there is always Catholic Charities. And those people do a good job. It's just that the organized hand of charity can often appear as impersonal as a closed fist.

Michael probably had a keener grasp of what can and cannot be done for everyone, rich as well as poor. And so he did what he could and didn't sweat the rest of it. Michael seemed to follow two rules in his ministry. Rule one: Don't sweat the small stuff. And Rule two, Everything is small stuff. Danny laughed to himself as he recalled those two fatuous rules that by now had become classics.

But then in the face of death, maybe those two rules are the most practical. Danny knew he didn't believe that.

As he dwelt on Michael's death and on death in general, Danny decided he would go and visit Steve Rinko, his friend who was dying of liver cancer. He realized that it wasn't so much a matter of concern on his part and his own need to get another and different perspective. And what better person to get it from that someone who was dying.

He wondered if the members of Viri Lucis ever thought of their deaths. Somehow he thought one member did. Judging from Michael's final entry, Danny thought he felt a premonition, even a kind of death bed conversion, echoing throughout Michael's words.

Danny felt a pang of tragic sadness.

He went over to his car and removed the cable that had been plugged in to regenerate the electric batteries. He stood for a while taking in a deep breath of what had become the warming, sweet-smelling Spring air.

How many breaths did he have left? he wondered. The soft tissue of the warming air enveloped him like the embrace between friends bound together by the faintly unfurled revelations of a love deeper than emotions.

The warm Spring embrace was like a prayer offered unambiguously to a Majesty that creates a world, quiet yet intense in its continuous flow through generations of nature's cyclic sensations. A smile crept across Danny's face in slow motion like the curve of a wave before it breaks. It would be Spring again and there would be hope even for his friend, Steve, whose hope would soon blossom into the courteous grandeur of divine fulfillment.

He spoke the code that swung the driver's side of the bubble top open and up, got into his car, set the directional guidance system, spoke his code number to turn on the motor and headed for Steve Rinko's rectory. One of these days, he thought, I'll have to spring for an updated used car.

As he drove along he reminisced about his years of friendship with Steve. They had grown up together. Steve had been a few years ahead of him in the seminary but they had always remained close.

Sometimes their friendship had been reduced to Viewphone calls. It was often that way with priests. They got off on their own tight schedules and whatever time they had for themselves they sought isolation rather than each other's company.

That wasn't always true. There were times of enjoyable and in the case of Steve, boisterous get togethers. Stories were swapped. Jokes were told. And often very serious discussions took place about the work in the Lord's vineyard.

But unlike Religious priests, the diocesan priest's life was lived apart and more often than not alone. Even when there was an assistant pastor, the demands made on each priest were such that often the two priests carried on lengthy conversations with each other only at the weekly staff meetings. Sometimes too at meals.

Now that Steve was dying of cancer Danny wished he had spent more time with him over the years.

He sighed. He certainly didn't relish visiting Steve under these circumstances.

THE NAME AT THE TOP

"Good morning, Eminence," Douglas Haynes spoke respectfully to the Secretary of State, Camillo Cardinal Tamacci.

"Good morning," Tamacci responded curtly without looking up from his desk.

Haynes was aware that the Secretary of State did not like him or resented his proximity and habitual access to the Pope. As a result, Haynes tried to compensate by being especially courteous.

"What is it?" Tamacci sounded more than a little annoyed at having been disturbed. He moved a stack of printouts to the corner of his desk and stood up. Then without so much as looking at Haynes he turned and stared out the window. "Yes?" he said with disinterest dripping from his tongue.

"Your Eminence, the Holy Father has sent me to ask you to place a name on your list of poet collaborators."

"And what name might than be?" Tamacci asked as he turned around and looked at Haynes for the first time, his forehead arched in quizzical wrinkles.

"Father Joseph Walter Daniels of the Chicago Archdiocese," Haynes replied still with a respectful tone. "In fact, his Holiness wants Father Daniels name placed at the top of your list."

The face of Cardinal Camillo Tamacci, the consummate diplomat, went ashen.

"Is something the matter, Eminence?" Douglas Haynes asked registering genuine perplexity.

"No, no," Tamacci answered quickly as he regained his legendary diplomatic posture. "I suppose I was just puzzled by the fact that out of the thousands and thousands of priests in the world, our Holy Father would pick one and that one not even from here in Rome."

"You're wondering how he knew of him?" Haynes asked with his own brand of a diplomatic tone.

"Yes, yes." Tamacci seemed to lose it again as what sounded like a growl of impatience broke through his tone.

"Well, Eminence," Haynes said in a tone that conveyed a tiny bit of one-upmanship as though he were having difficulty hiding the fact of his inside information which he knew would drive Tamacci to the edge of his polished diplomatic veneer, "Father Joseph Walter Daniels is a former student of the then Professor Percussi.

"In fact, the Holy Father considers Father Daniels his premiere student. He is very fond of him. And since he is both a poet and an inner city pastor as well as a degreed theologian, the Holy Father thought he would make a fine first selection as a collaborator on the encyclical."

There was no hiding it. Monsignor Douglas Haynes was taking insufferable delight in relaying this inside information to the Secretary of State.

"And, your Eminence," Haynes again very respectful, "I was under the impression that the Holy Father was not confining the search for his collaborators to Rome but ..."

"Yes, yes, I know," the Cardinal growled, obviously angry at Haynes' presumption to tell him anything.

"May I leave now, Eminence?" Haynes asked as politely as the appearance of abject deference would permit to someone who had just beat the champion diplomat of the Vatican.

"Yes, yes," Tamacci waved his hand impatiently in a sign of dismissal.

"Good morning, Eminence," Haynes said as he gave a short bow of respect and withdrew.

Tamacci wondered if he had detected a smirk on Haynes' face. Thought better of it and decided he just imagined it, unnerved as he felt.

No sooner had Haynes departed than Tamacci waved his hand over his Viewphone and punched in the sacrosanct number. Then he thrust his hand over the phone deactivating it and just sat there staring as though he were having a vision. A vision of disaster.

Joseph Daniels, a protégé of the Pope? My God, what next? Daniels and the Pope sitting around drinking some of that damnable sherry the Pope likes so much. Daniels regaling the Pope with the tale of the note, Viri Lucis, the Mentor and God knows what else.

He could see himself being summoned. "Do you know anything about this, Camillo?" the Pope would interrogate him.

"No," he would lie with full diplomatic immunity.

"Well, find out yesterday, Camillo. I want a full report on my desk by sherry-time this evening. You know my dearest friend and confidant, Father Joseph Daniels? Wouldn't he just make a superb Undersecretary of State? He would be the first Undersecretary with the Red Hat.

"You know, Camillo, the Pope can choose his successor. Wouldn't Father Daniels here make a superb pope? I'll bet Viri Lucis would give him one hundred percent support. Especially since he has that note Viri Lucis so desperately wants.

"By the way, Camillo, you wouldn't happen to be the Mentor, would you? I understand it's someone high up on the hierarchical ladder."

Well, Tamacci thought, might as well make an appointment with the Mentor and get it over with. Premiere student! Why couldn't Daniels just be another brain-dead priest?

"Mentor," Tamacci spoke with a hurried and harried voice, "I need to see you at once."

"Camillo, my brother, you know I am always at your disposal. Come here immediately." The Mentor sounded so confident, so smooth, so obviously powerful.

Well, Tamacci thought, wait until he hears what I have to tell him. We will see how confident he is.

An hour later Camillo Cardinal Tamacci, Secretary of State, was ushered into the Mentor's inner sanctum with a flurry of abject respect.

"You Eminence," one of the priests said, bowing low, "the Mentor is still offering the Holy Sacrifice of the Mass. Would you mind waiting? It shouldn't be too long now."

Tamacci grunted as he sat down on the damnable wooden chair reserved no doubt for esteemed visitors to the Mentor's quarters.

It only takes me twelve minutes to recite a private Mass, Tamacci mused to himself. It takes the Mentor over an hour? Maybe he is a mystic after all. God knows, I hope he is.

"May I get you something to drink, Eminence?" one of the priests asked most politely. "Perhaps some cappuccino?"

"Yes, that would be nice," Tamacci replied placing his hand over left eye which was twitching uncontrollably.

Finally the Mentor strode into the room. For a man who was obviously overweight, he moved as smoothly as a ballet dancer. There was a certain delicacy about his posture which bespoke a buoyancy of spirit.

Camillo Tamacci stood immediately. "Good morning, Mentor," he said without any sign of subservience.

"Good morning, Camillo. Am I to assume you are here to report on your progress concerning our plans for Perez and Rawmanda?"

"Not exactly, Mentor." Tamacci sat down quickly fearing his legs would give out.

"Oh, then what is it, Camillo?" The Mentor sat down behind his huge desk that was covered with neat piles of printouts. He picked up the cup of steaming cappuccino and took a deep gulp without so much as wincing.

"Something else," Tamacci sighed audibly.

"Yesss …" the Mentor sounded wary and agitated.

Tamacci launched into his report of the Pope's plans. He told the Mentor of the plans to write an encyclical on the Mystical Body and how he was going to bring poets, pastors, ordinary lay people, theologians, both conservative and radical to the Vatican.

He told of the weekly televised messages downlinked to every home in the world. Of the Pope's plan to hold frequent media conferences where he would open himself up to questions from those sharks in the media. This, he said, he learned with no difficulty from that lightweight, O'Reilley, who was bouncing all over the place with the fervor of his new-found importance.

He mentioned the evaluations of all the Prefects of Congregations and most everyone else in the Vatican and how he was to come up with an evaluating instrument. How he learned from his spies in the

Banco Vaticano that the Pope was going to re-route funds to cover all these plans and how Shamansky was burning the midnight oil to come up with a plan to manipulate the money.

"All this is as interesting as it is innocuous," the Mentor replied with obvious indifference. "You've tied up better Pontiffs than Percussi. Just do it again."

"He told me," Tamacci whined, "that if his desk kept getting piled with nonsensical paper work, heads would roll."

"Hmmm, how efficient," the Mentor purred. "But aren't they all when they first take over the helm of the Barque of Peter?"

"There's something else," Tamacci coughed nervously.

"Well, what is it? Out with it." The Mentor was obviously losing patience.

You remember that list of poets I'm to draw up?"

"Yes," came the curt reply.

"The Pope himself has placed a name on the very top of that list."

"Go on," the Mentor seemed to be showing some interest.

"Well," Tamacci spoke hesitantly, "did you know that Joseph Walter Daniels is a published poet?"

The Mentor's head jerked up but he said nothing. His eyes drilled through Tamacci like two laser beams.

"And," Tamacci added with a bit of courage in his voice as if he was taking some pleasure in giving information the Mentor did not have, "this same poet-priest was once the premiere student of Professor Alessandro Percussi, our present Holy Father.

"And the Pope has just ordered me to put Daniels' name at the top of the list of those he will be consulting with about his encyclical."

The Mentor swept the cup off his desk and smashed it to pieces against the wall.

"Damnit!" he screamed as he stood up and began to pace furiously. "Goddamnit!!"

Tamacci viewed this uncharacteristic reaction of the man who was always in control — of himself as well as of others — with a growing feeling of delight. He had really pulled the rug from under the Mentor's smug self-satisfaction and his haughty indifference to his report.

"That's all we need!" the Mentor yelled. "Daniels hobnobbing with the Pope, filling his ears with unsubstantiated guesswork. But titillating enough to tweak the Pope's curiosity."

Tamacci put his head down as though signaling his anguished empathy for the Mentor but in fact he was trying to hide his glee at the Mentor's rage that seemed ready to explode into a romping episode of paranoia. What was that American slang he had heard? Oh yes, "Gotcha."

"Good God in heaven!" the Mentor continued to rant as he kept pacing. He suddenly reached out and knocked over a statue of the Blessed Mother. It was carved out of wood and no damage was done except for a few scratches.

"There is no place in the world where gossip is more contagious than in the Vatican," the Mentor spoke in a more controlled tone. "Gossip in the Vatican carries more weight than any *ex cathedra* papal pronouncement. Gossip is the *real* exercise of infallibility.

"We cannot allow Daniels to come to the Vatican, to have access to Percussi. We just can't." Now his tone had the customary sinister sound that Tamacci and others were used to.

"I felt exactly the same way," Tamacci sounded like he was cheering. But he just had to say something to keep himself from breaking out in a wide grin of obvious self-satisfaction. Not in all these years had he gotten to the Mentor as he had this morning. It was so gratifying to see him so unnerved. A deserved lesson in humility. A very needed lesson.

"Look, Camillo, you take care of Perez and Rawmanda. We'll see to Father Joseph Walter Daniels." The Mentor literally flopped on his chair and stretched out his short heavy legs as though he were trying to stave off some impending catastrophe.

Then as if talking out loud to himself, he said, "Right now the most pressing, the most imperative concern we have is to get that money, that half a billion dollars so that I can buy the document.

"I am the one with the true faith and that document in my hands will resolve every problem that could possibly block our progress.

With that document I will ride the crest to our blessed goal. You know that, Camillo."

"Yes, Mentor." Cardinal Tamacci stood. His eye was no longer twitching. His legs were as stable as those of the many stone statues that peopled the Vatican. He bowed. "I'll take care of what has to be done, Mentor." How he wanted to say, And you take care of Daniels if you can.

Tamacci bowed slightly and swept out of the room. He hadn't felt so much like a Prince of the Church in the Mentor's presence as he had this morning. He was jubilant. But he also knew he had a great deal of work to do both to accomplish the goals given him and at the same time to stymie the Pope.

Tamacci had barely left when one of the Mentor's Attendants entered. He was visibly shaken.

"Mentor, I have bad news."

The Mentor stood up and placed the palms of his hands flat on the dull desktop.

"Go ahead," he said. "The news this morning has been so bad that I doubt if yours could be any worse."

"The Sudanese assassins …"

"Go on," the Mentor rasped, his face like a sky full of dark, foreboding clouds.

"They took the half million dollars and …. and ran. They've disappeared."

The Mentor kicked the wastebasket across the room. "Never!" he shouted. "Are you positive?"

"Yes, Mentor."

"I should never have bothered with them. I should have entrusted the assassination of the American President to one of my own. I just couldn't take the chance of it being traced." He was seething.

"This is a trial," the Mentor said in a lowered tone that was as ominous as a loaded gun pointed directly at the Attendant's brain.

"God is testing me. I have been victorious in a more threatening trial than this. I will once again rise out of the tomb of apparent defeat into a new life of power. By the resurrection of Jesus I will."

The Attendant trembled. He knew well how the Mentor punished the messenger because of the message.

"We'll get back to this at another time." His sinister smile spread like a streak of lightning across his face. Once I have the document in hand .... We will take care of that heretical President of the United States.

"For now we must take measures to make certain that Father Daniels never arrives in Rome"

STEVE RINKO

As Danny continued to drive along, he glanced out the window. The pale sky was coming alive with pink rays wrapped like ribbons around the gift of early Springtime. He was still lost in memories of his lifelong friendship with Steve.

He always enjoyed Steve's raucous and often irreverent humor. His rowdy laugh you could still feel long after you left him.

Now his voice seemed so subdued, so weak as he tried to sound upbeat about his impending death. Steve, Danny thought, was the most refreshing person he'd ever known. Steve loved to shock others with his rather vulgar remarks.

Danny spoke the words, "Classical Music." His radio immediately responded, "Any particular composer?" "Mozart," Danny replied. At once the sounds of Mozart filled his car. He had about a forty minute drive to Steve's rectory.

Actually it was no longer Steve's rectory. The Cardinal had asked him to step down, resign. He then immediately appointed Donald Skarsic pastor.

Danny smiled as he remembered a remark Steve had made not too long ago when they were talking on the phone.

"Remember, Danny, how I used to say we should have had four years of psychiatry instead of theology to deal effectively with our people? Well, as I look back over my priestly years, I've changed my mind. We should have had four years of proctology since we've had to deal with so many assholes."

He recalled the day Steve had called him with the horrible news.

"Danny, they tell me I have liver cancer." He could hear Steve fill up. And then control his voice. They're giving me three to six months.

Danny had asked, "What about a liver transplant?"

"Who's gonna give me their liver?" Steve retorted now in full control. "You? Your liver's probably ten times worse off than mine.

Danny had laughed. He knew Steve wanted him to. "What about an artificial liver?" he had asked.

In a more serious reply, Steve had said, "Can't. The cancer has spread to other vital organs too. Funny how they've found a cure for so many kinds of cancer …." His voice trailed off.

As Danny turned into a narrow twisting road, he observed the double lines and stayed closely to the right. He wondered how many people ever stopped to think about the time and energy that went into making certain that these lines were properly centered on this winding road.

How much we take for granted, he thought. What a metaphor these lines were. If he didn't drive on the right side of the road, he would not have the freedom to move. There would be nothing but traffic jams and pile ups. Constraints are necessary for the exercise of true freedom. The problem is that too often constraints are used not for our freedom but for our enslavement.

Danny pulled up in front of the rectory. It sat back behind a semicircular drive. It looked more like 'real' home, as Steve once remarked, than one of those artificial houses called rectories. A home for unwed fathers, he had laughed loudly.

Danny rang the bell. The door became transparent. A voice said, "Father Joe! What a pleasant surprise!." The door opened.

A pleasant looking woman in her fifties stood inside.

"Hello, Annie," Danny smiled at the parish secretary. "How is he?"

"Not good, Father Joe. Not good at all. He's getting weaker by the day."

"May I go up?"

"By all means. It'll do him so much good to see you." Annie stepped aside and waved Danny past her.

Danny entered Steve's study to find him curled up almost in a fetal position in his huge armchair.

"Steve?" Danny walked over toward him thinking he might be asleep.

"Oh, hi-ya, Danny," Steve said in a quiet voice, barely audible. "Sit down, won't you?"

"How're you feeling, Steve?" Danny asked as he pulled a straight back chair up close to Steve.

"Okay, I guess. Just sort of waiting." Steve tried to smile.

Danny felt so uncomfortable. Steve was a shadow of his former self.

"Damn itching," Steve said. "I think it's the medicine. Don't know why I'm even taking any medicine. Doctor says it'll cut down on my pain. It does that but I can't get any sleep I'm itching so bad."

Danny didn't comment.

"It's good of you to come, Danny. How're you doin'?"

"Fine, Steve, fine."

"A slow death is interesting, Danny," Steve just introduced the subject as simply as talking about the weather. "It's like knowing the thief is coming and not being able to do anything about it. Sometimes I wish I just popped out with a massive heart attack or got stabbed. No time to think."

"But you do have time to get yourself ready, Steve. Time isn't your enemy."

"Right now, time isn't my friend either. It's like time's put me up for adoption and eternity is the adopting parent."

"Rather profound," Danny laughed.

"You're damn right. Profound. Never thought anyone would ever say that about me," Steve laughed back. It was such a weak laugh in contrast to the belly laughs Danny was used to.

"When you have time to think, to review your life, you get kinda profound, I guess," Steve continued as he shifted in his chair.

"I think I would rather have gone quick and the hell with profound. You know what I mean, Danny? Profound is for you poets. Me, I'm just a practical bastard. If it needs to be done, I'll get it done. No fanfare."

"You're the most practical person I've ever known, Steve," Danny said as he felt his eyes fill up. "And a very faithful friend."

"Boy, death is very real, Danny. Not ultimate but it is real." Steve came close to his usual boisterous laughter as he asked, "How's that for profound. Scaring the bee-jeeses out of you, ain't I?"

"Not really. I always suspected there was a lot more depth to you than you were willing to let on," Danny laughed back.

"You know, it's not the going that bothers me, it's the leaving. I get goofy ideas like I won't be around for the Superbowl."

"But you'll know who won before we will," Danny leaned over at patted Steve's arm. It was a bone. Steve had lost so much weight in such a short time.

"Well, a slow death gives you time for grieving. I was thinking, grieving's like aging. It's always there but it changes. There I go being profound again."

"You're right though, Steve. I think I spend a lot of time grieving without even realizing it. I've always been perplexed about my mortality. Wondering if everything I've been taught about the afterlife was true. I mean, who knows? Then I'm told it's a matter of faith. So I end up wondering about my faith."

"You should have been called Thomas. You have more doubts than a whore has customers." Steve tried to laugh again but just didn't have the energy.

"I won't burden you by telling you that I derive some consolation from Process Theology, Steve. But I do seem to believe that we keep becoming more of who we are after death. We keep growing and developing. A kind of endless evolution."

"No eternal rest? Shit, Danny, why did you have to go an spoil things for me with all your theological bullshit?" This time Steve did manage a laugh.

"Oh well, who knows?" Danny sighed. "Eternal rest or eternal becoming?"

"All through our priesthood," Steve seemed to be thinking out loud rather than talking directly to Danny, "we preach about being pilgrims, that this isn't our real home. But it's at times like this that it really hits home.

"All of sudden you begin to notice flowers. They become your friends. They welcome you only to say goodbye.

347

"You tell people in your homilies to look at things or other people as though for the last time, you know, trying to live in wonder. Now there's nothing else to do but look for the last time."

"What a wonderful way to prepare for death," Danny said sincerely. "To meet death filled with wonder. Wonder and surprise. I read somewhere that the best way to prepare for death is to sharpen your sense of surprise."

"Yeah, you think you got it all down pat and then you die and God shouts, 'SURPRISE!'" Steve just shook his head.

"I think that's exactly what God will shout, Steve. I've always believed that our God is a God of surprises. The problem's been that our religious formation was offered to us as a routine that only had to be followed like a recipe or the instructions on a doctor's prescription.

"God, as far as I'm concerned, is always surprising us," Danny continued. "An inspiration here, a challenge there. An unexpected word of thanks from somebody we don't even remember helping. A temptation to a particular sin we thought we'd conquered. These surprises go on all through life so why wouldn't God greet us with a surprise at death?"

"I always thought that surprise was what the parables were about," Danny sounded really enthusiastic at this point. "You know, the guys who worked only one hour being surprised to get a whole days wages."

"A hell of a surprise for the guys that bore the heat of the day," Steve laughed quietly. "I guess the biggest surprise when you're dying is to find out you're as replaceable as a word in a rewrite of a story. Danny, do me a favor, will ya? Take some of that cream and rub it all over my back. It's supposed to help stop this itching."

Danny got up as Steve pulled up his T-shirt. He began to rub the cream on Steve's back, again feeling Steve's bones like lattice work under his fingers.

"I remember a dear old lady I used to bring Communion to," Steve said. "She was in her nineties. I used to ask her how she was feeling and she'd always say, 'My feet are cold.' Then she'd laugh

348

and say, 'Maybe I'm dying from the feet up. Used to say three rosaries every day to stop abortion and euthanasia.

"Did I tell you that one of my doctors suggested assisted suicide? The son-of-a-bitch. 'It's legal, you know,' he said. Like legal is everything. Those bastards in the Supreme Court — they think they can change the whole moral landscape by saying something's legal. I wonder what kind of surprise God has in store for them.

"I think I shocked the doctor when I told him to go to hell. Told him that he could put me to death after he kissed his own ass. Called him a goddamn butcher. Maybe I gave him something to think about. I doubt it. Got me another doctor to see me through this thing.

"It's so easy to treat life as a throwaway until you know you're not going to have it in a short time, right, Danny?"

"Right, Steve," Danny continued rubbing Steve's back. "Living is dying. The only difference between you and me is that you know when your dying will become death. I keep living as though I have all the time in the world. But you never know."

"It's kinda sad, Danny, but I look at my life and it seems a pale reflection of my dreams.

"I guess we all start out thinking we'll make a difference and then something happens, the news that you have incurable cancer or some crisis you never expected and you sit and wonder what kind of a difference you ever made." Steve fell silent. In the old days, silence was as foreign to Steve as speaking hieroglyphics fluently.

Danny couldn't help but remember Muntz wondering about the same thing. What difference do we make with all our efforts and work? To Steve he said, "You've made a difference, Steve. Your efforts aren't just a ripple on the sea of history. You've brought the laughter of faith into people's lives. You've proven that you can be holy without being holier-than-thou. You've shown people that it's great to be human. As you said, no fanfare, just being your true self, your real self. You've made a difference."

"Sometimes I have this feeling of regret. I'm going and I'm not leaving anyone behind. You know, no children. No one with my genes. It's like I was here and I'll be gone and nothing." Once again, Steve just sat in the silence of his own thoughts.

"That's not totally true, Steve. You're leaving all the good you've done behind. All the lives you've touched …."

"Touched is the operative word, Danny. Oh sure, there'll be some who will feel bad for a while when I push off, what's it called, 'this mortal coil' whatever the hell that means. But there won't be anyone who keeps me alive in their memory. Like I said it's just a fleeting thought. Occasional not with me all the time."

"I guess," Danny said in a reassuring voice, "that it's at times like this that 'One sows, another reaps' becomes our only reality. You've done your sowing. Now there'll be others who will reap the harvest of what you've sown."

"That's a consoling thought and I thank you for it," Steve smiled.

Danny laughed quietly. "I remember Muntz used to say, 'Why should we care about posterity? What's posterity ever done for us?'"

"Yeah, that old geezer's still alive, isn't he?" Steve sounded for the first time a bit bitter. There was an implicit question like Why me? in his voice.

"Tell you one thing, Danny. When you're at death's door, a lot of things you thought were so very important seem really insignificant. But by then it's too late."

"I know. We ought to get our priorities in order a lot sooner," Danny replied.

"You think something's do or die," Steve continued, "like paying off the debt and now you wish you put all your energy into helping people live holier lives. Who the hell sets up our priorities for us, Danny?"

"It's the system, Steve. I've thought for a long time that saints are recognized as saints only after the Church catches up with their prophetic vision.

"Until then they were the mavericks, the rebels, the risk-takers who launched out into the deep, who traveled the uncharted road.

350

For the rest of us, well, we have just enough rules and regulations to keep us immature in our faith.

"If someone does manage to break through the boundaries of those rules and achieve spiritual maturity, that individual's a *persona non grata.* To the Church's credit, no one has ever been canonized for the heroic practice of propriety." Danny sat in what seemed to be brooding silence.

"I know this sounds strange coming from me, the supreme pragmatist," Steve said, "but I think we get so bogged down in the nuts and bolts of the organization, worrying about bills and collections that things become essential and people are left in a ditch on the roadside of life. What's that saying? We're to love people and use things but we do just the opposite.

"That's what I meant earlier when I said my life seems like a pale reflection of my dreams. How did that poem go? 'Boyhood dreams of long ago, saw an altar fair.' When we were ordained, it was all about people. But things were easier to manage, to measure."

Again Danny recalled almost the exact same words from Muntz. "I think you're being too hard on yourself," Danny tried to sound reassuring although he knew Steve had hit a raw nerve. "You're a legend as a people person.

"But I know what you're saying. We have such a magnificent mystical tradition in our faith. But it's untapped, perhaps even abandoned for the sake of rules and regulations, finances and real estate. Danny stopped rubbing Steve's back and went to the bathroom to wash his hands. He kept talking in a louder tone.

"I remember reading one of Thomas Merton's letters. In it he wrote and I'm not quoting him exactly but I do have his precise idea, 'I love all the nice well-meaning good people who go to Mass and want things to get better. But I understand Zen Buddhists better than I do them.' Then he posed this question, 'Is the Church a community of people who love one another or a big dog fight where you do your religious business seeking your friends somewhere else?'

"I never read anything by Merton," Steve said. "He was too heavy for me and so are you." Steve laughed a little laugh.

Danny stretched before he sat down again. "What I'm saying, Steve, is that if someone of Merton's stature felt that way, what about all those people who are searching for mystical experiences beyond or outside the Church?"

"Why should they have to when we have such a rich treasure of mysticism within the Church? Maybe we're afraid that if we do share the mystical tradition of our faith, we will have to let God be God. Maybe we're afraid that if we do, God will disrupt the finely honed organization we've erected to his honor and glory. Maybe even destroy it."

"Yeah," Steve agreed. "The Church should be the conduit for God's kingdom but you're right. We've made the Church God's kingdom and tried to make him its king."

"You know what surprises me, Danny?"

"What?"

"I thought for sure that at a time like this my prayer would be .... well, sort of mystical. And yet all I find myself saying is, 'Oh my Jesus' over and over. Sometimes I'll say, 'I love you, Jesus.' That's about it."

Danny was startled by what Steve was saying. It was almost the very same thing Muntz had said. Is it only when one is near death that the genuine desire for mystical experience becomes a reality? Or is the desire for mystical prayer an immediate preparation for an eternity with God?

"Who knows what mystical prayer is?" Danny asked as though he were grilling himself. "Spiritual writers have analyzed and compartmentalized it and glued it back together until it seems absolutely unattainable.

"Sometimes, Steve, I think we need our ordinary, everyday language to help us discover what our inherited sacred language isn't saying to us anymore."

"What do you mean?"

"Well, stories of ordinary events often bring us closer to revealed truth than all our heavy theological language.

"For instance, there's a story that comes out of the time when schools were beginning to be integrated here in the great Melting Pot.

"A young white mother was taking her little girl to her first day in a newly integrated school. She was very apprehensive, wondering how her little daughter would do with all the Negro students in her class.

"At the end of the day, the mother went to the school to pick up her daughter. The little girl ran into her mother's arms and shouted, 'Guess what, Mommy?' 'What, dear?' her mother asked with even greater distress at what may have happened to her daughter.

"'Well, I sat next to a little Negro girl in my class.' Filled with anxiety, her mother asked, 'And what happened, Honey?' 'Well, we were both so scared, we sat and held hands all day.'"

"That's a good one," Steve smiled. "I like it."

"My point is, Doesn't that story have a greater impact than some abstract statement like, Bigotry is a grave sin?"

"Yeah. And what are you saying? That we got to go into the everyday to find this mystical experience?" Steve asked, intently paying attention.

"Exactly. It's not in the high-sounding mystical words we've inherited but in the ordinary events that we find the mystical. You know, we say things like the Paschal mystery is our salvation. What does that mean to people?

"But when you say that what Jesus did for us is like the sign, 'We will crawl under your car oftener and get ourselves dirtier than any of our competitors,' people may begin to understand with greater realization what Jesus did for them.

"It's the same with prayer, Steve. Sometimes the most mystical prayer comes out of our contact with the most ordinary events or words in our daily lives. Think of some down-and-out parishioner you took time to talk to. There's where you'll find the gold nugget of mystical experience."

Steve made no response. Danny wondered if he had lost him. Maybe it was too heavy for him to grasp, given his present circumstances.

Then Steve smiled. "I remember Betty Kolhoss. She died a few years ago. Used to live with her widowed sister. Funny thing. She couldn't stand the smell of people. I mean everyone. She used to wear a mask over her mouth and nose. One of those surgical jobs.

"She used to kneel in the middle aisle during Mass with her arms outstretched. At first people were annoyed but they got used to it. She's spend her days walking around. Walking all over the place. Walking and walking.

"One day I asked her what she was thinking about when she was walking. 'Thinking about?' she says with an puzzled look on her face. 'Nothing. I'm just praying. I pray for all the people I pass, people in cars. I pray for rain or sunshine. In the winter I pray for all the people who have to live on the streets when it snows. I just pray.'"

"That's beautiful, Betty," I says to her.

"'Do you think I'm crazy?' she asks me. 'People say I'm crazy, you know.'

"'No,' I says. 'Some day we'll be celebrating Mass in honor of St. Betty of Chicago.'

"She took off her mask and smiled at me. It was a wonderful smile. Then she sniffed and says to me, 'You stink.'

"What a difference from this other woman who was in church before Mass. I stopped and asked her how she was. She says to me, 'I came here to pray not to talk to you.'

"Like you said, Danny, there's probably more mysticism in that story about Betty Kolhoss than in all the religiously inherited jargon about becoming more Christ-like."

More silence. Danny didn't want to say anything right away. It was a sacred moment.

Finally Danny said, "You're right, Steve. What does it mean to be Christ-like? Doesn't it mean to be welcoming and accepting of others, with no regard for their being different from us, just as you were toward Betty? Isn't that the core of mystical experience?"

"People," Steve was still remembering, "used to say, 'That poor woman.' I think she was the richest person I ever met. They called her 'Batty Betty.' She was probably saner that all those people who were well-adjusted instead of well-developed.

"You know, the ones that give the impression that they've got it all together while they worry themselves sick about their self-image or their self-worth. They're paranoid about whether they're better or worse than others. Betty never worried about that stuff.

"She was a mystic and the hell with all that crap about what your parents did or didn't do to you or whether you're insecure or lovable. You know how people are, Danny. Their whole religion is about how they appear. They are so preoccupied with themselves that Betty thought they stunk, I guess."

"So her mask was a reminder," Danny said, "that people should strip themselves of all their masks and disguises and take a good, hard, honest look at themselves."

"Yeah, be real," Steve agreed. I guess you can't really be a mystic unless you're real."

"No one is as real as you are, Steve."

"I guess mystical experience has to be worked at. It just doesn't happen, does it?" Steve asked.

"Just let go, Steve. Let it flow. The Whole Christ is in you and you're in the Whole Christ. Some spiritual writer from the 20th century said that if we're going to receive the Eucharistic Body of Christ, we have to be willing to swallow the Whole Christ — Christ and all the people that make up the Body of Christ. That's all there is to mystical experience. Let it be. Just experience it in your prayer, 'O my Jesus.'"

Steve laughed. "Maybe all I need is a mask on my face." Danny laughed with him.

"As far as I'm concerned," Danny continued, mystical experience could be as simple as Newman's 'Heart speaks to heart' without all the subdivisions and footnotes. Sometimes I think we've invented so many intellectual categories that we've robbed the heart out of our mystical tradition. We've taken the simple story of Jesus and turned it into dry theological speculative thinking.

"It's that routine business again, Steve. Some people find themselves so attached to their routine of spiritual practices that it's like digging deeper but always in the same old hole. They don't search around for other buried treasures.

"They need a more creative spirituality. One that challenges them to look for other areas, unexplored areas on the landscape of spiritual development. That's what you're doing right now."

"Boy you sure can get into profound conversations when you're talking to a theologian!" Steve was able to get out a hoarse laugh.

"As a theologian, then, let me assure you, Steven Rinko, that you are into mystical prayer.

"Thanks, Danny. That means a lot. I'm feeling tired now."

"Okay, Steve, I'll be back to see you again."

"Oh, Danny?"

"Yes."

"You will preach at my funeral?"

Again as with Muntz so now with Steve. "I'd be honored, Steve. Thank you for asking." But Danny experienced the same pain of imminent loss as he had done when talking with Muntz.

"Just don't tell the truth. People wouldn't be ready for it." This time Steve did let out a raucous laugh.

As Danny picked up his sweater, Steve made an excruciating effort to get up out of his chair.

"Stay," Danny ordered. He walked over, bent down and gathered Steve into his arms. They both began to cry as they hugged with sincere male-bonded affection.

"I'm okay, Danny," Steve whispered. "I'm ready."

Danny blessed Steve and then knelt and asked Steve to bless him.

As Danny drove home, his eyes still damp, he was lost in his thoughts. I envy you, Steve. How I envy your simple faith, your total trust. When you get there, pray for me, pray for me." How we take so much for granted, Danny thought. We seem to live our lives like glancing at a clock to get the time. We don't really notice the clock at all until something goes wrong with it.

We seldom live our lives in the present. We dwell in the past and bring all kinds of baggage with us into the present. Baggage filled with past failures, sins, disillusionments, hurts. And carrying this baggage around siphons off our energy for living in the present like water gurgling down the drain of a bathtub.

Or we dwell in the future composing negative lists of what ifs. What if I fail? What if I get sick? What if so-and-so says such-and-such to me? What if things don't pan out the way I expected them to? And this litany only intensifies our anxiety so that we don't even see the tasks at hand on this one God-given day.

As he drove along, he thought about what Steve had said about being at death's door and how things you thought were so important are really insignificant.

How time becomes a slave master, snapping the scathing whip of ceaseless demands that goad us into endless activity which drains our energy like an arterial wound gushing with the body's blood.

Danny's attention went back to the note again. It was becoming an obsession. Despite what Michael ordered, Danny thought, I'm wasting precious time holding onto that note, trying to track down Viri Lucis. Who cares? What difference does it make? I have more than enough to do at St. Matt's, helping people to become holier, as Steve had so simply reminded him.

I'll contact that pretentious Archbishop Brown and turn the note over to him. Celine can get me a lawyer and that will be the end of it. Danny felt himself relax. He even felt lighthearted. Steve was a blessing.

When Danny got back home his phone butler announced, "You have a message." It was a message from Monsignor Richards, the Cardinal's secretary.

"Father Daniels, please call me at once. It is urgent."

Now what? Danny wondered. He recited the number and clicked on his telescreen.

"Ah, Father Daniels. Thank you for getting back so quickly." Richards did not click on his screen. Just as well, Danny thought, I won't have to look at that officious face of the young careerist.

"The Cardinal asked me to call you. He would have called you himself but he's in a meeting," Richards sounded rushed.

"Ah …. Father Daniels …. the Cardinal has received word that you …. that is, that the Holy Father has personally chosen you to come to the Vatican and help him …. ah, to aid him in the writing of his encyclical." Richards was literally breathless.

"His Eminence asked me to convey his warmest congratulations." Was that awe in the young Monsignor's voice, Danny smiled. "Oh, and you will be getting an official statement from the …. the Secretary of State, Cardinal Tamacci. May I add my own congratulations. This is a unique honor not only for you but for our Archdiocese."

"What about St. Matt's?" Danny asked, ignoring the sugary obsequiousness of the now awestruck Domestic Prelate.

"Oh …. yes, yes, of course. His Eminence wanted me to assure you that he will make certain that St. Matthew's parish will be covered for the duration."

"Well, thank you, Monsignor Richards. It was so kind of you to take time out from your grueling schedule to prepare me for the letter from the Vatican. I would have certainly been taken off guard had I received it cold."

"Ah, you're …. welcome, Father Daniels. You are very welcome."

Danny waved the phone dead and laughed out loud. He just couldn't help himself. He had to get his syrupy dig in even though it was lost on the Cardinal's secretary. Bureaucrats are the quintessential literalists. He knew that Richards was waiting for the question, Why me? But he would not give him the satisfaction of asking. Danny laughed again. He'd call his classmate, Douglas Haynes, who was now the Pope's personal secretary and get the scoop from him.

He had to admit his own confusion at this honor and indeed it was an honor. Why would Professor Percussi choose him out of all the clergymen in the Church? He felt a shot of Adrenalin surging through his tired lifeblood. He was excited. He was thrilled. What an opportunity!

Later he would call Celine and Gene. He wanted to tell them of his decision about the note too.

Despite his feelings of exhilaration, Danny sat down and in a pensive mood began to review his visit with Steve.

How it always seemed to come back to the same discussion. Faith lived or religion practiced. Mysticism or legalism. Why did it have to be that way?

Thanks to the dichotomy between the sacred and the profane, mystical experience was always considered the preserve of the chosen few. The fact is, Danny thought, mysticism is the common fare of all.

When St. Paul said, "I live yet not I but Christ lives in me," he wasn't talking on behalf of the chosen few. What he was saying was common fare. It was meant for everyone. We all live yet not we but Christ lives in us.

If we truly lived our faith, then it would be faith and religion. The practice of religion would flow from the deep well of faith. Religion would be the transparency of lived faith.

He knew that when he was talking with Steve about people seeking mystical experience beyond the Church, he was thinking of Celine as a prime example.

He wondered if he would have enough input into Percussi's encyclical to get some of these ideas he'd been harboring for all these years into the final draft.

He remembered how one evening as they were walking to Celine's apartment from a small restaurant nearby, Celine told Danny that she belonged to that growing mass of Catholics between obedient Churchgoers for whom the slightest pronouncement from on high was law and those who had totally given up on any external practice of religion.

"I go to church not regularly but more often than not. I belong to a group that is neither persuaded nor particularly disturbed by each and every one of the Church's teachings as they are handed down by the present Administration in the Church."

Celine had a way of teasing. Danny wasn't always sure whether there was some very serious searching going on behind what seemed to be her off-handed questions.

They arrived at her apartment and Danny went in with Celine. Celine went into the kitchen and put water on for some coffee. She returned to the living room and sat down on the couch. Danny was already sitting in the easy chair.

"Tell me," she repeated her often asked question, "if Aborigines are able to get to heaven, is the Church essential for salvation?"

He tried to be honest. There could be no other way with someone whose mind was as incisive as a scalpel. "Perhaps not essential but from the gospel viewpoint it is necessary. Jesus not only founded a new way but commissioned his followers to preach that way to everyone. This is the command to evangelize. To lift up people from primitive or superstitious religious practices into the truth of the good news."

"Spoken like a textbook," she smiled.

"Let me put it this way, Celine. If we consider the Church to be essential to salvation, then all we have to do is keep the laws of the Church imposed on us to insure us of the salvation of our souls."

"What you're saying then is there is hope for the Aborigines." Celine laughed in a warm, ingratiating way.

"Of course," Danny replied. "If the Church is not essential to salvation, then we who belong to the Church have a serious obligation in spades to be living witnesses of God's universal presence in the lives of everyone and in all religious groups."

Celine got up and went to the kitchen where she poured two cups of coffee and then came back and handed one to Danny.

"What you're saying, as I hear it," Celine said, "is that we as witnesses must live our lives in such a way that all the ramifications of the gospel are fulfilled in us. To my way of thinking, that's a much more strenuous demand and challenge than merely belonging to the Church."

"So," Celine said, extending Danny's thought, "you can't be satisfied with just going to Mass. You're saying something like we have to be living signs of God's universal love out there where we work and play."

Danny was more than a little impressed with Celine's quick comprehension.

"Right. And we can't be satisfied either with just confessing the wrong we've done. There's also the good that we failed or refused to do. Someone said that we can't be satisfied with knowing the answers and going to church. We have to live the answers and be the Church."

"So," Celine stood up and stretched a little, "if you think of the Church as being essential, you could end up with nothing but the smug security of just belonging."

"It's either that or working tirelessly to be witnesses, living signs of God's saving power that extends to every member of the human race, all his sons and daughters," Danny replied.

"From my experience," he continued, "when people think of the Church as essential to salvation, they usually live with an otherworldly expectation not a this-worldly involvement. You know, let God take care of it, let God do it all. I just have to be a good, law-abiding Catholic."

As if the conversation had become a lot heavier than Celine had bargained for, she said teasingly, "Well if, as you are saying, the Church is not essential, then is the priesthood?"

He merely smiled at her. She was teasing and he was not going to get into the trap of defending his priesthood and eventually celibacy. He'd been down that path too many times. "You draw your own conclusions," he continued to smile at her. Besides, it had been obvious to him for some time that his feeling for Celine had been growing stronger.

Celine collected the cups and took them into the kitchen. She called out from the kitchen in a far less flippant tone, "It boggles my mind, "that women are still second-rate members of the universal Catholic Church."

She came back into the living room and walked over to the bookcase. She reached up and took a book down from the third shelf.

"Here," she said. "It's in one of Eugene O'Neill's plays." She flipped through the pages. "It's in *Strange Interlude*." She read aloud:

> The mistake began when God was
> created in a male image. Of course
> women would see Him that way, but
> men should have been gentlemen

enough, remembering their mothers, to make God a woman! But the God of Gods — the Boss — has always been a man. That makes life so perverted and death so unnatural. We should have imagined life as created in the birth-pain of God the Mother. Then we would understand why we, Her children, have inherited pain, for we would know that our life's rhythm beats from Her great heart, torn with agony of love and birth. And we would feel that death meant reunion with Her, a passing back into Her substance, blood of Her blood again, peace of Her peace!

Now wouldn't that be more logical and satisfying than having God a male whose chest thunders with egotism and is too hard for tired heads and thoroughly comfortless?

"What was it that Voltaire said?" Celine had asked rhetorically. 'God created us in his own image and likeness and we have returned the favor.' How ironic that *Mother* Church is top-heavy with a patriarchal administration which, in O'Neill's words, created God in a male image."

Danny could see that Celine was genuinely agitated. He decided that it would be futile to offer some feeble explanation. So he just let the matter hang there at that.

The important thing was to make certain that when he was dealing with women, he always made them feel that they were first rate members of the Church. He treated them with dignity and respect for their talents and used those talents as effectively as possible.

Once again if faith were truly lived, there would not be this discrimination against women. Just as body has been split from soul so division between men and women in the Church has been the norm. But the division isn't lateral, it's vertical with men occupying the places of power while women are expected to follow decisions made with little or no input.

As a result, God who is Wholeness is not the God who is being worshipped. How easily religion with all its trappings can become idolatry.

That night Danny had a recurrence of his dream. Once again he was standing in front of a burning forest. He heard Janie's voice from inside the forest, "Joooey! Come here!" He felt another presence. He turned and looked up at the hill. He saw a man dressed in a white cassock. This is what he missed the last time.

The man was holding a piece of paper in his hand. Could it be the note? In the man's other hand Danny saw what looked at first like a letter opener. No, it was a knife. He heard Janie again, "Joooey! Come here!" Then the man on the hill called out, "If you go into the burning forest, the flame will enter you, the flame, the flame."

Danny woke up with a start. He sat on the side of his bed, sweat drenched his entire body as though he had just stood in a cloudburst.

Time to analyze. The man in the white cassock. Pope? Could be. He had been wondering how high up in the Church Viri Lucis went. The paper. The note. Nothing unusual. He was fixated on the note and had just decided to turn it over.

The knife. Something, but what? Cutting through the Gordian Knot of the puzzle about Viri Lucis. A threat? Danger? Some kind of a warning. The flame entering in. Could symbolize so many things. The Spirit. Burning desire. Mystical experience. On the other hand, self-destruction through burnout.

Why Janie again? Why was she caught in the burning forest? Was she there beckoning him to some kind of purgation. Maybe his decision to give up the note would finally purge him of his obsession with Viri Lucis.

363

Dreams. Who knows? Why was he plagued by this dream at this time? He should be experiencing exhilaration over the news of being invited to Rome to work with the Pope. He tried to go back to sleep. Just fitful naps.

THE DOCUMENT

"Well, Joshua! Welcome back from the dark back streets of international intrigue." The older man laughed as he rose to embrace the younger.

"Manachem. It's good to be home. Iran is a hell hole."

"Yes. The world may look upon Palestine as the missing link in geographic evolution, but it is home. It is Yahweh's own garden." The older man laughed again.

"So tell me, what did you learn about this secret weapon the Iranians are supposed to have?"

"First, I learned that it is a document," the thin, wiry young man said.

"A document?" Menachem shouted in laughing disbelief. "A document is a weapon?"

Joshua got up and went to the sideboard. He poured two cups of tea, came back and handed one to Menachem.

"Our informant is quite the spinner of tales," Joshua smirked. "Are you sure you want to hear it?"

"My time is your time, Joshua," Menachem said as he sipped his tea. "Besides we paid enough for the information to allow an old man the happiness of listening to a story. Begin."

"Well, our informant recited his tale like a memorized legend. There are many gaps and when I asked him questions, he merely shrugged and continued as if he was annoyed that I was distracting him from his recital."

"And I'm sure, with your talents, that you will duplicate his recital verbatim," Menachem spoke reassuringly.

"I made notes," Joshua said with overt modesty as he fingered the papers in his hand. "Well, it all began after the Christians' so-called New Testament times with a secret sect called the Gnostics."

"I've heard of them but I don't know anything about them," Menachem was always most attentive when anything about the

Christians was being discussed. He prided himself on his knowledge about their beliefs if only to be able to refute them for his own peace of mind.

He shifted his burly body to get more comfortable. "Continue, please."

"Well, briefly, the Gnostic teachings went something like this: They believed they had secret knowledge or in Greek gnosis and thus the word Gnostic. The so-called gospel, they contended, was for the commoners and worthless for genuine salvation.

"According to them, the rabbi Jesus gave his closest followers, the Apostles, secret oral knowledge and this secret knowledge was transmitted only orally to others — the chosen, the spiritually gifted, the elite."

"We have had and still do have our share of elitists," Menachem interrupted. Menachem, like so many political and military leaders, was a secularist and attached little or no importance to the halakah (ritual law).

"I don't want to dwell on the Gnostics but one other of their teachings was the split between spirit and matter. The soul was essentially good, the body essentially evil. It has a lot of ramifications when marriage, for example, is the topic of discussion." Joshua laughed at the earthy implications he was nuancing.

"Anyway one of the Gnostics, a man by the name of David of Arimathea, had a private vision of Michael the Archangel. In that vision, as the story goes, the Archangel gave to David a secret incantation.

"If anyone performed this incantation, he would become the most powerful man on earth, the most powerful in the world. He would in fact be the one and only world leader."

"Or she," Menachem corrected. "Let us never forget that women too enjoy the idea of having unlimited power. I must admit I worry about religious practices based on pie-in-the-sky promises and cosmic threats. And I can't tolerate the fierce looking faces of the humorless religious either."

"Quite. There was a catch, however, and it was this: only the person with the true faith could recite the incantation to get all this power. If someone without the true faith did the ritual of this incantation, that person would die a most torturous death.

"Well, David of Arimathea did the unpardonable act. He wrote down his vision in Aramaic together with the words of the incantation. For that the Gnostics excommunicated him, ignoring what his vision was all about. For them it had to be oral teaching or nothing.

"Now comes a gap. A big one. A gap that spans over a thousand years."

"Not exactly a tight-knit story, is it?" Menachem remarked without any indication of frivolity or seriousness. "You have to wonder if the truth lies somewhere on the far side of madness, don't you?"

Ignoring Menachem's interjection, Joshua continued. "Apparently the document doesn't turn up again until during the first Crusade in around the end of the eleventh century.

"According to my source, a nephew of Count Raymond of Toulouse, Antoine Bisset, came across a Jewish rabbi while Jews were being massacred during that Crusade.

"As Antoine Bisset prepared to sever the rabbi's head from his body, the old man pleaded for his life.

"'Please, mighty warrior, spare my life. I still have so much more to learn.'

'Why should I care about your scholarly pursuits, you unbeliever?' Bisset threatened.

'I have something here to make it worth your while. It is a prayer that can make you and you alone the most powerful man in the world — the whole world!'

'If such a prayer exists, why did you not say it? You would now be the most powerful man in the world and would not be standing here waiting to meet your Yahweh.'

'I have no need, no desire for such power. I am but a simple rabbi.'

'Give me that prayer,' Bisset demanded.

'Here,' the rabbi reached into an a roll of papers and produced an ancient looking document — *the* document, as it turned out. He handed it to the Crusader, slyly smiling as he knew this butcher would surely die a most gruesome death if he ever tried to perform the incantation. No one of such violence could have the true faith.

The smile was still on his face as his head rolled to ground."

"Any record of the Crusader using the incantation?" Menachem asked, now fully enthralled with the story.

"If he did, it didn't work. Antoine Bisset certainly never became the most powerful man in the world. And he lived long enough to return home to Toulouse. Perhaps he never bothered to have the document translated from Aramaic to French.

"He does mention the document in his memoirs of the Crusade, as I understood from our informant. But apparently only as a souvenir of his great valor in lopping off the head of a poor defenseless rabbi."

"The Crusaders were such valiant warriors," Menachem sneered. "How easily people are seduced by the trivia of religion preserved in a plastic world of ornamental goodness."

"There is yet another gap," Joshua continued. "According to the tale of the informant, two or three centuries elapsed. Then one of Bisset's descendants, who had fallen on hard times, took the document to the Vatican Library. There he sold it to one of the curators for a mere pittance.

"Whether he told the curator what the contents of the document were or whether the curator ever bothered to find out is not clear. It seems that the document was placed in the stacks and forgotten."

"Some strange way to handle a document that purportedly offered such power," Menachem remarked. "You know, I've always tried to be tolerant of utopian dreamers. They may be the light shining into tomorrow, but this sounds like some kind of subversive mysticism."

"Isn't all mysticism subversive?" Joshua asked innocently.

"Joshua, why don't we leave this stuffy room and go outside for a walk while you continue with this intriguing story?"

They both went outdoors and walked away from the Kibbutz where they could be alone. Menachem greeted some children who were playing ball.

"Now then," Menachem said, "please continue." He said this with a smile which Joshua interpreted as a sign that Menachem didn't believe a word of the tale but found the story entertaining enough to want to listen to more.

"In 1945, near the end of the Second World War," Joshua was warming up to what he considered the best part of the legend, "a German priest who worked in the Vatican Library by the name of Hermann Gofner — I must admit, I myself am a bit captivated by the way these names have all been preserved — came across the document. Apparently he was literate in Aramaic and he translated the document into German.

"When he discovered what the contents were, he contacted a Nazi Colonel by the name of Franz Kueger. Gofner gave both the original and the translation to Kueger.

'Take these to the Fuhrer at once,' Gofner urged. 'These documents contain the secret of attaining all the power in the world. The one who recites this incantation will become the most powerful man on earth.'

'The Fuhrer has the true faith,' Gofner explained. 'By using this incantation he will be able to reverse the doom that is threatening the Third Reich and win the war.'"

"Come, Joshua," Menachem invited. "Let us sit here in the shade. There is a slight breeze and perhaps the shade will cool us."

They both sat down. "Please continue," Menachem said as he stifled a yawn brought on by the heat of the day.

"Well apparently Gofner was so enthusiastically persuasive that Kueger set out for Berlin immediately.

"But by the time he got to the border, Hitler was already in his bunker and any hope of victory for the Reich was hopeless. So Kueger joined the retinue of an S.S. General, Gerhard Hummel. And with Hummel he escaped to Argentina, taking with him the original and the translation of the document."

"We never did get Hummel," Menachem sighed. "Just as we were ready to close in on him, he committed suicide. May he rot in hell. When you survey the flatland of life, you find there are no villains or heroes, no saints or devils — just victims, most of them self-made."

"Kueger settled in Rosario, a seaport in the east central part of Argentina on the Parana River, about one hundred and ninety miles northwest of Buenos Aires. Hummel settled in Buenos Aires.

"Kueger married an Argentinean woman and worked as a fisherman. They had one daughter, Marissa.

"Life was good for Kueger. Years passed and his daughter, a beautiful young woman, at the age of twenty-two, married Caesar Lopez, an Argentinean archeologist in 1970.

" But then one night while drinking with a friend, Josef Hesler, Kueger, in a drunken state, began to brag about how he could be the most powerful man in the world if he wanted to be.

'I have a document — no, two documents — with this incantation to Michael the Archangel. If you perform this incantation properly and you have the true faith, you will be the most powerful man on earth.'

'Well,' Hesler scoffed, 'why haven't you done it? Why do you stink yourself with fish every day?

'Because, my dear Hessler, if you don't have the true faith, and you perform this ritual, you will die a most torturous death. That is right in the document. You'd have to be a madman to chance it. Anyway all I believe in is my family and the fish in the river."

Hessler, who was a devotee of the former S.S. General, Gerhard Hummel, went to Buenos Aires and reported Kueger's revelation to Hummel.

Not long after that, one night when Kueger was leaving the Bundsbar, a car pulled up and two men jumped out, grabbed Kueger and whisked him off to Hummel in Buenos Aires.

Marissa and her mother waited for two days. Then they reported Kueger missing. Nothing was done.

"Meanwhile General, now simply Herr Hummel, and his minions were busy torturing Kueger to force him to tell them where the documents were. The torture was excruciating.

"Finally Kueger broke and told them he had given the documents to his daughter for safe keeping. Hummel shot Kueger between the eyes.

"Two days later when Marissa went to visit her mother to find out if she had heard anything about her father, she found her parents house in a shambles and her mother lying dead in the middle of the kitchen floor. She called the authorities. Nothing was done.

"She called her husband and he met her back at their apartment. That, too, had been ransacked. There was a note on the wall inside the narrow hallway that led from the living room to the kitchen. GIVE US THE DOCUMENTS OR JOIN YOUR PARENTS.

"Marissa was terrified. He husband had put the documents into a safe deposit box with the few valuables they had.

"'I'll give them to whoever wants them,' Marissa cried. 'No,' her husband disagreed. 'Can't you see? You give them those documents and they will kill you — and me — as they did your mother and presumably your father, if we are to believe that scrawling on the wall.

'You know I've been thinking about going to Iran for that dig that is now in progress. I'll get our money and clean out our safe deposit box. You gather what we can carry. There is nothing to keep us here and one very urgent reason to leave — our lives.'

'But my father?'

'Your father is dead. We have to leave at once. Whoever these people are, one thing we know. They are cold-blooded murderers.'"

"All this over that document?" Menachem was incredulous. "Why is it that people live in the straight lines and squares of opposition instead of in circles of relationships?"

Joshua continued spinning the tale as he had heard it from his informant.

"Marissa and Caesar fled by night to Buenos Aires. They hid out for two days while they made arrangements to book passage on a freighter that was headed for Spain.

"On the night of their departure, as they were sneaking toward the ship, they were suddenly surrounded by four men carrying Lugers. Marissa screamed as one of the thugs grabbed hold of her while shoving his gun at Caesar.

"'Give us those documents,'" the man holding Marissa growled, "'and we will let you board the ship.'

Just then there was the sharp crack of a gunshot and the man who had grabbed Marissa fell quietly to the ground, a gaping wound in his forehead. Simultaneously the other three men were grabbed from behind and when Marissa looked again, all three were lying on the ground with their throats slit, blood pouring profusely onto the ground.

"A short heavyset man approached Marissa and Caesar. 'I am Otto Liemelch,' he said introducing himself as if they were at some social gathering. I was a corporal serving your father. Your father once saved my life. Long ago when you were still an adolescent, your father asked me to watch over you. Like a guardian angel.

'When I heard of your father's disappearance and your mother's brutal murder, I gathered my companions here and we followed you to Buenos Aires. We knew you were planning to leave the country and so we kept watch until you were gone.'

'Fortunately for us,' Caesar held his wife, comforting her, hoping she would not go into shock.

'May God go with you,' Liemelch smiled as he waved them off.'"

"Whether it's a true story or not," Menachem laughed, "it is certainly one of the best stories I've heard in a very long time."

"Oh, there's more," Joshua sounded as if he was becoming weary and could hardly wait to get to the end.

"Please, Joshua, do not give me the abridged edition," Menachem had that menacing tone when he wanted others to know he meant what he said. He stood up and stretched. Joshua remained seated and didn't particularly like looking up at Menachem as he continued.

"Marissa and Caesar made their way from Spain to Iran. It took them over a year and they arrived almost penniless. Caesar joined the excavators but he and Marissa were still hard pressed even for their daily sustenance.

"Finally Caesar talked Marissa into selling the documents. When they went to get them, all they could find was the German translation. The original was gone. They had no idea what had happened to it.

"Caesar took the German rendition to a scholar he had heard about and asked him to translate it into Iranian. The Iranians would be his market.

"Several weeks later when Caesar went to get the German and Iranian documents, the scholar had disappeared.

According to the story, the scholar brought his Iranian translation to an ayatollah who, when he was told about the contents, paid handsomely for the document. Later he had the scholar killed and retrieved his money.

"Now," Joshua took a deep breath, "here's where it becomes really interesting. You wondered about the authenticity of this document, Menachem? Well, this next episode is as much a part of the story as the printing on the document."

"Believe me, Joshua, I am all ears, as they say."

"This ayatollah — and surprisingly there is no name — performed the ritual and within two hours, died a most horrible death. He bled from his eyes, ear and nose. He went into traumatic shock and shook until his bowels burst through his anus and then his head caved in and he died. It is said you could hear his screams all the way to Jerusalem."

"When did this happen?" Menachem asked.

"Sometime in the late 1970s. Now we have another time gap. Apparently the document was locked up. It wasn't until about two years ago that it was rediscovered by another ayatollah, Ruhollah."

"Where in the name of all that is holy did this story come from, Joshua?"

"You see, Menachem, this story I've just told you is incorporated into the document. Apparently, for instance, Caesar Lopez told the scholar about his and his wife's misadventures as well as Marissa's father's tale. Part of Bisset's memoirs about his crusade is also included. And, of course, the story of the torturous death of the ayatollah.

"A servant of the ayatollah who now possesses the document told our informant. It seems that the ayatollah has surreptitiously put the document up for sale."

"Obviously the ayatollah is not buying into the tale of power," Menachem smirked again. "He'll just use it to line his own coffers if he can. But who in the name of all that's holy would even consider buying it?" Menachem sat back down and frowned. "Who in his right mind?"

"This is the clincher, Menachem. Our informant told me that someone in the Roman Church has put in a bid."

"You're kidding. I mean he has to be kidding. That's as farcical as the story you just told."

"The bid is for a half billion dollars." Joshua sat and for the first time smiled at the clouded, befuddled look on Menachem's face.

"And so," Menachem said in his official tone, "this is the new weapon the Iranians possess? What tripe! It's an interesting story as stories go but, Joshua, it's the craziest myth, the silliest fabrication, a hoax. Pure bullshit!"

"Maybe and maybe not," Joshua said solemnly. Menachem didn't know it he was putting him on or was he really serious?

"Suppose that that business about having the true faith was authentic. How many down through the eras may have tried the incantation and died like the story of that ayatollah? We just don't have any record of those deaths. Don't forget the huge time gaps in the story."

"Are you seriously telling me you give credence to this .... this superstitious yarn?" Menachem's skepticism was visible as the quake in his voice.

"No," Joshua replied sincerely. "I just find it a fascinating tale."

"So do I, Joshua. So do I. But that certainly doesn't make it authentic. It's rubbish."

"What do you think about someone in Rome wanting to buy it," Joshua asked as though he hated to see the closure on the topic.

"That, too, is pure bullshit. Although if ever there was anyone who would believe that he had the true faith, it would have to be someone as arrogant as a Roman Catholic.

"Still ...." Joshua was hesitant, his face empty of emotion, just his brown eyes fastened on the pages of notes he had jotted down from the informant's monologue. "I mean .... what if it might be ...."

"True?" Menachem shouted in disbelief, his usual placid look now screwed up in an expression of apparent horror at the very suggestion.

"Well …. the incantation would be …. be the most formidable weapon …." Joshua seemed to sense he was on dangerous ground.

"Listen to yourself, Joshua!" Menachem's volume was still as vehemently loud as a teacher trying to get across an obvious point to a slow learner. "You've allowed that stupid story to dislodge your logic." Menachem rubbed his broad forehead with his huge hand. "That story is as nonsensical as the one about a crucified carpenter rising from the dead."

"If you say so, Menachem." Joshua spoke with the reluctance of a child who still believed that a magic staff in the hand of Moses could slither like a snake.

"Joshua, please, don't tell a living soul how much money we squandered to get this information. Let's keep it our little secret, all right?"

"I certainly don't want to be held up to ridicule, Menachem. It will indeed be our secret — to the grave."

Joshua got up and walked away from Menachem still clutching his notes in his hand. He wished with all his heart that he had as little belief in the supernatural as Menachem.

Menachem continued to sit in the shaded spot. He hoped that Joshua's apparent belief about the authenticity of the incantation story would never be his.

As Joshua walked back to the kibbutz, he was lost in thought. He was an avid student of history. He believed that history which does not teach lessons is like a stagnant pond. All you see is the scum of the past.

Joshua always wanted to taste the refreshing waters of history's living lessons. The lesson history was teaching him at this moment was never to shove into oblivion even the craziest sounding claim to power. That's what his people did in Nazi Germany.

A history lesson ignored was an historical event bound to be repeated. The current lesson to be learned from this Iranian document is the old adage, To fail to plan is to plan to fail. He hoped the plan he was devising would not be lost in the maze of political expediency or in the cull de sac of ideological opposition. After all, better safe than sorry.

THE NEWS BROADCAST

Ever since the Cardinal's Secretary's call in the late afternoon Danny had been feeling an exuberance the likes of which he had not felt since his days in Rome when he was studying for his doctorate.

He felt intellectually stimulated, alive, challenged. He had gone to the attic and brought down three boxes of books and as many boxes of printouts. He was going through them marking off anything he could find on the Mystical Body.

He had also retrieved his own dissertation entitled, "The Process of God's People." He had investigated the ramifications of Process Theology on the Church as an institution. He had dealt with the title from Vatican II, The People of God, rather than the Mystical Body. Still his dissertation might prove useful. Anyway he had done it under the tutelage of Professor Percussi.

He smiled to himself as he allowed a spark of vanity to shoot through his enthusiasm. Had his dissertation played any role in John Paul IV's decision to write an encyclical on the Mystical Body? With more realistic humility, he decided he was really stretching it.

He wondered again just how much input he would have in the final draft of the encyclical. Of course, there would be many other theologians involved. And the final draft would have to pass muster with the Prefect of the Congregation for the Doctrine of the Faith.

Still he felt elated to have been one of those chosen. And he was looking forward to being with his old professor again.

The phone sounded. The phone butler spoke, "You have a call. Do you wish to go online or should I take a message?" "Online, please," Danny responded as he got up from his chair and walked over to his desk. It was Hank "The Flash" Covey, a regular parishioner who looked to Danny for personal and honest support in his legendary feats on the gridiron. Hank had been chosen first string tailback on the All American High School Football Team. He had rolled up more than a thousand yards more rushing than the player who was on the second team.

Danny clicked on his viewscreen. "Hi-ya, Hank. How's it going?"

"Hi, Father Joe. Father Joe, the coach from Notre Dame is coming here to see me. You 'member I was out there in November and February." Hank had been recruited by every major college in the United States and Danny was very proud of him.

"The head coach? Gary Westermann?" Danny asked enthusiastically.

"Yup."

"That's great, Hank.

"Father Joe, I always was thinkin' 'bout Notre Dame like I told ya. But I don't want to go to no college that's goin' make me no defensive back. I go as a runnin' back or I ain't goin'."

"I know, Hank. And I think you're right."

"Well, I don't want no head coach comin' here tellin' me he needs me on defense and think 'cause I'm a dumb black kid I'll go for it."

"Hank, how many times do I have to tell you that you're not dumb. I've told you there are all kinds of different brains. You have physical intelligence that's right up there in the genius category."

"Yeah but when it comes to talkin' and thinkin' things through, I ain't that bright. I just don't want to get pushed into nothin' widout somebody helps me."

"Okay, Hank, what can I do for you?"

"Will you be there wit me, Father Joe?"

"Hank, I'd be honored. When?"

"About four o'clock here at my house. A week from Thursday."

"I'll be there. With bells on, as they say."

"Gee, Father Joe, thanks a whole lot. My mom will be real happy. Goodbye, Father Joe."

"Goodbye, Flash." Danny was joined by Hank in laughter.

Hank's mom was, like so many moms in The Alley, a living saint. He prayed that Hank would do well enough to get into the pros and get his mother out of The Alley if she would go.

While he was there he decided to call Gene.

Trying to keep his excitement at a reasonable level, Danny told Gene about Richards' call.

"Wow!" Gene exclaimed. "That's fabulous, Danny! Did Richards tell you how you got chosen?"

"No. And I didn't ask him."

"Good for you. Do you know when you have to go? How long will you be over there? Who else will be with you? You'll probably be hobnobbing with the finest minds in the Church. And, if I know you, you'll be *the* shining light."

"A bit of an exaggeration, I'm sure," Danny said with proper modesty. "But I am excited at the opportunity."

"And well you should be. What an honor!" Gene, true friend, was genuinely proud. "Have you told Celine yet?"

"No, I'm going to call her as soon as we're finished talking. There's something else I want to tell you, Gene."

"What's that?"

Danny told Gene about his visit with Steve. He emphasized Steve's words which had been haunting him ever since. "Steve said, 'When you're at death's door, a lot of things you thought were really important are actually insignificant.'

"Even before I got Richards' call, I had made up my mind to turn that note over to Archbishop Brown and put this thing behind me. Who Viri Lucis is and what they're about is one of those insignificant things in my life. And now with this other challenge .... well, I've got to get on with my life."

"Danny, I really think that is the wisest decision you've made on this whole matter. Look, there are many wonderful priests in the Church. If there are some who are less than noble, let those in charge take care of them.

"Nobody's going to bring the Church to ruin. We have Christ's promise .... 'until the end of time' and we've got to believe that more than anyone else in the Church. I'm really happy you've come to that decision, Danny. Celine will be ecstatic when you tell her. I don't know which piece of news to celebrate more."

"Okay, Gene. I had better call Celine now. Goodbye for now. Talk to you later."

"Goodbye, Danny, and God bless."

Danny recited Celine's number and got a the butler voice recording telling him she was not available. He knew she would be at her office but didn't want to disturb her there. He left a message asking her to give him a call.

He went back to his books and scholarly printouts, paging slowly through them. What a wonderful day. A great conversation with Steve, his decision about the note, Richards' call, Hank Covey's call, his conversation with Gene, going through his books and printouts, the challenge of working with Percusssi. What a day!

That evening his phone sounded. It was Celine. Danny told her first about Richards' call.

"Oh, Danny, that's wonderful! That is truly the best news you've received in years. How happy and proud I am that you're finally being recognized. When will you have all the details?"

"I'm supposed to get a letter from the Secretary of State soon. I'll fill you in whenever I find out all that's involved."

"I just can't get over it. That the Pope should remember you from when you studied under him. How absolutely wonderful!"

"I have other news too, Celine."

"What's that?"

Danny told Celine about his visit with Steve. And about Steve's statement about what's important and what's insignificant.

"And so I've decided to let you get me a lawyer and get on with it. I'll turn the note over to Archbishop Brown."

Celine's reaction wasn't the same as Gene's. "It may not be legal in the strictest sense," she said. "On the other hand, besides you only Viri Lucis, Travine, Gene and I know about the note. I don't think your bishop friend had any inkling of what he was getting you into. I'm sure if he had known, he would never have asked you to do what he requested."

On a more encouraging note, Celine said, "I think you've made the right decision. Do it!"

"Thanks, Celine. I'll be talking to you later."

"Okay, Danny. And I want you know that I'm going to miss you while you're in Rome."

"Ditto in spades, Celine" Danny enjoyed using twentieth century slang.

The next morning, Danny got up and was surprised at how well he had slept. He went over for Mass and returned to the rectory hoping he'd hear from the Secretary of State that day. There was nothing. He'd just have to wait. Even for his classmate, Douglas Haynes, the wheels of the Vatican moved as slowly as the passage of centuries. Rome wasn't built in a day, Danny smiled to himself.

About a week later, Danny's phone sounded. It was Gene.

"Hi, Gene, what's up?"

"Do you have your NewsNet on?"

"Not yet." Danny said with a feeling of apprehension.

"Activate Channel 51A," Gene said without explanation.

"That junkheap on the sophisticated landscape of journalism?" Danny was more than a little puzzled.

"Activate it!" Gene ordered. "I'll talk to you later."

"Channel 51A," Danny called out.

He stood there staring at pictures of Celine and himself with their names printed underneath the pictures. Under the pictures, the headline caption read:

INNER CITY PRIEST AIDED BY LONGTIME
UPTOWN LAWYER MISTRESS.
LIVE COVERAGE

Danny was in shock. He slumped down into a kitchen chair. Staring. Numb from head to toe. For a long while he didn't hear the over voice. Then the words began to filter into his anguished brain.

.... who, according to a highly placed
official in the Roman Catholic Church,
has been having a clandestine affair
with Mrs. Celine Korbach for the past
six years.

Mrs. Korbach is employed by the prestigious law firm of Lambert, Hudson and Greer. She is married to George Korbach, a prominent entrepreneur in Chicago. According to the source, Mrs. Korbach met Father Joseph Daniels while she was still single and was doing charitable work for the residents of The Alley where Father Daniel's church is located.

Father Daniels has been pastor of St. Matthew's for about thirteen years. Neither one could be reached for comment. People contacted in The Alley were shocked at the news.

Then there were several pictures one after another of people Danny recognized as parishioners. It was all like a verbal typhoon. Danny could barely concentrate. Mrs. Johnson was pictured, saying:

We all love Father Joe. This is terrible. We know his friend, Celine. She's a wonderful woman. I just can't believe it.

Then there was Therese Lopez:

I think priests should be married. Then you wouldn't have something like this. My heart breaks for both of them. I have always loved Father Joe ever since I was a little girl when he first came here. I can't believe you people are doing this to him. He's such a holy man ....

Danny heard the voices but he no longer was able to hear what was being said. His eyes filled. Shock could not begin to describe what he was feeling. "Print!" he yelled. Then, "Off!"

He sat there in a mind-boggling stupor. Those bastards! The Viri Lucis! They're responsible. They promised retaliation. Poor Celine. And Danny began to shake with anger, crying silently.

He felt as though an artist whose palette was overflowing with black paint had slashed broad brush strokes of despair all over the canvas of his life.

He was devastated, humiliated, heartbroken as though someone had abducted his soul, exposed it to the jeers of a screaming mob and then chained it in the dark depths of Hell.

He felt invaded as if a barbaric horde had charged into the private sanctuary of his conscience and desecrated all that was sacred and meaningful in his relationship with God. His future, he knew, was crumbling like a sand castle in a hurricane.

Poor Celine! Oh my God. My God. What have they done? Viri Lucis! Those rotten lousy bastards! How in God's name could they put their Roman collars on in the morning? If he had given that goddamn note to Brown twenty four hours earlier, this would never have happened. Oh my God.

And the news report lied. They made it sound like there was an 'affair.' What will George think? Will he believe that he and Celine had only made love once.

He heard his phone. He looked over at it. It was Gene. "… or should I take a message?" the butler voice asked. "No response," Danny answered. He couldn't think never mind talk.

Celine was making her way to her office. She looked especially bright. She should. She was so happy for Danny.

She noticed strange furtive glances from the secretaries. What's up? she wondered. Something wrong? She sat down behind her desk. Her secretary came in. No usual cherry good morning. Her secretary looked gruesomely somber.

"What's up, Helen? Somebody die?" Celine tried to look pleasantly nonchalant.

"Did you see Channel 51A this morning?" Helen asked quietly.

"No. Why? I don't make it a practice to look at that gossipy slop that passes itself off as a news program."

"Well," Helen said as she called for a repeat, "you'd better have a look at this."

Celine sat staring. If she was reacting to it, there was no sign of it on her face except that it was as pale as whitewash. Then her hands began to shake. "Could you leave me alone, Helen?"

Helen left without a word and closed the door behind her.

The phone sounded. It was Margaret.

"I can't talk now, Margaret." Celine's voice sounded sepulchral.

"I understand, dear. But you're going to have to talk. I just want you to know I'm here."

"Thanks and goodbye."

In a wild rush of images, Celine thought of Danny, her job, her father, George. Oh my God, George! Had he seen? If so why hadn't he called? This was so unfair — so hideously unfair! There had been no affair!

How was Danny reacting. He was so happy yesterday and now this …. Had old man Lambert heard yet? All her friends who thought she was so straight laced? How was she going to leave her office? She would storm out. That's what everyone would be expecting.

Celine got up, grabbed her attaché case, flung open the door and stomped out past all the secretaries, calling after her to Helen, "Cancel all appointments for the day!"

When she got to the lobby floor and the elevator door opened, Celine was faced with a raging mob of reporters. They were screaming at her like starving vultures. Cameras zeroed in on her like a swarm of fireflies.

"Mrs. Korbach! Mrs. Korbach! Is there any truth to the report ….?"

"How long have you and the priest been lovers?"

"Can you give us a few words on this ….?"

"What's your husband's reaction?"

"Have you been fired?"

"Will you sue?"

"Where is your lover now? Have you been in contact with him?"

Celine pushed by them all, giving a few a good push as she stormed out. She was so angry at them she was able to hold back her tears of frustration and hurt.

Now that she was out of there, where would she go? There probably were reporters at her apartment too. Maybe there was some out of the way bar she could disappear into.

Disappear. That's what she wanted right now more than anything in the world. She wanted to be alone. All alone. Finally she ducked into a little dark bar, found a table and sat down.

The bartender called out, "What's your pleasure, lady?"

"Ginger water," she called back.

She paid him when he served her. Then he went back behind the bar, busying himself there. Celine crumbled in the seat and cried quietly and profusely. If the bartender saw her, he paid no attention.

After a long while, Celine got up and without a word left.

She began walking aimlessly up one street and down another. Sometimes she would stop and look at a display in a store window. Nothing was registering. She was as numb. A corpse. No feelings, no thoughts, no images. She walked for hours.

Finally she stopped and went into a little restaurant. She walked to the back where there were phones. She waved her hand over one of them, activated it, spoke her home telephone number, placed her credit card in the slot and waited. There was no viewscreen to click on.

"Hello," George gasped.

"George, it's me."

"Celine! Are you all right? Where have you been? I've been worried sick. Where the hell are you?"

"George, I want to come home," Celine said without answering his questions.

"Do you want me to come for you?" George's voice was tortured.

"No, I'll get a pod." Celine sounded flat and lifeless, dull and emotionless, weak and tired. Her words seemed to come from an anguished emptiness deep within her.

"Come right home, Honey. Are you all right?"

This time Celine answered. "I'm okay. Tired. Been walking all day."

"I'll be waiting for you, Celine. Please get a pod right now and come home."

"Goodbye George. I'll see you in a little while."

It seemed to take all her strength to flag a pod. One stopped. Celine got in gave the driver the address, sat back and for the first time that day she let herself go and relaxed. Still her mind was like a stage where the heavy curtains had been drawn closed and the lights extinguished.

When Celine entered her apartment her hair was wind blown. Had the circumstances been different, she would have looked comical. George rushed to her and threw his arms around her. He held her tight. "I was so worried. My God, I didn't know what happened to you. Celine. Why didn't you call me?"

"I don't know. I was so upset. I was embarrassed. Heartsick. George, that was a goddamn lie. There has absolutely been nothing between Danny and me except for that one time They lied. And they never tried to contact me before they ran that story. Oh, George, the reporters were all there when I got off the elevator. They were screaming questions at me. I was terrified. What's going to happen to me? To Danny?"

George continued to hold Celine, soothing her, saying nothing, just being there. She fastened her arms around his neck fiercely. He could never remember her holding him so tightly. Despite the tragedy of it all, George had never felt so reassured since the day they were married.

He loved Celine more than he could ever describe but he always doubted that she loved him with the same intensity. Now he believed she really did love him and under different circumstances he would have cheered and danced. As it was, he stood there letting her bury herself in his strength.

Finally, George whispered, "Come on I have some soup ready for you."

"I am hungry. Didn't eat all day. Oh, George, don't be angry."

"My God, Celine, angry is the last thing I'd be. I'm just so relieved that you're all right. I'm just happy I can be here to help you through this. But we'll talk about that later. For now, come and eat some soup. I also poured you a very dry martini."

For the first time, Celine looked at George. And as if to prove that miracles do happen, a weary smile etched across her lips. "I love you," she said almost shyly as though for the first time she was feeling what she was saying.

"And I love you, Celine, more than you'll ever know. We'll see this thing through. Don't worry. We'll see it through." George's eyes filled and he wasn't quite certain if they were tears of empathy for Celine's pain or tears of joy for her love

Danny had spent his day roaming around the rectory, tidying up, fixing this and that, staring out the window, sitting down and getting up to roam some more. Except for Gene's call early that morning which he didn't answer, there had been no calls. No one had come to the rectory. He had never felt so alone. So lonely. So helplessly frustrated. Do damnably angry.

His brain had shut down and his mind had been a blank all day. Just a throbbing ache in the pit of his stomach. He wanted to vomit the whole experience out of his life. But he couldn't.

He had fully expected to get a call from Monsignor Richards.

This time the viewscreen would be on. There he would be, that debonair caricature of clericalism, his eyes uncharacteristically squinting as though he were examining Danny under a moralistic microscope.

His smile beaming with self-righteous violence. His words measured out in the cadence of damnation like the merciless Cherubim at the gate of Eden.

Hello, Father Daniels, he would say in that peripherally polite tone of his. My, my, haven't we been having a busy life. Scholar and adulterer. How blessed we are to have such talent right here in our own Archdiocesan backyard. Nothing like serving the poor and screwing the rich.

I wonder what his Holiness will say when *I* report this tidy little mess to him.

Your Holiness, here is St. Nicholas and Don Juan spliced together like fantasy and horror films. I'm certain, your Holiness, that Father Daniels will make an immortal contribution to your encyclical on the place of women in the Church. If you want to put flesh on your encyclical, Father Daniels is your man.

May I recommend to your Holiness that Father Daniels write an appendix to your encyclical? Perhaps "Intimacy Among the Members of Christ's Body." Yes, that should do it. Or perhaps, "Discovering the Mystical Body In the Body of Your Mistress." Yes, that's even more tantalizing. Or what about "Lusting For Union Within The Mystical Body."

Your Holiness, may I recommend Father Daniels for the top spot on the world's honor roll of all-time hypocrites? He is so deserving.

Danny was snapped out of his fantasy by the sound of the back door signal. He went to the door. It was an old fashioned door that still had a peep hole. Danny peered through it and saw Joan Cromlic, his principal standing there.

That's all I need today. Some insurmountable problem at the school.

He opened the door. "Hi, Danny," Joan said in an especially consoling tone. "I'm not here on business. I just thought …. well, maybe you'd like some company. If not, just say the word. I'll understand."

"Come in, Joan. Maybe I do need some company but I don't know how much company I'll be."

"How are you doing?" Joan asked. Solicitude was all over her face as well as in her voice.

"Not too well, I'm afraid. I guess there are times when sanity is more a burden than a refuge. This happens to be one of those times, Joan."

Suddenly, as if for the first time, Danny noticed what a wisp of woman Joan was. Her graying hair was pulled back neatly into a bun. Prim and proper. Her thin narrow face always seemed strained as though she was continually wondering if what she was doing with her life was the right thing to do. Her shoulders were a bit stooped and she had to make an effort to look up at Danny.

Except that it would be an unkind stereotype, she looked the part of an aging spinster. Yet behind her round brown eyes there was always the unmistakable sign of power or perhaps of total dedication which is the most formidable power of all.

Danny had nothing but the greatest respect for her as a professional, as a human being and most of all as a Christian who truly lived her faith. He deeply admired her selfless love for the children she guided so carefully and challenged so hopefully.

"I've been praying for you all day ever since I saw …." Joan seemed as though she couldn't bring herself to mention the news report.

"Thank you, Joan. I appreciate it. I really do."

"What are you going to do?"

"I don't know. Wait around for the dropping of the episcopal shoe, I guess."

"Oh my, you do sound apprehensive. A little self-pity too?" Joan laughed quietly.

"How about a drink?" Danny tried to sound like himself.

"Sure. A dry martini if you have the makings."

Danny's eyes filled as he heard the words, dry martini. Celine's favorite drink. He turned his head to the cupboard. "Coming right up," he said with feigned cheerfulness as he pushed aside the cocktail glass Celine had brought for her martini. "Don't mind using a water glass?" he asked.

" As long as it's very dry, I'll drink it out of your shoe," Joan laughed again hoping to brighten up an otherwise very despondent atmosphere.

Danny poured himself a hefty slug of bourbon and ran a little water into his glass.

"I don't think it's self-pity," he said as he put both glasses on the kitchen table. "Although I wouldn't rule it out entirely. All day long, more on an subconscious level, I've been searching my life story. Reviewing, if you will.

"You know that I believe a life story is the seedbed, the 'stuff' of a person's spirituality, of one's mysticism, if that doesn't sound too pretentious."

"It's not. And I do know what you mean," Joan said. "I've heard it so often from you. You know, spirituality isn't something over there that you step into and out of like a jacket. Your favorite word, compartmentalization."

"Right. And the integrating force of your spirituality is your life story," Danny spoke seriously as if trying to reinforce himself with his own convictions.

"You once used the example of someone with low self esteem who comes to God not be challenged but to be babied," Joan said reminiscently.

"I really believe it," Danny said seeming to welcome the distraction of the conversation. "How can someone love others if she doesn't first love herself?"

"She could," Joan said, "end up hating others or the Church or God or her spouse and so on down the line. Her children and who knows?"

"All because she won't do anything to develop and reinforce self esteem," Danny said. "'Grace builds on nature' and that for me anyway means that a person's spirituality has to be rooted in a healthy psychology, as you also have heard me say so often.

"I can identify with that," Joan said as she reached for some chips. "I left religious life because I was finding that I was becoming more self-centered within the warm comfortable cocoon of the community. It doesn't have to be that way but that's the way it was for me. While community gave me a 'we' it was not giving me a 'me.'

"I had to struggle after I left to find the authentic me. And, in effect, that was and still is a struggle for self esteem. But that's what life stories are all about, aren't they? Struggle."

"It reminds me of the story," Danny said, "of the man watching the movement within a cocoon. He watched for several days but nothing was happening. So he bent down a slit the cocoon with his pen knife. The moth emerged underdeveloped and died."

Joan laughed because she had heard him tell that story many times and couldn't help but join in as both she and Danny recited the ending together, "It's the struggle that transforms the moth into the beautiful butterfly." They both had a good laugh.

"It's a tightrope walk," Danny said almost ruefully, "between self esteem and narcissism. A precarious balance between being totally down on ourselves and overcompensating by being braggadocios."

Danny took a swig of his bourbon. "It's Celine I'm worried about more than myself."

"Have you talked with her?" Joan asked.

"No. I thought I'd wait till later. Maybe tonight. I don't know what to say. God she doesn't deserve this. We did not have an affair, Joan.

"God, you know you've done something wrong, you repent, you believe God has forgiven you and then your past catches up with you as a prosecuting attorney and judge who condemns. We're just loving friends."

"*Just* loving friends?" Joan exclaimed. "A loving friend is the most precious gift God can give us."

"True." Danny could feel the ache in his heart like an abscessed tooth.

"I would like you to think of me as a loving friend," Joan said quietly.

"I do, Joan. You'll never know how much I appreciate what you are doing for the children.

Joan seemed to withdraw. Was she asking for more? Danny wondered. God, I hope not. Once was more than enough.

"Well, I had better be going," Joan said as she stood up and took her glass to the sink. The cupboard door was still open and she saw

391

the cocktail glass and wondered why Danny had pretended he had only a water glass. "I'll keep praying for you, Danny."

"Thanks. You *are* a loving friend," Danny said without getting up.

Joan smiled. That seemed to be enough for her. As she got to the door she turned around. "You've been on the margin for a long time," she said. "Don't let this push you over to the other side. Your questioning is the lifeblood of your faith — and of ours, too. And, Danny, take it easy on the bourbon." With that she was gone.

Danny sat staring at the closed door. She truly was a wonderful person. He felt embarrassed for thinking she might want more than being *just* loving friends.

About an hour later, Danny called Celine's apartment. George answered. Danny could see from the expression on George's face that he was absolute distraught. He was also abrupt.

"I don't know where she is. I don't know how she is reacting to this. I don't know when or if she is coming home. I don't know one damn thing." George's voice broke Danny saw the tears in his eyes.

"If …. when she does contact you, tell her I am so sorry. I …."

"I'll convey your message," George interrupted. "I'm certain it will be a tremendous source of strength." With that George deactivated the phone.

Danny was desolate. He wanted someone to embrace him, hold him, tell him he was loved. He stood there enveloped by the aloneness that was his life.

THE FALLOUT

At about ten o'clock that night, Danny's night signal on his phone awakened him from a sleep of emotional exhaustion. He got up from his chair and clicked on his viewscreen hoping to see Celine.

It was Monsignor Richards.

Danny was taken aback. Richards did not have the officiously sardonic look Danny had expected. Instead he seemed grim, even concerned.

"Father Daniels, you are to report to Bishop Casey at ten o'clock tomorrow morning."

The viewscreen went blank. No goodbye, see ya around. So much for concern.

Danny went back to his chair. He wouldn't even get to see the Cardinal. Don Casey had been in Administration all his life. He was there when Danny had reported as the Cardinal's secretary. Don Casey had never cared for Danny. Called him the 'fair haired boy wonder.'

Word was that Casey suffered from the bitterness of failed ambition. He just couldn't handle the fact that he had been passed over so often. That he never was given his own diocese. As Vicar General/Secretary for Clergy and Religious, he was said to thrive on the revulsion the priests had for him.

It would not be a pleasant meeting, Danny sighed.

Danny picked up a folder that was laying on top of a box. Inside he found a poem he had written and forgotten about. He read it.

BECOMING

I was asked, "Who are you?"
    I answered,
I am one who is becoming,
    still becoming,
      forever becoming.

I am becoming maturity.
I am becoming love.
I am becoming poetry.
I am becoming holiness.
I am becoming me —
        the most treacherous
        ascension of all.

I am a perennial coming to
        full bloom and dying
            and blooming again.
My process of becoming
is the rhythm of resurrection.

My force is against
        those who would say, "You are."
A declarative sentence like
        a barbed wire fence of limitation
        all around me.
No outlet, no growth, no process.
        A concentration camp
        of just being.

My force is against
        those who would pigeonhole me,
        shoving me into airtight categories
        where all becoming
        is suffocated:
            male, white, extrovert, high J.

They forbid me from becoming
        more female
        or black, tan, yellow, even polka-dot
        or becoming an introvert
        lost within the secrecy of my
        thoughts, feelings, reactions

or a high P
allowing life to wash over me
without manipulating it
with shorelines
or sculpting it into the waterways
of my dimensions.

Yet despite the external shackles
of brazen socialization,
or the internal prison
of inferiority or insecurity,
my name is still
"Forever Becoming."

I am a spark of infinity
and can stretch beyond
out there with no boundaries
into a universe of possibilities
where my becoming is the becoming
of that universe.

There are those who despise
actually despise
my becoming.
It threatens them and they do
what any human does
when threatened —
they destroy.

But I am a spark of eternity
and becoming
is my inheritance from
the divine imagination
and there is no destruction
but self-destruction.

My own deliberate choice

to cease becoming
to jettison
the divine
the infinite
the eternal
and merely be a lump of inert clay
waiting passively
for final decay
with no laughter to sound the echo
of my visit here
with no tear to mark
the ground of my being here.

But there will be no such choice.
I am one who is becoming
and I will laugh and cry my way
into the One who is eternal Becoming
who treasures me
as forever becoming.

"…. there is no destruction but self destruction," Danny repeated the words aloud. Maybe that was too idealistic, he thought. There *is* destruction from outside us. That news broadcast is a perfect example. Perhaps he should have written something along the lines that no matter what destructive forces may be marshaled against us, we do not have to give up control.

Who controls me? he asked himself. Do I control myself or do I allow others to control me? Doesn't my very becoming all that I can be, all that God wants me to become, depend on my taking control of who I am despite the negative violence that people use to curtail my freedom?

How can I be in control of this disaster? What can I do to help Celine to be in control? Tomorrow I face Casey. Tomorrow Celine will no doubt face the three Senior Partners of the firm.

We may not be able to control what those in power may do to us. But we can control our reactions. We can forbid them from plunging us into depression or despair. They may control the events of our external lives but they cannot destroy our interior peace unless we let them.

That is where we still have control. That is where we still have the freedom of choice. No destructive force can stop any of us from becoming all we can be. We may be forced to change the external circumstances of our becoming but that will never hinder or cancel our becoming. Who knows? In the long run the change of circumstances could enhance and propel our becoming.

The next morning Celine went to her office. George had been so reassuring that she knew she would be able, as Margaret had quoted Eleanor Roosevelt, to walk into the main office wearing an invisible crown on her head.

Late in the evening she had received a call from her father who shocked her by telling her he was with her all the way. That he would stand by her and if she needed any legal help, his firm was at her total service. They had spent over an hour on the phone talking about a variety of strategies she could use when, inevitably, she faced the three Senior Partners of the firm. Her father was good. Damn good.

When Celine entered the office she noticed that the secretaries were still casting sheepish glances at her. She went into her office and sat down at her desk as Helen, her private secretary, entered.

"Helen, get me the Scapperelli file please," Celine spoke in even, controlled words. Helen smiled as if to say, "Atta girl!"

Upstairs on the top floor the three Senior Partners were seated in Sylvester Lambert's plush office. He, John Hudson and Simon Greer were huddled around the upper end of Lambert's huge conference table.

Lambert was the oldest of the Senior Partners at seventy-two. His slick white hair contributed to the air of dignity he exuded. He was a man always in control. Hudson, the youngest of the three at sixty-three years of age, was a ferret-faced individual whose demeanor signaled intimidation. Greer, a corpulent man in his late sixties, always gave the impression of serene joviality. Underneath that guise resided the most ruthless of the three.

Together they reigned over the firm that boasted of thirty-seven partners and two hundred and three associates and innumerable paralegals. They were men used to power and the wealth that could assure quantum leaps into even more power.

"We don't need the other partners for this. The firm cannot handle this kind of public scandal," John Hudson was saying. "There are norms and she has violated one of the most basic. She has brought disgrace to the firm and opened us to public ridicule."

"And what exactly do you want us to do?" Simon Greer asked pleasantly. "Let us not forget for one moment that Celine is one of the most productive members of the firm."

"If we fire her, she'll sue," Sylvester Lambert offered what he knew the other two already recognized. "And her father is no small time lawyer. He's good. Very good."

"No doubt at all that he would represent her interests," Greer said.

"We could let her go …. ask for her resignation with a promise of a fine recommendation and a huge bonus," Hudson suggested. "Let her go work for her father."

"Or," Sylvester Lambert spoke softly, almost conspiratorially, "we could let her stay on and treat her as a paralegal. Make life too miserable to endure, as it were.

"It's a shame," Greer responded, "she has been one of the most productive we have," Greer repeated himself as he most often did to the annoyance of all involved. "Don't forget, we were even considering her for a partnership not too long ago."

"Well, that's out the tube," Lambert slammed his hand on the table. "One thing I think we are all certain of is that Celine Korbach will never be a partner in this firm."

"It's down the tube, Syl," John Hudson said, enjoying the moment of correction to the point that he added, "It's out the window. Down the tube."

Lambert ignored the correction. "She will never be a partner in this firm."

"I like your suggestion, Syl," Simon Greer said, trying to counteract Hudson's gleefully delivered correction. "Already three very ultra conservative clients called and asked for someone else to represent them other than Mrs. Korbach."

"I think it's time to send for Mrs. Korbach," Sylvester Lambert said. "It will be interesting to hear her side of the story."

Danny showed up at ten o'clock. He sat in the large waiting room for forty minutes. At ten forty, a secretary appeared and with an artificial smile, said, "He'll see you now, Father."

"Good morning, Don," Danny greeted Bishop Casey in the most neutral tone he could muster. He sat down without being invited to do so. He noticed that having addressed the bishop informally brought a look of displeasure to his face.

"Father Daniels," Bishop Casey began without any of the usual formalities, "we have a very grave situation here."

"Tell me about it," Danny had now assumed a flippant air. Consciously or not, he was being defensive.

"I must tell you, Father Daniels," Bishop Casey insisted on keeping the encounter as formal as a small group sitting through a string recital of the Viennese waltzes of Johann Strauss, "that I strongly suggested to his Eminence that you be suspended pending further investigation. But our Cardinal has a soft spot in his heart for you. Why, I'll never be able to fathom.

"You've been a maverick, to say the least. Your public criticisms of the Archdiocese for not caring about the poor is a matter of record. Your disregard for the policies and procedures of the Archdiocese is legendary in the worst sense of that word. And now this." Casey could not have shown more disgust if he had practiced for months.

Bishop Casey rose and walked away from his desk. He turned his back to Danny. "You will report as chaplain to the retired Poor

Clares near Dearborn Park. If nothing else, it should prove a nice change of scenery from what you've been used to.

Danny sat in stony silence, the last vestige of defensive flippancy drained from his spirit like blood poured out of open wounds.

"You will report there tomorrow." Bishop Casey seemed to take special delight in this announcement. "You had better get back now. You have a lot of packing to do in a very short time."

Not one question as to the truth or falsehood of the accusation. Not one sound of compassion. Not one word as to what the procedure of the so-called "further investigation" would involve. Casey turned around to face Danny. There was an unmistakable smile of satisfaction on his face.

Danny rose. "What about St. Matt's?"

"No longer your concern, Father Daniels." Casey's officiousness filled the office and wrapped Danny in a suffocating grasp.

Danny took three steps toward Casey until he was towering over him. A look of fear streaked across Casey's chubby face. Danny could feel him tremble.

"What about the school?" Danny's voice was like a steel blade. "What about the *school?*" he repeated.

Casey had lost his composure. He seemed to be in a state of shock. "That …. that is n-n-not my domain. That is the province of …. of Sister Regina Pacis." Casey was whining. Then suddenly he shouted, **"Get out of here! Now! Or I'll see to it that you are stripped of every vestige of your priesthood. Get out!"**

Danny turned and stomped out of the Secretary of Clergy's office. As he propelled his way through the outer office, he ran literally into Monsignor Richards. "I'm sorry," the Cardinal's secretary said as he regained his balance. Danny didn't know if he meant he was sorry about what had happened or because he had been in Danny's way. Danny didn't care. Without a word he went through the glass doors and out into the corridor.

"Celine," Sylvester Lambert sounded almost syrupy. "So nice of you to come up." Both Hudson and Greer nodded and smiled in agreement. "Please be seated. Would you care for some coffee?" Lambert continued in a soft soothing voice.

Celine shook her head no.

"May we say," Hudson's voice was his usually bottom line tone, "how distressed we all are at the unfortunate news release that appeared on NewsNet yesterday?"

"No sorrier than I am," Celine sounded totally composed although she was worried her stomach would do a leapfrog and they would hear the noise of the splash into the abyss.

"Needless to say," Greer sounded cheery which was always a bad sign, "this unfortunate incident does present the firm with, shall we say, a certain perplexity."

"I would agree with you," Celine replied with a steady, studied voice like the one she used in court when she feared her opponent might have her up against the ropes, "provided 'this unfortunate incident' is a matter of fact."

The three men looked at one another quickly and with matching startled expressions. "Are you saying that the news report is groundless?" Hudson asked incredulously.

"Have you seen any proof?" Celine realized she had them up against the ropes.

"Are you denying it?" Lambert asked, trying to duplicate his former sweet tone but failing.

"Do I have to deny or admit?" Celine was a good lawyer. "As preeminent members of the legal profession, you need not be lectured to on the right a person has not to incriminate herself. Furthermore, you are all aware of the distinction between allegation and proven fact."

"But," Greer repeated what he had said earlier, "we have already had clients call and ask for someone other than you to represent them."

"And you of course will give me their names and let me talk with them." Celine was so matter of fact that she knew the three men on the other side of the glass ceiling were experiencing deep discomfiture.

"Why, yes. Of course, Celine." Lambert was backing off. Celine smiled engagingly.

"You are this priest's friend, are you not?" Hudson seemed to be assuming the role of prosecutor.

"That is a matter of record," Celine answered quickly. "I'm certain that all three of you have friends with whom you do not have sex?" She let the question hang in the midst of their growing confusion as she recalled Margaret's image of the good old boys bragging about their sexual conquests in the locker room at the golf course.

"By the way," Celine said almost offhandedly, "if there is any sort of recrimination, know that I will sue. And I have my father's assurance that all his resources will be mine."

Celine knew she had won. Guts, she thought, that's all it takes. Guts and a professional poker face. What was it she and Margaret had often laughed about? Woman's intuition is nothing else but man's transparency.

"There is really no need to talk like that, Celine. About initiating a suit, I mean. There's really no reason. We are men of integrity." Lambert was a beaten whelp.

"Provided there is nothing to this matter," Greer was not beaten. Never would be. He was the threat.

"Is there anything else?" Celine smiled broadly. She always mystified her employers. So beautiful and at the same time so cleverly brilliant. No doubt about it, she was an asset to the firm.

"No, nothing more," Hudson spoke for all three senior partners. "Except to say that we're sorry you were made the victim of such an atrocious slander.

"Anyone of us could be slandered, isn't that correct, gentlemen?" Celine stood up, turned around and left. "Have a nice day," she called over her shoulder. She hoped she could make it out the door before she collapsed right there in front of them or threw up.

The three senior partners sat and looked at each other. "Let's put the matter on the middle burner," Lambert suggested. The other two nodded and left without further discussion.

Monsignor Douglas Haynes approached Pope John Paul IV quietly, solicitously.

"I'm afraid I have some disturbing news, Holiness," Haynes sounded as though he was deeply concerned that bad news would upset the old man far beyond his capability of bearing unhappy personal information.

"Yes, what is it, Douglas? And you don't have to wear that worried look. I am quite capable of absorbing a karate chop."

"Well, Holiness, this may be just that. Joseph Daniels was accused on public newscasting of …. impropriety with a woman."

"True?" the old Pope asked in a shaky voice that indicated he was not as capable as he boasted about absorbing karate chops.

"He's been relieved of his parish and sent to a retirement home for Religious Women as chaplain."

"I am so sorry to hear this, Douglas. And I am sure you are grieving as well." The Pope's voice seemed to be hiding tears. "He was the most brilliant student …. so promising."

"I can only hope it's not true," Douglas said with a deeply sad expression on his face. "So far as I've been able to ascertain, there has been no denial."

"Under the circumstances, Douglas, I think it would be wise to tell Cardinal Tamacci to remove Joseph Daniels' name from the list of collaborators.

Douglas bowed and left the Pope to whatever real emotions he was now experiencing.

Douglas tapped on Tamacci's door as he always did.

"Yes, Monsignor, what is it?" Tamacci was brooding over some printouts on his desk.

"Eminence, the Holy Father has instructed me to ask you to remove Father Daniels' name from your list of collaborators. It seems …."

"Yes, I heard," Cardinal Tamacci cut him off.

"You did?" Douglas was genuinely surprised.

"It's a matter of public scandal in the Archdiocese of Chicago," Tamacci said. "As a matter of fact, in anticipation I have already removed the name of Joseph Walter Daniels."

"Thank you, Eminence," Douglas said as he nodded to the Cardinal who showed no regret. Douglas wondered not how but why the Secretary of State would be in possession of such information.

No sooner had Haynes left than Tamacci contacted the Mentor

"Yes, Camillo, what is it?"

"Father Joseph Daniels will not be coming to Rome."

"Excellent, Camillo. Now we must concentrate on getting that note. I repeat, do anything that has to be done."

"But," Tamacci sounded like a wounded bear, "I thought that was to be handled at your end. I am still working on the Perez and Rawmanda things."

"So be it," the Mentor replied with sizzling disdain, "the note will be handled from here. And Camillo, be sure to take care of the Perez and Rawmanda 'things.' What I need right now is that document. Goodbye, Camillo."

Danny was surprised at how little of this world's goods he had. Other than his books and printouts there really wasn't much. Gene had told him he could store his books and printouts at his rectory. Gene had been genuinely upset when Danny told him he had to leave St. Matt's. "That goddamn Viri Lucis," he had said. "I don't know if I'm madder at them or at our dear Bishop Casey. We'll talk when you get here."

Danny piled as many boxes of books and printouts into his car as he could. Then he drove to Gene's.

"Is this all of them," Gene asked as he told his two sextons where to put the books.

"There's more. I'll have to make two trips." Danny stared at the boxes of books, remnants of a much happier time in his life. An essential part of his biography. Now they sat there like accusations of a wasted intellectual life.

"Are they packed?" Gene asked.

"Yes," Danny said in a distracted tone.

"Then I'll have Jed here drive over in his truck and pick them up," Gene nodded to the sexton who nodded back.

Gene led Danny upstairs to his study. It was well furnished in brown leather with a huge desk up against the windows. The book cases were not all filled and most of the shelves had piles of magazine printouts on them.

"You could use a drink," Gene said rather than asked. "Smooth?" he asked.

"With water and ice and just a thumbful, please," Danny answered.

"I guess I had tried to pretend to myself that they wouldn't use that information," Danny said as he took the glass of bourbon from Gene. "I probably assumed that if they did, they would have contacted the Cardinal. I never dreamed they would go public with their accusation."

"Have you talked with Celine?" Gene had asked.

"No, I called but George was anything but receptive to my call." At that time Celine had not contacted him either. "I'm really worried about her. I'm presuming she finally came home but I don't know for sure. I was hoping she would call me. It's such a rotten mess.

"So how was our Secretary for Clergy?" Gene asked with contempt oozing through each word.

"Well," Danny said, "he not only kicked me out of St. Matt's but out of his office too." At this Danny smiled wryly. "Told me he'd strip me of every vestige of my priesthood." Danny told Gene how he had threatened Casey with physical presence and of Casey's trembling reaction.

Gene laughed out loud. "God, I would have given two months' collections to have seen that."

"Gene, the school's a goner. Casey said it's in Regina Pacis' hands. She won't be able to wait to wash those hands of my school. Of everything, that bothers me the most. Next to what this mess has done to Celine, I mean."

"Yeah, it's hard to decide where the damage has had its most disastrous impact," Gene said sympathetically.

"I keep thinking," Danny sighed, "if they had held off just for twenty-four hours. They would have had the damn note and none of this would ever have happened."

Gene buzzed downstairs. "Mrs. Caulley, may we have a plate of cheese, please."

"Gene, what if I just stayed at St. Matt's?" Danny asked abruptly as if thinking of this strategy for the first time.

"They'd suspend you. You'd be powerless. It would do more damage than good. You can't fight Casey anymore than City Hall. And wouldn't Casey just love for you to disobey."

"Yeah, like an old prof I had in Rome," Danny said. "Any time he was making what he thought was a very important point, he'd squint his right eye shut. One day he took that pose and said, 'The Church will never tolerate disobedience. Always be obedient. First you go and then you resign.'"

"Do you think if you gave Brown the note, they might retract the story," Gene asked feeling naive as he did.

"Not a chance. Remember your word? Ruthless. These guys play hardball."

"What're you going to do? I mean about the note," Gene asked.

"I don't know. Right now that's the least of my worries."

"You didn't admit anything to Casey?" Gene was making an effort to get back to what was immediately worrying Danny.

"He didn't ask," Danny replied. "A high up authority in the Church said I did it therefore I am guilty until proven innocent. He did mention 'further investigation.' I'm not quite sure what that meant. Maybe he thinks he can ferret out other scandalous misdemeanors I'm guilty of."

"Maybe you should get yourself a Canon lawyer," Gene suggested. "Casey can be most formidable and that's in spades when it comes to you. He was always envious of you."

"And all this under the guise of religion. Preserving the honor and glory of the Church." Danny sounded bitter. "I do have a classmate from Rome who had doctorates in both Canon and civil law. He's in Biloxi, Mississippi Bet he'd love to get his teeth into something like this."

"Unless he's personally ambitious. With those two degrees he may have his eye on the miter," Gene countered and knew he was being negative at the very time he should have been grabbing at any straw of hope.

"Yeah," Danny agreed. "It's interesting how toothless ambition can be when it comes to taking a bite out of the institution."

"It's still worth the try," Gene tried to be reassuring in the face of his just having thrown a negative block in the way of Danny's hopes.

"Well, Danny roused himself, "I have to get over to my new digs." Then with a break in his voice, he said, "I won't even be able to say goodbye to my people — to the children. That's cruel, Gene. How can those who profess the love of Christ be so cruel? What's wrong with the system? I could go over to the school tomorrow before I leave. No, no, there would be too many questions. Those children don't need to be clobbered with more cruelty in their lives. Joan will handle it."

"It's not the system," Gene said pensively. "It's some of the people in the system. Sometimes I think our obsession with keeping the rules and balancing the books has robbed some of our confreres of the spirit of Jesus."

"And then there's the hang-up with purity or chastity," Danny added. "You can hate or destroy another person and it's confessed as a venial sin even though love is the essence of Christ's teaching.

"But we've made purity or chastity the cornerstone of our religious practice. If people examine their consciences and discover no sins against purity, they're not ready for confession. They're ready for canonization!"

"Danny, Danny, how often have I heard you say, 'We are all human therefore limited therefore imperfect'? Doesn't that go for our leaders as well as for the rest of us?"

"Yeah, it does. Sometimes I guess I am just as self-righteous in condemning the self-righteousness of others."

Danny got up and started to leave. Then he turned to Gene. "I'm so worried about Celine in all this. What should I do? Should I call her again?"

"Maybe you ought to wait a while. Or wait till she calls you," Gene suggested. "You don't know what's happening in her life right now. She has a much higher profile that you do. Prestigious law firm.

"A father who is a well known defense attorney. A husband who travels in the upper echelon of the business world. She herself an up and coming lawyer. She's dealing with all that and, I'm sure, she's just as concerned about you as you are about her. Give her some space."

"Even if she does call," Danny sounded rueful, "I don't know what to say except I'm sorry. If I had given Viri Lucis that note, none of this would ever have happened."

"Hindsight, Danny, hindsight," Gene admonished gently.

"But what if I've ruined her?" Danny was obviously agitated.

"Do you really think she'll dump this all on you?" Gene asked trying to help Danny to clarify his thinking. "I mean, consenting adults …."

"And the consequences," Danny shuddered. "Why is it that you repent and you believe God has forgiven you and yet there are those who insist on punishing you like Casey who was speaking for the Cardinal?"

"It might be," Gene offered, "that they are projecting their own unadmitted desires on you and punishing you for their guilt feelings. I don't know."

"I'll be in touch, Gene. And thanks again for being such a good friend."

"I would expect the same from you, Danny. You've got my prayers."

Danny left to go to his new 'appointment,' leaving behind the parish he so loved. In fact, he didn't realize how much he loved it until it had been taken away from him.

Celine sat at her desk staring at the Scapperelli file. Nothing was registering. After her meeting upstairs she didn't know whether to do a hi-five or vomit. She had won the first round but there may be fourteen more rounds to go. What is that saying? Win the battle and lose the war.

In the midst of her anguished ambiguity, in walked or rather pounced Margaret. Clad in wild colors of purple and pink with a black scarf, her red hair piled on the top of her head, her face twisted into a question mark, Margaret filled Celine's office like a high voltage charge

"You look like shit, Honey," Margaret flipped her evaluation at Celine like tossing a quarter in a Salvation Army bucket at Christmas time. "Let's spend the whole afternoon boozing and all that. You'd be surprised how messy atmospherics can seem so much more orderly and brighter through the vapors of a couple dozen martinis."

"Hello, Margaret," Celine said listlessly, noticing that Margaret's voice sounded like a muffler dragging along on a concrete highway. Probably had a few martinis already, Celine thought.

"Have you seen the Big Boys yet?" Margaret asked with obvious disinterest.

"Yes, and it went pretty well. Best defense is a good offense."

"Told you it'd be a slap on the wrist. So why are you looking lower than snake's sweat? You know the old saying, 'If you can't beat 'em, be condescending' and all that."

"I don't know," Celine responded. "I just feel so stressed out. I still have to contact three clients who want to dump me. If I persuade them to keep me on, that'll be a gold star on my forehead. But I don't know how long the Senior Partners will be tolerant if the media vultures keep swooping down on me."

" I can't stand intolerant people," Margaret spewed, not realizing her obvious contradiction. "Oh, Honey, you'll do it. You've got hot lava in your veins."

"And I'm so worried about Danny."

"Ah, the sepulcher doth open and out pops the haunting ghost. That man is like a cherry in your martini."

"He hasn't called. Then neither have I," Celine sounded weary. "I'm as paranoid as a lab rat. I think those media vultures have my line tapped."

409

"Oh, Celine, dearest, the media folks are off searching for another gruesome headline and all that. Right now your affair — excuse me — your love relationship has about as much attraction for them as a chapel in a whorehouse. The media vultures, as you call them accurately, will be scarcer than nuns at a porno flick."

Despite herself, Celine had to laugh. She got up from behind her desk and walked around to the front where she parked herself on the edge, her head bowed either in thought or anxiety.

"Remember, Honey, 'Yesterday's headline is today's yawn.' Besides I saw their Monsignor O'Henyeu, Communications guru for the Cardinal, on NewsNet this morning. He's pretty smooth for being a pompous ass. But he did do a good job spreading the horseshit freely about and all that.

"Why don't you take a look at it, Honey?" Without waiting, Margaret barked the order at Celine's televiewer. "Review. Channel 22 XL. Eight O'clock morning news."

Appearing on the screen was Chicago's Golden Girl, Dawn Sylva. With her was Monsignor Thomas O'Henyew, Archdiocesan Secretary for Communications and Spokesperson for the Cardinal.

> Sylva: Well, Monsignor, what do have to say about this vulgar story released today about one of your priests and a prominent married attorney?
> O'Henyeu: Dawn, I think you just hit the nailon the proverbial head. Vulgar. And that's precisely what it is. You know that news outlet better than I. But I won't go into that. They'd love to sue me.
>
> Sylva: Do you get many lawsuits filed against you for what you say?
> O'Henyeu: Well, Dawn, there have been some. But let me assure you that none of them has ever been won.

We have one of the finest law firms representing us. Lambert, Hudson and Greer ....

Sylva: But isn't that the law firm Mrs. Korbach works for?

O'Henyeu: Now that you mention it, yes. Yes, that's right. I must admit I didn't make the connection. You are an incisive reporter, Dawn. But, as I was saying, these law suits have never been won precisely because I am very careful in what I say in my official capacity. Never forget that I am speaking for the Cardinal. And he has to be most circumspect in all that I say. That's why I will not say anything derogatory about that character assassinating other news station.

Sylva: Are you saying that that report was false?

O'Henyeu: Well, now, I didn't exactly say that, did I, Dawn? No what I am saying is that most likely there will be a full and thorough investigation into these allegations. If they prove to be false, we may sue the station. Who knows?

Sylva: Are there many priests who get involved? You know, with women. I mean as far as you know.

O'Henyeu: For some reason women are attracted to priests ....

Sylva: Have any been attracted to you?

411

O'Henyeu: Now, Dawn, that would be telling, wouldn't it? Let me assure you that even though women do find me …. shall we say …. not unattractive, they know that they can get no closer to me than to a skunk.

Sylva: That's an interesting analogy. What do you do to keep them from enveloping you? Talk to them?

O'Henyeu: Oh yes. I talk to them and try to point out the beauty of celibacy. I talk about the need for all of us to maintain our proper places in our respective roles. Women are very open to logical explanations despite the popular myth that they are illogical. I find that when you speak to them man to man, they understand and comply. Most women know their place.

Sylva: Do you like the celibate life?

O'Henyeu: Certainly. It frees me to give myself to the work of the Lord. Now I am not saying anything against family life. That's wonderful too. What would we do without families? Why we wouldn't even be here. Still I like to think that all the people I deal with are my family. I look upon you, Dawn, as a daughter or a niece.

Sylva: But don't you get lonely? I mean after a hard day at the office, you come home and there's no one there. Nobody to share your day with.

O'Henyeu: We priests have a wonderful confraternity. Why I can call any one of my many, many priest friends and we'll go out for dinner, talk things over, offer support to one another. I doubt any married couple enjoys such camaraderie as we priests do.

Sylva: The best of both worlds?

O'Henyeu: Yes, I suppose you could say that. Not that I am in any way putting down the beauty of family life. As I said, where would we be without our families. Why, I get home to see my mother at least once a month.

Sylva: Funny, I never thought of you as having a mother.

O'Henyeu: Oh, yes. She's a wonderful woman. Always warning me about what I say on television. I tell her, Mother, you don't have a thing to worry about as long as I have such wonderful reporters as Dawn Sylva to interview me.

Sylva: Why, thank you, Monsignor. So you think nothing will come of this?

O'Henyeu: I should like to think that it will all be resolved within a week's time.

Sylva: Do you know the woman allegedly involved?

O'Henyeu: No.

Sylva: Well, thank you, Monsignor Thomas O'Henyeu, Archdiocesan Secretary for Communications. Now, back to you, Shirley.

413

"Whew!" Margaret said, "if ever there was someone of shimmering eloquent emptiness, it's that frustrated Shakespearean actor. You could even see that airhead, Sylva, trying to stifle her giggling and all that. But it didn't come off bad. Fortunately, all he does is talk about himself.

"Margaret, I envy your attitude. Doesn't anything ever bother you?"

"Everything, my dear. I've just learned to play the duck and let the water roll off." Margaret sprawled in her chair like an uncoordinated land crab.

"I know you don't want to hear this, Celine dearest, anymore than you want to inhale poison gas, but now is the time to sever whatever there is between you two and all that." Margaret used her prim tone which she did when she adopted the persona of counselor.

"He's been publicly disgraced, Margaret. And you want me to say, 'Well, Danny boy, tough shit. I'm off to the theater. Don't bother to call. Good luck and God bless.'"

"You haven't exactly been canonized yourself, sweetie. And you're not exactly out of the proverbial woods with the boys upstairs and all that."

"There is still something I have to tell him," Celine insisted.

"What? That your love is forever? What is it about your head that you continually want to offer it to the executioner's axe? Sometimes, if you don't mind my being blunt, you have all the sense of a cow flop in January."

"Margaret, you're not helping, if you don't my being blunt."

"Okay, okay. Live your tortured life on the rack of good intentions. By the way, how's George holding up?"

Celine waved her hand over the intercom. "Helen, could you bring in two cups of coffee, please? Sugar for my friend."

"George has been wonderfully supportive, Margaret. Far more than I deserve. He really does love me."

"Good." There was enough ice in Margaret's voice to freeze Arizona. "Sorry, Celine, I have this penchant for reaching out and nagging somebody."

"Please don't be angry, Margaret. I really do appreciate your concern. There are just some things about this situation ...." Celine left the rest of her words hanging in the empty space between her and Margaret.

"I'll be in touch, Honey," Margaret said as she gulped down the hot coffee without even wincing. "I'm not angry. Just agitated. You're so brilliant but so ...." Margaret stopped, letting Celine fill in the blank. Stupid or neurotic or misguided or hopeless or foolish or unreasonable. "I can't help myself. I only hope that 'something' you have to tell Danny is Goodbye. Remember, you may have won the battle upstairs ...."

"I know, I know. I'll talk to you later, Margaret. Thanks for coming by — and for your friendship."

Celine went back behind her desk and sat down, thinking about an aphorism she once heard Danny use. 'You can always be kind to people you care nothing about.' Margaret was truly a caring friend.

She waved her hand and activated her phone and viewscreen. She repeated Danny's number. Danny's viewscreen flicked on and she heard the phone butler's recorded voice, "Sorry, Father Joe is not here. Leave your name and number and he will return your call. And he has asked me to remind you that 'Diplomacy is the art of letting others have your way.' God bless."

Celine smiled. As far as the senior partners are concerned, I must be the quintessential diplomat.

Celine spoke slowly. "Danny, please call me. I'll be here in my office until about six. Then I'll be home. Hope you're doing all right. So far, so good for me." She deliberately tried to sound confident and composed, hoping that would help Danny whatever he was going through.

Celine sat for a while not knowing what to do. Then she walked over to her private file tube, placed her palm against the electronic eye and retrieved the poem Danny had given her at Bennie's. She had read it over and over. She never did make a copy of it as Danny had suggested. There was something precious about reading it in his own handwriting.

She sat down at her desk and read it once again:

A wistful willow swaying brushing
against the kiss of life, she thinks
beauty with her heart, her glistening
laughter draws tears of ecstatic love
from my worn hope.

And her eyes softly absorb me not
knowing, I'm sure, that they do —
just there, full and innocent, trusting,
giving totally present and gracefully
aware that, like the breeze of a
summer evening, what is between us
must pass gently and finally with no
harm done.

And so she fades back into her own
life smiling a fragile goodbye, leaving
me with the memory, the memory to
haunt my life, my dreams, my hope
long, long afterward.

She remembered how she had felt when she first read the poem
and now her eyes swelled with tears again. She thought of lines she
had once memorized. "Of all the words of tongue or pen,/ the saddest
are these: it might have been." The poem had been a heartbreaking
reminder of what might have been. And to this day the heartache
was still there.

Later in the day, Danny called Celine's office. Helen's very prim
countenance appeared on the viewscreen. "Hello, Danny," Helen
said. "She's been waiting for your call. I'll put you right through."
Celine's face appeared. She looked as self-assured as her voice had
sounded.

"Danny, are you all right?"

"How are you, Celine?"

"Oh God, I've been so worried about you, Danny. It's that damn Viri Lucis, isn't it? They're the ones who did this, aren't they? Those lousy bastards. And to think, you had made up your mind to give them that damn note." Celine, despite her look of confidence, was running on as she did when she was nervous. Not in total control.

"I've been worried about you too, Celine." Actually, Danny sounded more in control than Celine.

"Well, I still have my job," Celine tried to sound lighthearted. "At least for the time being. I threatened to sue them if they brought any recriminations. They're probably upstairs still arguing about what to do with me. I think I've got them under control. What about you?"

"They've kicked me out of St. Matt's. Until 'further investigation.'"

"Oh no! Can they do that? Aren't you innocent until proven guilty? They don't have anything to go on but that sordid report, do they? What will you do? Where will you go?"

"I'm being sent to a home for retired nuns near Dearborn Park. I don't know for how long. Maybe till they finish their further investigation. I don't know what's going to happen to St. Matt's. I'm worried about that, Celine. They don't know anything. Never even asked if the report was true. I really don't know how they operate on something like this."

"Is there anything I can do? Anything at all? Get you a lawyer?"

"Nothing right now. Maybe later I'm going to need a lawyer. Gene suggested I get a Canon lawyer. All I care about now is that you're okay. I called but George sounded very upset with me."

"He didn't tell me you had called. I guess he was too busy trying to give me solace and support. He must have forgotten."

"Well, for now, I look at this transfer as an extended retreat. Maybe I'll rest and write some poetry. I don't know."

"Danny, what about Rome?"

"Probably cancelled. Haven't heard yet. I probably wouldn't have had that much of an input anyway. I do need some time for myself. You know how it goes,, When you're too available to others, you can't be available to yourself."

There was silence between them as if neither knew what to say next. Or perhaps there was really nothing to be said. Then Celine spoke. "Look, Danny, when you get settled, call me. Under the circumstances we can't meet anywhere but we can talk."

"Right, I'll call you. You're sure you're all right?"

"Yes, I'm okay. Danny, there's something else." Celine paused as though she was trying to phrase what she was going to say accurately.

"What's that?"

"Don't give that goddamn note to them, Danny."

Silence.

"Did you hear me? Danny, Viri Lucis may have power within the Church but they're sheep when it comes to dealing with the powers of this world. They can be tracked down. I'm sure of it. They can be exposed for the rotten bastards they are. The note …. it's what we have to use against them."

"I'll call you as soon as I move and get settled," Danny said, not responding to what Celine had just said.

"When do you have to be there?"

"Today."

"My God, they don't give you time enough to think. Danny, don't run away and allow yourself time to become bitter, please."

"Right."

"Take care and I love you, Danny."

"Love you, too.

The connection went dead.

ARCHBISHOP PEREZ

Father Armando Ricci entered Cardinal Tamacci's office quietly and stood in front of the powerful Secretary of State in respectful silence.

Ricci was a small thin man with sharp features, a balding head and the stooped shoulders of one who was accustomed to being subservient. He had the forlorn look of a man who knew that whatever his ambitions had been, he was now resigned to being the chief gofer of this all-powerful bureaucrat who sat at his desk ignoring him. Finally Tamacci looked up.

"Well, Armando?" Tamacci asked without any sign of respect or affection. "When did you get back from the United States?"

"About an hour ago, Eminence."

"And it took you this long to make your report?" Tamacci spoke each word with emphatic impatience.

"Traffic ...."

"All right, all right. Just give me your report."

Armando Ricci looked down at the chair waiting for an invitation to be seated. None came. He continued standing.

"I made contact with the reporter, Louis Gabler. I detailed what was wanted. He agreed without hesitation. I gave him the fifty thousand dollars with the assurance that another fifty thousand would be his when the task was completed.

"Gabler said he would need a photographer as you had anticipated, Eminence. He said he knew one who was an expert. I gave Gabler fifteen thousand for the reporter with a promise of twenty thousand more at the end. The plot is under way, Eminence."

"I should like to think of it as God's will rather than a plot, Armando," Tamacci said with acid in his voice indicating his displeasure at Ricci's including himself in the universal affairs of the Church. Still Tamacci knew he had to have Ricci's loyalty and closed mouth, so he added in a softer tone, "Thank you, Armando,

419

you did a very fine job as always. I can always count on you. In fact, I'd be lost without you."

Armando Ricci smiled a thin smile of satisfaction as though the master had just thrown him a bone. He bowed, turned and left as quietly as he had appeared. Ricci loved this inner-circle intrigue. It was what kept him going. He had no idea why Archbishop Perez was being singled out for destruction. It was, as Cardinal Tamacci had said, "God's will."

San Antonio, Texas

"It was so good of you to see me, Archbishop Perez. I know you are a very busy man."

"What can I do for you, Mr. Gabler?" The Archbishop gave no hint of busyness. He was a short man in his mid-sixties. Despite the fact that he was overweight, he exuded energy. His eyes flashed beneath thick brows. He was totally bald and it was obvious he had the sides of his head shaved.

He moved quickly as he came forward to greet Gabler. He spoke quietly yet as someone who was used to power. There was an air of ordinariness about him. A certain humility. He laughed easily, sincerely. He was a simple, warm, attractive man.

"I am hoping you will allow me to do a story — a kind of vignette — on a day or two in the life of a busy bishop. I'd like to get behind the work to your personal values, your priorities."

Archbishop Perez laughed softly. "I'm afraid I'm not much different from my brother bishops. How did you come to choose me?"

"Well, you do have a reputation for working with the poor, illegal aliens, migrant workers, the marginalized, as it were. You're also Latino. And, if I may be so bold, you do have quite the reputation for being a liberal in these very reactionary times. I thought a portrait of such a man would make better copy than that of a less — shall we say, conspicuous — bishop."

"Something like a screaming headline?" Perez smiled. "I am flattered. I read the articles you have had published. They're good.

Balanced. I wouldn't want to come off as some kind of a wild-eyed fanatic in the cause of liberalism."

"Not at all, Archbishop." Gabler was poised and professional. "And I wouldn't get in your way. I would be only in those situations you wanted me to be in. And most of all I would clear everything I write, all the recordings and all photos with you. You'd have the final editorial say."

"Well, we could try it," the Archbishop said without any indication of being really flattered.

"I will also have a phototelevisor with me. He'll take still and video shots, if that is amenable with you." Gabler seemed now to have relaxed. He crossed his legs and was pumping his right leg as though to indicate that the sooner they got started the better.

"Yes," the Archbishop said simply. "The more I think about this, the greater the opportunity for me to advance some of my ideas of what Church should be today. It may be a source of blessing, this photo-portrait."

"And that's exactly what it would be. A photo-portrait. By the way, was that a quotable quote about getting your ideas on the Church across?"

The Archbishop laughed heartily. "Oh, there will be plenty of those, I'm sure. I am accused by my brother bishops of running off at the mouth too much. I just say what I think needs saying.

"I am, after all, an Archbishop. I have nowhere else to go. I'm on the top rung of my ladder. So why waste the precious few years I have left being circumspect and cautious? I can't expect others to say what I think needs to be said."

"There is, however," Louis Gabler began at once to demonstrate his ability to probe, "a strong rumor in some circles that you might be the next pope — the first American pope. I mean because of your reputation for involving yourself with the downtrodden and other involvements which I'm sure we will be discussing."

"That rumor is as farfetched as my Presbyterian counterpart here in the city being elected the next pope," Archbishop Perez said most seriously. "Why, I have yet to be elected to any important post by my own brother bishops in our national conference. If you want a quotable quote, use this, If asked, I will not run. If elected, I will not serve. It's not original but it serves the truth of my feeling on that matter."

Louis Gabler could not help but like the man. He had a way of drawing you into his inner spirit without your even noticing it. This portrait would not only be interesting, it would be fun. Why anyone would want to do this man harm .... But that's what he was getting the big bucks to do and do it he would.

"Shall we begin on Monday, then, Mr. Gabler?" the Archbishop asked.

"I am at your disposal, Archbishop. And, please, call me Louis. On Monday I will bring along Harry Myers, the phototelevisor."

"Fine. Until Monday at 9 A.M." Archbishop Perez extended his hand and both men shook hands warmly.

At 9 A.M. on Monday, Louis Gabler and Harry Myers were ushered into Archbishop Perez's office by a very bright and pleasant middle aged woman who served as the Archbishop's secretary. "He's been waiting for you," she said after they had introduced themselves to her. "My name is Suzanne. If there is anything I can do for you while you're here, please don't hesitate." They thanked her and entered Perez's office.

It was not the neatest office either of them had ever seen. Papers were stacked in various spots on his desk. News printouts filled one corner of the room. Books were overflowing on the chairs. The room itself was Spartan. A few knickknacks on the desk. Two paintings hanging on either wall. Nothing much else.

Archbishop Perez greeted Gabler and was introduced to Myers who seemed disinterested. He was dressed in jeans and a pullover. He hadn't shaved. His young face wore an old expression of boredom. He was the exact opposite of Gabler's enthusiastic attitude.

"I'd ask you to sit down but I want to leave immediately for San Juan clinic," Perez said as he invited both men by taking them by the arm and leading them back out of his office. "We'll be back sometime before lunch, Suzanne," he said to his secretary. "There's cheese and Jell-O in the refrigerator." With that he waved to her and hurried outside.

"This clinic," he explained as they drove along, "is for the very poor. People without any government aid. There's an elderly doctor there and three Sisters who care for these poorest of the poor."

"How do you find time for such a visit when you have this large diocese to run?" Gabler asked.

"I make time. I delegate a lot. I refuse to get buried under piles of paperwork although, as you must have noticed, paper serves as tombstones on my desk." The Archbishop laughed genially. Gabler joined him in his laughter. Myers did not. He sat looking out the window perhaps preparing for background shots.

"For me," Perez continued, "it has always been relating to people. Christianity is more a movement than a static organization. You can quote me. What do I care? My brother bishops don't think much of my opinions anyway and in Rome I'm kind of a *persona non grata*.

"Still I believe Jesus related to people always. He didn't set up a building and invite them to come to him. He went out to them. The Shepherd who searched. He was a visitor more than a welcomer. Yet his whole mission was one of interpersonal hospitality."

"That's good," Gabler said with enthusiasm. "Maybe even a bit explosive." It was obvious to Gabler that the Archbishop did not have that kind of maverick imagination that carves passageways into pastel never-never lands.

"It all depends on how you report it." Archbishop Perez smiled.

"I have your words recorded here," Gabler said as he held up a mini recorder. "I will try my best to let you do the talking with as little editorial comment as possible. I'll just set the scene."

"I don't know you, Louis, but I'm drawn to trust you," Perez replied. "I know you will do me justice."

When they arrived at the clinic they got out of the car and went in. The Archbishop was greeted not only with warmth but with joy.

"Okay, Harry," Gabler said, "start shooting. I want a lot of footage of this visit."

The visit from a journalist's point of view was fantastic. Shots of people's faces lighting up, smiling as the Archbishop moved among them, holding their hands, speaking softly, smiling. He was kindly, encouraging, bright, joyous and most of all respectful of each person.

Then he approached the old doctor as they were preparing to leave. He took an envelope out of his breast pocket and handed it to the doctor. "From someone who cares," Perez said. The doctor beamed. "For the poor," he said with subdued excitement. "For the poor."

As the three got into the car, Gabler was unexpectedly quiet. Also unexpectedly, Harry Myers was the one who suddenly seemed bubbly. "Got some great material, Archbishop." he exclaimed. "Some really good stuff."

"Just remember, Harry," Perez said solemnly, "this is not about me but about the people I serve."

Louis Gabler sat looking out the window. He knew he had one of the best stories he had had in a long, long time. He was upset. He would never be able to use it. It was so good.

For the rest of the trip back to the Archbishop's residence, they rode in silence. Gabler and Myers were obviously in awe of this man. Gabler wondered why anyone would want to destroy him. But he wasn't being paid to question. Just do what had to be done.

The rest of the day was rather routine. When Gabler and Myers were about to leave to go back to their motel, Archbishop Perez told them that that evening and tomorrow there would not be anything of much interest. But tomorrow evening he would have his monthly meeting with the Archdiocesan Lay Council at eight O'clock. "You'll have to be patient," Perez told them. "Some days are more interesting than others."

The next evening, Gabler and Myers sat in at the Archdiocesan Lay Council meeting. Archbishop Perez explained their presence and asked the members to just forget that the reporters were there.

Gabler turned on his recorder and also took copious notes. Myers kept his camera rolling with its recorder on too. At one point Gabler was annoyed with himself. Here he was going all out for a story he'd never use. But he most certainly had to keep up the appearances.

Archbishop Perez listened as the people around him supplied more than enough gripes about what was or was not going on in the Archdiocese or about certain priests or some school situation or about particular liturgies which were boring or off the wall.

The Archbishop took notes, asked some questions and in general was most attentive.

"Now," he said, "we will go around the table and I want each of you to mention at least one positive thing about our Church here in the Archdiocese."

They began. Some had much more that one instance of good things being done. Gabler could feel the atmosphere change. There was a vital optimism among the members of the Council.

The Archbishop closed with a brief statement about the mystical experience of living in unity within Christ. It was obvious that he had forgotten about the presence of the two reporters. He gave his blessing and asked for continued prayers.

The people gathered around him and stayed for another hour or so, chatting, laughing, telling stories. Gracious was the word that summed up the Archbishop's interaction with his people for Gabler. Or perhaps, love.

The next morning Perez invited Gabler and Myers to walk with him in the garden. "I have someone who takes care of the garden," he said, "but I care for the rose bushes myself. It gets me back to nature, to my relationship with creation, to the soil from which I came."

"What do you do with all that information you got from your Council?" Gabler asked as Myers videotaped the garden and especially the rose bushes.

"The matters concerning the priests I turn over to my Secretary for Clergy. The complaints about the liturgy and other pastoral problems go to the Secretary for Pastoral Renewal. And then at an Administrative meeting we will deal with our problems."

"And the positive input?" Gabler asked.

425

"That will go out in a monthly letter that I send to all households. Where there is no violation of confidentiality, I will also include references to some of the problems and what we are doing about them."

"The most important work I do is to keep people focused on the half-full glass." Perez sat down on a stone bench and stretched. He motioned to Gabler to sit with him while he let Myers do whatever it was he was doing with his cameras.

"That's not just proverbial — about the half-full glass — it's theological," Perez tried not to sound preachy especially since he was being recorded.

"You see, Louis, Jesus said, 'Behold I make all things new.' There can be no newness or renewal without hope. There can be no hope where there is the pessimism of seeing a half-empty glass.

"Hope and the future. That's what it's all about. The more we plan for the future, the more vital will our actions be in the present and the more we will draw upon the wealth of experience from the past."

"This is what you live?" Gabler asked.

"It's what I try to live," Perez sighed as though he was recalling the many criticisms about his being too futuristic. A crazed dreamer, he had been called. An ecclesiastical buffoon.

He knew he had a long way to go before some would ever experience the reality of being Christ's Body. Before faith would take hold and allow all the people to work to make Jesus prayer come true, "That they all may be one ..."

Then Perez turned to Gabler and said, "We need to keep our sense of humor alive. It's our sense of balance. Without humor, you can easily go off the deep end and plunge into the abyss of fanaticism. The only extreme allowed is that of loving service."

Gabler sat there pondering. If this man is for real, he is one of the most decently sincere men he had ever met. He is — Gabler searched for an appropriate word — holy!

"I want you to know, Archbishop," Gabler finally spoke, "that even though I'm approaching this as an objective reporter, I do admire you."

"Well, thank you, Louis. I do have my dark side though." Perez laughed softly.

The next day Gabler and Myers were in Perez's office when a young priest came in. From the conversation Gabler learned that the priest had been arrested for giving sanctuary to illegal aliens.

The priest gave the Archbishop a full report which was recorded with his permission. "Maybe you will help me with your report," the priest said to Gabler. The Archbishop made notes of the priest's report. "I'll see to that," Perez said. And, "I'll take care of that myself." And "I know who can handle this."

The meeting ended with the Archbishop asking the priest for his blessing. Perez knelt down while the priest made the sign of the cross over his head. Gabler knew instinctively that this was not being done for the camera.

On another occasion, Gabler sat in the back of the Archbishop's chapel while Perez prayed. Perez had told Myers he could capture this on film but asked that sound be eliminated. Gabler heard Perez sigh often, heavily at times as he prayed.

Later he told Gabler, "I pray for all my people many times each day. I don't know if my prayers are helping them but they are helping me to help them." They were sitting in the kitchenette sipping strong tea.

"I pray out of their suffering that they will forgive those who mutilate their lives. I pray out of their helplessness that they may rise to a new life of hope and energy to do for themselves what needs to be done.

"I pray out of the wealth of others that they may live simply that others may simply live, as the saying goes. I pray out of politicians' promises that they may be selfless in the fulfillment of their offices of trust. I pray out the pain of my priests that they will be wounded healers."

Gabler was visibly moved. This man was so simple, so honest, so unselfconscious. He was beginning to be torn between the integrity and authenticity of this man and what he had been paid to do in order to destroy him.

427

Archbishop Perez's faith was as pervasive as the blood that streamed through the veins of his body. He used his eyes like searchlights to look for those in need of recognition, for those whose broken lives needed mending, for those who lived on the margin of human existence and needed to be brought into the center of full Christian compassion. He used his ears like a tape recorder to play back the pleas for help hidden beneath the loud, familiar sounds of resignation.

After about ten days, Gabler approached Archbishop Perez and told him he thought he had enough material for an in-depth report. "I was wondering if maybe we could bring my visit with you to closure by going out for dinner? On me," Gabler laughed.

"I would be honored," Perez said sincerely. "You've been around so much and have been such a part of my day that I'm going to miss you."

"Shall I pick you up about six this evening?" Gabler asked.

"Fine. See you then. What about Harry?"

"Oh, he'll be around tomorrow to say goodbye. He's working on editing. A compulsive."

Later that afternoon, Gabler and Myers were huddled in the motel room.

"Don't worry," Myers was saying to Gabler. "I'll get the picture you need. Just do your part. You have to get him to reach across to you. Then you have to reach across to him. Spill a glass of water or somethin' and then reach out and over to pick it up. Do it before he does."

"What exactly do you call what you're going to do?" Gabler asked with his typical newsman's inquisitiveness.

"It's called photocompudigitaliztion," Myers smiled, knowing that his verbal counterpart was lost. "It's a big word that means you can change a picture into anything you want it to be. It's illegal. And if you're really not good at it, it can easily be detected. But I'm the best.

"I'll get his hand caressing yours. And the look on his face will be a long tortured plea."

"Good. I picked out the table you wanted and reserved it," Gabler sounded almost sad.

That evening as Perez and Gabler sat across from one another enjoying a cocktail and making small talk, Gabler announced, "In remembrance of our meeting, I've brought you a gift."

"You really shouldn't have," Perez said, a bit embarrassed that he had no gift in return.

Gabler took out a small package, wrapped in silver and placed in front of himself, a few inches to the left of his plate.

"Go on, take it," Gabler laughed. "It can't be the first time you've ever received a gift."

Perez reached across the table to pick up the small package. *Click!*

He opened it and knew it was a box containing a ring. What he didn't expect was the beautifully shaped amethyst set in gold.

"I'm astounded," Perez said in both a shocked and grateful tone. "This is far too much for you to spend on me, Louis. My birthstone. How can I thank you? Let me buy dinner, at least."

"No, dinner's on me," Gabler said as he reached for his glass of water, knocked it over and immediately reached out to retrieve it. *Click!* "I'm terribly sorry," Gabler said in exasperation. "Did I spill any on you, Archbishop?"

"No, I'm fine except I'm still flabbergasted over this beautiful ring."

The next day, Gabler and Myers bid farewell and left Archbishop Perez's residence. Both hugged Perez as they left and the Archbishop had tears in his eyes. "Do come back," he said. They both agreed that they would return for an informal visit.

Four days later on both NewsNet and GlobeNet, there was a shattering report by Louis Gabler about Archbishop Perez's homosexual advances made on the reporter.

The picture from the restaurant left nothing to the imagination. Perez was clearly depicted in a most compromising position. He was shown caressing Gabler's hand from across the table and his face held the expression of someone who was pleading.

Gabler explained how he was doing a story on the Archbishop and how several times the Archbishop had made homosexual advances. He further explained that he asked Harry Myers if he could possibly get a picture to back up his allegations. Myers had. "…. and this is the picture you are now viewing.

"I feel compelled in conscience to reveal this matter since Archbishop Perez is held in what turns out to be undeserved esteem. Besides, he told me that he had aspirations for the papacy. I really liked the man and I feel terrible at having to release this story."

Gabler's voice sounded sorrowful. And his face was one enveloping look of regret. But he was the reporter through and through, telling a news story that had to be told, giving the facts, speaking the truth.

The viewer had to wonder how Louis Gabler could possibly get through this. But he was a pro and he did his job well.

Archbishop Perez sat frozen in front of his telecomputer. His face sagged with utter disbelief. Tears rolled down his cheeks. He trembled from head to toe. His heart breaking, his mind filled to bursting with the question, Why? His emotions shifted rapidly back and forth between grief and anger.

He had been betrayed. But why? Betrayed by someone he had taken into his confidence, shared his innermost beliefs with, befriended. Why? How could he do this? Why did he do this?

He had been set up right from the start. Why?

Later that day, Father William Markle, Archdiocesan Assistant Secretary for Communications, appeared on NewsNet with a brief statement.

"Archbishop Perez denies without qualification the allegations made earlier today by Mr. Louis Gabler. The Archbishop assures his people and the whole community that he never was and is not now a homosexual in tendency or in action. He categorically denies that he made any such advances to Mr. Gabler.

"He further asserts that he never made any statement about his wanting to be Pope. He is absolutely perplexed and devastated by these allegations but forgives Mr. Gabler and Mr. Myers. Archbishop Perez has no intention of resigning."

By the time of the evening newscast, prominent laypersons from the Archdiocese, known for the ultraconservative stance and their continued opposition to Archbishop Perez, appeared denouncing him and demanding his resignation.

There were a few others who spoke on behalf of the Archbishop but they were obviously poor people with no standing in the community.

Two priests were interviewed. They both stated bluntly that there was absolutely never any indication in word or action of homosexuality in Archbishop Perez's lifestyle.

One priest was asked, "Could it be a case of his staying carefully in the closet?" The priest was taken off guard. He stammered and ended up muttering that it could be possible. It was obvious from the anguished expression on his face that he no sooner said this than he realized what a horrible mistake he had made.

He tried to say something else but the reporter cut him off with a "There you have it. Back to you Tom." "Thank you, Shirley. Well, this has certainly shaken up the Archdiocese of San Antonio, if not the whole of Texas or perhaps even the entire American Catholic Church. And now to a heroic fireman who rescued a little girl's kitten from a tree …."

"It's done, Mentor," Cardinal Tamacci reported with confidence oozing through each word. "It should only be a matter of a brief time until Perez resigns."

"Excellent, Camillo. And now for Rawmanda in Africa." The Mentor sounded genuinely delighted.

"I'm meeting with Matubu, his finance man, within the week." Tamacci deactivated his phone. This would be much easier. Matubu would have no trouble falsifying the books. His Eminence, Cardinal Rawmanda, would be revealed as a pilfering criminal. A Swiss account would be opened in Rawmanda's name. It didn't matter how much was in it. No one could divulge that information anyway. But what would be discovered was the fact of the account.

But Tamacci's meeting with Matubu would never take place.

VINDICATION

Father Armando Ricci approached in his usual respectful manner but he was obviously upset.

"Eminence. Eminence!" he all but shouted.

Tamacci jerked his eyes open and sat up.

"Armando, did you pay those two hoodlums off? Did you drive them to the airport? Have they left Rome? I didn't want them here in the first place."

"Eminence, I have …. well, the news …. is not good."

"What are you saying?" Tamacci asked with a studied indifference developed over the years of diplomatic maneuvering. He stood up and stretched lazily. Something he would do only in the presence of his most trusted minion. "News …. not good? What do you mean? Nothing has gone wrong with the plot against Perez?"

Ricci could not help but remember how he had been reprimanded for using the word plot. What had happened to God's will? "No, Eminence, rumor is that he will be resigning within the next two weeks. 'Pressure from Rome' and so on.

"It's Gabler. I paid him his second fifty thousand dollars. He just sat there and laughed at me. 'This is big time,' he said to me. 'You represent somebody with hefty clout in the Roman Church. So, my friend, I want one million dollars. So does my accomplice, Harry Myers. One million a piece. You can deduct the money you've already given us, if you want.' And he kept on laughing. A horrible laugh. A threatening laugh."

"Is he out of his mind?" Tamacci flopped down into his chair. All signs of indifference gone like snow in first springtime rays of the sun. He looked like someone had just kicked him in the groin.

"He may be demented, Eminence, but he is deadly serious." Ricci winced waiting for the explosion of Tamacci's legendary temper.

There was none. Instead Tamacci got up and walked slowly around his desk, then he stared Ricci squarely in the eyes. In a steely, subdued voice that was far more frightening than an explosive scream, he said, "So he thinks there's someone with hefty clout, does he? Well, we will just show them both how hefty the clout is."

Then the explosion. It was not Cardinal Tamacci's expected blazing temper. This time the Cardinal, it appeared to Father Armando Ricci, had lost complete control. Even when he was furiously angry he always maintained the substratum of his diplomatic objectivity. A cool center in the flames of his temper.

This time, however, Ricci thought Tamacci had become as demented as he accused Gabler of being. There was no sign of the restraint that his commanding authority and his years of training in the diplomatic corps had always graced him with.

"Armando," Tamcci screamed in a shrill voice, "arrange for these two penny-ante gangsters to come here to my office at once. Right here! In my office! We will scare the living greed right out of them."

Within the hour, Gabler and Myers sat in the office of Cardinal Tamacci, Secretary of State of the Holy Roman Catholic Church. Gabler's face was a visible sheen of arrogance. Myers hung back, dutifully impressed with the power structure of the Vatican. Tamacci's trained eye saw the weak link immediately.

Tamacci began in the polished tone of a weathered diplomat. "Gentlemen, I have summoned you (he emphasized the word, summoned, to bring the full force of his power to their attention) to discuss our contract. You, I am given to understand, want to violate this most sacred covenant."

"There's nothing sacred about what you had us do to Perez," Gabler was fighting for the advantage. His tone was cavalier, even disdainful. His obvious message was, You're not going to intimidate me.

Undaunted by this show of bravado, Tamacci spoke quietly as one who had all the power. "Now I want you both to know, and mark the seriousness of my threat, that I will see you both destroyed. Neither of you will ever work again in your respective fields. Archbishop Perez's disgrace will look like a canonization contrasted with what

433

I will do to you two." Raising his voice, he suddenly shouted, "Do you hear me? Do you understand?

"I am Cardinal Camillo Tamacci, Secretary of State, of the universal Catholic Church with powerful contacts throughout the world. Mine is no idle threat. I have paid you, Mr. Gabler $100,000 and you, Mr. Myers, $35,000 to bring about the ruination of Archbishop Perez.

"And that is all either of you will get. Not one cent more." Tamacci almost seemed irrational, his anger was totally out of control. He was doing everything in his powerful position to threaten and intimidate the two men sitting in front of him.

Gabler appeared to have lost the last trace of arrogance like someone who had just been flogged to the point of death. Myers seemed to be trembling. At least he was twitching.

Without a word, they both got up, turned and walked out like two men heading for death row.

"I think you put the fear of God in them," Armando Ricci, who had witnessed the whole draconian scene, spoke in what could not be described as anything but fear.

Outside Gabler and Myers stopped in the middle of St. Peter's Square.

"I didn't think the bastard would come through with a million a piece," Myers said matter of factly.

"Nor did I," Gabler agreed. "But it was worth the try. The pompous wop was so caught up in the throes of his own power that he didn't even suspect the hidden camera and recorder. We'll show him power, Gary. We'll show him. We have nothing to lose by recanting and exposing that officious bastard. In our line of work there will always be job opportunities. Let's see how his contacts 'throughout the world' will react to what we have on him.

"In a way I'm glad it turned out this way, Harry. I really did like Perez."

"But," Myers objected, "that doctored picture is illegal."

"So Perez is going to sue you?" Gabler responded contemptuously.

Four days later, all over GlobeNet were the pictures and statements of Camillo Cardinal Tamacci.

In a lengthy interview, Gabler broke down and cried convincingly for the audience. "That Cardinal paid me to destroy one the holiest men I ever met. I lied. I'm ashamed. I just couldn't live with it. My conscience has had me up for nights on end. Archbishop Perez never once made any kind of inappropriate gesture toward me."

Then to cover for Myers, Gabler said, "In that picture, the Archbishop was merely extending his hand in friendship. A friendship I betrayed. He is absolutely innocent. I publicly beg his forgiveness. I was carried away with greed."

One reporter called out, "Do you have any idea why you were hired to frame Archbishop Perez?"

"How would I know?" Gabler answered and then added, "I'm not Catholic."

The reporters, who were as used to cynicism as they were to proclaiming human perversity, laughed out loud at Gabler's last response.

John Paul IV paced furiously, the printout from GlobeNet crushed in his right hand. Monsignor Douglas Haynes just stood there dumbfounded. Finally the Pope stopped. "Monsignor Haynes," he said in his most commanding papal voice, "will you be so kind as to summon his Eminence, Cardinal Tamacci, here? At once!"

A few minutes later, Camillo Tamacci entered the Pope's presence. He was cowering. He had aged twenty years. It was evident he had been crying. Ruin was carved all over his face. He was so pitiable. But the Pope was far too angry to feel pity, to feel anything but rancor.

"Why?" John Paul asked with utter disgust. Then he shouted, "Just tell me why? What in the good God's name possessed you? Why would you, of all people, want to harm a good man like Perez? Why? Why? Why?"

By this time the Pope had exhausted himself. He began to cough and brought his handkerchief to his mouth to hide the blood. He hobbled over to his chair and sat down still coughing uncontrollably.

Tamacci stood there in front of the Pope. Head bowed. Audibly whimpering.

In an almost sinister tone, the Pope asked, "Just tell me, Camillo."

Tamacci said nothing. Just stood there trembling.

"Camillo Tamacci, I hereby take from you every vestige of ecclesiastical honors. You will spend the rest of your life in penance at the monastery at Monte Casino. You are to have no outside contacts. You will be under constant surveillance.

"The official announcement will be that you retired due to ill health. God knows, you have to be one of the unhealthiest men in the Church today. In the meantime I will try to weather this storm you created for my papacy. You are dismissed."

At that the former Prince of the Church, the former Secretary of State, wept out loud. "Camillo," the Pope said in what sounded like a compassionate tone, "count your blessings. I could have excommunicated you." With that Tamacci ran, stumbling, from the room.

"Douglas," the Pope said gently, "activate GlobeNet, please."

Appearing on the screen was the diminutive, heavy set, benign looking Archbishop Perez' surrounded by reporters.

"I should like to say," the Archbishop said in an even tone, "that I am deeply relieved. I have always tried to devote my priesthood to the service of God's people. Although I do not understand, I do forgive Mr. Gabler and Mr. Myers and anyone else who was involved." He deliberately excluded Tamacci's name.

"It will take time, I know, to feel this forgiveness. There is no such thing as instant reconciliation. But in my will, I forgive."

A reporter asked, "Do you think your reputation as a liberal had anything to do with this?"

"If caring concretely and individually makes me a liberal, then so was Jesus Christ a liberal and him they crucified."

"Are you running for Pope?" another reported called out.

"Absolutely not. I have no ambition but to serve wherever I am assigned."

"But you are a progressive?" a well known reporter asked his question in a tone that told everyone present that as reporters go, he was a celebrity.

"It's difficult to answer such a question. Words like liberal, conservative, radical, traditionalist and progressive can have so many meanings for as many people who use them. I know that I am tired of the autocratic sarcasm of so-called progressives and the behind-the-back vindictiveness of so-called tradionalists.

"If living the gospel makes me a progressive, then so be it. At the same time I would like to think that the gospel is in the best of our sacred tradition."

The screen faded from Perez to an earthquake in Japan. "And now to a really serious tragedy," the anchor said.

"He handled himself very well, don't you think, Douglas?" the Pope asked.

"Very well, Holiness. Very well. God bless him."

The Pope looked up suddenly at Haynes still standing. "I'm sorry, Douglas, please be seated.

"I've been thinking ever since this broke — about Tamacci, I mean — I'll need a replacement. You have your ear to ground and you're in and out of a lot of these offices. Whom would you recommend?"

"I think the Undersecretary is most suitable, Holiness. He is very capable, has the experience and most of all, he is loyal."

"Yes, yes. He is all that. You are thinking along the same lines as I was. Good! Then it's decided. My Secretary of State is you, Cardinal Haynes."

"But, Holiness, I don't have the experience. I am no professional diplomat. I …."

You're a brilliant man. You will learn and learn fast. You can take courses in Public Relations as I am doing. You have noticed the change?" For the first time that morning, the Pope smiled that contagious, almost whimsical, smile he was now becoming famous for. "Will two weeks be enough to get your family and friends here for the ordination and Red Hat?"

"Yes, Holiness. I'd like, if you don't mind, to make a retreat."

"Take whatever time you need, Douglas. And meditate on not running for Pope," this time the Pope actually laughed and then began to cough.

Haynes got up, poured a glass of water and took it over to the Pope.

"Thank you, Douglas," the Pope said still gagging. "You will have to think of a replacement for yourself too."

"Yes, Holiness and thank you for your confidence in me."

With that the soon-to-be Cardinal Secretary of State bowed and left.

Camillo Tamacci stood staring out his window seeing nothing. What would he do now?

Nothing. The Pope made that quite clear. Go to Monte Casino? Where the Mentor held court?

That damn Mentor! He's responsible for my fall from power. Damn him. I was right. He's insane!

The thought of suicide flitted through his mind. He shook his head as if the physical fury could rid him of the thought. What to do? Oh my God, have mercy on me! He fell into his chair, put his head in his hands and cried, his whole body shaking like a twig in a hurricane.

What would the Mentor say? Who cares? Nothing he could say would equal the abject disgrace he was feeling. Anyway he was of no further use to the Mentor. He would throw him away like used tissue.

Tamacci got control of himself. Enough to call Ricci's name through the intercom. Ricci appeared almost at once. "Would you start packing my things, Armando?"

"Pack them yourself, Tamacci," Ricci sneered. Then he turned on his heal and stomped out.

Tamacci sat there stunned. The news had probably spread throughout every cubbyhole in the Vatican.

His phone signaled. As soon as he glanced at the viewscreen and saw no picture he knew who it was.

"Well, Camillo," the voice of the Mentor sounded like distant thunder, "you've really botched it this time. What in God's name made you expose yourself to those two hoodlums you hired? And then you didn't even sweep them for bugs. You with all your experience! My God, you were taken in like a first year theologian who doesn't know his knees from his ass.

"You actually brought them here to the Vatican? Why didn't you contact me? It could have been arranged to end both their lives — and the blame could have been dumped right on Perez's doorstep. What made you think you could act on your own without even filling me in, never mind getting my permission?

"Stupid! That's what you are, Tamacci. Stupid"

Camillo Tamacci could hardly bear to listen. He had more than his share of humiliation for a lifetime. He didn't need this berating form this paranoid schizophrenic. He should have told the Pope everything. Why did he bother to keep his Oath of Secrecy?

"Now you've done more damage to our cause than I care to calculate. I'm forced now to move faster to retrieve McCann's money. I need that document now. With its power I will be able to reverse the damage you've caused. You've really done it, Tamacci

"The word is that Percussi has stripped you of everything?"

"That's true. You should be able to identify," Tamacci sneered.

"Where has he sent you to do penance?"

"Monte Casino."

"Then do me a favor. Stay away from me. I never want to see you again," the Mentor snapped harshly.

Camillo Tamacci had had it. *"You go to hell!"* he bellowed and swept his hand over his phone.

"What do think of this Tamacci thing?" Gene asked Danny the morning of the day the story broke on GlobeNet.

Danny sat looking at Gene's image on the viewscreen. "The media are having a field day with us aren't they?" Danny sounded glum.

"No doubt about it, Tamacci's one of them. He's a groupie," Gene said.

"Do you think he might be the Mentor? Danny asked hopefully.

"Don't know. Could be. He is or was a man of immense power. But why in the hell would he go after somebody like Perez?"

"Maybe Perez knew something about Viri Lucis and was threatening to go public," Danny offered.

"Then why didn't he?" Gene asked.

"Right. I don't know why Viri Lucis went after him. He's supposed to be a beloved bishop."

"He is known for being a liberal. Would that have anything to do with it?" Gene asked.

"We're fishing, Gene. All we know is what the rest of the world knows. Tamacci was exposed and Percussi acted."

"Which proves the Pope isn't one of Viri Lucis, doesn't it?"

"I never thought he was," Danny said defensively.

"My God, if Tamacci is a member of Viri Lucis, its power reaches up to one of the highest offices in the Church," Gene almost had awe in his voice. "Viri Lucis is power."

"But the Tamacci episode doesn't get us any closer to Viri Lucis."

"Maybe Viri Lucis will fall apart now." It was Gene's turn to sound hopeful.

"We'll have to wait and see, I guess," Danny replied with less hope. "One thing for sure, a big chunk's been taken out of the armor of Viri Lucis' anonymity."

"Okay, I'll be talking to you. Give Celine a call and see if she has any insights." Gene's image disappeared from the screen.

Danny thought he would call Celine later. He just wanted to process the information from GlobeNet for a while.

BANISHMENT

The first morning after Danny arrived at the convent/retirement home, he sat in his chair which faced the east. There was a wide window opposite him. As usual he rose before sunrise.

As he stared out the window, he saw the sun in its early morning rise. On this morning the sun was a globe of gold, almost blinding, resting on his window sill yet 93 million miles away.

He sat entranced at the sight of the first glimpse of sun, seeing it but hearing nothing. And yet this star, as one poet had described it, was a "roaring nuclear furnace."

It climbed the ladder of minutes, rays expanding yet pinpointing its brilliance through his window so that he had to lower his eyes. It was the nineteenth century poet, Gerard Manley Hopkins' "brown brink." The burnished appearance of sunlight.

The canvas of the sky overflowed with lavish colors. Danny was drawn into the presence of the Artist who painted this luxurious sunrise on this morning.

Danny meditated on this wondrous gift. Who am I, Lord, that you should care for me? I am not precious. I am priceless here in the midst of the vastness of the universe. This must be my perspective when horrible problems and petty annoyances plague me.

Sunrise, he smiled comfortably despite the soul-wrenching torment he was going through, had done its daily chore and it is once again day. A new day, a new lease on life, a new opportunity, a new challenge.

In the light of day, he prayed, I celebrate the Creator Spirit with the childlike wonder that says, Do it again! Do it again!

Later Danny came back to his room after having celebrated Mass for the Sisters. The elation of the morning sunrise had all but evaporated. Once again he was feeling dismal. At a time like this, he thought, you look for a sign. Some sign no matter how dim. A sign to tell you there is hope. Something to catch and cling to so that you won't be lost in the darkness of despair.

But there is no sign. Or at least none that you can see. And suddenly in a moment of grace, it dawns on you, through some mysterious shift in you wavelength, that the dismal time itself is the sign. And you smile at your anxious doubts and relax for a while in the confidence of hope.

This hope invades your feelings of loneliness which seem to hang over you longer than you can bear. And as you listen to your heart more for its silences than words, you find a new feeling.

The feeling that loneliness is not isolation but a preparation for extending yourself more fervently, more generously to others, offering your emptiness as your gift, drawing from others in return whatever can fill, whatever can sweeten.

He smiled again as he remembered the bromide, When you're locked in a cellar, look for the wine. What wine could he discover? What possible positive element was there in all this?

He sincerely believed that being positive or hopeful or optimistic was a skill. Yet he felt so drained of energy that he couldn't put the skill into action. Depression, no doubt. He had a lot of work to do on himself if he was to get through this.

He recalled a thought that helped him get through so much: It's not so much what happens to you but how you interpret or react to what happens to you that makes you unhappy, bitter, joyless, depressed or, on the positive side, cheerful, optimistic, hopeful, loving.

Things don't change, we do. It was back to, If you want to change your life, change your attitude. He'd have to work on his attitude. What was going on in his life right now was being filtered through whatever attitude he had.

Changing your attitude sounded so simple. It was the toughest thing in life to do especially when negatives were penetrating you from all sides. Why is it so easy to be negative and so hard to maintain a positive attitude?

Probably because our environment is negative. From childhood you absorb all these negatives. Someone said that for every thirty affirmations a child hears, there are four hundred negatives. The world situation is one gigantic negative. There are positive things going on, good people doing good things. But it's the negatives that grab the headlines.

And through this all, you need to work tirelessly, endlessly to maintain a positive, hopeful, optimistic attitude. Then when you succeed in doing so, there are always those who mock you for looking at life through rose colored glasses or being out of touch with reality or being superficial or not taking the problems of life seriously enough. There are always those who would pull you down to their level of despair or at least their negativity.

He walked over to his desk deciding once again to try to do some therapeutic writing. He thought he'd work on some poems about awareness and wonder as roots of the mystical experience of holy indifference.

Lately he had been overwhelmed with the feeling of rejection as though he had been deleted like a word from a telecomputer. He felt sealed off like having the door of a burial vault slammed closed on him.

For Danny holy indifference was an attitude that winged its way over worldly possessions like the birds of the air. It concentrated on the development of inner beauty like the lilies of the field. Holy indifference meant holding the objects of his desires in an open hand, never clenching them in the tight fist of possessiveness or selfishness.

Holy indifference, as Danny understood it, said, If I have something, fine. If do not have it, that's fine too.

How do I live holy indifference in a situation like this? he wondered. How can I honestly say, If I have the feeling of inclusion, fine. If I don't, that's fine too? He had always believed in holy indifference. Now he was realizing once again that practicing holy indifference toward things was much easier than toward the need for approval.

He recalled a verse by the French poet of the early twentieth century, Apollinaire:

> Come to the edge.
> No, we will fall.
> Come to the edge.

No, we will fall.
They came to the edge.
He pushed and they flew.

The other time he experienced this challenge to live holy indifference with similar anguish was when he and Celine had broken off their relationship. To be holy indifferent to the love he cherished had been the most strenuous struggle of his life. He did it then. With God's help and some creative writing he'd do it again.

He wrote his poems in longhand. It gave him a feeling of touching his words, of being inside his words. It was like incarnating himself in the words he wrote. Later he would transfer his poems to a telecomputer.

He thought about the Sisters he had just left in chapel. They were such a prayerful group of women. If nothing else, he thought as he poured himself a cup of coffee and sat down, being here should put me back into contact with the mystical experience of my faith.

He couldn't perceive in these Sisters any of the anguish he felt in prayer. They seemed so at peace whereas his prayer was for the most part a tumultuous battle. It was as though they had knocked and the door had been swung open wide for them. He, on the other hand, was forever searching, seeking without finding.

Sometimes the harder he tried to pray, the more elusive contact with God became. He wasn't always sure that he was speaking to God. Was he just thinking? Talking to himself? At other times, he would try to talk to Jesus friend-to-friend. Often that worked. But then that kind of prayer seemed sort of one-sided.

He wanted a depthful experience of God. He wanted to be immersed in God. Sometimes he tried to address his prayer to the Trinity dwelling within him. Still he wasn't sure if he was just addressing his so-called prayer to himself instead of the Trinity within.

Perhaps it was a lack of interior harmony that made him feel his efforts at praying were so useless. Or maybe he was still filled too much with himself. He had problems with balancing his cooperative efforts with letting go.

He sincerely believed that when he prayed for guidance he was to try to figure things out as a way of cooperating with God's inspiration. He had always been skeptical about people who implied that they had some kind of a direct line to God. He thought of them as dangerous. Those who really believed that God spoke to them, giving them detailed advice or making their decisions for them always seemed a bit fanatical.

He remembered a comedian saying, "These people who get on public access TV and tell everyone God's been talking to them. How come if God's talking to them, he doesn't give them network time?" Danny smiled.

He still fervently believed that you had to love others thoroughly and honestly if you were going to say you loved God. He had tried all through the years to love the people he served. He remembered having conversations with Gene on the matter of loving people.

They were the same questions that plagued him every time he tried to analyze the dynamic of loving. He had asked himself these questions so many times: Where and how and if the emotions played a part in the kind of love you should have for others as a priest? Or was it just a matter of willing their good and trying to help them move from being good to becoming better? Or helping them get a meal and a place to sleep?

Was love an abstraction? And all you had to do is say, "I'm doing this out of love for you?" Or should you feel something? And if so, how often should you feel it? And what is the something you should feel?

Can a priest really love the people he serves while keeping his emotions securely locked away? Is that love? Love without emotion? Maybe we were trained to fear our emotions without even realizing it. Our emotions may make demands on us that we can't control. So we insulate ourselves.

We priests talk about loving all the people. Do we do this so that no one can get near us?

Or do we use our emotions to gain popularity? And if we do, doesn't that leave us with the same kind of emptiness we'd have if we had no emotions at all? Is loving all the people just a fabrication for duty?

Whatever this love for others is or is not, it should carry over into your prayer. He knew well the difference between seeking the consolations of God and seeking the God of consolations. He didn't really think he was after consolations in his praying. And yet he so often had the pestering intuition that something was missing.

Being here for however long it would be and as traumatic as it was leaving St. Matt's, could well be a blessing in disguise. An opportunity to grow into the mysticism of his faith. He prayed that this would be so.

It's far easier to define the word, faith, than to express the experience of faith in words. What he had said about others applied even more to himself: People don't live the gospel because the gospel terrifies them. And so they hide out in their piety, mouthing pious bromides, calling that their spirituality. At this point he could certainly identify with that sentiment.

Danny's phone sounded. "You have a call. Do you wish to go online or do you want me to take a message?" "Online," Danny responded to the phone's butler voice. He put down his cup of coffee, got up and walked over to his Viewphone. He waved his hand over it to activate it and clicked on his Viewscreen. He saw that it was Joan Cromlic, his principal.

"Danny," she sounded distraught, "I've just received the worst news."

"What is it, Joan?" Danny asked hoping against hope she was exaggerating.

"I just got word that at the end of the school year, they're going to close the school."

She hadn't been exaggerating. Danny didn't have the emotional stamina to cry out, "Why?" Instead, he said almost in a whisper, "Are you sure? Did you get a formal memo?"

"Not yet, but as they say, 'It's in the mail.' It's being faxed as we speak. One of Sister Regina's underlings called this morning and told me."

How can you pray to good God when some of God's people can be so despicable? Danny thought. To Joan he said, "Maybe they're just …." He stopped. Just what? Regina Pacis had planned this for years. He was the only one who stood in her way. Now he wasn't there any longer. He was here trying to get in touch with the mystical elements of his faith.

"I don't know what to say, Joan. I've even been forbidden to go back to St. Matt's. How is the faculty taking it?"

"Oh, Danny, I haven't told them," Joan began to cry. "How am I going to tell them? How do I tell the children? Their parents? I shouldn't have to do this." She was crying openly now.

"Joan, I'll Viewfax the Cardinal as soon as we hang up."

"Will you, Danny?" Joan pleaded. "Will you get back to me as soon as you hear anything? I'll sit on this until I hear from you. Oh, Danny, what are our children going to do if they don't have the school? Where are they going to get their values?"

"Take it easy, Joan. Pray." Danny felt the word itself was an admission of hopelessness. We always pray hardest when there's no hope.

"All right, Danny. I'll wait to hear from you. Goodbye."

"Goodbye, Joan. And hang loose." Somehow that advice seemed more realistic than urging her to pray.

Danny sat down and began to type. He wanted to make certain that what he said and sent to the Cardinal was as persuasive as possible.

> Your Eminence,
> I am speaking to you, priest to priest,
> to protest the closing of St. Matthew's
> school. Sister Regina Pacis has been
> actively involved in the plot to close
> this school for years.

For her to use the allegations against me as a pretext and opportunity to close this school is heartless and ruthless. It is, I add, a crazed abuse of power.

To punish these wonderful, hopeful children by withdrawing from them the most inspirational source they have for bettering themselves and drawing closer to God because of me is cruel, thoughtlessly narrow-minded and sinful.

These children have so little. Almost every one is from a one parent home. They have suffered so much but they find hope and love in their school.

If we as a Church are committed to the poor, the outcast, the marginalized, then these children are the most precious members of your flock. What will they think now and later in life of a Church that betrayed and abandoned them and walked past them lying in the wayside ditch of helplessness?

I beg your Eminence to reconsider this horrifying decision. I pray that your pastoral concern will be translated into the action of stopping this closing and binding up the wounds of these children who have been so fiercely battered by life.

Your Eminence, help me to believe
that the Church is the image of
Christ on earth and that the essence
of Christianity is truly relationality. I
beg you.

Danny stood in front of the Viewfax screen, snapped on the network uplink and delivered his message.

Monsignor Richards read Danny's plea, fascinated by the anguish of its tone.

He walked over to the Viewfax and deleted the message. Then he took the printout and thrust it into the IRM (Instant Recycling Machine). He waited for a few seconds and then took the new blank piece of paper out of the other end of the machine, folded it neatly and placed it in the inside pocket of his suit coat. A silly gesture, he knew, but it gave him a feeling of security. At the other end of the Viewfax, Danny went back to his chair and sat down. The feeling of discouragement sank into tangible depression.

What was it all about? Have we become so entrenched in bureaucracy that there is no longer the wonder of mystery, the joy of believing, the reason for continued hope? Is the Church as an Institution itself the crucifixion experience? Where is the resurrection? Is the structure more important than the people, the children?

These holy Sisters he was serving spent all day praying for the members of Christ's Body. But were their prayers moving those who make the decisions that impact on the lives of those members? Are we kidding ourselves by thinking that more things are wrought by prayer than anyone dreams of? Where are the cooperative efforts needed to make God's dream for us come true?

Danny could feel the beads of sweat tricking down the side of his face. He looked over at the peace lily the Sisters had put in his room. He got up, went over to it and fingered the flower as delicate as peace itself.

He wondered if there could ever be peace as long as egotism is rationalized as concern for God's people, as long as the reality is the obsession with proper procedure and legalistic structures.

Certainly the powers of the educational bureaucracy had fallen into a form of secular legalism as far as St. Matt's school was concerned. The rules and regulations of a properly run school take precedence over the most important mission of bringing these poor children to God who is the Source of their self-worth? Maybe the whole thing had less to do with living the gospel than it did with the fact that, in varying degrees, we are all neurotic as Celine had said.

Danny decided to go out for a walk before dinner. He needed the exercise. In fact, while he was here, he should start a regimen for regular workouts.

The clouds sat on the blue velvet of the sky like a crimson crown. Below the path where he was standing, the half yellow forsythias flirted with the shy bluebells in a disheveled garden patiently waiting to be noticed.

Farther out he saw sturdy birches slumbering in the security of ancient complacency except for their upper branches which floated in the easy breeze, nodding to the mystery of just being. The delicate leaves hung in the unshielded freshness of the early Spring's artistic creation.

Over to his left were the wrinkled brown stems of rose bushes bidding hello to a new cycle of life. The smell of early evening filled him with quiet exuberance.

As he walked along the path that led past the Stations of the Cross, he allowed himself to glance at each Station, not actually praying them but just being aware of what they symbolized.

Why, he wondered, isn't there in all the heavy rhetoric of moralistic imperatives the lyrical poetry of mutual sensitivity? Why don't we dance more to the miracle of eternal music?

Do we create our own frustrations out of our fears, our cautions, our separations? Why this addiction to the superficial? The rush of the fleeting moment's gnarled inspiration?

It seems at times, he thought, that we watch life slowly, persistently eating away, like an acid, at the surface of our self-enclosed world until the whole structure caves in on us leaving us standing helpless in the midst of our nakedness.

He came up to the Station depicting Simon the Cyrenian helping Jesus to carry his cross. Why was he indulging in such morbid thoughts? The closing of St. Matt's school. That's why. He was feeling his powerlessness. He needed someone to help him bear this cross but there was no Simon around. He'd have to search his own heart for some faith connection to get himself out of these depressing thoughts.

Danny thought for a while as he walked along. He came upon the ninth Station: Jesus falls for the third time. He stood staring at the Station. Jesus falling reminded him of the seed that fell to various kinds of ground.

He thought of the seed that fell onto good ground. How it took root, grew, flourished and produced a hundredfold of grain so that others could eat. He made a connection between this thought and the grains of wheat that became the one Bread that others might eat and be transformed into the Unity which is the Godhead.

He extended the metaphor of the seed. In his desire for mystical experience he had to avoid the cold glamour of being a self-anointed saint. He had to dwell in the warmhearted delight of being a sower of seeds whose harvest awaited other generations. He sighed heavily. "'One sows, another reaps,'" he said quietly to himself.

He continued walking slowly down the path breathing in the very early Spring air. It was so delightful. He realized how this beautiful, sweet-smelling air was a symbol of the music and poetry all around him. All he had to do is make the effort to sink his roots into this music and poetry and then grow so that others will be nourished with the mystical enthusiasm of creation.

He stopped at the thirteenth Station. Mary holding the crucified body of her Son in her lap. When he was a seminarian and the Stations were part of daily piety during Lent, the thirteenth had always been his favorite. It was so poignant.

It was called the Pieta. The meaning is reverence. There was Mary, brokenhearted beyond description but with a faith that could show reverence for God's will. What a beautiful thought. Out of the negative the positive is born just as out of Jesus' death comes new life.

In the mysterious paradox of God's dream for us, Mary's sorrow is our joy. He thought for a moment of the mothers in The Alley who had held the dead bodies of their sons — sons shot down in a drive by murder or knifed in a senseless brawl.

He stood there thinking about a question he had probed so many times before: why is it such an uphill struggle to maintain a positive attitude? He had been over the answers many times before too. Is it because of original sin which makes us so weak and limited?

Was it childhood training with all the negative messages that have been recorded on our memory undermining self-esteem? Is it all the failures we have endured in the normal course of living and relating?

He began to walk away. Whenever he started on this line of thinking, he always felt he was back to square one. Maybe the whole question came down to the fact that we want to be in control but fear controlling.

"I don't know," he said aloud. Then, "Dear God, please help me to understand." He thought again of a line he had used so many, many times, We are human, therefore limited, therefore imperfect. Then he thought of something a dear friend had said to him, "When I fail, I celebrate my humanness."

Danny turned and walked up some concrete steps toward the small dining room where he ate dinner alone. He didn't mind that. He ate alone for the most part all during his time at St. Matt's. He passed a statue of Jesus pointing to his heart. It was worn from the weather. Probably acid rain, he thought. Was the finger pointing to the heart a symbol of the ache of wanting to be one and the pain of separateness?

This God who draws fire from the embers of my memory and stokes flashing insights that burn within my heart is the God of passionate surprises. Yet we live with the security of legalism while the passion of living our faith awaits our courageous launching out into the deep in search of truth. And the surprises God has in store for us are never revealed. Routine is our saving grace.

Then, he thought, is it truth or brainwashing with what someone decides is the truth? Danny remembered his dear old Professor, Father Henning, saying, "There is *the* truth and then there is your truth and my truth, their truth and our truth. We filter *the* truth through our background, attitudes and personal value system so it becomes ever more difficult to say this is *the* truth."

"But what about Revelation?" one of the students had asked.

"Ah yes," Henning had answered, "but don't we say that the gospels, for example, are theological reflections? The filtering system again."

"And the Holy Spirit?" another student ventured.

"We pray for the Spirit's guidance and enlightenment. But even here are we able to offer the Spirit a clear channel, devoid of all ideologies, all vested interests, all personal and communal prejudices?"

"So," Danny had said, "it's lifelong seeking. For *the* truth, I mean."

"So it is," Father Henning smiled in reply.

He sat down at the table. One of the Sisters quietly served him a bowl of corn soup with crackers. Then came a pork chop with boiled potatoes, green beans and a small salad. He had a glass of water and a cup of coffee. He thanked the Sister and ate his meal.

Gene and Celine had been in continuous contact with Danny. Gene kept trying to reassure him. And Danny tried not to sound like a martyr dying for no cause. Just yesterday Gene called and told him a number of priests had signed a hand delivered petition to the Cardinal protesting the injustice of the way the allegation against Danny had been handled by Bishop Casey, Secretary for Clergy. The priests accused Casey of being ruthlessly vindictive.

"Then," Gene said, "Jeff Horan, a Canon and civil lawyer, has promised to represent you. He'll probably be in touch with you soon." Danny hadn't thought about Jeff. a good man and an excellent lawyer. He felt his spirits rise some at this news. Innocent until proven guilty, he thought.

Celine had tried to sound upbeat, chit-chatting about this and that for the most part. "Things so far," she said any number of times, "at Lambert, Hudson and Greer are okay. I think the Senior Partners don't know how to handle this and so they're pretending it never happened. I am still trying to win back a few ultra conservative clients but it looks good." Danny knew she was saying this so that he wouldn't be worrying about her.

"Damnit, Danny," she left off her morale building posture, "a secular institute like my law firm can react in a more humane way than a organization dedicated to following Christ. Sorry," she immediately added, "I guess I shouldn't have said that. It doesn't help you at all."

"That's okay," Danny had said. But he knew it wasn't. Not that she had said it but that what she said was so true.

"Have you heard anything," Celine had asked tentatively as though afraid of opening a wound, "about going to Rome?"

"I think that's been relegated to the world of What if …." Danny had replied, trying to sound lighthearted but not convincingly.

"We still have to discuss what to do about that damn note," Celine said. "I'll wait until you're ready."

"Okay," Danny agreed.

They bid farewell. That was his most recent conversation with Celine. Despite her efforts to the contrary, Celine, Danny knew, was very intensely anxious.

Danny sat down and called out "NewsNet." He'd watch the local news for a while before going to bed.

"Off," he commanded. He had seen enough news for this day. It was all so depressing. He didn't need to feel any more depressed than he already was.

He sat in his room, dark except for one flickering candle. He really wasn't tired.

He focused in on imaging. He pictured himself on a rough, country-like road. Up ahead of him Jesus was walking along. Alone. He speeded up his steps to catch up with Jesus.

Finally he caught up with Jesus. There were no words. Jesus stopped and turned toward him. Danny knelt. Jesus placed his hands on Danny's head. "Peace," he said in a soft, soothing voice. "Peace."

Then Jesus placed a hand under Danny's elbow and helped him up. Danny's eyes were filled but he felt such peace.

"You are my friend," Jesus said quietly but directly.

"Jesus," Danny responded almost breathlessly. "You are my friend."

"Come, follow along with me," Jesus said. "My peace is my gift to you."

"Thank you so very much," Danny said. "I need your peace so much."

Danny lingered for some time in this image, allowing the feeling of peace to pervade his whole being. Words were unnecessary. It was an atmosphere. A feeling. Deep down in his whole being. It was like a frozen frame.

After a while, Danny began to pray:

> Eternal Trinity, dwelling within me, closer to me than I am to myself, Father, Son, Spirit. All-powerful God, Creator of the vast universe, dwelling within me, I am yours. Totally, absolutely, without condition.
>
> Father, Son, Spirit, dwelling within me, I feel so alone. So devastated. I need peace and harmony. I believe you are with me. I believe the words of Jesus, "Behold, I am with you …." I want so much to be with you.
>
> Please inspire me with the insight I need to do what needs to be done or not done about Viri Lucis. I feel so insecure. So bewildered. So helpless. I need courage.

I want to love you with all my being and becoming. There are so many people suffering far more than I am. Help me to identify with them. Help me to experience Christ identified with them. Let me see each person as Christ, even the members of Viri Lucis.

Let the fire of your infinite love burn within me. May this love of ours, yours flaming in mine, touch all people but especially those closest to me. Celine. Gene. May it ignite a responsive fire in others like Bishop Casey whom I feel so resentful toward at this time.

Fill me with the experience of yourself dwelling within me. Allow me to be absorbed into you. Fill my loneliness with your presence. Transform my helplessness with your infinite power. Restore me to peace. The peace only you can give me.

Danny paused. He allowed his words to envelop him in wordless awe. He wanted to make room for the Indwelling Trinity just to be. He stayed that way for a long while. Then he continued:

Indwelling Trinity, Father, Son, Spirit, grant that I may have a truly mystical experience of you within me. Purge me of all my egotism. Of all that holds me back from giving myself to you as you give yourself to me, ever-loving Trinity.

My God and my all. My God and my all. My God and my all. Help me through this crucifixion I am experiencing. Let there be a resurrection. Bring good out of this horrible wakeful nightmare. I offer my all to you, even though it is so little, so tarnished, so ragged, so unacceptable. I give you my all. Transform me. Enlighten me. Strengthen me. Calm me. Make me a fruitful branch on the Vine who is Christ.

Eternal, all-powerful, all-loving, all-knowing God within me, Father, Son, Spirit, I am so unworthy. Yet you created me in your image. Let me image you to others with a quiet, confident, trusting, hopeful zeal. Here in this place at this time, let me dwell within you more and more. Renew me. May I burn brightly with your glory no matter how much of a smoking ember I have allowed myself to become.

Father, Son, Spirit, my people. They are still in my care even though I am removed from them physically. I am with them in spirit. Through my prayer give them strength. They are good people in horrible circumstances. Return them to me, I beg you. Until then, fill me with peace. Not the peace of resignation but the peace of initiative.

Help me to use this time to renew my dedication, to strengthen my commitment, to grow in my faith. Help me to live the faith value of forgiveness especially toward the members of Viri Lucis. Touch their hearts with your loving truth that they may do all in their power to live the gospel.

Lord, Indwelling Trinity, bless these dear Sisters. Watch over my children. I would lay down my life for them. You know that. Keep our school open for them. I want them to grow in their love for you, in their dedication to your living Word. Bless us all. Grant me peace. Challenge me in my faith.

Father, Son, Spirit, dwelling within me and in all others, there are times, as you well know, when I am tortured with my desire to love you unconditionally, to love you more than I have or do. Times when I am torn apart with doubts leaving me with only scraps from your bountiful table. Times when I suffer because I want to love in you all the people in my life and beyond. With a real, felt love.

Indwelling Trinity, increase my belief in your presence within me so that in those times when you seem distant or even absent I will know you are living within me and no one can take you from me. Within me, loving, strengthening and healing me. Through me may others who come into contact with me experience you.

Jesus, my friend, I accept your peace. Your friendship. Let your peaceful friendship help me to work through my doubts about what I am to believe in. Let me believe in you, our Father, our Spirit living within me. Jesus, my friend, be with me as I bear this cross. Forgive me as I forgive those who devastated me and damaged the work I was trying to do. Forgive me the many times I have stood before you in serene deceptiveness.

Eternal indwelling Trinity, fill the torment of my emptiness with selfless love. Give me the experience of the emotional meaning of life. Rid me of the superficial nostalgia preserved in the clichés of the past. Let my prayer be creative excursions into you, the Unfathomable of eternity.

May my love be a yeast in the sacred, friendly bread I share each day in Eucharist. Help me to look through the broken bread of the altar and find the broken hearts of the streets. In the

> quiet of morning Eucharists, may your
> thundering turmoil disturb my apathy,
> challenging me to look through the
> windows of others' eyes and see you,
> the hungering Christ. May I bleed in
> my heart when I encounter others'
> wounds.

Danny paused again. He was feeling peace. He remained wordlessly with his prayer for a long time and then continued:

> I feel so alone right now. Yet in the
> depths of my aching I want to respond
> to your call to constant restlessness.
> I want to abandon the complacency
> that comes from doing a little good
> here and there. Grant me a ravenous
> appetite for the multiple possibilities
> of each moment you give me. Free
> me from my alabaster piety. Push me
> off the pedestal of my self-satisfying
> virtue, my growth-inhibiting good
> works.

> Eternal Trinity, loving Father,
> sacrificial Son, inspiring Spirit, within
> me, closer to me than I am to myself,
> help me to find beauty in ugliness, the
> miraculous in the ordinary, the sacred
> in all.

> Help me to be still in wonder and awe.
> Wordless in the presence of Mystery
> who is you.

Danny stayed still for some time, there in the shadows of the flickering candle. Then slowly he got up, stretched and yawned, and blew out the candle. He felt tired. He needed sleep. He wondered how the Cardinal was reacting to his plea. Maybe he won't see it until tomorrow. Tomorrow would be a new opportunity.

THE THREAT

Despite his plan to devote his time at the convent to prayer and writing, Danny found the days of the past three weeks dragging into one another like the colors of nature slowly blending into the beauty of Spring.

The analogy broke down, however, since the appearance of Spring was a delight whereas his stay here was a like the dark night of the soul. He longed for the involvement he had had at St. Matt's.

He had to admit that Easter here at the convent had been a one of the most beautiful spiritual experiences he had had in his life. The Sisters' fervor and joy had been contagious. Danny had preached on the theme of life out of death. Jesus, he had said, did not rise from the dead. Rather he rose out of death into new life.

Just as there is life out of death, so hope rises out of despondency, love out of rejection because of the resurrection power of Christ in our lives. He knew he had been preaching more to himself than to the Sisters, but the feast of the Resurrection had been for him as refreshing and rejuvenating as a month-long retreat. For a while he was able to hold onto the hope of the Resurrection.

As Danny was working on a poem or more accurately, dawdling, his phone sounded. "You have an incom …." "On line," Danny said impatiently. He got up and went over to it. He was surprised to see George's face.

"Danny," George said without a greeting, "I don't know how to put this delicately. Do you know where Celine is?"

"Where Celine ….? George, what do you mean?"

"You don't know, then?" George sounded panicky.

"No, George, I don't know. I won't be delicate either. Would you mind telling me what this is all about?" Danny sounded exasperated.

"She …. she's been gone for almost three days. I'm going crazy, Danny. She left for work and we were to meet for dinner at seven.

She never showed up. I finally came home and waited. Nothing. Not that night nor any day since.

"I've called all over the place. Danny, she never showed up for work that last day I saw her. I've called the police. Nothing. I'm going out of my mind."

"What can I do, George?" Danny was shocked at the sound of his own voice. It shook with terror. "Do you want me to come over?"

"No," George said firmly. "Stay there just in case she calls. Danny, if she does call you, tell her how upset I am. Tell here I love her. God, I hope I didn't do anything. She seemed fine when she left for work ...."

"If I hear from her, George, I'll have her call you at once. And, George, if you hear from her, please, give me a call."

"Okay, thanks." George was gone.

Danny paced back and forth, trembling with fear. What was this all about? Had she been in an accident? No, there would have been identification. She wouldn't have gone somewhere — to her sister's or her parent's home without telling George. Where could she be? What has happened to her?

Danny finally sat down. Emotionally drained. There was nothing he could do but wait. Waiting would be the most cruel experience of his life. Maybe he should call his friend, Lou Mc Dermott. No, he was in homicide. Lou would have called him if ....

The very thought of the word, homicide, filled him with renewed fear. No, that couldn't be possible. Why would anyone ....? Viri Lucis? "My God," Danny prayed aloud, "not that. Please, dear God."

Later that evening around eight O'clock, Danny's phone sounded. He flicked on his viewscreen. From the other end there was no image. Just a voice.

"Good evening, Father Daniels. There is someone here who would like to talk to you."

With that the image of Celine appeared on the screen. She was tied to a chair. Her mouth was sealed with tape. The expression on her face was pure horror. Her left eye had been bruised. It looked like a ripe plum had been smashed against it.

463

Danny swayed and grabbed hold of the edge of his desk. He thought he was going to throw up. He could barely breathe.

"Oh sorry," the voice said, "I guess she can't talk to you under these, may I say, benign circumstances." There was a diabolical joviality in his voice. The screen went blank but the voice continued.

"The note, Father Daniels. The note. Now here's how it's going to be. For every day of delay, we will send you a memento. First, Mrs. Korbach's eyes, then her tongue, next her breasts, hands and feet, one at a time. By the way she hears what I'm telling you. You give us the note and we will give you your sweetheart intact. We will give you to four o'clock tomorrow afternoon to give us your decision."

"You don't have to wait," Danny half screamed. "You can have the note!"

"Fine. Then we will contact you at ten o'clock tomorrow morning to make the arrangements." The line went dead.

So it was Viri Lucis after all. Danny immediately got in contact with George.

"Danny! Have you heard from Celine?" The hope in his voice was palpable.

"Not directly, George …."

"What do you mean? What …?"

"George, Celine's been abducted."

"Oh my God," George moaned. "Abducted? Who? Where?"

"They want the note. I told them they can have it. They're going to call back at ten tomorrow morning to give me the arrangements.

"They will return Celine?" George asked, the fear rising in his voice. "Unharmed?"

"Celine for the note," Danny tried to sound self-assured in an effort to allay George's fears.

"George, I'm going to call my detective friend, Lou Mc Dermott…."

"We don't want the cops in on this! They might …. kill … oh, God!"

"George, I just want to get some direction, some insight into this. We've never dealt with anything like this."

"I want to come over first thing tomorrow morning," George said in a determined tone.

"I'll be expecting you, George." With that the conversation ended.

Danny called Lou Mc Dermott at his precinct. He was at home. Danny called his home.

"Haallo, Danny. What has you calling me at this hour?"

"Lou, you've heard of the disappearance of Celine Korbach?"

"I did hear somethin' about it, yes."

"Well, we've found her. I mean she's been abducted. They've been in contact with me."

"Why you? Why not the husband? What do they want? How much? Is it about that news report about you and her?"

"Lou, I hate to do this to you but I've got to see you right now. I've got to explain some things to you. I need your professional advice. Desperately."

Mc Dermott could hear the desperation in Danny's voice. "Okay. How about we meet half way. You know Hope's Grill and Bar?"

"Yes."

"I'll see you there in about a half hour."

Danny and Lou met and went into the Grill section of Hope's.

"Now what's this all about?" Mc Dermott asked slowly as though he was preparing himself not to believe a word Danny told him.

Danny sat there, after they had ordered coffee and doughnuts, and told Lou the whole long and gruesome story. He began with Michael's murder, went on to the will, the note, Archbishop Brown's visit, pertinent excerpts from Michael's diary, Viri Lucis, the Mentor, Tamacci which Lou was familiar with from GlobeNet. He told Mc Dermott his suspicions about Pope Charles' death, Michael's murder, Leno's heart attack. He told Mc Dermott how he, Gene and Celine had been ….

"Playing detective?" Mc Dermott interrupted.

"Trying to put the pieces together," Danny finished.

"Interesting that you waited till now to tell me any of this. Especially when you knew I was up to my arse investigating the bishop's murder."

"I'm sorry, Lou, but what I …. we have is all speculation. Except for Celine's abduction and the trade off for the note.

"So why are you coming to me now?" Mc Dermott sounded annoyed.

"Lou, there is going to have to be some kind of contact made between what I think are members of Viri Lucis and me. Without risking Celine's welfare, is there anything you can suggest …."

"To grab these guys? I don't know. Maybe I can get a couple of our men to trail them and pick them up after Celine is safe. I don't know."

"Lou, I don't want a couple of your men. I want you."

"That's not my bailiwick."

"It's got to be you. I don't want anyone in on this who might put Celine in the slightest jeopardy."

"I'll see what I can do. You'll have to let me know what arrangements …."

"What arrangements should I make, Lou?"

"You say the note's in the bank? Okay. Tell these bastards to pull up in front of the bank at a specified time. Tell them you'll slip the note through the window as Celine gets out of the car. In the meantime, our car will be parked where we can put a laser tracer on their car. With that gimmick, we can't lose them. I'm going to have to get clearance for this."

"Oh, God, Lou, get it. Please! I want to make as certain as possible that Celine's safe. And …. and besides this could be our chance to get information on Viri Lucis. These people, whoever they are, will have to be small potatoes but they still should know something."

"We know they're kidnappers," Danny continued to make his case. "They must be apprehended for that. And if they are murderers too, then that *is* your bailiwick. If they can tell you about Michael — the bishop's — murder, wouldn't that be the break you've been looking for? If Viri Lucis is as ruthless as we, that is, Gene, Celine and I, suspect, they should be exposed and stopped. It's not just a Church thing."

"All right, Danny-boy, as soon as they make contact, you call me."

"Lou, what if they don't go for our scenario?"

"They want that note, don't they? You can call the shots. Be firm."

They finished their second cups of coffee and left.

The next morning at ten sharp Danny's phone sounded. Again there was no image on the screen.

"I want to see Mrs. Korbach," Danny said in an imperial tone.

Celine's image appeared on the screen. This time she wasn't tied to the chair. She was sitting on a couch but her arms and legs were still bound. There was no tape across her mouth but she was not looking directly into the viewscreen.

"All right, Father Daniels, now for the arrangements...."

"No. You listen. I will make the arrangements. You had better copy them down because I'm only going to tell you once."

"Feisty, aren't we? You must have had a good night's sleep."

"Now listen," Danny was using the sternest voice he could muster. "Be firm," Lou had told him. "What kind of a car are you driving?"

"A black Mercedes."

"At one o'clock tomorrow afternoon, pull up in front of Stanson's Bank. Find out where it is yourself. At exactly five minutes after one, I will exit the bank and come to the car. You will lower your window on the passenger side. Before I put the note through the window, you will let Mrs. Korbach out of the rear seat of the car."

"And what if you don't hand us the note?"

"Don't be a fool!" Danny shouted. "If I don't give you the note, what's to stop you from abducting her again?"

"All right. We'll follow your scenario. But with this exception. It will be at one o'clock today not tomorrow."

Danny said nothing. He could feel his pulse pounding. He couldn't tell this rat he wouldn't have enough time. But would he have enough time for Lou to get in place?

"Okay," Danny finally said. "One o'clock this afternoon."

"By the way, Father Daniels, once we have the note, you are expected to take the will to Ralph C. Mackin and Associates immediately. We will be in contact with that firm within twenty-four hours after getting the note. Do I make myself clear?" the voice rasped.

"Yes," Danny answered. "Ralph C. Mackin and Associates."

"One more thing, Father Daniels, if police are involved, we'll come back and this time you can bid eternal farewell to your mistress."

The phones went dead. Danny wanted to get a hold of Lou immediately not only so that he could get rolling but he wanted this all out of the way before George arrived which would be soon.

Danny spoke Lou's number and got him at once. He told Lou the arrangements and how the abductor had insisted on this afternoon. Mc Dermott didn't seemed fazed. "We'll be there ready for the chase."

Danny told Lou about the threat on Celine's life if police were involved. "Not to worry. We'll nab whoever they are. There won't be any chance of retribution." Lou sounded in control which was most reassuring for Danny.

There was a knock on the door. Danny opened it and George stood there looking like he had just finished a one-man attack on the Citadel of Evil.

After brief greetings, Danny told George about the arrangements, leaving out the part about Lou. He felt bad about doing it but he couldn't risk George disrupting the plan. He had to get Celine back safely and also have her abductors captured.

"I'm going with you to the bank," George insisted.

"All right, but just stay in the background. We don't want to arouse their suspicions. They could always drive off with Celine and make other, more stringent arrangements for picking up the note later. If they're in control, we have no way of knowing whether or not we'll get Celine back." Danny knew that would be the winning argument. George agreed.

At 11:45 A.M. Danny and George left for the bank. It was about a thirty-five minute drive. Danny wanted to make certain that he had plenty of time to retrieve the note and then wait for the Mercedes to pull up.

Although Danny was maintaining a calm exterior for George's sake, his heart felt like an ocean in a hurricane. The ripping claws of nausea were tearing at his stomach. He had a splitting headache. They drove along in somber silence. George's face looked like a low burning candle that had just collapsed.

They arrived at the bank at 12:30. The traffic had been slow. Danny got the note, put it in a fresh envelop and he and George sat down to wait. Three or four times George got up and went over to the door and looked out. At 12:55 they both went to the door.

George stood behind Danny. True to his word and despite his agonizing anxiety, George stayed in the background. In fact, Danny thought, George was the background. The avenging angel ready to strike and condemn if anything went wrong.

At exactly one o'clock, a black Mercedes pulled up in front of the bank where there was a ten minute parking zone. Danny could feel George's tension behind him just as he felt his own fear. What if something went wrong? What if something horrible happened to Celine? Would the men in the car dare to shoot him and Celine in broad daylight once they got the note? Why would they? They would have the note. That's all that mattered to them — except, Danny knew, they were psychopaths.

Danny looked for Lou's car. He couldn't see it. Then he realized he didn't know what kind of car Lou was in. Lou had assured him that the laser tracer was fool-proof. Once its beam made contact with the Mercedes, Lou could follow it "to hell and back."

Would Lou have enough time to flash the laser on the Mercedes? And if he did, Danny would have to wait for how long before he got word from Lou about the chase. Actually, Lou had told him, with the laser tracer there was no such thing anymore as a chase. "To hell and back," Danny thought.

At 1:03 Danny stepped through the doors of the bank. George stayed inside. Danny walked directly to the car. The window on the passenger side was zipped down half way. The windows were dark. Danny couldn't even see if Celine was inside. He stood and waited.

Then the rear door opened and Celine slowly and with some difficulty emerged from the car. When Danny saw that she was standing on the sidewalk, he pushed the envelop containing the note through the window. With that the Mercedes pulled out deliberately, without any show of being hurried and drove west on Grand Avenue. About ten or fifteen seconds later another car passed in front of him. It was Lou.

By this time George had come running out of the bank and enfolded Celine in his arms. She was trembling and she began to sob. "There, there," George said reassuringly. "It's all going to be okay." Danny just stood there looking down the street where the two cars had disappeared.

Finally George let go of Celine and she turned to Danny and collapsed into his arms. "Thank you," she whispered over and over. Danny was shaking more than Celine. Tears were streaming down his cheeks but he could say nothing.

THE CHASE

George hailed a Pod and the three of them got in. They instructed the driver to take them to Lou's precinct station where they would wait for him. George studied Celine's blackened eye and murmured, "Sons of bitches!"

"It looks a lot worse than it feels," Celine said in a distant voice as though she was talking about someone else. "They did this to me, they said, to impress Danny with the seriousness of their intent. George, I was frightened beyond human stamina. I thought they might ...."

"There, there," George said, almost feeling foolish for using that word. "It's all over. They'll never bother us again."

Danny sat looking out the window. Anger was consuming him like a ravenous cancer.

The fanatical hypocrisy of Viri Lucis. Their scheming hatefulness. Their ruthless disregard for human life. And all this under the rubric of religion. In the name of God. They were waging a "holy war" on God's own people.

He prayed that Lou would capture whoever was in that car. Then he would send the note to Archbishop Brown but only after Brown and his cohorts knew that they couldn't control his life or the lives of those he loved — of the one person in the world he loved more than life itself.

The desk sergeant told them where Lou's office was. They found it, went in and sat down after they moved bundles of papers from two of the chairs. The office looked like Lou, Danny thought. Carefree yet in some strange way organized. He saw a picture of Lou's former wife and his two daughters on the desk. Priests are not the only ones who should be celibate, he thought. The blinds were drawn and the room had the eerie feeling of a prison. Celine fell asleep almost at once, he head resting on George's shoulder.

Lou and Detective Paul Ramirez cruised along at a comfortable speed. They had the Mercedes in sight and the laser was fastened to the escaping car. Suddenly the Mercedes made a sharp left turn into oncoming traffic, barely slicing past the cars heading east. Lou had to wait and then he gunned the motor and sped across the left lane. The Mercedes had speeded up but Lou was able to catch up with it at a safe distance. Then the Mercedes made a sharp right.

"Lou, I think they made us," Ramirez said sternly.

"Damnit, Paul, they must have a laser-check. Talk about state of the art kidnapping."

"They do," Ramirez pronounced solemnly. "Our laser's out. Who said the old time chases were gone forever?" Ramirez snorted. "Step on it, Lou."

The Mercedes took another right. The street was lined with mostly empty buildings. It looked like a Hollywood prop for a ghost town. The Mercedes slowed. Lou touched his brake. Then suddenly the back door of the Mercedes flew open and a man jumped out, running.

"Go after him, Paul!" Lou commanded as he jammed on the brake. Ramirez, despite his weight, was out of the car like a sprinter.

Lou stepped on the accelerator full force as the Mercedes sped onto the John F. Kennedy Expressway. Lou tore after the Mercedes in and out of clumps of traffic. Then the Mercedes headed toward an off ramp. Lou swung over to the right lane, cutting off a car on his right and just missing it by a thread.

When Lou came down the ramp, he was surprised to see the Mercedes pulled off the road. Lou pulled over about twenty yards behind. He got out of his car with his gun drawn. He stopped and shouted, "Okay, you in the Mercedes, get out! Hands in the air!" Nothing.

Then there was a shot. Lou hit the ground, gun pointed at the car. He was shivering. Nothing. Lou waited. Then he shouted again, "Out of the goddamn car!" Nothing.

Finally, carefully, Lou stood up and crept to the right side of the Mercedes. He edged up on it. He couldn't see through the heavily tinted windows. "Shit!" he groaned. Then he eased his way back around the rear of the car. He stopped and made his way back to the passenger side. He tired the door. Locked.

He remembered the other man had jumped out the back door. Maybe the driver forgot to lock it or maybe the lock was automatic. Probably was. He tried the door. It was unlocked. Slowly he opened it. He held his gun in front of him. "Freeze!" he screamed.

Back at the precinct office, Lou sat behind his desk with his feet up. He was a small man and wiry. He had beady eyes which Danny thought he had developed to advertise himself as a detective. His nervous energy was exhibited in a spasmodic twitch in his left shoulder. He was forceful in a dispassionate sort of way.

There was a carelessness about his demeanor that hid the intensity of his concentration. Without appearing to do so, he observed every nuance of word or gesture. Most of the time he was sullen, not in an antisocial way, but more as lost in introspection as though his chief detective work was searching for clues to the meaning of his own existence.

Sitting there he gave an accounting of his chase in an almost lackadaisical way. "When I looked into the car," he said, "the son of a bitch had blown his goddamn head off. Splattered all over the place," Lou's face was a tableau of disgust. "Ramirez lost the other guy. Couldn't keep up with him."

"Did the driver have the note on him?" Danny asked quietly.

"Didn't have a damn thing on him," Lou replied in total frustration.

"That means the other one had it," Danny said as though speaking out loud to himself. "Good, now they'll have the damn note. I'll go to that lawyer first thing tomorrow morning. It'll all be behind us."

Danny looked over at Celine. She was still asleep. Danny felt George's glare brandishing anger at him for what he had caused happen to Celine. "It'll all be behind us," he repeated.

"I sure would have liked to nab one of those creeps," Lou said moodily. "They may be the only lead to the bishop's murder I would have had."

"Maybe," Danny whispered. "Maybe not."

For the next few days, after he had taken the will to the designated lawyer, Danny remained at the retirement home. He had heard nothing from Viri Lucis. He prayed they were off his back.

473

Jeff Horan had visited him and seemed rather optimistic about his case in Canon Law.

"Bishop Casey fouled this one up good," Horan had said. "The Cardinal won't back him if he thinks for one moment that his reputation will be besmirched in any way. He's too old to even delegate a confrontation with Rome. The whole thing's hearsay. And Casey didn't even ask you if there was any truth to the allegation. Neither will I. That's not the legal bone of contention here. Procedure is.

Danny had asked Horan what his chances were for going back to St. Matt's. "That is not for me to say," Horan answered. "They could let you go back as a form of reparation or they could send you somewhere else as a thrust of their control. You'll just have to wait and see."

THE LETTER

The next morning Danny sat watching the news but it was a blur of information. He wasn't concentrating. He was plunged into the swamp of self-pity. In his overwhelming mood of feeling sorry for himself, his thoughts wandered to his mother who died ten years ago next month. Maybe he was thinking of her because his mother had always been a visible force of stability for him.

He got up, ended the transmission from NewsNet and went over to his telecomputer. He decided he would write a letter to his mother.

Dearest Mother,

I am writing to you to thank you and tell you how much I love and admire you. So often the tapestry of memory is spun from the weavings of afterthought. I want you to know that your death lives within me not as a memory but as an incarnation of my own mortality and as the touch of eternity.

Your death evokes my realization that stars fall, fires dwindle, exuberance fades to a sigh and life departs. It is not cruel fate. It is the luxuriousness of mystery.

When I think of you it is as though in my heart the air is silent, the sky is formless but not foreboding, the raging waves lap languidly and I am at peace. I still feel the tender grief

475

visited on those whose laughter at life is turned to tears over death.

When Dad and I were bonding so closely, you remained in the background of our manly affection. You were so patient with both of us, so supportive and never, never envious of the father-son bond that was being forged through our mutual interests like baseball and fishing.

Yet it was you who taught me, as well as I could learn, the need to be gently affectionate. You did this with the beauty that danced on your fluttering eyelids or gyrated softly, subtly in your graceful body language.

From you I did learn about the music within all creation, a harmony, a unifying motif and you taught me to play my own interior notes delicately with concentrated delight. When I was enjoying one of my unpredictable fits of depression, you were always my exuberance. You showed me by the way you lived that inside each dying of hope there is a moment of resurrection, a reason to rise up to a new life of perseverance.

How often after a day of strenuous activity with Dad, you and I would sit together on the evening porch in the transparent silence of love. How I recall that behind your beautiful face there was a magical world luring me into the depths of your delightful presence.

As you did your gardening you taught me to let my soul stand astounded not so much at what was new but at how the familiar can unveil fresh insights. In Chesterton's words, you showed me how to stare at the familiar until it became strange so that I would live in wonder and awe at all of God's gracious creation.

I learned from you that God is fertile, that his is the universe and a rosebud, a star and a new born babe. All a lavish mystery. I remember your reverence toward the thin skin of earth's shyness where underneath lay the voluptuous womb brazen enough to continue birthing a sustaining planet.

It was from you I learned that in the gardening of the heart the surface had to be broken open if ever love was to grow. You taught me that in the gardening of the heart the weeds of failure and disillusionment had to be uprooted. That in the gardening of the heart I needed to be rooted in Mystery despite the swirling winds that blow and bend me to the grindstone of the mundane.

Thanks to you I do not have to go my lonely way, a spendthrift of the treasures of love and enthusiasm, wonder and ecstasy which you bequeathed to me. You shared each of your joys with me as though each one were a flower placed delicately in a bouquet of bursting color.

It was you who taught me that words were like precious diamonds to be examined thoroughly and treasured lovingly. It was because of you that passion flows through my words rather than forcing my words to be manufactured off the assembly line of my mind.

Because of your influence I honestly believe I am today a gracious singer of poems, a humble weaver of tales who will never wander aimlessly without fantasy through the ragged poverty of reality. Still often I sit with my pen poised while the world shouts, "Hurry up!" and I put my pen down and wait.

I must confess to you, Mother, that often too I pen my words with aching fingers that throb with the fear that I will feel what I write. There are times when the poetic fires burn low and all I feel are the thorns of anguish, the pangs of emptiness. This is not your legacy. Rather it is I who dwell in the anxieties and problems of life for they are the mysteries that make my life excruciatingly creative.

You lived the greatest gift of our Creator: the freedom to be unique. And you were unique among people who merely flirted with the mystery of life's goodness, never coming into contact with it. You penetrated the mystery, touching its core.

The way you lived your faith, the values of the gospel you embraced in their totality, revealed to me that Christ's power is tumultuous passion and that a broken heart is an open space for the Spirit to enter. I think that is why today I refuse to give into the miserliness of legalistic book- keeping and risk the passion of mystical abandonment.

You taught me so well that imagination is not a stepchild of the mind, ignored and unappreciated, while logic is hailed as the crown prince and memory, the spoiled princess.

With you everything in life was haloed, all the music was the flutter of cherub's wings and all sunrays formed a crown of gold for earth's bowed head.

Mother, I am going through some inexorable sadness right now, misery of laser-beam intensity. God who is silence itself is my life. All is night. I still seek to discover and deal with my own truth and to affirm others' possibilities. But it is most difficult at this time.

I remember you telling me to watch the birds of the air, look at their graceful sweep in the sky and learn a most important lesson: lighten up. It's a lesson I have yet to learn.

In the vast spaces of my fantasies, I am a hero. But in this earthen particle I call my self, I am merely a human tiptoeing along the tentative paths of life.

Can I plant my anguish in the soft soil of my frail hope and wait for the surprise of blossoming peace? I don't know. My imagination leaps and fantasies prevail over reality and I wonder if disillusionment is the fate of passion.

Sometimes I think my world has been reduced to a rock pile within my heart. I look to God, the divine Architect of love, to build a cathedral there where my world can find worshipful inspiration.

There is frost on my love, a crisp despair. I have given to the point of a life-draining heart. And I am too weak not to expect a return. Why is it I close myself off, like a sleeping bird, from all affection offered me and then by day take flight from those who love me? In the darkened theater of my imagination, I watch reruns of my desire for love worn out by cruel denial. God help me. And forgive me, Mother, if I am whining.

I have broken with the stereotype of sanctity that kills all spontaneity. I seek a faith that is open rather than a religion that fashions only defense mechanisms. I can say to you in all honesty that my faith experience always validates the human and never denies it.

I am well aware that I miss the sacred in the gospel when I don't feel the pull of the gospel's social demands. The sacred occurs when I enter fully into the flow of life.

I still frequently lose my way in the wilderness of the insignificant and I experience a kind of romantic anguish in ignoring unpleasant realities. I fear that I will develop the skill of domesticating Jesus until he becomes no more than a household pet.

Pray for me, Mother. Pray that in the groundswell of my heartbreak I may learn wisdom. Pray that I may not remain alone in visionless, wordless isolation where survival is terror and emancipation is hollow despair.

I remember so clearly how your words, your silences, your glances, your life were a resurrection within me like the full bloom of a summer rose. You were the soother of pain, the sustainer of drooping hearts, the rejuvenator of mournful discouragement, the co-sufferer with those crushed by life's imponderable adversities. You were truly a twilight saint.

The gift I give you, Mother, is as ancient as the Eden Garden, as new as fresh cut flowers, as timeless as an immortal soul: my love.

You indebted son,
Danny

THE RIOT

Two weeks later after he had finished dinner, Danny went to his room and called for NewsNet. "On. NewsNet," he commanded. "Channel 22 XL," he said as he sat down on the comfortable VibeLounge chair the Sisters had provided for him.

Suddenly he sat bolt upright.

There on the screen he saw Tom Aimes, the Black leader from The Alley. He was being interviewed as he stood in front of a burning building.

"We were having a peaceful demonstration," he was saying, "until those damn police came storming in here to maintain law and order. They started to shout orders, scream at us and then they pushed a few people. After that all hell broke loose. The one thing we didn't want was for thugs from another area to come here and disrupt our vigil. But when the cops started a riot, these hoodlums poured in and …. well, you're seeing the results."

Dawn Sylva of 22 XL faced front. She looked frightened. Was it real or was she dramatizing for the sake of ratings. You never knew. Most of these journalists and commentators attended some kind of a drama institute along with their journalistic preparations.

"Here in The Alley," Dawn was using her strained but sultry tone giving the impression that this was a momentous story and she was the star who was breaking it, "what began as a peaceful demonstration protesting the removal of Father Joseph Daniels as pastorate of St. Matthew's Catholic Church has exploded into a violent state of anarchy." Dawn swept her hand in an arc behind her to draw attention to the burning building as if anyone could have possibly missed it.

Danny couldn't believe his ears. Protesting his removal? He never gave it a thought ….

"Mr. Tom Aimes," Dawn continued, "the leader of the Black/Hispanic coalition, as you just heard is blaming the riot on the Chicago police and on arsonists and looters from outside The Alley.

"The residents of The Alley have always been known for their law-abiding behavior," Dawn sounded quite sympathetic. "If anything, they have asked for more police protection from the thugs, as Mr. Aimes called them, who moved into The Alley and caused this havoc. The residents here certainly did not expect the kind of 'protection' they got from the police earlier this evening.

"The question from these residents now is, Could this pillaging by hordes of looters have been contained if the police had not withdrawn after the initial skirmish broke out? According to a spokesperson for the police, they were not prepared for a riot. There had not been any plan or a sufficient commitment of resources.

"The attempt on the part of the police to restrain the crowd that they, the police, had stirred into a furor and to make arrests, even before outsiders rushed into the melee, resulted in rock throwing. The outnumbered police retreated and the rioting roared out of control …."

"Bring Father Joe back here," a white lady, who had pushed herself into camera view, shouted. "Tell that Goddamn Cardinal his palace is next if he doesn't send Father Joe back here." She was about to shout something else but got shoved out of the way by an unseen person.

Dawn Sylva was visibly shaken. It was obvious from her expression that she was deciding whether or not to leave. Just as obvious she was getting instructions to stay.

Danny sat glued to the screen. He couldn't believe what he was hearing and seeing. He felt the appealing ambivalence of elation and embarrassment. This was a horrible triumph. Then he settled into an appalling anxiety for the welfare of these people, dwellers of The Alley. If only he could talk to Tom Aimes ….

What remains mystifying," Dawn seemed to have regained her composure, "is why the police did not send for backup. Why did they stay in their fallback position especially after the outsiders came and began to set fires and to loot?"

Next on camera was deputy fire chief, Emil Austin. "We have the fire trucks," he explained with an air of disinterest. "But we don't have the police escorts. I'm not jeopardizing my men. Fighting fires is dangerous enough without having to worry about getting mangled by a crowd of frenzied looters.

Suddenly more police arrived. The full force rushed after a few of the straggling looters as the mob moved down the street to a Thrifty store. The police grabbed these stragglers and then the mob of looters turned and began to shout defiantly at the police who freed the few men they were holding.

"As we stand here in the midst of this ongoing destruction," Dawn Sylva's voice had reached the pitch of screeching, "you're forced to wonder how much damage, how much lawlessness, how much human tragedy is going to be allowed before someone on the police force takes charge and tells his men to rid the area of this makeshift minority of looters." She was into it now. She knew she was occupying front and center stage. Her words were flowing smoothly and colorfully. The ratings would skyrocket.

Danny could see that the people who lived in The Alley were dispersing. This is not what they had come here for. Tom Aimes was standing on the steps of St. Matt's shouting something but he couldn't be heard. Perhaps he was telling the people to go to their homes.

As they broke up and began to move out, the looters seemed to disappear.

"We have with us now," Dawn was saying, "from our studio, the Mayor. Mr. Mayor, what can you say about how this perverse tragedy has been mishandled?" Dawn was brash beyond derision. She knew she had the Mayor in the hot seat and she was going to turn up the heat as far as it would go.

The Mayor, a quintessential politician, had no trouble turning the grisly scene that was appearing in homes throughout Chicago into political clichés. "If it weren't for this liberal permissiveness that is tearing away at the very fabric of our society," the Mayor said with proper middle class rectitude, "this would never have happened.

"The people who live in The Alley are good people …."

"But," Dawn interrupted the pious homily geared to salvaging whatever votes could be garnered for the next election, "the police are responsible for turning a peaceful demonstration into a riot, are they not?"

"They are most certainly not, Dawn," the Mayor replied with serene reserve. "The law enforcement officers of the great city of Chicago are dedicated to the preservation of law and order. As I understand it, they were just trying to make sure the demonstration did not get out of hand," the Mayor smiled for the camera. "A few fanatics responded irrationally …."

"But what about these arsonists and looters who came here to, well, in effect, to destroy The Alley?" Dawn interrupted again. She would get a bonus for her tenacious grilling of this lackluster, major foot-dragging leader of the great city of Chicago.

"The police have been given orders to hunt down each and every one of those looters," the Mayor responded with a vehemence that he hoped would hide the perception that he was a genial bumbler. "And you have my word that they will all be brought to justice."

The camera shifted to scenes of firefighters doing their best to turn the flaming buildings into smoldering ruins. The Mayor's overvoice could still be heard. "I have nothing but pride and the greatest respect for our stalwart civil servants both of the police and fire departments. It's the insidious hypocrisy of some members of City Council who refuse to give the go-ahead to hiring more such noble and selfless human beings to guard the great city of Chicago."

It was obvious from Dawn Sylva's expression that she wanted to bring this interview to an end as soon as possible. But that was a decision that had to be made at the studio. As if reading her expression, the studio bureaucrats signaled her. "Thank you, Mr. Mayor," Dawn spoke in a sweet tone of professional expertise.

"As has happened in other inner city riots," Dawn's matter-of-fact voice could readily be heard over the high-tension noise of the firefighters, "Black owners of businesses were quick to hang BLACK OWNED signs on their places of business, hoping to ward off Black looters. And, as in other such riots, the signs had been ignored by looters and arsonists."

The camera shifted just in time to catch a gang of looters grab one of the firemen. They threw him to the ground and began to kick

486

him unmercifully. He cried out for help but apparently his fellow firefighters did not or chose not to hear him.

An anguished Dawn Sylva, who had by this time become a major part of the news story herself, shouted, "Where are the cops? Where are the cops?" As was evident from the screen, the cops were nowhere to be seen. Then there was a loud gunshot and the fireman on the ground was seen bleeding from his left shoulder. Finally there was a volley of tear gas. The looters scrambled away and then the firefighters began to choke and run from the area leaving the fires to burn.

"Chalk up another astute maneuver to the noble and selfless members of our police force," Dawn spat out the words in thunderbolt irony. If nothing else the riot would be the occasion of ensconcing Dawn Sylva among the top ten sorcerers of the mass media sophisticates.

Then she herself fell victim to the tear gas and began to choke as she bent over as if to escape the fumes but without success. But Dawn Sylva was a trooper. She raised her head, tears streaming down her face and gasped, "And that's it from here, in The Alley where the removal of a priest has been the *cause celebre* for a brutal riot."

The anchors appeared. "That was a special broadcast brought to you from Channel 22 XL. Now back to our regular programming in progress."

Danny sat stunned. At least Dawn had not mentioned his name a second time. Still he wondered how many Catholics who usually sat on the sidelines of apathy would be churned into anger against him for being the 'cause celebre' of such devastation. He wondered too if the Cardinal had seen the hideous scenes and heard the corrosively cynical report of superstar, Dawn Sylva.

The next morning even before Mass, Danny commanded Channel 22 XL to activate. There was a young man standing amid the ruins of a part of The Alley, doing a second day report. Typical of such reporters, he was properly somber and his rich baritone voice was sepulchral.

"In the beginning," he was saying, "the demonstration was one of righteous indignation directed at the Cardinal of this Archdiocese for removing Father Daniels from St. Matt's, an old and venerable parish, known for its involvement with the poor and needy due in large part to the delicate sensitivity of Father Daniels.

"You may recall that just recently Father Daniels was accused of having an affair with well-known attorney, Celine Korbach. From the information we can get, Father Daniels was removed from his pastorate here in The Alley because of this highly publicized scandal."

Danny could feel his stomach squeeze into knots, his legs were shaking and perspiration began to pour off his forehead. He slumped down in his chair, paralyzed. Was Celine watching this? George? The Cardinal?

"For nine hours," the reporter continued, "hatred ruled the streets here in this ghetto.

"For the most part it was not the residents of The Alley who were responsible for the mayhem that shocked Southside last night. It was the gangs from other areas who charged into The Alley and opportunistically used the demonstration to loot and burn.

"One man who was watching the looters was gunned down and is now in the hospital in critical condition. A car careened out of control when the driver was shot and killed by a sniper. Eventually fire fighters had to put on flak jackets to protect themselves."

The reporter paused and then in a solemn tone announced, "Dawn Sylva of our station, who so courageously stood here last night and reported on the riot, had to be smuggled out of The Alley lying down on the back seat to avoid gangs of young black and Hispanic men who were hurling rocks and setting fires. She is now at home recuperating and taking a deserved rest. Everyone agrees she is a true heroine.

"Thomas Aimes, a black leader in the community, said that he could not tell how many of the local residents participated in the riot. But he added that the rage exhibited last night had been building up for a long time. He said that is no excuse for those who came here and tried to destroy The Alley.

"Still he cited cases where Blacks had died from choke holds and of one man who had been stopped in a routine traffic check and had his head shoved through a plate glass window. To quote Mr. Aimes," the reporter glanced at his notes, "'As Father Joe constantly pointed out (Aimes was referring to Father Joseph Daniels, the former pastor of St. Matt's), there is grave injustice being perpetrated here in The Alley. An injustice that is intensified by the benign neglect of city officials. Last night,' Aimes continued, 'that neglect was responded to with violent aggression.'

" From what we have learned from Mr. Aimes, the peaceful demonstrators intend to come back here this evening. This time, however, we have been informed by highly placed officials, the police will be out in full force. One official who asked that he not be named is reported to have said and I quote, 'If there is so much as a crossed eye, the whole damn bunch of them are going to end up in jail.'"

Danny would get hold of Tom Aimes immediately after Mass. He had to do all he could to put a stop to this demonstration even if he had to go against Bishop Casey's order and go down to The Alley himself.

"Whether or not there will be a repeat of last night, we will just have to wait and see. Dawn Sylva will be here this evening. That's about all there is here in The Alley, the morning after the riot. Back to you, Jim."

Just then his phone sounded, "Excuse me. You have a call. Will you go on line or should I take a message?" "On line," Danny replied.

On the screen appeared Monsignor Richards. "Good morning, Father Daniels," Richards said with almost phlegmatic courtesy. "His Eminence would like to see you immediately."

"Tell him I'll be there after I celebrate Mass for the Sisters. And, Richards, tell his Eminence, that I will wait fifteen minutes and if doesn't see me by then, I'm out of there. Got that?"

Richards was taken totally aback. "Yes, I ... I got that," he blushed.

489

Danny was ushered into the Cardinal's office immediately.

"Ah, Father Joe," the Cardinal smiled. "Please do come in. Take a seat. Would you like some coffee?"

"No thank you, Eminence," Danny replied with due respect.

"These allegations …. may I ask what your answer was to Bishop Casey?"

"He never asked," Danny said flatly.

The Cardinal sat in stiff silence. Then, "He never asked? I did receive a letter signed by several priests indicating that Bishop Casey had mishandled your …. Well, the truth is that I haven't yet got around to speaking with Casey. Perhaps that is why he never reported his conversation with you to me. Did he assume the allegations were factual?"

"Perhaps." Danny was noncommittal.

"So, what this is saying to us is that you were transferred without any admission of guilt?"

"And with a dire promise of a full-blown investigation," Danny couldn't help but feel a bit self-satisfied.

"Tell me," the Cardinal's tone was firm but his expression was compassionate, "if I were to ask you about those allegations …."

"I would answer that what might have been true does not mean it's true now. It was never, I repeat, never an affair. And I would add that if God forgives, who are we to condemn and punish? Maybe it's the difference between faith and religion."

"Still fighting that battle?"

"Till death, Eminence. If I've learned anything in my priesthood, it's that the rote memorization of religious formulas which reinforce our comfort and security is not the faith Jesus calls us to.

"Faith is the shocking realization that God is unexplainable Mystery. And all the good we try to do just draws us closer to Mystery. We cannot reduce Mystery to our rules and regulations, our expectations and manipulations. Sorry if I sound pompous but this is what I sincerely believe."

"Whither have we drifted and, if so, how far?" the Cardinal murmured. "Perhaps it's time for Bishop Casey to experience true pastoral service on the front lines. Monsignor Cappelli's parish is still open. Yes, that sounds like a fine suggestion. Thank you.

"Did Monsignor Richards inform you that your services are no longer required in Rome? The result of another assumption."

"No, he did not," Danny answered severely. "I should have thought that nothing would have given him more pleasure. Unless he thought that by keeping me in the dark, I would grasp at any ray of hope as in no news is good news."

"I don't think he's like that," the Cardinal sounded defensive.

"I guess," Danny said, "when you work close up with somebody, you stop seeing the pimples on his face and soon they no longer exist. By the way, Eminence, did you get my fax about St. Matt's school?"

"No, I did not."

"Then most likely it was intercepted. Maybe we're back to the same pimply-faced individual. If so, the most charitable interpretation is that he wanted to preserve you from becoming embroiled in such a minor matter." Danny was pushing hard. This was his opportunity to deal directly with the Cardinal, bypassing all his lackeys.

"You can be sure I will talk to him — on the carpet!" The Cardinal did nothing to hide his displeasure.

"When I was a young Archbishop, I thought you would one day be my successor. Did you know that?"

"No."

"That was what? Some twenty-five years ago. A lot of water over the dam, as they say. I've been thinking about you since that …. that tragic occurrence, that horrible report was made. You've dedicated yourself in a way I would never have imagined back then."

"Well," Danny countered, "as the twentieth century writer, Elie Wiesel, said, 'Our lives don't belong to us alone. They belong to all who need us desperately.'" Danny felt totally relaxed. The conversation was reminiscent of the ones he used to have with the then new Archbishop so many years ago.

"Yes, yes and there are so many who need us desperately." Again the Cardinal sat in thought as silent as the hushed adoration of the Sisters Danny was currently serving.

491

Then the Cardinal spoke. "I am very proud of what you've done with your priesthood. It hasn't been a perfect record but it is a record of genuine zeal. I must admit that for the longest time I thought you were wasting your talents being at St. Matthew's.

"I don't feel that way anymore. You have used your talents well. Here I am surrounded by people whose pimples, to use your image, are self-serving ambition. I guess it goes with the territory, as they say.

"Did I tell you I have copies of your books of poetry?"
Danny shook his head no.
"Perhaps before you leave you could autograph them for me?"
"I would be honored, Eminence."
"I don't understand all of the poems but there are enough I do understand to make the reading worthwhile. I suppose my symbolic consciousness, as you call it, is not as finely tuned as yours. You have been selfless in your priestly work. I am proud of you."

"Not all that selfless, Eminence. More visibly selfless than thoroughly selfless, I guess. I do crave a return from my people for what I try to do for them. More so than genuine selflessness would countenance."

"Don't sell yourself short, Father Joe. We all need to be affirmed for our efforts. God's affirmation works through people. I'm so sorry that that honor of working with Pope John Paul has been denied to you. Did I tell you he called me personally?"

"No."

"Yes, and he had some very good things to say about you. He considers you the most brilliant student he ever taught. Did you know that?"

"I knew we enjoyed the same kind of intellectual curiosity. And he has shaped my thinking — and my questioning."

"I want you to know that I will intercede on your behalf with the Pope directly and ask him to reconsider. I truly believe you have something very important to contribute."

"Thank you, Eminence. I considered it less an honor that an opportunity."

"I'm certain you did. We have such dreams of making a difference
...."

Danny felt the admiration for the old man that he had had when
he was newly ordained and the new Archbishop was so full of
dreams and plans. Was worry about making a difference integral to
the priesthood? Danny wondered. Probably not. Most people want
their brief stay in this world to be seen as significant in some way
or another.

But there was Muntz, Steve, himself and now the Cardinal all
questioning whether or not they had made a difference, left the
world a little better. Maybe it's false humility that dictates this kind
of doubt.

"You have made a difference, Eminence. You have done things
that will live on after you. Can anyone ask for more?"

Circumstances, Danny thought, had distanced the Cardinal. His
office had placed him on a pedestal or more accurately had sent him
into orbit over and above the people he led. Over and above their
lives of quiet desperation and punctuating joys.

"I have had calls from some pretty important people, Father Joe.
The Mayor several times and one from the Governor. They want me
to do something to stop any further riots in The Alley."

Danny sat in respectful silence. Still he was feeling the thrill of
anticipation. He had had an intuition when Richards called him. He
prayed that his intuition would prove true.

"Do you have any suggestions, Father Joe?"

"I could go back immediately, Eminence."

"Would you? As a personal favor to me? It's not just those phone
calls, mind you. I personally do not want to see these — my people
there suffer. I really don't."

"I believe you, Eminence."

"I tell you if you go back, I will come and celebrate Mass there
before the month is over."

"Thank you. I'm certain the people will be very proud to have
you. There's something else, Eminence. The school. Sister Regina
Pacis has informed the principal that the school will close at the

493

end of this school year. She told me personally that she had your preordained approval on all her decisions."

"More pimples?" This time the Cardinal managed a smile. Danny could tell he was enjoying the image. "Things get away from me. People too. I promise I will look into this matter. I will personally talk with Sister."

"On the carpet?"

"On the carpet." The Cardinal chuckled. "I wish you would give some thought to coming here and helping me. Of course, I don't have long. Mandatory retirement. How is that convent you're at?"

"A most wonderful place for prayer and reflection."

"Yes. I'd like that. You will go back to St. Matthews?"

"With all my heart. I'll go there as soon as I leave you."

"Fine. and give my people in The Alley my love and support."

"I will, Eminence. I most certainly will."

Danny asked for the Cardinal's blessing. As he was leaving, the Cardinal called out after him, "Don't forget your autographs. And, by the way, those allegations .... we all learn greater compassion from our failures and human weaknesses, do we not?"

"We most certainly do, Eminence," Danny answered with a grateful smile.

After signing the books, Danny entered the large outer office to be greeted by Monsignor Richards.

"Hope all went well," Richards said more as a question indicating he expected to be filled in.

"You'll soon find out." Danny couldn't help himself. His aversion to bureaucrats surfaced in his tone. Danny hurried out. He had to get down to The Alley and talk with Tom Aimes.

That evening the people gathered again outside St. Matt's church. The crowd was much smaller than the night before. The number of police was greater. Tom Aimes stood on the top step of the church.

"This evening, I am very happy to tell you, we have Father Joe back with us." The crowd's response was not enthusiastic. Then Aimes announced, "The Cardinal has sent him back to St. Matt's." The crowd went wild with cheers and hoots and all kinds of other

494

vocal noises. Finally Aimes got them quieted down. "I want you to listen respectfully to Father Joe," he commanded.

Danny got up. The crowd cheered again. Danny waited for them to quiet down.

> I want you to know how happy I am
> to be back. (Cheers).
> I know it was not you who brought
> destruction to The Alley last night.
> (Mumbled agreement).
>
> The Cardinal has asked me to bring
> you his love and support. (Silence).
> You need to know how much I want
> your love and support. And I love
> you.
>
> (Cheers).
> We will rise from the ashes around
> us.
> (Cheers).
> We may stumble down the corridor of
> hope from time to time but the wisdom
> you have from your experience I
> know you will share with one another
> and we will reach the end of the dark
> tunnel.
> (Sounds of agreement).
>
> I want you to know that the Cardinal
> is reviewing the decision about
> closing the school. And I believe he
> will reverse that decision. (Cheers
> and wild applause).
>
> God loves you. God is always and
> forever faithful to you. In the darkest

hour God is there for you. He is with you. God has created you out of the clay of the earth and placed a spark of divine love in each one of you.

Your lofty spirit challenges me to conquer the poverty that has been unjustly visited upon us here in The Alley. (Cheers).
Your love warms a cold universe and bestows heartiness in this heartless world.

Will you join me in restoring The Alley?
(Loud shouts of yes).
Will you live in peace with one another?
(More shouts of yes).
Will you now join me in prayer?
(Silence and bowed heads).

Oh Lord, you are the Shepherd who leads us, your flock.
Lead us now into the Promised Land of peace and cooperation.
Roll back the sea of violence that threatens to envelop us. Help us to forgive those who have harmed us and tried to destroy the land you have given us. Help us to make The Alley a place of caring love, joyous support and selfless hope. Amen.

(A shout of Amens).

Now will you go to your homes so
that if those who want to destroy us
come back, the police will be able to
keep them under control?
(A chorus of yes went up from the
crowd).

The crowd dispersed. Quietly. Dawn Sylva watched. "It looks like there will be no riot tonight," she said into the camera. She looked somewhat disappointed as though she had lost her chance at an Emmy. Then she perked up.

"Father Daniels! Oh, Father Daniels." Dawn rushed up to Danny, breathless. There's an Emmy in this young woman's future, Danny thought.

"Father Daniels, can you give our viewing audience a few minutes, please?"

Danny stopped and looked directly at Dawn. She could have been a model, he thought. "Yes, a few minutes," Danny responded pleasantly.

"Do you think the riots are over now?"

"There was only one riot. I don't think there'll be a repeat as long as the police keep the looters out of The Alley. The people ...."

"What do you think of last night's riot?" Dawn interrupted.

"It was a tragedy. The residents of The Alley were the victims not the perpetrators of that riot and ...."

"Are you back for good?"

"According to the Cardinal, yes."

"How important do you think your presence here will be in preserving the peace here in The Alley?"

"It's not just my presence. It's the presence of other leaders like Tom Aimes. And the presence of people of good will like the residents of The Alley. But we also need the presence of city officials ...."

"Thank you, Father Daniels."

Dawn looked intently into the camera, her brow knit in somber reflection. No smile. All concern. In a hushed tone like that once

497

was used at golf tournaments, she said, "Well, there you have it. That was Father Joseph Daniels, the reinstated pastor of St. Matt's ghetto church.

"As you heard, he is convinced that his presence here will forestall any further rioting. The people greeted him like a returning hero. And he humbly accepted their welcoming coronation.

"This is Dawn Sylva coming to you from the smoldering rubble here in The Alley. Back to you, Joan."

Later that night Danny sat in his office feeling very content. Danny called Celine. The phone's butler tone responded. "Mr. and Mrs. Korbach are not able to answer your call. Would you like to leave a message? Or would …." Danny waved the phone dead.

Next he called Gene. He expanded the screen's view to display his office.

"Danny, you are back at St. Matt's? I saw you on 22." Gene's disbelief was countered by his elation.

"Back for good, Gene. This morning his Eminence sent for me and in his inimitable round about way asked me to go back. Quell the riots. Stop the embarrassment."

"I can't believe it. He must have been getting some pretty hefty pressure. I'm not taking anything away from you, Danny, but under the circumstances …."

"Yeah, well I guess the Cardinal didn't get any calls from the Governor or Mayor about the story about me and Celine," Danny managed a weak laugh. "As you saw on 22, I met with a crowd of people as soon as I got back. Talked to them. Promised we'd restore what was burnt. I hope I didn't promise more than I can deliver.

"The Cardinal did some promising himself. He said he'd have a 'discussion' with Sister Regina Pacis about her decision to close the school. I think it'll stay open for the foreseeable future."

"That's great, Danny! Really great. How was the Cardinal? I mean about the story …. you and Celine?"

"I would say compassionate. Furious with Casey. Quelling the riot may have been my redemption."

"Thank God that's …. I'm happy for you. I'm so glad you're back where you belong.

Speaking of schools, I have some very good news too."

"What's that? I get so caught up in my own little bailiwick that I don't even ask you how things are going. I'm sorry. What's the good news?"

"Well, remember Teacher X?"

"It'd be cold day in hell till I forgot about her."

"The good news is that her husband's been transferred. At the end of this school year she's history."

"A double thank God for that one, Gene."

"She's been a devil right up to the end. She's tried to rally the faculty to have the Principal ousted. Insinuated that he was a possible pedophile. Based her accusation on his hugging the little ones. They love him. My God, can you believe that?

"We had to have a damn full-scale investigation. It turned out to be an absolute sham. No proof. No instances. The faculty was in a state of shock. Just lousy rotten innuendos and gossip.

"But she sure stirred up one hell of a storm. My Principal was a basket case. I had the diocesan lawyer inform her that if she persisted, she'd be sued for defamation. She's backed off at least publicly. I had to hold a town hall meeting with the parents. I had the lawyer there at the meeting. He cleared it up legally. But you know how it is. Cleared but under suspicion. My Principal is heartbroken.

"Danny, how can someone like that be so convincing about her deep piety and be so goddamn diabolical at the same time?"

"You said it before, Gene. She's a religious psychopath. She needs professional help like Frankenstein's monster needed lightning."

"One good thing. The faculty has rallied in support of the Principal and they're avoiding Teacher X like the plague. I wish I could toss her out this minute and not have to wait for the end of the school year. The lawyer agreed with me. He thinks she's a sociopath. Devoid of all conscience. Absolutely no sense of responsibility. Frankly, in less sophisticated terms, I think there's a connection missing between her idle brain and her ever-wagging tongue."

"There's nothing more formidable or treacherous than self-righteousness reinforced by psychosis," Danny said in agreement.

"It sort of gives you an insight into how a gang like Viri Lucis could exist."

"It seems to me," Danny went on, "that the self-righteous who proclaim themselves good Catholics unwittingly admit that they are not even good Christians.

"It's satanic, Danny. You know, the real sadness comes not from the fact that 'good Catholics' attack others they consider less worthy or even out-and-out sinners.

"The sadness, the tragedy is that they are convinced that their attacks are based on their deep religious beliefs and that they have a divine right to attack. Well, we have the summer and then she'll be gone, spreading the 'good news' somewhere else." Gene let out a heavy sigh. He really was feeling exasperation over this woman, Danny thought.

"Yeah, if she hates herself, as she apparently does," Danny said, "and refuses to admit it, then she'll go on disguising her hatred of others with the most noble of virtues."

"I only hope she's the exception." Gene's face looked like a knot.

"Problem is there are too many exceptions." Danny sounded sour.

"Well, anyway, I'm glad you're back, Danny.

"I've got to get a list of people who were hurt last night. I'm going to start visiting them as soon as possible. Thank God only one person was killed. But then that's one too many."

"Keep in touch. Things are looking up all around."

Danny called Celine again. This time she was at home. He related the good news to her and she was ecstatic.

"I feel like making a novena of thanksgiving," she laughed. "I saw you on TV. That Dawn Sylva is a real dip. I think she's a few brain cells away from being retarded. But she is a beauty."

"Yeah, her summary was right out of fantasy land. Also the Cardinal promised to come here and have Mass in the near future," Danny told her.

"That's great."

"Wait till you hear this. He told me he's going to contact the Pope and ask him to reconsider. Whatever else, our old Cardinal still has clout in Rome."

"That would be just too wonderful …. Oh, Danny, I will pray for a reversal. You deserve it. And you would make such a fabulous contribution. I know you would."

"Thanks. And I might add that the Cardinal said the same thing."

"I'm so happy that you were able finally to meet with him. Talk to him personally instead of through those sycophants. Did he …. say anything about …. the allegations?"

"He was most compassionate. Truly. My estimation of him is at an all-time high. I hope it's not due to self-serving reasons."

"It's not. Danny, as you know, I'm not given to pietisms but I sincerely believe God wants you at St. Matt's. I really do believe that."

"I only hope the Cardinal counteracts the decision about closing the school."

"He will, Danny. He owes you. Big time. Look, after you're settled, I'll …. George and I will have you over for dinner. Okay?"

"Wonderful. I've got to get out to the Sisters and pick up my stuff. They were very kind to me and they'll be praying for me."

"Take it easy. Talk to you later."

Danny sat for a while thinking about the riot, the damage, the increased burden for the people, their hopelessness perhaps.

There are moments, he realized, perhaps fleeting moments, when you get a glimpse ever so momentarily that skin is not black or brown or yellow or white. It's just skin and you feel comfortable in yours and comfortable that others are in theirs without explanation or apology.

It's then that you feel the unity of the human family, the challenge to make that feeling universal and real. You know that you've not always been as involved in the work for unity as you should be.

But that is no reason for capitulating to failure. In fact, it's all the more reason to try harder, to share your experience. You know possibilities can be real and that's what keeps you going. It's called hope.

Even in those times when you have tried to bring about greater unity and failed, you need to be alert to human finitude. You need to realize that you are not a supernatural force in the lives of others but that you are just another struggling pilgrim on the way.

You may not like swallowing your vulnerability but unless you do, you will have to eat the frustration that turns the milk of ideals into the sour cream of defeat.

You give yourself some breathing room. Some distance until you can convince yourself that others have freedom of choice and are responsible for the choices they make. You are not here to be a messiah for others.

You are more like John the Baptist pointing to the Messiah. You have to come to grips with the reality that there will be times, perhaps more times that you'd care to count or experience when you will stand at the edge of your desert with your promises caught in your throat. All you can do at those times is watch others walk away from you as they did from Jesus. And you let them go. You let go of them knowing that your ways are not always God's ways.

Danny opened his telecomputer. "Calendar," he commanded. "The only thing you are committed to, Danny," the telecomputer spoke in that tinny voice that used to annoy Danny but now sounded so much like home, "is your appointment to meet with the coach of Notre Dame at Hank Covey's house on Thursday evening."

The next few days Danny devoted to meeting with Tom Aimes and other leaders. The riot may not have been repeated but there were many wounds to be healed. And Danny was the Samaritan stopping on the roadside. He also visited hospitals to extend words of encouragement to those who had been hurt during the riot.

In one room he found Concetta, the prima donna prostitute of The Block.

"How are you, Concetta?" Danny asked her.

"Okay, I guess. Don't you go givin' me no shit about God punishin' me." Concetta was patently belligerent.

"I won't," Danny smiled, trying to establish some rapport with her.

"I wan't got by those guys from outside The Alley. My pimp did this to me. I tell him what you says to me and he go nuts. You watch yoself. He's one pissed off dude.

Danny decided this was not the time to go into a lecture about the benefits of giving up her chosen way of life.

"May I give you a blessing so you will heal faster?" Danny asked.

"Yeah, that be nice. He jus' broke my arm. That crazy son a' bitch."

Danny blessed her and was leaving quietly when Concetta called after him. "When I git out here, we talk, okay?"

"I'll be looking forward to it," Danny waved goodbye.

On Thursday evening of the following week, Danny showed up at "The Flash's" house. He was warmly greeted by Hank's mother who told him how happy the people of The Alley were to have him back. Hank bashfully introduced Danny to Coach Westermann.

"It's a privilege to meet you, Coach," Danny said with what amounted to reverence. Some people you reverence because of their achievements, others you're forced to reverence because of their position, Danny smiled to himself.

"And I've heard many wonderful things about you, Father," the coach responded sincerely and warmly.

They sat around and talked for a long while as Hank's mother, Martha, served snacks and sodas. Coach Westermann spoke in great detail about his program and where Hank would fit in as a breakaway tailback. Hank asked a lot of good questions. He told the coach about his girlfriend, Marcia, about his devotion to his mother and how he wanted to do well scholastically wherever he went.

Then at one point, Hank looked at the coach intently. "I've got to tell you this, Coach, in all honesty. I've been offered $30,000 just to sign a letter of intent by more than one recruiter."

"Sounds like the going rate," Coach Westermann smiled. "I'm surprised there wasn't a bidding war for someone with your talent."

Hank sat there. He wasn't sure what the coach meant. Was he going to offer more?

"Hank," Coach Westermann said, "we don't operate that way at Notre Dame. I want you at Notre Dame. I don't remember any player I've wanted more at Notre Dame. But you've got to come because you want to play for Notre Dame."

Danny couldn't help but notice how the coach repeated the name of the school. Each time it was like announcing the legend. It was like speaking words of magic. It had a sacred, hallowed ring to it.

Hank looked over at Danny. "Father Joe?"

"Do you think what those other recruiters are doing is honest, Hank?" Danny asked simply.

Hank sat there staring down at the floor. He was such a phenomenal athlete but he was still only a seventeen year old. Finally he said, "No, Father Joe, I don't think it's honest. But that's the way it's done. That's what's so confusing."

"That's why you've had the training you've had, Hank," Danny spoke softly as though he was worried about scaring Hank off. "All through high school, you've been an all-star. Yet Sunday after Sunday you served Mass for me. That made me prouder than anything you did on the gridiron. You've been such a special example for the kids of the neighborhood.

"You've heard me preach. You know right from wrong. And now it's decision time. You're the only one who has to live with you."

"Coach," Hank said, "I really do want to go to Notre Dame. You've promised me the one thing I want — to be a running back. That means a lot."

"It's up to you, Hank," Coach Westermann said smoothly. Notre Dame wants you and from what you're saying, you want Notre Dame. And I can promise this, too, Hank. You will earn your degree. That will be yours years after the cheering stops. I think you're Heisman Trophy material. And if you should win that honor, it will give you bragging rights. But it will not give you the self esteem of being a college graduate in your own right."

Danny was duly impressed and prayed that Hank would go to a school with a man of such integrity as this coach.

"I want an education, Coach," Hank said with intensity. "In fact I can see me going on for higher degrees some day."

"As I said, Hank, it's up to you," the coach repeated.

"Can I think on it, Coach? Not long. But I have to think about what Father Joe said about honesty. And I want to talk to my mom."

"Fine, Hank. I'll call you, say, within ten days?"

"That sounds good enough, Coach."

Danny excused himself. Repeated what an honor it was to meet the Coach. The coach told Danny, "If you ever want to come to Notre Dame and see Hank play, just give me a call." The coach winked at Danny. They shook hands and Danny told Hank to stay in touch. The coach and Hank walked Danny to the door and watched him walk down the street toward his car. Then the coach and Hank went back into the house.

"He's a good man, Hank," Coach Westermann said. "The best," Hank agreed.

Danny walked down the street. He had to park his car three blocks away.

While he was walking along, he found himself smiling. Earlier today he had received a formal invitation to come to Rome and work on the Pope's encyclical. The Cardinal had come through. There was also a personal note from Doug Haynes saying he was looking forward to spending quite a lot of personal time with Danny. Now the day was ending with Hank. "The Flash" had stimulated his hope. No, more than that. His optimism. Suddenly like a shock of revelation he realized as he never before had that there is good in the world. And that good will triumph. *Good will triumph!* It will!

Here I've been harping about living our faith, he thought, but I really haven't believed in God's power for goodness. Not with every pulse of my life. I've given lip service. Intellectual assent but not the kind of belief that rushes through my whole being like the blood in my veins.

If I really, totally believed in the possibility of goodness, I would constantly feel joy like the jolt of joy I'm experiencing right now.

Belief in the triumph of goodness is what gives you confidence to move in and out of horrible situations with peace and equanimity. No matter how bad things get, no matter how treacherous people are, no matter how much suffering there is, goodness will prevail. God's dream for us will come true.

Belief in the ultimate victory of goodness over evil is the stuff of genuine love. He really was feeling love! A personal love for all the people in The Alley as well as for the greedy rich and everyone in between. No one can take this from me, this love.

People fail. Some are cruel. But goodness will triumph. If just one person truly, fervently believes in the total possibility of goodness, his or her belief will become contagious. One person's belief in the goodness of people can open up so many others to their goodness. I must be that one person, Danny thought.

It's a matter of gentle persuasion. That's it. Gentleness not banging your head against every obstacle in sight. Obstacles are adventures in the making.

Life is good. God is goodness itself. Yes, he said to himself, for the first time since I can remember I am optimistic. I truly do believe. There is goodness all around me. All I have to do is mine for it.

My belief in the triumph of God's goodness in his people is how I can make a real difference. It's my lasting legacy. Goodness, like the Resurrection, rises out of death-dealing evil.

This is what hope is all about. And people want more than anything else to have a person of hope in their midst. They want someone who will gently assure them of the victory of goodness. This is life to the fullest.

He felt relieved as though a lifelong heavy burden — a cross — had been lifted from his shoulders. He felt released as though he had finally walked into the light at the end of his long dark tunnel of doubts and desperate longings for the experience of God, the infinitely generous source of all goodness.

He felt like the Creator God had drawn him into himself and together God and he were able to look at all that was created and see, in the words of Genesis, that it was good. His spirit so long trapped in despondency over the evil in the world was now like the birds of the air, flying higher than ever before.

He felt so free. So *free*! He had never felt this kind of freedom since he was a child with nothing to do but eat, sleep and play. He was experiencing a freedom as exhilarating as a free fall through space.

It was as though he had been freed from all the shackles of doubts, judgments, criticisms, disillusionments, hopelessness. Free from Viri Lucis and the Mentor as Celine's friend, Margaret would say, "and all that."

Danny suddenly realized that all the rules and laws he had so often found fault with had a true purpose: to facilitate openness to the Spirit dwelling within him. He felt like jumping, dancing, cheering, singing.

He was as elated as ... well, as the day of his ordination when everything seemed possible, when hope was as abundant as a hundredfold, when Jesus was as close as his heartbeats.

He remembered Martin Luther King's cheer: "Free at last! Free at last!"

Oh God, Danny prayed as he came to his car, don't let me lose this. Burn this experience into the fleshy tablets of my memory. Help me to believe — always and enthusiastically believe — in the triumph of goodness and the exuberance of freedom.

THE SHOCK

The chimes were counting ten in the evening. Celine was preparing for bed. Then the door signal sounded. She pushed the red button and the door became transparent. It was Gene.

Celine pushed the white button and as the door slid open, she crossed the room to greet Gene. They embraced and Celine said, "Well, isn't this a pleasant surprise," Celine sounded genuinely delighted. "You're not here for a census call, I hope. I haven't registered yet," she said teasingly.

"Hello, Celine," Gene said rather gravely. "Is George home?"

"No, he's away till Thursday. What's up, Gene?" Celine's frolicking manner suddenly subsided.

"Celine, there's been …. Danny was mugged earlier this evening."

"Where…. Is he all ….? How ….? Danny? What hospital?

"Celine, the mugger used a knife on Danny."

"What hospital is he in, Gene?" Celine's voice had reached the pitch of a screech.

"Celine …. Danny's …."

"NooooOOOO!" Celine screamed and then collapsed on the couch.

Gene moved toward the couch. He felt helpless. Celine was quaking with uncontrollable crying anguish. Finally she managed to ask, "How …. how did it happen? Do you know?"

"From what I've been told, Danny had gone to his friend, the football player's house. Hank Covey. He was with the head coach of Notre Dame. Apparently it happened when he was walking back to his car," Gene explained.

"Lou told me Danny was stabbed in the back and right through the heart. He said he didn't think it was a mugging. He said that from the coroner's preliminary observation, Danny was stabbed with a slender Italian dagger. A stiletto. Lou said muggers don't use that kind of a knife."

Gene fell into the chair beside the couch. Then he got up, went over to the couch, sat down and put his arm around Celine who was shaking like a vibrator and crying until Gene thought she might hyperventilate.

"Why? *Why?* **Why?**" she kept moaning over and over as Gene held her tighter as though he was fearful that she would literally fall apart.

"Gene, did Danny tell you about his recurring dream?"

"The one about the burning forest and a little girl named Janie? Yes, he told me."

"I'm thinking of the knife in one version of that dream. My God, Gene, was the knife in the dream some kind of a premonition?"

"I don't know, Celine. I really don't. Maybe."

"And what about the man in a white cassock? Did he tell you that?"

"Yes."

"Who wears a white cassock, Gene? Who? The Pope. That's who."

"You're not suggesting the Pope had anything to do with Danny's .... with his death? That would mean the Pope and the Viri Lucis .... Celine, that's a stretch beyond reason."

"I'm not suggesting anything. I'm trying to put some pieces together. What was the burning forest all about?"

"I don't know, Celine. Dreams .... Who knows what they mean? Dreams are open to as many interpretations as there are interpreters. I don't put much stock in them myself."

Still sobbing she exclaimed, "Goddamn!" She forced the word through clenched teeth, her eyes narrowed in contempt. "He was murdered by those self righteous pompous pious bastards!" She wiped at her angry tears. "He was murdered! Why? He gave them the goddamn note. Oh God, how could those self appointed guardians of orthodoxy do it?

"God damn their rotten souls into the depths of hell forever! They're so orthodox they wouldn't know Christianity if it kicked them in the balls!" She sobbed and sobbed while tears streamed down Gene's face.

Gene sat next to Celine and held her in his arms unable to say anything to console her. Celine was expressing with furious vehemence all the embarrassing hatred he himself was feeling toward Viri Lucis.

"What are we going to do, Gene? What? They can't get away with this."

"Do you want me to call your friend, Margaret?"

"God no! I couldn't take her for one second. Gene, call George. His number is in the telecomputer. Please."

Gene got up and walked to the phone. He waved his hand, activated it and spoke the number. At once George's image appeared on the screen. Gene could see part of the lavish hotel room where George sat.

"Gene?" George expressed more than surprise. "Gene, is something the matter? Celine?"

"George, Danny's been killed. I'm with Celine now."

George's face reflected absolute consternation as though he didn't know where to begin. "Is Celine …."

"She's totally broken up, George. We both are."

"How was Danny killed, Gene? What happened?"

"He was stabbed. Mugger or murder. Lou Mc Dermott's leaning toward the latter. Danny was stabbed with a stiletto."

"Gene, tell Celine I'll catch a Red Eye. I'll be there in a little less than an hour or so, if not sooner. Do you think it was Viri Lucis?"

"I have no doubt. Neither does Celine. We just don't know why."

George raised his voice. "Celine, honey, I'll be back as soon as I can." With that the screen went dead. Gene waved the phone dead.

Gene walked back over to the couch and sat down. "George will be here soon, Celine," Gene said, trying as best as he could to console her. Celine nodded. They sat for the longest time in total silence. Each one feeling the pain of loss. Each one searching for some word that would make sense of this brutal killing. All to no avail.

Finally Gene said, "I don't want to leave you alone. I'll stay until George gets here."

Celine, Gene knew, was drained. Listless. "You know, Gene," she said in a tired voice, "after Danny and I .... got back together as friends, I mean, except for the day the kidnappers released me, he and I never so much as hugged. Not even as friends, close friends. How much of life is a waste?

"I remember," Celine said through her sobs, "that story Danny told about an emergency call. A woman had died during the night. He said after the prayers and anointing, the family gathered in the kitchen.

"He sat down at the table with the woman's granddaughter. She was in first grade at St. Matt's. She was oblivious of the adults around her and was intent on filling in her coloring book. Then she looked up and said aloud to no one in particular, 'I hope Grandma's having fun with God.' Maybe Danny's writing poetry with God."

Celine burst into tears and began to moan loudly. "Oh, Gene .... Gene! How am I going to live without him? How are we ....? All those people. They depended on him. They loved him. I don't think Danny ever realized how much they loved him. Now for sure they'll close St. Matt's."

Celine rambled on. Gene sat beside her in frozen silence, allowing her to pour out her woe. Her heartbreak. The same heartbreak he was feeling so deep. Too deep for words.

"Just let anyone tell me that was God's will." There was fury in her voice. "Maybe it's God's will that your kitten dies but not this .... not this!"

Gene became worried. What was Celine talking about? Kitten?

"Danny would never say it was God's will. Never! He'd have said that human beings abused their freedom to defy God's will. Wouldn't he, Gene?"

"Yes. I think that's exactly what he would have said, Celine."

"If hatred consumes and destroys those who hate, I hope to God the hatred Viri Lucis has eats away at each one of them in the slowest, most torturous way possible. Inch by inch. Bone by bone.

I hope their leprous souls decay in the most excruciating suffering for all eternity."

Gene let Celine rant on. There was no sense in trying to reason with her. She had to get all this poison our of her system.

"Do they just go on, Gene? Viri Lucis. Defaming, destroying, murdering …. My God, can't the Pope do something? The Pope is …. was Danny's friend, his mentor. Danny was his prize pupil. His protégé.

"What about the Cardinal? Are all these powerful men helpless? Viri Lucis is a bunch of psychopaths and religion in their hands is the most dangerous weapon on earth. Under the guise of purifying the Church they'll pollute every soul in the world. They're the antiChrist. Maybe it's the end of the world."

"Celine!" Gene snapped loudly. He had to stop her. She was losing it.

Celine screamed. Gene thought the roar of her crying would bring the security guard running to her apartment. Then suddenly she stopped. The silence was like a funeral parlor.

Quietly, tentatively Gene said, as he put his arm around her again, "There are people who destroy what they're trying to save. Who destroy what they love. It's not just in the Church. It's not just Viri Lucis.

"Married couples do it regularly. Friends. The Military. Politicians. Some are misguided. Some are psychotic. But they all do more than their share of destruction. It's the original sin: Destruction of what is good, innocent and beautiful …."

" …. and parents. Don't forget parents," Celine cried quietly. "Parents who destroy their children trying to make their children the perfect incarnations of what they are not," Celine interrupted.

Good, Gene thought. At least she's on a reasonable wave length. "Did that happen to you, Celine …. an incarnation?"

In a monotone, Celine related what she had learned in therapy about her relationship with her father. Her dead kitten. Her father's pronouncement about God's will. How she had projected her unresolved emotional conflicts with her father onto the men in her life including Danny. How she eventually was able to open this baggage from her past and begin to throw out some of her deep-seated, unadmitted problems.

Gene sat and listened intently. Shocked that such an accomplished, self-sufficient woman who held out her beauty of body and spirit like a gift to everyone could have been tortured to the point of neurosis by a past she had not dealt with. No wonder Danny had been so caring of her.

Celine fell silent.

Gene wondered how many buried problems he had. Problems he hadn't faced. Whoever invented the idea of the Shadow Self made one of the most valuable, remarkable contributions to the survival of the human psyche.

But it's a contribution few ever bothered to accept and cash in on. People just don't want to face their darker, more despicable side — their Shadow Self. And so they are haunted by it on the unconscious level. But conscious or unconscious, it is a destructive force in their lives and in the lives of those with whom they have relationships. Those they love.

Maybe that's why the search for God is so often replaced by a quest for sanity. Maybe that's why letting go of past debilitating psychological damage is so essential to a healthy spirituality. And before the letting go there has to be an admission that the damage exists. And that's the *bete noire* of spiritual growth.

"Are you happy being a lawyer as your father is?" Gene asked, trying to get Celine to focus for the time being on anything but Danny's death.

Celine began to answer. It was less giving an answer to Gene's question than her remembering. She spoke about school. How she got with the firm she now worked for. She described some of the more interesting cases she had had. What her hopes were when she started to practice law. She described with almost harsh honesty her driving ambition. Then suddenly she switched gears.

"Sometimes I wonder if it's all worth it. I mean like Danny was always saying, we have to develop ourselves in all areas of our lives. But I think we zero in on one area or one talent or one ambition and forsake the rest. We grow vertically not horizontally. But like Danny said we're a garden not just a single flower.

"I remember when I was in law school, my father gave me this novel to read. He never said why — just gave it to me.

"It was called *Primary Justice* by a fellow named Bernhardt. It was tattered paperback. My father must have had it in his library for decades. Never said why he gave it to me to read.

"It was about this man, Ben somebody. He wanted to be a lawyer because he wanted to do the right thing. He worked for the D.A. for a while and then he got a hot-shot position with Tulsa's most prestigious law firm. He soon discovered that doing the right thing and representing a client's interests can be mutually exclusive.

"He still wanted to see justice done, to do the right thing, but he discovered that the law firm he worked for was no place to look for justice.

"A scene in the story depicts Ben's visit to his dying father, a doctor with whom he had less than a loving relationship …." Celine stopped as though she was becoming aware of why her father gave her the novel to read.

She continued, "The father/doctor said something to Ben like, 'I guess you were expecting some profound philosophical deathbed advice. Fine. I'll give you some advice. Don't get old. You spend your whole life going from one moment to the next. A happy moment here, a sad one there, hoping to stack three or four of the happy moments together. Trying to freeze time.'

"Then he said to Ben, 'But it can't be done. And then you're old and your life is like a book you read too quickly. All you can remember are a few scattered images and random thoughts. No sense of the whole.'

"At the end of the novel when Ben has been fired even though he was the one who tracked down the killer, he thought that perhaps somewhere in the midst of this fiasco he had done something right. Perhaps, he thought, it was all right to feel happy now. It would only last a moment. and what is life but moments?

"I remember thinking after I finished reading the novel that Ben's father, even though he was dedicated to healing, had no overwhelming purpose of life, no sense of the wholeness of living. His was a life of cynicism bereft of happiness. At least that's what I thought.

"Yet, as Ben found out in the end, there was a certain realism in his father's philosophy. Life isn't just one happy moment after another. There are the sad, the tragic times which we have to live through and deal with otherwise there would never be the happy moments to be enjoyed.

"And I think Ben found out that the happy times come when we do what is right — even if it costs.

"That's what Danny did, isn't it, Gene? He did the right thing and it cost him his life. Where the hell is the happiness, Gene? You do what is right and it's a tragedy? How many moments are we going to be able to stack, Gene? Danny didn't even have a chance to grow old."

Gene didn't respond. He took Celine's questions to be rhetorical.

Celine talked and talked about anything and everything, wandering from here to there with no apparent connections. Finally George arrived.

George rushed over to Celine and embraced her. "I'm sorry, Celine. I'm so sorry." Then he turned to Gene and they embraced in silence.

Gene excused himself knowing that George would be able to care for Celine in every way possible. On the way home Gene thought of Celine's reaction to Viri Lucis. She wasn't just being hysterical. What she said made ultimate sense.

Celine's recounting of the novel she had read reminded him of a line he had read in a novel some years back. "The mediocre can gain notoriety by slandering others." That is the expertise Viri Lucis had: slandering. For them it was all appearance. They detested substance. Here was Danny, a man of substance and the ones who wore the masks of hypocrisy did him in.

Viri Lucis had once again preserved the appearance of orthodoxy by eliminating — by murdering — someone whose authenticity was a brash challenge to all Viri Lucis stood for. Gene's mouth filled with the metallic taste of bitterness.

Anger struck him with the force of a thunderbolt. Too many people down through history have been murdered because of religion, to make religion the standard for judging anyone's orthodoxy.

How true it is that we should live each day to the fullest because we never know which day will be the last. What was it the twentieth century humorist, Will Rogers, said when asked if he had only forty-eight hours to live, how would he live them? "One at a time."

There was a stanza from the nineteenth century poetess, Emily Dickenson which Gene used sometimes in funeral homilies.

> Because I could not stop for death
> He kindly stopped for me.
> The carriage held but just ourselves
> And immortality.

At least Danny was preserved from what he feared most. The doubts that might torture him in a slow dying. God love him, Gene thought with profound depression, he never succumbed to the breaking of the spirit that ensures conformity.

Danny always tried to remind the Establishment why it was established in the first place. As some old Jesuit said, "We're a long way from Galilee." My God, Gene thought, Danny was right when he said we've taken all the wonder, mystery and poetry of our faith and turned it into the drab dogmas of religion.

Gene remembered that Danny used to say that it's all mystery and we insist on defining and pigeonholing it. He used to laugh, "Someone once said, 'The Spirit dwells within us like a stick of dynamite ready to explode' and here we are shuffling papers waiting for recognition and honors."

As Gene pulled into the garage, he wondered how he would ever get himself together for his postponed Parish Council meeting.

The next day Celine did not go to her office. She sat on the couch sipping coffee. Nothing but a blank mind, nowhere to go.

The door signal sounded. Celine pressed the transparence button. It was Margaret. Celine pushed the open button and the door slid open as she stood up.

Margaret entered and walked slowly, tentatively as though she were making her way to Celine on a tightrope. Then suddenly she threw her arms around Celine. "I'm so sorry. I'm so sorry," she kept repeating like a clicking metronome. "George called me. It was on NewsNet this morning. I'm so sorry."

Celine's face looked like it belonged on Mt. Rushmore. Her eyes were as dry as desert sand. Margaret sat down on the blue settee catty-cornered from the rose colored couch. Celine went into the kitchen to get coffee.

She came back, handed the cup to Margaret and sat down on the couch. Without any prelude, she began to tell Margaret in a lethargic monotone about Viri Lucis, the note and the whole psychotic event. Margaret sat in silent, intense attention throughout the entire recital.

When Celine finished, Margaret whispered, "My God."

"Dearest, dearest Celine. I had no idea …. I knew something horrendous was going on when you were kidnapped but …. Your life has been one hell on earth. My God, Celine, the whole thing is like bobbing for apples in a bucket of mud," Margaret loved to use that metaphor. "You must feel like you're trying to hold a dozen corks under water at the same time."

Margaret stared at Celine. Her face was a sullen as a dark storm cloud. "Honey," Margaret tried to soothe, "just remember that a negative reaction is the psychic equivalent of the bars of a prison. Please don't let yourself get into a turtle-in-a-shell depression."

Then in her typical fluttering way, Margaret said, "Dear, there's no problem so tragic that it can't be run away from. May I suggest you treat this tragedy with the Law of Raspberry Jam?"

"What's that," Celine asked with no indication of real interest.

"The wider you spread it, the thinner it is," Margaret didn't smile. Then in a more serious tone: "Honey, I don't want to be a Chicken

517

Little alarmist but are you safe? I mean with all that happened to you, being kidnapped and all that.

"I don't know," Celine responded apathetically. "I guess so. I really don't care."

Margaret was visibly disturbed by Celine's attitude. She didn't know how to deal with it. "Did you see this morning's NewsNet report?" Margaret asked.

"No."

"Well, there's something you need to hear. The Golden Girl, Dawn Sylva, interviewed that quintessential bullshitter, Monsignor O'Henyeu. Those two should take their act on the road." Then Margaret barked in that tone that sounded like a gurgling sink, "Review. Channel 22 XL, eight O'clock morning news."

O'Henyeu's face looked like a fist made out of Silly Putty. Dawn Sylva looked gorgeous as always. "She must get up at midnight to put herself together," Margaret all but sneered. "She's half flesh, half celluloid in her cotton candy finery."

> Sylva (purring): Monsignor O'Henyeu, how is the Archdiocese dealing with this second murder of one of its priests?
> O'Henyeu: Well, Dawn, I can tell you on the record that the Cardinal is crestfallen. We are cooperating with the homicide division of our stalwart police force. Everyone is praying.

"God," Margaret exclaimed, "he's a one man Tower of Babel. A psychic invalid."

> Sylva: I suppose Father Daniels' death will end the investigation into those allegations about his affair with Mrs. Celine Korbach?"

"Now here's the part. Listen," Margaret whispered to Celine.

> O'Henyeu: Actually, Dawn, that was
> a horrendous rumor begun by media
> people of far less credibility than your
> revered newsgathering organization.
> It was rubbish. And, as you know,
> Dawn, Father Daniels was reinstated
> to St. Matthew's by the Cardinal
> himself. It just goes to show you what
> damage irresponsible news reporting
> can do, doesn't it, Dawn." (He looked
> like he was holding a Royal Flush).

"You really needed to hear that, Honey," Margaret said.
"Who cares now?" Celine spoke through clenched teeth.

> Sylva: So what will happen to St.
> Matthew's now, Monsignor?"
> O'Henyeu: No decision yet, Dawn. I
> myself have been thinking of applying
> for St. Matthew's. I think I could bring
> a public relations expertise to the
> ghetto. With that skill I would be able
> to 'urge' the haves of our Archdiocese
> to contribute to the have-nots. I must
> tell you that I have not made this
> sacrificial offering official as of this
> moment. But I'm certain that the
> people of The Alley would be glad to
> hear that their best interests are being
> considered by no less than the upper
> echelon of the Archdiocese.
> Sylva: Would you give up being the
> Secretary for Communications then?

O'Henyeu: Oh no. Not at all. Being pastor of St. Matthew's is certainly not full time ministry – no offense to our beloved brother, Father Daniels. But just the other day the Cardinal told me how much he depends on me to get out all the vital information of the Archdiocese to the media. Now I must tell you that I in no way feel indispensable but if the Cardinal feels that way, who am I to argue?

Sylva: Do you think there is some connection between the murdered Father Daniels who was executor of the will of the murdered Bishop McCann? Or is it just a coincidence?

O'Henyeu: Neither, Dawn. Although I must tell you that the two murders have the priests of the Archdiocese quaking.

Sylva: Have you received any death threats lately?

O'Henyeu: Oh, I can't go into that, Dawn. Although I must tell you that all my public exposure makes me the most vulnerable. I try not to tread on anyone's toes but when you speak the truth as I always do, there are those neurotically paranoid people who imagine their feet have been crushed under the weight of my public statements. I can only say, If the shoe fits ….

Sylva: We seemed to have drifted away from the murder of Father Daniels. Do you think that the murderer will be captured?

O'Henyeu: No doubt. What with our
fine law officers ....

Sylva: But they are still looking for
the one who killed Bishop McCann?

O'Henyeu: That murder should be
solved any time now, Dawn.

Sylva: It should? I haven't heard that.
The last time one of our reporters
asked, the police stonewalled.

O'Henyeu: Well now, Dawn, you
know the police have to be tightlipped
about their progress.

Sylva: But you just said they're on the
verge of solving the murder. Doesn't
that tip their hand?

O'Henyeu: Well, Dawn, all we can do
is pray that justice will be done. Now
I must tell you that I have to be getting
along. A lot of work yet to be done in
the Lord's vineyard, you know.

Sylva: And there you have it.
Monsignor O'Henyeu has informed
us that the murder of Bishop McCann
is all but solved. You heard it here
first on 22 XL.

"Sorry to have put you through all that," Margaret said
sympathetically.

"I just can't believe they were talking about Danny's murder. It's
like a doom-ridden nightmare." For the first time since Margaret's
arrival, tears flowed from Celine's eyes.

"Do you want me to stay with you, Honey?"

"No thanks, Margaret. I'd like to be alone. I have some serious
thinking to do. But I do appreciate your coming over. Really I do."

Margaret got up, bent over and kissed Celine on the cheek. "I'll
pray for you," she said with total sincerity. Without looking back
Margaret left.

Celine went into the kitchen, emptied Margaret's cup in the sink and poured herself another cup. She went back into the living room, went over to the desk and took out a notepad and pen. She went back and sat down on the couch.

Cardinal Rudolf Krantz entered the Mentor's room. He was unmistakably a man whose imagination was hopelessly sterile from habitually exploiting it for selfish gratification. His face wore the steadfast pain of someone who was unable to balance the forces of intellect and emotion, action and receptivity, self-assertion and cooperation.

Despite his almost infinite self-assurance, his eyes seemed to flicker with the coded suspicion that in the end, he would discover that his life had been a vacuum. "Why did you have Father Daniels killed?" he asked with no sign of respect in his voice.

The Mentor smiled benignly. "He was still a threat. Our brother, Father Daniels, was a dangerous mixture of tenacity and unpredictability. He could have taken a copy of that note to our American lawyers. Even though it would have no legal standing, the process could have been slowed. I need that money *now.* The Iranians are not going to wait forever.

"Besides, Rudolf, we have learned that Daniels has been reinvited to Rome to work on the Pope's imbecilic, idiotic encyclical and lest you forgot, our brother, Father Daniel's classmate and friend is the current Secretary of State thanks to that numbskull idiot Tamacci. And Daniels would have had immediate access to his former teacher and friend, Alessandro Percussi, our reigning Pontiff. It was just a matter of tying up loose ends."

"I am not in accord with, as you say, your dispatching these people to their eternal reward. I want you to know this." Krantz was obviously angry. "If just one of these .... these 'dispatches' is traced back ...."

"Rudolf, where is your trust in God?" The Mentor was using his most persuasive, soothing tone. "Do we not believe that God will provide? Do you not believe that what we are doing is God's will? Certainly you do not want to become weak and fearful in our mission. Not after all we have accomplished."

Krantz stood up. The Mentor always smiled when he looked at Krantz. He was a dwarf of a man who tried to cast a long shadow. "You know I put my trust in you. We all do. It's just that ...." Krantz stopped. "I have a meeting to attend." With that he turned and left.

The Mentor sat with a furrowed brow. He turned to his most trusted Attendant. "He bears watching," he said simply.

Later that afternoon, Celine contacted Gene. As Gene looked at her on the viewscreen, he noticed her composure. She spoke in a flat, uninflected voice.

"Gene, I've been thinking. The only lead we have is Monsignor Travine. We suspect he is a confirmed homosexual. Remember Danny's hunch about Travine? That he may have had a string of 'contacts'? I have a plan. Can you meet me at Sheridon's? Say around four?"

Gene waved his hand over his watch to check his calendar of appointments. "Yes, I can meet you," he said.

"Till then." Celine disappeared from the screen.

At four o'clock, Celine and Gene were seated in a booth. They each ordered a glass of Bitter Lemon. Nothing to eat.

"I want you to know," Celine began, "George wants me to back off — back out of this whole horrible quagmire. He said to let Lou handle it. Fat chance he'll find anything. The only route we can go is through Travine. Whether you're with me or not, I'm going ahead with my plan."

"Before I make a decision," Gene said without a trace of annoyance, "maybe you'd better tell me your plan."

"I'm sorry, Gene. Here's what I'm proposing. There's a private detective who works on contract for my father's firm. His name is Jim Solesky. He's good. I've decided to hire him to shadow Travine. We may get something on him or we may not. But it's our only chance. In fact, I've already hired him."

"What does he intend to do? This Solesky fellow?"

"I've invited him to join us at four thirty. Are you with me?"

"As you said, what alternative do we have?"

"Gene, I want them to pay. They murdered Danny. They're going to pay in spades." Celine had now assumed a bitter tone. Perhaps, Gene thought, more wrathful than a woman spurned is a woman bent on vengeance.

They sat not speaking, waiting for the arrival of Jim Solesky.

At about four thirty-five, a man arrived at their booth. Jim Solesky looked to be in his early sixties. Rotund would have been a comical understatement. He sat down without a greeting, huffing and wheezing instead of breathing. His tie hung loose around his neck and looked like it had been to a smorgasbord marathon.

His jacket was motley and seemed to be a metaphor for his lifestyle. He was bald except for a few strands that made hair-raising more than a figure of speech. His bulbous nose looked like it had permanent residence in the neighborhood cafe.

Jim Solesky, Gene thought, was everything you would not look for in a sharp, efficient and dependable investigator. But Celine had assured Gene that Solesky was like a bulldog. Once he sank his teeth into an investigation, he would never let go. He would tear the problem open until the answer was as evident as the conclusions of a research paper.

"I don't give no guarantees," he said as Celine was introducing him to Father Gene. "I'm honest. If I don't think I'm gettin' anywhere, I'll tell ya. But it depends on how long you want me to keep at it. How much you want to spend. As I told you, Celine, I'm givin' ya a break. A hundred and fifty a day plus expenses. The expenses ain't much."

Gene thought of a few questions he wanted to ask but then thought better of them. He said nothing. Celine arranged to have Solesky start right then and there. "I don't want you off on some other caper while you're working for us. Do you understand?" she warned.

Solesky nodded. "Ain't had a case in three weeks. Don't expect they'll come pourin' in now all of a sudden."

BAZUN'S REPORT

Jacquin Bazun, S.J., Superior General of the Society of Jesus was ushered into the Pope's presence by Cardinal Douglas Haynes, Secretary of State.

"Your Holiness," Bazun smiled warmly.

"Jacquin," the Pope smiled back. Haynes started to leave. "No, Douglas, please remain with us. I would like you to hear Jacquin's report with me. It will make it easier later when we have to discuss it." Haynes took a seat across the room as if to study both men.

"Well, Allesandro, I do have something to report. It's so preposterous that I hesitated to bring it to your attention. One of our men who operates in Iran …."

The Pope gave a short laugh. "You Jesuits," he coughed into his red handkerchief, "everyone else in the Church is involved in ministry but you *operate!* Well, go on. What did your 'operative' report?"

"There's a document the Iranians have which supposedly contains an incantation to Michael the Archangel. Supposedly anyone with true faith who offers this incantation will become the most powerful person on earth. Someone who does not have the true faith and performs the incantation will die a most brutal and torturous death."

The Pope looked over at Haynes as though to say, Why is he bothering us with this?

Bazun went on with the entire history of the document. How it was a product of a Gnostic named David of Arimathea, taken during the first Crusade. How it ended up in the Vatican Library, was given to a Nazi soldier at the end of World Was II and how it ended up in the hands of the Iranians. It was a riveting story and Bazun told it with histrionic dramatization.

"And now the reason I am bringing this to your attention." Bazun paused for effect. "Our man in Iran reported that someone — someone presumably high up in the Vatican bureaucracy — has made a bid to the Ayatollah who currently has this document in his possession. He wants to buy it!"

Consternation darkened the Pope's face. "Who in God's name would be stupid enough to believe this fairy tale?"

"You're right, of course," Bazun replied. "Our man who is in the 'ministry' of archivist in the Vatican Library, old Father Pierre Lamieux, said he knew nothing of such a document. At first. Then he did some lengthy research.

He discovered that there had been the transaction between a descendant of Antoine Bisset and a curator of the Library. He came across a notation that the curator had purchased the document as a further proof of the fanaticism and heretical teachings of the Gnostics

"Anyway," Bazun continued, "the report of someone — someone with power and financial wherewithal — wanting to buy this document peaked our interest. There may be — I repeat, *may* be — some kind of secret organization here in Rome. We can't get a handle on it yet. Our men are still investigating. Right now it's only rumor. If there is such an organization, it is a very well kept secret."

Once again the Pope looked over at Haynes who, through the whole of Bazun's recitation, had kept a blank stare on his face, displaying nothing. "What do think, Douglas?" the Pope asked. "Camillo Tamacci? Could he belong to this secret organization?"

"I think the matter of the incantation is rubbish. As for a secret organization, it is possible. Anything is possible in the Vatican. Tamacci? Could be. I think Jacquin's operatives should continue ferreting out any information they can." For the first time Haynes smiled as he used the word, 'operative.'

The Pope turned back to Bazun. "Thank you so much," he said. "And, by the way ...."

"There's something else, Alessandro." Bazun looked very uncomfortable. "And this is not a fairy tale."

"What is it, Jacquin?" The Pope seemed to Haynes that at this time to be doing all in his power to control his cringing anticipation.

"Holiness, one of our men who works closely with the American C.I.A. — I might as well admit it — who is undercover for us *in* the C.I.A. found out that there was or is a plot to assassinate the American President."

"My God, Jacquin, what does that have to do with the Vatican?" Pope John Paul IV exploded in violent panic.

"Again, the rumor part of this report places the ones who hired or tried to hire the assassins here in the Vatican. The C.I.A. is pursuing this 'lead.' There is even talk that the plot might be laid right here on your doorstep."

"My God .... my God," the Pope whispered. "Are you telling me that the American C.I.A. suspects *me* of plotting to assassinate the President of the United States?" This time the Pope's face was twisted into tortured anguish.

"Not you personally, Holiness. But perhaps one of your ...."

"Tamacci?" The Pope erupted. "Do you think it could be *Tamacci?"*

"Not enough information yet. But it is someone who has high ecclesiastical power here in the Vatican. At least that's what the C.I.A. calculates." Bazun was passionately horrified as he related the findings to the Pope.

"Has the plot been foiled?" Haynes asked in a subdued, almost nonchalant, tone.

"As far as we can ascertain, the hired assassins took the down payment and disappeared," Bazun replied. "But the Americans think that there might be another attempt. So they're going to come here and comb this place for any possible perpetrators. They may even want to talk to you, Alessandro."

"Splendid!" the Pope exclaimed with slashing rage. "Can you see the headlines? POPE QUESTIONED IN ASSASSINATION PLOT AGAINST U.S. PRESIDENT."

"I'm certain the interview will be conducted in the most discreet manner, Alessandro." Bazun's assurance was lukewarm.

"All I can tell them is about my own suspicions of Tamacci. Should I do that? Tamacci will deny. But the news people could get a simplistic, a biased headline out of that. The damage it could do to the Church …." The Pope's voice trailed off into a dismal doomsday silence.

"Inasmuch as it is only a suspicion, Holiness," Haynes finally broke the silence, "and you do not have concrete proof to name Tamacci, I don't think you have to mention his name"

"I agree with Douglas," Bazun said quietly. "The C.I.A. has some facts and a lot of conjectures. If they want to come here and investigate, then let them investigate. There's nothing that says you have to aid them. It's their job. Let them ferret out what they can."

"Glory be to God," the Pope's voice was lowered to a hushed prayer. Silence filled the room for what seemed like eons. Then the Pope in a lighter tone said, "As I was saying, Jacquin, bring Father Pierre around sometime. There are some authentic documents I would like to peruse."

"Always the scholar," Bazun laughed out loud.

"Yes, and often I wonder why," the Pope smiled.

"May I be so presumptuous," Bazun said, "as to remind his Holiness that Jesus said we will produce a harvest of thirty or sixty or one hundred fold? It seems that he doesn't expect one hundred percent success all the time. He'll be satisfied with our sixty or even thirty percent."

"If I may," Haynes joined in, "in baseball in the United States, if a player has a batting average of .300, that is, if he only hits the ball three times out of ten, he' considered a superstar.."

"It is certainly worth my meditating on," the Pope responded. "These two images. I need to trust more. And I thank both of you for reminding me of that. The tension of living the gospel is between our desire to be perfect and the messiness of life."

Douglas Haynes was duly impressed. Here was this man who was considered one of the scholarly geniuses in the Church so childlike and transparent in his humility.

Haynes had heard Cardinal Krantz at their meetings call John Paul IV a do-nothing Pope. "All we have to do is wait for him to die so that we can get on with the business of doing away with all these unorthodox liberals who are destroying the very fabric of the Church," Krantz had said.

"It is a time when we all need to trust more," Bazun said. "Whatever is going on, we are not certain what God is demanding of us. We have to trust that even though we are slow growers, we are growers. And we have to trust that a little progress is still progress."

The Pope turned to Haynes as he moved to escort Bazun out. He spoke softly as though he were whispering his most intimate sins in the confessional.

"Douglas, go to Tamacci. See if you can find out anything about a secret organization here in Rome or anywhere else for that matter. Don't mention the assassination plot. Not just yet.

"There's something about that Perez matter that is still gnawing at me. Why would Tamacci, the Secretary of State go after Perez? Tamacci who thought only in terms or world events. Did he really go after Perez on his own?

"If there is such a secret organization and if Tamacci belonged to it, wouldn't his attack on Perez make more sense? Perhaps he was ordered to do this? That is, if he himself was not the head of the secret organization.

"I would be willing to bet my infallibility that Tamacci knows something, if not everything, about this matter. Of course, I am not a betting man. And anyway infallibility is not mine to bet with. It belongs to the Church," the Pope exhibited his mischievous smile.

"Come to think about it, why doesn't infallibility serve as a source of revelation on a secret group in the Vatican?" The Pope managed another slight smile at his own attempt at humor in this diabolical situation.

"Holiness," Douglas finally spoke up, "if such an organization does exist, doesn't' that mean that the Vatican itself may be under assault? Your sacred office and even you personally?"

"I hate to even think about that, Douglas. Get over to Tamacci as soon as you can, please."

"I'm on my way, Holiness."

"Jacquin, thank you so very much. I mean that sincerely."

"I am sorry that it had to be such …. a disturbing report, Alessandro." With that Jacquin Bazun began to take his leave.

"You will keep me informed?" The Pope sounded exhausted. "Here I am planning one of the most stupendous public relations onslaughts and I find myself under assault."

"As soon as I hear anything. Perhaps our 'operative' within the C.I.A. will maneuver his way into being the one who visits with you. We shall see." With that Bazun bowed and left.

Three hours later, Haynes reported back to the Pope.

"Total denial," was Haynes very brief but comprehensive report. "Tamacci said he had no idea under heaven what I was talking about. It was a sullen confrontation from his side. He seems incurably bitter. Maybe it was because I was the one who was accosting him. I'm certain he is nurturing a volatile resentment against me."

"A stone wall, eh?" The Pope appeared too tired to be outraged. Or was he going through the agony of disappointment at Tamacci's refusal to talk. Douglas wasn't sure.

"Do you think if I brought him here to talk to you face to face ...." Douglas's voice trailed off, allowing the obvious suggestion to the Pope to sink in.

"I'm afraid, Douglas, Camillo's loyalty is not to me," the Pope sighed.

" Holiness. Perhaps Father Bazun will be able to track it down for us .... for you, I mean," Douglas corrected himself.

"'Us' is most appropriate, Douglas. I consider you my *alter ego.* I depend on you to keep reminding me that all that is urgent is not important. For better or worse, we are defined by the mutual problems that confront us."

"And the joys," Douglas smiled. "The victories .... we have to be victorious. Christ is with us until the end of time and ever after. We are all bonded together by God's dream for us. What divides is the way we respond to that dream.

"But, Holiness, that's what you are here for. To help us to respond with unity not uniformity. It is obvious to me that you are already involved in fostering a creative response by bringing together so many diverse people to help you with your encyclical."

"True, true, Douglas. But it is such an overwhelming task: the bitterly unreconciled, the anachronistic reactionaries, the stubbornly unalive, the outraged fence-sitters, the arrogantly indifferent, the joyless progressives, the controlling intimidators, the pretentious moralists — my God, Douglas, how can I ever be a sign, not to mention, an enabler of unity."

Douglas broke the heavy seriousness of their exchange by laughing out loud. "Sorry, Holiness, but I couldn't help but think that you certainly didn't leave anybody out of your facile litany."

"It was quite imaginative, wasn't it?" The Pope sounded like he was giggling. "Maybe that is how I should address the encyclical. Using all those categories I just mentioned." Now the Pope was laughing. "Or maybe I should just address it, 'My dear Dissidents,' and no one will feel left out.

"Still, Douglas, I have to make whatever efforts I can. Otherwise my papacy will go down in history as a tragic chronicle of sins of omission."

During his lifetime Alessandro Percusi had been preoccupied with sins of omission. He worried that people were in the habit of confessing what they did wrong but ignored the good they could have done and did not do.

He knew sins of omission were due sometimes to the shrug of the shoulders in blazé indifference and at other times to the sub zero hearts of raw callousness. Whatever, too many who prided themselves on admitting the sins they committed were as detached from the needs of others as mannequins.

He thought that people didn't want to get involved because the ditch on the roadside of life was no antiseptic clinic and if they stopped they would most assuredly be up to their elbows in the mess of binding the bloody wounds of those beaten by the frustrations of life and robbed of their rightful dignity as human beings.

Too often people allow their past negative experiences to become a straightjacket rendering them immobile as they selfishly dwell on their own plight, actually enjoying wave after wave of self pity.

In their sins of omission people pull the plug on the generator of affirming aid and as a result the sparks of enthusiasm in others never burst into the flames of zeal.

And yet he knew that personal involvement, doing the good that had to be done here and now, was the golden clasp that held together all the links of human relationships. The question that he faced was how he, the Supreme Pontiff, could get personally involved?

"Well, Douglas," the Pope said recovering himself, "let us wait to hear from Jacquin Bazun. I'm sure he will come up with something. Then we can move in on Camillo Tamacci. If we have proof of the existence of some subversive group, Tamacci will cave in."

The image of Cardinal Krantz appeared on the Mentor's viewscreen.

"Mentor," Krantz said in a controlled but bristling tone, "just for your information. The American C.I.A. will be swarming all over Rome looking for the perpetrators of the plot to assassinate of the American President. You promised me you would leave him alone."

"I promised you I would not follow my original plan about having his niece accuse him of pedophilia, Rudolph."

"But you went ahead and spawned a plot to have him assassinated?" Krantz was losing control. "You did this without consulting me …. us?"

"Rudolph, Rudolph, be at peace. No one will trace this back to us…."

"May I strongly suggest that you pray fervently that that will be the case, Mentor?"

"Thank God for you, Rudolph. You do enough worrying for all of us. God bless you and thank you for informing me." The Mentor waved his phone dead.

The Mentor turned to his chief Attendant. "Prepare. If those American barbarians get too close, we will give them Tamacci. Make certain that the trail will lead clearly to him. Fabricate the proof and make it air tight.

"And prepare the injection. If we do have to throw Tamacci at them, I want him to be totally unable to remember anything. All they'll have is a blithering idiot, which he already is. But we can't take any chances that he will reveal anything."

"At once, Mentor," the Attendant bowed and left.

"Only use the injection if they get close," the Mentor ordered. "I prefer that Tamacci suffer his humiliation for as long as possible."

Once again the Attendant nodded as he left.

C.I.A. agent Richard O'Leary approached Pope John Paul IV with uneasy reverence. He knelt and kissed the Pope's ring. Pope John Paul was seated behind his desk.

O'Leary was not a tall man. Perhaps five feet ten or eleven. He was wiry in a way that gave the impression that he was a man of extensive physical strength. His blond hair was thinning. His blue eyes sparkled and although he had not smiled, the creases around his lips indicated that his smile would be magnetic. He was a handsome looking man in his mid forties.

The Pope stood up and made a gesture of raising O'Leary from his kneeling position.

"Please," the Holy Father invited, "sit down. You are C.I.A. agent Richard O'Leary. I have heard much about you and your work from Father Bazun."

"Your Holiness," O'Leary was obviously uncomfortable, "Father Bazun has informed me of all the information that is available to date. I might add it's more information than we at the C.I.A. were able to gather."

"And your reason for coming to me?" the Pope asked in a neutral tone.

"*Pro forma*, your Holiness. I was able to have myself designated as the one to …. to interview you on the assassination plot."

"As you know, Father O'Leary, I know little about it. I have some suspicions but that is all they are. Were I to share them with you, I would be guilty of the sins of rash judgment and slander, would I not?"

"Yes, your Holiness, you would be. However, I must be able to give a report to my superiors at the Central Intelligence Agency. Perhaps a few words that I might quote?"

"And if I deny any knowledge of an assassination plot, would you superiors believe me? They, as I understand it, believe that We have access to more international information than any other 'organization' in the world. Is this not true?"

"True," O'Leary responded guilelessly.

"You may state in your report that The Vicar of Christ has been informed of a secret group within the Church. That no proof has been proffered. That I have been informed that an assassination plot against the President of the United States was perpetrated by someone possibly from this secret group or someone high in the Vatican chain of command. That no proof has been forthcoming as of the time of your interrogation.

"That we like you are investigating these allegations but, as you Americans always like to advertise, the party or parties in question, if they exist at all, are innocent until proved guilty. I believe that accounts for all my knowledge on the matter as, no doubt, your Superior General has already told you."

"There is the matter of Camillo Tamacci, your Holiness."

"You may certainly go to question him. I doubt if you will get any further information from him. In fact, you will get less than what I have admitted to."

"Thank you, your Holiness. I think I have enough from you for my report."

"You are one of Father Bazun's 'operatives,' are you not?"

"Yes, your Holiness. No one at the C.I.A. knows about my being a Jesuit priest."

"I understand that you have a doctorate in criminal law and one in psychology."

"And," O'Leary smiled for the first time — a sheepish grin — a doctorate in Liberal Arts."

"You certainly must be a prized member of the Agency. You Jesuits certainly do prepare well for your ministry or 'operations' as the case may be."

"Yes, we do. And I *am* a most trusted member of the Agency."

"What would happen to you if the Agency found out that you funnel information back to your General Superior?"

"Probably be tried for treason, you Holiness."

"Then you are at grave risk."

"Yes, your Holiness."

"But with your obvious superior intelligence you feel you can keep your secret from the members of the Agency?"

"That is my daily prayer."

"It will also be mine, Father O'Leary. Each day. For, as you know, whatever information you are able to give Father Bazun will come to me. Such information will help me in my decision-making processes. So, you see, my son, you are very valuable to me."

"Thank you, your Holiness. I only hope I will be of service to both my Church and my country without betraying either."

"Kneel now and I will extend to you my blessing so that you can get that report in on time."

Richard O'Leary, C.I.A. agent and Jesuit operative, knelt and blessed himself. He then rose, bowed and left the august presence of the Vicar of Christ on earth.

THE HOMILY

On the evening before his funeral, Danny's body lay in state at St. Matt's. The funeral was scheduled for eleven O'clock the next day. From eight to eleven-thirty that night, people processed by the coffin. As Danny's executor, Gene had made all the arrangements. He had been told that the Cardinal would be there. Gene stood in the back of the old church watching — and praying.

Gene was amazed at the number of people who came to pay their respects. For the most part the people were from The Alley. Poor people, people of all kinds of ethnic and racial backgrounds. But, Gene noticed to his surprise, there were quite a number of well-dressed, apparently well-heeled people too.

One such person, a man who bore himself with unpretentious dignity, stopped on his way out to speak with Gene. "I never met Father Daniels," he said, "but I read his poetry. There are a lot of us here this evening who loved his poetry. How does God allow someone with so much to offer, someone who could have enriched our lives even more ....?" The man walked away shaking his head.

The next morning Gene stood to give the homily to an overflowing crowd.

> I want to begin this morning by telling you about Father Joe's will. Most of you know that Father Joe or Danny, as we, his closest friends, called him — and if you don't mind, I'd feel more comfortable referring to him as Danny — he was the executor of Bishop Michael McCann's will.
>
> Many of you also know that Bishop McCann was a very wealthy man in his own right. As executor of Bishop McCann's will, Danny stood to gain

anywhere from 20 to 30 million
dollars.

In his very simple will, Danny
bequeathed all his money to St. Matt's
parish and school. One third to the
parish and two thirds to the school.
In his own words, 'This money is to
be used only and exclusively for St.
Matt's parish and school and for no
other purpose.' I might add that any
money I receive for acting as Danny's
executor will be likewise given to St.
Matt's.

Gene stopped. He glanced over at the Cardinal but his head was
sunk in his chest. Gene took a deep breath. It was apparent he was
trying to get control of his rush of emotions. Celine and George were
sitting toward the rear of the church. She too took a deep breath and
fought back tears. George looked straight ahead, mixed emotions of
jealousy, regret and affection plagued his heart.

"I want you to give some thought to our taking a cruise for a
month," he had said to Celine. "I'll give it some thought," she had
replied. But right now all her fierce obsessive energy was on Jim
Solesky's investigation. Gene continued.

I could go into a long litany about
Danny's, your Father Joe's, dedication
to the people at St. Matt's here in The
Alley. But you know that better than
I. I would rather talk about him as a
man of faith.

Danny's faith was his greatest treasure
and his most poignant torture. Faith
for him was not simply a matter of

total acceptance. Rather his faith was always a search, a seeking. His was a questioning faith that led him sometimes into severe mystical experiences and at other times into a sea of perplexity like a boat without a rudder.

Most of the time his faith was an adventure where the divine and the human intersect as mystery. Rarely was his faith a safe port in the storm of life. Danny was the most brilliant person I have ever known. Yet on one occasion he said to me, 'The more I study, the more I realize how little I know. The more I reflect, the more I question.'

There was a sincere humility in his seeking. A realization that there are no easy answers like those which the superficial practice of religion provides. He was neither a liberal or a conservative. He was a radical believer in the values of the gospel. And this was what set him apart. He would not make any compromises with the demanding challenges of gospel living.

This was his lifelong battle: living our faith as opposed to practicing our religion. He saw religion without faith values as being pious and at the same being selfish, prayerful and yet indifferent, penitential and yet uncompassionate, orthodox and yet self-righteous. He saw with clearer vision than anyone I know that it is possible to take care of our own selfish spiritual security and foster our own delusions about God. Yet he also saw that because we use religious language, we can presume to call this faith.

How often I heard him say and you did too that faith was more than being good according to rules and regulations. He said that living our faith is a clarion call to heroism.

It takes heroism to stand up for gospel values in our culture which ignores or sneers at those values. This is why he so strongly advocated living our faith in a countercultural way.

How often he said that when our culture proclaims that if you turn the other cheek often enough, you face will look like a ragged doormat, faith teaches that if you turn the other cheek always, your face will look like the face of Christ. How he struggled to help people to live Christ's vision of faith rather than their own version of religion.

Because of his deep but troublesome faith, Danny, your Father Joe, was always seeking in the messiness of life for the power of poetic insight.

He invested the commonplace with enchantment. He refused to seal the meaning of life with the language of fainthearted piety. He sought the grace of a gentle exploration of beauty as he served his God who has the inexhaustible capacity for surprise. Danny, your Father Joe, lived the belief that not succeeding was far better than not trying at all. And he dedicated his priesthood to helping people to practice a religion that was infused with faith values.

In his seeking, he clung to the gospel image of the Widow's Mite. He believed with all his faith filled heart that each one of us can make a contribution, no matter how small, to the overall impact for good in the world. He also believed in the Jesus saying, 'One sows, another reaps.' He was convinced that what he was doing would bear fruit some day somewhere. That it was not his immediate concern as to when or where or who would get the credit. He said repeatedly, 'You can get a lot of good done if you don't worry about who gets the credit.'

His was an open-ended abandonment to the unpredictability of God's challenges coming to him through the people he served so willingly, so zealously, so selflessly. He was a genius who never used his intellectual gifts to manipulate others or make them feel inferior. In fact, his true genius lay in the fact that he was able to learn from everybody and anyone. For him the fact that people were there and were human entitled them to his caring love and generosity. He said to me, 'I have never met anyone who did not want to be loved or to love — no matter how they try to deny it.

Danny didn't laugh very much. Perhaps he was too haunted by the injustices in the world, too close to them. He was not an idealist but a realist with ideals. But his very realism put him in open conflict with the wickedness and the blatant maliciousness of the world around him. He was forever engaged in the struggle against the enemies of life such as bigotry, exploitation, abortion, excessive competition, the haves having too much and the have-nots never having enough.

Danny, your Father Joe, was a seeker. He spent his life seeking the truth as it had meaning for him and those he served here so lovingly. He sought the beauty of God's creation in the midst of human deprivation. He was a seeker of the meaning of life and the significance of our relationships with God who is the bond of love in all human relationships.
He believed that even after death, it would not be eternal rest

541

that was granted but a restless seeking
out of the depths of
God's infinite mystery.

In his seeking, in his questioning
— even in his doubting, Danny, your
Father Joe, constantly strove to cut
through the respectable excuses for
bigotry, to heal the blindness of self-
righteousness and break the mood of
sublime self-sufficiency. He tried to
reach those who had withdrawn into
self-enclosed piety by being prophetic
enough to disturb their comfortable,
well-fed virtue.

How many clenched fists he forced
open into praying hands we will never
know. He wanted for himself and for
others the ability to see their faith
values in an acutely imaginative way.
This is what made him such a sensitive
poet. And how he loved the children of
St. Matt's and of The Alley! How he
loved their wide-eyed questions. And
the hope he felt in their innocence. He
lived for their future. Now because of
his bequest, their future is secured. St.
Matt's school will be the finest in the
entire Archdiocese.

Someone asked me last night, Why
would a good God allow this to
happen to such a person who still had
so much to offer? Danny's answer
would have been, God did not allow
this to happen. God grants us the

greatest gift of all, our freedom. He even gives us the freedom to abuse our freedom. My death, he would say, is the result of such an abuse. And now we celebrate Danny's total, absolute freedom to continue exploring the mystical depths of the God he loved and served so well in the people entrusted to his loving care.

Danny, your Father Joe, ached always in his search of the mystical experience of his faith. It was the beauty and torture of his whole life. His vision was too expansive, too radical for one human being to bear, to realize. Yet it was when he encountered those whose lives had been torn with the crude lashes of disillusionment and repression that he felt the trembling vibrations of the mystical in life. For him life itself was a mystical experience. For him each person was a fragment of God's mystical revelation.

Let me conclude with a poem he was working on the day he .... the day he died: This flame, this flame, burns within me burns uncontrollably, irrepressibly then burns out leaving me with the blister of memory the wrinkled torment of what has been.

In this lifetime, this wink of eternity, what must I leave behind in this world of floating sensations of heartrending

543

illusions to enter into the vastness of
a wilder dream?

I am on my way to deep silence there
are no words now only the feeling,
the unutterable feeling. In the fluid
world of emotion images, like fish in
the deep, are all graceful are all silent
and I know in the Mystical we call
Love, in this life, hope is forever
the beginning of the end — an eager
hope pleading with cosmic Beauty to
once again be incarnate in my welling
dread that love may be too fragile to
enfold.

Gene left the pulpit and went to the Presider's chair. He was visibly drained. The sadness on his face as obvious as the perspiration on his forehead.

Celine wiped the tears from her eyes. She sat lost in her own thoughts, oblivious of the rest of the Mass. Sadness had been supplanted by vengeful determination, sorrow, by vindictive retaliation.

She couldn't go to communion. She knew that the raw hatred she felt toward Viri Lucis was not — could never be — a tribute to Danny's memory. It might well be her unpardonable sin. That would be up to God.

All through the Mass, the Cardinal wore a somber expression. During the homily his head was bowed. At the end of Mass, he stood up, walked with effort to the pulpit and with tears, said in a weak voice, "I loved this priest."

The same was not true of Monsignor Richards who was still smarting from the dressing down the Cardinal had given him. After Mass Gene thanked Richards for coming. Richards, with the off-handed indifference of a well-schooled bureaucrat said, "I didn't come. I was sent. And may I say I enjoyed the revisionist history in your homily."

Gene took back his extended hand and whispered, "Will there even be anything in your life worth revising?" With that he left the sacristy.

THE CONFRONTATION

After ten days of surveillance, Jim Solesky called Celine. "Nothing," he said. "Man's as clean as a new bar of soap."

"Keep at it, Jim," Celine ordered with an urgency she didn't even know she had. "It's our only lead. Stay with him."

"Gotcha," Solesky said.

The following Thursday, Solesky contacted Celine. "We may have hit pay dirt," he said in his laconic manner.

"What?" Celine exploded. "Wait a minute, Jim." Celine pushed a button. Gene's image appeared on a split screen. "Hello, Celine. Hello, Jim," Gene said. He was greeted in return.

"Go on," Celine said to Jim.

"Well, I trailed Travine and a handsome companion to Dreamland Motel. Bungalow 11 last evenin'. I stayed there about five and a half hours. I snapped some pictures of them goin' in."

"That's not enough," Celine scolded. "We need more than that."

"It'll be handled," Solesky said with no emotion. "I'm gonna plant a video bug, hopin' he'll use the same bungalow."

"How will you do that?" Gene asked.

"Don't worry. I'll do it. If I git anything, I'll git back to ya." With that Solesky disappeared from the screen.

"What do you think?" Gene asked Celine.

"I trust Jim implicitly," Celine reassured Gene.

"Okay," Gene said. "Until we hear from him."

"Gene, I didn't have the chance — no, that's not true. I didn't — I couldn't bring myself to say anything to you about your homily. I'm really fighting bitterness the likes of which I never knew I was capable of. Your homily was exquisite. You captured Danny ...." Her voice failed at the mention of the name. "It was just beautiful. If you will, I'd like copies of his last poems. I think I'll get them published."

"Thanks, Celine. It was the most difficult thing I've ever done in my life — that homily. And I will teletype his poems to you. I forgot to mention that Danny left you all his notebooks and discs. I'll get them to you as soon as I can. Keep in touch."

"Will do, Gene."

On Friday morning Solesky meandered into the manager's office of Dreamland Motel. He was dressed in overalls with a plaid shirt. He wore a heavy imitation leather belt with all kinds of tools hanging from it.

"Got a call about the shower in 11," he said with drawling indifference.

"I don't know nothin' about no shower," the clerk spoke in a hurt tone as though he had been excluded from the most important decision ever made in human history.

"Here's the order sheet," Solesky spoke as if he couldn't care if he had to work or go on a coffee break. He handed the fake order to the clerk.

"Oh, okay," the clerk snapped. "Here's the key to 11. Just make sure you bring the damn thing back."

"Right," Solesky droned. Solesky sauntered to number eleven.

Once inside, he moved quickly. He turned on the shower and let it run. Then he took out of his leather pouch a tiny circular visor button. It was flat and plain. In fact it looked like a piece of mirror. He fastened the button to the mirror over the desk in the middle of the room. He wiped it thoroughly until it was indistinguishable from the mirror.

Then he took out an electronic video monitor. "On," he said. Then, "Record." He walked slowly back and forth in front of the mirror. He lay down on each bed. He then took a small TV receiver out of his pouch. "Play," he said and watched himself walking back and forth and lying on the two beds. Now all he had to do was wait for evening. Every evening until the prey and a friend showed.

On Wednesday evening at five O'clock, Solesky muttered, "Pay dirt!" As soon as Travine and companion entered bungalow 11, Solesky gave the appropriate order to the monitor. He had unlimited recording time. Solesky had nothing else to do so he curled up and went to sleep. Two hours later he woke up, grunted, snorted and stretched. He looked down at the monitor. The red light was still blinking which meant the machine was still recording.

Enough, he thought. Time to have a look. "Rewind," he commanded. Then he spoke at the receiver, "Play." He watched for about ten minutes and then exclaimed with more excitement than he had felt in the last twenty years, "Pay dirt!"

Solesky drove over to Celine's without bothering to call. Celine called Gene. Gene said he was leaving at once. George poured Solesky a heavy drink of Scotch. Celine paced back and forth, waiting for Gene. All Solesky would say was, "Paydirt."

When Gene arrived, the four of them sat down. Solesky pushed the wire into the televisor receptacle. George said, "Play." They sat and watched. Celine watched for about five minutes and then turned away. George got up and went to pour himself a drink. Gene and Solesky continued to watch.

"There!" Gene shouted. "There! Travine's face in full view! Full view!! No doubt who it is. We've got him!"

Celine turned back when she heard Gene shout. She too saw Travine's face. Gene motioned to Celine and she said, "Off."

"I always prided myself," Celine said to no one in particular, "on being very liberal about people's sexual preferences, but I never ...." She hesitated not knowing what she was feeling or how to express it.

"Next stop," Gene said with determination, "Monsignor John J. Travine's apartment."

"I'm going with you, Gene," Celine sounded just as determined.

"I hope," George, who had been standing behind the couch, spoke solemnly, "I'm not hearing vengeance here."

"I don't think ...." Gene began.

"It's justice," Celine interrupted. "And sometimes justice is hard to separate from vengeance. It depends on who is guilty of the injustice." Even as she spoke she felt embarrassed. Her bitterness has taken hold beyond control and she knew George was very upset with her. But she persisted. "Danny was murdered and justice has to be served." She spoke without emotion. Matter of fact.

Celine got up and took the video wire out of the televisor set. "You have copies?" she asked Solesky.

"Didn't have no time. Will get them for you by tomarra."

"Good," Celine walked over and stood in front of Gene who was seated on the far end of the couch. "When do we go to Travine?"

"What about tomorrow evening? Chances are he won't be busy on a Friday night since he doesn't do weddings," Gene replied.

"How ironic," Celine almost snarled. "Tomorrow evening it is. We go unannounced?"

"Unannounced," Gene agreed.

At seven O'clock on Friday evening, Monsignor Travine saw through the transparent door Gene Shilling and a woman he assumed was Joe Daniels' mistress. He pushed the button and the door slid open. He walked toward them. "What is it you want?" he asked in a cultivated, suave voice. He was clearly a man who had never turned down the volume of his own vested interests.

"We want to see you," Gene answered in a neutral tone.

"You didn't call ahead for an appointment." Travine countered.

"The business at hand won't take long," Celine was sharp.

"Come in then although I think common courtesy would have dictated your calling for an appointment," Travine was annoyed.

"John, this is Mrs. Celine Korbach," Gene bowed slightly toward Celine.

"Oh yes, Father Daniels' *friend,*" Travine sounded haughty.

"You'll never know how much of a friend, Monsignor," Celine rasped.

"Let's get down to business," Gene spoke with the efficiency he used to use when he was in the marketplace. "John, please activate your televisor wire server. We have something to show you."

For the first time, John Travine looked like he was clutching for control. "What *is* this?" his question sounded more like a plea. He walked over to the other side of the room. "Televisor/Wire Server On," he spoke the words with definite hesitancy in his voice.

Celine went over and pushed the video wire into the receptacle. She turned and glared at Travine. She called out, "Play." Travine went around his desk and sat down, pushing his chair into a reclining position facing the televisor, feigning a smug look of invulnerability.

As he watched, he sat up straight, peering, squinting. His face grew as pale as whitewash.

He began to tremble. "Where did you get ….?" His voice trailed off as he sat there staring. Then suddenly he screamed, "Off!"

John Travine's face was bathed in sweat. He couldn't control his shaking. He stood up, then bent over and vomited into his wastebasket.

As he stood erect, his eyes stood wide open in terror. His lips were bloodless. The classic features of his smooth, handsome face crumbled into jagged fragments of despair. His regal bearing shriveled into the cringing anxiety of an abused child.

Travine was a caricature of the urbane, self-assured sophisticate whose elaborate posturings had won him so many favors from so many admirers. His charming fluency with which he had persuaded Churchmen in high places of power to trust and like him froze into a desperate, marble-like muteness.

After several long minutes, trying to regain his composure, he whimpered, "What do you two want?"

"Simple," Gene said in a most clinical tone. "Everything you know about Viri Lucis."

Travine fell back into his chair. "I don't know …."

"Or this goes to every station on NewsNet, even GlobeNet," Celine spit out the words like bullets.

Travine turned his chair away from Celine and Gene and stared out the window. Celine went over to the couch and sat down, striking one of her lavish poses, freed from any hint of the fashion-plate stereotype. Gene continued to stand in the middle of the room. "Well?" he said in the most sinister voice he could muster.

Travine turned back, looking at neither of them, just staring out into space. Finally he began to speak, "What I know about Viri Lucis ...."

"No, no!" Celine shouted at him as she got up from the couch and rushed over to the desk. "You write down what you know in your own handwriting," she commanded severely. "And remember we know enough that we'll know if you're lying.

Travine picked up a pen and looked at it as if seeing a pen for the very first time. He began to write, his hand trembling.

"Stop!" Celine commanded. "Don't write one word until you get control of yourself. We will not accept anything you write unless it is written in your own hand without the tremors.

Travine sat for a while clasping his hands together. He took several deep breaths. He did not look at either of them but stared down at the blank sheet of paper on his desk, looking like he was about to write a suicide note. He began to write in a steadier hand:

Viri Lucis was founded in 2016. It has adopted the ancient spirituality of the Ardentes. Viri Lucis is dedicated to the reintroduction and preservation of the orthodoxy of the holy Catholic faith inherited from Jesus and his Apostles. Viri Lucis is bound by oath to fight against and destroy all heresy in the Church and any hint of heretical teaching as well as all heretics, that is, anyone who is unorthodox in belief and practice.

There are high ranking prelates within Viri Lucis. Cardinals Rudolph Krantz, Prefect of The Congregation for the Doctrine of the Faith, Reginald Modenna, Prefect of The Congregation for Bishops, Jerzy Yukablonski, Primate of Poland,

Owen O'Rourke, Archbishop of St. Louis, U.S.A., Archbishop Brown, Secretary of the Supreme Council of Pontifical Missionary Works and, until recently, Cardinal Camillo Tamacci, Secretary of State. There are others of less noteworthy status such as myself.

Viri Lucis is headed by the one we call the Mentor and is divided into five levels: Electi, delegati, operati, Viri and attendantes. Leno Cappelli was of the operati. Michael McCann of the delegati. Cardinals form the electi. Attendantes are the ones who do all the Mentor's gofer work. I am among the Viri. When I become a bishop, I'll belong to the delgati. Recruiting is done through promises of advancement within the Church.

The goal of Viri Lucis is to gain total control of the Church. It is financed mainly through Archbishop Brown's Council of Missionary Works and through donations from other members. Michael McCann was the most generous donor. He was promised the Red Hat in return for his generosity. In his will he left most of his fortune to Viri Lucis. But because he rebelled against the decision to dispatch Pope Charles to his eternal reward for his blatant acts of heresy, he himself was likewise dispatched. The same is true of Leno Cappelli.

Father Daniels too was dispatched but
I do not know the reason.

Viri Lucis is mandated to perform
stringent acts of mortification and
penance and prayer. Each member is
to purify himself that he may purge
the Church of all heretical practices or
even what appears to be unorthodox
beliefs and practices. The members of
the Viri Lucis believe that it is God's
holy will to use any means to achieve
this purgation. Each member takes
a vow of absolute obedience to the
Mentor and a vow of absolute silence
about the workings, membership and
goals of Viri Lucis, both of which I
am at this time violating.

Viri Lucis is the new leaven in the
Church and intends eventually to *be*
the Church. God's will is made known
to us through the Mentor.

He signed it, Monsignor John J. Travine and dated it, May 27,
2031. Travine handed the paper to Gene who had remained standing
while Travine wrote it. "Will you give me the wire now?" Travine
pleaded.

As Gene took the paper and walked back to the couch, he said,
"Not even if Hell freezes over." Gene sat down next to Celine and
they both read what Travine had written.

Then Gene got up and went back to Travine who was still seated
behind his desk looking like he was going to faint. "The name of the
Mentor," Gene demanded.

"I don't know his identity. As God is my witness ...."

"The name or the video wire goes to the media," Gene
threatened.

Travine took the paper back and wrote below his signature, Antonio Franscara is the Mentor.

Celine, who had followed Gene over to the desk, watched Gene's face blanch as he read the name.

"One more thing, Travine," Gene said harshly. "We know from Michael McCann's diary that he told you he was quitting Viri Lucis. He informed you before he let the Mentor know. Did you inform Viri Lucis of Michael's decision?

"Micahel was going to withdraw from Viri Lucis," Travine whined. "I'm a nobody. I was inducted into Viri Lucis only because of Michael. If Michael quit, I would have been discarded like so much garbage.

"I knew if I called and reported what Michael had in mind, they would prize my loyalty. It was a way of assuring my future. As a matter of fact, it's in the workings now for me to be named an auxiliary bishop. They were really pleased."

"You're disgusting," Celine's voice was like a snake's hiss. "You profess to preserving unblemished truth and orthodox practice in the Church. All you're really interested in is your own calculated ambition."

"I didn't know they were going to kill Michael. Oh, God," Travine cried openly, "that was the last thing I wanted. I thought they'd just try to persuade him to stay." He sat and cried. Gene thought it must have been the first time he was able to demonstrate his agony over Michael's death.

Celine was far less empathetic. "Bishop McCann's blood is on your hands, you fastidious bastard," she hissed again. "You loved him so much you could hardly wait to get your boyfriend into bed," she spit the words at him as she motioned with her head toward the televisor.

"Let's go," Gene said abruptly. They both turned and walked out leaving Travine quivering, tears pouring out his eyes like a waterfall, moaning out loud, "My God! My God!"

As they were getting into Gene's car, Celine asked impatiently, "What? Who?"

"Antonio Franscara," Gene answered. "My God, he was right under our noses."

"Who in God's name is Antonio Franscara?" Celine almost shouted to try to jerk Gene out of his apparent state of shock.

"The deposed Pope Peter II," Gene jeered. "I remember some things about him. Let's go back to my place and check with the CompuIntel."

Back in Gene's apartment, Gene gave orders. "CompuIntel, on."

"Yes, Gene, what can I do for you?" the CompuIntel asked in a pleasant tone.

"Good evening," Gene said. "This is my friend, Celine."

"It is a pleasure to meet you, Celine."

Celine didn't bother answering.

"CompuIntel, Roman Catholic Church History," Gene ordered.

"What era, Gene?" the CompuIntel asked politely.

"Current. Pope Peter II." Gene directed.

Within seconds the name appeared on the screen and the CompuIntel asked, "Recitation or Printout, Gene?"

"Recitation first then printout, "Gene replied.

The mellow tone of the CompuIntel's voice began. "Pope Peter II, Antonio Franscara. Born on February 22, 1963 in Rome, Italy. Sixty-eight years old. His parents ...."

"Computer, just the information on his reign as Pope, please," Gene said.

With that a picture of Pope Peter II appeared on the screen. A man with thick white hair. The skin on his face was carved in deep wrinkles. The eyes had an hysterical glare. Yet strangely the overall impression was of a grandfatherly civility. "This picture was taken in 2016," the CompuIntel supplied. "Do you want a printout of the background material, Gene?"

"No thank you."

"Antonio Franscara was elected to the Papacy on August 19, 2015. He was considered one of the most brilliant minds in the Roman Catholic Church and a mesmerizing charismatic leader. He spoke several languages fluently. Do you want to know which ones, Gene?"

"No thank you."

"He began to reorganize the Vatican for greater efficiency. This efficiency included his taking all power to himself. No one was to make any decisions without his approval. Two months into his papacy on October 23, 2015, he excommunicated liberal theologian, Louis Natchez. This brought great praise from the tradionalist and conservative elements of the Church.

"Two months later, on December 23, 2015, he issued the Decree of Errors condemning such heresies as Mass in the vernacular. Do you want a complete list of the errors, Gene?"

"No thank you."

"It is a rather lengthy list. I will give it to you in the printout."

"Thank you. Please continue."

"In this Decree, Pope Peter II excommunicated one hundred and seventeen theologians and thirty-six bishops who supported these theologians. This caused great consternation throughout the Catholic world.

"Two Cardinals, one from the United States and one from Belgium, protested and were summarily dismissed from their posts. Do you want a list of the theologians and bishops who were excommunicated, Gene?"

"No thank you."

"To continue, then, on March 30, 2016, Pope Peter II placed three African dioceses under interdict as well as all the Belgian dioceses. On April 15, 2016, the Cardinals from around the world met in council in Rome to begin proceedings to depose Pope Peter II.

"During the next three and a half weeks, two of the most outspoken Cardinals, Welsey from Great Britain and Suzusaki from Japan died under mysterious circumstances. Their deaths were attributed to food poisoning. No autopsies were performed.

"On May 6, 2016, the Cardinals issued a Solemn Decree of Deposition effective immediately. He was the first Pope to be deposed since Pope John XII in 936 although Pope Benedict IX was forcibly removed from office in 1044.

" All but five Cardinals signed the Decree. The five who did not sign argued for compromise, asking that if Pope Peter II would rescind his excommunications and interdicts, he might remain on the Throne of the Vicar of Christ. Do you want a list of the names of the Cardinals who did not sign, Gene?"

"Yes please."

"Cardinals Camillo Tamacci, Rudolf Krantz, Reginald Modenna, Jerzy Yukablonski and Owen O'Rourke. Do you want further data on any of these, Gene?"

"No thank you."

"Pope Peter II is now known as Peter the Excommunicator."

"CompuIntel, where is Antonio Franscara now?" Gene asked.

"He resides in the monastery of Monte Casino where he spends his days in prayer and penance. His successor, Pope Pius XIII stripped him of all ecclesiastical honors and laicized him. Pius XIII restored some order by rescinding Peter's excommunications and interdicts. Do you want to know more about Pope Pius XIII, Gene?"

"No thank you. CompuIntel, that will be all."

"It was very nice meeting you, Celine. Sleep well, Gene." The CompuIntel closed down.

"How can something like this happen, Gene?" Celine sounded like she was about to burst into tears.

"If you check Church history, you'll find any number of aberrations," Gene answered in an off-handed manner. "But this is one aberration we can put an end to," he said with renewed intensity.

"How are you going to do that?" Celine asked and the word, you, was not lost on Gene.

"I'm going to contact Danny's friend and classmate, Cardinal Haynes who is now Secretary of State. And I'm going to pray with all my heart that he is not a member of Viri Lucis."

"His name wasn't on Travine's list," Celine observed.

"A lot of other names weren't on his list either. I'm sure you noticed that the five Cardinals Travine did name are the same ones who refused to depose Peter II," Gene added.

"Lends veracity to Travine's statement," Celine said in a preoccupied tone. "Gene, I've decided to take that month-long cruise with George. I have a lot of thinking to do. Reevaluate my life. I'll take a leave from my firm. I don't know if I'll even come back to it."

"I'm glad, Celine," Gene said. "You need to distance yourself from …. all that's happened. And maybe you can make some part of this cruise a kind of retreat. I've been worried about the bitterness I've seen in you ever since Danny …. Bitterness will only eat you up, destroy you."

"I'll give you my itinerary before I leave in case you want to get in touch with me about how things turn out — or don't, Celine said, ignoring Gene's reference to her bitterness.

They hugged. "You're a beautiful, most precious woman," Gene said quietly.

"I only hope to God that we — you — can put an end to these fanatics. These goddamn murderers," Celine spoke harshly, again ignoring what Gene had said about her bitterness.

THE VATICAN CONNECTION

Cardinal Douglas Haynes entered his office. He saw the flash on his phone indicating a confidential call. He smiled. All his calls were "confidential." "Message," he ordered and saw the image of a priest appear on the viewscreen.

"Your Eminence, I am Father Gene Shilling, a priest in good standing in the Archdiocese of Chicago. You have probably heard by now of the death of your friend, Joe Daniels. I am …. was a very close friend of Danny's too.

"The police are straddled between a mugging and murder. I believe I have proof that Danny was murdered." Gene held up a piece of paper and Douglas Haynes could see handwriting on it. "In a way it's a signed confession. But it also deals with another very urgent matter about a secret organization within the Church.

"I do not want to fax it to you. I would prefer to hand deliver it. I really believe the Holy Father should read this. I'll leave that up to you. Please let me know about your decision as soon as you can, your Eminence." Gene's number appeared at the bottom of the screen.

Cardinal Haynes called out the number and delivered this message. "Gene, I am Doug Haynes. I did hear of Danny's death and was heartbroken. By all means come to Rome as soon as you can. Bring your document and we'll discuss it. And thanks for getting in touch."

Gene felt hope as he listened to Haynes' message. Yet he was still being nagged with questions as to where Douglas Haynes fit in. A member or not? If a member of Viri Lucis, Gene's life could be in danger. He would make preparations to leave at once.

Cardinal Douglas Haynes sat staring at Gene's image. "Printout," he ordered. It would appear, he surmised, that forces were closing in on this "secret organization." First Bazun and now Shilling. What and how much did Gene Shilling know? What was this "signed confession?"

He'd have to wait until Shilling got here before he decided what to do. He left his office and went outside for a meditative walk even though the weather this June had been especially humid. He'd take a shower later.

The next morning Gene boarded an XM 542 at seven O'clock at O'Hare. The plane was Super speed Transit that traveled at Mach 9. It took only an hour to fly from Chicago to Rome. An hour later the plane was landing at Da Vinci airport in Rome. It was 3 P.M. Rome time. The hot towel of humidity wrapped itself around Gene's face. Perspiration beaded his brow like Braille characters spelling out the word, Discomfort.

But it was the discomfort within at the thought that he might run into the stone wall of Vatican intrigue that caused him to sweat even more. What if Douglas Haynes was a member of Viri Lucis? My God! What if the Pope himself ….? And if so, it could not just be a matter of his not being believed or of being diverted. His life would be in jeopardy. Danny was the most recent victim. He could be next. His heart was pounding like a volcano ready to erupt.

He checked into La Scalia hotel, called Haynes' office and made an appointment with his secretary for 9 A.M. the next morning. Again Gene whispered a fervent prayer that Cardinal Haynes was not a member of Viri Lucis. So much was riding on that. Everything.

"All we know, Mentor," the Attendant reported, "is that Father Shilling arrived here at three O'clock this afternoon and that he has an appointment with the Secretary of State sometime tomorrow. We don't know why he is here."

"What threat can he be?" the Mentor asked in a dismissive tone. "Even if he should tell Haynes about the existence of some secret organization called Viri Lucis or shows Haynes a copy of the note, Haynes would immediately ask for proof. Unlike Father Daniels, Shilling is a total stranger to Haynes.

"Daniels would have used his friendship to persuade Haynes to launch a full scale investigation even without any concrete proof. And as I have said before, Daniels would have had friendly access to the Pope who, despite the reports of Daniel's fornication, still held Daniels in highest esteem. Shilling doesn't have anywhere near that kind of clout. Haynes would be far more disposed to Daniels than to Shilling. We have nothing to be concerned about.

"Even if Shilling should mention Brown's name — that bungling idiot — or Travine's — that spineless wimp — and Haynes should call Brown in, Brown would deny and demand proof. It would be the word of Brown, a preeminent official in the Church against the word of a nobody priest, an unknown to Haynes. Where would that leave Haynes?

"Daniels could have accused Brown face to face and that could have at the least raised suspicion. Haynes is new to his office. And from what I understand he is not a risk-taker.

"Besides, soon I will have performed the incantation to Michael the Archangel. Then there will be no power on earth that can oppose me. The Church will be under my absolute control and under my control of the Church I will rule the world.

"Shilling is not the threat that Daniels would have been. But he still bears watching. We cannot be too careful now that we are so close to our ultimate and indisputable power."

The next morning at 9 A.M. Gene was welcomed by the Secretary of State, Cardinal Douglas Haynes, a fellow American.

"Gene, I'm so glad you could make it in such a short time," the Cardinal smiled.

"And I'm happy that you were willing to see me on such short notice, your Eminence," Gene replied graciously.

"It's Doug, Gene," the Cardinal continued smiling.

"Doug," Gene repeated.

Haynes seemed taller on the viewscreen than in person. He was a pleasant looking but not especially handsome man who didn't seem a bit impressed with the high office he held. He was not as muscular as Gene but he appeared to be a man of energy and yet there was a contemplative aura about him. His slate gray eyes were deep set and shrewd with a hint of playfulness dancing around the corners.

He was the type who immediately made you feel comfortable, relaxed and welcomed. His smile was like a hazy sun gently bathing you in its rays. He seemed like a man who could maintain his balance between the comic and the tragic of life's paradoxes. Gene liked him at once but still wondered if he was a man of integrity or a member of Viri Lucis.

"Your Emin …. Doug," Gene began at once, "have you ever heard of an organization called Viri Lucis?"

"Can't say that I have. Would you care to join me in a cup of espresso?"

"Yes, thank you." As Gene sipped the hot coffee, he told Haynes about Michael's will, the note, Archbishop Brown's visit, Leno Cappelli's sudden death, Celine's abduction, the escape of one and the suicide of the other of the two men who had kidnapped her, Danny's tormented pursuit of Viri Lucis and his murder. He told Haynes about Travine and how he and Celine had blackmailed him into writing and signing the confession.

"That's enough of a preface," Gene said. "Here is Travine's statement." He handed the sheet of paper to the Secretary of Stated. "I've made copies," Gene said as he prayed that Haynes would be the channel to the Pope. Gene got up and walked over to the window. The heat was steaming up from the ground outside and Gene watched the vapors.

Douglas Haynes read Travine's statement carefully as though he was deciding with each word whether or not to show it to the Pope. He finished, took off his reading glasses, sat back, turned his chair toward the window where Gene was standing and stared too.

Gene walked back to his chair and sat down. Haynes swiveled back and looked intently at Gene. "This is …. My God, Gene …." He fell silent. Then he began again to speak. "It's just so incredible. I mean it. It's too much. My God, will anyone believe it?"

He's one of them, Gene thought, feeling desperate, feeling despair.

"I will take this to the Holy Father at once," Haynes said abruptly as though he had just made a snap judgment.

"And I am on my way to see Archbishop Brown." Gene announced with similar abruptness.

"Why, Gene?" Haynes asked. "Once I give this to the Pope, it will all be in his hands."

Gene felt doubt again. Was Haynes really going to take Travine's statement to the Pope? To Haynes, Gene said, "I want to confront the Mentor — Peter II. I want to see him sweat. I want to tell him the Pope knows. I want to accuse him of Danny's murder."

"But first," Douglas Haynes asked, "come with me. The Holy Father can ask a lot of difficult questions. I'll need you to be there to fill in the gaps."

"Fine," Gene replied. Thank God, he prayed within himself, Douglas was not a member of Viri Lucis.

Douglas Haynes spoke into the intercom. He spoke in Italian. Gene had no idea what he was saying. The two left Haynes office.

"Your Holiness," Douglas Haynes said softly, "this is Father Gene Shilling from the Chicago Archdiocese. He was a very close friend of Joseph Daniels."

"I am very happy to meet you, Father Shilling," the Pope smiled. Then his face darkened. I was so sorry to hear about Joseph. What a waste. We must have faith. Put our trust in the Lord's overall plan."

Gene stood there awestruck by his proximity to the Vicar of Christ. The Pope standing erect in his white cassock looked like a tower or perhaps more appropriately like a lighthouse, high and alone in all the world. The only light to guide the slow-moving pilgrim vessels laden with human hopes and encrusted with the grime of human sin.

The Pope seemed to have aged since his election or perhaps the pictures had been doctored. But he had such dignity, such presence. Yet there was a gentleness that invited confidence and affection.

All Gene could do is murmur, "Your Holiness," as he knelt to kiss the Pontiff's ring. The Pope reached down and put his hand under Gene's elbow as a signal for him to rise. To Gene the Pope said, "Cardinal Haynes has informed me that you have brought with you a …. shall we call it, a most incriminating document?"

Cardinal Haynes nodded to Gene to indicate that he should speak. Gene gave the same prelude to the Pope as he had to Haynes. "It's a secret criminal organization within the Church," Gene concluded. After he had finished, Haynes gave the Pope Travine's statement.

"The organization Bazun was telling us about?" the Pope asked Haynes.

"I believe so, Holiness. Perhaps you should sit down to read this," Haynes suggested.

Pope John Paul took the paper and walked over behind his desk. He sat down and began to read. As he read there were audible groans emanating, Gene thought, from the depths of the man's soul like the cries of Christ on the cross.

When he had finished reading, the Pope sat perfectly still, staring across the room. He had turned to stone. After several minutes he looked over at Gene who was standing next to Haynes.

"This is true?" The Pope gasped as he went into a coughing spell that lasted for so long that Gene was surprised that Doug Haynes didn't run for a doctor. When he stopped coughing, there were tears in his eyes and his hands were shaking. Haynes had moved over next to him. "I am sorry," Haynes said. "I knew this would upset you but I was convinced you had to read it."

"That explains Tamacci's …. Tamacci's …." the Pope waved his hand, "…. what he tried to do to Perez."

"Please, Holiness, let me get you a drink of water," Haynes' concern was palpable.

"Krantz? Modenna? *Franscara!!* **Franscara!!**" the Pope shouted. "Since 2016? Fifteen years? How many others are there?

Gene wished he was anywhere but here. He really shouldn't be witnessing the Pope in this way. And yet the Pope was only human. Gene's desire for vengeance against Viri Lucis gave way to heartbreak for John Paul IV.

Then Gene was shocked when the Pope addressed him directly in a demanding tone. "Father Shilling, is this all we have?" as he held up Travine's statement. "How do we know Monsignor Travine's allegations have any weight at all?"

"Holy Father," Gene began, "this is only a statement. It is not in itself proof. I thought you …."

" ….would supply the proof?" the Pope interrupted. "Am I to call Cardinal Krantz in here and accuse this most loyal defender of the faith of complicity in these horrendous crimes based on the word of some young Monsignor who was blackmailed into writing this?" The Pope was upset, angry and sounding weaker as he again held up the paper and then threw it down on his desk.

Gene's only answer was the look of consternation on his face. The Pope was right. He couldn't go around accusing high ranking Churchmen of what amounted to ecclesiastical treason.

He felt hopeless, helpless. He had been so sure that Travine's confession would carry so much more weight. Haynes was right. The Pope could ask some very incisive questions. But where were the answers?

The Pope fell silent. Haynes stood next to him. A worried look twisted Haynes' face into a shock of perplexity. Suddenly the Pope looked up and then in an uncharacteristic gesture for a man of such exalted dignity he slapped his hand flat on his desk.

He shouted, "Douglas, get Tamacci over here! I'll bribe him with giving the Red Hat back to him if I have to. He is the one man who can be cajoled into giving verification to Travine's statement. He's the weak link."

Gene followed Haynes out of the Pope's office. Perspiring. To have been grilled by the Supreme Pontiff!

"Gene," Doug Haynes said in a soothing voice that told Gene the man was in total control, "why don't you hang out in my office or go for a walk in the garden. If Tamacci signs off on Travine's confession, I'll let you know immediately."

"Thanks your Emin …. Doug."

Cardinal Haynes led Camillo Tamacci to the Pope. Doug couldn't help but feel sorry for this man who was a shadow of his former powerful, disdainful self. Now Tamacci crouched and shuffled along, his head bent forward. He was a pitiful sight. It was hard for

Doug to think that a short time ago Camillo Tamacci had been the second most powerful man in the Church.

"Ah, Camillo, my brother, come in," the Pope greeted Tamacci with a sincerity that bespoke forgiveness but not dispensation from the penance inflicted on him. "I have something I want you to do for me. You're the only one who can help me."

"Anything, your Holiness, *anything,*" Tamacci responded almost in a whimper.

"I want you to read this," the Pope said as he handed him the handwritten paper.

Tamacci squinted and then reached into his black cassock pocket for his glasses. He read it and as he did, tears began to roll down his cheeks. He finished and looked up at the Pope who was waiting patiently.

"Is it true, Camillo," the Pope asked gently.

Tamacci began to shake and then he cried out, "Yes, Holiness, it is true! Every word of it! I don't know about Father Daniels' death. I …. I haven't been active in the …. Franscara has repudiated me. Holiness, he is mad!" Tamacci sobbed uncontrollably. The Pope walked around from behind his desk and put his hand on Tamacci's shoulder. "There, there, Camillo. Now here is what I need you to do for me."

"Yes, Holiness, what is it? Whatever it is …."

"I want you to give me a signed affidavit verifying the accuracy and truthfulness of Travine's statement. Here sit down at my desk."

Camillo sat down and without a hint of hesitation picked up the pen and began writing.

> As a member of Viri Lucis, I, Camillo Tamacci, have read the statement of John Travine and I attest to the validity and truthfulness of his statement.
>
> Viri Lucis does exist and the deposed Peter II, Antonio Franscara, is the head, the Mentor of the movement known

as Viri Lucis. The men mentioned in Travine's statement are all members of Viri Lucis and the criminal acts are also true.

Krantz. Modenna, Brown and I formed the core of power in Viri Lucis under the leadership of Antonio Franscara. Franscara alone is responsible for the deaths of the men mentioned and others. We had nothing to do with those decisions.

Franscara is obsessed with purchasing an incantation to Michael the Archangel from the Iranians with the half billion dollars from Bishop McCann's estate. He believes this incantation will make him the most powerful man on earth. He truly believes this. We questioned his sanity but continued our loyalty to him as our Mentor.

We really believed in purifying the Church of all heretical beliefs and practices and restoring it to its pristine orthodoxy. During my time at Monte Casino I have become reconciled with God. Now I beg your Holiness' forgiveness.

I swear by God and all his holy angels and saints that I am telling the truth.

He signed it, Camillo Tamacci, Priest. June 4, 2031.

"Fine, Camillo, fine," the Pope said as he read the affidavit. Douglas, please witness this and then see to it that Camillo, our brother, gets back to the monastery. Again, thank you, Camillo."

"Your Holiness," Tamacci said looking at the Pope for the first time, "I am so very sorry. I was so misguided. So personally ambitious. Thank you for allowing me to do penance."

Doug signed the affidavit. Douglas Card. Haynes. June 15, 2031.

The Pope smiled as Haynes led Tamacci out. He didn't even have to bribe Tamacci with the Red Hat. Penance does transform a man, the Pope thought through his smile of satisfaction.

FACE TO FACE

Doug slipped into his office. "Gene, Tamacci has verified Travine's statement. I would imagine all papal hell's going to break loose in a relatively short time. If you still want to go see Brown, I'll call over and tell him to extend every courtesy."

"Thanks, Doug."

"Anything for our mutual friend, Danny," Doug's face assumed the gloom of a mortician. "And, Gene, be careful. Franscara is a madman."

"Doug, I've been thinking this whole thing over. Why are people so hateful? And worse, why is their hatred so often masked with such ruinous piety? What is it about them that they can cover their hatred with such rationalizations like 'God's will,' or 'For the glory of God,' or 'To preserve the faith'?"

"I don't have answers for you, Gene. But I know that it's not just the obvious hatred that explodes in so-called 'Holy Wars.' At least that kind of butchery is known for the hatred that propels the hateful into the irrational bloodbaths that have drenched the earth since the time of Cain and Abel."

"Far more subtle and yet just as real and barbaric," Doug continued, "is the hatred of good, church-going people, decked out in the finery of absolute orthodoxy, reinforced by the jots and tittles of rules and regulations. And they use these jots and tittles to measure, judge and condemn everyone who differs from them."

"God, Doug, you sound so much like Danny. I know what you're saying. It's the kind of hatred that says, If you do not agree with my legalistic interpretation of God's love, you will be excommunicated from the Church. You are not only unworthy, you are a scandal and we are here to expose you, convict you, exclude you and destroy you. And God will give his divine stamp of approval to our actions."

Gene entered Archbishop Brown's spacious office filled with trinkets and exquisite paintings and busts of recent popes. He walked over the plush carpet and, when Brown signaled him to do so, he sat down, facing Brown across his huge ornate oak desk.

"And who is this that the Secretary of State himself asks for special consideration," Brown was as blazé as a politician who had just won a landslide election.

"As Cardinal Haynes told you, I am Father Gene Shilling of the Archdiocese of Chicago. You visited there earlier this year — Father Joseph Daniels?"

"Ah, yes. A very nice visit indeed, as I recall."

"Needless to say," Gene spoke as someone who was in total control, "Father Daniels told me about your demand for the note."

"I haven't the slightest idea what you're talking about." Brown became visibly defensive, slipping into the legendary Romanita.

"Be that as it may," Gene responded evenly, "I want you to take me to your Mentor, Antonio Franscara."

"Mentor? Franscara? I haven't the slightest notion …." Brown was becoming flustered as Gene broke in on him.

"Cut it, Archbishop. It's over I have a statement here from one of your members, John J. Travine. He names names and yours is one of them. He also outlines the purpose of Viri Lucis.

" Viri Lucis? The Mentor? What are you talking about? You come in here with all this gibberish …."

"As I said, cut the nonsense. Tamacci has signed as affidavit verifying Travine's accusations. You yourself have done quite a bit of pilfering to help finance Viri Lucis."

"I don't know what …."

"The Pope knows. Why else do you think Douglas Haynes called you? As we say in the States, the shit's going to hit the fan fast and furious."

Brown sat quite still obviously calculating how he could cut his losses, Gene thought. His mouth was moving but nothing was coming out. His face was as scarlet as a Cardinal's robe. "What do you *want?*" Brown finally whispered, groping for some semblance of control.

"Take me to the Mentor — and now! And don't bother calling ahead." Gene was in command.

Gene walked into the dark paneled room. A huge desk sat in the room like an impassable barricade. There was a lamp on the desk that cast an eerie glow on the man who presided like a judge behind it and a garish crucifix.

There were two wooden straight back chairs placed in front of the desk that seemed to signal curt dismissal rather than a warm invitation to linger. There was a window in the wall behind and to the left of the desk allowing a bright beam of light to fill a third of the room.

A graphic painting of the crucifixion hung darkly on the wall opposite the desk. To the right of the desk was a gigantic telecomputer obviously the latest state-of-the-art production.

Spartan would have been a ludicrous understatement. The entire room gave the impression of a bunker where an indomitable Field Marshal was directing his troops toward final victory.

Gene had a momentary dizzying feeling he could only name as nightmarish. Beads of sweat crept down his forehead like inchworms. He refused to wipe them away for fear he would draw the attention of the man behind the desk to the anxiety he was feeling. Perhaps that man would think that the perspiration was due to the weather outside. The man behind the desk sat in a black meticulously pressed cassock. Gene knew from the picture that it was the Mentor, Antonio Franscara, the deposed Pope Peter II. Three priests with the most dour faces Gene had ever seen stood nearby at attention it seemed.

Clutching the envelope that contained Travine's statement, Gene made a conscious effort to appear composed and in charge. Then as he looked at the man behind the desk, he thought of Danny and was filled with angry courage. He walked over to the desk and sat down without a word.

Antonio Franscara, the former Pope Peter II, was a formidable man. Big in physical stature and gargantuan in psychic energy. His face was as severe as a scorched desert. His eyes smoldered with power and intimidation. His snow white hair receded from his high forehead and gave prominence to the spectral appearance of his overhanging nose.

Franscara did not look his 68 years. He looked older. But then there was the feel of energy which, like electronic impulses, snapped out at anyone he was glaring at. This made him seem younger. He had the air of a sleek panther. Quiet but ready to leap at a moment's notice. Able to kill with one crushing chomp of its terrifying jaws.

He sat in his chair leaning over his desk, crescent-like, his arms like long sloping slats hanging from the small boulder that was the upper part of his back. He may have the air of a panther, Gene thought, but he looks like an ape.

His whole demeanor spelled one word—domination. His presence created fear and submission. There was about him a mesmerizing charism which made Gene feel that it would be impossible to deny his slightest wish not to mention a direct command. The whole atmosphere was as sinister as the torturous rack of the Inquisition, as suffocating as inhaling poisonous vapors.

When Franscara spoke, Gene sensed the ruthlessness of a confirmed fanatic who could strike terror in even the most stalwart of hearts. Slowly, deliberately. "You are Father Eugene Shilling." It sounded like a condemnation to death by lethal injection.

Gene drew upon his anger. In a stern, threatening tone, he said firmly, "You are responsible for the murder of my friend, Father Joseph Daniels as well as Pope Charles, Bishop Michael McCann and Monsignor Cappelli and God knows how many others.

The Mentor burst into fiendish laughter. "You God-forsaken nobody. You come in here and accuse *me?* With no proof. What is easily asserted is easily denied, to quote the Scholastics.

"Cut the charade, Franscara," Gene spoke through clenched teeth. "I have proof."

"You Goddamned imbecile!" Gene wasn't sure if the explosion was due to his accusations or his using the Mentor's last name with studied disrespect. Gene handed him the envelop.

The Mentor slit it with a diamond studded letter opener. He read it slowly. As he read, Gene studied him.

The Mentor was bent over at his desk. The desk was absolutely clear. The only other object on it, besides the lamp, was a horrifying crucifix, probably of Spanish origin. His dark eyes were sharp as though penetrating right through to the core of Gene's soul. His very presence seemed an attempt to evoke fear in everyone he dealt with.

The Mentor's rigidity as he sat in his chair reflected the moroseness of his inflexible moralism, Gene thought. The deep creases in the skin of his face told the tale of a man of arrogant worry about his self-appointed mission in life. His eyes, as he continued to read, blazed judgment.

He was, Gene surmised, a man who had spent his entire life enforcing the laws of God and the rules of the Church with the precision of a Pharisee and with absolutely no love and more often than not with barbaric cruelty. He appeared to be the kind of churchman who did everything by the book and nothing by the heart.

He looked like a man who lived in a perpetual state of self-righteous indignation. Gene wondered if you could pry open a genuine smile of delight on his face even with a crowbar. It seemed to Gene that the Mentor was consumed with madness fueled by hatred.

He knew he could be wrong in his appraisal. Still the Mentor's voice was a whiplash, his eyes gleaming like an executioner's axe. Gene got the impression — and it was only that, an impression — that the Mentor was capable of crystalline savagery.

The Mentor finished reading Travine's statement. He looked up at Gene and smiled hideously. "You call this *proof?*"

"Camillo Tamacci has signed an affidavit in the presence of the Holy Father, witnessed by the Secretary Cardinal of State verifying what is written on that paper." Gene surprised himself at his ability to maintain boardroom composure.

"As we speak," Gene continued, "some of your henchmen like Krantz and Modenna are being rounded up. Gene turned to Brown. "When you get back expect to be greeted by the Swiss Guard. And you, Franscara" — he used his last name deliberately to display his utmost contempt and disdain — "will be dragged out of here by force if necessary."

573

The Mentor leaned forward menacingly. "You have seen the reference to the incantation to Michael the Archangel." he said with the confidence of a poker player whose last dealt card was a fourth ace.

Gene sat perfectly still. Waiting to hear what the Mentor would say.

The Mentor explained the incantation fully with all the historical background but conveniently deleted the curse that anyone who performed the incantation without true faith would die a most gruesome death.

"So you see, you stupid ass, I and I alone have the totality of the true faith," Franscara shrieked. "When I perform that incantation I will be the most powerful man on the face of this earth. All I need is McCann's half a billion dollars. Even as we speak, that money is on its way here."

"You actually believe that fairy tale?" Gene was genuinely shocked.

"I am the one of the true faith. I alone. All through the centuries this incantation has been meant for me."

As Gene stared at Franscara the thought struck him that the Mentor had put himself in the place where God used to be. Compared to Franscara, Rasputin was a Santa Claus. "You're insane," Gene spoke with disgust.

"Didn't they accuse Jesus of being possessed?" the Mentor asked with lofty scorn.

"Isn't first century possession twenty-first insanity? If I am insane, it is with the insanity of a righteous God who condemns all the sane people who destroy religion with crazy innovations, stupid updating and spineless compromises with the satanic world.

"I alone and only those loyal to me have divine orthodoxy. If that is insanity, then, yes, I am insane. But keep in mind that the two sanest people on earth were the ones who committed the original sin."

"I take back what I said about your being insane," Gene countered. "Insanity relieves you of responsibility. You're not insane. You are diabolical. It's not the world that's satanic. You, Franscara, are Satan."

Gene's voice was calm which gave his statements all the more power to slice into the very marrow of Franscara's conscience.

Franscara leapt from his chair. "How dare you speak to me with such intolerable disrespect," he screamed. "You nothing! Take him!" he commanded his Attendants as he picked up a paper weight and smashed it against the crucifix on his desk. "Throw him out of here but make certain his broken bones will remind him of his imbecilic confrontation."

Two Attendants grabbed Gene but Gene was too powerful for them. He broke loose from one and smashed his fist into the nose of the other who shrieked in pain. Then he turned and socked the other on the jaw sending him sprawling to the floor.

"Grab him! Grab him!" the Mentor kept shouting." Seize him, you fools!"

Just then the door to Franscara's study flew open. An Attendant rushed in breathless. "Mentor! Mentor!" Everything stopped as suddenly as a blown fuse. Gene froze trying to catch his breath. Even the priest with the broken nose stopped squealing. Silence filled the room like the dry air in a sauna.

The Attendant fell to one knee. "Mentor," he cried out, "I have the worst possible news. Terrible. Horrible news."

"What?" the Mentor growled. "What news? Out with it, man! What is it?"

The Attendant rose, trembling. He knew well how often the bearer of bad news felt the wrath of the Mentor. "Mentor, the Israelis ...."

"Yes, yes," the Mentor barked.

"The Israelis have purchased the incantation from the Iranians! They paid one and a half billion dollars!"

The Mentor looked like someone had just shot him in the stomach. He stumbled backwards and fell into his chair. His eyes stared vacantly as though at a future that no longer existed.

After a while Archbishop Brown ventured, "This means .... you will never .... Oh God! the incantation is forever out of your reach!"

The Mentor sat there as if in an impenetrable trance. Finally he looked up. "Even if I have to wait …."

"You're forgetting something, *'Mentor,'* Gene sneered. "The only waiting you will do is in a jail cell, waiting to be judged by a God who is infinitely sane." Then with a voice like an Arctic wind, Gene said, "You're finished, Franscara, you murdering bastard and so is Viri Lucis."

"Well," Gene said jauntily, "looks like there's nothing more to keep me in this august company. See you at the trial, *'Mentor.'*" Gene turned and pushed his way through the Attendants, past Brown, who looked suicidal, and left.

Gene knew he shouldn't feel the exhilaration that was bubbling up within him. It was the exhilaration of vengeance. But he couldn't help it. My God! he thought, Viri Lucis has been destroyed. Who would have believed it? That man who plotted to be the most powerful man on earth has been reduced to a pile of helpless rubble. Strangely the metallic taste of bitterness was gone. He would report back to Doug Haynes.

CARDNAL KRANTZ

Cardinal Rudolf Krantz, Prefect of the Congregation for the Doctrine of the Faith, entered the Pope's study exuding self importance. Douglas Haynes was struck by the sheer aura of power Krantz projected. He may not have been the Grand Inquisitor in name but he most certainly was in commanding presence. Standing only at five feet four, Krantz had a way of filling a room. Doug wondered if Krantz wasn't the quintessential example of a Napoleonic complex.

Cardinal Krantz sat down immediately without being invited to do so. His eyelids were heavy veils either concealing himself from the probings of others or shutting out those he disdained which encompassed anyone he did not approve of including the present reigning Pontiff.

"You wished to see me?" Krantz asked with no show of reverence while totally ignoring the Secretary of State.

"Yes, Rudolf and thank you for coming at so short a notice. I know you are a very busy man."

"The work at the Congregation is a twenty-four hour job, Holiness. I am only too happy to serve the Church in my capacity as Prefect. Error is the atmosphere of the Church these days."

"Rudolf, I want to share something very disturbing with you," the Pope said not betraying any emotion whatever.

Krantz looked like he was about to be ordered to drag out the rack and stakes. "What is it you have for me?" Krantz asked. Doug thought he could see the Prefect licking his chops.

"Here," the Pope said as he handed Krantz Travine's confession, "read this."

Krantz read the statement and said nothing. "Now," the Pope said, "read this." He handed Krantz Tamacci's verification.

"This is preposterous!" Krantz shouted. "I demand to face my accusers."

"You are, Rudolf," the Pope replied with such an ease that Doug was filled with admiration at his superhuman self-control. Had he been the one confronting Krantz, Doug thought, he would long ago have allowed the anger he was feeling spill over into the most vituperative language he was capable of using.

"I, the Vicar of Christ, am accusing you," the Pope said as he began to pace rapidly in front of Krantz. "I've already had Modenna here and he, like Tamacci, has confessed. There is no need of your continuing the lie you have been living these past fifteen years as a member of Viri Lucis.

"You have been fanatically dedicated to the restoration and preservation of orthodoxy. I now accuse *you* of being unorthodox insofar as you have violated every radical demand and value of the gospel."

Krantz sat with his jaw down to his chest. His face had crumbled into utter bewilderment.

"You have been doing nothing but preserving and enhancing your own personal power born of the most insidious, self-serving kind of ambition. And you have done this in the name of all that is sacred. In the name of God and his holy Church." The Pope kept pacing even though he began one of his torturous coughing spasms that always sent a chill of alarm through Haynes.

"I want you to know ...." Krantz began.

"Shut up and listen, Krantz," the Pope swung around and glared at the Prefect. "Don't make me lose my temper," he said more quietly.

"You are the kind of hypocrite Jesus denounced without qualification," the Pope continued speaking louder and pacing faster. "You are guilty of complicity in the most heinous crimes of murder. Were it not for the embarrassment it would cause the Church, I would have you arrested.

"As it is you will resign from your office. You will have your letter of resignation on my desk within the hour. You will return to Germany and reside for the rest of your life in a monastery I will designate. I will not make it public but officially you are hereby stripped of all ecclesiastical honors. I will allow you to celebrate

Eucharist privately but you never again to preach or write. Nothing public. Do I make myself unmistakably clear."

Krantz was too stupefied to even nod his head. His whole cleverly constructed universe of power was crashing down on him.

"Modenna will return to Africa and work in a leper colony. The same punishments have been meted out to him as to you. Brown who is a confirmed embezzler will go back to England and be laicized. Yakablonski and O'Rourke have been summoned to Rome. Douglas has set up a timetable so that all this will not happen at once. But no matter when the deadlines are, everyone will be divested of all his power and authority." The Pope stopped momentarily to catch his breath.

"But you, Rudolf are the first to go. And you may thank me and God that you are not going to prison where you most deservedly belong. You men, entrusted with such sacred and high offices, are a scandal and you have broken my heart. I should excommunicate all of you."

With that the Pope stopped pacing. He stood in his usual erect position and stared at Krantz who was slumped forward with his head buried in his chest. The Pope went behind his desk and sat down.

"Besides your letter of resignation, by Vespers, you will have on my desk two other documents. One, the list of all the members of Viri Lucis and two, as your last official act, a statement turning over to me all the monies accruing to Viri Lucis from Bishop McCann's estate.

"This money will help me in my efforts to place the Church in the best light of public relations — something you have made a most formidable task. If ever any of this got out, it would take the Church a millennium to undo the damage you and your so-called Viri Lucis have caused. And, Krantz, if this ever does get out, you will spend the rest of your life in prison."

For the longest while Krantz sat sunk into the mire of humiliation. Then suddenly he jerked his head up. His face was a spreading blotch of red and black wrath. "You fool!" His voice was as menacing as a wild animal's growl. "You God-forsaken fool! You are presiding over the death of the holy Roman Catholic Church and you are too stupid to recognize it.

"You may judge me and use your powers to dismantle all the good I have accomplished. You may humiliate me to the point of total powerlessness. But one day you will stand before the judgment seat of God. And you will be condemned for all eternity."

"That demonstrates how little faith you have, Rudolf," the Pope said in a steady voice. "Jesus has promised to be with his Church until the end of time. It cannot be destroyed from outside or from within. It will never die. What has died here today is your faith in your own fanatical power. You have been gathering not for Christ but for yourselves and now all you have is a handful of ashes to be scattered to the winds. 'Whoever does not gather with me scatters.'"

At this point there was another about face. Krantz began to wail so loud that Doug thought he would be heard throughout the entire Vatican. Krantz's whole presence was a flood of tears. "I'm sorry, I'm sorry," he kept repeating in pleading anguish. And then, "Forgive me, forgive me." It was as if his last ditch effort to assert the validity of Viri Lucis' sanctimony had been a psychological suicide mission.

The Pope nodded to Doug who went over to Krantz and helped him to his feet. As he led Krantz from the room, Doug could not help but think how the power of this man had shrunk to match his physical size. A small man in stature and now in significance.

When Doug returned, he said, "Holiness, you just mentioned using McCann's money to bolster the image of the Church. May I presume to remind you that a week from tomorrow the poets and theologians will be gathered here to begin their collaboration with you on your encyclical?"

"Thank you, Douglas. With all that has transpired lately, I could have forgotten the most important task of my Papacy. I want to have an all inclusive statement prepared for them." He paused and coughed slightly this time. Then with eyes that looked as sorrowful as a mourner at a graveside, he said quietly, "How sad that Joseph Daniels will not be among them."

Then with a sudden infusion of enthusiasm, the Pope said, "Douglas, I so want this encyclical to help ease the tensions and heal the divisions within the Church — and the world, if at all possible. Do you think it is possible?"

"I know it's a bromide, Holiness, but anything is possible. We make the efforts needed and trust in God's graciousness."

"Perhaps," the Pope smiled, "we should trust more in God's sense of humor. I think sometimes that God so loved a good joke he created us. Still a sense of humor is a sense of balance.

"I want the encyclical to have stories in it. And poetic imagery. All backed up with sound theology that isn't apparent or dry as dust. I do not want a drab dissertation. God knows we have had more than our share of those. Maybe a few humorous stories would also be to the point."

"I remember," Doug said, "a line from one of Dann .... Joseph Daniels poems. It went, I think, 'God plays in the sandbox of our creativity.'"

"Ah, yes, Joseph.... In the end, he was truly a martyr, wasn't he?" The Pope looked out the window at the heat steaming up from the roofs and shuddered.

"May I say, Holiness, that I am truly impressed with your approach to this encyclical. I would have thought that you would have preferred a more highly sophisticated approach. I mean with your academic background."

"The intellectual approach?" the Pope replied. "Maybe that has been our problem. We address people's minds and ignore their emotions, their passion. Jesus appealed to our imaginations.

"He didn't use highbrow language as difficult to understand as a message written in ancient Sanskrit. The gospel is a passionate dramatization of God's love for us. It is simple and yet so profound that the most unlearned person and the greatest scholar can find a challenge there.

"For the most part we have done the gospel the disservice of translating it into abstract philosophical theories. The gospel doesn't move people. It's a challenge and we have made it a source of personal security.

"Sometimes I think we have made the gospel a reinforcement for people's psychological problems, their unresolved emotional conflicts. Does that sound too harsh?"

"Not at all, Holiness." Doug was truly enjoying listening to the Pope thinking out loud. "The gospel can be used as a cover-up or as an escape from a person's or a community's reality."

"Yes, yes," the Pope spoke again with the enthusiasm of a scientist making a long sought after discovery. "And I want this encyclical to be a means for the gospel to make intrusions into people's defense mechanisms. I want it to stimulate people toward a stripped down honest response.

"The kind of response they would make standing before the judgment seat of the all-knowing God where there can be no masks, no pretenses, no defense mechanisms, no psychological escapes or cover-ups.

"The gospel is communal and we have brainwashed our people into thinking it is private. A me-and-my-God spiritual experience. You know, as long as I keep the rules and say my prayers, who cares that God is the cry of the poor? The plea of the abandoned? The appeal of the emotionally displaced?

"Excuse me, Douglas, I do go on, don't I? A privilege of the elderly, I suppose. Especially the elderly who hold total power." The Pope laughed out loud. "But these are some of the ideas I want to get across to the gathering next week.

The Pope began one of his coughing spells. He pulled out his handkerchief to cover the blood that was coming out of his mouth. Doug trembled and wondered how long they would have this good and holy man with them. He offered the Pope a glass of water which he refused with his hand raised up.

The Pope spent time catching his breath after coughing for over five minutes. Finally he said, "I so want this encyclical to be something people, ordinary people, can read and enjoy, ponder and put into practice.

"There are so many people out there who are seeking peace of mind. Seeking justice or the meaning of their lives and relationships. Seeking truth and integrity and hope. They seek psychological balance and emotional health in a world mad with falsehood and inauthenticity.

"Douglas, you and I live in our own little worlds. Our needs are taken care of. We go to our apartments after a hard day's work and we can relax. Mothers and fathers come home from work and have to deal with nurturing their children, work at their own relationship with each other. Prepare meals, help with homework, settle squabbles among their children, forgive and support one another.

"My God, Douglas, we have certainly given short shrift to our wonderfully heroic laity, haven't we?

"I am going to make certain that I canonize a good number of ordinary, holy laypeople before my reign is over. Make a note of that, please, Douglas. And remind me to trim back that canonization process, too, will you?

"We have a lot more saints than the bureaucrats over at The Congregation for the Causes of Saints are willing to admit. They don't make these people saints. These people become saints by cooperating with God where they are, doing what they're supposed to with selfless love. The bureaucrats only declare them worthy of canonization. I wonder how many of them are saints?"

The Pope smiled and then began to laugh. "That would be an interesting study, wouldn't it? How many of the canonizers have ever been canonized?" He laughed heartily.

"Then," the Pope continued with his previous thought, "there are those who seek power and control like our brother, Franscara. Or they seek wealth and luxury at the expense of millions of the downtrodden. Or they seek a piety that is holier than the Church. And again, like Franscara's piety, it tries to destroy the Church.

"Everyone is seeking something and ultimately they are all seeking God," Haynes spoke softly.

"You know, Douglas," the Pope said in a confidential tone, "I fear open-ended abandonment to the unpredictable. I like things set out like a lesson plan or a curriculum."

"And yet, Holiness, you have been an inexhaustible source of surprises since you took over the Chair of Peter."

"Well, I know that in my efforts to seek the truth, I have to be hospitable to clashing views," the Pope poured himself a glass of water, missing the glass Haynes had already poured. He stood holding the glass in his hand. "But how do I use the grace of a gentle exploration of truth?"

"I'm not certain, Holiness. Unlike you and your pursuit of the truth, I find myself catching only erratic glimpses of the truth. Maybe I am not motivated enough. I get lost in the details of my daily duties."

"I know what you mean, Douglas. Life, our work and all the rest seem to be nothing more than endless distractions. I really didn't want this position, you know. I really didn't. No false humility. Just fact."

"But we have to trust, don't we, Holiness? I mean we do believe in Providence. I believe God wants you here at this time in history."

"For however short a time, eh? We've had too many popes in too short a time. Five in thirty-one years. It doesn't bode well for continuity."

"But you are here …. now. That is what is important."

"Yes but there are times when I genuflect and wonder if I will fall flat on my face — metaphorically speaking, of course. I don't want my statements and especially my encyclical to be relics from the past when they should be manifestos for the future."

"I am certain, Holiness, that what you say and do will be a legacy for future generations. I think we all have to take stock from time to time to find out whether we are merely functioning or are committed to a sacred mission."

"If we — I — am so committed, Douglas, then I want, I must gather people's lives, hopes, struggles and joys into my heart. Make them dramatically present to myself. But my problem is this: Can I articulate the feelings, the needs, the dreams of the diversified membership of the Church called the People of God?"

"I think we have to show compassion to ourselves, Holiness. I think we all want to live our faith in such a way that it touches human possibilities. As for myself, I've never been too courageous.

I suppose that's why I hide behind my work — controllable things. The path of least resistance."

"You will rise to the occasion, Douglas, as I am doing with whatever courage is needed at the time. And don't worry about courage for tomorrow."

"'Sufficient for the day is the trouble therein'?" Haynes smiled.

"Today is all that God gives us, Douglas. As you get older you appreciate that more and more. And in this day, this one day that is allotted to me, how do I come to God without looking for the quick jolt of instant insight? How do I approach God without bringing with me my solemn professionalism?"

Pope John Paul IV looked truly perplexed. And Cardinal Haynes was just as puzzled. He thought that by the time you reached the Pope's age these kinds of questions would all have been answered. Now here he was listening to the Supreme Pontiff of the universal Church still plagued by questions that should have been settled long ago.

"How," the Pope continued his questioning, "do I deal effectively — no strike that — affectionately with those who are painfully unaware about their defensive Catholic subcultures? Like the persistent, tragic ritual hatreds of ethnic groups?

"What can be said of a religion that cultivates a lofty disinterest, even an other-worldly disdain for the grotesque injustices that are tearing our world apart? A religion that tolerates grave injustices and brutalizes the human spirit? Is this what Christ envisioned?

"Yet in my own inherited brokenness I vacillate between a detached pity and a temporary intensity.

"We must do all we can, Douglas, to follow the lead of our saintly predecessor, John XXIII. We must throw open the windows of the Church. We must stop being a Church of maintenance and become a Church of missionary outreach.

"We have to allow debate, even if the debating is disagreeable. How else can we move from being an inward-looking Church fearful of change to an outward-looking Church, full of confidence in the Spirit?

"I am convinced more than ever of the deep faith of the majority of our people. But this huge reservoir of good will dry up if our people are convinced that they have no voice, that they are not being listened to." The Pope paused. Douglas Haynes spoke.

"As I mentioned, I myself tend to overintellectualize to escape feeling the cruelty of life, the futility of the struggle. In fact, I wonder sometimes if I have any experience of the emotional meaning of anything." He remembered Danny talking so long ago about the emotional meaning of life. "Are my efforts to respond to God's call all will and no imagination?

"I suppose I could very well be accused of not being a listener. But as you implied, Holiness, how can we possibly re-evangelize if we don't know where our people are in their faith journey? I will make you a promise right here and now. I will serve as your ears. I will be honest and I will not tell you only what you may want to hear. My solemn oath on this."

"I thank you most sincerely, Douglas. And I accept your offer to be my open, objective ears and an honest tongue." The Pope smiled sympathetically. He got up from behind his desk and walked over to Haynes. He put his snow-white hand on Haynes' shoulder. "We have to persevere in making our prayer daring explorations into the uncomfortable, accepting all the challenges Jesus continues to hurl at us. Action will follow. That I have learned over the years."

Both men, the Pope and the Secretary of State, stood in silence. They looked at each other squarely and honestly. The mutual admissions of vulnerability were forging a bond of deeper trust between them. A trust that would serve as a well of courage they could both drink from.

"There is no doubt in my mind," the Pope spoke softly, "that you will achieve great things, Douglas, as a preeminent shepherd of the People of God. Who knows what the future holds." The Pope winked and then turned to the work awaiting him on his desk.

Douglas could see that the Pope wanted to be left alone. So he quietly bowed and left, happy that the Pope had plunged into the future rather than dwelling on the sordid events that had just transpired and drained him of so much of his energy.

Douglas had never felt so reassured. He had the Pope's total trust. That's all he wanted.

Pope John Paul IV sat at his desk staring vacantly at the mounds of paper in front of him. Suddenly he was jolted by an unseemly thought. The last man he gave his unqualified trust to was Camillo Tamacci.

EPILOGUE

Gene went back to the Vatican, made his way to Doug's office and told him about the Israelis buying the incantation. "Franscara completely fell apart and lost all control," Gene said. "It was like he was pulled into the vortex of despair. In fact I'm concerned about what he might do. He is a man of immeasurable and preposterous ego."

"I'll get someone over there at once," Doug replied. Then Doug filled Gene in on what had transpired between the Pope and the various members of Viri Lucis.

"What are you going to do now?" Doug asked Gene.

"Later today I want to talk to Celine. She's in England. She and her husband are taking a month's cruise. I want to fill her in. Let her know that the matter with Viri Lucis has been settled. I only pray that that will help her get over or at least get through her bitterness."

"She must have loved Danny with unbelievable passion," Doug mused as though wondering what it would be like to experience such intimate love from a woman.

Gene nodded and Doug understood that anything more would be an invasion of the most sacred privacy. "She is a wonderful woman." That was all Gene said. Then, "How is the Holy Father doing?"

"I'm amazed at his resiliency," Doug said. Then he told Gene that they would have a complete list of all the members by the end of the day and how the Pope made Krantz sign over Michael McCann's money to him personally.

"Of course, the executor's money will go to Danny's estate. And from what you told me it will be put to the best possible use," Doug added.

"May I tell Celine about what steps the Holy Father took to put an end to Viri Lucis?" Gene asked.

"From all that she contributed to bringing as end to this whole matter, my answer is yes. Ask her to keep it in strictest confidence except for her husband. By the way, talking about contributions, the

Holy Father would like to see you before you leave. He wants to thank you and give you a blessing. We could go in now."

"I'd be most honored," Gene said simply.

"I don't mind telling you that the Holy Father feels deeply indebted to you."

Together they entered the Holy Father's presence.

"I will be forever in your debt, Father Shilling," Pope John Paul IV smiled pleasantly as he came around his desk. "And to our mutual friend, Father Joseph Daniels. He died a martyr's death. My prayers go with you." Gene knelt and received the Pope's blessing. "Thank you, your Holiness," he whispered.

"One more matter, Gene." Pope John Paul IV smiled and there was a twinkle in his eye. "I have the two volumes of poetry Danny had published. If there are other poems, would you please send them to me? I know I will be able to use many of his poetic insights in my encyclical."

"I will be privileged to send them to you, Holiness."

"And please give my blessing to your people whom, I understand, you serve so well and with true zeal."

"Thank you, your Holiness," Gene said in a steadier tone. Doug led Gene out into the hall. "My thanks too, Gene," Doug said sincerely. "I think we both memorialized Danny's life and death in an inimitable way." They shook hands, then embraced with the love they both felt for Danny and Gene left.

Gene placed a call to Celine in England.

"Hi, Gene." As Gene looked at Celine in the Viewscreen, she looked wonderful. Rested and as radiantly beautiful as ever. The drawn angry look on her face was gone.

"Hi, Celine."

"How'd it go?"

"Celine, it's all over. It's over." Gene repeated his words as though to make certain that he himself understood their impact.

"What happened to Franscara?" Celine asked.

"The Pope was going to excommunicate him ...."

"You mean he isn't?"

"He can't. Celine, Franscara committed suicide. Poison."

"Good," Celine said without any emotion in her voice. "I guess God's mercy is still a mystery to me, Gene, but when I think of little old ladies worrying about going to hell because it snowed two feet and they missed Mass and that bastard getting away with everything he did because he was most certainly insane …."

"Celine, let God be the judge. Find peace. Let it all go."

"What about Brown and the others?"

"Brown's to be laicized. Krantz and Modenna have been stripped of all their honors and power. Krantz goes to a monastery in Germany and Modenna to work in a leper colony in Africa. I suppose something similar will happen to Yakablonski and O'Rourke.

"The Pope will have a list of all members by evening time today. From what Doug Haynes said to me earlier today, the Pope will make certain that there will be no possibility of Viri Lucis rising from the ashes. All Michael McCann's money, except what goes to Danny's estate, will now go to the Pope.

"According to Krantz, Viri Lucis wasn't that large. Just a growing number of clerics who were fanatical enough to think they were holier than the Church. Men who were manipulated into believing they were the saviors of the Church. A tragic tale.

"A very stupid tale, Gene. I only wish Danny …."

"…. could have lived to see the end of Viri Lucis?" Gene ventured to complete Celine's thought.

"No, I wish Danny could have found fulfillment in helping his friend Pope Percussi write his encyclical. I feel so bad about …."

"…. about your love for Danny and his for you?"

This time Gene was on target. "Yes," Celine said quietly.

"Never feel bad about your love for Danny, Celine. In the end it was the most self-sacrificial love I've ever witnessed.

"Gene, why did Danny have to die?"

"Somebody said, some philosopher, I guess, that to say, 'I love you' is to say, 'You will never die,'" Gene almost whispered.

"Thanks for that, Gene. Thank you so much."

"Enjoy the rest of your trip, Celine. I'll see you and George when you get back."

"Goodbye, Gene, and again thanks for all you did for Danny — and for me."

"Goodbye, Celine."

After her conversation with Gene, Celine walked around the suite where she and George were staying. Then she stood looking out the window. London stretched out before he but she saw nothing.

George had gone out for a walk through the storied streets of London, taking an umbrella with him, of course.

Celine walked away from the window and went into the bedroom. She threw herself across the bed and lay there thinking, wondering, hurting.

Could there have been a different way? she wondered. Had there really been a need to track down Viri Lucis? Couldn't Danny have just let it all go? Given the note up at once and forgotten about it?

Could there have been something different for them? For Danny and her?

Was all this *really* God's will? A love denied? A loved one murdered? A despicable group of men who in their fanaticism to preserve the Church would have destroyed it? A Church that would now continue along giving whatever leadership fallible, weak human beings can bring to it?

Was this God's will? And if so, what kind of God is it? The word, it, shocked her. What kind of God is *it*? Is God after all just a projection of our needs, our helplessness, our unfulfilled dreams, our extravagant hopes, our resented dependency?

And what was left for her now? A dull, predictable life with George? Social events as empty as a body without a soul? A job that lavished wealth while it robbed you of satisfaction?

Would that be God's will too?

What kind of a God creates you and then abandons you to the misery of a brief stay on earth only to await death as the release from uncontrollable helplessness? From the anguish of living what might have been and what never could be?

"Oh God, oh God," Celine moaned aloud.

What was it Danny had said to her one time? Only those who can see the invisible can do the impossible. Dear Danny, he always had a maxim for every occasion.

What was the invisible behind all the visible events of the last months — the last years? God is certainly invisible. How do you see the invisible God? She remembered Danny's suggestion.

We see God in the results of his activity. In the dough that rises, God is the invisible yeast. In the tiny mustard seed that becomes home for the birds of the air. In the loaves that multiply in the very act of being divided. In the crucifix that becomes the Sign of the Cross. In all those images we see God who is Action itself.

Celine knew she didn't have the theological background or spiritual development to probe the mystery of what Danny had told her. She just had a phenomenal memory.

And what was the impossible she could do?

Is all of life what her father had told her when her kitten died? It's God's will. Is life just one long act of resignation?

Not if she believed in what Danny stood for. What Danny did with his life's energies, his mystical probings, his hunger for a God who could never be consumed, with his death.

Somehow life is the Widow's Mite. A lot of small contributions. And life is the willingness to trust that someone else, somewhere would reap what your contributions had sown. Wasn't that what Danny meant in all his talk about living our faith instead of merely practicing our religion?

What was left for her?

Somehow she had to memorialize Danny by living her faith, no matter how strong or weak it is. By carrying on his work for those in need. By getting involved in what Danny called the messiness of life.

She could live quite comfortably on George's income. She would not return to the firm. She would volunteer her skills and experience to those who cannot afford legal services. She would work to rectify unjust laws and inhumane social conditions.

She'd have to explain this to her father. No! No, she wouldn't explain at all. She would just tell him if and when he asked.

She would continue Danny's quest for meaning wherever that quest might lead. As he used to say, The wise person is not the one with the right answers but the one with the right questions. And, like Danny, she could not expect easy or retread answers. Like him she'd have to learn to dwell in the questions, to learn to love the questions, as the poet Rilke put it.

She thought for a moment that she could feel Danny's presence. To say, I love you, is to say, You will never die. Danny would never die as long as she lived.

Suddenly she wished George would come back to the suite as soon as possible. She needed him. Desperately.

Gene went back to his hotel to pack. It's over, Gene thought. *It is over.* The Pope was in charge. Viri Lucis was in ruins. The Vatican, indeed the Church, had survived another assault.

As he packed, for the first time he allowed the fullness of his sorrow over Danny's death to overwhelm him. Tears flooded his eyes. "It's not entirely over," he whispered to himself. "There is still the grief."

Gene checked his watch. It was two o'clock Thursday afternoon Rome time. He had plenty of time to check out of his hotel and catch his five o'clock flight back home. He'd get back at 9 A.M. Thursday Chicago time. He would also have enough time to get ready for his parish council meeting Thursday evening.

END

ABOUT THE AUTHOR

T. R. Haney has published several books on Christian spirituality. This is his first novel.

Printed in the United States
22841LVS00002B/61-72